BY JENNA GLASS

The Women's War
Queen of the Unwanted

QUEEN OF THE UNWANTED

THE
WOMEN'S
WAR

QUEEN OF THE UNWANTED

JENNA GLASS

DEL REY  NEW YORK

A Del Rey Trade Paperback Original

Copyright © 2020 by Jenna Glass
Map copyright © 2019, 2020 by David Lindroth Inc.

Published in the United States by Del Rey,
an imprint of Random House, a division of
Penguin Random House LLC, New York.

DEL REY and the HOUSE colophon are registered
trademarks of Penguin Random House LLC.

The map by David Lindroth was originally published in slightly different form in
The Women's War by Jenna Glass published by Del Rey, an imprint of
Random House, a division of Penguin Random House LLC, in 2019.

LIBRARY OF CONGRESS CATALOGING-IN-PUBLICATION DATA
Names: Glass, Jenna, author.
Title: Queen of the unwanted / Jenna Glass.
Description: New York: Del Rey, [2020] | Series: The women's war; 2
Identifiers: LCCN 2019038086 (print) | LCCN 2019038087 (ebook) |
ISBN 9780525618379 (trade paperback; alk. paper) |
ISBN 9780525618386 (ebook)
Subjects: GSAFD: Fantasy fiction.
Classification: LCC PS3602.L288 Q44 2020 (print) |
LCC PS3602.L288 (ebook) | DDC 813/.6—dc23
LC record available at https://lccn.loc.gov/2019038086
LC ebook record available at https://lccn.loc.gov/2019038087

Printed in the U.S.A. on acid-free paper

randomhousebooks.com

2 4 6 8 9 7 5 3 1

Book design by Elizabeth A. D. Eno

To all the women who've had the courage to say #MeToo. The world is changing—albeit slowly—thanks to you.

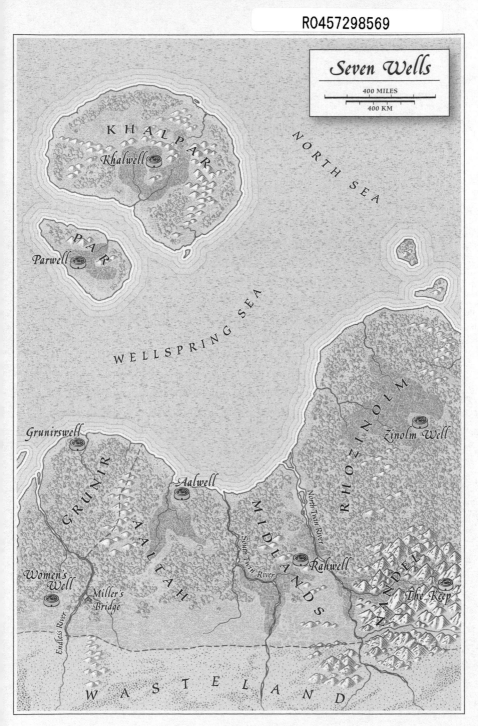

Seven Wells

400 MILES
400 KM

KHALPAR
Khalwell

PAR
Parwell

NORTH SEA

WELLSPRING SEA

Grunirswell

GRUNIR

AALTAH

Aalwell

MIDLANDS

North Twin River

South Twin River

Rahwell

RHOZINOLM

Zinolm Well

ZANDEL

The Keep

Women's
Well

Miller's
Bridge

Endless River

WASTELAND

Part One

THE ABBESS

CHAPTER ONE

From the moment he'd seen the results of his aptitude testing at the age of thirteen, Jalzarnin Rah-Griffolm had set his sights on one day being named the Lord High Priest of Khalpar, and he had never for a moment doubted his destiny.

He had been appointed to the office and joined the royal council at the respectable age of forty-five, and the king had favored him with several land grants and titles that he had not even thought to hope for. No life was without its setbacks and disappointments, but Jalzarnin knew he'd suffered far fewer than most. He could almost hear his late father railing at him, urging him to be satisfied with what he had. Lord Griffolm had even gone so far as to accuse his son of impiety for his outsize ambition.

But though he suspected there had been at least a kernel of truth in his father's accusation—Jalzarnin was admittedly not the most pious man to have held the office of lord high priest—he was not especially inclined to curb that ambition. Which was what brought him here to the anteroom of the king's private study, when a more prudent man—some might even say a *wiser* man—would keep a safe distance from a monarch who had a distressing habit of replacing members of his royal council with little to no provocation.

He paced anxiously, awaiting permission to enter as his father's voice continued to whisper discouragement into his ear. Given that the king was so apt to dismiss members of his royal council, Jalzarnin could never rest secure, unlike the lord high priests who had come before him. If he sat back and enjoyed the privileges of being on the council, he might all too easily find that seat pulled out from under him. There were plenty of other ambitious priests eager for his position.

The study door opened, and the king's personal secretary stepped out. "His Majesty will see you now," he said with a sweeping gesture.

Jalzarnin took what he hoped was a quiet steadying breath, pushing any doubts deep inside, where the king could not glimpse them. Then he stepped into the study and bowed low, surreptitiously studying the king's countenance for some hint of his current disposition.

Jalzarnin wouldn't be so crass as to describe King Khalvin as moody, but one could never tell which days he would be receptive to the opinions of his advisers. And as Jalzarnin had come with the specific intent of overstepping the bounds of his authority, he risked souring his relationship with his liege if he did not tread with extreme care.

"I hear you wish to speak to me about the appointment of a new abbess," the king said abruptly, the corners of his mouth tugging down to hint at his displeasure with the topic.

Clearly he was not in one of his more receptive moods, and Jalzarnin fought to hide the flutter of apprehension in his belly. He reminded himself that even when he was irritable, King Khalvin was a wise and thoughtful king. Jalzarnin's interference in a matter that should be none of his affair might annoy him, but that annoyance would pass if he realized his lord high priest's suggestion would benefit the kingdom.

"Yes, Your Majesty," Jalzarnin said.

"Perhaps I am getting forgetful in my old age, but I was under the impression you were my lord high priest, not my trade minister."

The sarcasm was far from a good omen; any other of the king's advisers—even his lord chancellor—would have taken the unsubtle hint and found an excuse to retreat. But Jalzarnin had not attained his position by being timid.

"Ordinarily, I wouldn't think to interfere with the trade minister's decision," Jalzarnin said. The trade minister was the lowest-ranking member of the royal council, and it was his job to oversee the Abbey of the Unwanted and appoint a replacement when an abbess died. Overseeing the Abbey of the Unwanted was hardly a glamorous responsibility—despite the substantial income the Abbey provided to the Crown's coffers—and it should have been beneath Jalzarnin's notice.

"But these are not ordinary times," he continued, "and we men of conscience must do whatever needs to be done."

The king's frown deepened into a scowl of displeasure. It had been nearly a year since the Abbess of Aaltah had cast the devastating spell that had cursed the Wellspring and changed the very nature of Rho, the element of life. Everything in the king's neatly ordered world had been turned on its head, all the carefully sculpted rules of society disordered in ways it was still difficult to conceive. There were those who were already beginning to view the current situation as normal. Fixed and unchangeable—and maybe even *right*. But King Khalvin was not among them.

"I don't see what that has to do with which whore is in charge of the Abbey," the king said with a curl of his lip. He was a genuinely devout man, who believed wholeheartedly in the sanctity of marriage vows. The whores of the Abbey were technically supposed to service only unmarried men, but it was an open secret that they would service anyone who had the means to pay. If the Abbey weren't such an integral part of life for the nobility of Khalpar—and if it did not provide such a ready source of income for the Crown's coffers—the king would likely have abolished it altogether.

Jalzarnin shifted uncomfortably. The king was in a worse humor than he'd thought. Impatience nearly crackled in his every small gesture, and his index finger was tapping softly on the edge of his desk. Jalzarnin wished he could have presented his proposal at a time of his own choosing, when the king was in a more suggestible frame of mind. But not even members of the royal council could approach the king willy-nilly.

Jalzarnin steadied his nerves by picturing Mairahsol gazing up at him, her eyes full of the calm confidence and strength that had first drawn him to her. She'd been confined to the Abbey since she was nineteen. Her face had been disfigured by an especially violent case of pox—one she claimed was brought on by poison, which Jalzarnin was inclined to believe—and yet she was one of the shrewdest, most intelligent women he'd ever met. He couldn't honestly say he believed she could undo the Curse, but it wasn't out of the realm of possibility.

"All my research has led me to believe that we will need women's magic if we are ever to undo the Curse that Aaltah bitch cast," Jalzarnin said. "And our best hope of finding a cure is to put the most magically gifted woman in the Abbey in charge of the effort. Even if she is not someone who would traditionally be considered for the position."

The king was singularly unmoved by this assertion. "I still fail to grasp why we are having this conversation. Surely if you feel honor-bound to stick your nose into the trade minister's business, you should take up the subject with *him*."

Jalzarnin wondered just what had put the king in such a sour mood. He was rarely *this* unpleasant, even when annoyed. "Of course, Your Majesty," he said with a bow of his head. "I did raise the issue with Lord Prindar, but he was . . . concerned that you would not approve of a break with tradition." To say the trade minister was "*concerned*" was putting it mildly. Prindar had flatly refused Jalzarnin's suggestion, despite the obvious practical advantages. And Prindar would likely have an apoplexy when he discovered Jalzarnin had gone over his head and brought the matter to the king.

"I am a great believer in tradition," the king said, an unmistakable warning in his voice.

"And if we can but undo the Curse, our longstanding traditions can be restored and life returned to normal." Jalzarnin was pinning all his hopes on the king's oft-stated yearning for the old ways.

To his delight, there was a thawing of the peevishness in the king's expression as he studied the face of his lord high priest. The crease between his brows eased, and there was a spark of calculation and interest in his eyes. Catching the king's interest was not always desirable, but it was at least preferable to the annoyance he'd radiated previously.

"You have someone in mind."

It was not phrased as a question, but Jalzarnin answered anyway, fully aware that he was stepping into a trap. "Yes, Your Majesty."

"Because you are so well acquainted with all the abigails that you know which is the most . . . How did you put it? 'Magically gifted'?"

Jalzarnin felt the heat in his face and cursed his body for the betrayal. He had known before he'd set foot in this room that he was opening himself up to criticism by speaking of his familiarity with the Abbey. His patronage was a blatant violation of his marriage vows, though he and his wife were both content that he should take his pleasure elsewhere. He told himself he was not ashamed of the arrangement, but his obvious blush said otherwise.

Jalzarnin bit down on his reflexive need to defend himself. Nothing he could say would reduce the king's censure, but it wasn't as if the king did not already know of his frequent visits to the Abbey. The discreet "married man's" entrance was supposed to be a secret, but the king's spy network was more than capable of seeing past such pedestrian attempts at subterfuge. It was in the king's best interests to know of any scandals his royal council might spark, and Jalzarnin doubted there was a single member of the council about whom the king did not know at least one embarrassing secret.

Deciding his best course of action was to ignore the censure completely, Jalzarnin spoke as though he had not heard it. "There is one abigail whose gift clearly exceeds that of any of her sisters."

The king's nose wrinkled in distaste at this discussion of women's magic. "I cannot see how the ability to create love potions and fertility aids is of any significant advantage to the effort to undo the Curse."

Jalzarnin acknowledged this opinion with a nod. "And a year ago, I would have been similarly skeptical." Women's magic paled in comparison to men's, its power so paltry that magically inclined women were not tested and assigned magical ranks as men were. And, of course, it was forbidden in polite society for women to practice magic at all. Women's magic was the sole purview of whores, practiced only in the Abbey where polite society could ignore it—an open secret not much different from the "married man's" entrance. "But it has become clear that women's magic has more strength than we had originally realized, and the Curse has increased the power of that magic exponentially. And as the Curse was created using some bastardization of women's magic, I have begun to believe that only women's magic can reverse it.

"The woman I have in mind—Mairahsol Rah-Creesha—would rank as Prime or maybe even Master based on the number of elements she can see. As far as I can tell, no other woman at the Abbey would test at better than Gifted. It would behoove us to have a woman such as Mairahsol leading the effort to undo the Curse."

"And yet Lord Prindar is reluctant to appoint her?"

"She is young," Jalzarnin admitted. "Not yet thirty." Tradition held that the abbess should be selected from among the most senior of the abigails who were still of sound mind and body.

The king started slightly, finally recognizing Mairahsol's name now that he was no longer imagining a crone. Her fall from grace had been very public, despite her family's best efforts to keep it as quiet as possible. Most people looked upon her with horror and disdain for how she'd ruined both her own family and the family of the man she'd once thought to marry, but Jalzarnin couldn't help but admire the courage and iron will that she'd shown.

The king shook his head, his lip curling once more as he thought back on the scandal that had rocked the kingdom a decade before. "You would put *that woman* in a position of authority?"

"There are no innocent maidens in the Abbey," Jalzarnin argued.

"But there are few as notorious as Mairahsol Rah-Creesha! I can certainly understand why our trade minister would object to bestowing such an honor upon her."

"Is being named abbess really such an honor?" Jalzarnin asked. "She would have authority and rank within the walls of the Abbey, but to the rest of the world, she will still be an Unwanted Woman.

"Because she is so young and untried," Jalzarnin continued, "her fellow abigails do not listen to her and will not accept her suggestions when it comes to researching a cure for the Curse. If she was appointed abbess, they would have no choice but to listen and to do as they are told. It is our best chance."

The king was agitated enough by the unconventional suggestion that he rose from his chair and crossed the room to the hearth, gazing into the fire as his brow furrowed in thought. Jalzarnin swallowed his impulse to advance further arguments, confident he had presented a convincing case. There was very little King Khalvin wouldn't do if it meant undoing the Curse.

"Can you assure me," the king asked, still staring into the flames, "that you are thinking about what's best for the kingdom and not about what's best for your cock?"

Jalzarnin's face heated again, but he was not surprised to find the king knew about his . . . dalliance with Mairahsol. The king knew he was a frequent visitor to the Abbey, so of course he also knew which of the abigails Jalzarnin favored.

"She is mine however and whenever I want her," he responded simply. "I have no need to woo her or cajole her, and she is not in any great demand." Most men would look at her pockmarked face and turn their attentions to the more comely abigails in the Abbey. "I gain no personal advantage by suggesting her promotion."

Of course, that wasn't *strictly* true. Mairahsol would happily allow him into her bed—even without payment—whether she was abbess or abigail. But as much as he enjoyed bedding her, he was far more interested in her other formidable talents. Her ability to sniff out secrets and spy on her fellow abigails—and, more important, their customers—had already saved Jalzarnin's place on the council once. If she had not overheard Lord Deenan admitting to his taste for young boys, that ambitious and well-thought-of priest might have succeeded in his plan to curry favor with the king and supplant Jalzarnin. Men were forever talking more than they should in women's beds, and that one incident had driven home exactly how Jalzarnin could take advantage of the situation.

But several months ago, Mairahsol had made a misstep and been caught eavesdropping. The late abbess—who had made it clear she detested Mairahsol—had punished the poor woman so severely that Mairahsol had refused to undertake any more intelligence gathering missions on his behalf. Having seen the welts and bruises left by the beating, Jalzarnin could hardly blame her. However, if she was the abbess, she would have access to a great deal of information without having to be sneaky at all. And if she was caught spying, she would not be subject to punishment.

He did hope she had the necessary skills to craft a spell to reverse the Curse—and he was well aware that much of the glory of such a spell would spill over onto him, for the king would remember his wise counsel—but her skills as a spy were valuable to him regardless.

The king let out a soft snort of laughter as he shook his head and turned back to his lord high priest. "You are not made for subterfuge, my friend," he said, but the sourness and annoyance were gone from both his face and his voice.

Jalzarnin stiffened and had to bite back a sharp retort. "There is no subterfuge, Your Majesty," he protested in as mild a tone as he could manage. Ulterior motives he could admit to, but that wasn't the same as subterfuge. And though he'd been King Khalvin's lord high priest for going on a dozen years, he would hardly term himself the king's *friend*.

The king ignored the protest. "I will have a word with Lord Prindar. Perhaps we can appoint young Mairahsol on a provisional basis. Give her, say, six months to demonstrate her ability to lead the Abbey and make progress toward a cure. If in six months' time, she has shown herself up to the task, we can discuss making it a permanent appointment."

Jalzarnin bowed deeply, letting out a silent sigh of relief. He had come into this meeting expecting either unconditional success or utter failure, but this partial success was satisfactory. Mairahsol might not be able to reverse the Curse in six months—or at all, for that matter—but he had a great deal of faith in her ability to convince the king she was making progress, whether she was or not. And if the worst happened, and she failed, at least he would get six months' worth of intelligence out of her.

"Thank you, Your Majesty," he said, anxious now to escape the study as quickly as possible. He was almost out the door when the king's voice stopped him in his tracks once more.

"Out of curiosity," the king asked softly, "was there any investigation into the death of the previous abbess? I understood her to have been in excellent health, and her age not terribly advanced."

Jalzarnin turned back toward the king, keeping his face as expressionless as possible. "There was nothing suspicious about her death that I know of," he said, which was nothing but the truth. "It is not unheard of for the heart to give out even in a seemingly heathy woman of her age. I could look into it further, if you'd like." He prayed the king would turn down his offer, for while there was nothing outwardly suspicious about the death, he had to admit to himself that it was . . . convenient. And that the abbess had been terribly unkind to Mairahsol.

If Mairahsol had anything to do with the abbess's death, Jalzarnin would never dream of holding it against her. Indeed, he might applaud her for once again having the courage and will to avenge herself. But all the same, he would prefer not to know.

"That won't be necessary," the king replied, but there was a glitter in his eyes that said he'd seen much more than Jalzarnin was comfortable revealing. His unpredictable moods made it easy to underestimate him, but the king was nothing if not observant.

This time, when Jalzarnin made to leave, the king let him go.

CHAPTER TWO

In the first few weeks that followed the death of her daughter at the hands of her half-brother, Sovereign Princess Alysoon made no attempt to pretend she was anything resembling a rational human being. The grief and the rage—and the crushing guilt at not having protected her child—transformed her into a being of pure emotion and stole her ability to eat and to sleep. She did not leave her home for days at a time, and the weight dropped off her until her dresses hung limp from her gaunt frame. Occasionally, her lady's maid, Honor, coaxed some food into her and badgered her into lying down for jagged bits of restless sleep. Honor also did her valiant best to keep Alys's royal council from troubling her with any demands, and for three full weeks after the funeral—a singularly soul-destroying ordeal, for they had no body but only a head to consign to the cleansing flames—Women's Well functioned, more or less, without any input from its sovereign.

Eventually, however, her brother—and lord chancellor—Tynthanal grew weary of making allowances.

Alys was slumped in her usual chair by the fireplace—which was unlit on this warm late-summer day—when she heard Honor's raised voice coming from the sitting room just beyond. Although Alys had spent most of her days in a fog of alternating numbness and paralyzing grief, some part of her had known she would not be allowed to hide in her den and lick her wounds forever. In point of fact, she was no doubt lucky Tynthanal or one of her other council members hadn't burst in on her already.

Alys straightened in her chair, blinking in the dimness of the room, for she had lit no luminants. Honor's voice took on a pleading tone, but heavy footsteps approached the bedroom door anyway.

"Alys, I'm coming in," Tynthanal announced, and there was no room for argument in his voice.

Alys sighed delicately and smoothed her skirts, trying to drag her mind back from the abyss. She was not ready to face the world yet, wasn't sure she ever would be again. But even as the grief tried to drag her back down, she realized she could not remain comfortably inside her self-imposed tomb forever. Delnamal had killed Jinnell not because of any special ill will toward his niece, but because he'd known how deeply it would hurt Alys. It was likely he even had hopes that it would destroy her utterly, and if she did not somehow find a way to reclaim her life, she would be letting him win.

Tynthanal hesitated a moment at the door—either because he was hoping for an invitation or because he thought Alys needed that critical moment to prepare herself. Then, the door opened and he stepped inside. With the covered windows and the lack of luminants, he appeared as nothing more than a dark silhouette, framed by the doorway. Honor hovered anxiously at his shoulder, one hand stretched out toward him as though she might physically hold him back, though she had more sense than to try.

Tynthanal muttered a curse under his breath, then strode to one of the windows and yanked the curtains open, letting in a blinding beam of desert light. Alys squinted and raised her hand to shade her eyes as Tynthanal crossed to the other side of the room and opened more curtains. Alys wasn't entirely sure what time it was, though she vaguely remembered Honor had brought her some lunch not all that long ago, so it was probably the early afternoon.

"I'm sorry, Your Royal Highness," Honor said from the doorway, wringing her hands anxiously. "He wouldn't take no for an answer."

Honor looked so distraught that Alys experienced a stab of guilt. She imagined she'd been snappish and unpleasant, and though Honor no doubt fully understood her state of mind—and shared her grief, for she had loved Jinnell—that didn't mean Alys's behavior hadn't been hurtful. No effort of will could dredge up anything resembling a smile, but Alys hoped she managed an expression that was at least reasonably pleasant.

"No apologies necessary," she said, then had to clear her throat, her voice as rusty as if she'd just rolled out of bed. "You couldn't keep him out indefinitely."

Honor bobbed a quick curtsy, then retreated. Alys told herself that as soon as Tynthanal left, she would have to seek Honor out and give the woman an apology of her own. It could not have been easy caring for her over the last weeks, and yet Honor had not once complained or gotten impatient with her. Alys doubted she would have handled the situation with the same grace had their roles been reversed.

She turned her attention to Tynthanal, who stood by the window and shook his head at her. A lifetime of dressing in military uniform meant he never quite looked himself in the traditional civilian garb of doublet and breeches, but the mourning attire—without all the extra embellishments and color—looked more natural and comfortable than the ornamental dress of a traditional court. His skin was dark enough, both in natural coloration and from countless hours spent in the sun, that the black did not make him look pale or wan. There was a pinched look to his face and shadows under his eyes, but aside from that he looked very much like himself. Grief had not turned him into a hollow, shadowy vessel as it had Alys, and she had to fight down a sudden urge to snarl at him for looking so normal.

Tynthanal had, of course, loved Jinnell, but he was her uncle, not her father. There was no reason to expect his grief to be as transformative as Alys's own. And the Principality of Women's Well was much better off that way, for Alys was sure her brother had been taking care of all sorts of business in her stead, giving her as much time to grieve as he could afford.

"You're going to tell me I have to snap out of it," she said, her voice a little firmer this time.

Tynthanal blew out a heavy sigh and scrubbed a hand through his hair, which based on its state of disarray had received similar treatment countless times throughout the course of the day. "I was going to be a good deal less insensitive than that."

She nodded and pushed to her feet, stifling a groan. She'd been sitting still for far too long, and her joints complained at the sudden demand for movement. Rarely had Alys been as aware of her age as she was right now, and she subtly stretched and shifted her weight, trying to shake off the stiffness. Her neck made nasty crackling sounds as she tilted it first to one side, then the other. Fog still clung to her mind, her thoughts sluggish and dulled, but she knew that if there was one thing that could help restore her to some semblance of her usual self, it would be planning Delnamal's downfall.

"But the message would have been the same," she said. "And you're right. I cannot sit in my room forever."

"No," Tynthanal agreed gently. "There are people who need you. And you need them just as badly."

The words, so innocuous on their surface, triggered another pang in Alys's chest. Of all the people who needed her, her son, Corlin, should need her the most. And yet despite the fact that he lived in her house, she had barely seen him since the day of the funeral. That was in part her fault, for having not ventured out of her room, but she had told Honor that Corlin was the one person who was allowed to interrupt her grieving whenever he wished. He had not once taken advantage of this permission, and when she sought him, he was almost invariably out, doing who-knew-what. She'd neglected her duty as a mother and failed to question his absences—something she should rectify as soon as Tynthanal left.

"I will attend tomorrow's council meeting," she promised. That would give her almost a full day to prepare herself for the demands she was sure to face once she returned to pubic life and resumed the business of being the Sovereign Princess of Women's Well.

Tynthanal's shoulders slumped with relief. Clearly, he'd come expecting a fight.

"But before that," she continued, "I want to speak with you and Lady Chanlix. In private."

Tynthanal's brows drew together in an expression somewhere between confusion and alarm. Alys assumed he and the grand magus were still sleeping together, and she knew Chanlix was worried Alys would frown on the relationship. Tynthanal had never seemed to share Chanlix's concerns, but the wariness in his eyes suggested perhaps he'd merely kept his concerns deeply hidden.

"May I ask what about?"

"I would like the Academy to begin work on a new Kai spell—on an unofficial basis."

"Ah," Tynthanal said, having no trouble following Alys's thoughts without further explanation. "You want to find a way to send a deadly spell via flier."

The spell the former abigails of Women's Well had developed using women's Kai was something completely unprecedented. With the spell they'd named Vengeance, a woman who possessed a mote of Kai could use that Kai to send a flier winging to her enemy, and, if the flier found its mark and broke skin, the hapless victim would be rendered permanently impotent. It was a devastating spell, and one that was very difficult to guard against. Alys had tried to strike Delnamal with it, using a mote of Kai donated by Chanlix, but the attack had been foiled. And now that he'd had Jinnell put to death out of pure spite, Vengeance was too mild a spell to fit his crimes.

"I would prefer to murder Delnamal as slowly and painfully as possible with my own hands," she growled as the rage in her belly swelled and threatened to overwhelm her. "But my chances of reaching him with a flier are far higher, and I want him dead sooner rather than later."

"Understood," Tynthanal said with a bow.

Mairahsol let out a contented sigh as she snuggled closer to Jalzarnin, enjoying the afterglow—but also enjoying the plush mattress as well as the softness of the sheets. She remembered vaguely that the bed she'd slept on growing up had been even more luxurious, with silken sheets and feather-stuffed pillows, but after ten years of the rock-hard cot in the junior abigails' dormitory, the beds in the Abbey's play-rooms felt like the pinnacle of decadence. A decadence she'd experienced all too rarely, for her pockmarked face meant she had never worked the Abbey's pavilion. Until a chance encounter with the lord high priest had, for reasons she did not understand, changed her life.

Jalzarnin ran a hand through her hair—an affectionate gesture she suspected few men who visited the Abbey would bestow on the abigails who serviced them. She was not naïve enough to believe him in love with her, but she was sure at least *some* of that affection was genuine. He'd been equally tender with her even before she'd shown her usefulness to him as an amateur spy, and his outrage when he'd seen the results of the beating the late Mother Wyebryn had ordered had been awesome to behold. She'd been afraid his rage would motivate him to act rashly, but he'd eventually calmed—never realizing how much of himself he had revealed to her in that rage.

"I have some good news for you," he said when both their pulses had lowered and Mairah was so comfortable she was beginning to drift off to sleep.

His words banished any hint of sleep, and she sat up with a cry of excitement she could barely contain. He had, of course, believed it was *his* idea to try to have her appointed abbess, but she had conceived the plan herself even before the fateful beating that had won him entirely to her side. She'd barely allowed herself to hope he would follow through on his promise to advance her cause to the king, and even now she tried to temper her enthusiasm.

It was nearly impossible to believe her plan could have worked when she'd had so many obstacles to overcome. Not only had Mother Wyebryn been in good health and expected to rule the Abbey for another decade or two, but Mairah herself had been the woman in the Abbey *least* likely to succeed her. There was the question of her age, of course. But more damning was the fact that she had not a single friend within the Abbey's walls. Mother Wyebryn and her cronies—especially the hateful Sister Norah—had had it in for her since the moment she'd first donned the red robes, and they had made it clear to every other abigail in the Abbey that befriending Mairah was a sure path to misery. But then, for whatever reason, Lord Jalzarnin had shown Mairah favor, and she'd begun once again plotting an epic, if improbable, revenge.

Knowing the effect it would have on her lover—or at least *hoping* she knew—she had allowed herself to be caught when supposedly spying on his behalf, thereby securing his loyalty through a combination of guilt and self-interest.

Yet even with Jalzarnin's help, her plan would have had no chance of working if she hadn't exaggerated her powers of foresight.

There was no question in her mind that she could see more elements than any other woman in the Abbey, but as a seer, she was almost entirely untested. Based on her bloodlines, she *should* have some natural abilities. However, when she'd tried her first seer's poison—the mildest one available, just to test her tolerance—the pain and the misery it caused her was so wretched she'd vowed never to take another. Almost worse than the ravages of the poison was the punishment—and ridicule—heaped on her by Mother Wyebryn when Mairah had recounted what she'd seen. She'd been called a liar and a fraud and beaten soundly for what was termed her hubris. And yet now it seemed her vision—which had shown her sitting behind the abbess's desk while still a young woman—had been true all along.

"You spoke with the king!" she exclaimed, her heart rate shooting all the way back up as her breath nearly froze in her lungs. "Why did you wait so long to tell me?"

Even *she* had doubted the veracity of her own vision! But even so, she had confided in Jalzarnin, embellishing her vision with additional details to suggest she might use her power as abbess to undo the Curse. And whether because she was an exceptionally skilled liar or merely because he'd wanted so badly to believe her—likely a combination of the two—he'd been convinced. No longer would she sleep on a miserable cot in a dormitory filled with snoring women! Never again would she be forced to fast—or take a beating—anytime one of the senior abigails took exception to her tone of voice, or the expression on her face, or the thoughts they imagined she was thinking.

Jalzarnin laughed. "You know me, dearest. I do enjoy the savoring of joyful anticipation." He waggled his brows at her, and she laughed with delight.

It was true that he was a master of foreplay. So much so that he always purchased two hours of her time instead of the traditional one.

"I can't believe it," she said wonderingly, covering her mouth with her hand as she shook her head. It had been a long time since she had felt anything resembling genuine joy—the glee she'd felt when Mother Wyebryn had blithely drunk the poison Mairah had slipped into her wine didn't count—but that was what she felt now. "How did you manage it?"

He propped himself up on his elbow, smiling at her as his eyes glowed with satisfaction and pride. "I told you the king would do anything if he thought it might undo the Curse. I was not exaggerating. It makes sense that it would take women's magic to reverse what the Abbess of Aaltah did, and it therefore makes sense to have the most magically gifted abigail leading the effort. The king saw that logic as clearly as I do."

It sounded more like wishful thinking than logic, as far as Mairah was concerned. The Curse that the Abbess of Aaltah had cast was unthinkable in its scale and power. The woman had sent out fliers all through Seven Wells, explaining that the Curse had been generations in the making and that the three women who'd died in its casting were the only ones who had any idea how it was accomplished. It had affected the Wellspring—the source of all magical elements, which were said to be the Creator's seed. And it had changed the most common of all elements: Rho, the element of life. It seemed the worst kind of hubris to imagine anyone could simply reverse it. Not in this lifetime, at least. Not that she'd ever allowed any such sentiment to see the light of day.

"The trade minister will come by the Abbey tomorrow," Jalzarnin continued, "to deliver the official decree. This is the last night you will spend as an abigail."

It was all Mairah could do not to leap out of the bed and dance for happiness. From the moment she'd set foot inside the Abbey—no, from the moment she'd started down the path that had led her here—

she had considered her life all but over. Becoming abbess wouldn't come close to restoring the life she'd had before her ruin, but it was a far cry from the miserable drudgery she'd resigned herself to.

"At least, as long as the king has reason to hope you will succeed in reversing the Curse," Jalzarnin finished, draining all that joy and replacing it with cold horror.

"What?" she cried, hoping he didn't mean what she feared.

He sat up and put a comforting hand on her thigh, giving it a squeeze. "Don't panic, dear one. You will be named abbess on an interim basis, but the office will become officially yours in six months' time."

"Six months?" Her voice rose to something near a shriek. "You expect me to reverse this impossible spell in *six months*? Are you mad?" Her fellow abigails already despised her. She could only imagine how they would feel about her after she'd been their abbess for six months. If she should be removed from office and returned to their ranks . . . She shuddered. Hard to imagine she could be treated worse than she was right now, but she was certain that was exactly what would happen.

"Of course I don't expect that," Jalzarnin soothed. "And neither does the king. All he wants is to see signs of progress. He wants to be reassured that my recommendation is sound and based on logic, not emotion." He grimaced briefly. "He is not unaware that I have formed a certain degree of attachment to you, and though I believe he trusts me and trusts my judgment, he is a careful man."

Mairah folded her arms over her breasts—a gesture that was protective, rather than modest. She'd survived being ruined once—and it was a ruination she'd made a conscious choice to accept—but she wasn't sure she could survive it a second time.

Jalzarnin drew her into his arms, and though she didn't resist, she didn't melt into him, either.

"Do you have any idea what you're asking me to risk?" she murmured, trying not to think about just how much more miserable her life could become. Perhaps it would be wiser not to try than to risk trying and failing. Not that she supposed Jalzarnin was exactly *asking* this of her. He had already spoken to the king, after all, and the king had already decided to appoint her.

"You *will* be named abbess permanently," he said, his voice ringing with conviction. "Of that I have no doubt. You are gifted in so many ways." He released her, then cupped his hands around her face, forcing her to meet his earnest eyes. "You deserve so much more than life has given you. I can't give you everything you deserve, but I can give you this chance. Remember, all you have to do is convince the king you have made progress. I *know* you can do that!"

Mairah swallowed hard, forcing down her fear. Jalzarnin was the lord high priest—presumably the most devout man in all of Khalpar. He and his fellow priests preached that the Curse was an abomination, an insult to the Creator's will and a blight on all humanity. And yet right now, he didn't sound like a man in the grips of a pious fervor, desperate to restore the natural order.

"And will *you* be satisfied?" she asked. "If I appear to show progress but don't actually reverse the Curse?"

Jalzarnin smiled ruefully. "I'm a realist, darling. I don't think a spell that was generations in the planning will be reversed quite so easily as our king and many of my fellows wish. I also think that the Creator allowed it to happen, and that therefore it may very well be His will after all. But of course I am not a fool and have no intention of sharing these sentiments with anyone but you."

Mairah nodded and bit her lip thoughtfully. It was not an unqualified victory, and the dangers involved were immense. But Jalzarnin had given her hope where none had existed, and for that she could only be grateful.

"You will be a magnificent abbess," he said, gazing at her like a man infatuated.

Mairah smiled and practically glowed with the praise—despite her natural skepticism. She was under no illusion. She recognized the depths of his ambition and was well aware that he viewed everyone around him through the lens of his own self-interest. But one thing she knew: compared to her, he was a rank amateur.

CHAPTER THREE

Corlin looked startled when Alys swept into the dining room, leaping to his feet so fast he almost knocked over his chair. He had not been home when Tynthanal had visited, and apparently he'd had no inkling that Alys had decided to emerge from her room. Guilt gnawed at her once again, and she wondered how many meals he'd eaten at this table in solitude while she'd surrendered herself to grief. He was grieving, too, and though she doubted her ability to comfort him, the least she could have done was keep him company.

He'd never been the demonstrative sort, her son, so Alys was not surprised that he did not fling himself joyfully into her arms, though his stiff and very proper bow felt strangely accusatory.

"Your Royal Highness," he said in greeting.

Protocol demanded that even her closest family members bow and greet her formally when in public, but there was no one else in the room at the moment, and she was sure she was not imagining the chill in his voice and bearing. Her throat tightened, and she had the momentary urge to turn and flee the room. She fully understood why Corlin was angry with her, why he blamed her for Jinnell's death. After all, she blamed herself, too, even if logic insisted there had been nothing she could have done to save her daughter had she remained home instead of traveling to Women's Well.

Alys sucked in a deep breath and stiffened her spine. She was done with running away.

"I'm sorry I've been . . . absent for these last several weeks," she said. "It was terribly selfish of me, and . . ." Her voice trailed off as Corlin refused to make eye contact, his gaze fixed on something just above her right shoulder. She felt as if she were looking at a stranger— one who clearly did not like her very much.

Wishing she could think of something to say to make it better, she took her seat at the head of the table. Corlin remained standing until she was settled, once again freezing her out with his overly proper court etiquette. A footman entered the room and served the first course, a clear broth redolent with the scent of locally grown herbs. Despite her emergence from her room, Alys had not come close to recovering her appetite, and she knew she would have to force herself to finish even this lightest of all dishes.

She glanced at Corlin, who sat ramrod straight in his chair and stared at the wall. He did not reach for his spoon. As an experiment, Alys picked up her own spoon and dipped it in the broth, stirring it around as if waiting for it to cool before sipping. Corlin's hands remained in his lap as she slowly lifted the spoon to her mouth and took a delicate sip.

As soon as she took that sip, Corlin's seeming paralysis was broken and he set to the soup with gusto.

Alys shook her head and put the spoon down with a firm thump. "I get the message that you're angry with me, Corlin," she said. "You needn't work quite so hard at it."

He paused with his spoon halfway to his mouth. His gaze shifted briefly in her direction before he remembered how vitally important it was that he not make eye contact. With a start, Alys remembered acting in a similar manner to her own father more than once over the years. She had never forgiven him for divorcing and disgracing her mother, and she had never been shy about letting him know that. Corlin had learned from the best how to deliver a very effective cold shoulder.

He put the spoon down and stared straight ahead, apparently riveted by the dining room wall. "I know you were too busy to notice, but I'm now fourteen."

Alys flinched, her heart giving an unpleasant thud. She'd sunk so deeply into her sea of self-pity and self-indulgence that she had actually forgotten her own son's birthday! It was unconscionable, and she could hardly blame him for being angry. Surely she should be able to mourn the death of one child without neglecting the other.

"I'm so sorry—" she began, knowing that no words could take away the hurt she had caused, but Corlin wasn't interested in hearing her apology anyway.

"I'm of age to join the Citadel now," he interrupted. "I have already spoken to Lord Jailom about it, and he assures me I will be accepted as long as I have your permission."

Alys was struck speechless, staring at her nearly grown son and seeing instead the chubby, cheerful toddler who'd once clung to her skirts. But there was a hint of peach fuzz on his cheeks, and the subtle broadening of his shoulders and chest showed he'd spent a considerable effort honing his swordsmanship as he drilled with the soldiers of the Citadel. She had initially been against him training with the soldiers, but learning to wield a sword was an essential part of any young nobleman's upbringing, and she'd eventually decided there was no harm in allowing him to learn from the best.

"Is that where you've been all this time?" she asked.

His eyes narrowed and the muscles of his jaw worked. "You've barely stuck your head out of your room since the funeral," he said, his voice full of sharp edges. "How would you know whether I've been anywhere other than here?"

A footman peeked in the door, saw that neither Alys nor Corlin had finished their soup, and vanished again.

"I'm sorry I've been so neglectful," she said. "I wish I were a stronger person, wish I could have found the will to . . ." She blinked rapidly as tears threatened. It was all she could do not to bolt from the room and dive back into the darkness and safety of her bedroom. The condemnation in Corlin's eyes was more than she could bear when her soul was still so terribly fragile.

"Do I have your permission?" Corlin asked. "Lord Jailom said I could start immediately. He needs all the cadets he can find if we're to have a real army someday."

"You're the crown prince," she said, grasping for an excuse. If Corlin joined the Citadel, that meant he would leave home and live in the barracks. Women's Well was, of course, a very small principality, and the Citadel was within easy walking distance of her house—just as it would be from her palace, when that building was completed—and yet she felt certain that if he moved away, she would lose him for good. "Joining the Citadel is meant to be a lifetime commitment, which is fine for a second or third son, but not for an heir." Not to mention that there were few things she wanted less than to have her son become a career soldier—especially in a time that was almost certain to see war.

"Lord Jailom says there is precedent," Corlin insisted.

Alys was going to have to have a word with her lord commander for putting this idea in Corlin's head.

She sighed, suspecting it was very much the other way around. But Lord Jailom had apparently done nothing to discourage it—and she'd been too busy licking her wounds to put an end to this before it began. The thought of Corlin going into battle made her feel dizzy with panic, though of course cadets—especially the youngest of them—were only called into battle in the gravest of emergencies.

I can't lose you, too, she thought, but she had the good sense not to put the sentiment into words.

"Just because there is precedent doesn't mean *you* should do it," she said. "You never much enjoyed—"

"It doesn't matter what I enjoyed in the past. I *need* to do this. I need to know how to fight. I need to be ready when the time comes."

"You will not fight!" she snapped, panic making her words come out sharper than she intended.

Corlin shoved his bowl away, sloshing lukewarm soup onto the table. Anger rolled off him in palpable waves, and Alys barely recognized the sweet, mild-mannered child she had raised. It was natural that a boy his age would begin to rebel against his mother, and it was also natural that he should be angry after everything he had gone through and everything he had lost. But the intensity of that anger scared her—and made her wonder what he would become if he could not let go of it.

Maybe joining the Citadel would be the best thing for him. Maybe the drilling and sparring would give him a much-needed outlet for the rage that currently had nowhere to go.

"You don't even care what I want, do you?" he snarled. "You've decided to keep me tied to your apron strings because you think that will somehow make up for leaving Jinnell and me alone, and I have no say in it."

Alys put a hand to her stomach as if to stanch the bleeding as his words stabbed into her. He'd chosen her softest, most vulnerable spot, and the pain was so vicious she had to close her eyes to contain it.

For a moment, the room was silent, and all Alys could hear was the ringing in her ears as the world threatened to crush her. Then Corlin heaved a loud sigh.

"Forgive me, Mama," he said. "I didn't mean that."

But of course, he had. She had trusted that her children would be safe in Aalwell, never imagining that her father might die in her absence and her half-brother ascend the throne. She'd trusted her father to protect his grandchildren, which he certainly would have, had he lived. Alys could not have anticipated her father's death, but she still should not have left her children unprotected so long. She would carry the guilt of those decisions for the rest of her life.

Forcing her eyes open, she regarded her son. She did not want him to be a soldier, even temporarily. But perhaps it was about what he needed rather than about what she wanted.

"Are you sure you want to do this?" she asked, hoping there was no quaver in her voice. "A soldier's life is not an easy one, even when he is but a cadet."

Corlin snorted. "But I was never destined for an easy life, now was I?"

"No. I suppose not." Alys had never considered her own life particularly easy, but she'd had no idea how much harder it would become after her mother cast the spell many referred to as the Curse. She would do anything in her power to protect her son against the repercussions, but no, his life could never be easy. "If you're sure this is what you want, then you have my permission."

Queen Ellinsoltah of Rhozinolm stood before the mirror in her dressing room and smoothed her hands down the skirt of brilliant blue silk that draped her hips, emotions rioting in ways she had never expected. Behind her, Star, her lady's maid, hummed approvingly, plucking at her belled sleeve so that it lay just right.

"It is so lovely to see you wearing a proper color once more, Your Majesty," Star said. Then, unable to stop fussing, she reached up and adjusted the jeweled snood that restrained Ellin's hair.

Ellin blinked at her image in the mirror, hardly recognizing herself. "I had not realized how . . . accustomed I had become to wearing black," she murmured, and was surprised to find her eyes stinging with tears. One year ago yesterday, she had lost her mother, father, uncle, and grandfather all in one terrible, terrifying evening. It felt almost like a betrayal to lay her mourning clothes aside.

Star patted her shoulder gently. "Just because you no longer wear black does not mean you no longer mourn. Today will be difficult, but it will get easier as time goes on."

Ellin turned to her maid with a wry smile. "I very much doubt that," she murmured. She would grow used to wearing color again, just as she had somehow grown used to being the queen. But with the end of her official mourning would come a new and daunting set of obstacles.

"You are up to the challenge," Star assured her stoutly.

"Which one?"

"All of them."

Ellin couldn't help smiling in genuine affection. It would perhaps be inappropriate to call Star her friend, but that was the space she occupied in Ellin's heart, regardless of the difference in their stations. "If only my royal council had as much confidence in me as you do."

As was nearly always the case, her first order of official business this morning would be presiding over the meeting of her royal council. They were nominally more cooperative since she'd used magic she'd acquired from Sovereign Princess Alysoon to brutally murder her cousin Tamzin when he had tried to launch a revolt in the midst of one of their meetings, but there was never a day when she didn't remember how easily her lord commander and her lord high treasurer—managers of the money and the military that supported the Crown—had been swayed by Tamzin's rabble-rousing. They might have abandoned their open resistance at Tamzin's death, but that hardly made them her most ardent supporters. And today she could no longer use her mourning as an excuse to delay some difficult conversations.

"They don't know you as well as I do," Star said. "You are a formidable queen, and those who don't know it yet will soon learn the truth." She frowned. " *'Soon'* being a relative term, if you insist on hiding in your dressing room."

Ellin made an unladylike face. "I'm not *hiding*."

"Then why are you still here? You've been dressed for a good quarter hour already."

"I'm sure that's an exaggeration," Ellin said, "but your point is taken." She quickly touched a hand to the gold circlet that rested on her brow, patted her hair, then realized that while she might not be *hiding* exactly, she was certainly *dithering*.

Turning from the mirror, she finally emerged from her dressing room, leaving the royal apartments and making her way through the palace halls until she reached the council chamber. As befitted a monarch, she was always the last to arrive at these meetings. In the old days, before she had made an example of Tamzin, she would enter the room to find the traditional tray of refreshments well and truly picked over. These days, the tray contained only dainty—and quite delicious—seed cakes, and everyone waited until she had arrived and given them permission to sit before taking one. In the first few meetings after they'd seen what her spelled ring could do to a man whose stomach contained those seeds, they'd been hesitant to touch the cakes. Then her lord chancellor—her one true ally among her advisers—had boldly taken a cake and finished it off in a couple of bites. The others had much more reluctantly followed suit, some of them practically gagging on what had once been considered a treat.

No one had forgotten the danger those seed cakes represented, but the ritual eating of them had become commonplace enough that there was no longer any choking or gagging. Ellin even took one for herself—they really were *quite* delicious—although her memory of Tamzin's death was as visceral and unpleasant as theirs.

Dabbing at her lips to ensure no seeds were left clinging, she turned to her lord chancellor. "What is first on our agenda today, Lord Semsulin?" she asked.

It wasn't truly a question, for of course she and her lord chancellor had discussed their strategy well in advance of the day her official mourning ended. Since the moment she had ascended to the throne, her entire royal council had been obsessed with the prospect of her marriage. Her cousin Tamzin had been the most insistent that she marry with all possible haste and hand the throne over to the more capable hands of a man. Specifically, himself.

When she'd cast the spell that killed Tamzin, she had made it clear that she had no intention of ceding her throne to her husband, but the question of her marriage was still very much an open one.

Semsulin's habitually dour expression lifted momentarily at her pretended innocence, but he did not go so far as to smile. "I believe now that your mourning period has ended, we must discuss your marriage prospects."

Lord Kailindar—who was both her uncle and the man who had succeeded Tamzin to the office of lord chamberlain—raised both his bushy eyebrows in inquiry. "Prospects? As in more than one?"

Semsulin lifted one shoulder in a half-hearted shrug. "Well, it seems unlikely that we will have more than one candidate on the table, but I'm sure Her Majesty is open to suggestion if there is some-one we have missed."

"I am open to suggestion," she confirmed, though she wasn't sure

that was entirely true, "but if that suggestion is anyone other than
Zarsha of Nandel, there must be a corresponding suggestion for
other ways we can induce Sovereign Prince Waldmir to renew our
trade agreements." Her grandfather, King Linolm, had nearly a decade ago convinced Prince Waldmir to accept a trade agreement that
was highly favorable to Rhozinolm, but relations between their two
lands had cooled over time. Waldmir's daughter had married the
Crown Prince of Aaltah, and nothing Rhozinolm had been able to
offer, aside from Ellin's hand for Prince Waldmir's nephew, had
swayed him to renew those agreements on the same favorable terms.

Now that King Delnamal had divorced Prince Waldmir's daughter, it was not impossible that *some* form of agreement could be managed without her marrying Zarsha, but certainly not on favorable
terms. Although Waldmir had signed the previous agreement with
Linolm, and it had all been done in perfect good faith, Waldmir had
come to feel he'd been taken advantage of, and he had brought that
sense of offense to the bargaining table every time.

Ellin had long ago gotten over her violent—and admittedly
unfair—dislike of Zarsha, and the thought of marrying him no longer filled her with dread. He was both a canny adviser and a good—if
distressingly complicated—friend. But though she doubted she
would find any other candidate a more pleasing choice, she did not
much enjoy the feeling she would marry him simply because there
was no better option.

"Are we certain a marriage to Zarsha would prompt Prince Waldmir to renew those agreements?" her trade minister inquired. "The
match is . . . highly unusual, and Prince Waldmir might find his nephew's marriage to a sovereign queen as some form of subjugation."

It was an objection that no one had ever raised before, and Ellin
felt an uncomfortable prickle of anxiety. Zarsha had been more than
willing—*eager*, even—to enter into a marriage with a woman who
would forever outrank him, but he was not a typical Nandelite. In
that backward—but very powerful—principality, women were entirely subservient to the men in their lives, lawful property of their
fathers or husbands. Zarsha could never be accepted as a king in
Rhozinolm, so there was no question of ceding her throne to him on

marriage; but would his uncle be insulted that he was offered the title of prince consort instead?

"Zarsha has never suggested there would be any difficulty," she said, though it was hardly a definitive answer. She had yet to catch Zarsha in a lie, but there was no doubt in her mind that he kept a good many secrets. He had as much as admitted that a part of his purpose for lingering in Rhozinolm had been to act as his uncle's spy.

"I have met Prince Waldmir," Kailindar said, "though only the once. He might feign insult in hopes of improving the terms of any agreement we might make, but my impression is that he is at heart a practical man. He hoped his grandson would one day sit on the throne of Aaltah, but now that King Delnamal has divorced his daughter, he cannot help but be tempted by our offer."

He turned toward Ellin. "As I am already acquainted with Prince Waldmir, and as your closest living relative, I believe I should represent the Crown on your behalf."

She frowned at him. "It was my impression that when arranging a marriage for the king, the king speaks for himself. Am I mistaken?" She hoped the expression on her face conveyed innocence rather than suspicion. Although Kailindar had supported her against Tamzin, he'd done so because he was *against* Tamzin, not because he was *for* her. Under ordinary circumstances, he, as the bastard son of the late king, would be sitting on the throne of Rhozinolm instead of Ellin, and she didn't entirely trust his motives.

Kailindar resisted the urge to point out that she was not a king, though the thought was writ plainly across his face. "That would ordinarily be the case," he confirmed. "However, I am concerned that a man like Prince Waldmir might not enter into negotiations in good faith if you negotiate on your own behalf."

"You mean because I am a woman," she said, having no patience for subtle insinuations.

"Yes," Kailindar answered unrepentantly. "Keep in mind, the man is little more than a barbarian warlord, and the principality of Nandel is hardly a bastion of enlightenment when it comes to their treatment of their women. I mean no disrespect to you when I suggest Waldmir might hope to take advantage of you."

Several members of the council—predictably—nodded their agreement, and Ellin fought down a surge of annoyance. Every time she allowed herself to believe she was finally earning their respect, she would receive some unwelcome reminder that she was still "just a woman."

"I'm sure Her Majesty is more than capable of looking after her own interests," Lord Semsulin said, and Ellin had to suppress the urge to flash him a grateful smile. The urge was quickly quelled when he continued. "However, it might be to our advantage to humor Prince Waldmir's prejudices. The need to renew the agreements is pressing, and though I have absolute faith that he will eventually come to respect our fair queen, we can ill afford the time it would take to establish the necessary environment of mutual respect."

Under the table, Ellin clenched her hand into a fist, nails biting into her palm as she fought not to allow her sense of betrayal to show on her face. She understood Semsulin's point—and she might even have to admit that he was likely correct, for the trade agreements were set to expire within a month—but it stung nonetheless.

Their eyes met briefly, and she could read the apology in his gaze. She knew the battle was already lost, but she swore to never again allow men to negotiate her fate without her consent. She turned to Kailindar.

"Very well, Lord Kailindar," she said. "You may contact Prince Waldmir and begin the negotiations. But you are to enter into no agreements without consulting me first. Is that perfectly clear?"

Kailindar bowed his head. "Of course, Your Majesty."

She searched his face for any hint of deceit or rebellion, but saw nothing. She did not *want* to trust him with negotiations that could so greatly affect the course of her own life, but with even Semsulin warning her against entering into those negotiations on her own behalf, she had little choice.

CHAPTER FOUR

Mairahsol stepped into the abbess's apartment—*her* apartment—and couldn't resist breaking into a delighted grin. For ten years, she'd slept in a dismal dormitory on a sagging cot surrounded by ten or fifteen other women. No privacy or personal space, no comfort, no dignity. Every abigail, no matter the station in life she had enjoyed before entering the Abbey, had the same bed, the same threadbare covers, the same thin pillow, the same oft-mended robes.

The abbess's apartment was a far cry from the luxury of her childhood home, having only two rooms and furnishings that were little better than mismatched castoffs. But it was something that was uniquely *hers*.

"Is there anything else you need, *Mother Mairahsol?*" asked Norah, the abigail who had escorted Mairahsol to her new quarters. The disdain that colored the woman's tone was surprisingly satisfying.

Mairahsol smiled at the older abigail, who'd had every reason to believe *she* would be the new abbess. How the respectful title must burn in the old woman's throat! She and her cadre of self-righteous crones would choke on it every time they were forced to utter the words.

"Now that you mention it, Sister Norah, I think the rooms could use a good scrubbing." She wrinkled her nose. "It smells like old lady in here."

Fury flared in Norah's eyes, and her mouth dropped open in shock at the disrespect of the old abbess's memory. Not so long ago, Mairahsol would have been denied meals—or perhaps even beaten—for daring such an insult. In fact, she *had* been. Ordinarily, she'd managed to keep her opinions to herself, but in moments of weakness she had not been able to resist the desperate need to lash out. The price of her incautious words could be read in the scars on her back.

Now, she could say whatever she wished—within the walls of this abbey, at least—and anyone who didn't like it would have firsthand knowledge of what it felt like to have a leather strap taken to vulnerable bare flesh. She was not a cruel person by nature, but she nevertheless looked forward to her first excuse to exercise her new power. There were so many women in this abbey who had mistreated her, and the satisfaction of returning the favor was positively delicious to contemplate.

The fury in Norah's eyes was quickly overtaken by a shimmer of tears, which she blinked furiously to clear. The older abigails had all worshipped the late abbess, and their grief at her passing was as sincere as it was revolting. Mairah couldn't imagine how *anyone* could have felt affection for the spiteful old hag.

"Have you no sense of decency whatsoever?" Norah asked, her voice hoarse with suppressed grief.

"Careful, Norah," Mairahsol warned, savoring the moment. "I'm the abbess now, and if you don't speak to me with the proper respect, there will be consequences."

Norah stiffened her spine and met Mairahsol's eyes. "Don't pretend you won't find excuses to have me punished even if I grovel at your feet."

Mairah's smile broadened. Over her twenty-nine years of life, she had honed her skill for revenge to an art form, and the prospect of paying Norah and her crones back for all the years they'd scorned and abused her was sweet indeed. The only thing sweeter would be never to have to avenge herself again, but life had taught her there were always more people waiting for a chance to be cruel.

"Don't pretend you haven't earned it."

Norah snorted. "You have always played the part of the innocent victim, haven't you? I've never been able to tell whether you are play-acting or whether you actually believe yourself blameless."

Mairahsol clenched her teeth, hating that this old woman still had the power to hurt her. Docking Norah's meals or having her beaten might eventually take that power away from her, but such things took time. Perhaps Mairahsol could engineer a more permanent solution—as she had for the old abbess. But that, too, would take time, for another sudden and unexpected death in the Abbey so soon might arouse suspicions.

"I believe it is time you embark on a fast, Sister Norah," she said. "Three days, though the duration could be extended if I do not find you appropriately contrite."

Norah showed no sign of surprise or even dismay. But then Norah had never been forced to go hungry for three days, did not appreciate just how severe the hunger pangs would become as she stood at the wall of shame in the dining hall and watched her sisters eat their fill.

"Of all the women in this abbey," Norah said softly, "you are the only one who made a conscious choice to condemn yourself to this life. You are *not* a victim, no matter how much you pretend to be."

"*Five* days."

Mairahsol finally had the pleasure of seeing Norah flinch. It was convenient that the old bitch had given her such an easy excuse to flex her muscles. As the rest of the abigails saw their sister suffer, they would understand that the tables had turned, that Mairahsol was no longer vulnerable to their cruelty and machinations. She would finally, *finally* be treated with respect. She had no idea how to go about reversing the Aaltah woman's Curse, but she had no intention of ever letting go of her new title. One way or another, she would convince the king she was making progress. And she would never sleep in the abigails' dormitory again.

Alys strode down the main street of Women's Well at a pace just short of a run, the men of her honor guard following silently on her heels as if afraid to draw her attention. She imagined her rage was a nearly visible aura around her, and she half expected the townsfolk to run for cover as she stormed past. Her heart pounded against her rib cage, and her damned stays squeezed so tightly she could hardly breathe.

She had never wanted her son to be a soldier, and now she wished she had never allowed herself to be persuaded to let him join the Citadel. She had resisted because she had feared what might happen to Corlin in the regrettably likely event of war. What she had *not* expected was for her son—who had already been through so much and suffered so cruelly at the hands of his uncle—to be beaten by her lord commander, the man she had entrusted with his care.

The town of Women's Well was less than a year old, but it was growing so rapidly that it would soon be large enough to call a city. The abundance of elements produced by their impossible Well lent itself to all sorts of spells that were good for building and growth, making it possible to erect buildings in less than half the time it would take elsewhere. The street down which Alys traveled had not so long ago been a barren track in the dust, but was now a tree-lined avenue busy with traffic, all of which moved quickly to the side as she and her entourage hurried past.

The Citadel of Women's Well was a far cry from the venerable Citadel she had known during her life in Aaltah. Much smaller than its counterparts in older, more established lands, the hastily constructed barracks and training facilities were almost entirely built of wood, for stone was more expensive to acquire in this remote territory. There was no proper wall separating the Citadel from the rest of the town, merely a low fence. Townsfolk sometimes gathered around the fence to watch the soldiers drill, and Alys was painfully aware of the scene she caused as she passed by.

It was in the Citadel's main building that Alys expected to find

Jailom, her lord commander, and her already hurried footsteps sped even more when she burst through the door, ignoring the startled guards who attempted to greet her. The lord commander's office was situated directly across from the main entrance, and Alys was so furious she did not even bother to knock before throwing the door open, a torrent of angry words poised to spill out of her mouth.

The words died on her lips when she stepped into the room and found herself face-to-face not with her lord commander, but with her brother. Tynthanal was leaning against Jailom's desk, arms crossed in a posture that suggested he'd been waiting for someone.

Alys blinked and made a quick assessment of the situation. Jailom was not an idiot. He was fully aware of what Corlin had gone through as a virtual prisoner in Delnamal's brutal care. He also knew that Alys, having already lost one child, was fiercely protective of her son. He had known news of the beating would bring Alys to his doorstep—and he had chosen not to be present when she arrived.

She shook her head and glared at her brother, who had once been Jailom's commanding officer. "I never took Jailom for a coward," she growled as she slammed the door behind herself, leaving her honor guard to wait uncomfortably in the hall. Her hands shook with pent-up rage, and she wanted to howl at the unfairness of being deprived of her target.

Tynthanal stood up straight and uncrossed his arms. She could not read the expression on her brother's usually open face, and somehow that enraged her even more.

"Where is he?" she demanded. And she swore to herself that if Tynthanal told her to calm down, she was either going to scream or resort to physical violence.

"He and I both agreed that this was a conversation best kept among family," Tynthanal said, his voice maddeningly level.

"He doesn't get to make that decision! He chose to have my son beaten, and now it's time for him to face the consequences. This does not concern *you*."

"It doesn't concern me as the lord chancellor, but it *does* concern me as your brother and Corlin's uncle. And also as a lifelong soldier, who received a fair number of beatings himself as a cadet. It is of vital importance to military discipline that all cadets be treated as equals, and Corlin earned his thrashing."

"How dare you!" Alys spat, and to her shame she felt tears welling in her eyes, her chest and throat aching with the effort to hold them back. It was beneath her dignity as the Sovereign Princess of Women's Well to weep like a heartbroken child, and yet she feared that was just what she was about to do.

Tynthanal rubbed his eyes and looked tired. "I'm sorry, Alys, but I saw the other boy, and I can assure you Corlin most definitely deserved to be punished. Unless you want your son to turn into a vicious petty tyrant like our thrice-damned half-brother."

Alys swallowed past the aching lump in her throat, still fighting to keep the tears at bay. She'd been told Corlin had been punished for getting into a fight, but her indignation and her protective instincts had been so instantaneous and overwhelming that she hadn't asked for any details of the incident. Corlin was a sweet boy with a generous dose of courage and a good heart. The thought of him becoming a "vicious petty tyrant" was absurd.

Tynthanal shook his head and sighed. "He's just so angry," he said. "He should not have allowed the other boy to bait him so easily, but that isn't what I find most troubling about the incident. Corlin was still throwing punches when the boy was unconscious. He had to be pulled off by three older cadets."

Alys's mouth dropped open in shock, her anger temporarily forgotten. "I can't imagine Corlin . . ."

She let the words trail off. It was true that she couldn't imagine the Corlin she'd known before Jinnell's death savaging a boy who was unconscious. But the time since Delnamal had ordered an innocent girl's execution had unquestionably changed him. The boy blamed himself in a way that was simultaneously understandable and completely unfair. Jinnell had made the choice to put herself in danger to keep her brother safe, and it was hardly Corlin's fault that she had paid the ultimate price for her courage. How Alys hated that the world expected even young boys to somehow be responsible for protecting the girls and women in their lives.

"Beating him isn't the answer," she said, feeling like she was returning to solid ground. "Delnamal thought it was, and it only made him more stubborn." She shuddered as she remembered the shape Corlin had been in when he'd escaped from the palace and arrived in Women's Well, his body brutalized by multiple beatings inflicted by the sadistic tutor Delnamal had assigned to him.

"I agree," Tynthanal said, to her surprise. "Fear of a beating will not teach him to control his temper. But teaching him that he can beat another boy unconscious with no repercussions is not a viable alternative, and Jailom cannot allow the other cadets to perceive that Corlin is somehow untouchable and not subject to the same discipline as everyone else."

Some part of her recognized that Tynthanal's argument was perfectly rational, but the burning need to protect her remaining child made it impossible to view the situation in a logical manner. All she knew was that her son had been hurt, that she had once again failed to protect him.

"I don't care what he did," she said, tears now slipping down her cheeks despite her best efforts to suppress them. "I will not have my child brutalized."

Tynthanal had been patient up until now, but it seemed he couldn't resist rolling his eyes at the accusation, giving her anger new strength.

"He was not *brutalized*," he said. "He was punished. There is a difference."

Alys's hands were clenched, nails digging into her palms as she sought to regain some semblance of control over herself. "You don't understand!" she accused, her voice coming out strangled as her throat tried to close up. "You don't have children."

Tynthanal flinched at that—a subtle expression that nonetheless hit her as sharply as a slap, shocking some of the anger out of her. She grimaced and closed her eyes, forcing as deep a breath as her stays would allow.

"Forgive me," she said. "I didn't mean that the way it came out."

Tynthanal could not sire children. Perhaps during his long years as a career soldier and affirmed bachelor, he had felt no great loss at the prospect. But as a high-ranking civilian nobleman, his unmarried and childless status was remarked upon in a way it had not been when his home had been a barracks. He could not help but feel the pity of those few who knew why such an eligible bachelor remained unmarried, and the mingled curiosity and censure of those who didn't.

"I know you didn't," Tynthanal said, but she knew her brother well enough to see the shadow of pain that remained in his eyes. "And I *do* understand. I'm here because Jailom and I already had this same argument, before I stopped thinking of Corlin as my nephew and started thinking of him as a cadet. If he's to remain at the Citadel, then he must do so as a cadet, not as a prince. And that means enduring discipline when he has earned it."

Alys shuddered and hugged herself. "I never wanted him to be a cadet," she said, which of course her brother already knew. Corlin was destined to succeed her as the sovereign of Women's Well, and the military would one day serve *him*. He did not need to be a fighter himself, and if she had her way his education would take a very different direction.

"But you let him come to the Citadel because you knew it was best for him," Tynthanal said gently. "If you force him to withdraw, he will resent you for it."

She wasn't sure it was possible for Corlin to resent her any more than he already did.

"If it makes you feel any better," Tynthanal said, "Jailom gave Corlin the choice to withdraw from the Citadel rather than endure the beating. Corlin did not hesitate to pay the price for his bad behavior and promised it would not happen again. I believe he is genuinely sorry for what he did, but it remains to be seen if his desire to remain at the Citadel is stronger than his anger."

The fight went out of her, and Alys sank down into one of the chairs in front of the commander's desk. Closing her eyes, she put a hand to her belly and drew in a deep breath, searching for a calm she wondered if she would ever feel again. How she wished she could turn back the clock and return to the halcyon days before her mother had cast the Curse. Her life had never been simple, but in some ways she'd felt very much more in control of it in the days when she was nothing but a mother and a nobleman's wife. And no pain she had ever faced in her previous life—not even the death of her beloved husband—could compare to the agony of losing her daughter. And yet as the Sovereign Princess of Women's Well—and as Corlin's mother—she hadn't the freedom to wallow in her pain, to withdraw from life until the world somehow became tolerable once more.

"We're all doing the best we can," Tynthanal said softly. "Corlin is young and resilient, and he's surrounded by people who care about him. He may not always appreciate our care or the forms it takes, but we will get him through this. He will never be what he was before." He sighed. "But then neither will any of us."

CHAPTER FIVE

King Delnamal of Aaltah scowled over the report he had requested from his lord commander. The damn thing told him what he'd known all along: Aaltah was not prepared for sustained military action. The late King Aaltyn had slowly let the ranks of his military forces, both on land and at sea, shrink over the years since Aaltah had last been at war, and the defection of an entire company of soldiers under Tynthanal's command had only made the situation worse.

"This is outrageous," Delnamal said with a shake of his head.

Lord Aldnor stood before Delnamal's desk at stiff military attention, but seemed to stiffen even more at Delnamal's harsh tone. Delnamal reminded himself that it was not the lord commander's fault the late king had allowed their military to dwindle to such a degree—although some of the blame for the defection of Tynthanal's men lay on Lord Aldnor's shoulders. Surely it was the lord commander's duty to ensure that his men were more loyal to the Crown than they were to any commanding officer!

"We are near the limit of what the budget will allow, Your Majesty," the lord commander said. "I can afford to recruit perhaps fifty more men to replace those we've lost, but after that we will be at capacity. Unless our budget were to be increased, of course."

Delnamal shoved the report aside irritably. There were few prospects less appealing than trying to pry more money out of his royal council. Already the lord high treasurer was grumbling about the loss of revenue the royal coffers had suffered when Delnamal had ordered the old Abbey razed and sent all the abigails away. He realized now— way too late, of course—that the Abbey had been one of the Crown's most profitable ventures, operating on a very low budget and with impressive revenue. He had instituted a new abbey—the men of Aaltah needed *somewhere* to send their unwanted women—but without the guidance of more senior abigails, their ability to produce the most powerful potions and spells was limited. And because the Curse had made it inadvisable to take a woman who was not willing, the Abbey's most profitable commodity had all but dried up.

"Well, we need more men if we are to subdue the rebels my cursed half-sister leads," he said, fists clenching at the idea that the woman *dared* to style herself a sovereign princess. He refused to call that pathetic encampment in the Wasteland a principality, just as he'd refused to call it by the name others insisted on using. It was a gathering of outlaws and traitors, not the fucking Principality of Women's Well! There were only *seven* Wells in the land of Seven Wells, and the abomination that had sprung up the previous year was merely a pimple on the earth's surface.

"I'm not certain that's the case," Lord Aldnor said.

Delnamal gave his lord commander the kind of glare that would send most men scurrying for cover, but Lord Aldnor was not so easily quelled.

"We might have prevailed when we marched on Women's Well the first time," Lord Aldnor continued, showing no sign of having noticed his king's disapproval, "had we left a sufficient garrison behind to discourage Rhozinolm from attacking."

Delnamal clenched his fists, blood pounding in his temples. The lord commander had advised him not to march on Women's Well with such outrageous numbers, but Delnamal had brushed off the man's concerns in favor of the grand show of force. There was nothing in Lord Aldnor's voice or expression that could be read as *I told you so,* but Delnamal was sure that sentiment existed behind the coolly professional façade. Not that Delnamal had any intention of ceding the point.

"We *might* have prevailed, you say," Delnamal snarled. " 'Might' isn't good enough. We need enough men to be *certain* to prevail."

Lord Aldnor nodded. "Understood. But those men would need to be armed and trained and housed and fed. The council may be persuaded to increase the Citadel's budget, but you don't need me to tell you how strained our treasury already is."

"No, I don't!" Delnamal snapped, for of course the lord high treasurer complained ceaselessly during council meetings. The effort to rebuild after last year's devastating earthquake and flood had drained the treasury, and it would be years—if not decades—before Aaltah's wealth was restored. "And unless you can provide some helpful recommendations, I suggest you take your cloud of doom and leave."

Lord Aldnor took Delnamal's cutting words in stride, his face showing no sign of anger or even annoyance. Delnamal wished he himself could learn to keep his feelings so deeply buried that others couldn't see them, but it was a skill he'd never acquired.

"I would recommend that we look to our allies to provide naval support, should it be needed," Lord Aldnor said. "Khalpar's navy is more than a match for Rhozinolm's. A few of their warships added to our fleet should be enough to discourage Queen Ellinsoltah from attacking while our troops are on the march."

Delnamal grunted a noncommittal answer. By all rights, he ought to be able to count on support from Khalpar. He was King Khalvin's nephew, after all, and the very reason Delnamal's father had married his mother was to forge an alliance between their two kingdoms to save Aaltah when they were losing a war to Rhozinolm. But Delnamal could not bring himself to trust Khalvin the way his father had.

"So what happens when the traitors are defeated?" Delnamal

asked. "Are we to host Khalpar's navy indefinitely? We would *still* need more men to withstand an attack from Rhozinolm."

"It's far from certain that Queen Ellinsoltah would follow through on her threats as long as Aaltah is not an easy target. Especially when she cannot get at us by land without invading the Midlands."

"As if either of our kingdoms has ever let the Midlands serve as an impediment to our wars," Delnamal scoffed.

The lord commander acknowledged the point with a shrug. There had been countless wars between Rhozinolm and Aaltah over the centuries. The Midlands was an independent principality just now, but it had been annexed by its neighboring kingdoms so many times that even its sovereign prince must consider the condition temporary.

"There's also Nandel to think about," Lord Aldnor added. "Rhozinolm's trade agreements with Nandel will expire before our own, and if they are unable to reach a new agreement . . ."

Then they would be so badly hamstrung they could not possibly go to war. If Shelvon of Nandel had only given Delnamal the heir he was due, he could have counted on Nandel's continuing strong support—so much so that he might have convinced Prince Waldmir not to renew his agreements with Rhozinolm at all. But now that Delnamal had divorced Shelvon and married another—and that it seemed possible Waldmir's nephew would become the Prince Consort of Rhozinolm—it was his own trade agreements that were most vulnerable.

"You've given me much to think about, Lord Aldnor," Delnamal said. "I still feel it necessary to build our military, but I will consider all the options."

Lord Aldnor looked relieved, and Delnamal was glad to have finally silenced him. However, the lord commander was much mistaken if he thought he had accomplished some kind of victory over his king. Lord Aldnor's suggestion involved relying on another power to protect and supplement Aaltah's military. If Aaltah was to stand strong in the face of all potential adversaries, it must do so on the basis of its own strength.

The Citadel's ranks would swell, one way or another. And if the

lord high treasurer—or any other member of the royal council—
objected, there were other, more loyal men who would be overjoyed
to accept the office.

Star had just taken Ellin's hair down and was about to begin the
nightly ritual of brushing the kinks out of the long tresses when there
came a knock from behind the tapestry against one wall. Star gave a
huff of exasperation and picked up the brush.

"Don't let him in," the maid advised. "That man needs to learn
that you are not at his beck and call."

Ellin laughed. "You are in danger of becoming prim, dear one."

Star sniffed. "I am *not* prim. I just feel he should treat you with the
respect you deserve and not come knocking on your door at all hours
of the night."

Ellin opened her mouth to argue, then shut it again. Zarsha had
shown himself more than trustworthy, and though it was perhaps
true that he took advantage of the intimacy of shared secrets, she had
no desire to turn him away. All of which Star already knew. She was
merely being protective, as was her wont.

The knock sounded again, polite and patient. Not demanding entrance so much as requesting it.

"Let him in, please," Ellin said.

Muttering softly to herself, Star lifted the edge of the tapestry to
reveal the door hidden beneath. She slid back the bolts, expressing
her continued disapproval by not then opening the door. Zarsha hesitated a beat, then pulled open the door himself. His eyes twinkled
with good humor as he flashed his most charming smile.

"Good evening, Star," he said with a bow of his head that might
be taken as either respectful or mocking.

"You have to stop doing this," she said boldly. It was entirely improper for a servant to speak that way to *any* nobleman, much less a
member of the royal family of Nandel.

"Star!" Ellin scolded, taken aback by her maid's behavior. Star had
always seemed to like Zarsha—even in the days when Ellin herself
had despised him—so this sudden enmity was shocking.

Star was unrepentant. "You have no parents to look after your best interests, so I will have to do it myself," she said to Ellin, then gave Zarsha a narrow-eyed glare. "And if you want what's best for our Ellinsoltah, you won't object to those who love her trying to protect her."

Zarsha dispensed with his usual easygoing smile. There was no hint of annoyance or anger in his expression, which instead looked grave and uncommonly serious—at least for him. "I don't object. She is lucky to have you. But there are many things she and I cannot speak about in public, and it would arouse far too many uncomfortable murmurs if she were seen to grant me too much official access during the day. I am not popping in for the pleasure of your lady's company." The mischievous grin returned, his foreign blue eyes—which Ellin had once thought disturbingly cold—dancing. "Well, not *just* for the pleasure of her company, at least."

Ellin doubted Star was completely mollified, but she subsided with a soft grumble. "You will let me know when you are ready to continue preparing for bed?" Star said, half question, half order.

"Of course," Ellin confirmed, then fell silent as Star slipped out of the room.

"She used to like me," Zarsha said when the door had closed behind her.

"She still does. She just thinks you're being overly familiar. Which you are."

He smirked. "I've *always* been overly familiar. It's part of my charm."

Ellin smiled despite herself. "But you really shouldn't come to my room unexpectedly so often. She was fine with it when we knew you were coming, but . . ."

"If you didn't expect me to make an appearance on the evening of your first day out of mourning, then that is evidence of a certain lack of foresight on your part," he said dryly. He gestured toward the chairs by the fireplace. "May I sit?"

It was a peace offering of sorts, for he rarely observed the formalities when they were alone in her room at night. "Yes, let's sit," she agreed, realizing he was right. She should have expected him. She had wanted a little time to think and process the discussion of her royal council before speaking to Zarsha, but of course he had known the topic of their marriage would be broached today and was eager to learn how it had gone.

They each took a seat before the warm glow of the fire, and Ellin regarded her would-be bridegroom with assessing eyes. He had never suggested Waldmir might find it offensive for his nephew to take the title of prince consort to a sovereign queen, and Ellin couldn't help wondering why that was so. Did he simply not think it was a problem, or had it been a willful omission in an attempt to present marriage as a reasonable and trouble-free solution to the problem of the trade agreements?

She was firmly convinced that Zarsha was a good man, and he had made an outrageous number of accommodations for her over the course of their on-again, off-again courtship. And yet she was always painfully aware of his hidden layers, of his not-always-clear motivations. He did such a good job of presenting himself as open and honest that she sometimes almost forgot he had a spy's skill for subterfuge.

She could approach her questions subtly and diplomatically, but so far she had found that with Zarsha, the best strategy was usually directness, lest he manage to steer the conversation in the direction he desired.

"My trade minister brought up a potential obstacle to a marriage agreement that I had not previously considered," she said.

Zarsha raised his eyebrows and looked genuinely interested, no hint of shifty-eyed guilt on his face. Not that she would expect him to give anything away so easily.

"What might that be?" he inquired, and she told him.

To her astonishment, Zarsha laughed.

"Why is that amusing?"

He shook his head. "Because it involves some misapprehension of a close, personal bond between myself and my uncle that would cause him to be insulted on my behalf."

"You have made it quite clear you and your uncle are not overly fond of each other," she pointed out.

"That is, perhaps, understating the situation. I believe it would actually give him a great deal of pleasure to think of me as some kind of kept man, groveling at the feet of my wife."

"Why?" she asked, not for the first time. She had received from him only vague and unsatisfactory responses, but now that the possibility of marriage seemed more immediate, it behooved her to press. She would marry Zarsha for the good of her kingdom, but if she was going to allow this man into her bed—and maybe even into her heart, though she wasn't sure if she could ever lower her guard enough to allow such a thing again—she needed to know more about him than he had so far been willing to reveal.

"I've told you why."

"You've told me he doesn't like you because you're nosy. That is hardly a detailed explanation, nor does it explain the level of enmity you're describing now. What is there between you?"

Zarsha was rarely one to squirm, but he did so now, averting his gaze. "I know things about him that he would rather I did not. Things that he fears I might one day use against him."

"Blackmail, you mean?"

He nodded. "He is a cruel and ruthless man, my uncle. If I had not . . . taken measures to protect myself, I would have found myself in a secret grave by now. He hates me for what I know, for the fact that it gives me a certain level of power over him. However, I am still his nephew, still a representative of the royal family of Nandel. He can hate me all he wants, but he cannot disown me. He might see my marriage to a woman who outranks me as some kind of insult to my manhood, but he could easily separate the insult to *me* from any insult to Nandel. I can guarantee that he won't make an agreement easy, but any pretense he makes at feeling insulted is just that: a pretense."

Ellin was struck by the suspicion that there was something Zarsha was leaving out of the explanation. Something other than the very obviously omitted details. She couldn't put a finger on what made her feel that way, for his demeanor seemed unremarkable, despite a degree of visible discomfort.

"What is it you know about Prince Waldmir that he is so anxious to keep hidden?" she asked, though surely if he had intended to tell her he would have done so already.

She was not surprised to see Zarsha's shields go up, his expression becoming guarded.

"It is not a secret I am free to share. I am not loyal to my uncle personally, but I am loyal to the office of the sovereign prince, if that makes any sense."

"What good is blackmail material if you aren't willing to share it?" she pressed.

"I said Waldmir *fears* I might use the information against him, not that I *would*. He is not a man inclined to trust anyone, not even family." He frowned. "Maybe even *especially* family."

She shook her head and leaned back in her chair, still convinced she was being lied to. Or at least being provided an incomplete accounting of the situation. "Are you saying that giving this information to me would be giving me something I could use against your uncle?"

He groaned and squirmed a bit in his chair. "The subject is ridiculously difficult to talk about without specifics, yet I cannot give you those specifics. I understand why you want them, and I understand it is not for idle curiosity, but my life—and the lives of other people I care about—depends on my continued silence."

Ellin chewed her lip as she digested the cryptic response. For all the conversations she'd had with Zarsha, she couldn't remember him ever before making reference to caring about anyone in Nandel. She hadn't realized how odd that was until this moment. Just how many secrets was he hiding, anyway?

"Who are these people you care about who might be endangered if you break faith?"

Zarsha rubbed his eyes—an unusually vulnerable gesture for a man who so prided himself on his self-possession. "Let it go, Ellin. Maybe when we are bound by the vows of marriage, I will feel free to tell you more, but I can't even guarantee that."

"But—"

"I know *many* uncomfortable secrets about *many* people. Yourself, for example."

Ellin flinched at the unwelcome reminder. It was possible that with Tamzin dead, a revelation of her lack of chastity might do little material damage to her reign, but it would certainly undermine her moral authority.

Zarsha leaned forward and put his hand over hers, but she pulled away from the intimate gesture.

"You can trust me with your secret," he said earnestly. "Just as my uncle can trust me, whether he is willing to do so or not. I know my silence has made you doubt me, but it is the very reason why you should not."

She met his gaze, trying for all she was worth to see behind his façade. "There is more to this story than you are telling me," she accused. "It is not just a case of omitted details."

"Be that as it may, I have said all I am willing to on the matter. When I am your husband, my first loyalty will be only to you, and that may free me to tell you more. But for now I am naught but a representative of a foreign court, not bound to you by anything save what I hope is mutual affection."

Ellin had no choice but to accept his refusal, though she had to admit it stung in a way that might not be strictly logical. His friendship had meant so much to her over the difficult last year that she had perhaps presumed a level of intimacy that did not exist. It was an important reminder of why he had always been a most complicated friend.

CHAPTER SIX

The worst thing about having Mairahsol as the new abbess, Norah thought as her stomach rumbled with hunger, was no longer being able to meet in the abbess's apartment. She was careful to tread lightly as she made her way through the darkened halls of the Abbey toward the kitchen, which would be empty at this hour of the night. She had no fear that the door would be locked against her—the new abbess had more than enough ways to enforce her punishment without physically blocking Norah from the food—but the meeting would feel far more furtive and dangerous in a room that was meant to be public. Grief for Mother Wyebryn squeezed her heart, and she wondered how they would function now that they no longer had the leadership—and protection—of the abbess.

Norah entered the kitchen to find a dozen of her sisters gathered round a single lit candle in the far corner. She had no doubt that they would all be punished if Mairahsol were to discover them gathering like this, but it was a risk they would all have to take if they were to continue honoring the Mother of All as they had each been called to do.

She closed the kitchen door and hurried to join her sisters, who were whispering anxiously amongst themselves and welcomed her into their circle with hugs and words of support. Sister Ide offered her a crust of bread that she had secreted within the folds of her robe, but Norah refused with a shake of her head—and a growl of her belly.

"If Mairahsol has any reason to believe I have cheated, she will not hesitate to force a purgative on me," she said with a grimace. Considering Mairahsol's spiteful love of revenge—even against the most minor of perceived offenses—it was possible Norah would be forced to drink purgatives anyway, but she would avoid the additional misery if she could.

Sister Ide gave her hand a squeeze of sympathy. "It is an offense to the Mother that *that woman* has been named abbess," Ide hissed, and the other women all mumbled their assent. There was no woman in the Abbey more roundly disliked than Mairahsol, and to have her suddenly vaulted to the most honorable position of abbess was intolerable.

"She cannot last," Norah said with a shake of her head. "She might have convinced that lover of hers that she can reverse the Mother's correction, but he and the royal council will soon learn that her own assessment of her power is greatly exaggerated."

There was no denying that Mairahsol could see a great number of elements, but her claims of power were hard to verify. Just because she *said* she could see elements no other women in the Abbey could see didn't mean it was true. And though Mairahsol clearly had a seer's talent—as evidenced by the ridiculous vision she'd reported and no one had believed—she had not a seer's courage. She would not have drunk even that first mild poison had Mother Wyebryn not forced it on her, and she'd certainly shown no inclination to subject herself to the experience a second time.

The woman was a fraud, and when the lord high priest learned that he had been duped, she would trade the abbess's apartment for a dismal cell in the dungeons. If her head remained attached to her body, that is.

"Don't underestimate her," Ide cautioned. "She has already shown that she is willing to do *anything* to hurt those she feels have wronged her. And I'm sure every woman here falls into that category."

More nods and worried murmurs.

"We are taking a grave risk even meeting like this," Ide continued. "If she should find out there's a group of Mother of All worshippers in the Abbey . . ."

Norah could not deny that it was a concern. The membership in their sect—she refused to think of it as a cult, no matter what the priests might call it—had swelled since the casting of what so many referred to as the Curse. It seemed the plainest sign imaginable that the Mother of All was unhappy with the ways in which Her children had chosen to live their lives. Mother Brynna, her daughter, and her granddaughter had clearly been guided by a divine hand, for their ability to cast a spell that would affect the Wellspring itself was well-nigh unthinkable. And what hand would guide them to free women from the betrayal of their own bodies except that of the Mother of All?

"We took risks even when we met in Mother Wyebryn's apartments," Norah said, hoping she did not look as worried as she felt. It was something of an open secret that the Mother of All was worshipped throughout the kingdom of Khalpar, but the practice was officially outlawed. Some kings of Khalpar had been happy to ignore it and pretend it didn't exist, but King Khalvin was not one of them. Worshipping the Mother of All was especially risky for women of the Abbey, who had been disowned by their families and therefore had no protection should the authorities decide to crack down on the "heresy."

King Khalvin could well decide to reassert the authority and superiority of men by executing women who dared claim that the Mother had given birth to the Creator and was thus both His predecessor and superior. It wouldn't be the first time a king of Khalpar had ordered a purge.

Ide's unattractively thick eyebrows drew together in a severe frown. "That was hardly the same and you know it. There's a reason there are only a dozen of us here tonight."

Norah couldn't blame her sisters for being afraid. When Mother Wyebryn had passed, everyone assumed Norah would be appointed abbess and they could continue to meet and worship under the abbess's protection. In some ways, being virtual prisoners of the Abbey worked to their advantage, for there was no chance of their meetings being witnessed by a priest or some overly pious servant with a big mouth.

"If you're looking for guarantees of safety," Norah snapped, "I can't give you any. We are both Unwanted and outlaws, and there is no safety to be had for any of us. If some of our sisters are too timid to worship the Mother of All without the illusory protection of the abbess's apartments, then they are cowards and were never true believers to begin with."

Many of the abigails flinched from her anger, and Norah closed her eyes to calm herself. She couldn't help feeling she had failed her sisters when she had not been appointed abbess as expected. It was her duty as Mother Wyebryn's chosen successor to protect her sisters, and yet with Mairahsol as abbess, she couldn't even protect *herself*. The injustice of it all made her want to lash out.

"Forgive me, sisters," she said. "I have no cause to take out my anger on you."

"What shall we do, Mother Norah?" Sister Melred, the youngest and most timid of the gathered abigails, asked in a tremulous voice.

Norah let out her breath on a long sigh, feeling calm return as she released the anger and fear that had built in her chest. Whether she was abbess in the eyes of the law or not, she was abbess within this worship circle. That meant it was her duty to lead, which required her to demonstrate confidence even when she didn't feel it.

"First," she said with a gentle smile that she hoped would take any sting out of her words, "you should refrain from calling me Mother Norah even in private. Make a habit of it and you might let it slip at some inopportune moment."

The abigail blushed and bowed her head. "My apologies."

"None are necessary," Norah assured her, then turned her attention to the full gathering. "We are needed now more than ever. The

lord high priest has maneuvered Mairahsol into the position of abbess because he believes that the two of them working together can
undo Mother Brynna's spell."

"Surely that's impossible," Ide said, but there was an unmistakable
tone of questioning in her voice. She *wanted* to believe it was impossible, but she was not sure.

"We all read Mother Brynna's letter," Norah said.

The late Abbess of Aaltah had sent fliers to all the kingdoms and
all the principalities explaining just what her spell had done—and
explaining that the spell had been generations in the making and that
the only three women who knew how they'd done it had died in the
casting. Mother Brynna—who by all accounts had been a gifted seer
as well as an extraordinary magic user—had stated unequivocally that
the spell could not be undone. Norah saw no reason to disbelieve the
claim, no matter how desperately the men of Seven Wells wished
otherwise.

"Even if the spell *could* be reversed," she continued, "I hardly
think *Mairahsol* could manage it. She is not half so clever and powerful as she believes. However, I do worry that she has just enough
power that any attempts she makes to undo the spell could have serious consequences. We cannot stop her from trying. But we can certainly impede her progress, and I believe it is our duty to the Mother
of All to do whatever it takes to keep her from succeeding."

"She has been named abbess for a probationary period," Ide
mused. "If she does not succeed, she may be removed from the position."

More than one face lit with a touch of glee that Norah might almost term malicious. There was not a woman in their circle who had
not on occasion been unkind to Mairahsol, but the girl had brought
it on herself. She was a vicious, scheming pretender, and there was
only so long she could hide her true nature from her lover and the
king.

"I don't want anyone to take untoward risks," Norah said. "But
perhaps we can arrange for Lord Jalzarnin to overhear a few damning
snippets of conversation when he visits the Abbey."

Sister Ide smiled. "You mean the kind of conversations that might plant a doubt in his mind as to the authenticity of her claims of power?"

Norah smiled back. "Just so. And if we do all we can to ensure that she shows no signs of anything resembling progress, those hints may take root and grow. With any luck, we may succeed in discrediting her long before her six months are up."

Norah couldn't honestly say she believed it would be that easy. For all that she hated Mairahsol, she had to admit that the woman had a kind of animal cunning that made her supremely dangerous. But even the most dangerous of animals could be killed by a skilled and determined hunter.

Gracelin's heart fluttered with nerves as she reached the end of the only real road in the town of Miller's Bridge and saw the guard post that sat on the banks of the river, blocking the bridge that led out of the town—and out of Aaltah. Sensing her nerves, the donkey planted its feet in the middle of the road and tried to pull the rope from Gracelin's hands.

"What's wrong, Mama?" little Forest called from the back of the cart. He'd stubbornly insisted he could walk even when her eyes plainly showed her he was exhausted. She'd then assigned him the "important" task of making sure none of the small flat of seedlings fell over as the donkey cart jolted over the rutted road. He was only five, but the sharp look in his eyes told her he'd seen right through her even as he'd obediently climbed into the cart.

Gracelin forced a smile she did not feel. "Nothing," she said, then clucked her tongue and gave the gentlest of pulls on the donkey's lead. The animal was more easily convinced than her son, plodding forward and taking them both closer to the terrifying unknown. She took a deep breath to steady her nerves, reminding herself how little there was left for her here in Aaltah. It would be hard enough for a woman her age to find a job to support herself when she had no marketable skills, but even if she *did* find work, there was no one to care for Forest. She cursed her husband for dying so young without having made any provisions for her future or the future of their son.

About two days from the border, Gracelin and Forest had fallen in with a small caravan of travelers who were heading toward the promise of Women's Well, and she couldn't help fearing the lot of them would be turned away. Not one among them needed more than a single donkey cart to carry all their worldly possessions—most didn't even have that much—and all were dressed in much-mended clothes that were only sometimes clean. Nearly all the adults were women, widowed or unmarried or cast off by their husbands, and there was a palpable aura of desperation that clung to each and every one of them. Even the people of Miller's Bridge—hardly a wealthy or noble community—looked upon their ragtag caravan with mingled expressions of distaste, disgust, and pity. Why should Women's Well accept them?

But they had all heard the rumors: Women's Well had huge, empty expanses of fertile land that needed tending, and Sovereign Princess Alysoon was open to accepting common folk—even women without husbands—into her fledgling principality. Only the most desperate would risk leaving the security of Aaltah for a principality that was so small and vulnerable and likely to be torn by war. But Gracelin had to admit she was indeed desperate.

Gracelin and her donkey cart were near the front of the caravan as they approached the bridge that led out of Aaltah. A bridge that was newly outfitted with a guardhouse, about which the members of the caravan had also heard rumors. Those who sought to leave Aaltah for Women's Well were considered the dregs of society, and as far as the Crown was concerned, it was of no consequence if they suffered and died in their poverty. And yet with the possessiveness of a dog that refuses to give up its well-gnawed bone, the Crown also objected to its poor abandoning it.

A large man in a stained and ill-fitting uniform stepped from the guardhouse to block the way, scowling fiercely at the caravan. Gracelin quailed inside, feeling small and vulnerable and strangely guilty. She had to remind herself that she was not doing anything illegal as she stiffened her spine and came to a stop in the dusty road. Behind her, the rest of the caravan fell silent, and Gracelin realized she was no longer just *near* the front.

The guardsman sauntered up to her as several of his fellows left the guardhouse and took up positions blocking the bridge.

"What have we here?" the guardsman asked, peering into the cart, which held everything she owned. There was one small sack that held all her clothing and Forest's, and one small trunk that held her housewares and the few toys her husband had made for Forest. Aside from that, there was a rickety table, a pair of wooden chairs, a rolled-up, threadbare rug, and the flat of Aalwood seedlings.

Forest, usually a friendly, gregarious child, shied away from the large, scowling guardsman. Gracelin had often found her son an excellent judge of character. She gripped the donkey's lead more tightly, glancing nervously over her shoulder. The other members of the caravan had formed a somewhat less than orderly line behind her and were watching with interest and trepidation.

"Where are you headed?" the guardsman asked inanely.

It hardly seemed likely that the question was genuine—the road only led to one place—but she answered anyway, keeping her gaze demurely lowered while trying not to look *too* timid and deferential. "We're going to Women's Well."

"That so?" he inquired, then spat. He pointed at the flat of seedlings. "With contraband, no less."

Gracelin's heart jumped, and it was all she could do not to gasp in indignation. Her voice came out tighter than she would have liked, for she hated to let the guardsman see any hint of vulnerability. "My late husband worked in an Aalwood grove. The landowner sent that flat of seedlings as a condolence when he heard of my husband's death." In truth, the seedlings and a bag of seeds had been sent as "payment" in lieu of her husband's last wages. While the seeds and seedlings were technically valuable, they were of little use to Gracelin, as their value wouldn't be realized until the trees matured. Even if Gracelin had owned land on which she could plant them, they would bring in no money for at least fifteen years—by which time she and her son would have starved to death. She had worked the Aalwood groves herself as a girl and a young woman, but no one would hire her now that she had a small child in tow.

The guardsman glared at her with obvious suspicion, though she suspected it was all an act, meant to unnerve her. Unfortunately, it was working.

"I kept the landowner's letter of condolence, if you'd like to see it," she volunteered.

He hawked and spat again, then gestured at the trunk in the back of the wagon. Forest, who was sitting on the trunk with his thumb in his mouth, flinched at the gesture. To her surprise, the guardsman gentled his voice.

"I need you to open that trunk and show me what's inside," he told her, then looked at Forest. "Why don't you get down from there and stretch your legs, little man?"

Gracelin thanked the Mother that the guardsman apparently had a soft spot for children. And that she herself was not especially young or pleasing to look at. She imagined this brute and his fellows would behave even more churlishly with a woman they found tempting. She could only hope that their little caravan was of sufficient size to protect the handful of younger, prettier women in their midst.

"Come here, Forest," she beckoned when it seemed the boy might not obey. Still sucking his thumb, Forest exited the cart and hurried to her side, grabbing a handful of her skirts. She laid a hand on his head, hoping to soothe his nerves despite her own turmoil as the guardsman rummaged through the trunk and her sacks. Looking for valuable "contraband" he could appropriate for himself, she supposed, though he was sorely disappointed in what he found.

Leaving their belongings in disarray, strewn in the bottom of the cart, the guardsman seized the flat of seedlings and heaved them out. "These won't do you any good outside of Aaltah," he told her. "Might as well leave them behind."

She gritted her teeth against a protest. It was true that Aalwood trees refused to grow outside of Aaltah. The seedlings would likely wither and die within days of leaving their native land, and the seeds in the pouch she kept tucked in the pocket of her traveling dress would not sprout. But they were *hers* nonetheless.

The guardsman gave her a challenging stare. "The king has decreed that anyone who leaves Aaltah for Women's Well is no longer a citizen of Aaltah and may not return, on pain of death. I would advise you to take your seedlings, turn this wagon around, and go home."

Gracelin's jaw dropped. Always when she'd thought of leaving, she'd comforted herself with the idea that if she could not find a place for herself in Women's Well, she could return to Aaltah and be no worse off. Never had she imagined her decision to be an irreversible one.

"Shall I put the seedlings back?" the guardsman inquired impatiently, eying the line of people behind her. He looked at his fellows who were blocking the road, jerking his chin to indicate they should let her pass.

Gracelin bit her lip, but the moment of indecision lasted less than a second. If she stayed in Aaltah, she didn't know how she would put a roof over her head and food on the table. At least in Women's Well, she might have a *chance* at a better life for herself and her son.

And if Women's Well refused to grant them entry? What then, if Aaltah would not permit them to return?

With a minute shake of her head, she took Forest's hand and started forward. All she could do was throw herself on the mercy of Sovereign Princess Alysoon. There might not be Aalwood groves to tend, but she could hope that a principality that valued women as Women's Well was rumored to would find some use for her.

The guardsman grunted in satisfaction as he set the flat of seedlings aside—Gracelin figured he was in for a rude surprise when he tried to sell them and found out how little they were worth at this point in their life cycle. And she felt a certain dangerous thrill of satisfaction knowing he had not bothered to search her person and therefore had not confiscated the pouch of seeds.

There was no reason to believe those seeds might grow in Women's Well. None.

Except that so many things that seemed impossible turned out to be possible after all in that land of women's magic. So despite Gracelin's best efforts to keep her hopes from growing to unrealistic proportions, she found her heart soaring as she crossed the bridge into her unknown future.

CHAPTER SEVEN

The kings of Rhozinolm had a long tradition of setting aside a little time each week to hear petitions from commoners. Ellin's grandfather had held these audiences in the grand receiving room, where he sat upon his throne on a raised dais. The room was filled with eager would-be petitioners and eagle-eyed palace guards, and those who wished to speak with the king had to be willing to share their business with everyone in the room.

Ellin knew for a fact that her grandfather's method of hearing petitions was specifically designed to make him seem accessible while discouraging any but the boldest of commoners from making demands on his time, so she had moved the audiences to a small and informal parlor. Petitioners were asked to wait in a comfortable reception area until it was their turn to meet with her, and while she couldn't grant them absolute privacy for security reasons, there were only two guards inside the room. She was certain she did not see as many petitioners as her grandfather had, for the intimacy of the audiences invited longer conversation, but those who came to her showed every sign of appreciating her attention and discretion.

The audiences were unquestionably wearing—no one asked to see the queen without bringing a story of woe that tugged at her heartstrings and made her wish she could right the injustices of the world with a snap of her fingers—but Ellin never once considered curtailing them, and she heard as many petitions as she possibly could each time.

Her day's audience was nearing its end, for which she felt guiltily glad, when a young woman in a tattered brown cloak was shown into the parlor. Ellin smiled in a way she often found soothed the nerves of those who were in awe of her, meeting the young woman's eyes with warmth that belied her weariness.

Ellin blinked and frowned as the guardsman who had shown the woman in retreated, for she looked vaguely familiar—and younger than Ellin had taken her to be on first glance. A girl, rather than a grown woman.

The girl delivered a deep and graceful curtsy, the movement practiced and easy. "Forgive me, Your Majesty," she said, and even her voice seemed distantly familiar. "I'm afraid I'm here under false pretenses."

One of the guards took a hasty step in the girl's direction, but Ellin sensed no threat from her, so she waved him off. He continued to hover instead of retreating to his post, but he did not lay hands on the girl.

"I feel as if we have met before," Ellin said, trying and failing to place that face and that voice.

"We have," the girl confirmed. "Three years ago at my sister's coming out ball."

Commoners did not have coming out balls, and when Ellin stopped thinking of the girl as a commoner, her face and voice finally came into clear focus. "Norbryn!" she exclaimed suddenly, sitting back in her chair.

The girl had made quite the impression at the time, for at thirteen years old, she was far too young to attend a ball. Which hadn't stopped her from making a brief appearance, much to her parents' consternation. Ellin remembered her mother muttering darkly that Norbryn was bound to end up in the Abbey someday. And yet it was her prim and proper sister, Leebryn, who had been condemned to the Abbey earlier this very year for failing to give her husband a child. Ellin shook her head, for it seemed Norbryn had not taken her sister's example to heart.

"Does your father know you're here?" Ellin asked, already knowing the answer.

Norbryn raised her chin defiantly. "No. He would not allow me to bring my petition to you the proper way, so I had to get creative."

The guard gave Ellin an inquiring look, silently offering to remove the girl, but Ellin shook her head ever so slightly. He took a step back and assumed an expression of stoic indifference.

Ellin gestured Norbryn into a chair. "I don't imagine your father will be best pleased to discover your creativity," she murmured, and Norbryn winced delicately.

"No, he will not," the girl confirmed. "But it is worth enduring whatever punishment he gives me if I can help Leebryn." She blinked rapidly, but Ellin saw the sheen of tears in her eyes anyway.

"I cannot intervene," Ellin said regretfully. "Someday, I hope that I will be able to change the laws that allow a husband to send his wife to the Abbey against her will, but that day is not yet come."

Honestly, Ellin dreamed of a day when she could abolish the Abbey altogether, as Alys had in Women's Well. But with her fledgling principality and her devoted citizens, Alys had luxuries that Ellin did not. Ellin had convinced her royal council to outlaw the practice of forcing women of the Abbey into prostitution, but she knew she had only succeeded because the fear of women's Kai made the prospect of rape unappealing. Abolishing the Abbey altogether was not possible in the current climate and with her shaky grip on her throne.

Norbryn dabbed at the corner of her eye, nodding. "I understand that you cannot order the Abbey to release Leebryn or order her husband to take her back. But because of the changes you have already made to our laws, I am hoping you will not condone my sister being forced to sell her body at the pavilion."

Ellin frowned in puzzlement. She could imagine no other law Norbryn might be referencing save the outlawing of forced prostitution. "I don't understand. No one at the Abbey is being forced to work the pavilion anymore." She was aware that the pavilion still operated, though the treasurer frequently grumbled at the reduction of its income, but the women who worked it did so by choice. They weren't exactly *paid* for their efforts, but those who worked the pavilion were given additional creature comforts. The situation was far from ideal, but it seemed to Ellin a decent first step.

Fire flashed in Norbryn's eyes. "Tell that to my sister!" she snarled, then gasped and covered her mouth with her hand. "Oh! Please forgive me!" Her eyes watered, and her breaths came tight and shallow as she tried to control her anguish.

Ellin, at first taken aback by the response, felt a tug of pity. She did not know exactly what was behind Norbryn's pain and anger, but there was no doubt in her mind that it was genuine and heartfelt. "There's nothing to forgive," she assured the girl. "Now tell me what is the matter. I take it you have been in contact with Leebryn?"

Society expected women who were condemned to the Abbey to be entirely cut off from their friends and family, and such was often the case. But Ellin was hardly surprised to find that Norbryn had not disowned her sister as she was meant to.

Norbryn nodded. "Our father has forbidden me to contact her, but . . ." She sighed heavily. "She's my sister still. And I love her."

"I understand." No one especially close to Ellin had ever been sent to the Abbey, but she imagined she herself would be unwilling to cut ties in a similar situation.

"When Leebryn first entered the Abbey, the abbess assured her she did not have to work the pavilion," Norbryn said. "But she could earn 'privileges' if she agreed to it."

"Yes," Ellin said. "That is the compromise my royal council devised."

Norbryn's chin jutted out. "Do you know what is considered a privilege in the Abbey?" The fire was back in her eyes, and this time she made no apology.

Ellin's heart sank as she realized she had not fully thought through her elegant solution to the problem of the Abbey. Nor had she followed up to see how that solution was being implemented. "Tell me," she prompted, bracing herself.

"Any food other than just enough gruel to keep you from wasting away. A cot. A blanket. A full night's sleep. A rest break. A day off from work when you're ill."

Ellin could only gape in horror.

"Leebryn says the abbess and the trade minister kept taking 'privileges' away one by one, testing to see at what point the denial of those privileges would generate Kai in women who submitted. It seems that as long as the deprivation doesn't lead to physical harm, there is no Kai generated, however reluctant the abigail might be."

Tears rolled down Norbryn's cheeks unchecked, but she held her head up proudly. "Leebryn refuses to submit, and . . ." Norbryn hiccuped. "She's suffering. *Please*, Your Majesty. Help her."

Ellin took a long deep breath in hopes of keeping her temper in check. She wanted to show Norbryn only compassion and save her fury for those who deserved it, but no calming breaths could tame the fire that coursed through her veins.

"You have my word that none of this is happening with my consent or prior knowledge," she said through gritted teeth. It sounded disturbingly like an excuse, and yet she could not for a moment allow Norbryn to believe her sister was suffering on Ellin's orders. "I *should* have known," she continued, shaking her head at her own naïveté. The trade minister had been one of the most vocal opponents on her royal council to the decision to outlaw forcible prostitution in the Abbey, egged on by the lord high treasurer who'd despaired at the loss of profits involved. She had trusted that her orders—which the council had agreed to—would be carried out as she intended, and that had been a foolish mistake.

"I will relieve both the trade minister and the abbess of their posts," she vowed, even while a part of her murmured that such a decision would not go over well with her council. Even Semsulin would probably suggest a reprimand would suffice, for the trade minister had not overtly broken any laws even while he violated their spirit.

Norbryn's eyes widened and her mouth fell open. "Y-you would do that? You would choose your Unwanted Women over a member of your royal council? I had only hoped that you would speak with him and tell him to change the policy."

For a brief moment, Ellin wondered if perhaps that was the wisest course of action. Norbryn would clearly be satisfied as long as her sister was not made to suffer or submit, and a stern talking-to would sit much more easily with the rest of her council.

But how would she ever be able to trust him again? It was no accident that Ellin hadn't known how he'd chosen to implement the new law. He'd been well aware that she would not approve and had done it anyway. She had a strong suspicion the lord high treasurer was also involved—the man had, after all, been willing to stand with Tamzin when her cousin had attempted to seize the throne. But she had no proof, and dismissing the trade minister would cause enough of a sensation already.

"What he and the abbess did was despicable," Ellin said. "I will not stand for it."

Norbryn sniffled and swiped at her eyes. "I don't know how to thank you . . ."

Ellin sighed. "It is I who must thank you for bringing this perfidy to my attention."

Ellin did not look forward to what was certain to be an ugly scene when she brought her decision to the council. But council members served at the will of the sovereign, and it was within her rights to dismiss any one of them for any reason. A fact of which she would remind anyone who objected too vociferously.

The woman Lord Jailom had escorted into Alys's office was clearly a commoner. Her clothes were faded from sunlight and washing, patched in several places, and the hands she held clasped nervously in front of her were calloused, the nails short and ragged. In many ways, she was typical of the steady trickle of immigrants who arrived in Women's Well nearly every day. Alys had set up a citizenship committee to meet with and evaluate new arrivals with strict instructions that

they turn back only those they believed were a danger to the popula-
tion of Women's Well. At least once a week the committee chairman
urged her to raise her standards, for practically every new arrival was
an impoverished commoner who brought nothing in the way of
riches or special skills. People who in their native lands would likely
be beggars—or worse.

Alys's curiosity was piqued by Jailom's decision to single out this
unexceptional-looking woman for an audience with the sovereign
princess. Jailom rose from his bow, and she did not like the worry she
saw in his eyes. There were far too many worries in her life these days.

"Gracelin here just arrived from Aaltah today," Jailom said. "I
wanted you to hear firsthand what she experienced upon leaving Aaltah."

Alys blinked in surprise at the woman's name, for it was an unusual
combination of common and noble. Jailom—no doubt having had
the same reaction to the name—explained without prompting.

"Her mother was a noblewoman who left her family to marry a
commoner."

"Ah," Alys said, nodding. It was not an especially unusual story,
though of course it was a terrible stain on the honor of the noble
family. And it *was* unusual for the child of such a union to be given
an elemental name, even in combination with a common name such
as Grace.

Alys turned her attention to Gracelin, who curtsied again, her eyes
slightly too wide. Alys smiled at her in hopes of calming her nerves.

"Welcome to Women's Well, Gracelin," she said, putting as much
warmth as she could into her voice despite the unease that Jailom's
ill-concealed concern inspired.

"Thank you, ma'am. Er, Your Royal Highness."

Alys had never thought of herself as particularly intimidating,
though she supposed she looked rather severe in her black mourning
attire. She tried to will the nervous commoner to relax, keeping her
smile firmly in place.

"Tell her what happened," Jailom coaxed gently.

"I came here today with a small group of travelers," Gracelin said.
"There was a guardhouse set up in Miller's Bridge, and they stopped

all of us. They went through all our belongings—such as they were—and confiscated what they called 'contraband.' My late husband worked in an Aalwood grove, and I brought a flat of seedlings I'd been given in lieu of my husband's last wages."

Alys grimaced ever so slightly at the cruelty of giving an impoverished woman a bunch of seedlings instead of the money she was due. She wondered if the cruelty had been willful, or just thoughtless—though it mattered little to Gracelin.

"The guardsmen confiscated the seedlings," Gracelin continued, "and they told me that if I crossed the border, I would not be allowed to return to Aaltah on pain of death."

An audible gasp escaped Alys's lips, and she finally understood the disquiet she saw in Jailom's eyes. Only in times of war did Aaltah forbid its citizens from traveling to another kingdom or principality. And even then, citizens might be turned back at a roadblock, but not threatened with death!

Gracelin stood up a little straighter, her chin lifting with a hint of defiance. "Very few of us turned back. I can't speak for the others, but I myself am more than willing to work for my living, and I will do whatever work is necessary." Some of her confidence leaked away. "If you have work that will still allow me to care for my son."

"We are happy to have you," Alys assured her. There was a great deal of land that needed to be worked, and the bounty of that land meant that even with the influx of people, it was not hard to keep everyone fed. "It's a shame about the seedlings. It would have been nice to see if they could grow here, but I suppose it isn't likely." Aalwood trees—prized not just for their strong, dark wood, but for the Aal that occurred naturally in them—grew only in Aaltah, though Alys imagined every other kingdom and principality had made heroic efforts to encourage it to grow elsewhere. Aalwood was Aaltah's top export, a pillar of their economy, for Aal was required for spells associated with movement.

Gracelin grinned, the expression brightening her eyes. She patted at the patched skirt of her traveling dress, then stuck her hand in a pocket and pulled out a tied handkerchief. "Well now," she said, laying the handkerchief on Alys's desk and tugging its corners open, "they took the seedlings, but they didn't search my person, and I saw no reason to inform them that I had also brought seeds."

Alys's eyes widened, and she shared another look with Jailom, who chuckled.

"You can see now why the committee chairman thought you should meet Gracelin," he said, and Alys nodded.

"There's little chance they will grow here," Gracelin said sadly.

"But we won't know until we try it," Alys responded. "I will lease you a small plot of land. Big enough for a house and a garden."

"B-but I have no money for—"

"You will pay for your lease with goods and services. A portion of what you grow will go to the Crown. And if by some miracle those seeds of yours take root, that lease will become a land grant, and a rather large one at that."

Gracelin's jaw dropped open in amazement, and she stuttered. "L-land grant?"

Alys smiled. There had been some grumbling on her royal council when she'd first suggested giving land grants to commoners who'd shown themselves especially valuable to the community, but the grumbling had been easily quelled. The nobility of Women's Well was made up almost entirely of the original band of abigails—who were of noble blood despite the disgrace that had sent them to the Abbey in the first place—and the men of Tynthanal's company, who were generally second, third, or fourth sons who'd never expected to be landowners in the first place. There was still more arable land than there were people to work it, and the nobles of Women's Well were not a greedy lot.

"If you can grow Aalwood here in Women's Well," Alys said, "then I would be a fool *not* to grant you the land you need for it." And in reality, Alys didn't think even a land grant would be a great enough reward for so monumental an achievement, but she would discuss that with her council when and if it became an issue.

Lord Jailom escorted Gracelin out, but Alys was not at all surprised when her lord commander returned to her office shortly afterward.

"We should institute some border patrols," Jailom said. "It's . . .

uncomfortable to think that King Delnamal set up that blockade and we knew nothing about it until now."

"Yes, it is," Alys agreed. "Although we haven't exactly determined where our borders are, so I'm not sure exactly what territory we should patrol."

Jailom shrugged. "The influence of our Well is fairly clear to see. We can just follow the line of greenery. I will see if we can post some markers. I believe one of our newer residents has some experience as a surveyor and mapmaker."

Alys nodded, but the thought of a border patrol—as necessary as it might be—gave her pause. "Your patrols must include only your most trusted men. I would not be at all surprised if Delnamal's soldiers tried to instigate trouble. Skirmishes along our border would do a great deal more damage to *our* military than they would to *his*."

Lord Jailom bowed. "I will make certain there is a senior officer assigned to each patrol, and I will make it very clear they are not to engage unless absolutely necessary."

Sister Zulmirna has the face of a horse, Mairah thought as the young abigail was shown into her office. It certainly wasn't on account of her looks that Zulmirna was so popular when she worked the pavilion, yet she had acquired a nice stable of admirers in her short time at the Abbey.

Since the discovery of women's Kai, the Abbey could no longer *force* its abigails to work the pavilion, but the magic that created women's Kai was not as subtle or discerning as the Curse itself. Women reluctantly working the pavilion to earn privileges and creature comforts that were not available to the others in the Abbey could hate every moment of a coupling and still not produce Kai as long as they had the option to refuse. More than once, Mairah had seen Zulmirna crying after entertaining a customer. She was also fairly new to the Abbey and so hadn't had time to form any close attachments to Norah and the rest of Mother Wyebryn's cronies. Which made her the perfect candidate.

Sister Zulmirna stood before Mairah's desk, her eyes demurely lowered and her hands clasped before her.

"You wanted to see me, Mother?" the woman inquired without looking up. She had a husky, sultry voice that made the question sound almost flirtatious.

"Yes, Sister Zulmirna," Mairah said with a smile that she hoped was winning and friendly, though she caught the flash of worry in Zulmirna's eyes and wondered why she bothered. Making friends had never been her strong suit. "Please sit down."

Zulmirna took a seat, her back rigidly straight, as if she were still wearing fashionably stiff stays. The hands she clasped in her lap were white-knuckled, and Mairah realized that already she was gaining a reputation that struck fear into the hearts of her abigails.

"Relax, Sister," Mairah said soothingly. "You're not in any trouble."

Zulmirna's shoulders lowered just a little, and she finally looked up. "Thank you, Mother." She tried a tentative smile. "I've been trying to figure out what I could have done wrong . . ." She let her voice trail off, less nervous than before, but still clearly wary.

"How are you settling in?"

Zulmirna blinked, surprised by the question. "Er . . . All right, I guess." She grimaced. "As well as can be expected, at least."

"You are in much demand at the pavilion."

Zulmirna winced delicately and chewed on her lip. Perhaps to keep it from quivering. There was no question that she found working the pavilion distasteful, and Mairah suffered a twinge of conscience that she quickly quelled. No one was *forcing* the girl to be a whore; she had decided that degrading herself was an acceptable price to pay for a couple of extra blankets and larger portions at mealtimes.

"I hear you entertained Lord Deenan last night," Mairah continued. Once upon a time, Lord Deenan had considered himself a potential contender for Jalzarnin's council seat. Knowing that, Mairah had made up a batch of Keyhole ointment—the formula for which she'd found in the Abbey's disordered archives. The Keyhole spell, which created a magical spy hole through which an enterprising individual could both see and hear proceedings behind walls or closed doors, was officially outlawed. So Mairah had done the Abbey a service by removing it from the archives. And she'd done both herself and Jalzarnin a service by using the spell to look in on Deenan as he enjoyed his perversions in one of the playrooms.

As luck would have it, Deenan had never figured out where Jalzarnin had gotten the information about his unsavory tastes—information that would ruin him if he made any attempt to supplant Jalzarnin—and therefore he continued as a loyal customer of the Abbey's pavilion.

"Yes, Mother Mairahsol," Zulmirna answered, unable to hide a grimace. Whether her distaste was for the work in general or Deenan in particular remained to be seen.

Mairah tried another encouraging smile, but the girl was back to staring at her hands in her lap, squirming with discomfort. "What did you think of him?"

Zulmirna stilled, and she met Mairah's eyes with a look of confusion. "Excuse me?"

"I'm asking your impressions of Lord Deenan. Do you think him a good man? A good priest?"

Zulmirna's mouth opened and closed a few times, but no sound came out. She would be no good to Mairah if she proved to be too absorbed in the misery of her position to pay close attention to her customers, or if she was too prudish to reveal uncomfortable secrets.

"I'm asking for your honest opinion of the man," Mairah said. "You will not be punished if you speak ill of him, and I assure you there is a purpose behind my questions. Now tell me: how did you find him?"

Zulmirna swallowed hard and squirmed some more. "He is . . . unnatural."

"How so?"

The girl's naturally dark face flushed darker still. "He . . ." She cleared her throat. "He asked me to pitch my voice higher. *Like a little boy,* he said." She shuddered with revulsion. "And he . . . he . . ."

"Go on," Mairah prompted gently, knowing full well just how Deenan liked his women, and pleased that Zulmirna seemed willing to confide in her.

"He took me in a way I did not realize a man could take a woman," Zulmirna finished miserably.

Still too prudish to put into words exactly what Lord Deenan had done to her, but then she was painfully young and new to the Abbey. Her inhibitions would lessen over time, and her answer had been candid enough to suggest she might be a useful spy.

"If there was a way you could spend half as many nights in the pavilion as you do now and still receive the full privileges such duty affords you, would you be interested?" Mairah asked.

There was no missing the almost desperate flash of hope in the girl's eyes. "Of course, Mother!"

Mairah nodded, taking a moment to savor the power she had to influence this young woman's life, to revel in the certain knowledge that Zulmirna would do practically anything she was asked to escape her duties for a few nights a week.

"What would I have to do?" the girl asked.

"Pay close attention to each of your customers. Men have a way of revealing their true natures—and of speaking imprudently—when they are in the throes of passion. You will report to me any quirk or perversion or any hint of impropriety they admit to during their time with you."

Zulmirna's eyes widened with alarm. "That sounds . . . dangerous."

Mairah shrugged. "Dangerous to *me*, perhaps, if I ever try to use the information you feed me. But no one need know how I learned it."

Zulmirna looked unconvinced. She might be new to the Abbey, but it didn't take long for the Abbey to strip away a woman's innocence and trust.

"If you're not interested, then we'll say no more," Mairah said with another shrug. "You will continue your duties as usual, and we will pretend this conversation never happened."

"I'll do it," Zulmirna said hastily. As Mairah had known she would.

Mairah smiled, delighted to know she would have a steady flow of information to feed Jalzarnin. The lord high priest might not be able to confirm her to her position as abbess, but he was by far her strongest advocate, and it behooved her to keep him very happy.

"One more thing," Mairah said just before dismissing the girl. "I would advise you against befriending or in any way confiding in Sister Norah and her circle of friends. If I ever hear tell that you are fraternizing with them, our arrangement will be null and void."

Zulmirna revealed not a hint of surprise. "I understand, Mother Mairahsol."

CHAPTER EIGHT

The business and governance of Women's Well could easily take up Alys's every waking moment, and often it did. Being constantly busy was a much-needed salve for the grief that hovered always on the edge of her consciousness, and free time—time to *think*—was her most hated enemy. Whenever her duties threatened to leave her idle for an hour or two, she fled to the Women's Well Academy, delving into the fascinating secrets of magic that had been forbidden to her—to all women, except those imprisoned in abbeys—for most of her life. Alys could not escape the grief that assailed her every night when she was forced to lie down and attempt the daunting challenge that was falling asleep, but she would shield herself from it with work or study the rest of the time.

At first, she'd had every intention of using her time at the Academy to work on crafting the killer Kai spell she'd imagined sending to Delnamal. But though her rage continued unabated, she'd allowed herself—most reluctantly—to be talked out of it. Delnamal was far from the most intelligent person she had ever met, but he was not so stupid as to not know she wanted him dead. She'd already tried to send the Kai spell known as Vengeance at him once—a spell that had regrettably been foiled. He would from now on wear an active Kai shield spell all the time, as if he were a warrior going into battle.

Even if there hadn't been that very practical objection—and even if Delnamal's mysterious death would not endanger the relationship between Women's Well and the rest of Seven Wells, for no sovereign was eager to deal with someone who assassinated their rivals—there was a part of her that was just as happy to wait. A long-distance Kai spell might end Delnamal's life sooner, but Alys wanted to be there when he died, wanted to see him terrified and suffering and helpless as she ordered his execution. Just as her daughter had been when Delnamal had heartlessly killed her in an act of pure spite.

There was always at least a modicum of guilt when Alys first crossed the threshold into the Academy, for she couldn't shake the feeling that her insistence on remaining in Women's Well to pursue her magical studies had left her children vulnerable and led to—or at least contributed to—Jinnell's death. But once she opened her Mindseye and began working with the copious elements the Women's Well produced, the guilt would fade into the distance, ever present, but at least tolerable.

The women of the Academy—the former abigails of Aaltah—had been working on an ambitious project over the last several weeks, one that Alys could hardly believe had never before been attempted: creating a compendium of women's magic. Alys had been shocked to hear that no such documents existed within any of the abbeys, that the abigails' knowledge of magic was passed down either orally or on bits and scraps of paper that were only haphazardly stored. Who knew how many spells had been lost over the course of history!

In the past, women's magic was considered too minor and unimportant to be worth documenting, while there were whole libraries full of spell compendiums for men's magic, documenting even the most obscure spells of questionable use. Alys was sure there was enough women's magic in the world—even before her mother's spell had unleashed a slew of new feminine elements that had opened up whole realms of possibilities—to one day have a library of their own. But to start with, they would have a single, incomplete tome.

Chanlix Rai-Chanwynne, who had once been the Abbess of Aaltah but was now Alys's grand magus, was certain other abbeys would have their own unique spells that were unfamiliar to her and to the women of her Academy, but for now, they would fill the compendium with every spell the women of Aaltah knew, and with every spell that was developed within the Women's Well Academy.

Alys was unable to escape her duties until well after the Academy had shut down for the night, but she was not entirely disappointed to find the building dark and deserted. There was something almost soothing to the silence as she lit a few luminants and picked up one of the leather-bound copies of the compendium-in-progress.

There was a desk in the corner that was reserved specifically for her use—although she had repeatedly told Chanlix she need not reserve anything—and Alys laid the compendium on that desk and settled in to see what had been added since last she'd paid a visit.

Many of the spells listed were of little or no interest to Alys—traditional women's magic that might have sold well in the Women's Market but was of limited practical use. Things like aphrodisiacs and vanity potions had their place, and Alys hesitated to call them worthless—for that was the very kind of dismissive attitude men had always taken toward women's magic—but she didn't see any innovative new ways they could be used to further the security of her principality, which was her stated purpose for the hours spent with her Mindseye open and her worldly vision dimmed.

The latest spells added to the compendium were focused on fertility and childbirth, and though they were unquestionably useful spells, they did not spark any particular hunger for knowledge in Alys's breast. With a disappointed sigh, she gently closed the book and pushed back her chair.

Then she remembered her unkind words to her brother, her unintentional taunt about his childless state. And she thought again about the handful of fertility potions that were documented in the compendium.

There was a general acknowledgment—at least within the abbeys, if not in the larger world—that if a couple was unable to produce children, there was a roughly equal chance of the deficiency existing within the man or the woman. However—and Alys double-checked the listings, just to make sure—every fertility potion available was meant to be taken by women. Alys wondered if that was because society preferred to lay all the responsibility for childbearing on women, or whether there had been concerted efforts to restore male fertility and they had failed.

There was no way of knowing if someone ever had researched the making of a male fertility potion. And it was always possible that some of the previously unknown elements that were now available thanks to the Women's Well would make possible what had once been unachievable. Or that breaking with tradition and combining masculine and feminine elements in the same spell would do what women's magic alone could not. Alys could think of no better way to apologize for her cruel words than to present Tynthanal with a potion that would allow him to become a father.

Opening the book once more, Alys flipped to the section on fertility potions to gain a better understanding of how they worked. She had learned a couple of them when she had first begun her magical studies, using the impossible book of magic her mother had left her—which she had subsequently destroyed when she realized her mother had foreseen that her actions would lead to Jinnell's death. The compendium showed that there were many more variations than she had expected.

All the spells contained a trio of key ingredients: Rai, which was the element most strongly associated with fertility; Sur, which made the effects of the potion permanent; and Shel, which was usually associated with spells for stamina and energy but which—for no reason anyone had yet been able to identify—was required to make the potion work.

The spells varied the number of motes of each element used—with only anecdotal evidence of which formula was most effective—and some included additional ingredients of perhaps questionable value. It was unclear from the abigails' notes whether there had ever been any systematic testing of these potions, and Alys wondered whether some of them were made with unnecessary elements simply to make them sound more complicated—and therefore, more powerful and expensive.

Alys decided to concentrate her own efforts on potions containing only the three basic ingredients of Rai, Shel, and Sur. Rai seemed like the most obvious and most vital, as it was specifically associated with fertility, but it was also the element most associated with women. In fact, it was so closely associated with the female that it was used in names to denote a child born out of wedlock—a child "belonging" to its mother rather than its father. A quick skim through the rest of the compendium revealed no spells intended for male use that contained Rai.

The door creaked open behind her, and Alys looked over her shoulder to see Chanlix peeking into the room.

"I saw the light," Chanlix explained as she entered and closed the door behind her, "and knew it could only be you."

Alys smiled at the woman who had—somewhat to her surprise— become both a friend and a mentor to her. They had very little in common, Chanlix having spent her entire adult life behind the walls of the Abbey, but they had steadily been learning the magic of Women's Well together, and an undeniable bond had built between them.

"But you decided to check inside just in case I was some marauding thief bent on mischief?" Alys teased.

"I decided to check inside because I saw no sign of an honor guard keeping watch. You are well past the days when you could wander our streets alone in safety."

Alys waved off the concern. "I live two doors down. I was hardly *wandering the streets alone*." She had been the sovereign princess for nearly half a year yet Alys still lived in a relatively small and comfortable house, although a more palatial residence was under construction. Personally, she would have preferred to remain in her house for the rest of her days, but living in simple comfort was not the best way to convince the rest of the world of the legitimacy of her rule.

"And if *I* knew the light and lack of guards meant you were in here alone," Chanlix persisted, "then so would anyone else who happened by. Surely you don't think Delnamal would scruple to send assassins after you!"

Alys grimaced, for of course Chanlix was right. Assassinating foreign sovereigns might be frowned upon, but as far as much of Seven Wells was concerned, Women's Well was a rebel encampment rather than a legitimate principality. Queen Ellinsoltah might take offense if Alys were struck down, but she would likely be the only one. And Delnamal would jump at any chance to see Alys dead. He would never forgive either her or Tynthanal for receiving what he saw as more than their fair share of their father's love, and the shame he felt at having been forced to withdraw his army from their borders had elevated his hatred to new levels.

"I know," she acknowledged. "I just . . ." She let her voice trail off and shook her head.

Chanlix grabbed a nearby chair and dragged it over to Alys's desk. "May I?"

"You don't have to ask when we're in private," she said, but was not surprised by the other woman's disapproving frown.

"Would you have sat without permission in your father's presence, even if you were in private?"

Alys let out a resigned sigh. "Please do sit down, Mother Chanlix."

Chanlix's frown turned to an almost-convincing glare, though she wasn't able to conceal fully the hint of amusement in her eyes. "If you were anyone else, I would take that as an insult."

Chanlix had never been comfortable with the title when she was the Abbess of Aaltah, and of course it was a highly inappropriate address for the Grand Magus of Women's Well—though there were few outside their principality who would consider a woman to be a legitimate grand magus.

"Good thing I'm not anyone else, then, isn't it?" Alys quipped.

"Yes. Now, what are you up to all by yourself at the Academy when respectable townsfolk are tucked away in their homes for the night?" Chanlix reached for the spell compendium, pulling it toward herself and arching her brows when she glanced at the pages. "Fertility spells?"

Alys couldn't decide if it was good fortune or bad that Chanlix had walked in when she was researching this particular topic. Alys fidgeted and searched for a distraction, feeling as if she was treading on uncomfortably intimate territory. But Chanlix was nothing if not astute, and she would likely guess Alys's purpose whether she put it into words or not.

"I was wondering if anyone had ever *tried* to produce a spell to reverse male infertility," she said, watching her friend's face carefully for any sign of distress. She and Tynthanal had been all but living together these past months, their relationship growing ever stronger as time passed. Alys would not be surprised if sometime in the relatively near future, the two might ask her permission to marry. It would be seen as a scandalous marriage by many outside of Women's Well—a king's son marrying a woman who had once been forced into whoredom for crimes committed by her mother—but Alys had no objection to the match, at least not in theory. As brother to the sovereign, Tynthanal's marriage had the potential to be politically useful—if he were capable of fathering children. His deficiency was not public knowledge at the moment, but anyone who seriously considered marrying their daughter to him would expect a bloodline test to be conducted, and that would show the marriage to be fruitless.

Chanlix nodded thoughtfully. "I was taught that it was not possible," she said, "and that implies that it has been tried. However, because it is common practice to consider the woman to be responsible when a union does not produce children, it's hard to know just how much effort was put into any research that might have occurred. I suspect it is a rare man who is willing to take the blame and drink a fertility potion."

"That's what I figured," Alys said with a wry smile. It was hard to comprehend how men could at once be eager consumers of women's magic and yet hold it in such contempt. Almost all men partook of some form of women's magic—if only by drinking a sleeping potion— and yet they invariably treated it as some sort of shameful secret.

"The only thing I'm sure does not work is for a man to drink any of those fertility potions," Chanlix continued with a jerk of her chin toward the compendium.

"You're sure because . . . ?"

Chanlix met her eyes, showing no sign of discomfort or embarrassment. "Because we tried them, just in case."

Alys did not consider herself a prude, and yet she couldn't help blushing. The less she knew about her brother's sex life, the happier she would be.

Chanlix laughed, reading her discomfort easily. "You do know your brother and I are sleeping together, don't you?"

"I like to at least pretend that your relationship is entirely innocent and platonic. It's just . . . easier that way."

Chanlix laughed again. "My apologies for making your life more difficult. But as you know, I am nearing the end of my childbearing years, and it seemed like a topic of some interest both to Tynthanal and myself. We had both resigned ourselves to a childless life, but he is not the sort of man who is too proud to explore the possibilities. I made several of the most common potions for him, but they have not had the desired effect."

"Perhaps there simply hasn't been enough time?" Alys suggested, but Chanlix shook her head.

"I performed the bloodline test on Tynthanal and myself before trying any potions, just to confirm we received the same results your mother reported." When Alys and Tynthanal's mother had been the Abbess of Aaltah, she'd tested Tynthanal's blood and discovered that he was unable to sire children. "Then I performed the test again after he'd taken a few doses of each potion, but there was no change."

"I'm sorry," Alys said, though she couldn't imagine what it would be like to have one's first child at the age of forty-four. Perhaps Chanlix was not entirely unhappy that she needn't take contraceptive potions when she lay with Tynthanal.

Chanlix smiled sadly. "I am, too." She reached out and ran her fingers over the neatly printed page of potions. "I had considered the possibility of doing some further research, maybe trying some different formulas, but it seemed . . . selfish. Few men would be willing to take a fertility potion, and we need the resources of the Academy focused on spells that will be more profitable for our principality."

There was some truth to Chanlix's words, for Women's Well was still in a precarious position. They had formed an alliance and trade agreements with Queen Ellinsoltah of Rhozinolm—an alliance that had saved them from Delnamal's army—but they needed as many inducements to trade as they could come up with. It would not be wise for their grand magus to be seen researching a spell that was not of more general use.

Alys, on the other hand . . .

"I have very little time to practice my magic these days," she said, "but that also means that no one is expecting me to develop valuable spells for commercial distribution." Not that she hadn't been instrumental in developing some extremely powerful and highly sought-after spells in the days before the governance of Women's Well had taken over her life. "I will see if I can come up with anything that might help."

"Thank you, Your Royal Highness," Chanlix said with a grateful bow of her head. "If anyone can find a solution, it will be you."

Alys stifled her reflexive need to reject what felt uncomfortably like flattery. However, the fact remained that she and Tynthanal had inherited a great deal of magical ability from their mother. Alys knew of no other woman who could see even half the number of elements she could see. She did not have the level of magical training Chanlix or the rest of the men and women of the Academy did, but her ability to work with such a wide variety of elements gave her a definite advantage.

Alys shook her head and frowned as all at once she realized the implications if she should succeed in creating a viable potion. She was sure her face lost just a little color, and she felt like an idiot for not thinking of it sooner.

Chanlix reached over and patted her shoulder in an affectionate gesture that might not have been strictly appropriate to their respective ranks, though Alys didn't mind.

"I do realize what it would mean if Tynthanal were able to sire children," Chanlix reassured her.

Alys met the other woman's gaze and saw both wisdom and resolve. "So you understand that he will not be free to marry you if his marriage can be used to diplomatic advantage."

Chanlix nodded. "I do." She smiled sadly. "I long ago gave up all hope of ever becoming a wife or a mother. If I can only have one of the two, I would rather be a mother."

Chanlix broke eye contact and looked away. At first, Alys assumed she did it from sadness, but then she saw a hint of what looked very much like guilt on the woman's face.

"Did you discuss this with Tynthanal before you made fertility potions for him?" Alys asked, already knowing the answer.

Chanlix fidgeted and said nothing. Alys groaned.

"Chanlix . . ."

"I know," Chanlix assured her. "I told myself at first that he had to have figured it out himself." She held up a hand to stave off Alys's rebuttal. "I am as capable of lying to myself as the next person. I think I always knew he hadn't realized the implications. I promise that if you come up with a potion you believe is worth trying that I'll make sure he understands."

Alys shook her head. "He will be furious that you didn't mention it before. Even if he really should have figured it out himself."

Chanlix managed a half-smile. "He's good at lying to himself, too." She quickly sobered. "But then men are not trained from birth to measure their worth by their marriage prospects as we are. He forgot his hand could be a commodity."

There was no hint of bitterness in Chanlix's voice. It seemed she had already made peace with the idea of being either an unwed mother or a childless wife. How Alys hated the unfairness of the world.

"Will you promise not to hate me if I'm forced to marry him to someone else?" she asked, her chest tightening in pain at the prospect. The Sovereign Princess of Women's Well should never allow friendship or even love to interfere with her duties to her principality, and yet Alys wasn't sure she had the strength to do something that might cost her her closest friend and her brother.

Chanlix dispensed with protocol entirely, rising to her feet and giving Alys a hug. "Of course I won't hate you," she said soothingly. She met Alys's eyes, and there was nothing but stoic resolve in her gaze. "I have always been a realist. Tynthanal is the son of a king and the brother of a sovereign princess. Men such as he have almost as little say in their marriages as women. If you haven't received any inquiries into his availability yet, then it is only because people believe Women's Well is doomed."

Alys grimaced, but it was no more than the truth. She expected that as Women's Well continued to grow and prosper, she would be receiving multiple inquiries into Tynthanal's availability. And even her own, though she had never thought to remarry after Sylnin's death, and the prospect made something within her recoil in horror.

"It is better for everyone if Tynthanal can father children," Chanlix concluded. "How could I possibly hate you for giving me the chance to be a mother?"

Alys smiled sadly. "And do you think Tynthanal will feel the same way if I succeed?"

She already knew the answer to her own question. All of his adult life he'd enjoyed the advantages of being a king's son along with the freedom that came with illegitimacy. He was fully accustomed to thinking of his life as his own, and as a lifelong soldier, he'd been far enough removed from the machinations of the court that he did not yet realize how his life had changed when he'd urged Alys to declare herself a sovereign princess.

"He is a good man," Chanlix said with conviction. "He will not be happy about it, but he will understand."

Alys remained far from convinced.

King Delnamal of Aaltah could not abide the sight of a red-robed abigail in the halls of his palace, and so he was not present when the midwife sent from the much-altered Abbey of Aaltah examined his bride of just over a month. He stayed shut up in the sitting room of his personal apartments, a decanter of brandy and a tray of sweet-meats by his side. He partook of both equally, not caring that both his wife and the dowager queen, his mother, would object. His girth was now such that a brisk walk from one end of the palace to the other left him exhausted and gasping for breath, and he doubted his ability to mount a horse—or the beast's ability to bear him. But that did not stop him from eating. The brandy—and at other times wine, whiskey, and even ale—was the only thing that made his days tolerable, and he cared not about his physician's dire warnings about the condition of his liver.

Delnamal couldn't have said whether his most earnest desire was that the midwife declare his wife expecting, or not. It was, of course, his duty as king to produce an heir—which difficulty had led to his divorcing his first wife, who had miserably failed in her own duty and then had the gall to flee from him and join forces with his enemy. He should want nothing more than the happy news that Queen Oona was already seeded with a boy who would one day succeed him as king. But he'd had an heir on the way before, and though his former wife's miscarriage of that child had angered him, it had also been something of a secret relief not to have to be a father yet.

It might be even more of a relief if he were to learn Oona was just late with her monthly. His hasty marriage to a widow with a small child still clinging to her skirts had seemed something of a dream come true when he'd arranged it. He had wanted to marry Oona since he'd been a pimple-faced boy of fourteen, and he had often cursed the fate that sent them each to marry another. It had seemed like the ultimate *fuck you* to that fate when he had become king and her husband had "surprisingly" fallen victim to a cutthroat in the street. She had come to his bed, and then he had married her well before her year of official mourning had ended—despite grumbled objections from his council, who argued a king should marry a virgin with a lofty title and hefty dowry, not a widowed mother from the minor gentry.

Having Oona by his side—and in his bed—was every bit as gratifying as he had expected. However, having Oona's brat in his home was an entirely different story. Everyone assured him the four-year-old was extremely well behaved, and Delnamal had as little contact with the boy as possible, but what contact he did have was enough to renew his conviction that he was not made for fatherhood.

He did not like children. And though his mother had assured him he would feel differently when he held one of his own, he remained unconvinced. He hardly had Oona to himself now, thanks to her brat, but he had more of her than he would have if there was a new infant in their home. He wanted—no, *deserved*—more than one month of her (somewhat) undivided attention.

There was a tentative knock on his door, the sound so soft and delicate it could only be made by one person.

"Come," he said, standing ponderously, heart pounding more with fear than excitement. It was a disgraceful attitude for any grown man, much less a king, but knowing that only made him more surly.

Oona stepped into the study, dropping a deep and elegant curtsy. She was still the most beautiful creature he had ever laid eyes on, even though she was no longer in the first bloom of youth. While his former wife had been homely and awkward, with no discernible sense of fashion, Oona was the kind of woman who drew the attention of all whenever she set foot in a room. Even now, after her visit with the midwife, she was exquisitely put together in a gown of cream and gold, her every hair in place beneath a net of gold and pearls.

Delnamal sucked in a deep breath while he drank her in with his eyes. He fought off the urge to reach for his brandy before asking "What was the verdict?"

Oona smiled tremulously and put a hand on her belly, a gesture so universal Delnamal could not miss its meaning. "I am going to give you a son," she declared, and the tears in her eyes were tears of joy. "He may arrive a little earlier than is strictly considered proper, but then it is not all that uncommon for babes to leave their mothers' wombs in less than the traditional nine months."

It was his own fault, Delnamal realized, and felt like smacking himself in the head for his foolishness. There had been a period of several months during which there was no Abbey of the Unwanted in Aaltah, and during that time, contraceptive potions had been hard to come by. He could have sent off for a supply from a foreign abbey, but he'd been far too impatient to have Oona in his bed, and his use of sheaths had been both inexpert and inconsistent.

"Surely you are glad of this news, Your Majesty?" Oona asked, and Delnamal realized he'd been scowling fiercely instead of receiving the news with the joy of a soon-to-be father.

"Of course, my love," he said, forcing a smile he was quite certain did not convince her. "What man is not overjoyed when he learns his beautiful wife is expecting his son?" *What man indeed?* he wondered. He put his arms around Oona and hugged her close so that she could not read any of the contradictory feelings on his face.

Oona settled into his arms, her head resting against his shoulder. She smelled of faintly floral perfume. "I so want to make you happy," she murmured softly.

He squeezed her a little tighter, kissing the top of her head, though she probably didn't even feel it through the netting and pearls. "You do," he assured her.

But it was a lie, and they both knew it. He was the King of Aaltah, married to his childhood love, beholden to no one, and with a son and heir on the way. And yet he was a far cry from being happy.

His people did not love him and never had. They had always preferred his father's bastard, Tynthanal, who was so fucking perfect at everything and had now rebelled against the Crown—and gotten away with it!

His council did not respect him. Although he had clearly had very good reasons for withdrawing his army from the Women's Well borders—what good would smashing the upstart "principality" have done if Rhozinolm's forces had sailed nearly uncontested into Aaltah's capital?—it was clear they laid the blame and the ignominy of that retreat squarely at his feet.

And his whoring bitch of a half-sister had not only revolted against his rule but also declared herself the sovereign princess of her worthless excuse for a principality. A principality! What a ridiculous delusion of grandeur for a glorified encampment that had once been the virtual prison of the banished abigails of Aaltah!

The truth was, he could never be truly happy while his half-brother and half-sister lived, and while they presided over that joke of a principality. Only when they and all the rebels who'd joined them were dead, their town razed to the ground, and their abomination of a Well sealed off and guarded so that none might be contaminated by it, could he possibly find happiness.

CHAPTER NINE

"You can't really be serious about this," Shelvon said as Falcor led her to the center of the garden behind her house.

Not that it was accurate to describe the house as *hers*. It was the house that she occupied, but it belonged to Sovereign Princess Alysoon. As did the clothes Shelvon wore, the shoes on her feet, and the food that she ate. The fact of so little actually *belonging* to her had never bothered her—had never even crossed her mind—when her living had been paid for by her husband or her father; as a woman of Nandel, she had always been taught that nothing, not even her body, belonged to her. But it felt strangely different here in Women's Well, where she had neither husband nor father to support her.

A great many other single women—former abigails—were supporting themselves by working at the Women's Well Academy. She envied them their self-sufficiency, even if she had not yet completely succeeded in getting over her discomfort at the idea of women practicing magic. Or of former abigails being treated as perfectly respectable members of society.

Princess Alysoon insisted that supporting Shelvon financially was the least she could do after all the risks Shelvon had taken to help spirit Corlin away from Delnamal, and yet Shelvon couldn't help feeling like a stray dog accepting scraps.

"Of course I'm serious," Falcor said jovially, smiling at her as his auburn hair caught the sun. "A little physical activity will do you good."

"Then perhaps I should learn how to plant a garden," she suggested, though she had no desire to root around in the dirt.

Falcor gave a regretful sigh. "I'm afraid I don't know the first thing about gardening, so I can't help you with that." He brightened and held out a sword to her. "I am, however, fairly accomplished with a sword. Now go ahead. Take it. I promise it won't bite you."

Shelvon regarded the unadorned hilt doubtfully. She thought back over the last several conversations they'd had, and she was quite sure she had never actually *agreed* to let him teach her how to use a sword, so she wasn't entirely sure what she was doing out here. She put her hands on her hips.

"Doesn't the lord chamberlain have better things to do with his time?" she asked, knowing full well he would not be deterred so easily.

He shrugged. "I would not have accepted the office if it meant I could no longer swing a sword. I have spent all my life with a sword strapped to my side, and I wouldn't know what to do with myself without it."

"I don't see what any of that has to do with *me*." Falcor had once been Princess Alysoon's master of the guard, but after he had helped Shelvon and Corlin escape Aaltah, he had been elevated to her royal council. "You can wear your sword without having to give lessons."

"Take the sword, Lady Shelvon. I believe you will enjoy it, else I wouldn't be offering to teach you."

She frowned at him. "I'm not sure *offering* is the word you're looking for," she quipped, but almost to her own surprise, she closed her hand over the hilt. "Oh!" she said when he let go. "It's lighter than I thought." She had expected to struggle with the weight.

"A quick man with a light sword makes quick work of a strong man with a heavy one." He drew his own sword, which she saw had little more adornment than the one he had given her. It was the sword of an honor guardsman, not of the lord chamberlain, but then if there was an iota of pretension in Falcor, she had yet to see it. "This is the pommel," Falcor said, indicating the round protuberance at the very bottom of the hilt. "This is the grip," he said, hand moving up and down the rest of the hilt. "The cross-guard," pointing at the tee of metal perpendicular to the blade, "and, as you will no doubt be shocked to hear, the blade." He flicked a fingernail against the length of sharpened steel, and she shook her head at him.

"Your teaching style could use some work."

"Rule one of longsword lessons: never criticize your teacher when he's holding a deadly weapon."

The man had the audacity to *wink* at her. She had known Falcor for nearly six months now—though admittedly not well until their harrowing flight from Aaltah—and she'd always known him to have a reasonably grave and serious demeanor. The man standing here in her garden *winking* at her was a stranger, but then he'd been trying to jolly her ever since he'd caught her crying in a low moment when she was lamenting how lost and alone she felt.

You don't have to work this hard at it, she wanted to tell him, but that seemed . . . churlish. And unkind.

"Hold it like this," Falcor said, and she watched as he wrapped the fingers of his right hand around the grip, and his left around the bottom of the hilt, over the pommel.

Shelvon did the same with her sword, feeling faintly ridiculous.

"What I'm going to teach you first is a drill, something you can do every day without needing a partner."

Shelvon sucked in her cheeks and tried not to laugh at the idea of her going through longsword drills every day—by herself, no less. She wouldn't have even touched the stupid sword in the first place if he hadn't half-bullied her into it.

Falcor laughed at her expression. "I said you *can* do it every day, not that I expect you will. With every strike, you—and, naturally, your opponent—will be trying to land a blow between here and here," he explained, indicating first his shoulders and then his hips.

"The guards I'm about to show you are designed to protect you from those cuts, though there is a way around every guard.

"Start in this position." He stood with his left foot forward, the sword held at hip level, pointed upward.

If Shelvon had thought she felt ridiculous just holding the sword, she wasn't sure how to describe how she felt trying to stand in the position Falcor was showing her. She had always been taught to keep her legs demurely pressed together, and the wide stance felt vaguely obscene. She was certain her pale Nandel skin revealed her blush of discomfort, but Falcor showed no sign of noticing.

"From there, you're going to bring your left hand up and across your body," he said, demonstrating what appeared to be a complicated maneuver that ended with his forearms crossed and the blade held above his head, pointing downward.

"You're kidding," she grumbled, but when he showed her a second time more slowly, she found that she could follow the motion. The sword didn't feel as light when held so high, and the position felt even more awkward than the last.

Falcor nodded approval. "It's all right if it feels a little unnatural at first. It will get more comfortable." He ignored Shelvon's unladylike snort of disbelief. "Now move back to first position."

He demonstrated, and she followed. Then he had her move back and forth between the two until the motion flowed more smoothly and did not feel so awkward. When she had mastered—or at least gotten reasonably comfortable with—those first two positions, he expanded her repertoire, teaching her each of what he called the basic guard positions and having her move from one to the other in quick succession.

Well, not so quick, at least not at first. It was all so awkward and foreign, and the movements were certainly not designed for the ease of ladies in stays and layered skirts. But after that first terribly self-conscious quarter hour, she started to get into the rhythm of the movement. After a half hour, Shelvon was sweating profusely as the sun beat down on them, her breath coming hard and her arms feeling heavy. Her entire mind was focused on the movements of her body, of getting each guard exactly right without having to readjust. There was no room for thought or worry, no room for self-doubt or self-consciousness.

They stopped when her arms and legs were quivering with fatigue and she could barely lift the sword anymore, no matter how light it had felt when she'd first taken it. Falcor gently took it from her, and there was no missing the pleased approval on his face.

"An excellent first lesson, my lady," he said. "And you may wish to take a restorative potion before you sleep if you hope to get out of bed tomorrow morning."

Still panting, only now beginnng to feel the aching tiredness of her muscles, she had to agree.

All in all, it had been a surprisingly pleasurable exercise, more calming than she ever could have expected for such vigorous action. But when Shelvon was back in her house—no, *the* house—drinking the restorative potion Falcor had recommended, the melancholy returned. It had felt good to play at swords, to let the physical activity quiet her mind. But the fact remained that she was adrift in life, a divorced woman outside the walls of an abbey, with no greater purpose than to exist. It seemed a poor and unsatisfying way to live.

A thrill shivered through Mairah's body when Jalzarnin was shown into her office. Always before, she had met him in the Abbey's playrooms, where she was fully aware that despite whatever affection he might feel for her, she was a commodity that he had bought. She was not so foolish as to think herself his equal, but now she at least had the luxury of choice.

"Lord Jalzarnin," she said with a respectful bow of her head. "How lovely to see you."

"And you, Mother Mairahsol," he said, his eyes twinkling despite the formal greeting. They both waited in silence for the abigail who had shown him in to depart and close the door.

Mairah expected him to cross the distance between them and take her in his arms the moment he could no longer hear the abigail's footsteps. Like most men, he found it difficult to have a civilized conversation until *after* he had slaked his lust. But though her circumstances were now very different than they had been the last time she'd seen him, she had every intention of indulging him still. After all, even when he'd paid for her services, she had quite enjoyed his skills as a partner.

"How do you like being abbess?" he asked. He smiled at her with all the warmth she had come to expect, and yet he did not embrace her and remained an arm's length away.

Mairah blinked, wondering if she had misjudged him. Perhaps now that he had succeeded in having her installed as abbess, he was no longer interested in bedding her. She was, after all, hideous to look at—as she had been told often enough that the insult had almost lost its sting. Perhaps he believed now that she was so thoroughly beholden to him, he need no longer bother with seduction to get what he wanted out of her.

He must have seen her confusion, for his smile warmed even more and he reached out and took her hands in his. "I no longer have to pay for you by the hour," he said. "We needn't rush into things."

She sighed with relief, reminding herself yet again that she was now the abbess and he was her guest, not her customer. "Then please do come and have a seat," she beckoned, directing him to the sofa before the fireplace. The sofa was something of an eyesore, clearly someone's cast-off, with dingy gray fabric and battle-scarred legs, but it was comfortable enough and felt like a decadent luxury compared to the hard wooden stools and benches she was used to.

"I am settling in quite nicely," she told him with a smile of satisfaction as she drank in the warmth of the fire. Elsewhere in the Abbey, fires were only lit when the cold reached dangerous levels, making the winter a season of constant chills and shivers. Mother Wyebryn had carried that tradition into her own office so that she was no warmer than the abigails who served her, but Mairah had done away with that practice first thing. It was barely autumn now, but already the comfortable warmth of the fire was welcome.

"The older abigails aren't giving you too much trouble, I presume?"

Her smile broadened even more as she enjoyed the memory of today's luncheon, during which Norah and a half dozen of her closest friends had been forced to stand hungry and drooling while they watched their sisters eat. The fasts Mairah had imposed on those who resisted her were saving the Abbey money, which she could then spend on more firewood to keep her office toasty.

"They are learning that there is a heavy price for disobedience," she said. "I expect that I will have broken them of any bad habits within a month, if I haven't already."

His eyes twinkled. "Mairah, my dear, you are practically glowing."

She laughed. "I won't pretend it isn't very . . . satisfying to give them some firsthand experience of what they put me through for all those long years."

"Of course it is," he said, nodding. "But I do hope you've been taking advantage of your new position in other ways, as well." He raised his eyebrows.

"Naturally," she assured him. He seemed to genuinely enjoy seeing her happiness, but she could never allow herself to forget that he had installed her as abbess for his own purposes. "I have tasked a select few of my younger abigails with reporting to me anything untoward their customers might reveal in the throes of passion. I have nothing of any great interest to report just yet, but one of those abigails has been cultivating a Lord Thanstal, with whom I believe you are acquainted."

Jalzarnin's eyes lit with excitement, as she'd suspected they would. Thanstal, one of King Khalvin's cousins, was quickly rising through the ranks of the priesthood. With his blood ties to the king, he was a likely successor to Jalzarnin, and if he decided he would prefer not to wait until Jalzarnin retired of his own free will, he might be able to persuade his cousin to appoint him as a replacement.

In short, he was just the sort of man Jalzarnin hoped Mairah could keep tabs on now that she was abbess.

"What a pleasant surprise," Jalzarnin said. "Considering some of the sermons I have heard from him, I would have thought him the sort never to set foot in such a den of iniquity as the Abbey."

There was no small amount of sarcasm in Jalzarnin's voice, and she returned it in kind. "Yes. It's so rare that someone who makes such a great show of piety is not himself as pious as he pretends."

Jalzarnin grimaced in distaste. "I cannot abide hypocrites. I have my faults, but at least I am man enough to own up to them."

Mairah nodded again, although she did find it amusing that Jalzarnin would rail against hypocrites. He might not make a great show of his piety, but he *was* still a priest, and there was no question that he would preach about the sanctity of marriage vows when prompted. Just as he would warn others to beware the terrible sins of ambition and avarice.

"I don't know yet how impious Lord Thanstal might be," Mairah said. "According to Zulmirna, his tastes in the bedroom have so far been unremarkable, but he does seem inclined to linger and talk once he's been sated. I will keep you apprised of anything interesting he might say."

"Yes, that would be helpful. Obviously, I can't hold his visits to the Abbey against him, no matter what the Devotional might teach about a man's duties to his wife."

"Obviously," she replied rather dryly. "But it's a rare ambitious man who does not have one or two secrets that might disqualify him from office were they to become public knowledge."

Jalzarnin shot a sharp glance her way, but she smiled and blinked innocently as if completely unaware of the subtle . . . well, not threat exactly, but maybe warning that she had just issued.

Alys stared at the scrolled parchment, sealed with cream-colored wax, that her lord chancellor was holding out to her. She was sure her face had gone pale, and her stomach rolled over in visceral reaction at the thought of so much as *touching* something Sovereign Prince Waldmir had written. She shook her head in urgent denial, glad Tynthanal had chosen to approach her in private with this message.

No one in Women's Well had expected any overtures from Prince Waldmir. Especially not Alys or Chanlix or Tynthanal, who had all been involved in sending him a Kai flier loaded with Vengeance when they'd thought it might protect Jinnell from his lust. If that flier had struck him, he would know exactly who to blame for it, no matter how nondescript it might have looked.

"Perhaps our flier never reached him," Tynthanal said. "It is a long way from here to The Keep, and fliers sometimes struggle to navigate the mountains and their storms. This is unexpectedly good news. He is reaching out from one sovereign to another when we had no reason to believe he would accept either our independence or your rule. He sits on the greatest supply of iron and gems in the entire world, and—"

"Enough," she interrupted. For months, Delnamal had tortured Alys with threats of marrying Jinnell to the monstrous Sovereign Prince of Nandel, and the man had become synonymous with what she had once thought was her worst nightmare. Now the thought occurred to her that if Jinnell had married Waldmir, she'd be alive right now.

She shivered in a chill that had nothing to do with the temperature in the room. Women's Well had shown little inclination to change with the seasons, the daytime temperatures ranging from comfortably warm to scorching. However, within an hour of the sun setting, there was always a bite to the air, and sometimes she lit a fire to combat it. She moved closer to the small fire in the hearth, holding out her hands to warm them, though the fire had no power to fight the cold that welled from inside her.

"I can't do it," Alys croaked, shaking her head again. "I can't negotiate with that man."

"Ultimately," Tynthanal said, "he is not the one who hurt Jinnell. Delnamal shoulders one hundred percent of the blame for that."

He tried once again to hand her the parchment, and she recoiled as if he held a venomous snake. "I know that," she snapped. "But I am entirely certain he would prefer to see Women's Well razed to the ground than enter into any kind of agreement that might benefit us. I have no interest in making contact with him."

"You are the sovereign princess," Tynthanal tried again. "Negotiating with people you can't abide comes with your title." He practically poked her in the chest with the scroll. She jerked away and folded her arms, tucking her hands underneath her armpits.

"Not him," she insisted. "I don't care if you think I'm being immature or irresponsible. I will not negotiate with the man who planned to force my daughter into marriage."

"Let's at least see what he has to say." He'd been coaxing and persuasive at first, but now his irritation was showing through, his tone becoming increasingly curt.

"I said no!" And because she knew he was not going to let up—and she had no intention of allowing herself to be persuaded—she reached out suddenly and snatched the scroll from his hand, throwing it into the fire.

Tynthanal's eyes smoldered, but at least he made no attempt to rescue the scroll from the flames. "You're right: I do think you're being immature and irresponsible."

"Then so be it." She crossed her arms once more and stared at the fire as the scroll quickly turned to ashes and disappeared.

Lord Creethan stared at Ellin uncomprehendingly, blinking like a man who was sure what he saw could not be real. Surely he had expected *some* unpleasantness when he'd received her peremptory summons, and when she'd questioned him about the Abbey, his discomfort and defensiveness confirmed he'd known perfectly well she would not approve.

"You may go," she told him, but she wasn't entirely surprised he remained rooted in place.

"Surely . . ." he started, then shook his head as if to clear the cobwebs. "I will, of course, discontinue any practices of which you disapprove, but—"

"No, you won't," she interrupted. "Your successor will."

"Your Majesty—"

"This is not a negotiation. I will not have a man on my council who has betrayed my trust, and there is nothing you can say that will change my mind." Which was nothing but the truth, for Semsulin had said everything he could think of to try to talk her out of dismissing her trade minister. Not that he approved of what Creethan had done, but he had rightly pointed out that dismissing a man of his

stature—and with his family connections—would be politically problematic.

"Punish him, by all means," her lord chancellor had counseled,
"but don't dismiss him."

Ellin had listened to Semsulin's wise words and had known he was
right. There were many on her council and among the nobility of
Rhozinolm who would not see what Creethan had done as any true
crime. They might acknowledge that it had been inadvisable for him
to do it behind her back, but she was sure many would privately
praise his ingenuity in wringing more money from the Abbey. After
all, the women there were already disgraced, considered no more
than whores, whether they worked the pavilion or not. Creethan and
his influential family would no doubt frame her decision as choosing
those Unwanted Women over a sage and respected adviser, and that
was unlikely to go over well with the rich and powerful men of
Rhozinolm.

But Ellin had imagined what it would be like to sit in council
meetings with Creethan, knowing what he had done and knowing
that he would happily scheme behind her back if that was what he
needed to do to have his way. Dismissing him might not be politically
expedient, but she could see no alternative. She could not trust him,
and his actions proved him to be the kind of human being she could
never respect. Therefore, he could not remain on her council.

"You can't mean it," Creethan said, his voice caught somewhere
between incredulity and outrage. "I have served the Crown since
before you were born. I maintain I was *still* serving the Crown when
I instituted the new policies—and that it would be folly to reverse
them—but you have made your objections abundantly clear. I will
change the policies, and we can—"

"I don't think you're hearing me, Lord Creethan. I said you were
dismissed, and I meant it."

The incredulity and outrage were turning into something darker
as he continued to stare at her. The muscles of his jaw worked restlessly, and both his hands were clenched at his sides. "This is foolishness! You cannot dismiss a member of the royal council for *doing his*

job!" This last was said at a near roar, and he took a step closer to her desk.

"Yes, Lord Creethan, I can," she said calmly. Out of the corner of her eye, she saw one of her honor guardsmen take a step closer to her. She couldn't blame him for his caution, for Creethan looked like he was on the brink of losing his tenuous control of his temper. It took an effort of will not to flinch back from what she saw in his face. "Every member of the royal council serves at the sovereign's pleasure," she reminded him. "I thank you for the service you have done to me and for your years of service to my grandfather, but I will not have you on my council any longer."

Creethan shook his head and sneered. "This display of feminine hysterics is unbecoming of a sovereign! The Kingdom of Rhozinolm would be better served if you were to step aside and allow your grandfather's true heir to take his rightful throne. He can marry you to the Nandelite, renew the trade agreements, and—"

"You're about one word short of a treason charge," she interrupted, her voice still calm despite the anger that coiled in her breast. She was sure that such sentiments had been voiced in private among her advisers and among the rich and powerful men of Rhozinolm. And she suspected her dismissal of Lord Creethan would give new strength to those whispers, which was likely why he had said it. An implicit threat that might persuade even Semsulin that she was making the right decision. "There is only one hysterical person in this room, and I assure you it is not I. If you think this is somehow furthering your case for reinstatement, you are very much mistaken."

For a moment, she feared she would have to order her guards to physically remove Lord Creethan. He looked like a man contemplating violence—an impression the obvious readiness of the guards reinforced. Her heart throbbed in her throat, and she struggled to keep all she was feeling from showing on her face. Her serenity in the face of his fury would do nothing to change his opinion of her, but she refused to show him even a glimpse of weakness.

"Let's just hope we don't all come to regret this," he finally said, in a tone that suggested a very different sentiment altogether. He'd worded it in such a way that she didn't quite feel justified in calling it an overt threat—and therefore slapping a treason charge on him after all—but she was very much aware that she'd made a powerful enemy.

I hope it's worth it, Your Majesty, Semsulin's voice whispered in her mind.

But Ellin felt sure that whatever the consequences, Lord Creethan did not belong on her royal council.

CHAPTER TEN

Mairah stared at the open vial of seer's poison in her hand, willing herself to just down it and stop thinking about it. It was only a little stronger than the first poison she'd taken so many years ago, which meant it was highly unlikely to kill her and should also grant her a longer, clearer, more thorough vision. Her long-ago first attempt to trigger a vision had turned out to be well worth the misery—she doubted she would even have *thought* to try for the position of abbess had she not seen herself sitting behind the abbess's desk—and yet so far she had not found the courage and will to take another. She remembered all too vividly the nausea and racking pain even the most mild poison had caused her, and everything in her body rebelled at the prospect of inflicting that on herself once more.

"It's worth a quarter hour of misery for a lifetime of comfort," she exhorted herself out loud. She had set her abigails to the tedious and almost certainly futile task of researching possible paths toward a cure for the Curse, but she could not entrust her future to such a flimsy hope. She *needed* something more, and triggering a vision seemed the most logical next step.

She raised the vial to her lips, smelling the acrid scent of the poison, which overwhelmed the alcohol in the base liquid. Even that scent provoked a visceral memory, one that made her stomach turn over and her throat close in protest.

What were the chances that the vision she triggered would show her the way to reverse the Curse?

Mairah snorted softly. Common sense told her that reversing the Curse was something well beyond her abilities. To be sure, she was magically gifted—more so than any other woman within the walls of the Abbey—but for all her ability to see a multitude of elements, she had never truly applied herself to the study of magic. What was the point, when her abilities only made her sisters more jealous and spiteful? She'd been studying and practicing since she'd become abbess, but six months was far from enough time to develop the expertise she needed, no matter how talented she might be.

Mairah lowered the vial of poison once more, though she didn't immediately put the stopper back in it. Her instincts told her a vision could not set her on the path toward reversing the Curse, but was it possible a vision would show her how to create the *illusion* that she was on the right path?

For what felt like the twentieth time, she raised the vial to her lips but could not force herself to drink.

If her goal was to create an illusion only, did she really need to put herself through the agony of a seer's poison? If she abandoned any thought of genuinely trying to undo the Curse and poured all her imagination and creativity into that illusion, surely she could come up with something that did not require her to suffer so.

Slowly, she lowered the vial once more, and this time, she shoved the cork back in, shuddering at the thought of her close call. There was no reason whatsoever for her to drink a seer's poison! All she had to do was *claim* she'd taken one and seen a vision that hinted at future success. A smile spread upon her lips as a plan began to take shape.

All but one of the seers in the Abbey of Khalpar were among

Norah's circle of friends. Mairah could demonstrate "progress" on her mission and punish her enemies at the same time.

Happily working out the details of the vision she would claim to have received, Mairah opened the vial once more and poured the contents into the chamber pot, sighing with relief.

Jalzarnin relaxed when he'd finished delivering his progress report to the king and the rest of the royal council. He'd half expected the king to begin demanding unreasonable progress in the effort to reverse the Curse, and he'd come prepared with a list of arguments and explanations for why it was too soon to expect results. It was Jalzarnin's opinion that the king had been having fewer good days than usual lately, his always erratic temper alarmingly easy to ignite. But the king had accepted his report without demur or complaint, and his demeanor seemed gratifyingly cheerful for once. Until it was the marshal's turn to report.

The marshal was the most junior member of the royal council, and one of the lowest ranking. He was responsible for all law enforcement throughout Khalpar, and even before he began speaking, he seemed ill at ease. Which did not bode well for his report, though Jalzarnin still hoped the king's good humor would hold up to some unpleasant news.

"We have reason to believe that the Mother of All heresy has been active in Khalwell as of late," the marshal said.

It was all Jalzarnin could do not to wince. As the lord high priest, he himself should have been the most scandalized of all the council members to learn that this heresy had cropped up yet again, but though he found it distasteful, in his heart of hearts he did not see how it mattered if a few misguided people got together and made up silly stories about the relationship between the Creator and the Mother. Certainly mankind gave the Creator more serious and troubling reasons to be peevish with them. Of course, the lord high priest could not afford to express any such sentiment, so he forced himself to scowl.

King Khalvin's eyes narrowed and his lips thinned, his scowl entirely unforced as he fixed the marshal with a steely stare. Jalzarnin doubted there was a man in the room who did not instantly see that the king's mood had plummeted with the mention of the cult that he seemed to regard as a personal affront.

"What reason might that be?" the king asked, each word articulated carefully.

The marshal swallowed and shifted in his seat, and Jalzarnin was glad not to be on the receiving end of that fearsome stare.

"The Watch found an old woman plastering tracts on doorways late at night. Disgusting filth that has no place anywhere in our fair city."

The king's lip curled in distaste. "I presume she is being questioned so that her fellow cultists can be dealt with? After all, there is no such thing as a single heretic."

The marshal's gaze dropped to the table, and his shoulders tightened. "No, Your Majesty," he said. His voice didn't quaver, but it was so soft and breathy there was no missing his fear. No one liked to give the king bad news, but the marshal was proving unbecomingly timid for a man charged with upholding the law. "As I said, she was an old woman. It appears her heart gave out at the terror of having been arrested."

All trace of good humor had vanished from the king's expression, and Jalzarnin bid a sad adieu to this rare good day, for he did not see the king's mood improving from here.

"She just happened to drop dead?" the king asked with a snarl. "What a happy convenience for her fellow heretics. Tell me, do you think it might be possible her sudden death was something other than an accident?"

The marshal glanced around the room, perhaps hoping another council member would intervene on his behalf. But of course no one was inclined to do any such thing. When the king was in this foul a temper, everyone hoped to escape his notice.

"There is no evidence to suggest—" the marshal started, but the king immediately cut him off.

"Did she by any chance open her Mindseye when she saw what

was about to happen? And did she perhaps activate some spell that might have made her incapable of informing on her accomplices?"

The marshal licked his lips, once again glancing around in hopes of rescue. No one would so much as look in his direction, much less meet his eyes.

"I do believe that was the case," he reluctantly admitted. "The men had no reason to see an old woman as a threat, so—"

"So no one considered that a woman about to be arrested for distributing heretical tracts might take some action to avoid being questioned?" the king asked, his voice rising. "What kind of training are your men receiving that they are incapable of reaching this logical conclusion and taking care to capture the woman alive? *I* would know to watch for suicide, and I've not spent a day on Watch duty! Are these men imbeciles?"

The marshal's face had lost all color, and though he opened and closed his mouth a few times, he seemed incapable of speech, maybe even of thought. Jalzarnin suspected that by tomorrow morning's council meeting, there would be a new marshal sitting in that seat. Most kings and sovereign princes made at least a token effort to maintain a consistent royal council, but Khalvin had made it abundantly clear that no member of his council was irreplaceable. He'd once confided in Jalzarnin that he felt it best not to allow his council members to become complacent, but Jalzarnin hardly felt the rampant paranoia his purges inspired was an improvement.

"It appears inquiries will have to be made," Jalzarnin said, taking pity on the marshal despite the man's obvious unsuitability for his position. "I will instruct my priests to keep a careful watch on their flocks. A few artfully placed questions to the right people will help us track down the root of this heresy."

The king glared at the marshal for a long moment before finally turning his attention to Jalzarnin. "It is the duty of the priesthood to ensure the piety of the people of Khalpar," he said. "I am disappointed to find there has been a resurgence of this cult right under your nose."

Yes, the king was now thoroughly sunk in one of his most disagreeable moods, but there was nothing to be done for it. Jalzarnin wished he'd known what the marshal was going to report before the meeting began—he could have counseled the man to let him handle the issue without troubling the king. It wouldn't have been the first time during his tenure as lord high priest that he had kept rumors of heresy from reaching the king's ears.

"My deepest apologies, Your Majesty," Jalzarnin said, and for the most part, he actually meant it. "I have clearly been lax in my duties, but I promise you—"

"Perhaps you are being distracted by the amount of time you spend at the Abbey," the king interrupted. "Surely the abigails do not require your services in their efforts to reverse the Curse."

"No, Your Majesty." Jalzarnin stifled a sigh. He had enjoyed having the freedom to visit the Abbey under the guise of gathering "progress reports" instead of having to slink in through the married-man's entrance under cover of night. But he'd never expected that luxury to last.

"Then I see no reason why you should still be visiting the Abbey with any regularity. Your time is better spent seeing to the moral fiber of our kingdom, don't you agree?"

"Of course, Your Majesty," Jalzarnin agreed, hoping his face did not flush an angry—and embarrassed—red. It was just like the king to suddenly blame Jalzarnin for some great uprise in heresy just because the marshal had reported catching a single heretic in the act. And if heresy was, in fact, on the rise, it was of even greater importance that Jalzarnin gather whatever intelligence he could on Lord Thanstal and any other potential rivals who might think to win their way to the office of lord high priest. He hoped Mairah's abigail was still coaxing Thanstal to talk, and that the man would reveal something sufficiently damning.

"I will need to speak with the abbess on occasion to monitor any progress she and her abigails have made toward reversing the Curse," he continued, "but rest assured that I will focus all of my energies on rooting out the heretics."

The king nodded briskly, although his expression remained sour and unyielding. He was far from appeased, and every man at the table would have to watch his every word and gesture for the rest of the meeting.

Kailindar Rai-Chantah was Ellin's uncle, and so it was not considered extraordinary or unexpected for him to pay a visit to her in the residential wing of the palace rather than arrange a more formal meeting during the day. However, he had never before done so; she was fairly certain he had not fully forgiven her for stripping him of one of his titles during her early days as queen. He was cordial enough with her, and had supported her during her confrontation with her cousin Tamzin—more because of his hatred for Tamzin than any deep affection for her—but she was under no illusion that he was one of her most ardent supporters. He'd made that abundantly clear when he'd cornered her shortly after she'd dismissed Lord Creethan from the council to tell her how childish and unnecessary that decision had been.

By nature a dour and taciturn man, he was not especially well liked by the other members of Ellin's council—which was fortuitous, as with Tamzin now dead, Kailindar would have ascended to the throne if Ellin weren't already sitting on it. His lack of popularity meant that he had little hope of convincing the people to rise up in his name—but that was true only so long as she maintained her own popular support. He might be calling under the guise of a social visit, but he wasn't fooling anyone.

She waited until a servant had poured wine for both of them and departed. Then she turned to Kailindar with some amount of trepidation.

"To what do I owe the pleasure of this unexpected visit, Uncle?" she asked. She was depressingly certain he would not have called on her for an idle or pleasant conversation.

Kailindar took a sip of his wine before answering. His hair had gone gray at least a decade ago, and he insisted on wearing a droopy mustache that made him look even more dour than he was. He had to drink carefully to avoid dipping his mustache in the wine.

"As you know," he said, frowning down at the wine instead of looking at her, "I have made the first overtures to Prince Waldmir about your potential marriage to Zarsha."

Ellin took a sip of her own wine, though she didn't especially want it. Her reign and her continued support—half-hearted though it might be—from her council all rested on her ability to secure the trade agreements with Nandel. She had hoped the negotiations would go quickly and smoothly—as if anything ever did!—but Kailindar would not be here if that were the case.

"There is a problem?" she asked, wondering if she'd made a mistake in accepting Zarsha's assurances.

"There's *something*," Kailindar hedged, frowning even more deeply. "I've received several messages from him via flier, and for a man who likes to present himself as blunt and plainspoken—and whom everyone considers little better than a barbarian warlord—he can be maddeningly cagey. He seems to be implying that Zarsha is not a suitable husband for a queen—either that, or that he desperately needs Zarsha to return to Nandel so that he can continue to fulfill his obligations to the Crown."

Ellin let out a short bark of laughter. "He desperately needs Zarsha at home, and yet when our original engagement fell through, he assigned him indefinitely as a 'special envoy' to Rhozinolm?"

Kailindar crossed his legs and took another careful sip of his wine. "He's not making much of an effort to be convincing," he agreed. "Everything he's said has been through implication, rather than outright accusation, but what was quite obvious to me is that Prince Waldmir does not hold his dear nephew in high regard."

A feeling that was clearly mutual—and understandable, if Zarsha was blackmailing him, or at least threatening to. She wished Zarsha would be more forthcoming about whatever the issue was between them. Zarsha had seemed to believe Prince Waldmir would be agreeable to the match despite the bad blood, and she didn't know if that was misplaced optimism, or a form of subterfuge.

"It is possible Waldmir is merely trying to extort the best possible deal out of us," Kailindar continued. "He presented it as a given that if the marriage were to happen, our trade agreements would be renewed on their current terms, but he also suggested your close alliance with Princess Alysoon—and your necessarily strained relationship with King Delnamal—might make the renewal of those agreements problematic for him."

"In other words, you think he's throwing up every objection he can imagine in hopes that we'll somehow sweeten the deal—even though nothing we've offered before, short of my marriage to Zarsha, has been enough to tempt him to renew the agreements."

"I think it's more than that. I think Waldmir genuinely despises Zarsha and does not want to see him come into a position of power. It is hard for a man like him to envision any woman, much less one as young as you, sitting on the throne and making her own decisions. He considers that Zarsha would be the true power behind the throne—which ordinarily would be an inducement to make the agreement—and he does not want that. I *also* think Waldmir has heard of your exclusive agreements with Women's Well and is more than a little uncomfortable with them. You know how Nandelites are about women's magic."

"I know how Nandelites are about women in general," she muttered, shaking her head. Most of the world regarded women's magic as something unclean, only to be practiced by women who'd been shamed and ruined and sent to the Abbey of the Unwanted. In Nandel, even the women of the Abbey were forbidden to practice magic. And respectable women were considered property of their husbands or fathers and had few rights under the law.

"Yes," Kailindar agreed. "We are unfortunately not coming into these negotiations from a position of strength. Not only do we have a woman on the throne, but we've allied ourselves with another female-led principality. A *rogue* principality, in Waldmir's view. Now we propose to make his despised nephew the power behind our throne—again, in *his* view."

Ellin wasn't sure if she was imagining enemies where none existed, but she could have sworn she heard a faint undertone of threat in Kailindar's voice. A hint that possibly the negotiations would be easier if she stepped aside and let a *man* take the throne? She narrowed her eyes at him, but saw no hint of Tamzin's cunning or ambition in his expression. That didn't mean they weren't there, however; it might just mean he was better at hiding them.

"Have you by any chance mentioned my dismissal of Lord Creethan in your discussions?" Ellin asked, letting the faintest hint of an edge enter her voice. If Kailindar was angry enough about that "childish" decision, would he use it to undermine the marriage negotiations? She was certain Waldmir would take the dimmest possible view of her decision to punish a member of her royal council in defense of the Unwanted Women of Rhozinolm.

Kailindar's eyes narrowed in annoyance. "Of course not. I'm sure he's heard of it by now—as I warned you, it has created quite the sensation—and I doubt it has made him any more favorably inclined toward you, but I'm not foolish enough to rub his face in it."

"What do you suggest I do, Uncle?" she asked, for it was a rare man who did not relish being asked for his sage advice.

Kailindar steepled his fingers, looking lost in thought. "First, I would suggest you persuade Zarsha to tell you what the issue is between him and Waldmir. We have always assumed you would be an even more attractive match now that you are queen, but if Waldmir hates Zarsha enough, it's possible that your marriage is no longer the key to renewing the agreements after all. I myself would have done *anything* to keep Tamzin from gaining the power of the throne, and if Waldmir feels the same way about Zarsha . . ."

Ellin opened her mouth to remind him that Zarsha was not going to gain the power of the throne, but of course reality wasn't the issue. Waldmir assumed Zarsha would have the true power if they married, and that perception might ruin everything.

When she'd finally gotten over her childish dislike of Zarsha, Ellin had found that he was kindhearted and true, with a whip-smart mind that had more than once helped her out of an impossible situation. There was far more to him than his charm and good looks—though he had those in generous quantities—and sometimes when he touched her, she felt a stirring of attraction she'd feared she'd never feel again when the man she'd loved had betrayed her.

It was hard to know her own mind when her thoughts and feel-

QUEEN OF THE UNWANTED

ings were aswirl, but she was fairly certain that she now actually *wanted* to marry Zarsha. She did not feel for him the fiery passion she had felt for Graesan, did not long for him with that same kind of aching need. But Graesan had betrayed her, and marriage to Zarsha would be far more pleasant than the vast majority of diplomatic marriages.

Yet under all that, there was another reason Zarsha was an ideal husband: he was a foreigner, and therefore there would never be any pressure for her to cede her throne to him once they were married. Such was not the case for any other likely prospects, and though she had succeeded to the throne with the idea that her reign would last a year or two at most, she found she was now disinclined to step down in favor of her future husband—whoever he might be.

Kailindar shifted in his chair, drawing her attention once more. "If Waldmir's reluctance to sanction this marriage turns out to be real, and not just another negotiating tactic, you will be forced to make some very difficult decisions. If, for example, Waldmir's true objection is to your close ties with Princess Alysoon, I hope you will think only of the good of Rhozinolm when you consider which of our trade agreements is the most vital."

"In other words, if it comes down to a choice between having trade with Women's Well and trade with Nandel, I must choose Nandel."

He nodded.

"And if it turns out Waldmir cannot countenance having Zarsha so close to my throne?" She gave him her most challenging glare, daring him to put his implications into words. Kailindar might not be popular, but at least he was *male*. If she could not restore the trade agreements with Nandel by making Zarsha her prince consort—and no one came up with another inducement that would work—then if he decided to challenge the legitimacy of her rule, he might very well win.

"I don't lust for the throne, Your Majesty," he said, holding up his hands in a gesture of innocence. He looked and sounded sincere enough, but trust was a luxury she could not afford.

"Are you certain, Uncle?" she asked in a dangerous undertone, and had the momentary satisfaction of seeing a look of unease cross his face.

"I want what is best for Rhozinolm," he said. "Even if I *did* lust for the throne, I'm not the sort of man who would endanger our kingdom to take it."

"So the council was wrong to think you'd go to war with Tamzin if they put him on the throne?"

"You are not Tamzin. I would argue that a war would have been the lesser evil than having him on the throne. And may I remind you that I eat one of those damned seed cakes at the start of every council meeting. If you think I'm a threat . . ." He lifted his shoulders in a gesture that was meant to look nonchalant.

Ellin was sure he knew as well as she that she couldn't afford to cold-bloodedly murder any more of her advisers. If Tamzin hadn't been in the act of committing treason when she'd killed him, she'd have ended up in a dungeon, queen or not. The ring she wore and the seed cakes her council members ate were nothing more than a ceremonial reminder, and she did not believe for a moment that they would prevent her uncle from making trouble if he so chose. Which meant that perhaps a different tactic was in order.

She needed to make certain he was fully committed both to arranging her marriage to Zarsha and to continuing to trade with Women's Well, and she suspected she knew just the lever to use.

"How is Kailee?" she asked. "I believe she has a birthday coming up?"

Kailindar stiffened and paled at the mention of his daughter by his first wife. The poor girl had been blind since birth, and though he'd consulted with the abbess of every abbey throughout Seven Wells, no one had been able to reverse the girl's condition. Some men would have sent the child to the Abbey as soon as the blindness was deemed incurable, and the older Kailee grew, the more polite society murmured. Worse even than the blindness itself was the appearance of her milky eyes. In an old woman, the milkiness would be dismissed as cataracts. But in a woman Kailee's age, the first impression was that her Mindseye was shockingly open. Even with her beauty and her impeccable pedigree, she was considered unmarriageable. And there was only one place an unmarriageable girl was meant to live.

Kailindar looked so stricken that Ellin instantly regretted the impulse to mention his daughter directly after having questioned his loyalty. He clearly doted on the girl, and how could he not take her question as a threat under the circumstances? A fact of which she'd been well aware before she'd spoken. She'd let her suspicions get the best of her and been needlessly cruel.

"Forgive me, Uncle," she said, refusing to lie by claiming innocence. "I wish no ill upon your daughter."

"But you can command me to send her to the Abbey, and you wanted to remind me of that fact. I was actually pleasantly surprised you did not bring that up when I opposed your decision to dismiss Lord Creethan. It seems I gave you too much credit." His voice was cold and bitter, and he would not meet her eyes.

The words stung, and Ellin cursed herself for mismanaging the conversation. He might have bristled and heard a threat no matter how she'd broached the subject, but she'd done so in a way guaranteed to make him shut down when what she needed was for him to open up.

"I would never command you to send her to the Abbey," she insisted. "You have my word on that. Kailee is sweet and kind and deserves all the love you can give her."

Kailindar was clearly unconvinced. "You wouldn't be the first person to suggest I should have sent her to the Abbey by now."

"Perhaps not, but you won't hear it from me." Even with the improvements she had forced down the Abbey's throat, it was little better than a prison, though its inhabitants were guilty of no crime. "I was rather thinking that perhaps I could help you find a husband for her."

Kailindar shook his head. "I will not have her married by royal decree."

Ellin sighed quietly. While she could technically command one of her subjects to marry Kailee, she was well aware that doing so would do the girl no favors. "That isn't what I meant." It was far too likely

that any man forced to marry her would swiftly divorce her and send
her to the Abbey, and while the sovereign had the right to order her
subjects to marry, she did not have the right to forbid them to divorce. "I merely wanted to ask if you would mind if I made some
inquiries on her behalf." In truth, she already had someone in mind,
but she was not yet ready to show her hand.

Kailindar stared at her in silence for a moment, no doubt trying to
guess her intent. That he was still hearing a hint of threat in her offer
seemed clear. "I can't imagine there is a man who would have her to
whom I'd be willing to entrust her," he said carefully. "But I have no
objection to you trying."

She nodded briskly. "Very well then. I will see what I can do. You
have my word that I will neither order you to send her to the Abbey
nor order her marriage if you and she are not agreeable to the match."

His gaze was still wary as he met her eyes. "And *I* give *you* my
word that I will always do what is best for Rhozinolm. It would never
even occur to me to sabotage the negotiations with Prince Waldmir
merely because I disagreed with one of your decisions. I hope you
believe that."

"I do," she said with somewhat more assurance than she felt. It
was hard to shake the feeling that he might be waiting in the wings,
secretly hoping for her to fail so he could usurp the throne for himself. But perhaps that was merely an insidious side effect to Tamzin's
scheming. Perhaps her cousin's greed for the throne had tainted her
view so much she could not trust her own instincts.

CHAPTER ELEVEN

Delnamal had never expected to *enjoy* being king—he'd seen the harried, stressful, complicated life his father had lived and had not envied the man—but he had never fully appreciated just how *tedious* it could be. The meetings of the royal council were the absolute worst.

He'd been attending council meetings since he'd turned fourteen, and when he'd been a boy, his father had had an annoying habit of quizzing him on the proceedings afterward to make sure he'd paid attention. But as a man, he'd happily let his attention drift whenever the topic was especially dull, and though he suspected his father had been aware of this dereliction of duty, he had never called Delnamal to the table over it.

Now that Delnamal was king himself, however, he no longer had the freedom to tune out the boring parts—which was, to tell the truth, most of it—and if he missed anything or someone had to repeat himself, he was well aware of the disapproving glances around the table.

Delnamal took a sip of his wine, hoping that little bit of movement would help wake him up as the trade minister droned on and on about the intricacies of one of Aaltah's myriad trade agreements. It seemed there were new ones coming up for renegotiation every day, and if there was a topic duller than trade, Delnamal couldn't name it. He really should rearrange the daily agenda so that the trade minister's report did not come directly after luncheon. With a satisfying meal digesting in his belly and several goblets of wine mellowing his mood, that droning voice was as soporific as a mother's lullaby.

He blinked and gulped down the rest of his wine, realizing that despite his best intentions, he'd been on the verge of falling asleep. The wine really was most excellent, and he gestured with his goblet for the page to refill it. The lord commander frowned as the page obeyed, but Delnamal pretended not to see it. If the lord commander expected him to sit through the remaining hours of the afternoon without the aid and comfort of a drink, he was much mistaken. Of all the members of his royal council, the lord commander—who had once been the commanding officer of Delnamal's revoltingly perfect half-brother—was the one who most often gave the impression he was measuring Delnamal against his former protégé and finding him lacking.

The world was pleasantly hazy around the edges, and Delnamal was wondering if he could maybe close his eyes for just a few seconds without anyone noticing, when it suddenly occurred to him that the room had gone silent. Blinking in the vain hope that it might clear the fog, Delnamal sat a little straighter, surprised to find that his shoulders had been slumped forward, his chin nearly touching his chest.

The council room remained silent except for the sound of uncomfortably shifting asses.

"Well, go on then," he said irritably, grabbing for his goblet once more only to find it empty. "I wasn't asleep. I was just resting my eyes." Someone coughed, and Delnamal looked sharply at the other side of the table, ready to tear into anyone who dared challenge his assertion. No eyes met his.

"Get me some goddamn wine, will you?" he barked at the page, who hurried to obey. "Now where were we?"

The trade minister—officious twit that he was—cleared his throat with far more drama than necessary. "As I was saying, Your Majesty, the new terms offered are not quite on the level of offensive, but they are only just short of it. That little queen of theirs is feeling her oats, I should say. She is trying to appear the tough negotiator, but she has perhaps overplayed her hand."

Delnamal wondered just how long he'd been asleep—for he must indeed have drifted off, because he had no idea which trade agreement was being discussed, nor what terms had been offered. What he *did* know was that the bitch queen of Rhozinolm was directly responsible for his ignominious retreat from the borders of Women's Well, and he was not about to allow her to insult him again.

"Ordinarily," the trade minister continued, "I would counter with an offer somewhere in the middle, but—"

"Cancel it," Delnamal interrupted.

There was an audible gasp around the room, and the trade minister looked about to faint from shock. Delnamal felt a stirring of misgiving—apparently, they were not discussing one of the minor trade agreements of the sort he was used to hearing every day—but he could hardly halt the proceedings now and admit he did not actually know what they were talking about. The lord commander was practically glaring at him, as if Delnamal were one of his cadets who'd spoken out of turn to a superior officer.

"Rhozinolm needs to be taught a lesson," he said, swigging more wine. "If they cannot be bothered to make a good-faith offer, then we cannot be bothered to make an agreement with them at all."

The trade minister, still pale, rubbed his hands nervously on the table. "Threatening to withdraw from the agreement is perhaps a somewhat extreme tactic of negotiation," he said carefully, "but it may well frighten the girl into making a more palatable offer."

Delnamal felt almost as if he were two people, both sitting within one body. One of him was absurdly grateful that the trade minister had handed him this opportunity to gracefully retreat—of *course* he had meant to say they should *threaten* to cancel the agreement, not that they should *actually* do so. The other did not appreciate having a member of the lower council putting words into his mouth, when he was quite certain the trade minister knew he had been entirely serious when he'd said to cancel it.

There was a brief struggle as his two minds battled for supremacy, and he wasn't even entirely sure what he had decided, but words came out of his mouth anyway. "I said cancel it. Rhozinolm has never been a friend to Aaltah, and now they shall reap the rewards of their bad behavior."

The silence in the room was deafening. Delnamal ignored it as he drained the rest of his wine and once again held up his goblet for more.

It wasn't until after the meeting was over that Delnamal learned which trade agreement he had so blithely canceled. Apparently, the merchants of Aaltah would now lose their supply of Zinolm wool, the softest and most luxurious wool available anywhere in Seven Wells. Zinolm wool was not a vital necessity, he assured himself. Certainly it was in high demand—his winter wardrobe was full of the stuff—and certain spoiled members of the nobility would be annoyed at the loss. But surely his people would not have expected him to bend over for that damned queen to get it for them. He had stood up for the sovereign dignity of Aaltah, and that was his duty.

The people of Aaltah would understand. As long as no one on his council spoke too freely about the exact circumstances under which he had canceled the agreement.

But they wouldn't, of course. Discussing council business outside the council chamber was strictly forbidden and could lead to charges of treason. He would make certain the council was reminded frequently of that point of law, and they would keep their mouths shut.

Ellin would have been happy never to set eyes on Lord Creethan again, especially after the atrocious way he'd acted when she'd informed him he would no longer be a part of the royal council. He claimed to want to apologize for his behavior, but Ellin suspected he was more likely hoping to convince her to reinstate him.

Her first inclination when he'd requested an audience, naturally, had been to decline. Semsulin, however, had urged her to accept in hopes of mending whatever bridges possible. Creethan's family had not been silent in their outrage over his dismissal, and she was certain the recent cancellation of the trade agreement with Aaltah would be laid at her feet—even though Creethan had still been the trade minister when the terms were being negotiated. She could not afford to seem petty or hold a grudge, Semsulin argued, and she reluctantly agreed.

Lord Creethan bowed with every semblance of respect when he was shown into Ellin's office, and when he rose, his shoulders were slightly hunched, his gaze downcast. If she had not seen his explosion of temper when she'd dismissed him, she might think him truly repentant, maybe even embarrassed by his misdeeds. But she could never forget the look of hatred in his eyes, and she knew his polite court persona was nothing but a mask to hide his true, vicious self.

"Thank you for agreeing to see me, Your Majesty," he said, darting an anxious look up at her face. He seemed fidgety and nervous, his hands plucking at the buttons of his doublet as he shifted from foot to foot.

Ellin considered politely offering him a seat to soothe his unease, but decided against it. She would greatly prefer the audience stayed as short as possible. "You said it was important," she responded. She attempted to keep her tone neutral, but she was fairly certain a chill crept into it anyway. Once, she had thought of Creethan as harmless, but that had clearly been a mistake.

His eyes narrowed ever so slightly, his gaze turning sharp. Perhaps her tone had held more than just a little chill.

"I thought perhaps you might want to reconsider your hasty decision now that Aaltah has canceled our trade agreement. You will need a skilled negotiator to smooth things over and get that agreement renewed. With all my years—"

"Lord Creethan, are you forgetting that the terms to which King

Delnamal objected so strenuously are the ones you yourself put forth?" she interrupted. "If your purpose for this audience is merely to beg for your job back, then you might as well save us both the time."

Creethan shook his head, casting off his polite mask entirely. "If you were capable of being a queen rather than merely a woman, you would see that you are driving us all to the brink of ruin!"

Ellin's mouth dropped open. As badly as he'd remonstrated with her when she'd dismissed him, he had not gone so far as to offer open insult. But he was not finished.

"Prince Waldmir won't agree to renewal of our agreements and now you've alienated Aaltah as well, all because you insist on supporting that traitorous nothing of a principality that is of no strategic use to Rhozinolm whatsoever!"

Ellin pushed back her chair and rose to her feet, fighting to keep her own temper in check. "You had best leave the room this instant," she growled. "You are coming dangerously close to treason. Again."

The tension was such that the guard by the door took a couple of steps closer to Creethan, ready to seize him and bodily remove him if necessary. Ellin couldn't fathom why the man had bothered to request this audience at all. He'd made only a token attempt to convince her to reverse her decision, and surely the opportunity to insult her to her face was not worth the indignity of being bodily tossed out of her office.

Creethan bared his teeth in a snarl. And suddenly, there was a dagger in his hand. "I am loyal to the Crown of Rhozinolm, and I will see its rightful king on the throne!"

Ellin stood frozen in place, hardly able to comprehend what was happening. The door guard had been approaching Creethan from his left side and reached out to grab his left arm to keep him from getting any closer to Ellin. From behind her, she heard the sharp intake of breath from her personal guard, followed by the unsheathing of his sword. But Creethan made no attempt to rush toward her, instead plunging the dagger into his own breast.

For a fateful moment, everyone in the room was too stunned to react. Creethan's eyes blazed with pain and victory. Then they went white and his hand released the embedded dagger to reach into the air in front of him.

"Down!" both guards yelled at her in tandem as her personal guard reached her side and gave her a mighty shove.

The fall to the floor seemed to take a quarter of an hour, giving her a clear view of what happened next as Creethan brought his seemingly empty hand to the hilt of the dagger, activating the Kai spell that was no doubt infused into the jeweled pommel. She could not see the spell itself, but she saw Creethan fling that hand in her direction, aiming the spell at her as she fell. And then she saw her bodyguard step between her and the spell.

Ellin hit the floor with a grunt. Above her, her guard let out a cry of pain, and Creethan shrieked in frustrated fury. The guard collapsed on top of Ellin, knocking the wind out of her and making her vision momentarily go black. She didn't think she lost consciousness, but by the time she could breathe again, the room was swarming with guards. Ellin caught a brief glimpse of the guard who had saved her life as he was pulled off her. Blood streamed from the poor man's mouth and nose and eyes and ears. More blood than anyone could survive losing, although another guard put his fingers to the man's throat to search futilely for a pulse. She sat up, her whole body shaking with reaction, and saw that Creethan lay on the floor, his eyes wide and staring and his lips twisted into a permanent grimace of rage.

"Are you hurt anywhere, Your Majesty?" one of the guards asked her, kneeling by her side and looking at her in obvious concern.

Ellin looked down at herself and realized she was covered in blood. A sob rose from her throat, and no effort of will could keep it contained.

"Get a healer!" the guard shouted, but she shook her head.

"I-I'm not hurt," she stuttered between sobs. "Th-this isn't my blood."

The healer was sent for anyway, and Ellin was too shaken and miserable to protest.

———

Ellin sat shivering before the fire in her sitting room, cradling a hot cup of tea in her hands. The fire crackled cheerfully, and Ellin suspected the room was actually uncomfortably warm, but she couldn't seem to shake the chill.

"No one could have foreseen Lord Creethan would do such a thing," Semsulin said in a tone that was no doubt meant to be soothing. Comforting words were not his forte.

Objectively, Ellin knew he was right. Creethan had shown a flash of ugly temper when she'd dismissed him, but nothing had suggested he was so infuriated as to kill himself to destroy her. How could he possibly have hated her that much? And how could she possibly have failed to realize it? A good man had *died* to save her because she'd been too blind to see the truth.

"Do you think he really believed he was acting for the good of the kingdom?" she asked.

Semsulin snorted. "I think he saw the comfortable life he'd built for himself collapsing before his eyes and couldn't face the future."

Ellin frowned deeply, hardly able to comprehend what had happened. Tamzin's attempt to wrest her kingdom from her had hardly come as a surprise, but Creethan's assassination attempt felt like some bad dream come true. "Surely it's an exaggeration to say his life was collapsing simply because he was no longer on the royal council," she protested.

"I suspect if we investigate further, we will find he'd been using his office for a great deal of personal gain. You will, of course, write up a posthumous writ of attainder on him. I would not be at all surprised if, when the Crown seizes his assets, we find he has accumulated far more wealth than we knew. And I also suspect we will find he was beholden to people who would have been . . . displeased with him for losing his influence. I don't believe his attempt had much, if anything, to do with what he perceived as the good of the kingdom."

Ellin took a sip of her tea. She wanted to put the cup down, but she was afraid that with her hands idle, she'd once again start rubbing her wrist where she'd found a drop of her dead guard's blood that had escaped her attention when she'd changed out of her bloody clothes. She'd thoroughly scrubbed it off already and had the irritated red patch on her skin to show for it.

"But still, to kill himself in order to kill me . . ." She shuddered. Her guards had been prepared for attacks both physical and magical, and she knew for a fact that while they were on protection duty they had shield spells activated at all times. But not *Kai* shields, at least not in the supposed safety of her own palace.

"He knew that was his only chance to succeed," Semsulin said. "Perhaps he feared his family would suffer for his misdeeds, and he thought putting Lord Kailindar on the throne would save them." His eyes met hers, and his voice took on a brittle edge. "And perhaps Lord Kailindar encouraged him to believe such a thing . . ."

Ellin put down her tea and sat forward, staring into the face of her lord chancellor and trying to read the thoughts behind his careful expression. She was not shocked at his suggestion, for it was obvious to anyone with a modicum of sense that Kailindar would be the greatest beneficiary in the event of her sudden and unexpected death. "So you believe Kailindar is behind the attempt?"

Semsulin met her gaze unflinchingly. "I would not dismiss the notion out of hand. Just because he doesn't display the same kind of naked ambition as Tamzin doesn't mean it's not there."

Ellin had not yet told anyone about her promise to make inquiries on Kailee's behalf, and she couldn't help wondering if her uncle had seized on what he'd taken as an implicit threat to his daughter's safety and used that as an excuse to remove her from the throne. But their conversation had ended on what felt like a cautiously positive note, and she could hardly believe he'd been contemplating regicide. Nor did he seem the sort to make such a precipitous decision without some sort of severe provocation.

Then again, Ellin had failed to see the depths of Lord Creethan's hatred, so perhaps her judgment was not to be trusted on this matter.

"I see no reason to believe Creethan was acting on anyone's authority but his own," Ellin said, though the words came out sounding more like a question than a statement.

Semsulin shrugged as if it hardly mattered. "Even so, it would behoove you to have Kailindar questioned."

She recoiled at the very thought. If he'd been affronted by her stripping of a ceremonial title, she could only imagine how he would react to being questioned about his possible involvement with an assassination attempt. "Only if I am willing to alienate him forever." She wasn't certain of her ability to win him over with a marriage for Kailee, but she *was* sure she would lose any possibility of goodwill if she humiliated him by having him questioned.

"If he's behind the attempt, then alienating him is hardly an issue."

"But—"

"Even if he's not," Semsulin interrupted in what was for him a rare breach of protocol, "we have to consider that Creethan's attack is a symptom of a greater issue. You have as yet not secured our trade agreements with Nandel, you have lost an important trade agreement with Aaltah—a loss that is not of your own doing, but whose consequences will still be laid at your feet—and you have allied yourself with an upstart principality that many believe will be utterly destroyed before long. It is all too easy to see other malcontents viewing Kailindar as a potential savior, and the assassination attempt makes you seem vulnerable despite its failure."

Ellin had not thought it possible to feel any greater chill in her soul. "Just what are you suggesting, Lord Semsulin?" she asked, although she knew the answer perfectly well.

Semsulin hesitated only a moment before he put his implication into words. "I'm suggesting that Kailindar may be a danger to your throne whether he was behind this attempt or not. There are many already who consider him the rightful king and who support you only because they aren't especially fond of him. The more discontented the people become, the more attractive Kailindar will become. Lord Creethan may have given you an excellent opportunity to rid yourself of a dangerous rival—*before* his popularity comes to exceed your own."

Ellin was well aware that many monarchs before her had managed to conveniently rid themselves of anyone who might conceivably prosecute a rival claim to the throne. No doubt some of those rivals had been legitimate threats, but there was little doubt many had been eliminated merely as a precaution.

"I'm well aware the suggestion is . . . distasteful," Semsulin said when her silence stretched out for too long. "Rest assured that I don't make it lightly. But it is my duty as your lord chancellor to point out the unexpected opportunity today's unfortunate events have provided you."

Ellin stared down at her hands. "What would my grandfather have done if he were in my place?" she asked softly.

Semsulin's reply was swift and unequivocal. "King Linolm was never an especially sentimental man. If he saw a danger to his throne, he would be quick to eliminate it in any way possible. Your father would have done the same, had he survived to take the throne. But this isn't a question of what others would have done in your place. You must make the decision for yourself. After all, you are the one who has to live with it. Keep in mind, however, the distinct possibility that Lord Kailindar *is* behind this attempt."

Ellin noted that her lord chancellor had a remarkable facility for presenting something as a decision she must make herself while making it abundantly clear which decision he felt she *should* make.

If she had Kailindar questioned, there was no doubt in her mind that the magistrate who did the questioning could find an excuse to call in the royal inquisitor. Just as she had no doubt that the inquisitor could be persuaded to bring about the desired conclusion.

"Shall I contact the magistrate?" Semsulin prompted.

Ellin took a long moment before she answered, though in truth she'd known her decision all along. Killing Tamzin in the heat of the moment when he was openly attempting to seize her throne and throw her in the dungeon was one thing. Manufacturing evidence that Kailindar had planned an assassination attempt against her, condemning him to torture and eventual attainder and execution, was quite another.

"Not just yet," she said. "I believe I may have another way to ensure his loyalty."

"Oh?" Semsulin said with a raise of his eyebrow. "What might that be?"

"Let me determine if my way is plausible before I go into detail."

"Even if he is entirely loyal, that does not preclude others from rising up in his name," Semsulin cautioned.

"I know. I'll just have to make sure that uprising would not have the desired effect."

Semsulin was frowning at her, not surprisingly. She waited for him to point out that the assassination attempt might never have happened if she had taken his sage advice in the first place and not dismissed Lord Creethan. She was sure the thought had crossed his mind, but the words did not cross his lips.

"We can make the whole question moot if we can somehow persuade Prince Waldmir to approve your marriage to Zarsha," he said instead.

She nodded. "Something that will likely be much easier to do if Kailindar continues to represent me in the negotiations and does so wholeheartedly.

"I will not have him questioned by a magistrate at the moment," she said decisively. "But I reserve the right to change my mind if I cannot reliably secure his loyalty. I will make sure he understands that."

CHAPTER TWELVE

Alys stared at the door through which Honor had exited, listening to her footsteps retreat and breathing deeply. It was an uncommonly early hour for her to retire for the night, but she'd heard Jinnell's name mentioned earlier in the evening, and that alone had been enough to sink her into melancholy. She'd held off the grief while in public by promising herself a good cry as soon as she could get away. Not that crying ever seemed to do much to relieve the pain, but she'd found that if she held it all in for too long, the tears would escape at inopportune moments.

When at last she could hear Honor's footsteps no more, Alys collapsed onto a settee, covering her face with her hands and weeping with abandon. The pain was like a breathing, malignant creature that resided inside her chest, constantly gnawing on her bones, squeezing the air out of her lungs whenever she allowed herself the briefest illusion that it might be easing up even a fraction. It was incomprehensible to her how someone, *anyone*, could intentionally cause another person this kind of agony, for she couldn't imagine inflicting it on even her worst enemy. She would happily kill Delnamal with her own hands, and it would not trouble her conscience one bit if she made him scream loud and long while she did, but she would not put even him through *this*.

She cried until her eyes had no more tears to shed and her body ached with exhaustion. Her breath still came in hiccups, and her nose remained stopped up no matter how many times she blew it.

From a silken purse that lay on her bedside table came a soft chirping sound that could only be the talker she made a habit of carrying with her at all times. She had a nice array of the little talking fliers in her office at the town hall, but the one she had paired with Queen Ellinsoltah's was the only one she habitually carried, for there was no alliance more important to the survival of Women's Well than that one.

Still sniffling, Alys retrieved the little talker from the purse with a baleful look. There was no point in keeping it with her at all times if she was going to ignore its call, but she was hardly in a state to be seen right now. Bad enough she was dressed for bed, but she did not need a mirror to know she looked a fright, with reddened nose and eyes making it obvious she'd been weeping.

The talker continued to chirp patiently as she swiped at her cheeks and dabbed at her nose. She grabbed a heavy black shawl to drape over her nightdress, though with her hair uncovered and braided anyone could tell she'd been ready for bed. Digging deep inside herself for a semblance of calm, she opened her Mindseye and plucked a mote of Rho from the air to activate the talker and complete its spell. When she closed her Mindseye once more, a faint image of Ellinsoltah hovered in the air before her.

Ellinsoltah was a lovely woman whose wisdom and demeanor belied her young age. She'd spent most of her life expecting to be nothing more than a nobleman's wife, and to have no graver responsibilities than running her husband's household, and yet she had handled her unexpected ascension to the throne with uncommon grace and poise, despite difficult circumstances.

There was no question she knew she had caught Alys at an inopportune time, but Alys was thankful the younger woman let her keep her dignity and did not openly remark on her appearance.

"Good evening, Your Royal Highness," Ellinsoltah said, the gentleness in her voice the only sign that she had noticed Alys's state of distress. "Forgive me for contacting you without warning, but I was hoping you and I could have a conversation in a more unofficial manner. It is nothing urgent, however, so if you'd prefer to talk at some other time . . ."

Alys would not risk offending Rhozinolm by putting Ellinsoltah off—even if she *weren't* immediately and thoroughly curious. She patted at her hair, thinking how few people had ever seen her with her hair uncovered—a thought that she quickly shoved aside, for of course one of those few people was Jinnell, and she did not need her mind to go down that path again.

"I am more than happy to talk, Your Majesty, if my appearance does not offend."

Ellinsoltah grinned, reaching up to touch the pearl-studded headdress resting on her tightly coiled hair. "It only makes me jealous that I am still pinned and coiffed myself. And please, call me Ellin. Let's keep this as informal as possible."

A conversation between two monarchs could only be so informal, but Alys owed her life—and the lives of just about everyone in Women's Well—to Ellinsoltah's decision to recognize and support her, so their relationship was already somewhat extraordinary.

"I will call you Ellin if you will call me Alys."

Ellin smiled and inclined her head. "Here we've negotiated a deal, just the two of us, without a council of advisers to complicate things."

Although Ellin clearly meant the words as something of a joke, Alys didn't think the quip was born entirely of humor. Then again, considering the struggles Ellin had had with her royal council, it wasn't entirely surprising that she'd make a joke at their expense.

"I'm sure our advisers mean well," Alys said, "but they can be tedious on occasion, I must admit."

Ellin started to say something, then seemed to change her mind, frowning. Then she shook her head and smiled ruefully. "We've had frank discussions in the past. Would you mind if I'm less than diplomatic for a moment?"

Alys raised her eyebrows. It seemed this conversation was going to be even more informal than she'd expected. She wondered if this approach was a sign of Ellin's youth and inexperience, or if it was all calculated to disarm. No doubt it would be wise to treat any contact with a foreign sovereign with some caution, but Alys wasn't sure she had the energy for such caution after her crying jag.

Ellin took her lack of answer for assent.

"My lord chancellor would probably expire in horror to hear me say this to someone other than himself, but while my royal council is no longer on the verge of open rebellion, I still don't have the level of support I would like."

Alys forced her weary mind to focus a little more closely, for she imagined there were few lord chancellors who would *not* object to their sovereign admitting such turmoil to a foreigner. Then again, Ellin was fully aware of the power she had over Women's Well, of how badly Alys needed her support. There was likely no one else in the world more apt to keep such knowledge to herself than Alys, and Ellin knew it.

"I'm sorry to hear that," Alys said, and it was true. She imagined Ellin's council—entirely made up of older men, almost all of whom had been appointed to their positions by her late grandfather—had a great deal of trouble adjusting to having a woman on the throne, and Ellin's tender age would only exacerbate the situation. "But I must profess to some puzzlement as to why you might share that with me."

No doubt it was because Ellin had some notion that Alys could do something to help, but Alys was at a loss to figure out how.

"You know that my uncle Kailindar is now my lord chamberlain."

"And that some would argue he has a stronger claim to the throne than you do," Alys said, nodding. The slight tightening at the corners of Ellin's eyes suggested that claim to the throne made her uncomfortable—as well it should. Tradition would highly favor the late king's bastard son taking the throne over his legitimate granddaughter, and there was little doubt in anyone's mind that Kailindar would have ascended the throne if not for his conflict with Tamzin.

Now that impediment was gone, and it seemed likely much of Ellin's council regretted having approved her claim.

Other than that faint hint of discomfort, Ellin did not respond to Alys's comment. "I need his support," she said bluntly. "And so do you, if we are to maintain our alliance and keep King Delnamal from marching on Women's Well again."

This time, it was Alys whose eyes tightened, though she tried to keep her expression as neutral as possible. "And you fear you do not have it."

Ellin shook her head. "Let's just say I have reason to doubt the depth of his loyalty under the present circumstances. There was an attempt on my life."

Alys gasped. It was likely every other sovereign in Seven Wells would find out about the attempt through their spy networks, but she doubted she would have heard about it until much later. While Tynthanal did still have some friends in Aaltah, the man who had once fed him the most information had been captured and suffered a traitor's death, leaving Women's Well uncomfortably close to blind.

"Obviously, the attempt failed," Ellin said with a little smile that was supposed to look rueful, although the smile took too much effort to be convincing. "I have no reason to believe that Lord Kailindar was involved, but even if he wasn't, the attempt may inspire others to contemplate the possibility that they might prefer his rule to mine. And my decision to ally with you is not exactly popular."

Alys suppressed a shiver of dread. If she lost the alliance with Rhozinolm, then Women's Well would quickly fall to Delnamal's army.

"There are those who have suggested to me that I can best protect my throne by eliminating Kailindar," Ellin said bluntly.

Alys winced, for though it was far from unusual for sovereigns to treat potential rival claimants to the throne harshly, it was not a topic that was habitually discussed so openly.

"I'm certain my crown would be safer if the malcontents did not have so easy a standard to rally around," Ellin continued, "and to be honest, no one would be surprised if I were to accuse him of treason, whether he's guilty or not. However, I believe I may have a more . . . creative—and humane—way to secure his cooperation."

Alys was nothing if not intrigued. "Oh?"

"He has an unmarried daughter who has just turned twenty."

Alys knew at once where this conversation was leading. Girls tra-ditionally went on the marriage market when they turned eighteen—though they were sometimes unofficially betrothed long before that. A girl from a royal family might be expected to marry later than an ordinary noblewoman, simply because of the diplomatic implications of her marriage, but with Lord Kailindar being a bastard, his daugh-ter's marriage would not have such dynastic import. If she was still unmarried—and even unbetrothed—at twenty, that likely meant she was in danger of spinsterhood. And Ellinsoltah would not be men-tioning her if the girl were already betrothed.

"She is a little old for Corlin," Alys said, although she felt certain it was not Corlin Ellin had in mind for her cousin. It wasn't com-pletely unheard of for parents to begin discussing marriage prospects for a boy of fourteen, but it would be unusual for him to marry until he was at least in his twenties.

"But you have an unmarried brother, do you not?"

"I'm . . . not sure I can help you in that way," Alys said, trying not to squirm. Tynthanal would not be happy with her if she shared the truth about his inability with a virtual stranger, and yet she wasn't sure how else to explain her reluctance.

Ellin raised her eyebrows in polite inquiry. "Is there a betrothal already of which I am not aware?"

"No, but . . ."

"But you worry that Kailindar's daughter is not worthy of him if she has not yet been betrothed at the advanced age of twenty." There was an edge in Ellin's voice now, a slight hardening in her expression.

"It's not that," Alys hastened to say, though in truth she couldn't help wondering what was wrong with Kailindar's daughter. There had to be something, for though her father was a bastard, he was a *rich* bastard, and her dowry should have been tempting. "It's just that my brother has a . . . strong attachment, and he would object to the prospect of marrying another."

"Even if that marriage might make it possible to protect all of Women's Well?" Ellin asked. "Kailindar dotes on his daughter, and if she were living as your brother's wife, he would do everything in his power to see that our alliance is maintained to keep her safe. It would go a long way toward securing my throne—and your principality—if the malcontents among my people don't see eliminating me as a way of eliminating our relationship with Women's Well."

It was a fair argument—and one Alys would definitely have to have with Tynthanal if she succeeded in creating a fertility potion for him. Having no reasonable counter, she decided to try deflecting instead.

"If Kailindar dotes on his daughter so much, why would he risk sending her to our embattled principality in the first place? Surely he has more enticing marriage prospects for her in the safety and security of Rhozinolm."

"But of course you've guessed that if that were the case, she'd be betrothed by now."

"So why isn't she?"

It was Ellin's turn to look uncomfortable, though her voice was as firm and certain as always. "Kailee is a lovely girl, kind and soft-spoken, and quite beautiful."

"But . . ."

Ellin raised her shoulders in a small shrug. "But she has been blind since birth, and no healer's spell or abigail's potion has been able to reverse the condition. People say she should have been consigned to the Abbey as soon as her blindness was discovered."

Alys winced in sympathy for the poor girl—and was thankful her father had not conformed to that expectation.

"She can come to Women's Well with a substantial dowry in addition to cementing the relationship between our two lands," Ellin continued. "I will freely admit her blindness is an impediment, but she would make your brother a good wife nonetheless. And who knows? Maybe your Academy will be able to help her in ways that our Academy and our Abbey could not."

"Let me think about it," Alys said. Ellin's eyes narrowed, but Alys continued before she could remonstrate. "There are potential problems with this arrangement that I am not at liberty to share. Surely it's not something that must be decided right this moment."

"No," Ellin conceded. "But the longer we wait, the greater the risk becomes. If we could perhaps arrange for them to meet? Even knowing there is a *potential* match could go a long way toward gaining Kailindar's staunch support—and making him a less attractive alternative to myself."

Alys chewed her lip, realizing she was in no position to refuse. Women's Well was too dependent on Rhozinolm's support, more like a vassal than a true ally. And Ellinsoltah's grip on her own throne was alarmingly weak. A marriage alliance with the man who was the greatest threat to Ellin's throne was the surest way to keep the people of Women's Well safe.

All she had to do to make that happen was create an effective fertility potion for Tynthanal, then convince him that he could not marry the woman he loved and must instead marry a blind girl.

"I will do what I can to remove the . . . impediments," Alys said. "I feel it would be unwise to arrange a meeting until I have succeeded, but rest assured I will work as quickly as possible."

Ellin looked grim. "One way or another, an impediment must be removed—and the sooner the better. I would far prefer to do it by marriage than death. There has been far too much death in my family recently."

Alys closed her eyes and sighed. She did not want to put Ellin in the position of having to kill her uncle—and likely ruin his entire family in the process—to protect their alliance. But even the most desperate father would be unlikely to marry his beloved daughter to a man who could not give her children, especially in a principality that teetered on the brink of war.

"I will do my best," Alys swore, imagining she would spend many sleepless nights at the Academy in the near future. And dreading the conversation she would have to have with Tynthanal.

Norah was shaking and weak—the result of yet another forced fast—as she made her way up the stairs to the abbess's suite of rooms. She was well aware that she would have more than an empty belly to complain about should Mairahsol discover her, but she couldn't ask any of her sisters to take risks she was not willing to take herself, and just being in possession of the little pot of ointment she carried was against not only the rules of the Abbey, but the laws of Khalpar itself. When she'd found the paper with the formula for the Keyhole ointment tucked in Mairahsol's office on one of the many occasions she'd been ordered to clean it, her first thought had been that she now had the power to ruin the false abbess. Just being in possession of the formula was a crime, after all. But she quickly realized the abbess could merely claim she had confiscated the paper from someone else, and so Norah had decided to make an entirely different use of her discovery. She'd memorized the ingredients so that now she could make the ointment herself.

The lord high priest's visits to the Abbey rarely lasted less than an hour, and Mairahsol rarely emerged from her rooms once he had arrived, so in all likelihood, Norah would not be caught. But that did not make the prospect of discovery any less frightening, and Norah's heart pattered nervously in her chest as she tiptoed across the landing to the closed door of the abbess's chambers. The door was solid enough—and tightly enough fit—that while Norah could sometimes hear voices from behind it, she could not understand what anyone was saying, even with her ear pressed against it. Hence, the need for the Keyhole ointment.

Standing in front of the door, Norah grimaced when she heard the echoes of a faint, rhythmic knocking sound—all too familiar within the walls of this abbey. Norah had thought that perhaps Mairahsol would stop entertaining the one and only client who had ever shown any interest in her now that she had gotten what she wanted out of him. But then again, a woman as repulsive as she in both face and personality was no doubt overjoyed at the attentions of a powerful and not-unattractive man such as the lord high priest.

Leaning against the doorjamb, Norah waited for the banging sounds to stop, having no desire to look in on the festivities. After decades in this abbey, Norah understood men in a way she never would have had she remained free. The lord high priest obviously took some perverse pleasure in lying with the pox-faced bitch, but that was not the primary purpose behind his visits to the Abbey. Of that, Norah was certain. And if she could learn what additional services the lord high priest received from Mairahsol, she might find the key to removing the scheming pretender from her undeserved position.

When the sounds of sex were replaced by the soft, nearly imperceptible murmur of voices, Norah opened her little jar of ointment, dipping her pinky into it and rubbing a tiny circle on the door. She opened her Mindseye and activated the Keyhole spell with three motes of Rho. The voices from within became clear, though she still had to strain to hear them. She closed her Mindseye and saw that the circle of ointment had made a small transparent spot on the door, as if a piece of glass had been inserted, allowing her to see inside the room—as if peeking through a keyhole.

Mairahsol and the lord high priest were seated on the sofa in front of the fire. She was reclining with her back propped against the sofa's arm, her bare feet resting in his lap. Her dead-straight black hair was loose and disheveled around her shoulders, her wimple nowhere to be seen. The lord high priest was still panting contentedly, one hand resting on her ankles while the other idly stroked the tops of her feet, the picture of intimacy.

They engaged in a few minutes of revolting pillow talk, then the annoyingly short-lived Keyhole spell wore off. Norah repeated the process of smearing on the ointment and activating the spell, and her view became clear once more.

She had to renew the spell three more times before Mairahsol and the lord high priest finally started talking about more interesting subjects.

"Have I now greeted you thoroughly enough to be permitted to ask you about your progress in reversing the Curse?" the lord high priest asked.

Mairahsol sighed with great satisfaction, simpering as if she still thought herself a desirable young debutante with a great future ahead of her. How the lord high priest could stomach the woman was beyond Norah's imagination.

"I believe you have earned that privilege, my lord," she said, and she had the audacity to flutter her eyelashes. Norah wished the Keyhole spell carried sound only, so that she would not feel obligated to watch as well as listen.

"Happy to hear it. So has there been any progress?"

"I believe there has," Mairahsol said brightly, and the lord high priest looked as surprised as Norah felt. The so-called abbess had ordered everyone in the Abbey who was not actively working the pavilion or the market to comb through the Abbey's archives in search of "useful information," but it was an obviously futile task, seeing as the Curse—or the Blessing, as those who worshipped the Mother of All called it—was a spell unlike anything ever cast or even imagined before. The Abbey's "archives" consisted of the scribbles and often incomprehensible notes of abigails past, not a true library of carefully catalogued information, which made searching through it an exercise in frustration. Some of the "documents" were centuries old, and there were hundreds of duplicates of the most commonly used spells. The thought that the cure for the Curse was contained somewhere in those archives was ludicrous.

"Nothing to get too excited about yet," Mairahsol cautioned. "I merely have found an intriguing possibility to follow up on."

"I can't tell you how pleased I am to hear that. Please, do tell me more."

Norah muttered a soft curse under her breath as the Keyhole spell wore off once more. It was outlawed because it was considered an intrusion of privacy, dangerous in the wrong hands. Norah would argue that it didn't last long enough to be truly invasive, and she suspected the men of the Academy had developed something with a longer duration for the use of the Crown's spy network. She applied another dab of ointment and hoped she'd made enough in the small batch to gather the information she needed.

". . . trigger a vision," Mairahsol was saying when the spell was active once again.

The lord high priest's face creased with what appeared to be genuine concern. "I have heard that the process is . . . quite unpleasant."

Mairahsol seemed unable to hold back a shudder, her arms crossing over her chest in a protective gesture. "It is far from enjoyable. But I will do whatever I must to show the king that I am worthy of the trust he put in me."

"To remain Abbess of Khalpar, you mean," Jalzarnin said in a teasing tone, though Norah thought she detected a hint of bite beneath the surface. The lord high priest did not strike Norah as a fool, so he had to know that Mairahsol's only motivations were spite and ambition. Perhaps he took offense that she would bother to pretend otherwise.

Mairahsol pouted, though the sparkle in her eye said she had not detected any undertone. "I can hardly be expected to find a cure for the Curse as a lowly abigail, now can I? I want nothing but what's best for my kingdom."

Jalzarnin smiled. "Naturally. Now tell me, did this vision of yours grant you any useful information?"

"I'd call it *hopeful* information. Only time will tell if it is actually useful."

"What did you see?"

"I saw myself activating a spell in a vial of potion and then pouring it into a seer's poison. I cannot say what was in that potion, because I could not see the elements in my vision. I then drank the poison, and before it took effect, I asked for a vision that would lead to the reversal of the Curse."

Norah was so outraged she had to clap a hand over her mouth to keep her protest contained. That was *not* how visions worked! One did not *demand* that the Mother give one a vision—even when one believed in the Mother as a deity secondary to the Creator—nor did one order up anything *specific* as if one were some peasant ordering beer at a tavern. Mairahsol might very well have had a vision—she had taken one of the vials of seer's poison from the stockroom—but she was as likely to have poured it into her chamber pot as to have actually drunk it, and she was clearly lying about what she said she saw.

"My vision ended after that," Mairahsol continued, "so I have no guarantee that the spell I saw myself casting actually *worked*. However, I can guarantee that I would not drink a seer's poison on a whim. Future-me had some reason to believe it was worth the suffering to drink that poison."

The lord high priest rubbed his chin thoughtfully. "It is true that the Abbess of Aaltah was known to be a gifted seer, and it seems reasonable that her ability to see visions materially contributed to her ability to cast that impossible spell. What do you plan to do from here?"

"I will require every seer in the Abbey to apply herself to the use and research of seer's poisons. Once I have gained a thorough understanding of the poisons that are currently available—and once I have gained as much information as possible from all the visions—I will attempt to develop a spell that will help direct visions in a desired direction."

This time, Norah couldn't contain her soft snort, but Mairahsol and the lord high priest were too absorbed in their conversation to notice. It was plain to anyone with eyes that Mairahsol was stringing the lord high priest along with yet another promise of the impossible. And that she had engineered an excuse to force her seers—almost all of whom worshipped the Mother of All beside Norah—to suffer through the triggering of frivolous visions just for her own cruel amusement.

The conversation quickly devolved into what was obviously the prelude to more sex, so Norah withdrew. She had heard nothing that would help her engineer Mairahsol's downfall. But at least she had gained reassurance that the false abbess was about to waste a great deal of time during her temporary tenure. Mairahsol might have convinced the lord high priest that she was making progress, but it would take more than that one false vision to convince the king.

Norah could not say she felt *reassured* by what she had heard, but she was at least mildly heartened. Mairahsol was no closer to being confirmed as abbess now than she had been when she'd first been installed. And time continued its inevitable march.

CHAPTER THIRTEEN

Mairah's heart pattered in her chest, and her palms were damp with sweat, though she hoped her face was appropriately impassive. One of the abigails shrieked in pain, writhing on her bed and clutching at her throat, where Mairah knew the poison burned like a swallowed hot poker. Another stifled a moan with a fist as tears and snot streamed down her face.

Eight seers lay suffering on the hard cots of the dormitory, their concerned sisters darting from cot to cot, holding hands and wiping sweaty brows. The room stank of vomit and the acrid reek of poison, and even some of the abigails who ordinarily would have known better cast looks of loathing and reproach Mairah's way, for of course it was by her order that the seers had taken the poisons.

The stink of the room was making Mairah's own stomach groan in protest, and she was surprised to find that each cry of pain triggered a twinge of guilt in her breast.

These women were her *enemies*, she reminded herself. Even Sister Sulrai—who alone among these abigails was not an associate of

Norah's—was a surly and unpleasant bitch for whom Mairah felt nothing but disdain. But even so, it was all Mairah could do not to flinch as Sister Melred, the most powerful of all their seers, who had taken the strongest of the poisons, began clawing at her chest and throat so viciously that one of her sisters was forced to restrain her.

Standing by the doorway near Mairah, Norah was openly crying, her hands clasped into white-knuckled fists as she watched. She must have sensed Mairah's glance, for she met her abbess's eyes with an expression of pure hatred.

Mairah again reminded herself that these women had repeatedly hurt and insulted her over the years she'd been trapped in the Abbey. They *deserved* to suffer for their cruelty.

Yet Mairah's conscience twinged again, for in point of fact Sister Melred—although she was clearly a member of Norah's inner circle—was sweet and quiet and in all ways inoffensive. This was not the pleasant revenge Mairah had had in mind when she'd given the order, but it was nonetheless a necessary step in convincing Jalzarnin—and through him the king—that she deserved to be named abbess permanently.

Guilt was not an emotion with which Mairah had a great deal of experience, and she couldn't say she cared for the feeling. She returned Norah's glare with what she hoped was a gloating smile.

"I bet you're thanking the Mother that She didn't make you a seer," she said. The jibe rang false in her own ears, revealing far more of her true feelings than she would have liked. However, Norah was too furious to notice such subtleties. From the look on her face, it was all she could do not to leap on Mairah and claw her eyes out.

Sister Melred wailed, loud and long, and Norah looked her way with undisguised anguish, momentarily forgetting her hatred. Mairah suppressed a shudder and decided there was no reason she needed to stay in the room any longer. It would take many long minutes for the poisons to run their course, and the seers would need time to recover afterward before they'd be strong and coherent enough to communicate.

"Let me know when our sisters are ready to tell me their visions," she ordered Norah, drawing the older woman's attention and ire once more.

"You don't even have the stomach to watch the suffering you have inflicted," Norah rasped, and there was no missing the challenge being issued.

Mairah was not ordinarily one to shy away from challenges. However, she feared if she remained in the room much longer, she might humiliate herself by letting her weakness show. It was best for all if the abigails beneath her saw her as entirely unmoved by their pain and suffering. The moment they formed the impression that she could be swayed to pity, the more they would take advantage of her and the greater the danger she would find herself in.

And so she ignored the gauntlet Norah had thrown at her feet and retreated with all the dignity—and haste—she could muster.

Norah sat by young Sister Melred's bed and hated Mairahsol with every fiber of her being. Today had been a travesty, a mockery of everything the Mother stood for—even for someone who insisted the Mother was secondary to the Creator. The Devotional managed to make it clear that the Mother was the lesser deity while still teaching that She was greater than any mortal and meant to be obeyed. To force every seer in the Abbey to down the strongest seer's poison she could tolerate in an effort to undo the Mother's Blessing was . . .

Norah felt dramatic choosing the word "evil" to describe Mairahsol's order, but she could think of no more appropriate term.

Sister Melred shivered and groaned, shifting in the bed as if trying to get more comfortable. Norah put a comforting hand on the young woman's forehead, which burned with fever. Poor Melred was the strongest seer in the Abbey, which meant she had taken the strongest poison of all. She was over its most dangerous effects, but she would be sick and weak for days in the aftermath. And since Mairahsol had gotten no satisfaction out of today's crop of visions, she would no doubt force the seers to drink more in the near future.

"I did not tell Mother Mairahsol the truth about what I saw," Melred murmured.

Norah started, for she hadn't realized Melred was awake. "Rest for now," she soothed. "You need to regain your strength."

Melred licked her lips, then grimaced when she swallowed. The poison had left blisters in her mouth and throat. "I will rest soon," she promised. "But I wanted you to know I lied."

Norah smiled as warmly as she knew how, hoping to put the young woman at ease in her pain. Only one seer in the entire Abbey was not a part of the Mother of All worship circle, and every one of them had sworn to reveal no vision that might aid Mairahsol's effort. Most had not needed to lie when Mairahsol questioned them, because their visions seemed to be of no use to the effort to undo the Blessing. Norah was not entirely surprised that Melred had been the exception.

"I know, sweet one," she said. "You needn't—"

"I saw her being confirmed as abbess," Melred said, and Norah recoiled instinctively.

"What?" she cried, very much wishing she had misheard.

"I don't know how it happened," Melred said, wincing in pain as she forced words through her ravaged throat, "but somehow she was confirmed."

Norah shook her head, horrified. Until her rational mind caught up with her emotions and she realized the full implications of Melred's vision.

"The Mother of All only shows us events it is within our power to affect," she said, speaking more to herself than to Melred.

"Yes," Melred whispered. "She believes we can stop Mairahsol."

Norah reached out and squeezed Melred's hand, giving her another encouraging smile. "And we will," she said with more assurance than she felt.

"How?" Melred asked, but her eyes were drifting shut as exhaustion and illness dragged her back down into unconsciousness.

How indeed?

First and foremost, Norah decided, she had to ensure that no seer at the Abbey in any way aided Mairahsol's cause. She did not believe that the Mother of All would grant a helpful vision to the single seer in the Abbey who did not worship her, but gods did not always behave in ways that mortals expected. The next time Mairahsol forced the Abbey's seers to take poison, Norah would make sure that Sister

Sulrai's medium-strength poison was replaced with the strongest the Abbey possessed. One that even Sister Melred did not dare to drink. Sulrai would not survive, and if Norah played her cards right, she could lay the blame for that death squarely at Mairahsol's feet.

Norah had on more than one occasion remarked that Lord Jalzarnin was not a stupid man, however blinded he might be by Mairahsol's questionable charms. An anonymous letter claiming that Mairah's "vision" was a hoax was unlikely to convince him, especially when he would suspect Norah of having sent it. But perhaps the trade minister might be more open to hearing what Norah had to say. Especially once Sister Sulrai lost her life in service to Mairahsol's delusions.

Sister Sulrai's family had offered no protest when her husband had condemned her to the Abbey for what he termed chronic disobedience, but Norah knew for a fact that they had not entirely disowned her as they were meant to. If Sulrai were to die from taking a poison forced upon her by Mairahsol, there might well be complaints that would inconvenience the lord high priest in such a way as to weaken Mairahsol's hold on him.

It wouldn't stop Mairahsol from continuing in her quest, and Norah was certain she and her sisters would need to do a lot more to prevent her from being confirmed as abbess. But it was a start.

Shelvon regarded the tightly scrolled message that had arrived by flier with the same enthusiasm she might have shown a venomous snake slithering through her parlor. Her whole body had jerked in surprised recognition when she'd broken the seal and seen the familiar handwriting. The scroll had fallen from her hands and rolled into the far corner, where it seemed to stare at her accusingly as she crossed her arms over her chest.

When her father, the Sovereign Prince of Nandel, had shipped her off to Aaltah to marry Delnamal, she'd thought that was likely the last she'd ever hear from him. Waldmir showed no signs of affection for any of his daughters, but Shelvon was certain she was his least favorite of the lot, thanks to her mother's attempt to assassinate him. She had served her purpose as a girl and a bargaining chip, but that was the extent of his interest in her, and she'd seen no cause to complain. Her father's interest was a dangerous thing, after all.

Which told Shelvon that there was no possible message in that scrolled letter that she could want to read. The only safe thing to do was shove it in the fire and pretend it had never arrived. Hands shaking—and angry with herself for allowing a roll of paper to scare her—she grabbed a pair of fireplace tongs, hoping that little bit of extra distance would help her find the courage to burn the damn thing without reading it.

She grabbed the scroll with the tongs and turned toward the fire. The paper was less than a hand's-breadth from the flames when an image came to her mind unbidden, of the combination of amusement and scorn that her father's face wore whenever he saw that he had frightened her. He obviously *enjoyed* frightening her, and yet he at the same time held that fear against her, considering it evidence that she was weak and unworthy, a far lesser being than any son would have been.

Had he known when he'd sent the flier to her that she would react with just this toxic combination of fear and revulsion? And did that mean she was unwittingly doing his bidding if she consigned the message to the flames without reading it?

Shelvon was so tired of being afraid. Fear was the first emotion she could ever remember feeling, and her father had made certain it was her constant companion growing up. Fear had ruled her marriage and kept her subservient and compliant no matter how badly her husband treated her. But she had conquered that fear when she'd fled Aaltah with Corlin and Falcor, when she'd risked her own life to save the life of an innocent. If she'd found the courage to do *that*, certainly she could find the courage to read a letter from a man who no longer had any power over her.

Wishing bravery came more naturally to her, she sighed and plucked the parchment from the tongs, setting them aside. Then, wincing in anticipation, she unrolled the parchment to find her father's peremptory message: a demand that she immediately return "home," where she belonged.

Shelvon wasn't sure whether to laugh or cry. Her father obviously thought she was the most pathetic kind of fool in existence. He did not mention his intention to shut her up immediately behind the walls of Nandel's Abbey, but she knew that was *exactly* what he had in mind. For a divorced—and therefore irreparably disgraced—woman anywhere except in Women's Well, there was no place *other* than the Abbey, where she would spend the rest of her youth as a whore until she was too old to be any use at all and would merely be an inmate waiting to die.

That was the life her father was ordering her to return to, and though he clearly had a low opinion of her intelligence, he surely didn't think her so stupid as not to know what would happen to her if she obeyed.

Not so very long ago, she might have believed she had no choice but to do as her father commanded. After all, according to Nandel tradition, he owned her now that her husband had not only put her aside but condemned her as a traitor. There was no question of any woman, much less one as disgraced as she, making her own decisions.

But she was far from Nandel, and though her father would be outraged that she was taking advantage of Princess Alysoon's charitable offer to support her, that outrage no longer had the power to intimidate her. Taking a deep, determined breath, she tossed the letter into the fire with no intention of responding.

It was one in what had become a long streak of acts of defiance, but it didn't make her feel any braver. Nerves roiled in her belly as she imagined what her father would do when he received no response. She wished she believed he would just let her go—it wasn't as if she *mattered* to him, after all—but she had the sickening suspicion he would not make it so easy for her. Waldmir did not suffer defiance from anyone, least of all his daughters.

Shivering despite the warmth of the fire, she lowered herself into a chair and tried very hard not to think about what her future held.

Alys stroked the three vials that contained what she considered the most promising male fertility potions she had put together during her stolen bits of time at the Academy. As with all magic and potions, the only way to know for sure whether these worked was to test them. She had been practicing magic long enough to feel confident that her potions would do no harm—though she had created corresponding antidotes, just to be certain—but she had put off telling Tynthanal what she was up to, and why, until the last possible moment. Although Chanlix had assured her she and Tynthanal had discussed the ramifications of a successful potion, Alys suspected that being destined for a marriage of state in theory was very different from knowing a potential bride had already been chosen for him.

Which meant she had to approach the upcoming conversation with her coat of emotional armor firmly in place.

Tynthanal bowed when he was shown into the informal receiving room in the town hall, where Alys would continue to attend to all affairs of state until the palace was habitable. Ever since he had intercepted her at the Citadel, she'd sensed a hint of wariness in him whenever they spoke in private. She'd assured him she'd gotten over her initial anger with him over his defense of Jailom—and it was true—but she had the feeling he did not fully believe it.

"You wished to see me, Your Royal Highness?" he inquired as he rose from his bow and the page who had shown him in closed the receiving room door.

The address was perfectly right and proper—especially while the page was in hearing distance—but she couldn't quite get used to it coming from her little brother. Of course, after he heard what she had to say, he might use forms of address she found even less comfortable.

Swallowing the knot of apprehension that had formed in her throat, Alys gestured to the chair before her desk. Tynthanal sat obediently, and his gaze darted quickly to the trio of vials half-hidden under her other hand.

"What are those?" Though his wary expression said he'd already guessed.

"Maybe nothing," she answered as she lifted her hand so he could see the vials more clearly. Each one was labeled with its key element, and if none worked on the first attempt, she would try a new formulation with more motes of the key element. "But I hope at least one of them will turn out to be a viable fertility potion for men." She pushed the vials across the desk toward Tynthanal, who suddenly seemed fascinated by the arm of his chair. He had shown himself exceedingly uncomfortable with any discussion of his inability to sire children—though perhaps that was only the case when in his sister's presence.

He cleared his throat. "Yes, er, Chanlix had mentioned you had promised to look into that."

"And she also mentioned what it would mean for your future if one of these potions were to work," Alys said, watching her brother's face closely. He seemed reluctant to make eye contact, and his index finger was tapping restlessly against the chair—a nervous gesture of which Alys suspected he was unaware.

He nodded, the muscles of his jaw tight. "She seems to think that if I become capable of siring an heir, you will then consider me a valuable commodity to be traded like prized horseflesh. I had trouble believing you would do such a thing to a woman who has given so much to you and to this principality. You would not forbid her to marry whom she wished after all that." There was no missing the warning in his voice.

Alys uttered a silent curse under her breath. Chanlix had led her to believe Tynthanal was at least grudgingly accepting of the reality of his position. Had she been willfully blind, seeing only what she wanted to see? And would she be as eager to have Tynthanal take the potions if she knew that Kailee Rah-Kailindar was waiting in the wings?

Guilt and trepidation made Alys's voice sharper than she would have liked when she responded. "You're not naïve. You know how important marriages of state are to the diplomatic status of any kingdom or principality." She took a moment to gather herself and cleanse the anger from her voice. "If Father hadn't divorced Mama, neither one of us would have had any choice as to whom we married. We are *lucky* that we've both experienced love, despite the heartache that love might bring.

"We need whatever alliances we can make, and there is no stronger bond than that of marriages within the royal family. I know that I myself will have to marry again when my mourning is complete, and I can guarantee you I do not look forward to the prospect after having been happily married to a man I loved for so many years.

"If you cannot have children, then I can withhold you from the marriage market as long as I am free to explain why, so that no one might take offense. But if you get Chanlix with child, then there will be no excuse I can give. You lost the right to have the final say in your marriage when I became Sovereign Princess of Women's Well—at your insistence, I might add. We must now both put the well-being of our principality before our own happiness."

She recounted her conversation with Ellinsoltah and the proposal the Queen of Rhozinolm had made. The longer she spoke, the more she explained, the stonier her brother's expression became, until finally her voice petered out. Her palms were damp with sweat, and she was uncomfortably aware of the hard thump of her pulse.

"So that's it, then?" Tynthanal said after a long and resentful silence. "You'd force me to abandon the woman I love to save Ellinsoltah the trouble of having to deal with a rival claimant to her throne?"

"You make it sound like some triviality," she retorted. "A man's life hangs in the balance, although I hope you know I would put your happiness above the life of some man I've never met. But don't you see that the issue would never have come up if Ellinsoltah had a firm hold on her throne? We owe our very existence to her willingness to protect us from Aaltah. If you marry Kailee, we will be assured of Rhozinolm's support even if Ellinsoltah is dethroned."

"Then offer Corlin in my stead!" Tynthanal snapped. "If this marriage of state is so important, it shouldn't matter that he's younger than his potential bride!"

Alys growled in frustration. She understood her brother's distress, and she wished there were another way out, but she was in no mood to deal with a temper tantrum. "Stop being a child!" she snapped back. "As you well know, he cannot enter into a legal marriage agreement for another three years. I would not want to trust the lives of everyone in this principality on a nonbinding verbal agreement, would you? Even *Delnamal* did his duty and married Shelvon when he loved another. Are you telling me you cannot measure up to *him*, of all people?"

She had the satisfaction of seeing her verbal barb hit its mark as Tynthanal flinched at the comparison. He *had* to see the truth in her words, and yet he refused to accept them. "So you're basically telling me I have to take your damn potions or else!" There was a hint of panic hiding behind the anger that flashed in his eyes.

Alys wondered how many young women had worn that particular expression over the long history of Seven Wells, how many had screamed and cried and begged to be released from unwanted marriages only to have their wishes ignored. Why should her brother be any different? And why did he have to make an already difficult situation even harder? "Yes," she bit out. "That's it exactly."

"Fine!" he snarled, pushing back his chair and standing up. "I'll take the 'or else.'"

He gave his chair an angry shove, then stalked out of the room without awaiting a response. When the door closed behind him, Alys let out a groan and propped her elbows on her desk, covering her eyes. She wanted once again to retreat to the darkness of her room and hide away from the world. Yes, the grief would have its way with her, but at least she wouldn't have to force herself to function, to face impossible decisions and painful conversations like this one.

She had not expected Tynthanal to take the news well, and she'd been more than prepared for a certain amount of resistance. In truth, she'd put the conversation off more than once as she had tried to shore up the emotional armor she'd needed to face it. But she had no plan for how to deal with an outright refusal.

In theory, she could *command* him as her subject to take the potions, but she wouldn't do that to him even if she thought he would obey. No, she would have to rely on Chanlix—as well as Tynthanal's deep-seated sense of responsibility for their principality—to change his mind.

CHAPTER FOURTEEN

Mairahsol sighed contentedly as she laid her head on Jalzarnin's shoulder. It had been more than a week since last he had come to the Abbey, and she had begun to grow concerned that he had tired of her. But there had been no missing his enthusiasm in the bed tonight, and when she'd looked deep into his eyes, she'd seen something more than lust. He wanted her still, but more than that, he *cared* about her. If he said he'd stopped visiting so frequently for the sake of discretion, then she had to accept it as the truth, even if it made her nervous that her hold on him was slipping.

"Only a week without you in my arms," he murmured, "and I feel like a man who's been adrift at sea for half his life."

She smiled and cuddled closer, stroking the sparse hairs on his chest as she inhaled the scents of incense and man that rose from his skin. "At least you have a wife at home to see to your needs," she teased, making a pouty face at him. "I have no one."

He snorted softly. "I can't even remember the last time my wife came to my bed. Which you know perfectly well, so stop pretending to be jealous."

It was true that Jalzarnin had told her all about his frigid wife in the early days of their relationship. She had even felt vaguely sorry for him. And yet even so, she *was* just a tiny bit jealous. His wife *could* have him, if she wanted, as often as she liked. His wife also lived in a fine home, with all the comforts that came with being married to the lord high priest. She had been beautiful when she was younger—or at least so Mairah had heard—and she was a well-respected lady who received more invitations to dinners and parties and balls than she could possibly accept. The stupid bitch had it all and didn't even know it.

"She doesn't deserve you," Mairah said, angry all over again at how fickle and unfair life was. "If *I* were the wife of the lord high priest, I would do everything I could to make him happy."

It was the life she'd dreamed of when she came out to society and caught the eye of a highly respectable gentleman everyone predicted would be lord high priest someday. Jalzarnin's wife had no idea how lucky she was, living the life Mairah should have had.

Jalzarnin stroked her hair and laughed softly. "I suspect if you had been wed to Lord Granlin, he would be dead by now and you in the dungeon or worse. You would never have put up with a pious hypocrite for a husband. And don't fool yourself into thinking he would have been true to you. A man who cheats on his wife will do so no matter who that wife is."

"Says the voice of experience?" she asked, then regretted the catty comment immediately.

Jalzarnin showed no sign of being offended. "It's not cheating when it's done by mutual agreement."

Mairah propped her head on her hand and peered at his face. "So you have never slept with a woman behind your wife's back?" It seemed . . . improbable at best.

He smiled. "I don't give her an itemized list of my affairs. There's a limit to how much she wants to know. But we do love each other, albeit in an odd way."

Mairah had no right to be stung at the revelation, and yet she was anyway. She did not *want* to love Jalzarnin, and she'd frequently told herself that her attachment to him was due to nothing more than practicality. It would be pure foolishness for an abigail—even the abbess—to allow herself to love a man when she could never marry him and had to hide their relationship. Especially a man like Jalzarnin. She believed he genuinely cared about her, but he was also using her and made little effort to keep his ulterior motives secret. But no matter how well she understood the boundaries of their relationship, there was still a part of her that desperately craved love, that wanted to come first in a man's heart.

Jalzarnin must have seen the hurt she'd tried to hide, for he gathered her into his arms and held her tightly. "The love I have for you is different," he assured her. "My loving friendship with my wife is a guttering candle next to the roaring flame between you and me."

She pulled out of his embrace, unwilling to be mollified so easily. She looked into his eyes, seeing nothing in them but earnestness and truth. "What is it you see in me?" she asked—a question she had frequently asked herself and yet had never dared ask him. She had always believed that his attraction could be entirely attributed to his perception of her usefulness, that he had courted her so that he could take advantage of her talents for eavesdropping and subterfuge. And yet sometimes when she looked in his eyes, she could have sworn she saw something more.

"Even if my face weren't ruined," she said, "what man—what *sane* man—would want to share a bed with a woman of my reputation? Especially the lord high priest, who has a wife of whom I could conceivably become jealous?"

No one could possibly forget what had happened to the last man who'd shared her bed and dared to make her jealous.

Lord Granlin had been a priest of the highest caliber, famously pious, and from a prominent family distantly related to the king. When Mairah and her then–best friend Linrai had come out, Lord Granlin had courted them both, drawing that courtship out over the course of a full season. Mairah and Linrai were both of sufficient station to make them attractive choices for a man who had his eye on becoming lord high priest. Both had immaculate reputations and would have looked appropriately resplendent displayed on his arm at parties and balls. Most importantly, both would come with dowries sufficient to pay off his family's debts, which were the only stain on his otherwise flawless public image.

In an attempt to give herself every possible advantage, Mairah had flirted rather outrageously with Lord Granlin and begun allowing him certain . . . liberties. Liberties that a man who hoped to be lord high priest, a man who was supposed to set a shining example of virtuous manhood, should never have taken advantage of. Nonetheless, despite Mairah's flirting, it was unquestionably Lord Granlin who had initiated her deflowering after telling her he had decided to offer for her. Some part of her had known it was unwise to take him at his word, but she'd been young and foolish and in love.

Before Lord Granlin got around to announcing their engagement—which he'd assured Mairah he would do promptly—Linrai must have sensed she was losing the battle and slipped Mairah the poison that had destroyed her face. Mairah could never prove the little bitch was responsible—the poison had left no trace that any healer could find—but all it had taken was one look at her supposed best friend's face when next they met for Mairah to know exactly what had happened to her, why her face was marred with pox that occurred nowhere else on her body and had never made her ill.

Lord Granlin had offered for Linrai immediately, and the two were married within the year. His debts were paid off, his family's standing—both financial and social—secured, and Mairah was sure the happy couple had all but dismissed her from their minds. But Mairah was not one to let such an insult go unpunished. She was back on the marriage market herself, but with her pockmarked face, she was unlikely to find a husband, and if she did, she was likely to find herself repudiated instantly on her wedding night when he discovered she was not the paragon of virtue her parents claimed.

Lord Granlin and Lady Linrai had destroyed Mairah's life. And she refused to let them get away with it. With the help of a simple aphrodisiac potion, Mairah had cornered and seduced Lord Granlin at a party being thrown in his honor—to thank him for his generous donation to the Temple of the Creator, no less. And she'd made sure that they would be caught, that all of Khalpar high society would know what he had done.

The humiliation had cost Lord Granlin any hope of becoming lord high priest, but Mairah's revenge had run even deeper than that. For having so publicly broken his marriage vows, Lord Granlin was obligated to return Linrai's dowry to her family in reparation for the insult. Overnight, Lady Linrai's "grand catch" had turned into an impoverished social pariah, and their marriage could never recover.

Mairah had known, of course, that she was ruining herself. She had thought long and hard about all the ways she could get her revenge, and had decided that this most perfect of all acts of vengeance was worth the sacrifice of being condemned to the Abbey.

Jalzarnin smiled tenderly at her, his eyes soft and warm even at this reminder of her ignominy. "Just because others scorn you for what you did doesn't mean *I* have to. High society might see a scandalous slut, but I see a young woman with an iron will and astounding courage." His smile grew even broader. "The *commitment* it must have taken . . ."

There was no missing the genuine admiration in his voice and face, and Mairah was struck momentarily speechless. She had never imagined it possible that anyone would not condemn her for what she'd done, and the idea that someone actually *admired* her for it was nearly incomprehensible.

"You don't even know why I did it," she murmured softly, for she had never spoken so openly of her past before, mentioning only that she suspected Lady Linrai of having poisoned her to win Lord Granlin's hand. Which would certainly justify—in some people's minds, at least—Mairah's malice toward Linrai, though not toward Granlin.

Jalzarnin leaned forward and kissed her lips, a light brush of affection rather than a prelude to sex. "Of course I know," he said. "Lord Granlin was—and still is, actually, though he struggles to attract prey in his reduced circumstances—a sexual predator of the highest order. You had your revenge on Lady Linrai the moment she bound herself to him as a husband, for I would not be surprised to hear his vows were broken by the time his wedding night was over. It does not take much imagination to think of a reason why you might have wished to ruin him."

Mairah chewed her lip, not at all sure what to think of this revelation. Did it make her feel better or worse to know that she was not the only woman to have fallen prey to Lord Granlin's charm? "But his reputation was spotless," she protested, thinking back to the shining beacon of propriety and piety he had been.

"It is easy for a man's reputation to remain spotless when he preys only on those who cannot afford to reveal what he's done. He might well have continued on to this day without consequences had he not so badly miscalculated when he preyed on *you*."

She frowned. "But then how do you know about it?"

"I didn't at the time of his ruin. I never did like him—and not only because I saw in him a potential rival, though I won't swear that did not factor into my opinion. But it always struck me that a man as conspicuously pious as he had something to hide. The *truly* pious don't feel such a pressing need for public display, you see. So I knew there was something rotten about him. I just didn't know what. But after his ruin, he developed a habit of drinking too much—and therefore talking too much. Society at large might not know the truth about him, but those of the priesthood certainly do."

Mairah shook her head wonderingly. To think that she and Lady Linrai had savaged each other for the great honor of marrying such a man!

"You did all of society a great service by revealing Lord Granlin for what he was," Jalzarnin continued. "All of society may not be aware of it, may not thank you for it, but I do. And I also know that someone with such single-minded determination and courage is just the sort of person who will find a way to reverse the Curse."

That was a topic Mairah was considerably less enthusiastic about discussing, for when she had first encouraged Jalzarnin to believe she could do such a thing, she had never believed her circumstances could depend on it to such a degree. She'd imagined trying her hardest, but failing, with the only consequences being disappointment and the lack of the generous reward she'd hoped to earn. She had *not* imagined that failure would see her returned to the rank of abigail after having made such a target of herself. Time was ticking away— far faster than she would have liked—and the "progress" she had claimed so far was not yet enough. She was well aware that her vision of herself sitting behind the abbess's desk had already come true and that the future beyond that was unknown.

"I will do everything in my power," she murmured, hoping to change the subject immediately. But Jalzarnin did not cooperate.

"You need to start showing signs of progress," he warned.

"I *have* shown progress," she insisted. "We are still working on that new seer's poison." She had feared an official inquiry, and per- haps a command to cease having her abigails trigger visions, when Sister Sulrai had perished in the course of her duties. Sulrai had come from a powerful family who had not completely disowned her despite her disgrace, and it would not have been entirely surprising if they had kicked up a fuss. But when the trade minister had questioned Mairah about the incident, she'd told him that Sulrai had overstated her abilities and had taken a poison stronger than she could tolerate. It seemed the only logical explanation for the woman's death, and Mairah had let out a sigh of relief when the trade minister had ac- cepted her word.

"You've shown a *potential* for progress," Jalzarnin corrected. "And that progress is subject to certain questions."

"What do you mean?"

Jalzarnin rolled over to face her, propping his head on one hand while his other idly stroked her hip over the covers. "Someone sent an anonymous letter to the trade minister, claiming that you are not a genuine seer, and that your abigail died because of your negligence and ignorance. Thankfully, I intercepted it in time, but I cannot guar- antee that will always be the case."

Mairah's body went cold, though she attempted to keep any alarm from showing on her face. She hoped the look she cast Jalzarnin was all outrage and offended dignity. There was no hint of doubt or sus- picion in his gaze, but she couldn't help worrying the accusations in that letter might affect him.

"By 'someone,' you mean Norah, of course," she said with a dis-

missive sniff. "That woman would stop at nothing to tear me down."
Her heart pattered in her chest, as if her own body was trying to
betray her. She hoped he couldn't feel her pulse through that hand
on her hip.

He kept his expression guarded, hiding whatever he was thinking
and feeling from her searching eyes. "There is no proof that the letter
is from Sister Norah," he said, "though of course your assumption is
most likely correct." The hand on her hip rose to her face, caressing
her cheek. "You have a unique talent for making enemies, my love."

Mairah bit back a defensive reply, but her eyes suddenly stung
with tears. "I had friends once," she said in a husky voice, as the lone-
liness she thought she'd conquered long ago stabbed through her.
"It was only once I came to the Abbey that everything went so
wrong." She swallowed hard as a lump tried to form in her throat. It
wasn't just her *life* that was unrecognizable in the years after the
Abbey gates shut behind her, it was her *self*.

"I did not mean to hurt you," Jalzarnin said softly, brushing a
finger across her cheek and catching a tear that had leaked out. "I just
want you to be careful. Once you have been confirmed as abbess, you
can do whatever you like to Norah and her friends. No one will notice, much less complain. But your position right now is too tenuous
for comfort.

"You can take away all of Norah's weapons by showing verifiable
progress in your mission," Jalzarnin said. "We need something more
than your vision, which, though encouraging, is not provable."

"I'll figure something out," Mairah assured him.

Which would be a lot easier to do if the progress she'd reported so
far had been anything other than a convenient lie.

When Kailindar was shown into one of the parlors of the royal residence, he looked as concerned as Ellin had felt when he had paid his
surprise social call, watching her face far too carefully as they exchanged the expected pleasantries. The moment word of Lord Creethan's assassination attempt had gotten out, the entire court had
been abuzz. She wondered how many of her courtiers—and how

many of her council members—were disappointed the attempt had failed. And she knew Semsulin was far from the only one to speculate about Kailindar's potential involvement. Just as she knew some of his detractors were gleefully rubbing their hands together in anticipation of his arrest.

Discreet investigation had shown that Lord Creethan had indeed been far more dependent on his income as trade minister than had been apparent on the surface. He'd made a brisk business of accepting bribes, and had become so accustomed to the arrangement that he did not bother to wait until he had delivered to spend his ill-gotten gains. Losing his position would have meant having to return money he had already spent to certain unsavory characters who would not have taken his changed circumstances as an excuse.

It was enough to convince Ellin that Creethan had been acting alone—a desperate and angry man who saw Ellin as the sole cause of his downfall. She had hoped that inviting her uncle for a meeting in the residence would put to rest any fears he might have that she was about to accuse him, but his obvious nerves said that hope had been in vain.

She offered him a glass of brandy, which she thought might put him more at ease, but though he accepted, he seemed to eye the fine liquor with suspicion.

"I haven't poisoned your drink, Uncle Kailindar," she said drolly, and at the informal address some of the tension finally left his shoulders.

He harrumphed, and if he smiled at her wit, his droopy mustache hid it. He took a polite sip of his drink, then set to swirling the liquid around the glass. "Excellent brandy, Your Majesty," he said.

Ellin rolled her eyes, though Kailindar was too entranced by the brandy to notice. She had never had an especially warm relationship with her uncle, but it had never felt quite this awkward before. She had planned not to speak of the assassination attempt, but it seemed perhaps it would be best to clear the air.

"Can you look me in the eye, Uncle," she asked, "and assure me that you had nothing to do with Lord Creethan's actions?"

He looked up from the brandy then and responded with no hesitation. "I swear to you on my life and my honor that I had nothing to do with it. I told you before that I do not lust for the throne, and I meant it."

She nodded. "I believe you," she said simply, and it was true. Both Zarsha and Semsulin had urged her to do away with him while she had the chance, and she knew both of them still harbored a suspicion that Kailindar might have had a hand in the assassination attempt. But though she sometimes distrusted her judgment about people, she was convinced Creethan had been acting out of his own rage alone.

"But . . . ?"

"There is no 'but.' I believe you, and that is that. If there were more to it than that, you would already be before the magistrate."

His hand tightened on the glass, and she saw a rare hint of fear in his eyes. Clearly he understood the difficult position the assassination attempt had put him in. Just as he knew his continued existence would always pose at least some level of threat to her. Which meant *she* posed some level of threat to *him*.

"I did not ask you here to talk about Lord Creethan's treason," she said. "I had a rather more cheerful topic of conversation in mind." She motioned him to a chair, and he sat. That he was still ill at ease was evident in every nuance of his body language.

"I may have found a suitable match for Kailee," she said, hoping her decision to tell him about her proposal was not premature. Alysoon hadn't actually agreed to it, but Ellin thought it best that she plunge ahead anyway. If the arrangement fell through, she would have to more seriously consider Semsulin's plans to eliminate Kailindar's threat, but for now she could at least try to mitigate it with hope.

Kailindar frowned and set the brandy aside. "And who might that be?" he inquired with undisguised wariness.

"Sovereign Princess Alysoon has an unmarried brother," Ellin said. "She and I have agreed that Lord Tynthanal might be a suitable match for Kailee. As I'm sure you know, he was once the Lieutenant Commander of the Citadel of Aaltah, and he is now Princess Alysoon's lord chancellor. He is very possibly the most eligible bachelor in all of Seven Wells."

Kailindar laughed at the admittedly hyperbolic claim. "If one discounts the fact that Women's Well is always one step away from being obliterated. And that he is the son of the witch who cursed the Wellspring. Aside from that, he is, I agree, eminently eligible."

"He's the brother and lord chancellor of a sovereign princess," Ellin argued. "He is the firstborn son of the late king of Aaltah. And while it might not matter so much to Kailee, I can assure you after having met him via talker that he is handsome enough to make girls of her age swoon. They would make remarkably beautiful children together."

Kailindar winced ever so delicately.

"Kailee *would* like to have children someday, wouldn't she?" she asked gently, knowing exactly what her uncle's wince had meant. He'd imagined a life of perpetual spinsterhood for her and had likely never allowed himself to think that she might one day have children of her own.

He groaned and blew out a breath that made his mustache flutter. "Of course she would."

"If you aren't going to send her to the Abbey, and the nobility of Rhozinolm will not offer for her, then her choices in life are . . . slim." It was nothing he didn't already know, but he winced again. "If she is to have children, she will have to marry someone well beneath her. Someone who would likely only take her because he needs the money from her dowry, and who might well mistreat her—or even send her to the Abbey himself, once he has the money.

"Or, she could marry Lord Tynthanal, who is every bit her social equal. And who lives in the one place in Seven Wells where she need never fear being sent to the Abbey."

"There are worse fears she might face living in Women's Well," Kailindar said darkly.

Ellin met his eyes. "Not as long as they have the full and unwavering support of Rhozinolm."

Kailindar lowered his gaze and shook his head. "Ah. Of course.

You would reduce my attractiveness as a rival by tying me to Women's Well."

She raised one shoulder in a subtle shrug. "We both know there are other very much less pleasant ways I could neutralize the threat you pose to me. I can't claim Kailee will be in no danger living in Women's Well—and it will be very important to her safety that we get those trade agreements with Nandel renewed—but she will have hope of a better life there."

There was a haunted look in her uncle's eyes that Ellin did not like, one that told her he was focusing more on the dangers than the rewards.

"It's also possible that the magic of Women's Well can give her sight," Ellin suggested, and for the first time saw a flare of hope in his face. "Do you not think it worth some degree of risk to give her a future that includes a husband and children and even, potentially, eyesight?" She did not put into words the flip side, the side of which he was clearly already aware: if there was ever any hint of a rebellion brewing in his name—even without his participation and knowledge— Kailee's future would be destroyed. Kailindar would be attainted and executed as a traitor, and all his worldly goods—any money that might support his family—would be forfeit to the Crown. Ending up in the Abbey would be the least unpleasant fate that might befall her under those circumstances.

"I will not command you to send her to Women's Well, nor will I command her to marry," Ellin said. "But I do ask you to consider sending her there to meet Lord Tynthanal and decide for herself if the match is worth the risk."

He picked up his glass of brandy and took a healthy swallow. More, she thought, to give him a moment to think than because he wanted the drink so much. She sat in silence, trying not to hold her breath.

Finally, he nodded, not looking at her. "I will talk it over with my wife," he said. "And with Kailee. But if you believe that Princess Alysoon and Lord Tynthanal are agreeable to the match, then it is my duty as a father to send her."

Ellin smiled to cover her own unease and hoped that whatever impediments stood in the way of Princess Alysoon officially approving the match would be swiftly and decisively taken care of.

Mairahsol had spent an astonishing proportion of her life as an abigail slinking around the Abbey's hallways at night—it was amazing how much useful information an enterprising abigail could discover when all her sisters were snoring in their beds—but this was the first time she had done so as the abbess. Most of her information gathering was now done through her small coterie, but tonight's excursion suggested she actually missed the work. Her heart raced with a thrill of adrenaline, just as it used to in her earlier days, and yet this time she had nothing to fear. No one would dare challenge her or ask her what she was doing, even should she be seen. All the excitement, without any of the terror and risk.

The Abbey's halls were darkened for the night, all the luminants—which would have been considered an extravagance at any other Abbey, but which were one of Khalpar's primary exports, and therefore relatively commonplace—extinguished. She carried a small, dim luminant in one hand, giving herself enough light to see by, but—she hoped—not enough to draw attention to herself.

Not, she reminded herself yet again, that she was in any danger, but she had hopes of catching her quarry by surprise.

She smiled in satisfaction. All those years she'd been shunned by her sisters, and now some of them would happily claw one another's eyes out to curry favor with her. Sister Zulmirna had turned out to be quite the accomplished sneak, and though Mairah had never instructed the woman to spy on Norah and her friends, she'd been pleasantly surprised when the young abigail had come to her with the news that some of her sisters were secretly worshipping the Mother of All.

"It's disgusting," the abigail had said with every semblance of truly believing it. "How can anyone question the presence and power of the Creator?"

Mairah had shrugged and answered without thinking it through first. "To be fair, they don't really question His presence. From what

I understand, they merely believe their 'Mother of All' gave birth to Him."

Zulmirna had looked at her with an expression of shocked disbelief. "But the Creator created *everything*. Including the Mother. Everyone knows that!"

Mairah had been raised in the same tradition as everyone else in Khalpar—and, truly, throughout the Three Kingdoms, except within small pockets of heretics—but she did not feel any particular indignation over the beliefs of the Mother of All worshippers. It seemed rather frivolous to argue over which deity came first, and it hardly affected one's everyday life. However, the cult was outlawed, and the king would be horrified were he to learn there were practitioners of that heresy within the heart of Khalpar's capital.

"Of course they do," Mairah had said smoothly. Perhaps Zulmirna had brought this information to her out of genuine outrage rather than as an attempt to earn an extra reward. "And I must thank you for bringing this heresy to my attention. Sister Norah and her followers are an affront to this abbey, and I will put a stop to their outrageous behavior immediately."

"Will you report them?" Zulmirna asked, and Mairah couldn't discern whether her voice held excitement or dread at the prospect.

Reporting them would certainly rid Mairah of all the most troublesome abigails in the Abbey, and it would be a more than satisfactory revenge for all the wrongs they'd done her. In point of fact, it would be *too much* revenge. Though Mairah liked to think of herself as ruthless, she would not wish a heretic's fate on anyone. Not even Sister Norah. However, the threat would certainly bring the bitch to heel.

"It is my duty as abbess to guide and correct the behavior of my abigails," she said, hoping she sounded both pious and benevolent. "I will have words with them privately and attempt to show them the error of their ways. If I am sufficiently persuasive, then no one but we two need know of their perversion."

"You are very kind," Zulmirna said, though the sharpness of her gaze said she was well aware that kindness had nothing to do with it.

"I am always mindful of my duties. And I will arrange to catch

Norah at one of her illegal gatherings, so that no one will ever suspect you of informing on them."

Zulmirna bowed her head respectfully. "Thank you, Mother Mairahsol. And might I ask you to further reduce the number of nights I am required to work the pavilion?"

Ah. So *that* was why she'd taken it upon herself to spy on Norah. Mairah told herself to keep Zulmirna's superior acting ability at the forefront of her mind, for she'd been halfway convinced of the girl's religious fervor, though she prided herself on her skepticism.

"I'm afraid I still need your services in the pavilion," Mairah had told her regretfully. "Especially now that Lord Thanstal has taken such a great liking to you." The king's cousin had yet to reveal anything that Jalzarnin could use to ruin him, but it seemed he opened up more and more with each visit. "But let me think on it. I'm sure I can come up with a reward you will find just as pleasing."

Zulmirna had been a bit sulky in her acceptance, and Mairah was fully aware the girl could become a problem if she was not kept happy. However, she could hardly regret recruiting her when she'd brought Mairah such useful information.

When Mairahsol turned the corner into the hallway that led to the kitchens, she immediately saw that the door was closed, and there was light showing from around its edges. The corners of her mouth turned up in a satisfied smile. Paying Norah back bit by bit for every ounce of misery she had caused over the years had been even more enjoyable than Mairahsol could have imagined, but humiliating her in front of her followers—and proving to everyone in the Abbey that Norah was too toxic to befriend—would be the coup de grace.

Mairah crept closer to the kitchen door. Someone—it didn't sound like Norah—was droning on and on, though Mairah couldn't make out the words. In truth, she had no interest in what was being said, although she intended to pretend the greatest possible offense at the sacrilege.

The abigail stopped speaking, and another voice took over. Still not Norah. Mairah frowned as she approached the door. She would consider her plan a dismal failure if she burst through the door only to find Norah had decided not to attend tonight's illegal gathering.

Instead of throwing the door open the moment she reached it, Mairah used a dab of the ever-convenient Keyhole ointment to peek inside.

When Zulmirna had told her that Norah was orchestrating meetings of the Mother of All cult, Mairahsol had pictured a half dozen or so of the old women of Mother Wyebryn's generation sitting around a table and complaining about how they'd suffered under Mairah's leadership. She'd assumed they occasionally discussed their beliefs as part of the Mother of All cult, but she'd been certain their main purpose had been to do what they could to undermine her.

Which might indeed be the case, although at the moment, the Keyhole ointment revealed the elderly Sister Ide reciting a passage that sounded like it might have come from the Devotional, if it hadn't referenced the Mother of All. And there were nearly two dozen abigails gathered round, hanging on Sister Ide's every word. Norah was there, too, smiling like a proud mother as she mouthed the words herself.

This was not some little gossip circle made up of Mother Wyebryn's favorite crones! This was a gathering of fully a quarter of the Abbey's inhabitants. Worse, as she remained crouched by the keyhole she'd created, listening and watching, Mairahsol heard someone address Norah as "Mother Norah." Norah rebuked the abigail, but Mairah heard ill-disguised pleasure in the old woman's voice.

The passage Ide was reciting told a story about the Mother's fall from grace that was very different from the one with which Mairah was familiar. According to the Devotional, the Mother had broken Her marriage vows to the Creator by bedding Their son, the Destroyer. The Destroyer had been cast out of the heavens, His impact with the earth creating the lifeless Wasteland. In penance for Her sin, the Mother had vowed eternal subservience to the Creator and decreed that all women should be subservient to men.

But according to this heretical version of the Devotional, the Creator had been jealous of the Mother of All's greater power and status. He was Her creation, beholden to Her and clearly lesser. She foreswore some of Her power to make Herself His equal, and yet still

He was not appeased. Until finally, She cast away a part of Herself, diminishing Herself as a salve to His wounded pride.

The heresy made Mairah uneasy, despite her distinct lack of faith. And now, when she pictured herself throwing that door open, she imagined not the shocked and frightened faces she had originally assumed, but the angry and determined faces of women who were more than ready to turn on her. With the prospect of questioning by the royal inquisitor before an inevitable death by fire, those women were more likely to tear Mairah apart with their bare hands than cower in terror. The punishment they would face for Mairah's murder would be nothing compared to what they would suffer should she reveal them as Mother of All worshippers.

Heart pounding with this sudden recognition of her own vulnerability, Mairahsol backed slowly away from the door. Bursting in on this meeting was clearly not an option, and she was going to have to put a great deal more thought into how she would make use of the information Zulmirna had brought her. But make use of it she would. One way or another, she was going to destroy "Mother" Norah. And any abigail who took the bitch's side against Mairahsol was bound to regret that decision very, very deeply.

CHAPTER FIFTEEN

Chanlix resorted to a touch of potion to remove the last of the puffy redness from her eyes, then regarded herself closely in the mirror and decided she looked presentable enough to be seen in public. She took a long, slow, deep breath before stepping out the door, making certain the last of her urge to cry had left her.

Tynthanal was the kindest, most honorable man she had ever met. He had never judged her for what she'd had to do as an inmate of the Abbey, had not treated her as a damaged woman. Nor did he act as though she were a lesser being because she had been born female. Because of all this, she had somehow not expected him to be so profoundly attached to the idea that a woman required marriage to validate her existence. While marrying him made a nice fantasy, Chanlix had never truly believed it was a possibility, and she'd been perfectly content with her role as his unmarried lover. She did not like the thought of him marrying another, of course, but she understood the necessity and was prepared to live with it.

"You do realize practically everyone in Women's Well knows I'm sleeping with you now even though we're not married," she'd argued when he'd railed against what he saw as Alys's ultimatum. "I have not been stoned as a whore nor perished of shame."

But Tynthanal had been past seeing reason and had shouted about the "terrible" shame that would befall her should his infertility be cured and she become pregnant without the benefit of a husband. As if *men* ever showed a lick of shame over the children they fathered—and most often abandoned—out of wedlock. Chanlix herself had grown angry, and harsh words were exchanged, words she'd regretted the moment they left her mouth.

It had been a good forty minutes since Tynthanal had slammed out of the house, too angry to bear any company but his own, and Chanlix had used those minutes to put her emotions in some semblance of order. There was no question in her mind that establishing an alliance by marriage with the chief rival for Queen Ellinsoltah's throne would give Women's Well a degree of safety and legitimacy that nothing else could. If there was any way they could make it happen, they had to seize the opportunity. Which meant that Tynthanal *had* to try those potions, and Chanlix was likely the only person who stood a chance of persuading him.

There was only one place Tynthanal might have gone in his search for solitude, and Chanlix followed the well-worn path that led to what had become their own special spot, a tiny alcove in the spring that housed the Well, blocked from view by the lush growth around the water.

As she expected, he was standing in the shallow, clear water, his shoes off and his trousers rolled to his knees. (Although he was no longer in the military, he often eschewed the civilian garb of breeches and doublet for his more familiar shirt and trousers.) The Well beneath the spring gave off a hum of power that was both soothing and invigorating, and many were the times the two of them had waded together in the quiet.

He turned at the sound of her approach, and though he couldn't manage a smile for her, there was at least a slight lightening of his scowl.

Without a word, Chanlix sat on a log—one she was quite certain had been appropriated from a building site, for there were no trees of its size yet in the land that had once been barren—and removed her own shoes.

"You'll ruin your dress," Tynthanal called as she inelegantly hiked up her skirts and waded in after him.

The shock of cold water drew a gasp from her throat, expected as it was, and the hum of power brought a small smile to her face. "It will give me an excuse to buy a new one," she said. For decades, she'd worn nothing but the red robes and wimple of an abigail, and it was a delight to be allowed to wear whatever she wanted—and have the money to spoil herself shamelessly with new dresses when the mood struck her.

She reached his side, escaped folds of her skirt dragging in the water, and for a few minutes they stood there together in peaceful silence. Since they had first come here and discovered the Well, they had spent many a stolen hour like this, sometimes talking, sometimes making love, sometimes just enjoying the peace.

Beside her, Tynthanal closed his eyes in what looked almost like physical pain. She let go of her skirts with one hand—they were already wet anyway—and put that hand on his shoulder, squeezing gently.

"I'm sorry I lost my temper," he said without opening his eyes. "I hope you know it is *Alys* I am angry with, not you." He finally shot her a sideways glance as if afraid of what he would see on her face.

"You have no cause to be angry with either of us," she chided. "Alys is doing what she feels is best for everyone. And she's not wrong. You *know* that."

The mulish expression that crossed his face was becoming frustratingly familiar. "I love you. I will either marry you, or I will marry no one at all. I will not drink Alys's potions. She can't force me to."

Chanlix wondered if he'd ever noticed he'd never actually *asked* her to marry him. He just assumed she was his for the taking—which, to be fair, she would have been under other circumstances.

"So I have no say in this?"

"You *can't* want me to marry another!" he protested in outrage.

"I don't *want* you to. But I would like to participate in the decision instead of having you make it for me. Whether you choose to take the potions or not, you are not the only person involved here."

He rubbed his hands on his trousers, an unusually nervous gesture for one so habitually self-possessed. "I just assumed . . ."

"Yes, that's the problem." Hooking her arm through his, she leaned her head against his shoulder. "I have endured more shame and humiliation than you can possibly imagine over the course of my life," she said, feeling his muscles tense with the admission although it was nothing he didn't already know. "If you imagine the prospect of being your mistress will cause me to faint away in maidenly shock, you are much mistaken. I would happily bear you as many bastard children as my body can produce while it still can, for I know you would love them just the same as any legitimate ones you might have."

"I imagine my *wife*"—he said the word as if it left a foul taste in his mouth—"would be less pleased with such an arrangement."

"She would join the great sisterhood of women who have learned to look the other way. Such is hardly out of the ordinary in any marriage, much less a marriage of state. If you're worried about my feelings, rest assured I would rather be your mistress with children than your wife with none." She tensed, fearing he would take that assertion as some form of rejection, but Tynthanal merely ground his teeth.

"I'm a selfish bastard. I want both."

She shook her head. "Honestly, Tynthanal, what good would it do us to marry and have children when we're teetering on the edge of destruction? If Queen Ellinsoltah were to become unable or unwilling to uphold our alliance—if, say, her council should decide Lord Kailindar was the rightful king—we would be doomed. I want to have your children—but only if I have reason to think those children would live to see adulthood.

"Try your sister's potions," she urged. "There is no point in wrestling through all this only to find she can't cure what ails you anyway."

"And if one works?"

"If one works, we talk about it again. You will listen to me, and I will listen to you, and together we will decide what's best for all involved."

He heaved a huge sigh. "And we both know what that is," he said, his eyes full of anguish. He put his arms around her suddenly and pulled her to him. She laid her head against his chest and heard the steady thump of his heart. "You deserve so much better than this," he whispered into her hair. "After everything you've been through, all you've suffered . . ."

"You can give me your love. And maybe, just maybe, you can give me a child. It's so much more than I ever hoped for."

He was silent for a long time, wrestling with his demons. As wonderfully understanding as he had been about her past, she knew that he had not completely shaken off the notion that a woman having a child out of wedlock was a source of terrible shame. Even in Women's Well, she was sure there were plenty of people who shared his opinion, and her life as an unwed mother—should she be lucky enough to have it—would not be easy.

"What you said before—that you'd rather be my mistress with children than my wife with none—that's been your position all along, hasn't it?" he asked. "Even when we had no specific reason to believe my marriage could save Women's Well from destruction. Having children means that much to you?"

She heard the plaintive thought behind the words: *Am I not enough?* "It's more that marriage means so little," she said, hoping to take any sting out of it. "If I have a man that I love, if I have his child, and if I am not shunned and scorned for it, then what need have I for a priest's blessing?"

His arms squeezed so tight around her that for a moment she could hardly breathe, and yet still she reveled in his embrace. "I cannot bear to cause you pain," he said in a choked voice. "Don't tell me it would not hurt you to see me wed another."

She pulled away and looked up into his eyes, willing him to see both her love and her acceptance. "It will hurt us both," she said. "And it's what we both signed up for when we set out to create Women's Well as an independent principality. I will do my duty. Will you do yours?"

Another long silence ensued before Tynthanal finally sighed and said, "I will drink the potions."

Smithson had never been so excited as he had been on the day when Lord Jailom had announced that the Citadel of Women's Well would break with all tradition and allow sons of commoners to join up as cadets. Smithson had been learning his father's trade—metalsmithing, of course—since he'd been old enough to hold a hammer, but had shown little aptitude for the work. He despised the heat of the forge, and the repetitive hammering bored him to distraction. He was forever burning himself or hitting himself with the hammer or breaking whatever piece he was working on.

His father had been almost comically relieved—and embarrassingly overjoyed to approve—when Smithson had asked permission to become a cadet, and the last six months of military training had been the most satisfying of his young life. Other boys his age complained of the strained muscles and the small hurts of sparring, but Smithson much preferred those pains to the constant burns and the occasional smashed finger.

Then, he'd been given the opportunity to accompany one of Women's Well's very first trade caravans on its long and very important journey to Rhozinolm, and he'd practically burst with pride. He'd received the assignment from Lord Jailom himself, who'd told him what a fine job he'd done during all the training exercises.

"Don't be so proud of yourself," Prince Corlin had sneered when he'd overheard Smithson telling his friends at the barracks about the assignment. "The lord commander is sending you because he can't do without his best men for more than a month, so he's found the most expendable warm bodies available."

Smithson had pretended to ignore the prince's jab—Corlin was always spoiling for a fight, and he didn't much seem to care whether he won or lost them. But when Smithson had set out with the caravan—which consisted of a single mule-drawn wagon, a driver, and two of the Citadel's most junior soldiers in addition to himself—the echo of those words was harder to ignore. And it hadn't taken very long for him to realize that in the future, he would prefer to do without such "honors" whenever possible.

The first day of travel was not so bad. The influence of the Well that had brought life to the desert Wasteland meant that the once barren, dry land was now green with life, the soil no longer rising in clouds of dust at every footstep. There was enough wildlife that for their first supper, the men of the small caravan feasted on fresh rabbit roasted over an open fire.

The second day was considerably less pleasant, as the Well's influence began to wane. Smithson had lived most of his life in Miller's Bridge, a struggling town in Aaltah that had eked out a barren existence on the very edge of the lifeless Wasteland. He was well aware of the Wasteland's nature, had lived with its influence never far from his mind, but months of comfortable living in Women's Well had somehow blunted the edges of his memory.

Aaltah had flatly refused to allow any travelers from Women's Well to use its trade routes, and therefore the caravan had no choice but to travel outside of Aaltah's borders, within the Wasteland itself. The parched land produced no life whatsoever, not even the dry, brittle grasses that peppered the very outskirts of the land Aaltah claimed as its own.

There was no water, of course, save what they had brought with them, and every mouthful of food was strictly rationed. They traveled at night, both men and mule taking shelter inside a cramped canvas tent during the hottest part of the day. By the end of the first week, Smithson had to tighten his belt to keep his pants up, and the skin of his face was peeling and itchy. He entertained longing thoughts of the comfortable warmth of the forge and the intellectual stimulation of hammering hot metal.

Impossibly, the second week was even worse. There was only so much food and water they could carry, and though Smithson had found their first week's rations inadequate, it was abundantly clear that they'd eaten and drunk too much. The mule's ribs were showing, and the creature's head drooped with perpetual weariness as it strained to pull the cart that was growing ever lighter as they used up the food and water.

Smithson wished Women's Well did not suffer from such a dire shortage of chevals. With a pair of chevals to pull the cart, they would not have needed to bring so much food and water, and they could have traveled the same distance in the span of just a few days. But chevals were powered by Aal, and the Women's Well did not produce any Aal. Nor did they have the metal necessary to build the cheval skeletons even if they'd had the Aal to power them. Those chevals that the principality did have could not be spared just to make the journey more comfortable for the caravan.

At last, the fortnight of misery was coming to a close. Once the caravan crossed the South Twin River, they would be in the Principality of the Midlands, which had granted Women's Well passage without demur. There would be water and food and even a bed to sleep in, for they had been granted enough coin to secure two nights' lodging to rest up after the ordeal of the Wasteland before continuing on the considerably shorter and easier road through the Midlands to Rhozinolm. The prospect was enticing enough that they did not set up camp at first light and instead traveled on, despite the ever-increasing heat.

Smithson's stomach growled loudly in hunger, and his mouth would have watered at the thought of eating his fill if his body had a drop of water to spare. The other soldiers' stomachs were no quieter, and they exchanged a few half-hearted jests as their pace picked up despite their exhaustion. Even the mule seemed to sense that the worst of the journey was almost over, its head rising and its nostrils flaring. Perhaps it scented the water of the river.

The caravan steered closer to Aaltah's border, although they would remain on the Wasteland side until they had crossed the river into the Midlands, just to make sure Aaltah had no cause to complain or excuse to seize their cargo, which consisted of potions and of pebbles containing the Women's Well version of a traditional Trapper spell. What was ordinarily a minor spell used by trappers to hide snares had, with an unusual combination of both men's and women's magic, become the most powerful concealment spell ever known, and therefore one of Women's Well's most valuable assets.

Smithson suspected the caravan's insistence on staying on the

Wasteland side of the border was due to an overabundance of caution. There was no sign of civilization in sight, no one to see if they were to veer just slightly into the land that at least held the *possibility* of life. Even the hardiest of border towns were built at least half a day's travel from the Wasteland, and it was hardly as if Aaltah had to guard against attacks along this particular border.

Even the banks of the South Twin River were barren on the Wasteland side, but Smithson could see in the distance where the stubborn life of the desert had turned the banks in Aaltah sparsely green. And at least once they reached the river, there would be plenty of water to drink. Nothing lived in the water that traveled through the Wasteland, but it was not poisonous.

Smithson was staring so fixedly at the water that when the soldier in front of him grunted and then collapsed to the ground in a cloud of dust, he did not at first have any idea what had happened.

"Down!" the other soldier shouted, running for the rear of the wagon to take shelter. The driver gave an incoherent cry of alarm and dropped the reins, diving into the back of the wagon amidst the boxes of trade goods.

For a moment, Smithson stood frozen in his tracks, his mouth falling open as his confused mind finally made sense of what he saw, of the bloody arrow point piercing his fellow soldier's chest. The arrow had gone straight through the man's mail.

Another arrow thunked into the side of the wagon, the sound startling the usually placid mule.

"Get down, you idiot!" someone shouted—Smithson was too dazed to tell if it was the soldier or the driver—and he finally came to himself enough to realize he was an easy target.

He dove headfirst into the dust, his body sliding until he was at least partially under cover of the wagon. He coughed as he inhaled a lungful of the dust he'd just stirred up. The mule brayed and lurched forward, dragging the driverless wagon with it. A gust of bone-dry wind blew a cloud of blood-scented dust into Smithson's face, and he coughed once more. The earth beneath him vibrated with the thunder of hooves. Squinting, his eyes gritty, he saw the band of horsemen, eight or ten strong, that had obviously been lying in wait, concealed by the banks of the river.

The mule wanted no part of those charging horses, and instead of going forward, it skittered backward, pushing a wagon wheel dangerously close to Smithson's head. He wriggled in the dirt, trying to keep himself centered under the wagon and away from the wheels. A cry of pain from behind him told him the soldier had not been as lucky.

The horsemen were on them within the span of a few heartbeats. One of them slipped expertly off his horse and grabbed the mule's reins. Smithson glanced over his shoulder toward the back of the wagon. The injured soldier had drawn his sword, but one of his hands was mangled from its encounter with the wagon wheel, and the weapon wavered unsteadily.

Heart hammering in his throat, Smithson drew his own sword as tears of terror burned in his eyes. He had no room to maneuver under the wagon, but the enemy horsemen now had the caravan surrounded. There was the twang of a bow, and the driver cried out in pain. Then another arrow speared through the soldier's throat, driving home how useless a sword could be—even in the hands of one who knew how to use it—when faced with bowmen.

Smithson gasped for breath, his lungs heaving with effort as he continued to take in more dust. He clutched tightly to his sword, expecting to feel the bite of an arrow any moment, despite the cover of the wagon.

A man in peasant's rags dropped to the ground on his knees and peered under the wagon at Smithson, keeping carefully out of sword range. Not that Smithson could find the courage to take a swing. For all his six months' training, he was obviously woefully unprepared for the true experience of battle, and he wished with a desperate ache that he had remained his father's apprentice. A sob rose in his throat.

The crinkles at the corners of his eyes told Smithson the man kneeling by the wagon was smiling, though the bottom half of his face was entirely hidden behind a kerchief. Despite his terror, Smithson couldn't help noting that although the man was dressed as a peasant, his feet were clad in what appeared to be brand-new boots, and the sword he held was a thing of beauty, its pommel engraved with careful precision. It was possible this bandit had stolen both the sword and the boots, but there was absolutely no way any self-respecting bandit would lay an ambush out in the Wasteland.

"What have we here?" the bandit asked. "Looks like a baby soldier."

Smithson heard the laughter and jeers of the other bandits—all of whom were appropriately masked, but all of whom also carried themselves with suspiciously erect posture—more like soldiers than bandits. Not one looked especially dirty or underfed.

"Are you willing to die to protect your precious cargo, baby soldier?" the bandit asked, patting the side of the wagon.

Of course, the only honorable answer was "yes." That was the assignment Smithson had taken on when he'd agreed to accompany this caravan, and it was what any brave soldier was honor-bound to do.

The man's eyes softened, and he tugged down his kerchief to reveal a face that under other circumstances Smithson might have described as kind. "There's no need for you to die here. Not even the most demanding of all commanders would fault you for surrendering under the circumstances. Drop the sword, and come out from under there."

Smithson's hands tightened on the sword. Unbidden, he saw his mother's face, saw her holding back tears as she sent him off to the Citadel, proud of him, but also afraid. Although she'd never come out and said so, he was well aware that she had not wanted him to become a soldier, had heard her and his father arguing over whether they should allow him to enter the Citadel. She had eventually been persuaded, but if Smithson did not return from this mission, she would probably never forgive his father for that persuasion.

The make-believe bandit sighed. "I really don't want to kill you. I am not in the habit of killing children."

Smithson tried to summon up some sense of affront over having been called a child, but he was too terrified to manage it.

He'd been so focused on the bandit who was speaking to him that he'd forgotten how many others there were. Someone grabbed his ankles and yanked. The unmasked bandit hastily stuck out a leg and planted his booted foot on the blade of Smithson's sword, keeping it pinned as Smithson was pulled out from beneath the wagon.

Being dragged kicked up a smothering cloud of dust, and Smithson's incoherent shout of alarm was cut off by a heaving cough. Grit coated his eyeballs, and he shut his eyes, sure the killing blow was about to land.

Whoever had his ankles let go, and though Smithson thought distantly that now was the time to make one last, desperate attempt to save his life by running, he couldn't seem to make himself move. He kept his eyes closed and tried to find some semblance of a soldier's dignity as he heard the heavy tread of footsteps approaching from the far side of the wagon. Still, the killing blow did not land.

"I told you I don't want to kill you, and I meant it," the bandit said.

Reluctantly, Smithson opened his eyes, blinking desperately to try to clear the grit. The unmasked bandit was squatting right beside him, holding Smithson's blade, but not in a menacing way.

"I don't feel inclined to give this back to you," the bandit said, "but if you stay right where you are until we are out of sight, then you will live through this encounter. I swear it."

Smithson swallowed hard. "I'm to trust the word of a bandit?" he rasped, though there was no doubt in his mind that this man was no bandit. He and his men were soldiers of Aaltah, and had been stationed near the river for the express purpose of disrupting any trade caravans from Women's Well.

The bandit grinned. "You can trust the word of *this* bandit." He stood up and dusted off his pants, which was a fruitless endeavor. "Stay where you are, baby soldier. We'll leave you your water skins and any food you have left. With some skill and luck, you'll make it back to your home all right."

Smithson imagined trudging for two weeks through the desert, carrying his own water and food, with no chance of obtaining more along the way. Try as he might, he couldn't see himself making it back to Women's Well.

"If it's all the same," he said, his voice shaking despite his best effort to sound brave, "I'd rather a quick death by the sword than a long and torturous one by the Wasteland."

The soldier shrugged. "I'll kill you if I must. But you can reach South Bend in the Midlands in less than a day. The people there would likely be more kindly disposed toward you than someone from Aaltah. They might even help you find your way home in one piece."

Smithson swallowed hard, half-afraid to let himself hope. He had a few coins in his purse, and he had as yet seen no sign that the so-called bandits were going to rob him personally. It might not be enough to buy him passage back to Women's Well, but it should at least be enough to allow him to send a message home and perhaps obtain new orders.

"Stay where you are," the bandit-soldier said again as he turned toward the wagon.

Smithson watched him, then regretted looking up, for he caught sight of his three companions, all dead. One of the other men climbed into the back of the wagon and tossed the dead driver out into the dust. Smithson's hands clenched into fists at the insult to the dead.

The bandit-soldier turned back to him, his face tight with what looked like anger. "I would see your dead sent off properly if I could," he said, "but I have my orders. I'm sorry."

Without another word, he jumped into the back of the wagon and rummaged through the boxes and bags there, tossing out the scant stores of food and water. He gestured his companion into the driver's seat as he himself climbed down and retrieved his horse. He gave Smithson a salute that was only half-mocking as he remounted and ordered his men forward.

When the dust of their passage cleared, Smithson was left alone—but alive—in the blazing heat of the sun. He was too shaky to stand at first, so he merely rose to his knees and watched the dust cloud head toward the river—and then turn sharply toward the Aaltah border.

Still coughing out dust and trying to blink it out of his eyes, Smithson tried not to look too closely at his dead companions as he gathered up the water skins and what was left of the food. It was a sin against the Creator to leave their bodies to rot, but he had no fuel with which to burn them. Guilt made his stomach heave as he checked each of their purses, collecting a few more coins to fund his efforts to return to Women's Well. Then, muttering a brief prayer under his breath, he grimly began marching toward the river once more.

CHAPTER SIXTEEN

Delnamal slipped out of the grand ballroom as soon as the dancing had begun. His father had always stayed to the very end of even the longest balls, not because he enjoyed them so greatly but because he was constantly surrounded by those who wanted just a little of his time, and he felt it his duty as king to oblige. Delnamal, however, wondered sourly if anyone had even noticed him leaving.

But it was silly of him to be surly over something that turned out to be so damned convenient. He did *not* want this particular meeting with Rhojal of Nandel to be public knowledge, and there were very few opportunities for a king to meet with anyone, much less an ambassador, without everyone knowing about it.

Ordinarily, Rhojal declined nearly every social invitation sent to him, for he had the typical Nandelite's disdain for what he considered frivolity. Most envoys and ambassadors from Nandel learned at least a few of the most popular court dances and participated now and again just to be polite, but Rhojal never had, so Delnamal had sent him a private invitation by flier to request his presence in the Rose Room for a one-on-one meeting.

There were palace guards stationed throughout the halls, but Delnamal had instructed them to stay away from the Rose Room, which had always been his father's favorite location for private meetings— although in his father's case, those private meetings had almost always been with friends and family, not for official business.

The luminants on the path between the ballroom and the residential wing of the palace had been dimmed or even extinguished to discourage guests from wandering that way, but the Rose Room itself glowed bright at the end of the hall. Delnamal entered to find Rhojal waiting for him as requested.

Rhojal was the epitome of everything Delnamal found distasteful about the people of Nandel. His hair was so blond it was almost white, and his skin tone was only a couple of shades darker. But it was his eyes that always gave Delnamal a case of the shivers. The blue of them was such a shock of brightness in the otherwise pallid complexion, and the expression in them was always so cold and forbidding that Delnamal felt certain he was being judged and found wanting.

Also typical of the people of Nandel, Rhojal considered color and ornamentation frivolous and unnecessary, even for evening dress. He looked like a black cloud of doom in the Rose Room, with its soft colors and its delicate floral motifs.

"Your Majesty," Rhojal said with a respectful bow. His voice was deeper than his spare frame led one to expect, but it went with his unrelentingly somber demeanor and dress.

Delnamal nodded to acknowledge the greeting, glancing around the room in hopes of finding some wine or brandy lying about, but as this was an unofficial meeting, no one had thought to stock the Rose Room with refreshments. He had made every effort to limit the amount of alcohol he consumed during the dinner, knowing he would need his wits about him for this meeting, but his body was no longer used to such austerity, and his nerves jittered and complained.

"Thank you for coming," Delnamal said, for he hadn't been certain the ambassador would meet with him under such irregular circumstances.

Rhojal's thin lips curved upward in the barest hint of a smile, which was what passed for an emotional outburst for him. "How could I refuse such an intriguing invitation?" Those too-bright eyes of his studied Delnamal's face with an intensity that bordered on rudeness.

"Shall we sit?" Delnamal invited with a sweeping motion toward a sofa and chairs near the fireplace. The fireplace itself contained no more than a couple of glowing embers, leaving the room uncomfortably cold. Delnamal would have called for a servant to stoke it, except the fewer people who knew about this conversation, the better. No servant in his palace would *dare* to discuss anything witnessed, no matter how unusual, but one could never be too careful.

Rhojal chose the hardest, straightest chair to sit on, and Delnamal felt sure he was being judged once again for his own choice of a plump, comfortable armchair. The chair groaned softly with his weight, and he made a mental note to himself to have it replaced with something sturdier. He was heavy, but he wasn't *enormous*. Not yet, at least, though he noticed with displeasure that his new doublet was straining over his middle once again.

"I must admit to a most unseemly degree of curiosity," the ambassador said, once again smiling that thin smile of his. "I've been ambassador to Aaltah for almost two decades, and not once have I been summoned to an unofficial—perhaps even clandestine—meeting with the king."

Delnamal fought to keep his expression neutral, for the other thing he despised about Nandelites was their damned directness. There was no gentle buildup, no coy word games, and barely even a nod to common courtesy.

"I would hardly call this clandestine," he said. "I could easily have come up with something more secret than this."

"Granted, Your Majesty. And yet you will admit this is a highly irregular occasion."

Delnamal clasped his hands together in his lap, wishing once again that he had a drink. Well and good to try to keep his head clear, but he should at least have drunk enough to take the edge off. He felt awkward and fidgety, and he was certain Rhojal was aware of it.

"It is," Delnamal agreed. "But then these are unusual times."

"That they are. And relations between our two lands are not quite what they were just a few months ago."

There he was being blunt again when a little careful phrasing could have made this conversation so much easier. But it was only to be expected from a man of Nandel, and Delnamal would do his best to respond in kind.

"I am, of course, most sorry to have disappointed Sovereign Prince Waldmir after having offered him my niece in marriage," he said. "But she was a traitor to the Crown, and thus was hardly an appropriate bride for His Royal Highness."

And, he thought with a complex mixture of emotions, she had apparently been well on her way to dying when she'd set off to meet Waldmir anyway. He'd thought her illness at the start of the journey had been a ruse to give Shelvon and Corlin more time to flee, but she'd been at death's door when she'd returned to Aalwell at his command. He would never forget the shock of seeing her dull eyes staring out of a face that was more bones than flesh.

He'd thought to end her suffering as soon as his healers had declared her past saving, and yet he'd hesitated, keeping her hidden and supposedly imprisoned, until her mysterious illness had carried her off. Only then had he brought in the headsman for her "execution."

He had never been fond of Jinnell—how could he be, when she was Alysoon's child?—but he was not immune to pity, and even a touch of guilt that it might have been the journeys he'd ordered her to undertake that had laid her so low. He would never know whether he would have eventually ordered her execution as a traitor as he claimed to have done.

Rhojal lifted his hands in a shruglike gesture. "Be that as it may, it is still an uncomfortable reality that you divorced Prince Waldmir's daughter and then executed his bride-to-be within an alarmingly short span of time. His Royal Highness is not to be blamed for thinking that perhaps Aaltah is not the most reliable of business partners with you at the helm."

Delnamal's fists clenched, and it was all he could do to keep his temper from breaking free. "There's directness, and then there's outright discourtesy," he growled through his teeth. "You are treading dangerously close to the latter."

"Forgive me, Your Majesty," Rhojal said, bowing his head. "I did not mean to give offense. But I see no reason to pretend that all is well when we both know that it is not."

Delnamal was half tempted to send the ambassador home and demand Waldmir replace him with someone who had at least a modicum of diplomacy. But considering how unhappy his royal council already was with him for cancelling the trade agreement with Rhozinolm, he could not afford to further antagonize such a vital ally. Nandel was the only source of iron and most gems on the mainland. Khalpar, as Aaltah's staunchest ally, could provide the resources, but the cost of shipping such heavy items over the Wellspring Sea was prohibitive even with the most beneficial of terms. There was a reason Nandel was so anxiously courted by those who thought them uncouth barbarians.

Swallowing insults and disrespect had never been one of Delnamal's most practiced skills, but he was determined to do it this time. He was well aware that Waldmir's nephew might marry the Queen of Rhozinolm, and that marriage might very well inspire Waldmir to decide he no longer needed to provide iron or gems to Aaltah. The bitch queen had already threatened to invade Aaltah if Delnamal did not withdraw his forces from Women's Well, and if they were to gain exclusive access to Nandel's iron and gems . . .

The possibility did not bear consideration. He would find a way to repair relations with Nandel, and together they would bring both Rhozinolm and Women's Well to heel.

"You are right, of course," Delnamal said, though the words cost him. He dared not look Rhojal right in the eye, for if he saw any hint of smugness or triumph, he might not be able to contain himself after all. "And that is the reason why I wanted to meet with you. You understand that my decisions about Shelvon and about my niece were both made with considerable thought and with unquestionable justification. It would not be appropriate for me to make any kind of formal reparations to Prince Waldmir under the circumstances."

He risked a glance at Rhojal's face now and saw that the ambassador was watching him with furrowed brow. The expression looked more like deep thought than anger, so Delnamal felt encouraged. At least the man was not assuming Delnamal was a half-wit who had no more to say than that.

"You perhaps are considering offering *in*formal reparations?" Rhojal prompted.

Delnamal smiled, imagining just how Alysoon would feel when she learned the fate of her pathetic trade "caravan." How long would Rhozinolm's support last if the promised resources never reached their destination? "I just happen to have come into possession of some very valuable magic items. A group of, er, bandits, apparently intercepted a caravan from Women's Well intended for Rhozinolm. The bandits brought their cargo into Aaltah, where my soldiers fought and defeated them. Naturally, they confiscated the cargo, but I am hardly inclined to send it on to its original destination."

If the "bandits" had attacked a caravan that was traveling through Aaltah with the appropriate permits, the law would have demanded the cargo be returned to its rightful owner. However, there was no law that said cargo illegally brought into Aaltah need be returned.

Rhojal grinned at him, his eyes lighting with a combination of humor and cunning. "Bandits, eh? I presume the caravan was traveling through the Wasteland, having been denied entry to Aaltah?"

"That is correct. The bandits must have heard that I'd denied the caravan entry and made a logical deduction as to what alternate route they would take."

"How fortuitous that your men were able to intercept them before they'd sold off their ill-gotten gains."

"Indeed. The caravan was not overlarge, but as the cargo consisted of spells that are not being made available to anyone else but Rhozinolm, it constitutes a major windfall."

"One that you are offering to share with Nandel."

"Oh, no," Delnamal said and was rewarded by a glower. He allowed himself the span of a few heartbeats to enjoy Rhojal's surge of anger. "I'm offering to turn the whole thing over to Nandel. As you said, there has been some significant strain lately, and I would very much like to smooth things over. In an unofficial capacity, of course."

Rhojal quickly regained his good humor, though he made a show of frowning. "We of Nandel haven't much use for women's magic," he said with a curl of his lip. "While I'm sure these spells are considered valuable by some—"

"You have my guarantee that you will find at least one of those spells more valuable than you imagine." His soldiers had informed him that the shipment had contained hundreds of pebbles infused with the Women's Well Trapper spell, which was strong enough to hide a building from view. Hell, Women's Well had hidden damn near their whole *town* when Delnamal had foolishly sent a company of soldiers to attack what he'd expected to be easy prey.

Besides, although Rhojal was spouting the official Nandel position on the usefulness of women's magic, Delnamal was sure that everyone in the cursed place used women's magic when it was convenient. Their Abbey might not produce spells or potions, but that didn't mean the men of Nandel couldn't get hold of them when they wanted to. The spark of greed in the ambassador's eyes said he was much more interested in those spells than his words implied.

"And of course," Delnamal continued, "I must remind you that these are merely a gift. If Prince Waldmir finds them useful, then perhaps he can see his way to forgiving some of the unfortunate events that have come between us. If not, then we are no worse off."

Rhojal seemed to be thinking things over carefully, though Delnamal couldn't imagine why. It was hard to extort anything extra from what was ostensibly a gift. But Delnamal decided to sweeten the deal—or at least plant a hint that the deal might be sweetened—anyway.

"I hope that Nandel and Aaltah can become fast friends once more. It will be much to our advantage to work together when Seven Wells now has two women who fancy themselves sovereigns. The world will be in need of steady men who can counter their feminine hysterics and put them in their place when necessary. And perhaps in the future we can once again try for an alliance by marriage." He beamed his best proud-father-to-be smile. "After all, I have a son on the way, and Prince Waldmir still has one unmarried daughter."

Waldmir's youngest was four or five years old—Delnamal couldn't remember exactly—but being both a Nandelite and illegitimate thanks to her mother's disgrace and divorce, she would ordinarily be beneath the notice of a king. Certainly she would not be the most advantageous bride for Delnamal's son, but any formal marriage agreement would be many years down the road. And hopes of that formal agreement could persuade Waldmir that he should favor Aaltah over Rhozinolm. Surely he'd rather see a grand*son* on the throne of Aaltah than a grand*nephew* on the throne of Rhozinolm. Neither Aaltah nor Rhozinolm would allow him to have both.

Rhojal nodded thoughtfully. "You have given us a lot to think about. I will gladly accept your gift on behalf of my sovereign prince. And I will pass on your thoughts of where the future might lead us."

Delnamal looked forward to reporting the success of this endeavor to Lord Aldnor. The lord commander had been highly reluctant to order his troops to disguise themselves and ambush the caravan, blathering on about honor and Aaltah's proud military tradition. His protestations had strayed dangerously close to outright refusal, and Delnamal had clearly seen that several of the other members of his council were similarly discomfited.

In the end, the council had voted to approve the ambush. Aware that it had been closer than he would have liked, Delnamal had decided to make his offer to Rhojal *without* discussing it with the council first. If Rhojal had declined the offer, the secrecy of their meeting meant his council would never have to know the offer had been made at all. But now that Rhojal had agreed, Delnamal could report the results in triumph. And perhaps now the lord commander and his supporters would stop pining after the late king and finally give Delnamal the support and respect he was owed.

The letter Lord Jailom presented to Alys was crudely written and rife with misspellings. She frowned at it.

"The boy was in training to be a smith before he entered the Citadel," Jailom explained. "I've arranged for those boys who need it to receive remedial lessons, but their reading and writing skills are a bit elementary at the moment."

Once she got past the atrocious handwriting and the misspellings, Alys realized that the *content* of the message was far worse than its form. It was all she could do to keep from cursing out loud.

"There's no question Delnamal was behind it," Jailom said. "When he denied us use of the trade routes, he knew that we would travel through the Wasteland, and he set up that ambush along the route he knew our caravan would take."

"Of course he did," Alys groaned, tossing the distasteful message onto her desk and leaning back in her chair. Thanks to Delnamal's border patrol and his refusal to let anyone cross into Aaltah from Women's Well, she had so far managed to make successful trades only with the principality of Grunir, and those only on the smallest of scales, for Grunir did not wish to incur Aaltah's wrath. The *only* reason Queen Ellinsoltah had managed to coax her council into making an alliance was because of the unique magic Women's Well could offer. If Women's Well couldn't deliver . . .

"And of course he'll *deny* that those were his men," she muttered.

Jailom nodded. "The caravan was not attacked within Aaltah's borders, and he will naturally make the case that he is not responsible for it. Only those who *want to* believe him will do so, but . . ."

"But no one is going to take up arms on our behalf over an accusation like this. And there are plenty of people who'd be all too happy to believe it anyway."

"Exactly."

It was easy enough to send small quantities of spells and potions to Rhozinolm via flier, but that hardly constituted a healthy trade relationship. She could, of course, send more soldiers to guard the next caravan. But unless she had enough chevals to shorten the journey, she couldn't afford to send too many good fighting men away for a journey that would last more than a month. Women's Well had so few soldiers to start with that they had little chance of surviving an attack unless every one of them was on the battlefield. And though Delnamal had backed down once before, she feared sending more than a handful of soldiers away would be tempting fate.

"Perhaps when next you speak to Queen Ellinsoltah," Jailom said, "you might suggest trading along a naval route instead."

She nodded absently, although that would be no easy feat. Rhozinolm had an impressive navy thanks to its many hospitable harbors, but Women's Well was land-bound. Perhaps Rhozinolm could send a ship to a port in Grunir, but that would require the cooperation of the Sovereign Prince of Grunir, who had so far been less than enthusiastic in his communications with Women's Well.

"I'll talk to Ellinsoltah about it. Maybe we can find another way." They would *have* to.

"And the boy?" Jailom said, nodding toward the letter. "He is stranded in the Midlands. He cannot travel home through the Wasteland by himself with no mount, and I fear sending him through Aaltah might endanger his life. I doubt that so-called bandit-soldier of his was meant to leave any survivors."

"If we send him funds via flier," she said, "can he purchase a cheval in the Midlands?"

"It would be expensive," Jailom warned, although she knew that. Because chevals required Aal, they were almost all produced in Aaltah, which meant any the boy could buy in the Midlands would be both imported and comparatively rare.

She sighed heavily. "We need more chevals anyway, and I'm hardly going to leave your cadet stranded after all he's been through." Not to mention that she'd already lost two soldiers and a civilian driver in this doomed trade attempt, and she had no wish to lose another man, even if he was just a cadet. "Let's send him the money and have him ride the cheval through the Wasteland. He won't kick up a fuss about riding a cheval, will he?"

Riding a cheval was considered unmanly, and there were some soldiers who would balk at such a thing, preferring their horses.

Jailom smiled grimly. "He's just spent two weeks traveling through the Wasteland on foot. Even the vainest of men would abandon their pride to get that journey over with in a matter of days."

Alys imagined her lord high treasurer was going to have a word or two to say when he learned of this extravagant expenditure. But he would abandon all thoughts of lectures when the council began to discuss the establishment of new trade routes.

CHAPTER SEVENTEEN

Norah rubbed her hands nervously on the skirt of her robes, her heart pattering as she stood outside the door of the abbess's office. There could be no benign reason Mairahsol had summoned her, although Norah had been doing her best not to draw the other woman's attention and ire. The spirit of rebellion that had fueled her when Mairahsol had first been named abbess had dimmed a great deal thanks to the constant punishments and fasts. She was still resolved to resist the abbess's attempts—pathetic though they might be—to undo the Blessing, but there was only so much misery she was willing to endure.

And yet for all her good behavior, she'd been summoned to the abbess's office yet again. She no longer felt as brave as she once had, and it was an effort of will to force herself to knock.

"Come in," Mairahsol called. Just the sound of the hateful woman's voice was enough to make Norah cringe.

Reluctantly, Norah pushed the door open and stepped inside. Mairahsol was seated behind her desk, and she watched with a predatory gleam in her eyes as Norah approached. Norah gritted her teeth. She had never thought of herself as the kind of person who would hate another, but the feeling that roiled in her gut just now felt very much like hatred. Even if she did not feel such a huge personal enmity toward Mairahsol, she would still hate the woman for her willingness—no, *eagerness*—to bow to the will of men and try to undo the Blessing the Mother of All had bestowed upon Her daughters.

"You wanted to see me, Mother Mairahsol?" Norah asked, though it cost her dearly every time she had to utter that title.

Mairahsol's eyes gleamed with an almost lustful expression. "Indeed. Do you know why?"

Norah racked her brain, trying to think of some way she had displeased the abbess without noticing. But she had avoided Mairahsol to the best of her ability and had barely set eyes on the woman over the course of the last week. She had been as inoffensive as it was possible to be. "No, Mother Mairahsol."

Mairahsol's smile broadened, became something closer to a baring of teeth. "You are aware that worshipping the Mother of All is considered heresy? And that heresy is a crime punishable by death?"

Norah swayed on her feet and feared for a moment that she might humiliate herself by fainting dead away. She had worshipped the Mother of All for most of her life, always knowing that it was a deadly risk. But somehow, after decades without discovery, she'd allowed herself to believe that she would never be caught. She tried to summon a denial, but there was no reason to think Mairahsol would believe one.

"A heretic's death is not an easy one," Mairahsol continued, making a face that was supposed to convey sympathy, though Norah doubted she'd be very good at it even if she weren't being intentionally insincere. "But I suspect that death by fire, as agonizing as it must be, is less unpleasant than the hours upon hours a heretic must spend in earnest conversation with the royal inquisitor." She shuddered theatrically. "I understand that it is necessary to root out all traces of the heresy, but the inquisitor's methods are *most* disturbing."

Norah couldn't breathe. She had been foolish and reckless, assum-

ing Mairahsol would not venture forth from her rooms in the night—
and that none of her sister abigails would betray her. She did not
know of a single abigail who actually *liked* the woman, but there were
certainly those who were all too happy to curry favor. It would be
bad enough if Norah herself were the only one who would suffer
for her mistake, but she had no illusions about her own physical
courage—or about the effectiveness of the inquisitor's terrible methods. Under torture, she would betray every one of her fellow worshippers, and they, in turn, would face the same fate.

A hand took firm hold of her upper arm, and with a shock Norah
saw that the abbess had risen from her chair and come around her
desk. Norah's head was spinning—she hadn't even seen the other
woman move.

"Sit down before you fall down," Mairahsol said, her voice sharp
with impatience as she all but shoved Norah into a chair. "If I were
planning to turn you in, I would not have bothered meeting with
you first."

Norah's chest still felt tight with panic, her pulse stuttering errati-
cally as her mind helpfully conjured images of the torments she would
suffer at the inquisitor's hands. She heard Mairahsol's words in a distant way, barely able to comprehend them.

"It's no secret that I despise you," Mairahsol said. "You and all
your sanctimonious, holier-than-thou friends. You've made my life
miserable for years, and I have every intention of paying you all back
in full. But even *I* have to admit you haven't done anything worthy
of torture and death."

Norah sucked in a deep breath as her rational mind attempted to
return from the deep, dark cave in which it had hidden. Clearly, Mairahsol wanted something from her. Norah could not but think it was
something she would very much not want to give her, but *anything*
was better than the fate that would be hers should the abbess turn
her in.

"W-what do you want?" she managed to stammer, terror still
tightening her throat.

Mairahsol leaned her hip against her desk, folding her arms over
her chest as she regarded Norah with a look of equal parts malice and

calculation. "Am I right in suspecting that you and the rest of your fellow heretics have been doing your best to obstruct my research? I would not recommend lying to me."

Norah swallowed hard, willing herself to be steady, to *think*. Her life, and the lives of all her dearest sisters, rested in her ability to stay calm and give the abbess what she wanted. It was certainly her intention—and the intention of her sisters—to obstruct Mairahsol's research whenever possible, but there had hardly been much need. As far as Norah could tell, the abbess had made no progress whatsoever and didn't even have a clear idea how to start researching. However, it would obviously not be wise to say so.

"We believe what you call the Curse is actually the Mother's Blessing," Norah said. Her voice came out raspy, as if she'd been screaming. "We feel it is for the benefit of all women and that it would be a betrayal of our faith to try to reverse it."

Mairahsol rolled her eyes. "Has your life improved so greatly since it was cast? Has *mine*?"

Norah looked up sharply, indignation making her incautious. "It isn't about you or me! It's about all women. And yes, I believe that many lives have been improved."

Mairahsol shrugged. "In theory, I suppose, though I've seen little evidence to support it. And all those who lost their lives in the earthquake the Curse caused would no doubt argue. Not to mention all the newly divorced women who have joined our numbers recently."

It was true that the Abbey was overflowing with newly discarded women who'd been divorced for failing to provide their husbands with children. But Norah had talked to more than one of those women and found them still thankful for the effects of the Blessing. Without it, they would have been forever trapped in their abusive marriages. And as hard as life in the Abbey might be, it was better than some alternatives. Norah herself had actually been thankful when her ex-husband had grown tired of her and decided to marry— and no doubt mistreat—a younger woman.

"But it is only because of the Blessing that abigails are no longer forced to work the pavilion," Norah argued. Not that Mairahsol could comprehend that particular horror, for Mother Wyebryn had

taken one look at her disfigured face and declared her exempt from
pavilion duty.

Mairahsol waved the objection off. "It doesn't matter. The king
has commanded us to do our best to reverse the Curse, and so that is
what we must do. And unless you want me to tell the lord high priest
that I have discovered a nest of heretics operating within the walls of
this abbey, you—and your cohorts—will from now on put forth your
best efforts. Is that understood?"

Norah very much doubted it was the king's orders that concerned
Mairahsol—it was her provisional status as abbess. Mairahsol had a
great many faults, but stupidity wasn't one of them. She might not be
as magically gifted as she'd led the lord high priest to believe, and she
certainly wasn't the gifted seer she made herself out to be, but she
knew that if she could not find a way to convince the king she was
making progress, she would be back to being just one more abigail in
less than three months' time.

"Yes, Mother Mairahsol," she answered, bowing her head.

"I want your seers making an honest effort to find a solution,"
Mairahsol continued. "It was through the efforts of a seer that the
Curse was cast, and it only makes sense that it is through the efforts
of a seer that it will be reversed."

Norah bit her tongue to keep from pointing out how faulty the
abbess's logic was. Anyone who had even a basic understanding of
women's magic should know that the Abbess of Aaltah's power was
unheard of. It was sheer folly to believe that Mairahsol—or anyone
else now living, really—could reverse such a powerful spell. It was
also folly to argue with Mairahsol, but that didn't stop Norah from
trying.

"But the visions we receive are granted by the Mother," she protested in what she hoped was a calm and level voice. Even those who
believed the Mother was a lesser deity who sprang into being at the
Creator's will generally thought that She was the source of seers' visions, so she was not speaking heresy. "Clearly the Mother guided
the actions of the Abbess of Aaltah—and of her predecessors. Which
means the Mother wanted the spell to be cast. Why should we then
expect Her to help us undo it?"

Mairahsol fixed her with an icy glare. "If She cares about you and about your heretical friends, then She'd *better* help. I don't want to turn you in, but I'm sure you know I will if I have to. If I am demoted to ordinary abigail, I will destroy you and everyone you care about. You know my history, so you know I am speaking the truth."

Norah did, indeed, know Mairahsol's history. The woman would stop at nothing to get her revenge if she felt she was wronged. In fact, she was so vicious she might even have been willing to proclaim *herself* a worshipper of the Mother of All if she thought her "confession" the only way to condemn Norah along with her. Fear curdled in Norah's stomach, for she truly believed that what Mairahsol wanted to do was impossible, just as she also believed Mairahsol would follow through on her threat.

"I don't personally care if you call upon the Mother or the Mother of All to help you," Mairahsol said, "but one way or another, one of your followers had better foresee a path we can take to undo the Curse. If we fail to make progress, I'll be forced to tell the king you sabotaged my efforts. I hope I have made myself *abundantly* clear."

"Yes, Mother Mairahsol," Norah gritted, caught between fury and terror.

"And, Norah," Mairahsol said, just as Norah thought she would finally be dismissed. "Rest assured that I will make sure your secret comes out should anything mysteriously happen to me. I am not a fool."

Unfortunately, that was true. So as much as Norah would like to begin plotting Mairahsol's gruesome murder, she knew she could not.

The building that would one day be the royal palace of Women's Well was coming along nicely, Alys thought as the chairman of the building committee guided her through the construction zone. She hadn't been especially eager to conduct an inspection tour—she trusted the building committee, and she was still ambivalent about moving out of her current house and into a palace. She'd have just as happily done without all the pomp and circumstance that came with being a sovereign, but she was well aware that most of it was not for the sovereign's benefit. She might feel just as much like a sovereign living in her comfortable little house as she would living in a palace, but the same could not be said of her people—or, even more important, of the other sovereigns in Seven Wells, with whom she needed to trade and negotiate.

All the other palaces in Seven Wells were built almost entirely of stone, but there was no quarry within easy travel of Women's Well, and as it was expensive to transport such heavy building materials over long distances, Alys had at first insisted her palace be built entirely of wood. Even that, however, was expensive, for the trees that had sprung up thanks to the influence of the Well were as yet too young for timber. Growth potions were helping them along, and Alys suspected that within a year or two, Women's Well would produce enough timber on its own to be self-sufficient, but they weren't there yet.

At the urging of both the building committee and her royal council, Alys had finally agreed that it was worth the expense of importing stone for the most public areas of the palace, with the residential wing constructed of the less expensive wood.

"How long until it is habitable?" Alys asked the chairman as he led her through the almost-finished first floor of the residential wing. The public areas—the throne room, the banquet hall, the official audience chambers—were nowhere near as advanced in their construction, but then the need for some degree of ostentation was bound to slow down the progress.

"It should be ready for you within a month, two at most. If you don't mind that there will still be work underway on the public areas." He looked at her anxiously, as if worried she might demand all construction be finished before she move in. She would have liked nothing better than to delay the move, but duty to her principality outweighed her personal preferences.

"No, I don't mind," she assured him with a token smile.

"Then you are pleased with how things are going?" he prompted, still looking anxious.

Alys tried to add some warmth into her smile, despite all her mixed feelings. This palace would not be anything like the one she'd grown up in, which had been centuries old and practically the size of a small city all by itself. That palace had been comfortable, to some extent, because it was familiar. This one would be far less grand, and she could already see that the rooms of the residential wing would be far more homelike. Perhaps because she had had her late husband's manor house in mind, rather than her father's palace, when she had described the rooms she wanted in the residence.

"I'm very pleased," she assured the chairman, who sighed in relief.

"Thank you, Your Royal Highness," he said with a bow.

Both his anxiety and his relief brought a little genuine humor into Alys's smile. He was taking a craftsman's pride in his work, and she was suddenly glad she'd agreed to the inspection.

Her smile faded quickly when she saw Tynthanal appear at the far end of the hall. There was no reason he would come to the palace-in-progress unless he was looking for her. And there was no reason he'd be looking for her if he didn't have something urgent—and likely unpleasant—to speak with her about. The look on his face confirmed her suspicion. He nodded at her, clearly willing to wait until she was finished with the chairman, but she doubted she'd be able to give the building plans the attention they deserved with him hovering in the background like that.

"Please excuse me for a moment," she said to the chairman while continuing to watch Tynthanal's face in search of a clue.

"Of course, Your Royal Highness," the chairman said with another bow.

"Wait here," she instructed her honor guardsmen, then crossed to Tynthanal and gestured him into one of the empty rooms. There was no door, and the emptiness made for echoes, but it was a relatively quiet location to speak with her lord chancellor—she was quite certain he was not here as her brother.

"What is it?" she asked in a voice just above a whisper.

"A messenger arrived from Grunirswell," Tynthanal said. He held up a small wooden box that she hadn't even noticed him holding. "The messenger was just a hireling, but he said he was hired to bring this to you by the captain of a Khalpari merchant ship."

Alys suppressed a shiver as she fought to keep her imagination from running away with her. The box was not big enough to contain anything truly dreadful . . . *Delnamal taking a burlap sack from one of his soldier's hands* . . . but it was clearly not a message of support and friendship.

Tynthanal opened the box before she could get too lost in conjecture, and she bent forward slightly to look inside. At first, all she could discern was a pile of wood chips and bent nails. Then she made out the shape of a bird's beaked head and one clawed foot, still curled around a tightly scrolled piece of paper.

Her shoulders sagged as she realized what she was looking at. "Our flier to King Khalvin," she murmured, poking at the scroll and seeing that the wax seal was unbroken. He hadn't even bothered to read her message.

"It isn't quite a declaration of war," Tynthanal said, shaking his head.

"But it's far from a declaration of friendship." The King of Khalpar could have chosen any number of ways to respond unfavorably to Alys's overture. With all the time that had passed since she'd sent the flier, she'd assumed he'd taken the easiest route and merely chosen not to respond at all. Or he could have simply sent the flier back intact. To have made such a show of destroying it without having read the message . . .

"It was never likely to work," Tynthanal said quietly. "You know how . . . traditional the Khalpari are."

She nodded. "Religious, you mean." She was well aware of how much more seriously the people of Khalpar took the teachings of the Devotional, which very firmly placed women in a role subordinate to men. According to the teachings of the Devotional, the Mother had cheated on Her husband, the Creator, with Their son, the Destroyer. The Wasteland was where the Destroyer had landed when His father had cast Him down to earth, and to avoid the same fate, the Mother had promised always to love and obey the Creator for the rest of Her existence. This subservient relationship between Creator and Mother was the model on which people were meant to build their own relationships. Such a model would not look kindly upon a female sovereign—especially one of an upstart principality built around a Well that had appeared in the Wasteland.

"Yes. Pair that with their obvious preference for Delnamal, and it is far from surprising that King Khalvin responded with hostility."

True, it was not. But it also meant that Alys had no chance of trading with Khalpar—even on the unfavorable terms that were the best she could have hoped for—for iron or gems. If she wanted to build any kind of an arsenal for her minuscule army, her only choice would be to deal with Nandel.

"Perhaps you were right all along," she said, hating the admission. "I should not have burned Waldmir's message without even reading it."

Tynthanal shrugged as if it hardly mattered, and she was more thankful than she could have said that he chose not to rub her nose in her mistake. He was still angry with her over her refusal to allow his marriage to Chanlix, but at least he was not cruel about it.

"Waldmir can't know for sure whether his flier successfully made the journey to Women's Well," Tynthanal said. "After all, they do fail sometimes."

It was true that a harsh storm could knock a flier right out of the sky, maybe even damage it enough that its spell died and left it nothing but an inert carved bird. And Nandel was very much a land of harsh storms.

"If you send him a flier and make no mention of having received one from him previously, he might assume it never reached you," Tynthanal continued.

She made a vague sound of assent, though she rather doubted Waldmir would give her the benefit of the doubt. His reasons for scorning women—and disrespecting someone claiming to be a female sovereign—might not be religious, as King Khalvin's were, but they were just as deep-seated. If not more so.

Hating the very thought of trading with the man who had threatened Jinnell's life and happiness, she reminded herself for the thousandth time that the well-being of her principality had to come before all else.

"I'll send Prince Waldmir a flier," she said.

Norah had spent several sleepless nights trying to figure out what—if anything—she should tell her sisters about Mairahsol's ultimatum. It was dishonest of her not to tell them of the threat that hovered over them all, but she did not want them to suffer as she was now suffering. She wasn't sure how she would ever sleep through the night again, as every moment of quiet stillness gave her mind the freedom to conjure appalling images of the long and agonizing death that would be hers if Mairahsol followed through on her threat.

It was on the third of those sleepless nights, when exhaustion dragged her to the edge of a restless sleep, that she finally saw how she'd allowed her fear to overwhelm her faith.

Norah firmly believed that the Blessing was the work of the Mother of All, and that She had no intention of allowing Her children to reverse it. But that didn't mean that She would not guide the faithful to safety.

Norah gently shook Sister Melred awake from a sound sleep in one of the junior abigails' dormitories. She covered the younger woman's mouth with her hand so that she wouldn't cry out, then put her finger to her lips when she saw Melred had awakened. Melred nodded, and Norah moved her hand.

Silently, Melred slipped out of the bed. Norah glanced around at the other beds, trying to see if anyone else was awake. Mother Wyebryn had been careful in her assignment of beds, grouping the abigails so that the Mother of All worshippers were together and could leave their dormitories without being betrayed by their fellow residents, but Mairahsol had, of course, inserted several of her spies in their midst. Norah had gotten very skilled at sneaking sleeping potions into drinks.

No one else stirred as Norah led Melred out of the dormitory. Melred yawned and rubbed her eyes, but she followed obediently and asked no questions as Norah steered her to the row of playrooms that was just down the hall from the dormitories. It was late enough at night that none of the rooms was in use. Melred raised a curious eyebrow as Norah carefully peered into the first room, making doubly sure that it was empty before entering.

There were no windows in the playrooms, so it was dark when Melred and Norah first stepped in. Norah lit one of the room's many luminants, revealing the plush bed with its rich counterpane of red velvet. The beds the abigails slept on were rock-hard and covered in coarse, threadbare sheets, but the beds in which they entertained the Abbey's clientele were a good deal more luxurious.

Melred closed the playroom door gently, then turned to Norah. Pretty and sweet-natured, Melred had spent many hours working in the Abbey's playrooms, and she had continued to do so after it had become no longer strictly mandatory. Norah herself had been too old when she'd first arrived at the Abbey to be forced to sell her body, yet still every time she stepped into a playroom, something deep inside her shuddered at the thought of what so many of her sisters endured. Just because they would no longer be beaten or starved for refusing to work the pavilion didn't mean those who still did so were happy with their lot.

Norah's discomfort must have been obvious, for Melred smiled at her mischievously. "Working the pavilion is not a contagious disease," she teased, "and I promise you won't catch it merely by setting foot in a playroom."

Norah was fairly certain she blushed like a schoolgirl. "I figured this would be a place we could talk without anyone overhearing or interrupting us."

Melred hid a yawn behind her fist, then sat on the edge of the bed, leaning back comfortably on her hands. "You are certainly being quite mysterious, Sister Norah," she said with no hint of anxiety.

Norah hated to shatter the young woman's peace of mind, but it was a necessary evil. Melred was already the strongest seer in the Abbey, and Norah felt certain she had not yet tested the limits of her strength. In all likelihood, she could survive the poison that had killed Sister Sulrai and thereby trigger the most powerful vision their Abbey had received in recent memory.

Reluctantly, cringing inside, Norah told Melred about Mairahsol's threat. The young woman blanched, and her hands crumpled the velvet counterpane as she absorbed the horror. Her eyes glittered with unshed tears, and her lower lip trembled.

"We are doomed, then," she whispered, bowing her head and clasping her hands in her lap. "We couldn't undo the Blessing even if we wanted to."

"No," Norah agreed, sitting on the bed beside her and putting a steadying hand on her back. "But I think we must have faith that the Mother of All will protect us."

Melred sniffled and brushed away a few stray tears. "But how?"

Norah's lips curved into a faint smile, for that was the same question she had struggled with the last three nights, and the answer was obvious—once she let the fear fall away. "Through a vision, of course."

Melred blinked, and her brow furrowed in thought. "But we've been triggering visions constantly since the abbess claimed we were going to invent some new seer's poison. And we've seen nothing that would advance her cause."

Norah nodded. "True. But our seers have been triggering visions never *intending* to ask the Mother of All for guidance. We were solely focused on impeding Mairahsol's progress."

Melred frowned doubtfully. "But the Mother shows us what *She* wants us to see, not what we ask for."

"That is true. And if She sees a way to protect us while leaving the Blessing intact, She will show us what we need to do." Norah reached into a pocket in her robes and pulled out a small vial of green-tinged liquid.

Melred flinched backward, as if afraid the poison would leap out of the capped vial and force its way down her throat. Norah shivered and hoped she was doing the right thing. Melred was a naturally obedient sort, and Norah knew her own rank—both within the Abbey in general and their worship group—meant the girl would do as she was asked, despite any misgivings she might have.

Being a seer, Melred was well familiar with the range of seer's poisons available in the Abbey, and she knew at a glance the potency of the green poison. She swallowed hard, staring at the vial in Norah's hand.

"I have never taken one so strong," Melred said, her voice little more than a frightened whisper. No doubt she was thinking of how badly she had suffered from the last powerful poison she had downed. As was Norah.

"I know," Norah replied gently. "I believe you can handle it, and we need as clear a vision as the Mother can give us. You are our best hope. But it is up to you, of course. I would not force you to drink it even if I could." Guilt stirred in Norah's center, for though it was true that Melred *could* refuse, the girl's nature meant it was a foregone conclusion that she would not.

Melred bit her lip as she tentatively reached for the vial. "I suppose death by seer's poison is preferable to the fate we face if the Mother of All doesn't show us a way out."

And if Melred did not have a vision that would steer them to safety, Norah wondered if she and all of her fellow Mother of All worshippers would be best served by drinking the Abbey's entire supply of seer's poisons to avoid arrest. It would not be an easy death. But it would be far easier—and quicker—than what they would suffer at the hands of the inquisitor.

Melred blew out a deep sigh, then opened her Mindseye, scanning the room for the elements she would need to complete the poison's spell.

"May the Mother of All guide and keep you," Norah murmured as Melred tossed back the contents of the vial and swallowed with a grimace.

CHAPTER EIGHTEEN

O f all the amazing and impossible spells that had been produced in Women's Well, the talking fliers—talkers—were
by far Alys's favorite. Ordinary fliers carrying letters had once
seemed a perfectly adequate means of communicating, though de-
pending on distance and wind patterns, they could take days to
reach their recipients. A conversation full of back-and-forths could
take weeks, if not months, to complete. And of course meeting in
person with anyone—especially a sovereign—who lived in another
kingdom was a far from simple affair.

Alys sighed quietly as she fed a mote of Rho into the talker that
was paired with the one she had sent to Queen Ellinsoltah. Much as
she loved the talkers, she wasn't overjoyed to be contacting Ellinsoltah under the current circumstances. A slow and almost impersonal
letter would have been a much more pleasant way to deliver bad
news.

Eventually an image of Ellinsoltah took shape in the air, floating insubstantially over the dressing table on which Alys had lain the talker.

The Queen of Rhozinolm was dressed for evening in a deep purple gown with a fashionably low-necked bodice and a matching headdress, both sparkling with diamonds and trimmed with pink-tinged pearls. Alys suffered a twinge of envy, for her mourning would allow her to wear nothing but black. She had flouted that convention only once, disrespecting her father's memory by wearing red and gold in addition to black when she'd parleyed with Delnamal to avert his attack. Her logical mind knew her decision had had nothing to do with her daughter's death—Jinnell had already been dead by the time Alys donned the gown—but she honestly wasn't sure if she could ever wear color again, even after her official mourning was over.

"Please forgive me for disturbing you at this late hour, Your Majesty," Alys said.

Ellinsoltah flashed her a warm and friendly smile. "No need for apologies, Your Royal Highness. I presume that someday, the novelty of your talkers will wear off, but that day is still far in the future. We have already spoken in person, as it were, more times than your father and my grandfather ever did throughout their long reigns. It is a marvel."

Alys smiled, thinking that with their predecessors' temperaments, it was just as well they had rarely met in person, else their kingdoms might have fought more than just the one war over the course of their reigns. "I suppose it is," she agreed, though by this point she had used the talkers often enough that she was dangerously close to taking them for granted. "Unfortunately, at this moment they are making it quick and easy for me to deliver bad news."

Reluctantly, she told Ellinsoltah what had happened to the trade caravan and the "bandits" who had attacked it. She hoped that the two of them had established a good enough relationship that Ellinsoltah would not think this was a lie meant to delay delivery, no matter how outlandish the truth sounded. She was sure previous kings, both of Aaltah and Rhozinolm, had more than once engaged in similarly dishonest dealings, but it was still an affront to the rule of law.

"I believe it's worse than you think," Ellinsoltah said grimly when Alys was done. "My ambassador in Aaltah reports that there appears to have been an off-the-record meeting between Delnamal and the Nandel ambassador. Apparently, Rhojal of Nandel made a rare appearance at a ball, and both he and the king were seen leaving the ball at approximately the same time and were gone for at least an hour."

Alys grimaced. She had had few dealings with the Nandelite ambassador when she'd lived in Aaltah, for she had avoided court intrigue to the best of her abilities, but she knew that he never attended feasts or balls except on the most momentous occasions. She very much doubted it was a coincidence that he'd decided to be sociable when Delnamal had a caravan of stolen goods he wished to unload. She wondered how much additional iron and gems he'd been able to purchase under the table. Thanks to their previously warm relationship, Aaltah was already well-stocked for war, but it did not bode well for either Women's Well or Rhozinolm if Delnamal was acquiring additional raw materials for weapons and spells.

"Needless to say," Ellin added, "my people—especially my council—are concerned about what that secret meeting might portend. Our sources tell us Aaltah is building its military despite the limitations of its treasury, and many see Delnamal's cancellation of our trade agreement as a direct rebuke of our alliance with you. If he should find a way to weaken us further by undermining our relationship with Nandel . . ." She shook her head. "There are too many in Rhozinolm who remember the ravages of the last war between our kingdoms."

Alys shivered, seeing all too easily the threads that could lead to the destruction of Women's Well. "If your council decides that your relationship with Women's Well is putting you at risk of war with Aaltah . . ." Her heart thudded against her breastbone in fear. It seemed she could not have chosen a worse time to break the news about the caravan.

"That is my fear," Ellin admitted. "However, I do not see how it would improve our situation if Delnamal were to seize control of your Well, so let me reassure you that I don't intend to cancel our alliance because of this setback."

Ellinsoltah might not intend that, but Alys wondered if the same could be said of her council. "If Aaltah and Nandel ally against us, then I don't see how we can survive." She felt as if she were about to start screaming and never stop. Her life consisted of one crisis after another, each one hammering at the raw and bleeding nerves of a mother still trying to survive the aftermath of her daughter's death. She took a shaky breath and reminded herself that she had no choice but to cope with everything life threw her way.

"We cannot hope to defeat Aaltah and Nandel in battle," Ellin agreed. "So we must defeat them before it comes to battle. Ours must be a different kind of war. A *women's* war. Our weapons are not swords and spells, but diplomacy and trade and creativity."

It was said with a great deal of confidence and conviction, and Alys couldn't help being stirred. But Ellinsoltah was barely twenty-two, and though she'd clearly matured quickly over the short span she'd been queen, she still saw the world with the idealism of youth. Alys feared her confidence was unfounded.

"To that end," Ellin continued, "it is more important now than ever that we arrange a marriage between my cousin and your brother. My lord chancellor is a loyal man whom I trust implicitly, and if we can make sure my lord chamberlain is heavily invested in the well-being of Women's Well, it is unlikely my detractors will have the support they need to unseat me. Have you made any progress in removing the impediments?"

"Yes," Alys answered smoothly, though so far the potions Tynthanal had tried had failed. Alys reasoned it could be considered progress that he had agreed to try them at all. And saying no was out of the question under the circumstances.

"Good," Ellin said. "I will send Kailee on her way immediately. Before I report the attack on the caravan, lest such news make Kailindar think twice about the arrangement."

Alys smiled, feigning an ease she didn't feel. There were so many reasons why Ellinsoltah might choose to sever her relationship with Women's Well, and so few for her to stay true. Alys had never been especially devout, but she was nonetheless tempted to pray to the Mother that one of her potions would work. She did not want her brother forced to marry a woman he did not love, but the marriage felt more vitally important every day.

"I look forward to meeting her," Alys said, making sure to keep her qualms out of her voice and smile. "And I vow to you that I will find a way to get a caravan to you as swiftly as possible. No amount of diplomacy and creativity will help us if I am unable to fulfill my trade agreements. I don't imagine Delnamal's imaginary bandits have retired from the field, and I haven't the men or equipment to send better guarded caravans. Even if you are willing to forgive my failure to deliver, I doubt other sovereigns would be as kind."

Ellinsoltah raised a brow. "You have trade agreements with other sovereigns?"

Alys felt a muscle twitch in her jaw and hoped Ellinsoltah didn't see it. The Midlands and Grunir had both sent ambassadors to Women's Well—although neither principality was yet ready to commit to a long-term trade agreement—and of course Ellinsoltah had sent one, as well. But so far, those three were the only ones to have acknowledged that the Principality of Women's Well even existed. She wouldn't trade with Delnamal even had he been willing to, and had not yet received a response to her belated overture toward Prince Waldmir.

"Not anything ongoing as of yet," she admitted. It was perhaps too open and honest an admission to make to a sovereign of a foreign kingdom, but she hadn't the energy to dissemble. Alys was sure the Rhozinolm ambassador had already sent his liege a full report. "I'm still awaiting official responses from Par and Khalpar, but if they'd been interested in trading, I would have heard from them by now."

Khalpar was too tightly tied to Aaltah to want to anger Delnamal by trading with Women's Well, and though Par was technically an independent principality, it was for all practical purposes a vassal state of Khalpar. If Khalpar would not deal with her, then Par would not, either.

"I have spoken with the ambassador from Grunir," Alys continued. "The sovereign prince is understandably reluctant to make any arrangement that might anger Aaltah, but he has agreed to allow our caravans to pass through and utilize his ports." For an extortionate fee, unfortunately, but Alys had few options if the land route was unavailable. "Despite the loss of the caravan, we have enough potions and spells to fulfill our agreement if we can find an alternative way to get them to you."

The reality was that with only the one trade partner, the Women's Well Academy already had a surplus of spells and potions. Alys and her council had agreed that the Academy should therefore spend the bulk of its time researching new magic.

"Send the caravan to Grunirswell," Ellinsoltah said. "I'm sure one of our merchant ships can find room in its hold for some additional cargo."

"Let's hope Aaltah does not suddenly have a plague of pirates off its coast," Alys said, for any ship traveling between Rhozinolm and Grunir would have to sail by Aaltah on the way. Piracy was a perennial problem and helped keep Aaltah's navy combat-ready at all times.

"Yes, let's," Ellinsoltah agreed with a grimace. "But as much as Delnamal might like to intercept another shipment, it would not be as easy to take a ship—especially one traveling along a well-used trade route—as to attack a handful of men traveling through the Wasteland."

Alys conceded the point with a nod, but wasn't entirely sure she'd put it past him to try.

"Take heart," Ellinsoltah said. "I believe Delnamal is already beginning to sow the seeds of his own destruction. I don't imagine that his decision to cancel our trade agreement is meeting with a great deal of support from his wealthiest and most influential citizens. And his attempt to meet with Ambassador Rhojal in secret suggests he might not be confident he has the full support of his council. I don't believe there's a single man on my own council who would not have an apoplexy at the thought of my meeting with a foreign dignitary without their foreknowledge and consent, and I hardly think Delnamal's will react much differently. A king whose royal council is not with him loses a great deal of his power."

Alys rubbed eyes that were suddenly tired, wishing with a painful tightening of her chest that she could have her old life back. Not so long ago, her only responsibilities had been to run her household and to take care of her children. She would give anything to go back to those days. She'd had no idea how carefree her life had been. This thought was predictably followed by the still-shocking realization that she would never see her daughter's face again, never hear her voice, never hold her . . .

Alys sucked in a deep breath, fighting to keep herself from falling off that emotional cliff. It was a battle she fought every day, and she wondered how many times she could face it before she went mad. She'd thought she'd known the depths of true grief when her husband, Sylnin, had died, but as agonizing as that pain had been, it was nothing compared to losing her daughter. And knowing that a staggering portion of the blame lay on her own shoulders.

"Is there anything I can do?" Ellinsoltah asked with conspicuous gentleness. One glance at her face said she understood exactly what had just happened.

Alys thought she might sink through the floor in humiliation, and she was glad she'd chosen not to invite any of her council to sit in on this conversation. She was the Sovereign Princess of Women's Well, and she could not afford to let her emotions run away with her—especially not in front of a fellow sovereign.

Alys swallowed a lump of grief that seemed lodged in her throat. "Forgive me," she croaked. "It sneaks up on me every now and again with no warning." She blinked rapidly, willing herself not to cry.

"There is nothing to forgive." Ellinsoltah's eyes had a faint sheen to them. "I am all too familiar with the ways in which grief launches its sneak attacks."

Alys let out a shuddering breath. Ellinsoltah did indeed have all too much experience with sudden, shocking loss. But even so, Alys ended the conversation as soon as she was able. Her grief was her own burden to bear, and while she could not hide it completely, the less of it she revealed to the outside world, the better.

Mairah had no inclination to offer Sister Norah a seat when she invited the older woman to enter her office. Norah's face glowed with fever, and her nose was bright red from frequent blowing, and Mairah didn't want her sneezing and coughing all over the furniture.

"Stay by the door," she ordered, leaning back in her chair as if that would prevent her from catching the ague that was plaguing the city of Khalwell this season. The Abbey's stock of cold tonics was so diminished that Mairah could not allow any but the most vulnerable of her abigails to take one. Norah was old, but hers was a healthy old age so far, and she seemed unlikely to expire from something so minor. "I do hope you have some good reason for bringing your contagion into my office."

Hatred flared in Norah's eyes, and Mairah half expected her nemesis to cross the room and spit in her face in hopes of making her ill. Then the hatred dulled to misery as a coughing spasm left her gasping for breath.

"Well, come on," Mairah said impatiently. "Say your piece and then get out." She frowned, and almost reluctantly added, "And then you should probably go lie down. I'll excuse you from work duties today."

The surprise that lit Norah's face was almost comical.

"Oh, don't worry, Sister," Mairah said with a sneer. "I still hate you. But I have enough sick abigails already without you spreading the ague throughout the Abbey." Not to mention that if Norah's condition worsened, Mairah might be forced to waste one of the Abbey's precious stock of cold tonics on her, for though she had broad rights to punish her abigails, the law required her to treat any life-threatening illnesses.

"Sister Melred has had a vision I thought you should know about," Norah rasped. With her savaged throat and her stuffy head, her voice was almost unrecognizable.

Hope flared in Mairah's heart, tempered by a huge dose of mistrust. She felt certain she had frightened Norah into compliance, but she believed the older woman was more than capable of trying to deceive her. Then again, since Mairah herself was merely looking for a way to convince Jalzarnin—and through him the king—that she was making progress, she was not overly concerned about truthfulness.

"I am intrigued," Mairah said. "Especially since Sister Melred has supposedly already tried three times to trigger visions and come up with nothing useful."

Mairah suffered a tiny twinge of conscience at Sister Melred's suffering. Having firsthand experience with the misery of taking a seer's poison—and having no particular dislike for Melred, who was quiet and unassuming—she knew what a hardship those repeated visions must have been. Then again, if she'd taken yet another poison at Norah's behest, that meant she was one of Norah's cultists. Mairah might not care that the girl worshipped the Mother of All, but she cared very much that she followed Norah.

Norah bowed her head—no doubt to hide another flash of hatred in her eyes. "She took a stronger poison this time."

"Is that so?" Mairah asked in a tone that made Norah flinch. "I was under the impression that she'd already taken the strongest she could handle. As I ordered all of my seers to do."

"She took the strongest we were *certain* she could survive," Norah responded. "She could very easily have died from the one she took this time. I presume even *you* would have found that . . . inconvenient."

Mairah studied the older woman's face, wondering just how deeply the hatred ran. Would Norah go so far as to murder one of her own followers in order to strike at Mairah? If a second seer died from drinking too strong a poison so soon after Sister Sulrai, then Mairah might be forbidden from continuing this line of inquiry.

"If another of my abigails should perish from a seer's poison," Mairah said, "rest assured that I will hold *you* personally responsible. I'm sure you can imagine what sort of unpleasantness would result."

There was no missing the flash of fear in Norah's eyes despite her bravely lifted chin. "You can't have it both ways, Mother Mairahsol. To comply with your orders, we must take certain risks. And Sister Melred *did* survive."

Mairah considered ordering Norah to fast once more for her impertinent attitude, but decided against it. "What did Melred see that you thought might be interesting?"

"She saw you and me, working together, but not here in our abbey."

Mairah felt a brief pang of longing. While she was not technically a prisoner in the Abbey and did occasionally venture outside its walls, it was far from a common occurrence. And she certainly couldn't imagine herself traveling outside the Abbey to *work*. Especially not with Norah, of all people. She tried not to let that spark of interest show, staring at Norah flatly and refusing to prompt her.

Norah sniffled loudly. "From everything Sister Melred described about her vision, it appears we were in Women's Well."

Mairah couldn't hide her surprise this time, her eyes widening as her whole body jerked. "Women's Well?" she said wonderingly, and was shocked by the strength of the sudden yearning that seized her. As a young girl, she had dreamed of seeing other lands, and her favorite fantasy had been that she'd marry a diplomat who would, over the course of her life, take her to each of the other kingdoms and principalities in turn. She'd abandoned that dream when she'd entered the marriage market and set her sights on becoming the wife of the man she'd hoped would be the next lord high priest, but it had hovered at the back of her mind nonetheless. Then, she'd been sent to the Abbey, and the dream had died entirely.

Norah nodded. "It makes sense when you think of it. That Well did not exist before the Bless—Curse was cast. Clearly it is at the heart of all the changes. What better, more likely place to find a way to reverse them? Especially considering it is also rumored to be a source of never-before-seen feminine elements!"

Even Norah, whose heart was clearly not in the effort to reverse what she'd almost called the "Blessing," sounded excited at the prospect of visiting the strange and mysterious Well that by all rights should not exist.

Mairah tamped down her enthusiasm. In a life that had for so long been so constrained, the idea of traveling to a new land and exploring its magic was undeniably tempting. However, it seemed terribly . . . convenient that Norah said *both* of them should travel there together. She narrowed her eyes and scanned the other woman's face for subterfuge.

"A suspicious mind might wonder if you are in fact trying to remove me from Khalpar so I cannot follow through on my threat to turn you in. That suspicious mind might even wonder if you intend some ill to befall me along the journey so that you can return to the Abbey and be installed as abbess in my place." It seemed unlikely Norah could hope to get away with murdering her abbess here in the Abbey, where she would be so clearly the prime suspect. But if they were traveling in foreign lands, Norah could knife Mairah in her sleep and then flee the scene of the crime with impunity. No doubt a woman like her would be welcome in the Principality of Women's Well, which seemed the sort of place where Mother of All worshippers would prosper.

"I am not a murderer," Norah retorted. "However much the idea might appeal to me in theory. Besides, I've known you for a long time. You would not go anywhere with me without ensuring you would have your revenge if I betrayed you."

Norah had certainly not intended her words to be flattering, but Mairah smiled faintly in satisfaction anyway. There was just a touch of grudging respect in her tone, and that sound was delicious to Mairah's ears. "You can't seriously believe either one of us would be allowed to leave the Abbey," she said with a shake of her head. "Not to go to *Women's Well*, of all places. I don't need to be a member of the royal council to know exactly what our dear monarch must think of the place."

Mairah had heard Jalzarnin talk about King Khalvin often enough to know that he was even more officiously pious in private than he was in public. To a man who believed women were meant to be subjugated to men in penance for the Mother's infidelity to the Creator, the thought of a principality where it was possible to have women both on the throne and on the royal council was a horror. Mairah did not follow the politics of the outside world beyond the occasional rumor that reached even into the isolation of the Abbey, but she doubted the king would deign to recognize Women's Well as an independent principality.

Norah shrugged. "I'll admit, the vision was surprising. But you know how visions work . . ."

Mairah frowned pensively. Conventional wisdom held that visions always showed a future that was possible—and that the woman who experienced the vision had the power to affect it. If Melred was telling the truth about what she saw, then some action of hers—like, for instance, telling Norah what she'd seen so that Norah would share it with Mairah—could cause it to happen.

"If the king truly wants us to do everything in our power to reverse the Curse," Norah said, "then he must send us to Women's Well. Maybe he will have no wish to do so, maybe the very idea of it will offend him. But for all that you are abbess, you and I both are nothing more than a pair of Unwanted Women in an overcrowded abbey that would barely notice we were gone. If he believes there's even the slimmest chance that a trip to Women's Well could help us find the key to reversing the Curse, why would he hesitate to do it? He has nothing to lose."

"I think perhaps that you are underestimating the toxic effects of male pride. He may not miss us if we're gone, and he may not care about our fates, but he *will* care if we convince him to send us to Women's Well and he later suspects he's been duped. And fear of that possibility may well cause him to deny us permission."

Norah held up both hands in a gesture of helplessness. "I don't know what else to tell you, then, Mother Mairahsol. I believe Melred's vision makes it clear what we have to do."

Mairah cocked her head to one side. "Don't you believe this Mother of All of yours is the power behind the Curse in the first place?"

"I do."

"Then why do you think She would show you how to reverse it? Do you truly think you and your little coconspirators are that important in Her eyes?"

Norah raised her chin. "I believe the Mother of All has a plan and that it does not involve reversing Her Blessing," she answered with unexpected frankness. "I believe the Mother of All has a different purpose in mind for sending us to Women's Well. But you don't especially care if we reverse the Curse or not, do you? You just want to be confirmed as abbess. In the mind of the king, the Mother of All doesn't even exist. He believes the visions come from a Mother who is subservient to the Creator and can do naught but His will. So when we tell him of this vision, he will believe the Creator wants us to be sent to Women's Well." A fierce smile briefly lit her face. "It will be neither your fault nor mine if it turns out he is mistaken."

Mairah tapped her fingers on the edge of her desk, thinking furiously. Jalzarnin would very likely agree that the vision had to be steering them toward a reversal of the Curse. The visions might not be sent by the Creator Himself, but the doctrine clearly considered them to be sent with His permission. But Jalzarnin would only agree if he believed Melred and Norah were describing a genuine vision, which she thought him unlikely to accept without confirmation.

"You may go now," Mairah said with a careless wave of her hand. "I will think on what you've told me."

Mairah was glad Norah's head was stuffed and the fever was perhaps taking the edge off her wits. For there seemed to be only one way to convince the king to send them to Women's Well, and it was best Norah not come to that conclusion herself until it was too late.

CHAPTER NINETEEN

When the rest of her council members and even the servants had cleared out of the room, Alys moved from her traditional seat at the head of the table so that she could sit directly across from Chanlix and Tynthanal, whom she had asked to stay behind. It could be no mystery to either of them why Alys wanted the private conversation, and she could read the tension clearly on both of their faces, although the tensions were of a different flavor.

The clench of Tynthanal's jaw and the flash of his averted eyes spoke of anger, which had continued unabated despite his reluctant agreement to try Alys's potions. Chanlix, on the other hand, chewed her lip and darted furtive, worried looks in Tynthanal's direction. That the two of them still loved each other was unquestionable, but Alys could not help noticing that they were no longer as easy together as they had once been.

"Kailee Rah-Kailindar is on her way," Alys said, and Tynthanal stiffened even more, his whole body tight and tense. Unable to bear her brother's poorly hidden emotions, Alys focused on Chanlix instead. "I presume you have seen no success with the potions as of yet?"

Without looking at him, Chanlix placed a calming hand on Tynthanal's arm. He did not pull away, but he didn't relax, either. "Not yet, I'm afraid," she responded. "But we have more yet to try. And we can quicken the pace."

"I don't want to risk making him ill," Alys said, remembering all too well what had happened to Shelvon when Delnamal had forced her to keep taking fertility potions despite their obvious failure. She had become thin and wan, her sleep shattered by the stimulant effects of the Shel in the potions.

Chanlix smiled at her ruefully. "As a former abigail, I am well aware of the effects of too much fertility potion. I promise I will take good care of him."

Tynthanal snorted. "I am perfectly capable of taking care of myself. If the girl is on her way already, then I must risk becoming ill if necessary. I'll take one every day if I have to." He met Alys's eyes for the first time. "I cannot pretend I am happy about my duty, no matter what Chanlix might prefer, but I will do it nonetheless."

"I hope you know *I'm* not happy about it, either," she retorted.

He sighed and rubbed his eyes. "I know, Alys. I know. But you've always been better at pretending than I have."

She shook her head slightly, reminding herself that he'd had a very different upbringing than she. His entry into the Citadel at fourteen meant that he had never learned the intricate steps of the court dance, which required a great deal of hiding true feelings behind a practiced smile.

"Kailee will have to take a roundabout route to get here," she said. "Aaltah, of course, has denied her passage, so she will have to travel by sea to Grunir. We have some time, but I don't know what we will do if she arrives and we have not cured your . . . condition. We have at least to some extent invited her here under false pretenses, and I don't imagine her father or Queen Ellinsoltah will be very pleased if we are forced to confess that."

"If we cannot find a cure," Chanlix said, "then our only option is to feign ignorance. If Lord Kailindar—and Kailee, of course—agree to the match, then we will test the bloodlines and profess surprise when they turn out not to be compatible."

"That might save us from the perceived offense," Alysoon countered, "but it would leave us no better off than we are now. With Ellinsoltah's hold of her throne in jeopardy and with the difficulties we've had in delivering trade goods, we become an unattractive ally, to say the least."

"So we find Kailee a different husband," Tynthanal said. "As long as she is here in Women's Well, Lord Kailindar will want to maintain the alliance, whether Ellinsoltah remains on the throne or he takes it himself."

He said it with little hope in his voice, for he had to know that if there were another suitable match for Kailee, he would not be in his current situation.

"There is no one else in all of Women's Well who would be a tempting match for a woman of Kailee's pedigree," Chanlix said. "I can count on one hand the number of unmarried gentlemen in our midst, and you are the only one of sufficient rank for a girl only two steps removed from the throne of Rhozinolm."

Chanlix was, of course, right. Women's Well had grown enormously since its foundation, but it seemed they only attracted those whose circumstances were desperate. Theirs was a land of poor and unwanted commoners, of people who could not find a comfortable place for themselves in one of the established kingdoms or principalities. Most especially, theirs was a land of women, for Women's Well offered freedom and opportunities for unmarried—or unhappily married—women that no other land could give. Alys had once bitterly referred to her mother as the "Queen of the Unwanted," but the moniker now seemed to apply to herself, as well.

"Then we must find some other means to keep her here," Tynthanal argued.

"I hope you're not suggesting reviving the reprehensible practice of keeping hostages," Alys said, glaring at her brother. The practice of keeping royal hostages had been outlawed across all kingdoms and principalities more than a century ago, though of course such arrangements still occurred in a less formalized—and unacknowledged—manner.

She was relieved at the look of horror on her brother's face. "That wasn't what I meant at all!" he exclaimed. "I merely meant we must find ways to tempt her with the freedom that could be hers here. In Rhozinolm, she will always have to fear being relegated to the Abbey, and here such is not the case. Surely that might make Women's Well attractive to her even if I can't be her husband."

Alys made a noncommittal sound that might be taken as agreement, but she very much doubted Kailee would have the freedom to choose her fate. Ellin said Kailindar doted on his daughter, and as such he likely wanted her happiness. However, as a father, he would want her safety even more. Without the legal protections and treaties that would come from an alliance by marriage between two royal houses, Alys doubted he'd trust his daughter's safety in Women's Well. By far their best hope of survival was curing Tynthanal's deficiency and arranging that marriage.

"If nothing else," Chanlix said, and Alys thought she could read the same thoughts in her grand magus's eyes, "we can at least try to find a cure for her blindness. It's probably too much to hope that Lord Kailindar would become our staunch ally out of gratitude, but it might at least win us some short-term goodwill."

"I suppose," Alys agreed doubtfully. "But we will all be better off if I can make that fertility potion work."

She hated the bleak look that colored her brother's eyes as he nodded his silent agreement.

Ellin opened the secret door in her bedroom, and Zarsha gave her his usual respectful bow—which on the surface was a little absurd for a man sneaking into a queen's bedroom at night.

"Do you not think it slightly ironic, Your Majesty," he said, "that after having thoroughly schooled me on my dreadful habit of instigating too many clandestine meetings in your room you should soon thereafter initiate one yourself?" This mouthful was said with a perfectly straight and serious expression that might almost have been convincing were it not followed by the habitual grin.

Ellin huffed and shook her head at him. "I believe it was Star who took you to task, and not I."

Zarsha cast a furtive look both left and right. "And just where might your lady's maid be at the moment?"

Ellin smiled at his familiar wit, hoping to keep her nerves firmly under control. Today's council meeting had convinced her that this conversation was of vital importance, but she was under no illusion that Zarsha would be happy with her when he found out why she'd asked him to her rooms.

"I told her I would ring for her when I was ready. I promise she will not burst through the door to swat you with a broom, though it might amuse me to watch her do so."

He laughed. "Don't think me such a gentleman that I won't use you as a shield to protect myself."

She laughed and gestured him to the pair of chairs by the fireplace. They had sat in those chairs often enough that even when she was alone in the room, Ellin hesitated to sit in the one she thought of as Zarsha's. Which might suggest she was allowing herself to become too comfortable.

There was a decanter of sweet cherry cordial on the side table, and Zarsha paused to fill a tiny glass and offer it to her before pouring another for himself. She realized belatedly that it had been some sort of a test on Zarsha's part, trying to determine the nature of her summons. Drinking cordials together suggested something of a social nature, and she was glad she had unwittingly agreed, for it should set just the kind of relaxed tone she desired. It was perhaps not especially sporting of her to try to catch him off guard, but she would need every advantage.

Ellin fidgeted with her glass, then took a small sip. Her mouth flooded with sweetness and the lovely tart tang that followed. She licked her lips, and then, still looking demurely at the liquor, asked the question she had never quite dared put into words. "I know we've danced around this a couple of times, but now that I am out of mourning and the question is no longer theoretical, I have to ask: why do you want to marry me?"

The question was something of a front, a way to step sideways into what she really wanted to talk about, but she was not disinterested in the answer. She was fairly certain Zarsha was fond of her—perhaps even more than merely fond—but she wasn't sure that fondness was enough to explain his single-minded pursuit over the course of more than a year.

Zarsha thought about the question for a surprisingly long time, turning the cordial glass around and around absently as he stared into the glowing embers of the fire, which had been banked for the night. Then he turned and looked at her, the intensity in those icy blue eyes of his nearly taking her breath away.

"I've known you long enough to realize that you won't believe me, but I'll tell you the truth anyway. I want to marry you because I'm in love with you."

There was a part of Ellin that wanted to believe that; however, she was not the starry-eyed girl she used to be, and life had already taught her that what you *wanted* to believe was rarely the truth. "You were willing to look the other way when I slept with another man. That is not something I can imagine a man in love would do."

Zarsha took another sip of his cordial. "It will come as no great surprise to you to hear that I, in my arrogance, was convinced I would win you away from him. I imagined it would be with the force of my personality and charm, not because he would act like a witless fool, but I had enough ego to consider myself capable of it." He looked up at her once more. "He was never going to be enough for you, Ellin. You need a man who can be your partner in life, who can be your equal in marriage, if not in rank. Graesan was not capable of that, could not see in you the things I did. That I *do*."

Her heart gave a gentle squeeze as she realized that, dear as Graesan had been to her, Zarsha was right. Graesan had had no grasp of—or interest in—the politics of the court, and though she was sure he had genuinely loved her as she had loved him, he had seen her as a naïve young woman in need of his protection, not as an equal. He had tried to kill Zarsha to "protect" his fragile, innocent queen from her own folly. Zarsha had many faults, but he'd never presume he had the right to make her decisions for her.

"He's doing fine, you know," Zarsha said. "I'm sure he's less than thrilled with his new position, but he is adjusting."

Ellin closed her eyes and ordered herself not to cry. That Zarsha had not only let his would-be murderer live but had even spirited him away to Nandel and provided him employment—all to spare Ellin the pain of her former lover's death—was an extraordinary act of kindness. But she wasn't certain whether sparing Graesan had been an act of love or merely another attempt to win her hand for his secret purposes.

"Love is about putting someone else's needs above your own," Zarsha added softly. "It's a concept very few truly grasp, but I believe in it with all my heart. I will be a good husband to you, Ellin. And I hope that someday you will come to love me as I love you."

He reached across the space between them and took her free hand in his, twining his fingers with hers. She felt no particular need to pull away, the touch of his hand like an anchor, holding her in the here and now.

She had allowed the conversation to drift, allowed Zarsha to steer it when she had meant to do so herself. It was necessary that she shutter her emotions and allow her intellect to direct her.

"Tell me something about yourself that I don't know," she said, aware the question was coming out of nowhere. But Zarsha would not be surprised by her attempt to change the subject at this moment. She gave him a shy glance from below her lashes. "I know so little about your life before I first met you."

Between the stilted courtship that had taken place between them when her father had contracted her to marry him over her objections and the need to fight to protect her throne, she and Zarsha had had very few truly intimate conversations despite having known each other more than a year now.

"I know your father was a diplomat," she continued, "and that you traveled with him from court to court, but I know very little else."

He gave her hand another squeeze, then let go and sat back in his chair. Ellin found herself missing the warmth of the contact. His eyes turned inward as he thought, and Ellin took another sip of her cordial to fight the urge to prod him. She did not want him to feel as if this were an interrogation.

"It is not uncommon for diplomats to travel to their assignments without their families," Zarsha said, once more staring into the embers. "In fact, I'd say that is the more usual practice, so that diplomats often see very little of their wives and children. I don't know for sure why my father chose to do it differently—I never could get him to give me a straight answer while he lived, and my mother professes ignorance. But I have my own guesses, built on snippets of information I gleaned over the years.

"I believe there was some competition between my father and my uncle for my mother's affections."

Ellin raised an eyebrow. "Surely the sovereign prince needn't fear competition from a younger brother."

"The rivalry began *after* my parents' marriage, not before."

"Oh."

"I think my father did not trust Waldmir to honor the bonds of matrimony, and that is why my mother and I and eventually my brother all traveled with him."

Which meant that the enmity between Waldmir and Zarsha had likely started when Zarsha was very young—possibly even too young to understand just why his father had such poor relations with his brother.

"That must have been . . . difficult," she ventured.

He shrugged. "I knew no different. And as I said, I had to piece together this theory from a series of hints. It was clear to me from a young age that there was tension between my father and my uncle, but my father would always deny it."

"So which courts did you grow up in?"

Zarsha smiled. "I spent at least a year or two in all of them, but I spent the majority of my youth living either in Par or Khalpar."

"As far away from Nandel as is physically possible, you mean."

His smile broadened, and there was no hint of bitterness in his eyes. "Indeed."

"Wasn't that . . . hard? To spend so much time away from home?"

He shook his head and finished his cordial, setting the glass down. "It was always returning to Nandel that was hard. I was brought up with the bright colors and gaiety of foreign courts, living always in homes that were opulent in comparison even to the royal palace in Nandel. I was used to temperate winters and easy travel. Every return to Nandel was a slap in the face. My parents both missed it when we were away, but I certainly never did."

That explained why he was perfectly at ease committing himself to a life in Rhozinolm when it was usually expected that a woman move to her husband's homeland rather than vice versa. And now it was time to try to nudge the conversation closer to its purpose.

"So how did you go from being a diplomat's son who was not especially fond of his homeland to serving as your uncle's spy in Rhozinolm?"

His eyes narrowed, his shoulders tensing, but she had the instant impression he was not surprised by the question, that he had perhaps seen through her from the beginning and known where she was leading.

"Are you under the impression that I don't know Lord Kailindar has been in contact with my uncle or that I don't have a good idea how initial inquiries were received?" he asked. He might have anticipated her line of inquiry, but his sharp undertone said he did not much appreciate her attempt at subterfuge. She might even have felt chastened, were it not of great importance that she learn whatever he was hiding.

"You would be a very poor spy indeed if you did not. And I don't think you're a poor spy."

"I never said I was a spy."

"You never said you *weren't*, either."

"All right, I'll say it now: I'm not a spy."

Ellin put down the glass of cordial, still more than half full. Zarsha had always made a point of not lying to her, of simply refusing to answer questions he could not answer truthfully. But this, she was sure, was an outright lie, and it was like a slap to her face.

Zarsha huffed and rose to his feet, turning his back to her slightly as he faced what was left of the fire. The fingers of one hand drummed restlessly against his leg, and he spoke to the embers rather than to her.

"I wanted to win you, and I knew I could not do it if I returned home to Nandel. My uncle is painfully aware of my propensity for learning secrets, and so I offered my talents in his service if he would appoint me as special envoy. He preferred placing his nosy nephew in a foreign court than in his own."

Ellin shook her head. "How does that make you *not* a spy?"

He turned back to her. "A spy works on his master's behalf to further his master's cause. *I* work to further *your* cause. I have sent sensitive information to my uncle—but it was all regarding Tamzin and Kailindar. I told him I was certain one or both would make a try for the throne, and I sent everything I could find about them. Tamzin, especially, had a lot of dirty little secrets. But I sent nothing about *you*, and I stopped sending any information at all after Tamzin died. Which is why my uncle is now especially unhappy with me. I have blatantly shifted my loyalties to you, and that is a bitter pill for a man of Nandel to swallow."

"Especially when you know sensitive information that he fears you will share," she said, nodding her understanding—although she still had the sense that there was more to the story.

"He is testing the waters. Seeing if he can remove me from the equation and sever the bond he has belatedly realized I have formed with you."

"But why do that when you have sensitive information about him?" she pressed. "Surely he fears that you might retaliate by telling his secrets."

Zarsha shook his head. "He knows I cannot, *will* not take the risk unless under the most dire of circumstances."

Ellin rose from her chair and came to stand beside him, both of them staring into the fireplace instead of at each other. She could no longer avoid the issue. "If we are to marry," she said quietly, "you will have to tell me what it is you know."

He shook his head again.

"You say your first loyalty is now to me," she insisted. "Prove it."

Rarely had she seen true anger on Zarsha's face, but there was no missing it now as he turned to her, the muscles in his jaw working, his brows lowered. "There is a limit to how many loyalty tests I am willing to take. If you don't believe in my loyalty now, after all the ways I've proven myself to you, then it is clearly an impossible task."

Ellin had to fight off the urge to cross her arms defensively, for though it was true he had demonstrated more loyalty than she could reasonably have expected of any man, she could think of no reason why he might insist so vehemently on keeping this one secret—except that it was something he didn't want her to know.

"How can it possibly hurt to tell me your uncle's secret? Unless *you* don't trust *me* to keep the knowledge to myself. If it is a secret of such significance that it will guide the course of nations—which it clearly is—then it is necessary that I know what it is. I am not asking out of idle curiosity or prurient interest. I am doing what I must and looking after the best interests of my kingdom."

Zarsha's hands were clenched into fists beside him, his whole body taut with conflict. His usually lively face was dark and shuttered, and she couldn't read all the emotions in his eyes.

Her heart pounded at her breastbone, and there was a substantial part of her that wished she could just drop the subject and let the secret—whatever it was—lie. If the thought of telling her bothered Zarsha this much, she did not want to put herself through the pain of hearing it. And yet she couldn't imagine marrying him with this hanging over them—assuming it was even possible for the marriage arrangement to happen, considering Waldmir's first reaction to the proposal.

"I'm sorry, Zarsha," she said. "I owe you more than I can ever repay. I might not even be alive right now, much less sitting on the throne, if it weren't for you. I will not say there can be *no* secrets between us if we are to marry. But this cannot be one of them.

"The council is beginning to lose patience with me." Which was perhaps something of an understatement. If it weren't for Semsulin—and to a lesser extent, Kailindar, whose support would almost certainly vanish if Alysoon's brother failed to marry his daughter—she suspected they would be only a step or two away from open revolt.

"The only reason they accepted me as queen was because they saw me as the only way to restore our relationship with Nandel, and if I cannot produce . . ."

He shook his head. "That doesn't explain why you are suddenly pressing this issue."

"I need to understand what Waldmir wants and why he's playing hard to get. My lord high treasurer today suggested that perhaps it was time to reconsider our decision to trade with Women's Well in case that might be Waldmir's primary objection to the match."

Several council members had given Kailindar odd looks when he'd surprised them by opposing the idea, for they did not yet know that Kailee was on her way to Women's Well for a potential marriage. But thanks to King Delnamal's erratic and hostile behavior, it hadn't been too hard to convince everyone that letting him seize control of Women's Well would be a bad idea. But if negotiations with Waldmir continued to drag on—or if it should seem Waldmir and Delnamal were inclined to form an alliance—the suggestion might gain traction, and even Kailindar's support might not be enough to defeat it.

"Don't cancel those agreements," Zarsha said. "I'm sure my uncle would be overjoyed if you did so—and that he has hopes his hedging might make it happen—but I promise you it is not necessary. All you have to do is stand firm, and he will eventually agree."

"That isn't good enough. Tell me what you know about him."

But once again he shook his head. "You cannot use the information to force his hand. My own life and the lives of people I care about will be forfeit if you do."

"Then I won't," she said softly. "But I have to know. You've made it too obvious that there's more involved than just protecting yourself and your loved ones. There's something you don't want to tell me, and though I'd like to trust you wholeheartedly, I'm afraid I just can't do that."

He groaned, reaching up to rub his eyes as if suddenly exhausted. "You're not going to let this go, are you?"

"I'm afraid not."

For a long time, he just stood there, his whole body clenched and tight as he struggled to find a way out. Then he huffed out a loud, heavy sigh.

Still looking at the fireplace, his voice coming out uncharacteristically flat, he said, "Waldmir's youngest daughter"—he cleared his throat—"may, uh, actually be mine."

CHAPTER TWENTY

Mairah was not entirely surprised when Jalzarnin received the news of Melred's vision with something less than unbridled enthusiasm, though she tried to present it as if she had full confidence in its authenticity. It did not take a seer's talent to predict the outcome of the conversation—even if Norah had been too dense to see it—but Mairah would make at least a token effort to avoid the inevitable conclusion.

"Since when has Sister Norah been so . . . accommodating?" the lord high priest inquired.

Mairah did not like the hint of suspicion she saw in his eyes, for she had the uncomfortable feeling it was aimed more at her than at Norah. Even more disturbing was the fact that when he'd entered her office, instead of giving her his usual warm greeting, he'd said immediately that he did not have time for anything more intimate than a simple business meeting. She couldn't help worrying that even as Norah was ostensibly making a genuine effort to aid Mairah's cause, she was undermining her with more secret letters behind her back.

"Let's just say I've given her a good reason to want to cooperate," she said with a conspiratorial smile.

But Jalzarnin was not in the mood to simply take her at her word. Instead of returning her smile, he frowned sternly. "I have neither the time nor the patience for word games today. Tell me why I should believe this a genuine vision. It sounds to me more like a desire to satisfy idle women's curiosity."

Mairah stiffened in affront. Just as well he wasn't staying for bed sport; she didn't imagine she'd be terrifically eager to indulge him in his present humor. And, though she didn't wish to admit it to herself, there was no small dose of hurt behind the affront. Jalzarnin had never spoken to her in that tone of voice before, and she feared she was losing his affection. How could she possibly remain abbess if she lost his support?

Jalzarnin sighed heavily and rubbed his eyes. "My apologies, dearest," he said. "The king is being especially peevish today, and it is unfair of me to take it out on you. It's just when I received your message, I'd rather hoped you'd have something that sounded more promising."

It was no secret that King Khalvin was on the moody side, but then that had been the case for as long as she could remember. Surely the lord high priest ought to be used to it by now. "The most powerful seer in our Abbey has put herself through considerable misery to find a solution to the unutterable horror of men not being able to force women to bear their children. What better sign of progress could you have hoped for?"

Mairah instantly regretted her words, but there was no way to take them back. It seemed Norah's impassioned argument for why the Curse was really the Blessing had affected her more than she'd realized. Jalzarnin's gaze sharpened, and she raised her chin.

"Be careful what you say, Mother Mairahsol," he warned. "It would be unwise to give anyone the impression that you see the Curse as anything but an abomination that must be reversed as swiftly and decisively as possible. The king overheard a group of serving women referring to it as the Blessing, and he has declared any such appellation heresy. He is eager to make an example of someone."

Mairah couldn't suppress a shiver of apprehension. If the king wanted heretics to burn as an example, he could hardly find more suitable victims than inmates of the Abbey, who had already long ago been disowned by their families. Mairah wondered briefly if her own family would object if the king ordered her to burn. Her mother and her older sister would grieve, she was sure—though of course she had set eyes on neither of them since she'd been shut up behind the Abbey walls. Her father and her younger sister, however, would likely be happy to join the throng to witness the public spectacle, for they had made no secret of how they despised her for ruining the family's reputation with her wickedness.

"That was not a threat, Mairah," Jalzarnin said, though it obviously had been. "I would never share anything you revealed to me in confidence." He grimaced. "Actually, I doubt I could ever find it in my heart to denounce *anyone* as a heretic. I became a priest out of a desire to help people, not condemn them to die in agony."

Mairah suspected his decision to join the priesthood had more to do with ambition than altruism, but she was hardly about to say so. "Then if I reveal a secret to you, will you promise not to speak a word of it to anyone?"

The only leverage Mairah held over Norah and her cohorts was her ability to reveal them as heretics, and she'd have preferred to keep that knowledge all to herself. However, having spoken too freely to Jalzarnin about her troubles with Norah, she could see why he would be skeptical—as she herself was—about Norah's attempts to help, and it seemed she would have to explain.

"I believe I just gave you my word."

Mairah bit her lip, surprised at how reluctant she was to say her piece. She *hated* Norah, and it should give her nothing but pleasure to reveal the woman's sins to the lord high priest—even if she couldn't entirely trust him to keep the knowledge to himself. What did it matter to her if Norah and all her friends died? They knew what they risked when they chose to break the law and worship their false goddess.

Annoyed with herself, she shoved her reluctance into a back corner of her mind. "I discovered that Norah is a Mother of All worshipper," she said. She regarded Jalzarnin's face closely, hoping to glean his reaction, but his expression remained determinedly unreadable. "She and a couple of the other abigails had not been putting their full efforts into helping me figure out how to reverse the Curse. I told Norah that if she and her followers didn't help me find a way, I would reveal their heresy. So you see, they have ample motivation now, which they did not have before. Which is why I believe the vision is genuine."

Jalzarnin shook his head, unconvinced. "It's not like a trip to Women's Well is some quick, overnight jaunt. There would be considerable expense involved in getting you there. The king certainly wouldn't allow the two of you to travel so far without an armed escort. Both to guard you and to ensure that you carry out your mission. And once you are there, you'll all need food and lodging for however long your work takes."

He shook his head again and leaned back in his chair, frowning fiercely. "I'm sorry, but it's just not possible. Even if we believe the seer's report is entirely accurate, the king would never agree to such an extravagant expenditure." His frown deepened further. "And why would Women's Well even allow you to come? Surely the last thing *they* want is for the Curse to be reversed!"

"They obviously could not be told our true purpose," Mairah agreed. "But I hardly think they would be surprised that women of other abbeys would be interested in learning more about their magic. I see no reason why they wouldn't—"

"The king's piousness is well known throughout Seven Wells," Jalzarnin interrupted. "I very much doubt anyone expects warm relations between our two lands. In fact, the king ordered a very . . . forceful refusal when the so-called sovereign princess attempted to establish a diplomatic channel. A sudden reversal would be suspicious."

"Women's Well is small and newly built," she argued. "Surely we could arrive bearing a gift of some sort that would tempt them to overlook any questions they might have about our intentions. They must be desperate for trade goods."

He waved that off. "Even if we could tempt them, we still have the insurmountable problem of persuading the king to send you."

"Well, find a way to surmount it!" Mairah snapped. "If he wants the Curse reversed badly enough, he'll send us. The Mother did not send Sister Melred that vision for no reason, and if it is the Creator's will that we reverse the Curse, then we must heed His messenger." She had little patience with all this talk of the Creator and the Mother, but she knew how to speak the language of the pious—especially once Norah had already shown her the way. "The Mother obeys the Creator, and we must obey the Mother. Isn't that what you preach and what the king forcefully encourages all his subjects to believe?"

Jalzarnin's gaze sharpened, and Mairah tensed. She had always taken pains to conceal her lack of faith from him. He might not make the grand spectacle of his piety that the king did, and he was far from perfect in his obedience to the Devotional, but she sensed that his quiet faith was more genuine than that of most sermonizing priests she had met. His gaze said he was weighing her and judging her for her too-obvious skepticism. But though her tone had been less than respectful, it was only the words themselves he addressed out loud.

"From the standpoint of doctrine," he finally said, "your argument makes perfect sense. *If* your seer is telling the truth about her vision. It seems you have reason to believe her, but your reason is one we cannot share with the king. He would never give credence to the visions of a confessed heretic."

"Then we must find some other way to convince him she's telling the truth," Mairah said, and something inside her shriveled. Even knowing where this conversation would inevitably lead, some part of Mairah had hoped it wouldn't be necessary. It was one thing to order Sister Norah to fast until she nearly fainted with hunger, and quite another to turn Sister Melred over to the royal inquisitor for questioning. Norah had earned her punishment through years of unkindness and petty torments, but Melred had never said or done anything to deserve what the inquisitor would do to her.

Mairah shoved away the memory of fleeing the room while her seers suffered under the effects of the poisons they'd drunk. At least, she reassured herself, she would not be forced to *watch* whatever the inquisitor did to Sister Melred.

Jalzarnin smiled, showing no sign that he noticed Mairah's discomfort. Or that he felt any similar discomfort himself at the thought of ordering the torture of an innocent. "I suppose that could be arranged," he said with a pensive nod. "We would not have any legal grounds to subject her to questioning, but I suspect if I explain the situation to the king, he will see the necessity of it and grant us a dispensation."

Mairah squirmed as she tried not to think about what Melred would suffer. But if it was a choice between allowing an innocent to suffer and suffering herself . . . Well, then that was no true choice. Besides, Melred was a heretic loyal to Sister Norah. She wasn't *really* an innocent, no matter how sweet-natured she might seem. "I'm not very well acquainted with Sister Melred," she said in a voice that held the faintest of quavers. "It's possible she would recant immediately under threat of torture."

"I wouldn't worry about that," Jalzarnin replied. Often in the past, she'd been warmed by how clearly he seemed to *see* her, to care about her thoughts and feelings, but if he noticed her disquiet, he showed no sign of it. "The inquisitor is very skilled at prying the truth out of people who would say anything to stop the pain. He is a true master at sorting truth from lies."

Mairah clasped her hands together tightly under her desk. She was under no illusion that Jalzarnin was an especially nice or kind man. He'd more than once demonstrated a ruthlessness Mairah had so far been unable to match. She would happily hurt those who had wronged her without feeling a hint of remorse, but Jalzarnin would just as remorselessly strike at those whose only crime was standing in his way. And yet he was still somehow generally well-liked and well-regarded, while Mairah was reviled and feared. The injustice of it burned.

Mairah fully intended to keep her thoughts to herself, but somehow she found herself speaking. "It doesn't trouble you at all? To order an innocent woman tortured?"

Jalzarnin raised his eyebrows at her, and the look on his face was one of genuine surprise. "Is that not what you had in mind all along when you brought this situation to my attention?"

"Yes, but . . ." Her voice trailed off helplessly.

He nodded and leaned forward in his chair, reaching one of his hands over the length of the desk. Reluctantly, she wiped a sweaty palm over the skirt of her robes, then laid her hand in his. His touch was not as comforting as it had once been.

"I take no pleasure in it," he assured her, squeezing her hand. "But it is the king's demand that the Curse be reversed, and I am the king's loyal subject."

She frowned at him. "I was under the impression you didn't agree the reversal of the Curse was such a pressing necessity." He had all but said that all she needed to do was give the *illusion* she might be able to reverse it.

He patted her hand. "It isn't my place to disagree. But truly it is for *your* sake that I would subject your abigail to the inquisitor. We both know that things will not go well for you if the king chooses not to confirm you as abbess." He squeezed her hand in both of his, the grip almost tight enough to hurt.

"But it is up to you, dearest," he said, releasing her hand and sitting back. "If you'd rather save Sister Melred the torment, then I will say nothing to the king about her vision."

Mairah swallowed hard. She was fairly sure Jalzarnin had just neatly sidestepped her question, for she still saw no sign that he felt any remorse or reluctance to order the torture of a young woman who had done nothing to deserve it. And he was also neatly shoving all the burden of responsibility onto *her* shoulders rather than his own.

If Sister Melred was to be tortured, it would be because of Mairah's decision, and for all Jalzarnin's seeming compassion toward her, he did not make any attempt to ease her conscience.

"With the king's temper as it is," Jalzarnin said, "I'm not sure your tenure as abbess will last the full six months if you do not show progress. You are too famous, my dear, and there are those in the city who find your elevation . . . unseemly. The king's ability to ignore their grumbling lessens the longer you fail to show progress."

"All right, already!" she snapped, folding her arms in a defensive gesture. "I understand what's at stake."

"So you would like me to bring this vision to the king's attention?"

Hating the feeling that she was being manipulated, Mairah grunted something vaguely like agreement. Her conscience would trouble her for a time, but she was certain she would get over it. And when she was abbess for good, she would find a way to make it up to poor Sister Melred.

Alys looked around in awe as Gracelin led her through the small grove of saplings that had sprung up in little more than two months' time. The sturdy, healthy-looking little trees were already waist-high, their dark green leaves plump with moisture. Beside her, Gracelin beamed like a proud mama.

"They're already larger than the seedlings that were confiscated at the border," she said. "I would have thought these yearlings if I hadn't planted the seeds with my own two hands."

Alys reached out and stroked one of the plants. There were only twenty of them—but that was twenty more Aalwood trees than could be found anywhere outside of Aaltah. This once-dead land had proven to be extraordinarily fertile since the Well appeared out of nowhere, and even without the help of growth potions, trees and plants seemed to grow faster than they did elsewhere.

"How long before these trees are old enough to produce seeds and be harvested?" she asked, trying to contain her excitement. If Women's Well could supply its own Aalwood—and thereby have access to Aal—they could become much more self-sufficient. She smiled to think how Delnamal would react when he discovered that Aaltah was no longer the only place where those precious trees could grow.

Gracelin shrugged, then put her hands on her hips and looked around. "If we were in Aaltah and had none of the special growth potions, it'd be about fifteen to twenty years before they'd be mature enough to start seeding."

That dampened Alys's happy glow. "So long?"

Gracelin grinned. Her face glowed with health and happiness, a far cry from the gaunt and worried visage she'd worn when Alys had first met her. "Aalwood trees are pretty fast-growing, actually. An oak tree doesn't start producing acorns until it's around forty. But I've seen some young oaks near the Well, and I can guarantee you that if they keep growing at the rate they have been, they'll be mature in far less than forty years. Add growth potions to the magic of the Well, and . . ." She made a sweeping gesture with her arm. "I wouldn't be entirely shocked if they started seeding by next fall. I think the Mother is trying to make up for lost time and bring this land fully to life as quickly as possible."

If Gracelin was right, Women's Well might be producing fliers to trade within a year, considering how little Aalwood was needed to make one. They could never compete with Aaltah in volume, but they could conceivably drive down the price of Aaltah's most vital trade goods. She might not be able to strike at Delnamal directly— yet—but small victories like this one could be the key to ultimately dethroning him.

Alys considered the woman who only a month prior had been a helpless widowed commoner with only the most dire prospects for herself and her son, and she knew the shocking decision she had made—the decision even her open-minded council had initially balked at—was the right one.

"Your service to the Principality of Women's Well has been of incalculable value already," Alys said.

Gracelin curtsied deeply. "Thank you, Your Royal Highness."

"I had promised you a land grant if your seeds took root, but I now find a land grant is insufficient thanks."

Gracelin's eyes widened, and there was no missing the sudden trepidation that shot through her. The poor woman was used to being mistreated by those whom she served, and she clearly worried that the land grant would be denied and replaced by something that was of no practical use to her—as had happened when she'd received her husband's final wages in the form of seeds and seedlings.

"I will arrange a formal investiture ceremony, but I have already written up the papers to name you Baroness Gracelin in your own right, with a commensurate land grant."

Gracelin gaped at her in much the same way her council had gaped at her when she'd first stated her intention. It was certainly not unheard of for a commoner who had rendered extraordinary service to the Crown to be granted a title and thereby enter into the ranks of the minor gentry, but as far as Alys and the rest of her council knew, this was the first such honor to be bestowed upon a woman.

"You shall be Lady Gracelin henceforth, and your son will be baron after you. Or if you so wish, you may change your name and your son's to the noble style."

"Change my name?" Gracelin whispered breathlessly.

"It is customary for a commoner to change his name—and the names of his wife and children—when invested with a title. Though I must admit, I rather like your current name," Alys added with a smile. "It seems to embody both your old life and your new one. Perhaps you can choose a similar styling for your son. Add an elemental suffix so that you may keep calling him Forest and yet signify his new status with his formal name."

The look on Gracelin's face said she was not fully comprehending Alys's words, that she was still too shocked by the unexpected pronouncement to think clearly.

"You needn't make any decisions now," Alys said gently. "The investiture ceremony will not take place for at least a month, and that will be the time to declare your new names if you choose."

Gracelin shook her head. "I . . . I don't know what to say."

"You needn't say anything, Lady Gracelin. I mean for Women's Well to be a land of opportunity, especially for women. I see no reason to treat a woman's service to the Crown as something less significant than a man's. And as I mean to pass the throne of Women's Well to my son, I see no reason why other women should not be allowed to pass their own lands and titles to their children just as men would."

Her royal council had all agreed that her reasoning was sound, but the decision made many of them uncomfortable even so. "I've heard some grumbling on the streets," Jailom had warned her. "Men saying that they are being supplanted by women here. They worry that there is no place for them in Women's Well, that they are an afterthought. Granting a woman a title in her own right will only play into that fear. I believe it's the right thing to do, but you must do it with your eyes open."

Alys was well aware there was some risk involved with this precedent. But she was also aware that people came to Women's Well *because* it was different, and that the men who most hated and feared women would have no interest in settling here in the first place.

Gracelin swallowed hard. "I imagine there are those who will be . . . unhappy with the situation. Who will think I am getting above myself if I claim to be a baroness."

"I'm sure there will be," Alys agreed. "Jealousy and resentment and resistance to change are all part of human nature, I'm afraid. But whatever resistance there may be, people come to Women's Well because they want their lives to change. With you, I will demonstrate to all that ours is a new land with new rules."

And, she hoped, those who were currently too frightened to pass through Delnamal's roadblocks would find the incentive they needed to make the leap of faith. Her motives for bestowing this title on Gracelin went beyond simply rewarding a new and useful citizen for her service.

The roadblocks showed that Delnamal was unhappy with the defection of even his poorest and most downtrodden people, and anything that made Delnamal unhappy brightened Alys's day. So she would do everything in her power to lure more of them away. Every little nibble would weaken Delnamal's position, deplete his labor force and the pool of able-bodied men and boys who could be conscripted into his army should his plans for war come to fruition. From what she could tell—which was unfortunately little, for Women's Well had no spy network to speak of—Delnamal was already a less-than-popular king, and she imagined his landowners would begin to grumble if their laborers suddenly had more appealing options than accepting whatever pittance they were offered.

Dethroning Delnamal with dozens of small diplomatic and economic cuts was perhaps not the most exciting and stirring of fantasies. Alys still dreamed of a more spectacular triumph, one that led to his death at her hands or by her order. But until such a time as she could make her fantasies come true, she would settle for the petty torments that might someday chisel his throne out from under him.

CHAPTER TWENTY-ONE

Jalzarnin was not in the least surprised by the king's fierce scowl, and he wondered once again if he was being a fool for allowing Mairah to persuade him to make this ridiculous proposal. Oh, there were sound doctrinal reasons why it made sense to heed the unfortunate seer's vision. Jalzarnin was under no illusion that Mairah had made her arguments from a position of faith, but once the royal inquisitor had thoroughly examined Sister Melred and declared that the vision was genuine, Jalzarnin had been convinced that sending Mairah and Sister Norah to Women's Well was the right thing to do. Just as he'd known that the king would not like the suggestion, no matter how much sense it might make.

"You realize you are asking me to treat with that daughter of a whore who has the audacity to declare herself a sovereign princess, do you not?" the king growled, sitting back in his chair and crossing his arms over his chest as if to ward off the very thought.

Jalzarnin bowed his head respectfully. "I do, Your Majesty. And I assure you I am just as appalled as you are by the very idea of it."

Although he was truthfully more appalled at how much risk he put himself in by bringing the king a proposal that was not to his liking.

In the beginning, his attempt to install Mairahsol as abbess and establish his own personal spy network had seemed worth the risk. And when he had succeeded in convincing the king to appoint her—even temporarily—he'd believed the danger had passed. He might suffer some stain on his reputation—and a reduction in the king's trust—if Mairah failed to justify her right to the office, but he could use any information she'd gathered for him to make sure any would-be rivals were thoroughly discredited before they could so much as make eyes at his seat on the royal council.

Everything had changed when Mairahsol had revealed that some of the abigails under her command were Mother of All worshippers. By associating himself so strongly with the Abbey, Jalzarnin inadvertently put himself in a terrible position. If the king were ever to discover that a group of heretics had been worshipping their false goddess right under his nose . . . Well, the consequences were unthinkable. He and Mairah both might even be questioned by the royal inquisitor, so tainted would they be by the association.

But if there was one thing Jalzarnin knew about Mairahsol Rah-Creesha, it was that she would do *anything* to avenge any perceived wrongs. If the king stripped her of the office of abbess, if he made her feel as if she had no hope of being confirmed, there was no telling what she might do. At this moment, when she saw in Jalzarnin a wholehearted ally and coconspirator, she had clearly not put any thought into what might happen if the news of Norah's little following came out, but if she found herself cornered, it would occur to her how damaging that information could be to Jalzarnin himself.

"Common sense tells us these women have made up this ridiculous story because they have been seduced by the idea of a principality where they would not be secluded in an abbey," the king opined. "They want the Crown to finance their escape, and they will disappear the moment they set foot outside of Khalpar."

Jalzarnin refrained from pointing out that the seer had not claimed to see *herself* in Women's Well. Even if she had falsified the vision, it would not have been for the sake of engineering an escape. He met the king's eyes with an expression he hoped was both earnest and entirely innocent. "That is why I suggested the abigail be so thoroughly questioned before giving her vision any credence. Please believe that I would never advocate sending these abigails to Women's Well if I did not believe it would serve the will of the Creator."

The king's scowl only deepened. "I cannot comprehend how the Creator would want this! That woman who calls herself sovereign princess will not simply allow two of our Unwanted Women into her territory without demanding significant inducement. Not after we so forcefully rejected her overtures. Do you seriously mean to tell me the Creator wishes us not only to negotiate with her but to *bribe* her into allowing our abbess access to that abomination of a Well?"

Jalzarnin lifted his hands in a helpless gesture. "It is not for we mortals to comprehend the will of the gods. Ours is merely to obey. And surely if granting our abbess access to the Well will allow her to reverse the Curse, it is worth the temporary discomfort we might feel at pretending acceptance of a principality that will soon be destroyed in the aftermath."

The king thought for a long time, every nuance of his facial expression and body language showing how much he wanted to reject Jalzarnin's proposal out of hand. Jalzarnin realized he was holding his breath and forced himself to relax.

The king was too devout to disobey the Creator's wishes, even when obedience involved a certain amount of personal discomfort.

"How sure are you that the visions these seers claim to have are truly granted by the Mother?" the king asked, fixing Jalzarnin with one of his sharpest, most appraising looks. "The Devotional never actually *says* that's the case."

Jalzarnin almost answered with a careless affirmative, but he paused before the words left his mouth. The Devotional made scant reference to the visions of seers, and it was only through inference and interpretation that the visions were believed to be sent by the Mother. The king could likely recite the entire tome by heart, having read the thing more times than any priest Jalzarnin had ever known.

"The priesthood concerns itself little with women's magic," he answered carefully, "of which these visions are but one example. I can cite several scholarly works that address the question, and the consensus has always been that the visions are the Mother's doing."

The king nodded. Knowing him, he'd likely read all the scholarly works ever written about the Devotional—at least all the ones that did not contain any heretical theories. "So you are willing to stake your reputation on that being the case? Because if I send the abbess to Women's Well, and she does not reverse the Curse, you can rest assured that you will no longer hold the office of lord high priest."

Jalzarnin swallowed hard. How had he allowed himself to get in this deep? He *did* believe that the scholars were correct in their interpretation of the Devotional, and therefore he had to believe that sending Mairah and Norah to Women's Well was the Creator's will. It was his duty not only as the lord high priest but as a man of faith to do the Creator's will at all times. But to risk the ignominy of being dismissed from the royal council, of being demoted back to just an ordinary priest? Did he have the faith to do that?

The king watched him closely as he wrestled with the warring dictates of his ambition and his faith. Finally, he sighed.

"I will stake my reputation on it," he said, trying to ignore the trepidation the words spawned.

In the end, it was not his faith that led him to make this declaration. It was the sure and certain knowledge that if he refused, he would eventually have to either suffer Mairah's revenge or kill her to protect himself. Neither possibility was tolerable.

"Very well, then," the king said, still looking decidedly unconvinced. "Be sure to inform our abbess that she will not be sent unchaperoned, and that she will not be given any opportunity to slip away. If she fails to reverse the Curse, she will return to Khalpar to face a treason charge. If knowing that, she still wants to go to Women's Well, then we will find some way to get her there."

"Why are you not dead?" Ellin asked Zarsha in a flat, dead voice. Of all the things she'd imagined Zarsha might be hiding, having fathered a child on his uncle's wife was not one of them. "Prince Waldmir obviously knows the child is not his, and he doesn't seem like the sentimental sort who would spare you from a treason charge." Or his wife, for that matter. Waldmir had already executed one of his wives, so he obviously did not scruple to do so.

"To be cuckolded in Nandel is a shame greater than you can imagine," Zarsha answered, his tone nearly as flat as Ellin's. "Waldmir had no desire to publicly declare his humiliation." Zarsha cleared his throat. "Also, Brontyn herself had a certain flare for learning secrets, and we laid the foundation of our own protection before we laid each other. For all my uncle's pride in his manly prowess, he is unable to perform his conjugal duties without the aid of a potency potion. It is entirely possible he would be unable to hold the throne were that fact to come out in public. Brontyn and I made certain that if we were to die—either by execution or by 'tragic accident'—that information would be made public."

"Unable to hold the throne?" she asked in incredulity. "I understand that in Nandel there is a great resistance to the use of women's magic, but surely that is an exaggeration."

"It's ridiculous, but no, it's not an exaggeration. If he cannot perform in the marital bed without the help of women's magic, then there are those who would argue he is functionally a woman. And you know a woman's place in Nandel society."

Ellin had always been well aware that Nandel was a forbidding and repressive place for women, and she had dreaded having to adjust to their expectations of womanly behavior when she'd thought she'd be living there as Zarsha's wife—his literal property. She had not, obviously, appreciated the true depths of Nandel's hatred of women.

"His enemies—of which there are quite a few," Zarsha continued, "would also argue his use of women's magic is the reason he has had only daughters, although I'm certain he did not always need the potions."

"So you and his wife willfully took advantage of this knowledge to embark upon an affair." The huskiness of her voice revealed some of her feelings, no matter how hard she tried to rein them in, but Zarsha either didn't notice or didn't care.

"It wasn't so cold-blooded as you make it sound. I had met Brontyn during my stay at court in Grunir. We became quite fond of each other during my months there, and I petitioned Waldmir for permission to offer for her."

Ellin knew the spike of jealousy in her heart was entirely hypocritical when Zarsha had so gracefully tolerated her love affair with Graesan, but such knowledge did not cause the jealousy to recede. Logic told her that Zarsha had to have had multiple lovers before he had offered for her hand, but she had not allowed herself to think that he might have previously *loved* another.

"Waldmir was unable to steal my mother from my father, but there was nothing I could do to prevent him from stealing Brontyn from me. She begged Waldmir to release her and openly wept at the altar. But he wanted her, so he took her."

"And you both conspired to punish him for it."

Zarsha shuffled his feet awkwardly. "We didn't think of it that way. We thought only of how we could have each other with as little risk as possible. But whether we allowed ourselves to acknowledge it or not, I think you are right. I think our affair had as much to do with spite as with love."

"So you loved her, then." The jealousy spiked again.

He rubbed his face with both hands, then ran one of those hands through his hair. "If I had loved her as I ought, I would have stayed far, far away. But I was too selfish to see that."

"And because of that, she is now a whore in the Abbey of Nandel." It was the fate of all divorced women throughout Seven Wells to be banished to abbeys, but the Abbey of Nandel had a uniquely unpleasant reputation. Better than a traitor's death, perhaps, but not by much.

Zarsha's whole body jerked. "I may have acted selfishly, but not *that* selfishly. When Waldmir discovered our affair, I threatened to tell all if he forced Brontyn into the Abbey. We reached a compromise wherein she was *sent* to the Abbey, but somehow never did arrive. She lives in Grunir under an assumed name now. I haven't seen her in years.

"Because of all I know about him, Waldmir doesn't dare strike out at me. The problem is that he hates me for it—and that he also has a hostage for my good behavior."

"Your daughter," Ellin whispered.

"Maybe," Zarsha said. "Only women's magic can answer the question of which of us fathered her, and though my uncle could get hold of such a spell, he has chosen not to. He doesn't really care, you see. He considers her tainted whether she's my child or not. And anyway, she's nothing but one more useless girl to him. So we each have a weapon against the other, and that makes for a never-ending game of cat and mouse.

"I should have told you the truth long ago, but the story does not reflect especially well on me."

"And you were not certain I would be as protective of the child as you are." She reminded herself that Zarsha had seen her commit cold-blooded murder—and an especially gruesome one at that—and therefore was very much aware of her capacity for ruthlessness.

"I know you would not recklessly endanger an innocent," he said. "But I also know you are a good queen, and that if Waldmir were to back you into a corner and you felt it necessary for the good of the kingdom, you would use every weapon available to counter him. I am putting my own life and the life of a helpless child in your hands by telling you any of this."

And truly knowledge was the most dangerous weapon of all.

"So it wasn't merely out of fear that I would not want to marry you if I learned you were an adulterer," she said acidly and had the satisfaction of seeing him wince.

He was silent for a long moment. "I won't pretend the thought never crossed my mind," he said, appearing to address the toes of his shoes. "I did not want you to think ill of me. I hope you'll find it in your heart to forgive my vanity."

"You should leave now," she said coldly by way of answer. "I suppose I'll come to thank you someday for reminding me not to believe someone is worthy of my trust just because he claims to love me." She should have learned that lesson by now, after betrayals by her father, her grandfather, and Graesan, all of whom had claimed to love her. And yet once again, she'd given her trust to a man who did not deserve it.

"I'm sorry," Zarsha said, his misery plain to see. But when she didn't answer, he obeyed her command and left her alone.

Jalzarnin stood on the dock and watched as Mairah's ship cast off. He kept his hands clasped casually behind his back, and tried not to look longingly at the railing by which she stood. He doubted anyone had believed his claim that he'd come to the coastal city of Tidewater to visit his ailing aunt—although he had, naturally, looked in on her—but he was making the lie all the more blatant by seeing her off like this. It was possible she was sailing out of his life for good, and he could not bear to let her go any sooner than necessary.

Even watching from the corner of his eye, he could see her obvious delight and excitement as the ship bobbed gently on the harbor's small waves. The wind blew her robes and wimple every which way and would doubtless fill the sails without the aid of any magic. How free she looked! Though, of course, it was just an illusion. The king had insisted that she and Sister Norah be accompanied by an "honor guard," but those men were not there for Norah's and Mairah's good. They would keep a close eye on both women, making sure they had no chance to escape or do anything that might embarrass their kingdom. And one of those guards had another, very much unofficial mission: if Mairah failed in her quest, she would never make it back to Khalwell alive.

Abruptly, Jalzarnin turned away from the ship, unable to look at Mairah even from a distance after the special arrangements he had made. Though really, it was for her own good. If she failed, the king would very likely take his frustrations out on her, and she might find herself spending the rest of her life in the dungeon. Right alongside Jalzarnin himself. Better for *everyone*, really, if she did not return, if she suffered some mysterious accident before anyone knew of her failure.

But of course she would not fail, he consoled himself. Everything he knew about doctrine told him that Sister Melred's vision meant the Creator wanted Mairah to be sent to Women's Well. And that meant she would find the secret to reversing the Curse. Then both she and Jalzarnin would rise into the king's highest esteem. She would be confirmed as abbess, and for a blessed while, he would not have to watch his back so closely.

The fear that he would never see her again was just a symptom of nerves, not any kind of premonition. Premonitions were women's magic!

He did not, however, like the uncomfortable feeling that too much of Mairah's success depended on Sister Norah. Mairah had warned Norah that she had taken precautions to ensure the Mother of All cultists would be exposed if something were to happen to her during the journey, but surely Norah guessed that Mairah had rested her faith in Jalzarnin. Which meant she might also realize that Jalzarnin could not afford to turn her in for fear the scandal would sink both himself and his family thanks to his association with the Abbey. If that was so, then Jalzarnin's special arrangement was nothing but a waste of good coin, for Mairah might not even live long enough to reach the mainland.

Vowing to himself that he would find some other way to avenge Mairah if Norah should betray her, he left the docks.

Part Two

THE MISSION

CHAPTER TWENTY-TWO

Kailee Rah-Kailindar arrived in Women's Well on a fine, temperate winter day that showed the fledgling principality to its best advantage, but though the sun was shining, Alys was struggling to hold on to hope. At Chanlix's urging, Tynthanal had been trying potions at such an accelerated rate that he was left sleepless and surly—and still unable to sire children. He seemed to Alys almost relieved at the failure, although he was fully aware of what this marriage could mean for all of them and promised to keep taking the potions until all hope was lost.

Kailee was escorted by her stepmother, Lady Vondelmai, and by a sizable entourage of guards and servants, as befitted a woman of her stature. After a stilted and formal greeting in the new palace's grand reception room—which Alys was aware was not as grand as that of any other palace in Seven Wells—Alys made the unconventional move of inviting Kailee to join her for an afternoon tea, just the two of them. Lady Vondelmai seemed at least mildly annoyed—and perhaps even suspicious—that she was not included in the invitation.

However, even at the formal reception, where very little of any real consequence was said, Alys could see Kailee's stepmother had a habit of speaking for and over the girl. If Alys was to have any hope of convincing Kailee to stay in Women's Well even if Tynthanal could not marry her, she had to learn as much as she could about her, and that she could not do under Lady Vondelmai's regard.

Alys waited nervously until her guards informed her Kailee had arrived and been made comfortable in the parlor of the royal residence. Butterflies fluttered in her stomach—as if she were about to meet her own suitor—and she couldn't stop herself from looking into a mirror and fussing at a few wisps of hair that had escaped her headdress before venturing forth. So much rested on young Kailee and the security she could bring to Women's Well.

A palace guard threw the parlor door open for her, and after one last deep breath, Alys stepped inside.

Kailee Rah-Kailindar was as beautiful as Ellin had described, with an elfin, heart-shaped face and a delicate but nicely curved figure. The only fault Alys could find was the short dotted veil that hung from her headdress and reached to the bridge of her nose. If the veil were lightly dotted net, it might have been fashionable, if a little matronly for a girl her age. However, it was heavy enough to hide all but the faintest shadow of her eyes. It was perhaps meant to hide her blind eyes, but Alys thought it drew even more attention to the strangeness.

"Thank you for joining me," Alys said as Kailee made an elegant curtsy. Alys had the impression her eyes were modestly lowered, though she could not tell for sure because of the veil.

"Thank you, Your Royal Highness," Kailee replied softly. Even her voice was melodious, and Alys thought it a shame that the noble families of Seven Wells dismissed her out of hand for her blindness. A girl of her beauty and lineage should have had her pick of Rhozinolm high society instead of living in constant fear of being banished to the Abbey of the Unwanted.

"I hope your journey was uneventful," Alys said.

Kailee smiled. "As uneventful as a journey over both land and sea can be," she said. "I'd never been to the sea before." The smile turned wistful. "I will remember the sounds and smells in my dreams for the rest of my life."

Having lived on the coast until she'd come to Women's Well, Alys had long taken the sea for granted, and she felt a slight pang of sorrow that she might never see waves crashing to shore again. Maybe someday in the distant future, it would be safe for her to set foot outside of Women's Well once more, but that certainly would not be the case anytime soon.

"Please sit," Alys invited, reflexively gesturing toward the sofa on which Kailee had been awaiting her, then grimacing when she realized the girl could not see the gesture.

Kailee sat confidently, not fumbling to find the sofa, and spread her skirts around her neatly. She was elegantly dressed in sea green silk studded with tiny seed pearls, the picture of feminine beauty and grace. And none of it would matter to Tynthanal, who would see only that she was not Chanlix. His greeting at the reception had been brief and painfully awkward, though Lady Vondelmai's insistence on speaking for her stepdaughter was at least partially to blame.

A tea tray was set out on the table before the sofa, and as Alys took her own seat, she saw that there was a mostly full cup and saucer in front of Kailee. Alys poured a cup of her own, making sure to make enough noise for Kailee to guess what she was doing. She smiled with satisfaction when Kailee picked up her cup and took a delicate sip.

"I hope you don't think it's terribly rude of me to meet you privately like this," Alys said. "I fear I might have unintentionally insulted your stepmother."

"My stepmother is insulted by my very existence," Kailee answered with shocking frankness. "I've heard her yell at my father more than once for not sending me to the Abbey, where she feels I belong. This whole journey has been a sore trial for her."

Alys blinked, startled, for everything about Kailee screamed of a demure and soft-spoken young woman well acquainted with the expected social graces. But no shy young miss would speak so plainly to a total stranger—especially when that stranger was a sovereign princess. Suddenly, she understood Vondelmai's reluctance to let Kailee speak, although she still did not approve.

Kailee might not see Alys's face, but she had no difficulty reading Alys's momentary hesitation, her smile turning impish in a way that reminded Alys uncomfortably of Jinnell.

"There's more than one reason my father considers me unmarriageable," Kailee said with a modest drop of her chin. "I've a bad habit of being uncomfortably plainspoken. My apologies."

"Nonsense," Alys said as her heart squeezed in her chest. Kailee had little in common with Jinnell, save a similar age and that one slightly impish smile, but suddenly Alys missed her daughter with a fiery intensity.

Not now, she mentally scolded herself, exasperated with the sneak attacks of grief that were now a constant part of her life. She cleared her throat, struggling to keep her emotions out of her voice.

"I don't consider frankness a flaw in a woman," Alys said, trying for a tone of droll humor. "I assure you, my father was often exasperated with me, but I find it preferable for a woman to speak her mind rather than force those around her to guess what she is thinking."

"Or allow those around her not to concern themselves with what she is thinking?"

Alys smiled despite herself. "Just so."

Kailee reached up and rubbed the bridge of her nose, where the edge of her veil met her skin. "If that is so, would you mind terribly if I fold back the veil? My stepmother insists I must always wear it down when in public, but the constant tickle is driving me mad."

"Be my guest," Alys said, bracing herself for fear the veil hid something hideous. Instead, she saw pleasingly almond-shaped eyes with a frame of lush lashes, though the pupils were a milky white that made it look like her Mindseye was open. Not so long ago, Alys might have taken those eyes as something shocking, but a woman with her Mindseye open was hardly an unusual sight in Women's Well. "The veil is not necessary here."

"I feel certain Lady Vondelmai will disagree," Kailee said with a rueful smile.

"I take it you and your stepmother are not especially close."

Kailee blushed deeply, her shoulders hunching ever so slightly. "Forgive me, Your Royal Highness," she said. "One consequence of being told from an early age that I am unmarriageable and bound for the Abbey is that I have never been as constrained by social niceties as I should be. I . . ." She shifted on the sofa, putting down her teacup and clasping her hands together in her lap. "I did not intend to speak ill of my stepmother. She has always been kind to me. She is just terribly concerned about being proper." Her impish smile made a return appearance. "Something at which I admit I am not especially skilled."

Alys suspected that under different circumstances, Tynthanal might have liked this girl quite a lot, for he certainly seemed to enjoy Chanlix's often tart tongue. Though if Alys couldn't find a fertility potion that worked, she supposed Tynthanal's feelings would be the least of her worries.

"You've come to the right place, then. Maidenly propriety is not the point of emphasis in Women's Well that it is elsewhere in the world. And it is because of that that I wanted to speak to you privately about a delicate matter which might ordinarily be deemed an inappropriate topic of conversation between two ladies."

Kailee smiled again. "In that case, it's a good thing you did not invite my stepmother."

Alys stifled another laugh, inspired more by nerves than humor. "So it seems. I don't know how much you've been told about . . . well, anything, really." Alys found herself picking at one of the seams on her skirt and clasped her hands together to suppress the nervous gesture. Not that Kailee could see her tension.

Kailee bit her lip. "I do know that there would be some risks involved if I were to marry your brother and live here. My father explained the potential difficulties, but he swore to me that Queen Ellinsoltah will see to the protection of Women's Well. I am not afraid."

The girl's face was possibly more expressive than she knew, for Alys could see the doubts that belied her confident words. It was no small thing to leave the safety and security of one's home to take up residence in a land that ran the risk of being torn by war.

"Neither your father, nor your queen, nor I can guarantee you safety from war," Alys said, "though of course we will all do our best to avoid it." Alys wondered what Corlin would say if he heard her say that, for it was abundantly clear that he both expected and *wanted* war with Aaltah as only a sheltered fourteen-year-old boy could.

Kailee nodded in acknowledgment. "I understand. But whether it comes to war or not, I have . . . prospects in Women's Well that I do not have in Rhozinolm. At home, the *best* I can expect is to live as a pitied spinster who must take pains not to be seen in public any more than absolutely necessary to avoid bringing shame upon my family. The other, perhaps more likely option, is life in the Abbey."

Alys shook her head bitterly. Her mother's spell had in so many ways changed the lives and prospects of women, freeing so many from the specter of forced marriages and rape. But it would take a great deal of time—likely generations, at least—before women would gain anything like the same freedoms as men. A blind nobleman would face a certain amount of pity and discomfort among his peers, but he would not be shunned, and would likely find a wife and a comfortable existence.

"It is worth a great deal of risk to me to escape the specter of the Abbey," Kailee said with a brave raise of her chin. "If anything were to happen to my father, I have no doubt my stepmother would send me away immediately. Not through any ill will, but because she believes that is where I should be."

Alys was already developing a thorough dislike of Lady Vondelmai.

Kailee bit her lip, then asked in a rush, "May I share with you a shocking and wildly inappropriate secret?" She appeared to hold her breath, her whole body taut with tension.

Alys blinked in surprise and no small amount of curiosity. She had a great fondness for women who spoke plainly, but it struck her as almost painfully trusting and naïve that Kailee would offer to share a secret of any sort with a woman she had just met. Both curiosity and statesmanship demanded she accept any secret being freely offered, and yet she felt honor-bound to protect this young woman who reminded her—rightly or not—of Jinnell. "I am honored by your confidence," she said carefully, "but I hardly feel I have had time to earn it."

"You are to be my sister-in-law," Kailee said. "I would not have you accept me as a suitable bride for your brother without knowing the whole truth. Whatever my father and my stepmother might wish." Her chin lifted with defiance and courage. Courage that made Alys feel doubly guilty for her own lack of honesty.

There's still a chance a fertility potion will work, Alys counseled herself to stifle her urge to admit the false pretenses under which she had invited Kailee to visit.

"It is no sure thing yet that we are to be sisters," Alys said instead. "I have promised all involved that you and my brother must enter into a marriage of your own free will, and it remains to be seen whether you will find yourselves compatible."

Kailee lowered her head demurely. "This marriage may well be my only chance to have anything resembling the kind of life I've long been told was impossible for one such as me," she said. "If your brother is anything less than an ogre, then rest assured that I want to marry him. And yet even so, I cannot do as I've been told and stay silent. I do not require my future husband to love me, but I want to have at least the chance of friendship and cordiality. A chance that will be destroyed if he later learns I have lied by omission."

Her chin came up once more, and though it was hard to read the expression on her face with those eyes, Alys was sure she saw both determination and trepidation.

"I was born with my Mindseye fully developed and open," Kailee said, "and I cannot close it. That is why I cannot see. So now you know the *full* reason why my stepmother is sure I belong in the Abbey."

Alys sat back in her chair and found herself at a loss for words. She had never heard of such a thing.

Kailee took a shaky breath. "I hope that here in Women's Well, where you seem to have a very different attitude toward women who practice magic, my condition will not be considered so shameful that I must keep it hidden from all."

"You practice magic," Alys said, certain her guess was right. How could Kailee *not* practice magic when she was surrounded by the elements all the time?

"A little," the girl admitted shyly. "I have no training, naturally, and the one time my stepmother caught me doing it she fainted dead away. Then she and my father had a terrific row about it and I thought surely he was finally going to send me away after all." She shook her head. "I don't think I could endure it if Lord Tynthanal were to learn the truth of my condition after we are married and revile me for it. Even if there is no Abbey to which he can send me here . . ." Her voice caught, and she let the words trail off.

In the face of Kailee's honesty, Alys impulsively decided that she could not continue to keep her own secrets. She took a deep breath and hoped she was not making a terrible mistake. "Neither your Mindseye nor your magic is an issue of any consequence to Tynthanal or myself," she said, choosing her words with perhaps a little too much care.

"Ah," Kailee said softly. "But there *is* an issue."

Alys nodded, then abruptly remembered the girl couldn't see. "Yes, as of now, at least." She shifted in her seat, as she always seemed to do when speaking of Tynthanal's condition. "I am hopeful we will soon find a cure with our unique magic. But as of now, it seems my brother is unable to father children."

Kailee looked so stricken that Alys almost regretted the impulse to tell her. If one of the potions worked, she could have avoided the unpleasant revelation altogether.

"I see," Kailee said softly, closing her eyes. She seemed to gather her thoughts and regain her equilibrium swiftly, her lips turning up into another rueful smile. "I have always heard that when something sounds too good to be true, it usually is. Now I see that it is the case."

"I truly am hopeful that we can cure his condition," Alys said rather desperately. "I will do everything in my power to make certain that you did not get your hopes raised in vain."

Kailee started to say something, then stopped. A frown darkened her pretty face, only to be quickly dispelled. "One consequence to my blindness is that people often act as though I can't hear, either. Perhaps they are trying so hard to ignore me and avoid any discomfort that they simply forget I am present. But I am not deaf, and I am not stupid, either. There are important reasons why this marriage should happen, none of which have anything to do with creating a blissful union.

"I do not blame you for the deception, any more than I blame my father and my stepmother for theirs, despite my decision not to go along with it. I swear I will not tell anyone what you have told me, and I will endeavor to give you as much time as possible to craft your cure. But as I suspect you know, my father will not agree to the marriage if your brother cannot give me children, even if I might be amenable."

"I suspected as much," Alys admitted. "Though after what you've told me, it seems there are more reasons than one why Women's Well would be the best place for you. The place where you could have the greatest freedom."

Kailee smiled. "You'll get no argument from me. But my father is far more concerned with my safety than with my freedom. I had to plead with him more than once to keep him from cancelling this visit because he is afraid for me. The *only* reason he finally relented was because he saw for me the chance to lead a normal woman's life here, to have a husband and children. Taking those possible children away would tip the scales once more."

Alys, of course, did not know Lord Kailindar, but she saw no reason to disbelieve Kailee's claim. Even with Rhozinolm's full and enthusiastic support, there was no denying that Women's Well would remain frighteningly vulnerable to attack, and a loving father would be justified in fearing for his daughter's life if she married into this particular royal family.

And, she realized with a sinking feeling, it was unlikely to matter how much Kailee might love Women's Well and want to stay. If her father saw danger in her future with too little potential gain, he would command her to return to Rhozinolm and safety.

The future of Women's Well rested firmly on Alys's ability to create a successful fertility potion. She grimly resolved that she would forego all but the absolute minimum of sleep to get that done.

CHAPTER TWENTY-THREE

Delnamal's relationship with the dowager queen had not fared especially well since he'd ascended the throne. She blamed him for the destruction of his first marriage, insisting Shelvon would have borne him an heir if only he had treated her better. And she could not disapprove more strongly of Delnamal's second wife, her Khalpari sensibilities insisting that kings must only marry virgin brides. The Devotional that was her constant companion did not specifically insist that widows never remarry, but it was nonetheless viewed as improper in the most traditional households. And of course many were scandalized that he had married her so soon after her husband's death, not allowing her to observe the customary year of mourning. The people of Aaltah might not obey the Devotional as slavishly as those of Khalpar, but there was no denying the wedding had offended a great many. And he could no longer be in the dowager's presence without seeing maternal censure in her eyes.

Accordingly, Delnamal spent as little time in her company as possible, but his choices right now were to speak with her or speak with the Khalpari ambassador once more. Figuring he was marginally less likely to murder the dowager queen with his bare hands than he was the ambassador, he chose to brace his mother in the dowager's apartments. There was a line of supplicants in the hallway outside her receiving room, for though she had no formal position of power, she took on her expected role of people's champion with the same dedication she showed for any of her other duties.

Delnamal ignored the bows and murmured greetings, his temper too brittle to deal with any unnecessary interactions. He did not wait to be announced, and he did not knock, and when he entered the room to find his mother gently rubbing the back of a sobbing pregnant woman, it was all he could do not to snarl. Belatedly, he thought that he should have sat down and had a drink, given his temper time to cool, before marching to his mother's receiving room. But the moment he'd read King Khalvin's sanctimonious message, he'd stormed out of his office—leaving his flummoxed secretary to stammer in helpless confusion.

The crying woman did not look up when Delnamal entered—perhaps she was blubbering too loudly to hear him—but his mother did. Her expression was that all-too-familiar look of disapproval that set his teeth on edge, and he wondered if he should have taken his chances with the ambassador after all. But no matter how much he might disappoint his mother, she could not do him political damage, which was more than he could say of the ambassador.

"I need a moment of your time," he said in a tone that made it clear he was not asking.

"Of course, Your Majesty," Xanvin said, putting her arm around the woman and helping her to her feet. "We will finish this conversation as soon as I am able," she said with infinite gentleness. The pregnant woman snuffled and nodded as Xanvin guided her into an adjoining room.

Delnamal frowned. It was plain to see by the woman's dress that she was a commoner, and it seemed to him unwise to allow a commoner to sit unattended in the dowager queen's apartment. "She should wait in the hall with everyone else," he said, but his mother closed the door behind the woman as if he hadn't spoken.

"What is it you need, my son?" she asked when she turned to him. As was often the case, she was wearing a miniature Devotional on a chain around her waist, and her fingers stroked its cover absently as she faced him.

It was not as warm a welcome as Delnamal had hoped for from his own mother, and he stood briefly on the precipice of losing his temper once and for all. But the dowager queen's serenity had a certain contagious nature, and he found himself calming almost against his will.

"I need you to write to your brother on my behalf," he said. He had not intended to put it so bluntly—the idea that a king should ask his mother for help with diplomacy was an embarrassment he could barely stomach, and if any of his courtiers should realize he'd done it . . . Well, he could only imagine how they'd snicker behind his back.

Xanvin's surprise showed only in a quick widening of her eyes. Then she cocked her head with curiosity. "There is a problem of some sort, I presume?"

Delnamal grunted in affirmation and glanced around the receiving room, hoping his mother had some brandy or cordial sitting around to ease the distress of distraught supplicants. Not that he was either distraught or a supplicant himself, but he needed a drink. Inconveniently, there did not seem to be any available.

"The problem is that Khalvin is a self-righteous prick who does not seem to understand what it means to be an ally." Which, he realized after it was too late to take the words back, probably wasn't the best choice of words to use with the self-righteous prick's sister. He expected an immediate rebuke, but his mother only smiled.

"I know how my brother can get when he feels he has the moral high ground," she assured him. "After all, I grew up with him. Now tell me what has happened."

"I asked him to lend us some naval support in the event that tensions with Rhozinolm should boil over. He wrote back to say that I should be spending my time on trying to find a way to reverse the Curse rather than preparing for war. As if he thinks we haven't *tried* to figure out how to undo it. And as if readying our kingdom for attack somehow makes us incapable of doing anything else."

"Do stop pacing, my son," Xanvin said, startling him.

It showed something of his mental state that he hadn't even realized he was pacing the room while he spoke. He came to a stop and blinked as if rousing himself from sleep. He looked all around once more, hoping to spot a decanter he'd missed, his need for a drink getting stronger with each passing minute. He suspected his mother knew perfectly well what he was looking for, but she did not acknowledge it.

"Khalvin is not like your grandfather," Xanvin continued. "If your grandfather had not been a king, he would have been a soldier. If Khalvin were not a king, he would be a priest. His focus will always tend toward questions of morality and piety. The Curse is an insult to the Creator the likes of which the world has never known, and Khalvin will see your difficulties with Alysoon and with Queen Ellinsoltah as petty squabbles of little importance in comparison."

Delnamal blew out a gusty sigh, for that was exactly the message Khalvin's letter had delivered. "But he's supposed to be our ally!" he protested. "That was the whole purpose of your marriage to Father."

Xanvin shook her head. "That was our father's purpose for contracting me to marry your father, but Khalvin was not party to that agreement." Delnamal stiffened and opened his mouth for an outraged exclamation, but she continued speaking without giving him the chance to interrupt. "I am not saying he will disregard the alliance our father made with your father. All I'm saying is that he has different priorities."

"Don't you have anything to drink around here?" he complained, for anything else he might have said would have been even more inappropriate. If he didn't get a drink soon, he was going to do something rash like wreck his mother's receiving room.

When Delnamal had been forced to march home with his army in shame, he had comforted himself with the thought that it was naught but a temporary setback. He'd imagined that within six months' time, he would have raised a sufficient force to crush Alysoon's supposed principality while still protecting Aaltah from Rhozinolm's retaliation. But so far, his royal council had seen fit to raise the Citadel's budget by such a pittance that it hardly mattered, Nandel was still playing at being insulted over his divorce of Shelvon—despite his efforts to make reparations—and his closest ally seemed entirely uninterested in lending him any aid. Not to mention the never-ending whining he kept hearing over his cancellation of one silly trade agreement with Rhozinolm.

His mother gave him a disapproving frown, and for a moment he feared he was in for a scolding after all—which would have tipped him into a full-out rage, he was sure. Luckily, she thought better of it.

"I'll have some brandy brought in," she said, ringing a bell to summon a servant.

Delnamal turned his back on the door, going to stare sightlessly out a window so the servant would not see whatever dreadful expression he was sure he wore on his face. He heard the murmur of voices, but his blood was pulsing so loudly in his ears he could not make out the words. Bad enough that his mother was seeing this pathetic demonstration of his weakness, but he could not bear to have the servants gleefully discussing it, spreading the word until he was a laughingstock. A grown man, a *king*, shouldn't *need* a drink; not the way he needed one right now.

He'd sunk so deep into his sea of self-loathing that he started when a glass of brandy suddenly materialized in front of his face.

"Drink," his mother said simply, and he could do nothing but obey.

He managed two delicate sips before he just couldn't help himself and downed the rest in one burning swallow. Xanvin plucked the empty glass from his hand. Unfortunately, she put it down on a side table instead of refilling it, but he felt calmer already with the familiar flavor on his tongue and the pleasant warmth the brandy left in his throat.

"If you want my brother's support," Xanvin said, "you must present your case in a way that feels compelling to him. He will have no interest in your squabble with Alysoon, and even a trade war with Rhozinolm—should it come to that—would strike him as trivial."

Delnamal scowled. He had never met his uncle—nor any of his other Khalpari relatives, come to think of it—but he was well on the way to despising the man. "Then he is no ally of Aaltah's, whatever he might claim."

Xanvin sighed delicately. "You are missing the point. If you want his aid, you must present your requests in just the right way. I am certain Khalvin does not approve of the idea of a woman sitting on a throne. The Mother swore eternal subservience to the Creator, and it is the duty of women to honor Her oath. If in your communication with my brother, you were to emphasize that your troubles are caused by a pair of women who are flouting the laws of the Creator by placing themselves above men . . ."

"Huh," Delnamal grunted, having never thought of either Alysoon or Queen Ellinsoltah in quite that light. Xanvin had made certain he'd grown up well-lettered in the teachings of the Devotional, and he was well aware of the penance the Mother had sworn after She'd betrayed the Creator in Their son's bed. But for all his mother's efforts, he'd never really *believed* the stories in the Devotional. Certainly he'd never taken them *literally*, nor had he developed any but the vaguest sense of faith. And yet for his mother and King Khalvin— and most of the people of Khalpar—the Devotional contained nothing but the literal truth, and it was the duty of every human being to live in accordance with its laws and teachings. There had never been—and never would be—even a *temporary* sovereign queen in Khalpar.

"I am not suggesting that he will have a sudden and miraculous change of heart," Xanvin warned. "You may not immediately get the aid you request, but with a little time and persuasion, he might very well decide that it is his moral duty to battle against the decadent and unnatural rule of women."

It galled Delnamal that he would have to wheedle and cajole his uncle into fulfilling his duties as the blood ally of Aaltah—but then it galled him to need the aid in the first place. "Will you write to him?"

he asked his mother. "I suspect you can make a more convincing religious appeal than I can."

"I will write to him. *If* you will join me for my nightly prayers. If you are going to court my brother's favor, then you had best make an effort to absorb the teachings of the Devotional."

He made a disgusted noise at the back of his throat. "I am well aware of the teachings of the Devotional." He must have read the damned book twenty or thirty times when he was growing up, at his mother's insistence. He'd kept hoping his father would intervene and insist he be raised as a man of Aaltah, to respect the Devotional without being enslaved to it, but he never had.

"Awareness and absorption are not the same thing."

"You will not turn me into a priest! If you don't want to write the letter for me, just say so and be done with it." And then he would command her to do it or she would find herself ousted from the dowager's apartments, reminding her that he was not just her son but also her king.

She shook her head at him reproachfully, her eyes sad and troubled. "I will write your letter. But—"

"No buts," he interrupted with a sharp hand gesture. "Thank you for your help and your advice. Now I am afraid I must take my leave before my secretary sends a search party to find me."

For half a heartbeat, it looked like Xanvin might try to press, but the teachings of her own beloved Devotional must surely have warned her it was not her place. Instead, she dipped her head in a courteous nod.

"Of course, Your Majesty."

Alys—flanked, as always, by her honor guard—followed the soldier through the halls of the Citadel and out the back to the cadet training grounds. The boys were gathered in clusters of similar age groups, each headed by an experienced soldier whom Jailom had assigned as an instructor. Her escort led her to a group of fourteen- and fifteen-year-olds, who were the youngest cadets at the Citadel. Spaced in even rows, all looking tired and sweaty in the scorching sun as they

moved through the positions of a sword drill, the boys must have
noticed Alys's approach, if only in their peripheral vision, but not one
spared her even a glance. Their instructor nodded approvingly, then
called a halt.

Alys had not announced her intention to visit the Citadel, but her
purpose was no doubt clear, for the instructor called out to her, "Are
you perhaps looking for Cadet Smithson, Your Royal Highness?"

One of the boys turned to look at her then, his eyes wide and almost alarmed looking. Alys smiled at him encouragingly. Her smile
faltered just slightly when she realized that Corlin was not among the
group as he should have been.

"If you can spare him for a few moments," Alys confirmed. "I
don't want to interfere with his training."

"Of course," the instructor said with a bow. "Cadet Smithson,
you are dismissed."

The boy looked terrified as he sheathed his sword and left his position in the formation. As soon as Smithson was out of the way, the
instructor barked at the rest of the cadets to stop gawking and get
back to work. Alys looked over their ranks one more time, just to
make sure she hadn't somehow missed her own son, but Corlin was
definitely not there.

Alys forced herself to smile again and put aside her unease as
Smithson approached. The sun had browned his skin almost as dark
as his leather jerkin, making a stark contrast with the white of his
wide eyes. He had returned to Women's Well the day before, having
spent some time recuperating in South Bend before journeying home
on cheval back. The cheval had made the return journey relatively
quick, but the boy still clearly needed more time to recover from his
ordeals. His clothes hung loosely on his frame, and his movements
were overly careful, as if he was still sore from the saddle. Alys doubted
he'd ever ridden a horse or cheval before, and she knew from painful
experience how uncomfortable the day after could be. She was
amazed that he was drilling on his first full day back—she'd have
thought the instructors would have given him at least a couple of
days to recover—but perhaps they had felt returning him to his usual
routine as fast as possible was best for him.

Alys's smile failed to quell the boy's nerves, and when he reached her, he bowed awkwardly. She knew that he was one of the commoner boys who'd been allowed to enter the Citadel, and though he had perhaps seen her from a distance before, he was not used to being in the presence of royalty. Other than Corlin, whom Jailom had insisted not be treated as royalty while within the walls of the Citadel.

"Y-your Majesty," he stammered when he rose.

"It's just 'Your Royal Highness,'" she told him. "'Your Majesty' is for kings and queens."

Beneath the browning of the sun, the skin of his cheeks flushed darker, and Alys wished her first words hadn't been to correct him. She still hadn't gotten used to people being intimidated by her, and she hadn't thought before she'd spoken. In the background, the other boys had resumed their drill, the stamp of their feet loud enough to ensure they would not have heard the interchange. At least she had not subjected him to public humiliation.

"I wanted to take this opportunity to thank you personally for your service to Women's Well," she said, perhaps a little hurriedly, hoping to smooth over any discomfort she might have caused. She would have liked to issue the boy some kind of medal or commendation, but Jailom had rejected the idea, saying the boy was too young to receive such military honors. She would settle—grudgingly—for awarding his parents an additional land grant so that they need no longer live in their tiny apartment above the smithy.

Smithson's mouth dropped open, his eyes widening once more, this time in surprise rather than fear. "B-but . . . I didn't do anything." He swallowed hard as the color drained out of his face. "I hid under the wagon." His voice shook ever so slightly as the shadows of remembered horrors passed before his eyes.

Alys's heart ached for the poor boy, who had seen his three companions slaughtered, and who had had every reason to believe he, too, would die. He was so very young to have survived such a trauma, and she would have liked to gather him into a motherly hug. She settled for reaching out and putting a hand on his shoulder, giving it a squeeze.

"You survived," she said. "Sometimes, that's all you can do. I can't tell you how sorry I am that your first mission turned out to be such an ordeal. I just wanted you to know that I think you are very brave for agreeing to accompany the caravan, and that I'm very glad you made it back safely."

The boy shivered under her hand, and the haunted look in his eyes stirred a combination of guilt and rage in her breast. It was an act of mercy that the "bandits" had allowed the boy to live, but they had put scars on his soul that no fifteen-year-old should have to endure. How she wished she could pay Delnamal back in kind!

"It's what I signed up for when I entered the Citadel, Your Royal Highness," Smithson said staunchly, raising his chin as he regained his self-possession. "I did my duty as a cadet." His face colored again. "As best I could, at least."

She squeezed his shoulder again, then let go. "Yes, you did. And I'm sure Lord Jailom has already told you that it was your duty as a cadet to return to us safely instead of throwing away your life in some vainglorious attempt to do the impossible." She knew for a fact that Jailom had had this conversation with Smithson already, and she hoped the boy had taken it to heart.

"Yes, he did, Your Royal Highness."

"You only have to call me 'Your Royal Highness' the first time you address me," she said. "After that, you can just call me 'ma'am.' Much less of a mouthful." She smiled at him once more, and he tried a tentative smile of his own.

"Yes, ma'am."

He seemed perhaps a little more at ease than he had when she first approached, but there was still considerable tension in his shoulders. Perhaps it was best to let him return to his duties. She hoped that in the long run, he would be pleased at having been singled out for praise by the sovereign princess, but at the moment, it was just making him uncomfortable.

"I'll let you get back to your drills now," she said, and there was no missing the relief in his expression. "One question before you go, though. Do you know where Prince Corlin is? I expected him to be drilling with the rest of you."

The relief disappeared immediately, and Smithson looked like he would very much like to be anywhere but here. Alys fought to keep her own unease off her face, for all it took was that one look to know that there was no innocent explanation for Corlin's absence. And that she should have asked one of the adults rather than this poor child.

"H-he's in the barracks, ma'am," Smithson said, his eyes suddenly locked on the ground.

Why on earth would Corlin be in the barracks at this time of day? she wondered. But at least she had the good sense not to ask Smithson.

"Thank you, Cadet Smithson," she said with as much warmth as her worry would allow. "That will be all."

Smithson couldn't quite suppress a sigh of renewed relief as he bowed to her once again, then hurried to rejoin his comrades.

The sensible thing to do would be to ask one of the instructors what was happening—or maybe even seek out Jailom, who would certainly know the answer—but Alys had not the patience to do things the proper way. Instead, she turned and headed toward the barracks on the other side of the practice fields. She was well aware of the gazes that followed her, and she wondered for a moment if one of the instructors was going to break away from his cadets to intercept her. There was some level of informality to her leadership style that might have tempted an instructor with an exceptionally bold heart to do so, but she imagined the look on her face was especially forbidding, so no one approached her. There was no good reason Corlin would be in the barracks instead of drilling with his fellow cadets, and she was trying to keep her temper in check while still preparing herself for the worst.

"Wait here," she commanded her honor guard when she reached the barracks door.

At first glance, the barracks appeared empty. There were no luminants lit, and though the windows admitted a fair amount of light, the room was full of shadows. Alys had never set foot in a barracks before, and though she'd known the living was austere, it still came as something of a shock to see the long rows of narrow, identical cots covered in dull gray wool blankets. At the foot of each bed was a small wooden chest for personal belongings—each identical, just like the beds—and there were no other furnishings in the room. It was clearly a place made for sleeping and nothing else, and anything that might identify an individual was tucked away into those chests. Alys couldn't imagine what a shock it must have been to her son's system to sleep in such a place when he had grown up in a comfortable manor house and had always had a room to himself. And servants to take care of such chores as washing his clothes and making his bed— chores that Alys was sure the cadets were responsible for themselves here at the Citadel.

As she walked more fully into the room and her eyes adjusted to the dimness, Alys finally saw that one of the cots at the far end of the room was occupied. She moved tentatively forward, picking out the shape of her son, fully clothed in his cadet's uniform, lying on his back on top of the covers. His hands were crossed over his midsection, and when he heard the swish of her skirts against her legs, he turned his head in her direction.

Alys stifled a gasp, her hand flying to her mouth as she was caught between the warring impulses to dash to Corlin's side and to run away so she need not see. His right eye was purple and swollen shut; his nose was conspicuously crooked, the bruising at its bridge extending all around his other eye as well; and his lower lip was fat and scabbed over.

Wincing and groaning, Corlin sat up and swung his legs over the side of his cot. "Please don't make a big deal out of this, Mama," he slurred, his good eye looking at her imploringly.

Alys's heart thudded painfully against her breastbone, and she clenched her hands into fists to fight the tremor of rage. Once again, her child had been brutalized. And she had allowed it. Had not insisted he leave the Citadel and come home to her when her maternal instincts had screamed her need to protect him.

"What happened?" she croaked, barely able to force sound from her throat. Her knees felt a little wobbly, so she took a seat on the cot across from him, knowing he would not welcome any attempt to sit beside him or take him in her arms as she ached to do.

Corlin shrugged, though his quick wince said he regretted the movement. "I got in a fight. And lost."

Her hands fisted in her skirts. "Did this have anything to do with the last fight you were in?" She should have asked Jailom to keep an eye on Corlin after that, for she doubted the boy he'd beaten had been much mollified by his punishment. Perhaps that boy also had friends who felt honor-bound to avenge him.

Corlin rolled his good eye. "What does it matter? Cadets get into fights sometimes. It happens."

Alys sucked in a deep breath. She wanted to rant and yell and weep, but Corlin would see any of that as an overreaction, and she could not bear to be further alienated from him. It was certainly true that boys had a nasty habit of getting into fights, but Corlin's ravaged face said this had been more than an ordinary fight.

"Why have you not been seen by a healer?" she asked, changing tactics. The Citadel had two healers on site at all times, and they certainly had enough spells to repair the damage of a beating. It was unconscionable that he was lying here alone in the barracks suffering!

Corlin met her angry gaze with a stubbornness that was visible even through all the bruises and swelling. "Lord Jailom has said that I can see a healer as soon as I tell him who did this to me." His chin jutted out even more strongly. "Which means I will heal the *natural* way."

Alys bit back her immediate retort, forcing herself to think before speaking. There were aspects of the male code of honor that had always infuriated her, and she hated that her son had grown up thinking that it was his duty to protect the boys who had hurt him.

"Boys who would do something like this to you might do the same to others," she tried, already knowing that her logic would not sway him. "Actions should have consequences, and—"

"They do." He indicated his body with a sweep of his hand. "You're looking at them. I am not blameless, and I will take the consequences like a man."

You are not *a man*, she wanted to say. *Not yet*. But of course she held her tongue.

"You don't need to protect me anymore, Mama," he said, his voice going strangely gentle, as if *she* were the one in need of comforting. "I can take care of myself."

She eyed his broken nose and swollen eye with undisguised skepticism. The corners of his mouth tipped up in a painful half-smile.

"As long as I don't tattle," he said, "things will be easier now between me and the other cadets. This . . . had to happen after . . . what I did." His gaze lowered, and though it was hard to read his expression with all the swelling and bruising, she thought he looked genuinely contrite.

In other words, he hadn't so much been in a fight as been jumped and beaten senseless by his comrades. She glanced down at his hands, clasped together in his lap, and saw that the knuckles were scraped and bruised. He might have been jumped, but he had definitely fought back. It was hard to know whether to believe his words or the messages of his body.

"Did Lord Jailom send you to try to get me to talk?" Corlin asked. "I had asked him not to worry you with this, and I'd thought he'd agreed."

"No, Lord Jailom has not spoken to me," Alys said—an oversight which she would correct before leaving the Citadel. This time, Tynthanal would not be around to intercept her before she had a chance to tell her lord commander what she thought of his tactics. Perhaps she would have to remind him that she was not merely Corlin's mother but the Sovereign Princess of Women's Well. "I was here to express my gratitude to Cadet Smithson on his return and noticed you were not present." She sighed heavily, hating the feeling of powerlessness that enveloped her. She desperately needed her son to be whole and happy, and yet not even the magic of their unique Well could accomplish such a thing.

"Do you still want to remain at the Citadel?" she asked, already knowing the answer. "You could come home."

Anger flashed in his eye. "Is that what you think of me? That after a little adversity I'll come crying home to cling to my mother's skirts?"

Taken aback by the ferocity of his answer, she could only sit there and gape at him. It had been as calm and civil a conversation as the two of them had had in a long time, and the temper had come on so fast it nearly took her breath away.

Corlin sighed and closed his eye. "Sorry. Sorry." He swallowed hard, and his shoulders lowered, though she had the impression he had forced them down rather than actually relaxed. He opened his eye again, and it was like he was wearing a mask of calm over the rage that still roiled within him.

"I am where I need to be," he said. "No one ever promised it would be easy, but I have no intention of letting a few toughs chase me away."

Alys refrained from telling him just how very tempted she was to use her power as sovereign princess to forcibly withdraw him from the Citadel. And though she managed to stand strong in the face of temptation this time, she did not dismiss the possibility that such might not be the case in the future.

CHAPTER TWENTY-FOUR

Despite her pragmatic attitude toward the possibility of Tynthanal marrying another, Chanlix had to admit she'd not been especially predisposed to like Kailee Rah-Kailindar and had been fully prepared to treat the girl with only the most distant courtesy when she could not avoid her altogether. It was certainly how Tynthanal had been acting since Kailee had first arrived—never discourteous, but not his usual warm and charming self, either. He took each new fertility potion with grim determination, and received the failures with a confusing combination of disappointment and relief.

Chanlix had had little chance to interact with her, but what she'd seen from the distance—and gathered from Alys's warm descriptions—was that Kailee was a fierce young woman with an indomitable spirit. Someone Chanlix could not help admiring, despite the strife her presence brought to Chanlix's heart.

While Chanlix couldn't help liking and admiring Kailee, the girl's stepmother was an entirely different matter. Lady Vondelmai made no secret of the fact that she disapproved of just about everything about Women's Well, and she had practically recoiled in horror when she'd realized that the Women's Well Academy was largely staffed by the former abigails of Aaltah. Chanlix would not have expected the woman to allow her stepdaughter anywhere near the place. Which was why Chanlix was so shocked when one of her spell crafters came to her office and announced that Kailee had arrived and asked to meet with her. Both curiosity and courtesy demanded Chanlix accept Kailee's request, so she agreed.

Kailee arrived at the office with a scowling honor guardsman nearly treading on her heels. "Wait here for me," she ordered as she crossed the threshold, and his scowl deepened.

"I cannot in good conscience leave you alone with—" he started, turning his scowl to Chanlix. Apparently, he shared Lady Vondelmai's low opinion of former abigails.

"Just what do you expect Lady Chanlix to do to me?" Kailee interrupted. As usual, a veil covered the top part of her face, but Chanlix could almost hear the girl rolling her eyes. "I have matters to discuss with her that are not fit for men's ears, and I can assure you that Lady Vondelmai would not consent to you being present to hear."

Chanlix crossed the room and stood by the door, wondering if she should interrupt with a greeting. The guard shifted from foot to foot, clearly uncomfortable with any mention of topics not fit for his ears.

"She said I should escort you and she made no mention that I should wait outside," he said, though it sounded as though he'd lost some of his conviction.

Kailee gave an exasperated—and not especially ladylike—snort. "If you imagine my stepmother would like you to hear me discussing women's issues in front of you, then you do not know her at all."

Chanlix was practically burning with curiosity, for she could not imagine what kind of "women's issues" Lady Vondelmai would allow her stepdaughter to discuss with the former Abbess of Aaltah. Kailee stepped over the threshold into Chanlix's office, and Chanlix waited to see if her honor guard would insist on following. He gave both women sneers of distaste, taking advantage of Kailee's inability to see his inappropriate behavior, then stepped to the side and crossed his arms over his chest.

"Please have a seat," Chanlix said, closing the door and putting a gentle hand on Kailee's arm to guide her toward a chair. Having seen Kailee in public before, Chanlix was aware that the girl walked with surprising ease and comfort for one who could not see. And having learned from Alys that Kailee's Mindseye was always open, she understood the origin of that ease. She could "see" people and animals, in a sense, because she could see the halo of Rho that surrounded all living things. Such sight would not allow her to avoid inanimate objects, but it did not leave her completely in the dark, either.

"I must admit to some surprise that Lady Vondelmai would permit you to visit the Academy," Chanlix said, suddenly wondering if Kailee was practicing a deception that would come back and haunt them both. "I was under the impression that she doesn't much care for our work here."

Kailee smiled as Chanlix took her own seat. "It has taken a campaign of several days to convince her," she said. "But she would love nothing more than to see me turned into a 'normal' and respectable young lady. For that to happen, my blindness must be cured, and for my blindness to be cured, I convinced her I must reveal to you—and only you—its cause."

It made perfect sense. Chanlix had already assigned several of her spell crafters to the task of researching cures for blindness so that they might try to produce more powerful versions, but then blindness wasn't exactly Kailee's problem.

"I presume Princess Alysoon has already shared with you the shocking secret behind why I can't see?"

Chanlix felt the flush of embarrassment in her face and could not muster the smooth denial that the question warranted. She did not wish to confirm that Alys had shared the secret given to her in confidence, but her moment of hesitation gave her away.

Kailee smiled again. "Don't worry, Lady Chanlix," she said. "I am not as ashamed of my condition as my stepmother would like me to be, and I told Princess Alysoon the truth while understanding that ours was not a simple conversation between two ladies that would be held in the strictest confidence. There is so very much at stake . . ."

Chanlix sighed quietly. Alys had told her that Kailee had a sharp and strategic mind and that she was far from some sheltered young miss yearning for a husband. "Yes," Chanlix confirmed. "She did tell me that yours is not a conventional blindness. We will still endeavor to cure it, but—"

"In actuality, I did not come here to talk about my sight or lack thereof," Kailee interrupted. "That was the excuse I gave my stepmother to get her to allow me to speak with you in private. I have lived my entire life without any worldly vision, and while I admit to some curiosity as to what that vision is like, I cannot miss what I have never had. Her dream is for me to become 'normal' and enter into a normal and respectable marriage back home in Rhozinolm. But her dream is not my dream. To have that 'normal' life, I would be required to cut myself off from magic. I imagine the only way to give me worldly vision is to force my Mindseye closed. I do not miss the worldly vision I've never had, but I *would* miss the Mindsight I've relied upon my whole life. Just as I would very much miss the ability to practice magic, even though I've had very little opportunity to do so in safety."

"I see," Chanlix murmured, finally realizing just how far from a proper young miss Kailee really was. And understanding why her stepmother might have urged her father to put her away. A spirited, plainspoken, unabashedly intelligent young woman might fit in very nicely in a place like Women's Well, but not so much elsewhere in the world.

"I cannot imagine anything I would want more than to remain here in Women's Well," Kailee continued, and though her eyes remained hidden, Chanlix could hear the incipient tears in her voice. "As much as Lady Vondelmai has tried to shield me from the 'corrupting influence' of this place, I am still perfectly capable of seeing the freedom I could have here. Just as I know my future is bleak if I am forced to return to Rhozinolm. I *need* this marriage. Without it, my father will never allow me to stay."

Chanlix swallowed hard to keep a lump from rising in her throat.

She could only imagine what it would feel like to walk in Kailee's shoes, to see freedom and acceptance dangled before her nose and have it snatched away from her at the last moment. She had come to Women's Well fully expecting to marry Tynthanal—and no doubt willing to overlook a great number of flaws in his character if necessary—only to find out that the union might be impossible. Chanlix understood Alys's impulse to tell Kailee the truth after Kailee had been so honest with her, but she herself might have chosen to keep the secret until all hope was lost to spare her any needless anxiety.

"We are doing all we can to make that marriage possible," Chanlix assured the girl.

Kailee nodded. "But it might not work, no matter how hard you try." Despite the veil and the blindness, Chanlix could swear she suddenly felt the girl's eyes boring through her. "If everyone involved is indeed trying."

"W-why of course we are," Chanlix stammered, strangely discomfited by the accusation that seemed to come out of nowhere.

Kailee raised her chin. "As I told Princess Alysoon, people have a tendency to speak more freely in front of me than they would if I were not blind. And because I am already considered all but unmarriageable, I can get away with a certain number of unseemly questions without doing any further damage to my reputation. I know that Lord Tynthanal would very much prefer to marry you than me."

Chanlix almost gasped, although perhaps it should not have come as so much of a surprise. She and Tynthanal had hardly made a secret of their relationship. It was not, however, a subject that would ordinarily be mentioned to Tynthanal's prospective bride, despite the expectation that she both tolerate and ignore any relations he had with other women, even once they were married.

It might be politically expedient for Chanlix to deny the relationship between herself and Tynthanal. After all, despite the expectation that a bride ignore infidelities, it was not unheard of for a bride's father to take offense at this insult to her sensibilities. But there seemed little chance Kailee would believe the denial, even if Chanlix could have forced herself to utter one.

Chanlix cleared her throat and fidgeted, unable to think of a single thing to say.

"Please don't be offended," Kailee begged, apparently misinterpreting Chanlix's silence. "I know it is my duty as a woman to pretend ignorance, and I certainly don't mean to shame you or complain. I just . . ." She sighed and lowered her head. "I am hoping that your love for each other is not interfering with your attempts to treat his condition," she finished softly.

Chanlix took a deep breath to steady herself. Everything within her revolted at the idea of discussing her relationship with Tynthanal with the girl he was supposed to marry. She was far from prim and proper herself, but it seemed . . . cruel to rub Kailee's face in it. And yet she seemed to have little choice.

"I assure you," Chanlix said, "we are trying our hardest to find a cure. I am not an especially gifted spell crafter myself, but Princess Alysoon is one of the most naturally talented crafters I've ever known. If anyone can produce a cure, it will be her. And I can personally attest that Tynthanal has drunk every potion she has given him. I won't say he has done it with any great enthusiasm, but we both understand that he is not free to marry at will. And if he must marry another," Chanlix finished impulsively, "you would be just the sort of woman I would choose for him. He would not fare well with a . . . more conventional bride."

To her surprise, Kailee laughed lightly. "'Unconventional' is one of the kindest descriptions I've ever heard used for me," she said. The smile quickly faded, and once again Chanlix felt as if she were being closely watched. "I want you to understand that what *I* want from this marriage is not what my father and my stepmother want. I have never aspired to a 'normal' woman's life as they see it. All I want is to live free from fear that I will be sent to the Abbey or hidden away from public view. The only way I can have what I want is to marry Tynthanal, but it is not *him* I want. I need the marriage because it is my only chance to remain in Women's Well, where I will not be shunned for my open Mindseye. I will not complain or be hurt or insulted if you and Tynthanal continue to love each other once we are married."

Chanlix wondered if Kailee would still feel the same way after the wedding, if it ever happened, but she knew better than to argue. Kailee's willingness to accept a loveless marriage made Chanlix's heart ache for her. "You deserve better."

"So do you," Kailee answered without hesitation. "And though I've barely spoken with him since I've arrived, I'll venture a guess that so does Tynthanal. But if we cannot get what we deserve, perhaps we can all get at least some of what we want."

"I promise we are all doing the best we can to create a cure."

"I believe you," Kailee assured her. "But I would like to propose tilting the scales further in our favor."

Chanlix raised an eyebrow, well aware Kailee could not see her expression. "And how do you propose to do that?"

"Do you agree that it is best for everyone involved if this marriage happens?"

It was certainly best for the people of Women's Well, and Chanlix could see that it was best for Kailee, as well. Sometimes what was best for everyone still wasn't good enough, but there was no point in railing against it when the other options held so little appeal. "Yes."

"Then I propose we not rest all our hopes on a fertility potion that may or may not be effective. I have little knowledge of how these things work, but I hope it is possible to falsify the results of a bloodline test."

This time, Chanlix could not keep her gasp of surprise contained. "You would marry Tynthanal even if he could not give you children?"

Kailee shrugged. "I told you exactly what I need from this marriage. I need all the official trappings—the legal papers and the protections and treaties that will make it appealing to my father—but I don't need a true husband. Even if one of your potions works, I'd prefer not to lie with a man who loves another."

"B-but . . . surely you want children someday?" It was true that not *all* women wanted children—no matter what "conventional wisdom" might claim—but for reasons she couldn't put her finger on, Kailee didn't strike her as one of them.

"I do," Kailee affirmed. "But it need not be right away. And—" She cut herself off abruptly.

"And what?"

Kailee clenched her hands together in her lap and didn't reply, for the first time looking as uncomfortable with the conversation as Chanlix had felt since the beginning. Which made it easy for Chanlix to follow her thought to its logical conclusion.

"And it need not be Tynthanal's?" she asked gently.

Kailee blushed and did not respond, but it was clear that was exactly what she'd meant. "Can the bloodline test be falsified?" she asked instead.

Chanlix smiled ruefully. "I could use an illusion spell to hide the true results, but I suspect that with the import of this particular marriage, your father—and perhaps even Queen Ellinsoltah—will politely request to have the results verified in Rhozinolm. Even the most powerful illusions we can conjure here wear off eventually."

Kailee nodded. "Which means you will need me to switch the sample before it is sent off to Rhozinolm for its second test. I'm sure you can obtain a blood sample from another man, one that will give us the test results we need."

Chanlix could scarcely believe they were having this conversation—or that Kailee would go to such extraordinary lengths to ensure her marriage to Tynthanal. "You would do that?"

"If it would allow me to stay here? Absolutely. It would still be best, naturally, if one of your potions works. There would certainly be risk involved in trying to switch the samples."

A chill went through Chanlix thinking about just how disastrous it would be if they were caught trying to falsify the results. As kindly disposed as Queen Ellinsoltah might be toward Women's Well, she could hardly help but take the gravest possible exception to such deceit.

"But that risk would be worth taking, for all our sakes, wouldn't you say?" Kailee asked.

Chanlix could not help but agree.

Princess Alysoon understandably had a full social calendar on top of all her official duties, and Shelvon had debated whether to request an audience at the town hall or attempt to find a more informal setting during which to talk to the sovereign princess. Having never thought herself particularly skilled at the art of court maneuvering, Shelvon had settled on an official audience, and been granted one almost immediately.

She curtsied deeply as soon as she was shown into Alysoon's office, her heart hammering in her throat. "Your Royal Highness," she said in greeting, hoping her nerves did not show in her face or voice, though she feared that might be the case.

"Come in, Shelvon," Alysoon said with a welcoming smile that Shelvon read as entirely sincere.

For as long as she had lived in Women's Well, Shelvon had studied her former sister-in-law's face for any sign that she might have overstayed her welcome. Now, she also looked for hints that her father had made good on his threat and demanded Alysoon send her "home."

But Alysoon seemed pleased to see her, crossing the room and even offering a quick and obviously affectionate embrace. Shelvon had to resist the urge to cling, for she had known very little true affection over the course of her life.

Alysoon's smile faded when she pulled away. "Is something wrong?" she asked.

Shelvon forced a smile and tried to shake off her sense of foreboding. If the sovereign princess were thinking of shipping her back to Nandel, surely some sign of that would show in her bearing or tone.

"No, ma'am," Shelvon said. "Everything's fine."

"How many times have I asked you to call me Alys when we're in private?" the sovereign princess scolded gently. "You are my sister in my heart, and that has nothing to do with your marriage to Delnamal."

Some of the tension left Shelvon's shoulders. Sometimes, it was impossible to imagine that the princess could be as kindly disposed to Shelvon as it seemed. Even knowing that she had had no choice in marrying Delnamal, Shelvon herself felt guilty and tarnished by the association. How could Alys look past that with such ease?

And yet, although Shelvon was sure Alys was more than capable of deception, she found herself believing her.

"Thank you, ma'am—" Shelvon cleared her throat. "Thank you, Alys."

Alys smiled at her once more, then frowned slightly as she glanced around her office, which was very clearly laid out for formal discussions of business, not social interactions. The only places to sit were the chairs around the desk. Instead of retreating to the comfort of her usual chair behind the desk, Alys turned the two chairs in front of it to face each other, then sat in one and indicated Shelvon should take the other.

"I gather you're here for some official business," Alys said, "because *surely* you know that you can call on me socially." She gave a self-deprecating shrug. "Within the natural constraints of my schedule, of course."

"Yes, of course," Shelvon said, though she was pretty sure she was blushing. Even when she'd been the Queen of Aaltah, Shelvon had never felt comfortable presuming to call on people socially. She was about as unsocial a creature as existed, her tongue always tied in knots. She was well aware that the people of Aaltah considered Nandelites to be little more than barbarians, and everything about her— from her blond hair to the guttural accent she had never managed to shake to her skin that was noticeably pale even when tanned by the sun—screamed her Nandel heritage.

Shelvon shifted uncomfortably and tried for a rueful smile. "You may be aware that social engagements have never been my strong suit."

"I'm well aware that others have made you feel that way," Alys replied staunchly. "But I like to think that you and I have gotten on just fine in the past." She leaned forward and put her hand on top of Shelvon's, giving it a squeeze. "You can call on me, Shelvon. Whenever you like."

Shelvon feared she might burst into tears, for it was true that Alys had never treated her like a barbarian, nor had she seemed annoyed by her former sister-in-law's awkward and halting conversational skills. Shelvon would do anything necessary to cement her place here in Women's Well, because the idea of being sent back to Nandel was unthinkable. Despite her fears, despite her discomfort with her confusing social status, despite her uncertainty over what her future would bring, Shelvon was happier adrift here in Women's Well than she had ever been before in her life, and she would not give it up without a fight.

"Thank you, Alys," she said again. "But I do actually have official business to discuss, so scheduling an audience seemed appropriate."

Alys nodded and leaned back in her chair. "Very well, then. What official business shall we talk about?"

Shelvon bit her lip, aware that the request she wished to make was wildly improper. So much so that she couldn't force herself to blurt it out without preamble. "There have been quite a number of weddings here in Women's Well since we declared our independence," she ventured.

Alys cocked her head, her gaze intensifying. Shelvon suspected the sovereign princess quickly saw where Shelvon intended to lead this conversation.

"Indeed there have," Alysoon said, but she made no other comment. She might have already guessed what Shelvon was going to ask, but she apparently did not intend to ease the way for her.

"Even women who were once abigails have married," Shelvon continued.

The corner of Alysoon's mouth twitched in a smile that was quickly suppressed. "To perfectly respectable gentlemen, no less. It seems that without an abbey to confine them and hide them from the eyes of the world, many of the women who were once considered Unwanted have found they are very much wanted after all."

"Some of those women have been married before."

This time, Alysoon couldn't suppress the smile. "I know the concept of a woman remarrying after a divorce is terribly foreign to much of the world, but men have been doing it for a very long time. Frankly, it's never made much sense to me that the same was not true for women."

And yet the idea had not even occurred to Shelvon until that first wedding. All her life, she'd been taught that if a man divorced a woman, she was fully to blame for the disgrace and that no one else would even consider marrying her. The Abbey had been a terrible specter, but it had also been the only place she could imagine a divorced woman living—until she had come to Women's Well and seen another way.

"So, do you think . . . ?" For all her determination, Shelvon found she could not finish the question.

"That you might remarry?" Alys finished for her.

Shelvon didn't dare meet the sovereign princess's eyes as she nodded, her hands bunching in her skirts with anxiety. Her palms were sweating, and she hoped she wouldn't leave embarrassing wet spots in the fabric.

"I see no reason why not," Alys said, her voice still soft, as if she were afraid Shelvon might bolt if she spoke too loudly. "If you *wish* to remarry, that is. I cannot imagine marriage to Delnamal would make you overly inclined toward the institution."

Shelvon grimaced, for Alys spoke no more than the truth. Her marriage to Delnamal had been miserable from the beginning, although she was keenly aware that other women were mistreated more than she had ever been. The idea of subjecting herself to a man's attentions once more—especially in the marriage bed—was far from appealing. However, being sent back to Nandel was even less appealing, and a marriage might save her from that fate. After all, if she were to marry again, her father would no longer see her as his own property but as her husband's. Assuming he would accept a second marriage as legitimate, but that was a whole other question.

"If my choices are to be an abigail or a wife, I would prefer to be a wife," she said, but the sovereign princess frowned at her.

"Who says you have to be either one?"

Shelvon shrugged, reluctant to tell Alysoon the real reason for her sudden determination to remarry. "What other role is there for a woman in this life?" she asked. "I cannot simply go on as I have been."

"Whyever not?" Alysoon asked with what seemed like genuine puzzlement. "You have a right to a life of your own, one that you build for yourself. You need not shackle yourself to a husband you don't want. You are no longer a child who must marry at her father's say-so. You are more like a widow, who can choose to remarry or not as she pleases." Alys curled her lip. "Would that you were a widow in reality."

As a widow herself, Alysoon had so far seen no need to remarry, and Shelvon had not heard the slightest hint that such a thing was even under consideration. But then the sovereign princess was a good deal older than Shelvon and would not face the same societal pressure to marry, even when her mourning for her daughter was done.

Not that societal pressure had anything to do with Shelvon's need to find a husband. Realizing that Alysoon would likely not be inclined to help arrange a marriage she was convinced Shelvon did not want or need, Shelvon had no choice but to tell the truth.

Shivering inside at the memory of her father's letter, she shored up what courage she could find and met the sovereign princess's gaze. "My father has demanded I return to Nandel. He says that is my proper place now that I no longer have a husband, and by Nandel law he has every right to compel me."

To her surprise, Alys laughed. "You are not in Nandel, my dear. I don't see why you should be subject to Nandel law."

"My father sees things differently. I am his property, and he wishes to have his property returned. He has no reason to think I would not immediately obey his command, but even so he hinted that if I do not come back voluntarily, he will make demands of *you*."

Alysoon looked unimpressed by the threat. "He can make whatever demands he wishes," she said. "I would not give you up for all the precious gems and metals he can produce."

Shelvon had no doubt Alysoon meant what she said. But though Women's Well was so far managing to keep its coffers full through the sale of the unique magic it could produce, the fact remained that their tiny principality had frighteningly little in the way of natural resources. The life-giving magic of the Well was slowly turning the land fruitful, but it did not give rise to sudden iron or gem deposits. And so far, Alysoon had no trade agreements that would bring in such necessities, for Nandel was the primary source of iron and gems for all of Seven Wells. The only other place in Seven Wells where iron and gems were produced was Khalpar, and Khalpar was unlikely to trade with Women's Well when King Khalvin's nephew was the King of Aaltah.

"If I remarried," Shelvon said, "then my father might not demand my return at all. He certainly doesn't want me to come home because of his abiding affection for me. It's an affront to his pride that his divorced daughter is out in public instead of hidden away in an abbey. I doubt he would approve my remarriage, but if I had a husband, he would feel less compelled to force me to return to Nandel."

Alysoon shook her head. "He *can't* force you to return. I will not allow it, and he's certainly not going to march on Women's Well over the offense."

For all of Nandel's warlike reputation, the sovereign princes of Nandel had never attempted wars of conquest, content to fiercely protect their mountainous territory from all would-be invaders.

"Be that as it may, you can avoid any potential conflicts with Nandel by marrying me off."

Alysoon sat up straighter in her chair, and there was a sudden hint of indignation in her eyes. "I am not *marrying you off*! If you find a man whom you would like to marry and who is amenable, then by all means petition me for permission, as is customary for any citizen of such standing as yours. But you are a grown woman, and your life is your own. It is not for me to force you to marry whomever I choose, and it is not for your father to demand your return to Nandel."

"But—"

"The answer is no," Alysoon said firmly. "If your father wants to make an issue of it, he can take it up with me."

Shelvon wasn't entirely certain if the fluttering sensation in her breast was from disappointment at having been turned down or relief. She could hardly claim to be eager for remarriage. But she also knew her father in ways that Princess Alysoon could not. Once he realized that his disgraced daughter was rebelling against his command, getting her back to Nandel would become a matter of some urgency for the sake of his manly pride. And Sovereign Prince Waldmir was not one to suffer insults to his pride without making the offender pay dearly.

CHAPTER TWENTY-FIVE

Chanlix put her arms around Tynthanal and hugged him tight. He remained stiff for the duration of a few heartbeats, then sighed heavily and returned the embrace.

"I hate this," he said softly, and there was a wealth of anguish in his words. Chanlix had never fully appreciated how much he'd been pinning his hopes on the fertility potions failing—until she'd told him of Kailee's offer and taken away his only excuse not to go through with the marriage.

"I know you do," she said soothingly, "but please try to look at the larger picture. We will secure an alliance that Rhozinolm cannot easily withdraw from, and we can love each other with Kailee's blessing. She is happy to cede the physical and emotional bonds of matrimony to us as long as the marriage gives her the chance to remain in Women's Well. We each get what we want from the arrangement."

Tynthanal stiffened again in her arms, and Chanlix cursed herself for not thinking her words through before she spoke them. He had made it very clear he was *not* getting what he wanted, and she was well aware that her acceptance of the arrangement hurt him. Sometimes, she sympathized with his pain. And sometimes, she felt exasperated that the legal trappings of marriage meant so much to him.

She pulled back and looked into his eyes, willing him to let go of his stubborn need to make her into his definition of a respectable woman. For all that he had never scorned her for her past, his insistence on marriage made her wonder if he was as accepting as he seemed to be.

Tynthanal reached up and stroked her cheek, the caress so tender it sent a shiver through her whole body. His touch never failed to move her.

"Kailee might be willing to accept our relationship," he said softly, "but don't allow yourself to believe the marriage won't change things for us. We will not be free to have each other whenever we want, and we will have to keep up appearances to avoid undue scandal."

It was all Chanlix could do not to roll her eyes. "The gentry of Women's Well—what there is of it—has better things to do than wallow in salacious gossip. I grant you we will need to be more discreet than we have been—especially if one of those potions finally works and you get me with child—but I'm not suddenly going to wither away in shame at being your mistress, and Kailee does not need to be protected from some distressing truth."

"Are you sure you still want me to drink the potions?" he asked. "If it is no longer strictly necessary to make the marriage happen . . ."

Chanlix hesitated before answering, gaining control of her impulse to snap at him, for she'd made it clear from the beginning that she wanted his child even if she could not marry him. "Yes, I want you to keep drinking the potions," she said, hoping her exasperation didn't show in her voice. "It will be easier for all if we don't have to fake the results of the bloodline test, for one thing. And for another, I still want your child. We've been over this."

He nodded, his eyes troubled and sad. "Maybe we have. But I don't think having a child out of wedlock will be as easy for you as you believe. Women's Well may not be like the rest of the world, but we are not wholly removed, either. A woman with a child and no husband will not face an easy path."

Chanlix smiled and shook her head. "And when has my path ever been easy?" She chuckled. "Frankly, I don't think I'd know what to do with easy if I ever faced it." She reached out to squeeze his hand. "I will face whatever adversity there is to come, and I promise you it will not break me. So tonight, you will drink another potion and make love with me. And tomorrow, you will put in an official offer for Kailee's hand."

He grunted an unconvincing agreement, and Chanlix worried that if one of the potions should finally work, she would have yet another argument on her hands. It had been clear to her from the beginning that he himself did not have any particular desire to have a child— whether because he'd gotten so used to the idea that he couldn't or for other reasons, she didn't know. He would drink the fertility potions and try his best to give her a child only because he knew *she* wanted it. For the first time, she wondered if it was fair of her to ask this of him, if her desire to have a child superseded his desire *not* to have one.

It was an unsettling thought, and one she vowed to revisit if one of the potions worked.

Ellin hadn't fully appreciated how heavily she'd come to rely on Zarsha as a friend until *he* became the source of her troubles and she had no one to confide in. Once upon a time, she'd had a large circle of friends, girls of an age who laughed and gossiped with one another as they attended the myriad social events that consumed the highest-ranking nobility in Rhozinolm. They had whispered conversations in corners and secret gatherings in abandoned hallways, supporting one another and even crying on one another's shoulders when life was at its most unkind.

But one by one those young ladies of Ellin's acquaintance had been married off, and though some of them still lived in the capital city of Zinolm Well, the natural process of drifting apart had already begun even before Ellin became queen. Which meant that now she had no one to help her make sense of everything Zarsha had told her, no one to help her find reason within the storm of emotion his confession had stirred in her.

For three days, she'd managed—for the most part, at least—to keep herself so busy and distracted that the only time she thought about her heartache was when she laid her head on her pillow each night. It helped that Zarsha made himself scarce, considerately giving her time and space. Just as it helped that the marriage negotiations were currently at an impasse, though she would have to decide soon whether to prod Kailindar into making another overture.

But the moment she'd set eyes on him at the night's gala ball—an event the special ambassador from Nandel could hardly be expected to miss—she'd lost her equilibrium. She'd put her foot in her mouth more than once, and her attention had wandered dangerously. She'd finally decided that for once, she would allow herself to bow out a little early, no matter how undiplomatic her exit might seem.

Star's eyes were full of concern. "Are you feeling ill, Your Majesty?" she asked. "I can send for a tonic if you'd like."

Ellin forced a smile. "No, no. I'm fine. I'm just tired tonight." Her yawn was as forced as the smile, and it was instantly clear Star was unconvinced. Hoping she could avoid any further questioning, Ellin quickly exited the sitting room and headed for the dressing room so that Star could begin the long process of preparing her for bed.

Of course the hasty exit gave Star further reason to believe something was wrong.

"I've known you for a long time," Star said as she began unpinning her bodice. "You are quite adept at hiding your feelings from others, but you can't hide them as easily from me." Star's attention seemed entirely focused on her work as she spoke, and Ellin ordered herself not to be fooled by the evident lack of scrutiny. Star could read her reactions perfectly well without having to peer into her face. Ellin was actually surprised that Star hadn't noticed her turmoil over the last few days.

"I'm fine, Star. Really." But even she could hear the faint rasp in her voice that made a liar out of her.

Star laid aside a length of lacy trim she had removed from the bodice. Still she made no attempt at eye contact as her deft fingers removed even more pins. "I know there are things you can't talk to me about." She frowned. "*Many* things. But you know I can be trusted with secrets."

That was certainly true, for Star had actively helped Ellin arrange her trysts with Graesan, and Ellin had never once worried that her secret would be betrayed.

Ellin gave her lady's maid a wan smile as Star finally finished detaching the bodice and set it aside. "I would trust you implicitly with my own secrets," Ellin said. "But some secrets aren't mine to share."

This secret was definitely one of the latter. No matter how angry she might be with Zarsha.

Star patted her shoulder affectionately, then began unlacing her stays. "You can tell me about it without sharing details. Something's been eating at you for days. I didn't ask because I assumed it was affairs of state that troubled you. But I recognize that look on your face tonight. If Zarsha has hurt you somehow, I can assure you he will still bear the signs of my wrath when he is old and toothless. If I allow him to live that long."

Ellin swallowed a laugh, even as she winced at the thought that she was so transparent.

"Don't worry," Star soothed. "I can only see it because I know you so well. The men of your court likely haven't noticed anything's wrong, much less attributed your troubles to Zarsha of Nandel."

"So you mean to tell me I have a particular expression on my face reserved entirely for the troubles Zarsha causes me?"

Star gave her a droll look. "Let's just say I know troubles of the heart when I see them."

"Zarsha has no claim to my heart," she protested too quickly, insisting to herself that it was true.

"Yours may not be a classic romance, but I can plainly see you've given him at least a sliver of your heart over the course of your acquaintance. And I'd say that was only right and proper, seeing as he's the man you're going to marry."

Ellin shook her head. "That may no longer be the case."

The stays came free, allowing Ellin to draw in a deliciously deep breath. She closed her eyes and put her hand on her belly, concentrating on filling her lungs and finding her composure. Star respected her need for quiet, stifling the curiosity that no doubt had her burning to ask questions. Instead, she carefully removed Ellin's skirts and underskirts, leaving her dressed in only her chemise.

Star slipped a robe over her shoulders, and Ellin obediently slid her arms into the sleeves, shivering slightly as the cool silk settled over her skin. Her composure was still deeply hidden, but Ellin opened her eyes anyway and took her seat before the dressing table so that Star could begin working on her hair.

"Is it an affair of state that has you questioning your future with Zarsha?" Star asked, removing the headdress and snood that had covered Ellin's hair for the evening. "Or is it something more personal?"

"You are very persistent," Ellin grumbled, sure Star already knew the answer to her own question.

Star laid her hands gently on Ellin's shoulders, and their eyes met in the mirror. "You are very dear to me, and I don't care if it's improper for me to say so. I can see that you're hurting, and I can't pretend not to."

To Ellin's surprise, there was a sheen of tears in Star's eyes. Her heart squeezed with affection for her maid, who had at times during her youth served almost as a surrogate mother, when Ellin's own mother had lacked sympathy for her daughter's heartaches. Not that Star would be flattered by such a statement, as she was nowhere near old enough to be Ellin's mother.

Ellin reached up and covered one of Star's hands with her own. "You are one of the most kindhearted people I've ever known," she said, her own voice growing hoarse with tears she refused to shed. "I can't tell you what happened between Zarsha and me, but I learned something about him that I'm having a hard time swallowing."

Star began unpinning her hair, perhaps hoping the semblance of normalcy would calm both their emotions. Then she asked exactly the question Ellin least wanted to face.

"And if he had no claim on your heart, as you said, would whatever you've learned be hurting you quite so much?"

A hint of a sob rose from somewhere deep in Ellin's throat, and it took all her will to keep it contained. She knew Star would think no less of her if she broke down and cried—it wouldn't have been the first time Star had comforted her through a bout of tears—but she refused to let Zarsha have that kind of power over her.

"Maybe not," she rasped. "But he has made it abundantly clear only a fool would trust him with her heart. I refuse to be a fool!"

Ellin wanted to scream in frustration, as much with herself as with Zarsha. It was *ridiculous* of her to be heartsick over a relationship Zarsha had had in the past, even if that relationship had produced a child. Did she really expect a man of his age to be the male equivalent of a virgin bride? And it wasn't as if she'd believed him when he'd claimed to love her.

"I can't pretend to be an expert on the subject," Star said as she began brushing Ellin's hair, "but from what I can see, love makes fools of us all, men and women alike. You can't have all the pleasures of love without risking its pains."

Ellin crossed her arms. "I've had my fill of the pains already."

In the mirror, she saw Star shrug. "Did you prefer it when you were contracted to marry him against your will?"

"Of course not!"

"So you would prefer a husband to whom you might give your heart. Which means you must risk *giving* your heart if you are to have the kind of marriage you want."

Ellin avoided looking at herself in the mirror, not wishing to see the sour expression she no doubt wore. "Or maybe my father was right all along, and I should regard my marriage as nothing more than an affair of state and leave romantic fantasies to those with better taste in men."

"Just because things didn't work out with Graesan doesn't mean you should give up on romance entirely. I wasn't surprised that you outgrew Graesan, but Zarsha I thought was in every way your equal."

"I didn't *outgrow* Graesan," Ellin said peevishly.

"He was a sweet young man who doted on you and showed you affection when few others in your life did. But he did not have the keen mind and imagination and courage you need in a husband. Zarsha has all of those things."

"And the sordid past to go with it."

"Says the queen who was sleeping with her secretary."

Ellin scowled, but it was hard to argue Star's point. Not that that stopped her from trying anyway. "Zarsha knew about my past, but I didn't know about his."

"He knew about it because you told him in the spirit of honesty so that you would not go to your marriage with secrets?" Star asked with false innocence.

Ellin ground her teeth, for of course she *hadn't* told him about her affair with Graesan. He had somehow learned of it on his own, and he had never once thrown it in her face. Then again, she and Graesan hadn't had a *child*.

"My point is," Star continued, "that if you're going to insist your husband be perfect, you will go to your deathbed a spinster. You have to know there are few men who would be suitable husbands for the Queen of Rhozinolm. Perhaps you should take another look at Zarsha's actions with that perspective in mind. You have choices now you would not have had a year ago, but they are not unlimited. Zarsha may have hurt you, but he's also been a friend, and a loyal one at that."

Ellin heaved a sigh, for of course Star was right. Her choices were few, and if not for Zarsha's help and friendship, she might have ended up forcibly married to her cousin Tamzin. It was not reasonable of her to be so angry or so hurt.

A little of the tension eased out of her as she decided that just this once, she didn't *have* to be reasonable. Maybe tomorrow, or the next day, or even next week, she would set aside her childish hurt feelings and focus on her responsibilities as a queen. But for now, in the privacy of her own dressing room with only Star to witness it, she would indulge in a good, old-fashioned sulk. And she would *not* feel guilty about it.

Lady Vondelmai had insisted upon overseeing the bloodline test that Chanlix was tasked with performing, but it was clear she had done so out of a sense of duty to her stepdaughter and not due to her eagerness to act as witness. She could not be any more obvious about her discomfort with the practice of women's magic had she tried. Her whole body was stiff, her arms crossed over her chest and her shoulders hunched as if she was trying to protect herself from some taint that hovered in the Academy's air. Chanlix would have been amused at the lady's prudishness had it not been for the tension that roiled in her gut.

She was perfectly confident in the illusion spell with which she infused the vial that would be used for testing, but she was a great deal less confident in Kailee's ability to switch out the second sample that Lady Vondelmai meant to send on to Rhozinolm via flier for confirmation of the first test. The girl claimed she could do it, but it seemed a tricky endeavor for any girl who was not a practiced pickpocket—much less one who could not see.

Then there was the pressure of Tynthanal's rigid and poorly disguised unhappiness. He made a gallant effort to speak warmly to Kailee despite his turmoil, but Lady Vondelmai apparently feared her stepdaughter would say something inappropriate and spoke over her at every opportunity. Which did no one's nerves any good, although Kailee endured it with good-natured aplomb, no doubt used to it.

Hoping to get the procedure over with as quickly as possible, Chanlix beckoned for Kailee to give her her hand. For a moment, it looked like Lady Vondelmai was going to remonstrate, as if the thought of a former abigail touching her stepdaughter would somehow sully her, but she held her peace.

Kailee obediently held out her hand—drawing yet another scowl from Vondelmai, who had to notice that her blind stepdaughter had seen the gesture thanks to the halo of Rho that surrounded Chanlix's hand—and Chanlix pricked her finger. Kailee neither winced nor made any sound of discomfort as Chanlix squeezed a drop of her blood first into one vial, then into the second.

Despite his departure from the military, Tynthanal continued to perform the sword drills that had been part of his daily ritual since adolescence. His callused hands were reluctant to give up the needed blood—and Chanlix was too squeamish to poke him very hard—so he took the needle from her hand and jabbed himself with more force than necessary to get the blood flowing. His blood mingled with Kailee's in first one vial, then the other. He held one of those vials out to Vondelmai and one to Chanlix. Vondelmai wrapped her vial in a handkerchief for safekeeping.

Chanlix withdrew a couple of drops of bloodline testing potion from a bottle, then opened her Mindseye to add the Rho needed to complete the spell. She heard Vondelmai fidgeting with the vial and the handkerchief, taking a needlessly long time to secure them so that she need not see Chanlix with her Mindseye open.

Chanlix suppressed a smile, for she'd been mildly concerned that Lady Vondelmai might notice her reaching for more than one mote of Rho so that she could activate the illusion spell in the vial at the same time as she activated the bloodline spell. Closing her Mindseye, she swirled the potion and the blood around in the clear vial.

Like all the members of Alysoon's royal council, Chanlix at all times wore a ring with an active illusion-shield spell in it—it seemed a wise precaution in a land where new illusion spells were developed at such a rapid pace—and so she did not expect to see her illusion work. She fully expected that both she and Tynthanal would see the fluid in the vial remain the stubborn shade of watery red that said the two bloodlines could not form healthy children together, which meant that she had to watch Vondelmai to see when the illusion took effect.

At Vondelmai's brisk nod, Chanlix looked at the vial in her hand once more—and almost dropped it. Across the desk from her, Tynthanal's face lost a touch of its healthy color, and his eyes widened.

Sucking in a deep breath—and trying for all she was worth to keep her shock from showing on her face—Chanlix stared at the vial full of milky white fluid.

"I will send the second sample to Rhozinolm immediately," Lady Vondelmai said. Chanlix had the impression the woman would have been just as happy to forego the second test and have the wedding before the day was out. Mostly because she herself was so eager to leave Women's Well and return to the world that she knew in Rhozinolm. There was certainly no evidence that she would miss her stepdaughter.

Chanlix felt the weight of Kailee's eyes on her from behind her veil and had to remind herself that the girl could not see her face or read her expression. However, Kailee likely *could* read the results of the test, for the mingling of those blood samples and the bloodline spell would have created a small burst of Rho, indicative of the potential for new life.

Kailee's joy was plain to see, as was Tynthanal's dismay, but Lady Vondelmai was too self-centered to notice the rioting emotions of those around her. She quickly steered her stepdaughter out of the office, no doubt in a hurry to retreat from the den of iniquity, leaving Chanlix and Tynthanal alone together.

Without a word, Chanlix opened her Mindseye once more, glancing at her illusion-dispelling ring to make certain its spell was active.

It was.

Then for good measure, she deactivated the illusion spell in the vial by removing its Rho. She was not surprised when she opened her eyes to see that the liquid in the vial was still white.

All this time, she had assumed her bloodline tests with Tynthanal had failed because of *his* condition; never once had she considered that she herself might be the problem. Tears burned her eyes, and her throat closed so tight she could barely speak. She blinked rapidly and tried not to let her devastation show in her voice.

"It seems you weren't the only reason our bloodline tests failed," she said, then had to swallow hard to keep from crying. "Perhaps I am too old already to bring a healthy new life into this world." Her monthlies were still regular, but there was no question that she was of an age when children were harder to conceive. Or perhaps she had been barren all her life.

Tynthanal looked at her with great tenderness and sympathy. He rose from his chair and came around her desk, drawing her to her feet and into an embrace. She clung to him, breathing in his comforting scent while refusing to allow her tears to spill forth. "I'm so sorry, dearest," he murmured into her hair.

There was a small, mean part of her that questioned just how sorry he really was—it was clear that he hadn't much wanted the bastard child she'd been so yearning to give him—but even in her pain, she kept that nasty voice silent. And she reminded herself once again that she was the Grand Magus of Women's Well, that she loved and was loved by a man whom she never could have dreamed of being worthy of while she'd toiled in the Abbey of Aaltah. In the grand scheme of things, despite her disappointment, Chanlix had very little to complain about.

But for once, that very reasonable argument did little to ease her soul.

CHAPTER TWENTY-SIX

More than once on the journey to Women's Well, Mairah had cursed King Khalvin's impatience. She had not traveled outside the city of Khalwell since she was thirteen, and even then it had only been a brief jaunt to a cousin's estate, a mere three days' travel from home. She had never even *seen* the sea except in paintings and books, much less gotten onto a ship and traveled across it. Never could she have guessed how much she would love the experience, how deeply she would savor standing on the deck while the ship cut through the waves, the wind whipping through her robes as she breathed deep of the salt air and watched the gulls float above them in escort.

She wanted that journey to last forever, despite her need to quaff potions against seasickness with every meal. Norah looked positively green even with the potions and spent almost the entire trip prostrate in bed, but perhaps that was just an excuse to stay as far away from Mairah as possible. The enforced proximity of their travel was hardly improving relations between them, and Mairah was certain that

Norah dreamed of shoving her overboard. Which was why she made sure to remind the other woman nearly every day that she had plans in place to get her revenge should anything happen to her. She did *not* tell Norah that her plan was based on having already told the lord high priest about the Mother of All worshippers in the Abbey. She trusted Jalzarnin to avenge her should anything happen, but she did not want to deal with Norah's hysterics if she learned her secret had already been revealed.

As much as Mairah enjoyed the sea journey, it came to an end far too quickly, for the king had sent them on a magic-powered cutter that made the eight-hundred-mile journey in about six days. A lumbering cargo vessel would have suited her better, but the king had insisted she travel with all possible haste. He had not spoken to her personally, of course, but he had had Jalzarnin warn her that she would have only one month in Women's Well to find a cure for the Curse. If she failed, she would no longer be the Abbess of Khalpar.

She tried not to dwell on what would happen if she failed. She would still have ample blackmail to keep Norah and her friends from preying on her as they once had, but she didn't see how she could bear to go back to life as an abigail. In fact, if the deadline approached and she did not believe she could succeed, she might very well try to plot an escape, though the thought never failed to send a shiver of panic through her. She had no money, nor had she ever had to fend for herself, especially not in a foreign land. If she managed to escape the guards that watched her with suspicion even when she was trapped on the ship, where would she go? She *had* to succeed.

Regretfully disembarking in Grunir, Mairah and Norah had been immediately bundled into a rickety covered wagon hitched to a pair of ragged-looking chevals. The chevals were obviously intended for cargo rather than passengers. Even the cheapest chevals for carriages had at least some rudimentary decoration and were kept mended and in good repair. These two were nothing but wood and metal frames loosely covered by odds and ends of leather that was worn through in spots. Mairah gazed with longing at the much more comfortable and elegant carriage that had been reserved for Solvineld Rah-Solvin, who had been sent by the king as an official envoy to Women's Well.

It was Solvineld's responsibility to ensure that Women's Well allowed them to cross its borders, and a man of his wealth and stature could hardly be expected to ride in a cargo wagon.

As ugly as the chevals were, they were fast, dragging the wagon through the rutted streets at a pace that threatened to shake Mairah's flesh off her bones. The men of her escort had clearly experienced cheval rides of such speed before, for they braced themselves easily on the hard benches and looked unperturbed, whereas she and Norah clung to their seats with white-knuckled hands. There were no windows to look out of, and Mairah's perch on the bench felt too precarious to allow her to lean forward and see out the back of the wagon. She'd been under no illusion that she was going on a sightseeing tour, but she still would have liked to have seen more of Grunir than its harbor. She wondered if Solvineld's carriage had been spelled to ease the bumpy ride, but answered her own question immediately. He was no doubt reclining in comfort and ease while she and Norah—and their guards, who had probably been sent as some kind of punishment duty—suffered.

So great was the king's desire to have the Curse reversed that he had ordered the escort to travel straight from the harbor to Women's Well without a stop for the night—which was why he'd chosen to spend the money on chevals, which could travel indefinitely as long as they were supplied with a steady stream of Rho.

Mairah had spent many a miserable night during her life as an abigail, but none so miserable as that single night of travel by wagon. Powered by magic, the chevals were sure-footed enough to run full speed through the darkness. They would go around any ruts or holes in the road that might cause damage to themselves or to the wagon they pulled, but since they were designed for cargo—and sturdy cargo at that—they had no care for the comfort and safety of their passengers. The wagon jolted and juddered and bounced ceaselessly, and anytime Mairah made the mistake of relaxing or starting to doze, she paid for it with a new bruise or scratch. They stopped only for brief rests to stretch their legs and relieve themselves or grab a quick bite to eat.

The sun was just beginning to peek over the horizon when the wagon clattered over a wooden bridge, and about a quarter hour after that, the wagon slowed and then finally stopped. Mairah could not see what was going on outside, but she heard the whinny of real horses, and then a deep male voice called out in Continental. Mairah had been taught basic Continental as a girl—facility with the most commonly spoken language in Seven Wells being a mainstay of any young Khalpari's upbringing—but she'd never had a great ear for it, and having not spoken or heard it in more than a decade, she could not understand a word that was being said, even if she understood the gist of it. They were being challenged at the Women's Well border, just as they had expected.

Outside, she could hear Solvineld descending from his comfortable carriage.

"We have business with your sovereign princess," Solvineld called in Parian, and Mairah winced. Solvineld was fluent in Continental—else he would be a pathetic excuse for an envoy—and his insistence on speaking his own tongue was a none-too-subtle insult. He was tasked with smoothing the way for Mairah and Norah to enter Women's Well to fulfill their mission, but this was hardly an auspicious beginning.

"Is that so?" the soldier asked in passable Parian—no doubt disappointing Solvineld. "May I inquire as to your name and the nature of your business?"

Solvineld launched into the story that had been crafted to explain Mairah and Norah's visit. He claimed that Khalpar was experiencing a devastating blight on one of its most prized exports: plums. He'd even brought a sack full of blighted plum pits as proof. He claimed that the blight was spreading and that neither the Academy of Khalpar nor its Abbey had been able to find a cure. They were coming to Women's Well in desperation, hoping that the unique elements available here could produce the cure they so desperately needed.

It was at this point that he called for Mairah and Norah to come out of the wagon for an introduction. Mairah's whole body ached, and she was so weary she wasn't sure how she would find the strength to clamber out of the wagon. Even the men of the escort looked worn out. Norah, the oldest of them all by at least two decades, had fared worse than any of them and was so stiff that she fell to her knees when she tried to rise. Mairah felt so wretched herself that she unthinkingly gave Norah a hand up, forgetting their hatred for each other.

The two of them nearly tumbled out the back of the wagon, no doubt looking—and, unfortunately, smelling—as wretched and pathetic as they felt. The light was still bluish with dawn, and there was a mild nip in the air as Mairah stretched as subtly as she could and forced back a yawn.

Solvineld, looking perfectly groomed and well rested, stood before a party of three armored soldiers, two of whom remained on horseback while their captain had dismounted. In the distance, Mairah could see a few more horsemen heading their way. The captain's body language was relaxed and easy, but while his men refrained from putting hands to sword hilts, it was obvious they were more than prepared for trouble, their eyes watchful and suspicious.

Solvineld looked over his shoulder and gave both Mairah and Norah a disdainful look before giving their names to the captain. Mairah noticed that he introduced them as "Mother Mairahsol and Sister Norah" without indicating which was which, as if they hardly mattered, then turned his full attention back to the captain.

"Her Royal Highness made no mention that she was expecting visitors from Khalpar," the captain said pleasantly. "I'm afraid you've caught us at something of a disadvantage, for we have no welcoming committee prepared to greet you."

Mairah glanced at the half-dozen or so soldiers in the distance who were getting steadily closer. In the interest of common courtesy, King Khalvin *should* have sent an envoy—or at the very least a letter of introduction—in advance of their party. Perhaps he'd feared they would be denied entrance, and that their presence at the border—and the gifts they bore—would increase their chances of being allowed in.

"What a pity," Solvineld said. "I suppose our flier must have gone astray." He pulled a scrolled parchment from his doublet, holding it aloft. "I carry with me a letter of introduction from our king," he said, then gestured to his man-at-arms, who reached into the carriage.

The captain showed no sign of alarm, although his mounted men both tensed, hands shifting nearer to swords. They did not relax when the man-at-arms withdrew a small but obviously heavy chest and held it out to Solvineld. The envoy handed the scroll to the captain, then opened the chest to display the selection of jewels it held. For the first time, the captain showed something more than formal and impersonal courtesy, his eyes widening as the gems caught the rising sun's rays.

"King Khalvin does not wish us to be a burden on the resources of Women's Well," Solvineld said, and he was unable to contain the faint whiff of distaste in his voice. "He is more than willing to compensate your principality for the expenses of our visit and for any aid and guidance you might lend our abigails in their mission to cure this dreadful blight."

The rest of the horsemen finally arrived, and they joined their fellows in fully blocking the road. The surrounding land was dense with low bushes and shrubs and the occasional small tree, making it entirely impassable both to the wagon and to the carriage.

The captain graced them all with a courteous bow. "I must beg your pardon," he said, sounding truly apologetic, "but I'm afraid I must request my sovereign's permission before I can formally invite an armed party such as yours to enter Women's Well."

Solvineld sniffed, and for a moment Mairah feared he was going to say something irreparably insulting that would doom their chances. However, as undiplomatic a diplomat as he appeared to be, he was not completely obtuse. "Of course," he said with a thin smile. "Please do take the letter of introduction and our gift to your sovereign. We will rest and break our fast while we wait."

Mairah wanted nothing more than to sink into a bed—she'd have welcomed even the Abbey's miserable cots at the moment—and sleep until the following dawn, but clearly such was not to be. The captain sent one of his men back to town with the letter and the chest, and Mairah and her companions settled in to wait.

Alys stared at the chest of gems that lay on the table in front of her while her hastily summoned advisers filed into the council chamber. Lord Jailom read aloud the letter of introduction his captain had delivered from the Khalpari delegation, and as Alys tore her attention away from the gems and studied the faces of her council members, she could see they were all easily as confused as she by the sudden overture.

"Well," Chanlix said into the uneasy silence, "they clearly aren't here to research a cure for their 'plum blight.'"

"No," Alys agreed. Not after King Khalvin had so forcefully rejected her attempt to establish diplomatic relations with Khalpar. "But what can Khalvin hope to accomplish by sending the Abbess of Khalpar to our town?"

"They *have* to be spies of some sort," Jailom said with a shake of his head.

Alys raised an eyebrow at him. "Do spies usually arrive bearing gifts like that one?" she asked, gesturing at the chest of gems. Enough gems to more than double what was currently available to their Academy. "Just imagine what kind of spells those gems would hold." Gems were capable of containing far more elements than mere stone or metal and could therefore hold more complex and powerful spells.

Jailom shrugged. "It is a *bribe*, not a *gift*. And we can be certain they did not arrive here with goodwill in their hearts."

"No," the lord high treasurer agreed. "They merely arrived with enough gems to fulfill some of our trade agreements with Rhozinolm by flier."

Alys nodded, for it was well within the abilities of fliers to carry small items such as gems, thus avoiding the expense and danger of the long trade route through Grunir's harbor. The spell Alys had developed to provide immunity to magic—including illusion magic—was large enough to require a gemstone to hold it, and the lack of gems had so far curtailed their ability to use it for trade, despite what she was certain would be an eager demand.

"But at what cost?" Jailom insisted. "And why did they send their abbess, of all people?"

"They're here because they hope they can reverse our mother's spell," Tynthanal said, speaking up for the first time. "That's the only thing I can imagine that would motivate Khalvin to make overtures to us."

Alys closed her eyes and sighed, for he was undoubtedly right. Khalvin had sent his abbess because he believed women's magic was the key to undoing what many in the outside world called the Curse. The small group of Mother of All worshippers who had settled in Women's Well called it the Blessing, and the name had stuck in their small principality.

"They can't do that," Jailom protested. "Can they?"

"No," Chanlix said with absolute conviction. "I don't doubt they believe—or at least *hope*—they can. But Mother Brynna stated un-equivocally that the spell cannot be reversed, and I see no reason to doubt her. She was the most gifted seer I've ever heard of, much less known. If it were possible for her spell to be reversed, she'd have foreseen it, and she never would have cast it in the first place."

Alys closed her eyes again, this time for a very different reason. She had yet to come to terms with just how much of the future her mother had known when she'd cast her spell. Her heart overflowed with pain and rage at the knowledge that her mother had foreseen Jinnell's death, had deemed Alys's precious daughter an acceptable sacrifice for her concept of the "greater good."

She felt a hand on her arm and knew it was Tynthanal's. She tried so hard to keep her grief private, to project the image of the strong and stoic sovereign.

"I agree with Chanlix," Tynthanal said. "I cannot imagine that this abbess has the power to accomplish so monumental a task. Not even the magic of Women's Well can do that."

Alys opened her eyes and forced her emotions into the back-ground. Her heart pounded in her throat at the effort, but she man-aged to keep her voice level. "I tend to agree," she said, eying the gems once again. "But I also believe it would be folly to treat the delegation as if they were harmless. We must make certain to have each member of the delegation carefully watched at all times. And they must submit to a thorough search—each and every one of them—before they are allowed to leave, in case they are here to steal our magic." She glanced at Tynthanal. "We'll have to search them ourselves," she said, for she and her brother were both of an Adept level that would allow them to spot elements no one else in the town could see. "With both of us looking, they will not be capable of slipping anything by us."

"So you mean to let them in?" Jailom asked dubiously.

She stared at the jewels that winked and glittered in the chest. "Those gems are too precious to pass up." Which, of course, was why King Khalvin had sent them.

Jailom nodded. "I would be a poor lord commander if I did not point out that we can just keep them. We easily have enough men to turn the delegation away."

Tynthanal—who had been Jailom's commanding officer before they'd both joined the royal council of Women's Well—gave him a disapproving look. "We are not thieves. And the last thing we need is to provoke Khalvin into launching an attack against us."

"I know that," Jailom responded mildly. "But we must consider that Khalpar is our enemy already. Our very existence is likely a provocation to them." He gestured at the chest. "That may seem a fortune to us here when we have no other access to gems, but it is a paltry amount to a kingdom with its own natural supply."

Jailom smiled at the glower Tynthanal sent his way. "I'm not advocating an attack. I'm merely pointing out that it is an option."

"Thank you," Alys interrupted before the debate could continue. "I am still inclined to accept the delegation and exercise a great deal of caution. We must prepare rooms for them in the inn."

"And perhaps install a watcher in the room adjacent to the one we give the abbess," Chanlix suggested. "If she is going to try to undo the spell, she will have to do all of her work behind closed doors, and we should make certain she is not unobserved."

Alys nodded.

"I'll have a word with the innkeeper," Jailom said. "I imagine we can offer him and his staff some inducement to keep us apprised of their observations. The more people we have watching, the less likely we'll miss something."

"And I'll make certain to introduce myself to the abbess and assess her abilities—and her commitment to her mission," Chanlix said. "I, for one, cannot imagine how a woman who has spent any time in an abbey would wish to undo your mother's spell."

Alys shrugged. "Surely you've met some of the ladies my step-mother brought with her from Khalpar," she said, for the Abbey of Aaltah would have seen several of those ladies through pregnancies. "They take the Devotional far more literally than we do, and they believe women exist only to bear children for their husbands. Even if she's suffered under that doctrine, the abbess may well believe it."

Chanlix smiled with a hint of calculation in her eyes. "We'll see how those beliefs fare when she sees the alternatives that are possible here in Women's Well. If there are any cracks in her devotion to the ways of Khalpar, I will find them."

"Fair enough. But keep in mind that she will be forced to return to Khalpar when her days here are over. King Khalvin would never allow one of his Unwanted Women to escape the Abbey."

Chanlix sighed. "No, I suppose not. Maybe it's cruel to rub her nose in a life that can never be hers even if she wants it. But I believe—or at least I hope—that change is coming to the abbeys. There is only so long they can cling to the old ways now that women have more options in life. If nothing else, I can send her home with the seeds of revolution in her heart. That can only help women in general—and Women's Well in specific—in the long run."

CHAPTER TWENTY-SEVEN

Mairah was practically dead on her feet when, just as the sun began to set, the Khalpari delegation was finally invited to enter Women's Well. She barely saw the tiny inn her escorts bundled her and Norah into, and when she arrived in the room she was forced to share with Norah—for King Khalvin was happy to offer the Crown's money to speed the journey, but he'd insisted on frugality in everything else—she collapsed onto the bed and fell asleep fully clothed.

She had never slept so hard and deeply in her life, and she didn't awaken until the sun was high in the sky and hunger drew her to the inn's bustling common room. Norah was still snoring in her bed when Mairah exited the room to find two of the four guards who'd accompanied them from Khalpar standing watch outside. For their "protection," no doubt.

She descended the stairs and found the other two guards sitting at the common room's bar. Mairah felt immediately oppressed by their presence. They both pretended to be intensely interested in their food, but she was nonetheless aware that they were watching her out of the corners of their eyes. And that they had *not* been sent for her protection.

She took a seat at a small table in a corner as far away from the guards as she could get, mightily sick of their company. The cads had complained frequently about having to escort abigails who were too homely, in Mairah's case, or too old, in Norah's, to service them as they felt they deserved for the inconvenience of the trip. Never mind that they were being *paid* and that guarding caravans of cargo was their usual job.

Mairah was enjoying a bowl of excellent stew when the inn door opened and a middle-aged woman walked in. She was unremarkable in most ways, her face forgettable and her blue dress not especially fashionable, although even from a distance Mairah could see the quality of it. Mairah was already looking away again, ready to return her concentration to her meal, when her mind caught up with her and she glanced sharply upward again.

Unremarkable the woman might at first have appeared—except for the golden medallion that was pinned to the bodice of her simple dress. A medallion that marked her as the Grand Magus of Women's Well!

Mairah's spoon plunked back down into her bowl, and she found herself staring in the most embarrassing manner. She'd heard, of course, that the Women's Well Academy included both men and women in its ranks—an unheard of situation, when elsewhere in Seven Wells women's magic was confined to the abbeys or, in the case of Nandel, forbidden altogether. But no one had seen fit to tell her that the grand magus was a woman, and it had never occurred to her to ask.

The grand magus picked Mairah out of the sparse crowd easily— she was the only one wearing the red robes of an abigail. Smiling in greeting, her expression warmer than those Mairah was used to having directed her way, the woman crossed the room toward her. For her part, Mairah was still staring and gaping, her mouth having gone dry with something akin to panic, though she could not explain why that should be.

The grand magus reached the table, her smile still firmly in place, forming deep crow's feet at the corners of her eyes. Her face was deeply tanned, which would have made her look like a peasant if not for the fine silk dress and a pair of sapphire earrings that dangled from her lobes.

"You must be Sister Norah," the grand magus said in heavily accented Parian, reaching out her hand to shake like a man. "I'm Lady Chanlix, the Grand Magus of Women's Well."

Belatedly, Mairah pushed back her chair and stood, tentatively placing her hand in Lady Chanlix's. She'd never shaken anyone's hand before, for it was contrary to the customs of Khalpar to do so. Then again, it was contrary to the customs of anywhere in the world for a woman to be a grand magus.

Mairah forced a smile of her own, hoping she did not look as immediately flummoxed as she felt. "Actually, I'm Mother Mairahsol," she said, though it felt rude to contradict this great lady. She was momentarily surprised at Lady Chanlix's knowledge of Parian, but then she remembered that the Dowager Queen of Aaltah—and no doubt a number of her ladies—was from Khalpar, and therefore it would have behooved the abigails of Aaltah to learn the language.

Lady Chanlix's eyes widened in surprise, and Mairah was glad to know that she was not the only one who had been unprepared for their meeting. Of course without prior warning, there was no reason for Lady Chanlix to think a woman of Mairah's age could possibly be the Abbess of Khalpar. Norah looked far more the part, and Mairah was glad the older woman was still abed, for it would have been discomfiting to hear her addressed as if she were abbess.

"Forgive me, Mother Mairahsol," Lady Chanlix said, the surprise still evident in her eyes. "Not so long ago, *I* was the youngest abbess I had ever heard of, but I think you've beaten me by at least a decade."

The shocks just kept coming. *The grand magus* had been an abbess? It was unthinkable that *any* woman should be grand magus, much less a woman who had once been confined to an abbey. Mairah had heard tell of the occasional abigail who escaped an abbey, but it could only happen if a powerful lord was willing to marry her and plunge himself and his family into disgrace for doing it.

"You used to be an *abigail?*" Mairah asked, feeling sure she must have misunderstood somehow. Perhaps Lady Chanlix's Parian was not as well-honed as it sounded. The social ruin of being banished to an abbey was a wound from which no woman could possibly recover—at least that was what she'd always thought.

More crinkles formed at the corners of the grand magus's eyes. "For more than two decades," she confirmed. "You will find the customs and practices of Women's Well are far different from what you are used to in Khalpar. Or elsewhere in Seven Wells, for that matter."

Mairah certainly didn't think of herself as conservative or prudish, and yet she'd already been thoroughly shocked by what she'd learned. She had an unsettling feeling that there were plenty more surprises to come, and once more she cursed the king's impatience. Her mission would have been so much easier if she'd had time to prepare in advance. She felt slow and stupid from the long and uncomfortable journey, unsure how to handle all this new information.

Lady Chanlix reached out and touched Mairah's hand briefly. "You will enjoy your time here with us," the grand magus said. "It is a life I never could have imagined for myself when I was first sent to the Abbey."

Mairah swallowed hard, fighting down the tiniest hint of panic, for even if all went impossibly well and she found a way to reverse the Curse—or at least found a way to convince the king she had a hope of it so he would allow her to remain abbess—she would return to Khalpar to be shut behind the Abbey's walls once more.

"It is an extraordinary accomplishment," Mairah said, trying to quell the longing that instantly welled in her soul.

Lady Chanlix smiled. "I've found that a great many extraordinary accomplishments are possible in Women's Well. I'm sure we will be successful in finding a cure for your, er, plum blight."

The sparkle in her eyes said the verbal stumble had not been on account of a lack of proficiency in Parian. She and her sovereign princess were well aware that the plum blight was merely a pretext. Either they were confident the true mission would fail, or they were so desperate for a shipment of gems that they'd felt obligated to take a gamble.

"I do hope so," Mairah responded with as much enthusiasm as she could muster.

"When you've had time to settle in, I would like to show you around. If your abbey is anything like mine was, you've had little chance to explore outside its walls. I'd love to give you a taste of that freedom while you're here."

Lady Chanlix looked her up and down quickly with a staged frown. "But not until you've met with the seamstress." There was a too-knowing look in her eyes when she smiled. "We have no abbey here in Women's Well, and a woman's worth is not judged by her usefulness to men. Princess Alysoon has generously agreed to send over a couple of dresses for you and Sister Norah to wear during your stay. A seamstress will bring them by within the hour and alter them as necessary."

Mairah gaped at the other woman like an idiot. "W-what?" she stammered.

"There are no Unwanted Women here in Women's Well," Lady Chanlix said firmly. "The red robes are neither necessary nor appropriate."

Mairah's eyes strayed to the two guardsmen, who were still sitting at the bar and were now openly watching her. She could only imagine their outrage at seeing her and Norah dressed as ordinary women. They technically had no authority over her or Norah, but she'd spent enough time in their presence to know they would not let that stop them from showing their disapproval—with their fists, if necessary. But the thought of wearing a *dress* . . . Any dress, even the plainest, would feel like an unparalleled luxury after years of wearing the shapeless robes.

"We will make it clear to your escort that Princess Alysoon has forbidden the wearing of robes," Lady Chanlix said gently. "No blame will fall upon you or your abigail."

Mairah wasn't sure whether a royal decree would dissuade their loutish escorts from expressing their displeasure, but it was clear she didn't have much choice but to lay her robes aside for the duration of her stay.

Chanlix was smiling at her warmly, her expression guileless, but it was not hard to see that she was trying to seduce Mairah with the possibilities of Women's Well. Perhaps she—and Princess Alysoon—hoped Mairah would be so enchanted with the place that she would neglect her true mission. Or perhaps they intended to disrupt the mission more openly by offering her a lure they believed she could not resist.

A lure that she *must* find the will to resist, no matter how tempting the grand magus might make it sound. She was the Abbess of Khalpar, and the title curtailed nearly as many freedoms as it granted. She was not some nobody abigail who could disappear and not be missed or pursued. She did not doubt that her "escorts" were under orders to prevent her from escaping at all costs, else the king would never have agreed to send her in the first place.

"You are very kind, Lady Chanlix," she said. "We will set aside our robes for the sake of being good guests, but we are still Unwanted Women, and it will be best for all if we keep to ourselves as much as possible. We do not wish to embarrass our kingdom by making public spectacles of ourselves."

Chanlix's eyes met and held hers for a long moment, and Mairah cringed inside, for she was sure the grand magus read the longing in her. Then Chanlix inclined her head.

"The offer remains open," she said. "Let me know if you change your mind."

Mairah smiled despite the worry that brewed in her core. In her past, she had shown herself all too easy to seduce, but this time, she would stand strong in the face of all the temptations Women's Well offered.

Because whatever those temptations might be, Mairah knew they were out of her reach. She was the property of the Crown of Khalpar, and the guards that kept so careful a watch on her were a constant reminder that she was in effect a prisoner of the Abbey. It wasn't as if Women's Well could afford to shelter her if she took it into her head to refuse to go back to Khalpar. If she were somehow able to escape those guards, she would have to flee to Aaltah or Grunir—with no money, little knowledge of the area, only the most clumsy comprehension of the language, and, thanks to the pockmarks, a far-too-recognizable face.

Returning to Khalpar as an ordinary abigail who had failed her mission would be terrible—returning as a captured fugitive would be far, far worse.

"We have to stop meeting like this," Chanlix said, smiling and shaking her head at Kailee, who had walked brazenly into her office, with no sign of an escort or chaperone. It seemed her stepmother had finally lightened her grip on the reins now that the engagement was official, though Chanlix suspected Lady Vondelmai had no idea how much Kailee was taking advantage of that freedom. There was, as always, a wisp of veil attached to her fashionable hat, but the wisp was tucked up out of the way.

Kailee laughed lightly and took a seat before the desk, moving with surprising ease for one who could not see. "No doubt Lady Vondelmai is even now having a case of the vapors with no idea why. I've precious little time left to torture her before I become officially someone else's problem, so I must take advantage of what I have."

Chanlix laughed despite herself, for it was said with not an ounce of malice, only humor. "So to what do I owe this unexpected visit?" she inquired. "I presume you are not here *solely* for the purpose of shocking your stepmother."

"I admit not," Kailee said, still grinning. "I have come to you with a proposition that is almost guaranteed to turn her hair gray overnight. Or at least it would if she ever found out about it."

Chanlix regarded the young woman warily. "And what might that be?"

"In a town as small as this," Kailee answered in easy Parian, "it is hard to miss the arrival of the delegation from Khalpar. Tynthanal told me both why they *say* they're here and why you all *think* they're here."

Chanlix was momentarily taken aback that Tynthanal and Kailee appeared to have had an actual conversation, although that was hardly surprising considering they were engaged. Theirs might be a sham marriage, but now that Tynthanal had finally accepted the inevitable—and that Lady Vondelmai had relaxed her vigilance—it seemed the future bride and groom were trying to get acquainted. It was likely a testament to Kailee's powers of persuasion that she'd managed to pry sensitive information from Tynthanal. Although in truth her mind was so sharp there was little doubt she'd have figured all of that out on her own and only asked him to confirm what she already suspected.

"Is there a reason we are suddenly speaking Parian?" Chanlix asked.

"I've heard that the abbess does not speak Continental," Kailee replied. "As I am adept at languages, I thought I'd offer to tutor her while she is here so that she need not feel too isolated."

Chanlix switched the conversation back into Continental. "I'm sure your stepmother would be overjoyed at your charitable offer and would not for a moment balk at the thought of you spending time with someone who is even as we speak an Unwanted Woman, whether she wears the robes or not."

"That is why I've concocted an alternative explanation for her ears."

Chanlix groaned softly, feeling just the slightest hint of sympathy for Lady Vondelmai. Chanlix certainly didn't *like* the woman, but she imagined acquiring a stepdaughter like Kailee had been quite the challenge. "I'm sure you have nothing but the most noble intentions," she began, choosing her words carefully.

"I do," Kailee said before Chanlix could finish the thought. "You are going to be hosting the abbess here at the Academy, and she is going to be spell crafting. I don't imagine she would brazenly and openly work on a malicious or dangerous spell here, but it seems to me it would behoove Women's Well to keep a very careful eye on her activities."

"Which is why we are putting her in a room with the novices, whose instructor will monitor the abbess."

Kailee nodded. "While still attempting to teach her class. Which means she will be in danger of missing something. She can't have her Mindseye open all the time, and her attention will perforce be divided. Whereas *my* Mindseye is naturally open all the time, and I can watch what the abbess is doing. Unless she is stupid, she will suspect me of spying on her, but she can't legitimately claim offense under the circumstances."

Chanlix had to admit there was some truth to Kailee's argument, though she was far from fully convinced. "So you're planning to give her all-day, every-day language lessons?"

She was not surprised that there was more to Kailee's plan than that, for it was clear the girl had put a great deal of thought into her proposal. "Well, that's where the alternative explanation I plan to give my stepmother comes into play. The language lessons are merely a pretext to engage the abbess in conversation. I will tell my stepmother that I am coming to the Academy to work with your spell crafters toward finding a 'cure' for my blindness."

Chanlix leaned back in her chair and regarded Kailee with amazement. "Your supposedly more palatable explanation will be that you're doing magic?" she asked, her voice rising with disbelief.

"Well, I will be purposely vague about what it means to 'work with' your spell crafters. And yes, ordinarily the very thought of my setting foot in the Academy under any but the most dire circumstances would drive her to hysterics. But in her mind, my blindness *is* a dire circumstance. The thought that we might be able to cure it—especially before I have been wed to Tynthanal—will be a temptation she cannot resist.

"She is not a stupid woman, and she knows full well that extracting me from the marriage would be exceedingly problematic now that the agreement has been signed, but that will not stop her from dreaming of a 'better' future for me. She is pleased beyond words that we have found a man who will have me, and she feels that marrying me to Tynthanal is by far my best prospect as things stand. But she does fear for me living here in Women's Well, and she would be far happier to arrange a less exalted but safer marriage. She does love me, in her own way."

That was hardly the impression Chanlix had formed, but she refrained from saying so. After all, Kailee knew Lady Vondelmai far better than Chanlix did.

"I will endeavor to get to know the abbess," Kailee continued. "Maybe figure out what she's about. As I have mentioned, people tend to speak more freely around me than they probably should, so who knows what she might let slip? And I will use my study as an excuse for my extended presence in the Academy. Putting me in the room with novices will make perfect sense, and it will be useful for me to learn magic anyway. I will keep careful mental notes of what the abbess does and learn to recognize the elements as we go."

Kailee's argument was logical enough, and yet the idea of using an innocent young woman as a spy was more than a little unsettling. "Again, I know that your intentions are good, but this proposal of yours seems to me . . . unsafe."

"It's not like I will be creeping about in the shadows," Kailee argued. "I'll merely be sitting in the same room with the abbess, in full view of everyone. There is no danger in that." She leaned forward in her chair, her expression one of earnest entreaty. "I mean to be an asset to Women's Well. I have spent all my life being hidden away and regarded as a burden on my family. I am to be wed to a man who does not want me and who, for all his kindness, cannot help resenting me. If I cannot bring real value to the marriage, then I can at least bring value to my new home."

"You bring value just by being here," Chanlix said, and meant it. But she knew too well herself what it meant to be unwanted—or, in her own case, Unwanted—and she could not help but sympathize. "I will have to run the idea by Princess Alysoon before I can say yea or nay."

Kailee gifted her with a smile that lit up her whole face. "Thank you, Lady Chanlix!"

"I make no promises," Chanlix warned. But she and Kailee both knew that Alys would not pass up this opportunity.

Delnamal stared at his trade minister, the pleasant buzz of his after-luncheon brandy swept instantly away. Surely he'd been allowing his mind to drift into flights of fancy, as he was wont to do during the most tedious parts of council meetings. He could not possibly have heard what he thought he'd heard.

"They what?" he asked, his voice so loud and sharp the trade minister flinched, and the rest of the council shifted uncomfortably in their seats.

"They're growing Aalwood trees," the trade minister repeated timidly. "From all reports, it's only a tiny grove so far, but the trees are growing at an astounding pace."

"They should not be growing at all!" Delnamal insisted. "Aalwood trees grow only in Aaltah." How he wished saying the words would make it so. History taught that any number of attempts to grow Aalwood outside the influence of Aaltah's Well had failed miserably. Planted seedlings died, and seeds failed to germinate, and no amount of growth potion or careful tending made the least bit of difference.

He glanced around the council table and saw that every one of his councilors bore a similar expression of horror as they contemplated the possibilities. Aaltah's economy depended on its abundant supply of Aal, and Aalwood was by far its most prized export.

"I needn't tell you what a disaster it would be if Women's Well became a viable alternative source of Aalwood," the trade minister said. "Especially if they were to undercut our prices."

"No, you needn't tell me!" Delnamal snapped. He turned to glare at his lord high treasurer. "*Now* do you see why it is so vitally important that we increase the budget for our military? We cannot just sit idly by and allow that counterfeit principality to threaten the livelihoods of every man, woman, and child in Aaltah. We *must* crush them, and we must do so without leaving ourselves vulnerable to invasion from Rhozinolm. For that we need more men!"

As terrible as the news was, it had a hidden benefit as well, for instead of remonstrating with him, the treasurer merely nodded his silent agreement. Unfortunately, the lord commander was not as immediately accommodating.

"Lack of budget is only one concern," Lord Aldnor warned. "As well defended as we found Women's Well the last time we marched, they will be at least doubly so now. To have enough men to defeat them while still holding off Rhozinolm, we would have to conscript a great deal more men, and yet having a large number of conscripts in the city while we are not actively at war is . . . not ideal."

His lord commander was right, of course, but such objections were hardly helpful under the circumstances. "What would you suggest we do, Lord Aldnor?" he asked, hoping he did not sound quite so frustrated as he felt. All his life, Aaltah had been at peace, and though he was sure his father had had to handle many a diplomatic crisis, the stakes had never been so great as they were now, nor the cost of failure so dire. Why did things have to become so difficult now that he'd ascended to the throne? "Alysoon will not rest until she destroys us, and if she can't do it with her pathetic excuse for an army, then she will try to do it by undercutting our trade agreements. We can't simply sit back and do nothing."

There was a long and uncomfortable silence in the council chamber. A silence that left Delnamal seething, for he could well imagine what most were thinking, which was that it wasn't Aaltah that Alysoon was bent on destroying, it was Delnamal. And that it was he himself who had created an implacable enemy when he'd tossed Jinnell's head at Alysoon's feet. Not a man at the table was aware that Jinnell had already been dead at her beheading and that Delnamal had merely been taking advantage of the unfortunate situation.

"I fear you have the right of it," Lord Aldnor said, interrupting the lengthy silence. "No matter how fast the Aalwood trees grow, Women's Well will not offer us any significant competition in the near future, but the knowledge that they might do so is enough to make us vulnerable all on its own. The conscription will begin as soon as I have funds available."

It was not the most satisfying of victories, but at least now there would be some palpable progress toward the goal of wiping Women's Well off the map. Combine an overwhelming army in Aaltah with the ongoing difficulties Alysoon would have adhering to the terms of her trade agreement with Rhozinolm, and it was possible Women's Well would lose what support they had and become easy prey. Especially if Delnamal could use the hope of a marriage between Prince Waldmir's daughter and Delnamal's unborn heir to keep the Queen of Rhozinolm from marrying Prince Waldmir's nephew and renewing their alliance. With Waldmir firmly on his side, providing Aaltah with iron and gems while cutting off Rhozinolm's supply, Aaltah would be positioned for a swift and decisive victory.

CHAPTER TWENTY-EIGHT

Mairah was not a bit surprised to find that the grand magus had made room for her and Norah at a workbench in one of the Academy's small side rooms as far away from the main workspace as possible. Nor was she surprised that they were not left unattended in that room. A small class of fledgling spell crafters studied under the tutelage of an elderly ex-abigail, who spent much of the day with her Mindseye open. It was impossible to gauge the direction of that unfocused gaze, but Mairah was certain the teacher's attention was focused squarely on herself and Norah.

Lady Chanlix had kindly provided Mairah with a single sheet of parchment depicting the unique Women's Well elements she believed would be most helpful in the quest to cure the supposed plum blight. Although the list would be of little real use to her in her true quest, she was nonetheless thankful that the grand magus had thoughtfully written the descriptions of the elements in Parian. She studied each one carefully, for though she and Norah had no need to cure the

plum blight, their days at the Academy would be spent feigning research into the issue. Even if she'd seen no sign of anyone watching,
she would have had to assume that they were being carefully scrutinized at all times, which made the charade necessary, if annoying.

"Let's see how many of these we can each see," she suggested to
Norah after they'd looked over the page of eight new and unique
elements. Norah gave her a sidelong, surly look that Mairah had no
trouble interpreting. She rolled her eyes. "I'm not trying to lord anything over you," she said, although she fully expected to find a significant disparity in their abilities. "I'm just being practical."

Norah grumbled something under her breath, but Mairah ignored her and opened her Mindseye.

The instant her Mindseye was open, Mairah let out an embarrassingly loud gasp of amazement. She was physically closer to a Well
here than she had been when she'd worked her magic at the Abbey of
Khalpar, and so expected the density of the elements to be greater.
But she'd had no idea how *much* greater, how the air would be so
alive with motes she felt momentarily smothered by them all.

"So many," she heard Norah whisper beside her, though the old
woman likely saw less than a quarter of the number Mairah did.

Was the Women's Well truly putting out more elements than the
Well in Khalpar, or was it just that the high concentration of feminine
elements here made it seem that way? She had no way of knowing,
but for several minutes, she could do nothing but sit there with her
Mindseye open and stare around her at the bounty.

Every feminine element she could name was visible in that vast
cloud, and there were a reasonable number of neuter ones as well,
though far fewer than she was used to seeing in Khalpar. She was
taken aback, however, by the number of elements she *didn't* recognize, which made her realize just how stingy the list Lady Chanlix
had given her truly was. She easily recognized and located each one
on the list, but there were so many others . . .

"How many on our list do you see?" she asked Norah when she
finally recovered some of her wits.

Norah didn't answer at first—no doubt guessing that Mairah

could see far more and reluctant to admit her own shortcomings. "Three," she finally admitted, the discomfort in her voice making Mairah smile.

Mairah remembered seeing all those volumes of leather-bound spell compendiums on the shelves of the main room and wished she could run back in and crack one open. Not that she expected she would be allowed to do such a thing. It had been impossible to miss the hush that had fallen as she and Mairah had been hurried through the main workshop into the seclusion of this back room, nor had she missed the way the spell crafters covered their notes against her curious eyes as she passed.

Searching for a patience that had never been one of her virtues, Mairah reminded herself that not so long ago, no one had known of the existence of any of these elements, much less their functions. If the former abigails of Aaltah could work out how to use them in a few scant months, then surely Mairah could learn enough to suit her purposes in the time she'd been given.

There were quite a lot of abigails working on it, Mairah's gloomier and more practical side murmured. *And they had many months to experiment whereas I will have only one. And they'd not had to spend their daylight hours pretending to tackle a task that did not need tackling.*

"Between the two of us," she said to Norah a little too loudly, trying to drown out the voice of her own doubt, "I have every confidence we'll find a cure for the plum blight in no time."

Internally, Mairah winced at her admittedly ham-handed statement. While she doubted anyone in the room truly believed she and Norah were here to cure a plum blight, there was no reason to make the subterfuge any more obvious than necessary.

Wondering how she would ever get through the long days of playacting, Mairah closed her Mindseye and began scribbling some notes about which elements might work together to cure the imaginary blight.

Mairah wanted to scream from the skin-crawling feeling of being constantly watched. She could hardly take a step without tripping over one of the surly guards from their delegation. There were always at least two of them dogging her heels, and though they were supposedly meant as "protection" for the delegation, their constant scowling vigilance made it clear to everyone that their true purpose was not so benign.

And of course, it was not just the guards who watched her with such attention and suspicion. Mairah suspected some of the "novices" were aiding in their teacher's surveillance efforts. Every time she looked up from her feigned work in the Academy, she found at least two sets of eyes fixed on her, and she felt those gazes even when she looked away.

It was only in the night that Mairah could dedicate herself to the task of securing her position as abbess. Ever since Norah had revealed Melred's vision of the two of them working together in Women's Well, Mairah had turned the problem over and over in her head. She'd quickly dismissed the possibility of *actually* trying to undo the Curse. It was true that if there was a secret to undoing it, that secret might lie in Women's Well, but Mairah saw no point in throwing herself at a seemingly impossible task. Convincing the king she had the *potential* to undo it seemed a far more attainable goal. Besides, she had already set up certain expectations when she'd told Jalzarnin about her fabricated vision. She had claimed to see herself combining a secondary spell with a seer's poison to trigger a vision on a specific topic, so that was what she had to accomplish.

The task she had set herself might be easier than curing the Curse, but it was still far from simple, even with the vast array of elements she could see here in Women's Well. She felt certain many of the elements she did not recognize would be helpful to her task, but so far her hopes that she could steal the occasional forbidden glance at any of the Women's Well spell compendiums had been in vain.

Suspecting that Princess Alysoon would not leave her and Norah completely unobserved even when they were in the privacy of their room at the inn, Mairah did her nighttime spell crafting under the cover of one of her bedsheets, draped over the simple writing desk that was wedged under a window. Perforce, her first night of work—and, she was certain, many thereafter—would be spent trying to figure out what some of the unfamiliar elements could do. It was necessary work, but she was achingly aware that the king had given her a ridiculously short amount of time to perform what was surely a miracle.

Frustration chewed at the edges of Mairah's self-control, and it seemed like she spent the entirety of the next day swallowing snappish responses and reminding herself that murdering Norah would bring a death sentence upon her own head. There was no missing how much Norah enjoyed Mairah's dilemma. No doubt the old hag dreamed sweet dreams of Mairah's downfall at night when her head hit the pillow.

Inspiration struck Mairah on the morning of her third day at the Academy. She'd so far been able to recall only the tiniest smattering of vocabulary from her girlhood lessons in Continental—which was a sore hindrance to her efforts to learn snippets of forbidden knowledge by eavesdropping. She had a brief, offhand thought that perhaps a modified version of a memory-enhancement potion would help bring more of those lessons back to mind and realized, suddenly, that such a potion might be *exactly* what she needed to convince the king she could craft the spell she had described. What she wanted was to create a vision of a past event—which could at least loosely be termed a memory.

Mairah cursed herself for not thinking of this idea the night before, when she could have explored the possibilities. Now she would have to spend all day researching a cure for a make-believe plum blight when she finally had a promising lead!

While she sat stewing at her workbench, trying to keep her impatience in check, a young woman she had never before seen suddenly appeared in the doorway. She was walking arm in arm with one of the novices, her eyes milky white—though why she was walking around with her Mindseye open was a mystery. She was an extraordinarily beautiful young woman, dressed in a gown of peach-colored silk embroidered with tiny white flowers. Mairah suffered a pang of envy, for though after years of wearing nothing but robes, she enjoyed wearing the simple dresses Princess Alysoon had so graciously gifted her, she coveted that gown with an unreasoning hunger.

A pretty gown would do nothing to fix that face of yours, a voice that sounded very much like Norah's whispered nastily in Mairah's mind.

She would have wrenched her attention away and opened her own Mindseye to get back to work if the novice hadn't led the newcomer to the workbench at which she and Norah sat.

The novice said something in Continental that Mairah couldn't understand, although she gathered from the gestures and hearing her own and Norah's names that they were being introduced. Norah, who'd been absorbed in her fake work, blinked to clear her Mindseye, seeming to notice the other women for the first time.

"Thank you," said the stranger in the peach gown to the novice—that much Continental even Mairah could understand—smiling graciously while still keeping her Mindseye open. She then turned that smile toward Mairah. "I'm pleased to make your acquaintance, Mother Mairahsol," she said in fluent Parian. "I am Kailee Rah-Kailindar, and I am also a relative newcomer to Women's Well, so I thought I'd arrange an introduction."

The novice looked uncertainly between the two of them, and across the room, the instructress closed her Mindseye and frowned in their general direction. For a moment, Mairah thought the woman was going to demand that Kailee leave, but then she seemed to think better of it.

"Pleased to meet you," Mairah said, at a loss for how else to react. Why was Kailee walking around with her Mindseye open? And, if she was a respectable young woman, as her dress seemed to indicate, why was she arranging an introduction to an abbess?

Kailee laughed lightly, helping herself to a seat across from Mairah. She leaned conspiratorially across the table, dropping her voice. "If anyone asks, I've kindly offered to tutor you in Continental so you don't have to feel so isolated here. I've always had an ear for languages. I can speak Mountain Tongue as well, although I'm told my accent is amusing. I don't know if you've ever heard Mountain Tongue in Khalpar, but it's full of sounds my throat has trouble making."

Mairah shared a mystified look with Norah, having no idea what to make of all this.

"Er, that's very kind of you, Lady Kailee," Mairah stammered.

"*Miss* Kailee still," she corrected. "I'm to be married in two weeks' time, but I'm not a Lady yet. I suppose they really are keeping you cut off or you'd probably have heard of me by now. I'm the granddaughter of the late King Linolm of Rhozinolm, and I'm here to marry Lord Tynthanal, who is Princess Alysoon's brother."

"I see."

"And if you could speak Continental, you'd probably have heard already that I am blind." She pointed at her milky eyes. "I'm not being intentionally rude by keeping my Mindseye open while speaking with you."

It was only then that Mairah noticed the unusual flap of peach silk fabric attached to the underside of Kailee's fashionable hat.

As if she could see the direction of Mairah's gaze, Kailee reached up and pulled the little veil down, covering her eyes. "My stepmother would be furious if she knew I was walking around without this, but everyone has assured me that here in Women's Well, the sight of my eyes will not offend. So I've been enjoying the little freedoms that offers me." She tucked the veil back up under the hat again, then cocked her head and seemed to be studying whatever she could see of Mairah through her Mindseye. "The only person I've ever met from Khalpar until now was the tutor who taught me Parian, and he was so extremely tiresome that I felt I *must* meet another, lest I assume everyone from Khalpar was just like him."

Mairah was surprised to find herself smiling. The girl's good cheer was infectious, though a disapproving cough from Norah suggested the old woman was not so easily charmed—which only made Mairah like Kailee more. Mairah imagined Norah found Kailee too forward for her stodgy tastes.

"Then I shall endeavor not to be tiresome," Mairah replied, shooting a droll look in Norah's direction, "though there are those who would consider 'tiresome' too complimentary a term for me."

Kailee laughed, and Norah scowled. "In which case you and I are destined to become fast friends," Kailee said. "My stepmother calls my loquaciousness tiresome at least once a day, and has a selection of sharper terms to use for variety."

"It is very kind of you to offer to teach us," Norah said, making only a token attempt at courtesy, "but we have a great deal of important work to do and cannot afford to waste our time with frivolity. We will have no need to speak Continental when we return to our abbey, and we can make do with what we know while we are here."

"Nonsense!" Kailee said cheerfully, drawing a gasp of outrage from the old woman. "The best way to learn a new language is to immerse yourself in it." She said something in Continental that Mairah did not catch, then switched back to Parian. "I just said that I need not interrupt your work to tutor you. I need merely speak to you and allow you to ask me questions in return."

Mairah would have loved nothing more than to accept the offer—especially in light of Norah's opposition—but despite the girl's infectious charm, Mairah knew better than to take her overture at face value. There was no reason a well-brought-up young woman—the granddaughter of a king, no less—would volunteer to give language lessons to a pair of visiting Unwanted Women merely out of the goodness of her heart. She had almost certainly been recruited by Lady Chanlix to act as an additional spy in the room—and a convenient one, with her Mindseye perpetually open.

"I'm afraid Sister Norah is right," Mairah said regretfully, hating to express agreement with Norah on anything. "We must concentrate on our work, and it is difficult to concentrate while talking."

If Kailee was insulted to be so rebuffed, not a hint of it showed in her face or voice. "I have no wish to interfere with your important work," she said, only the tiny hint of a half-smile adding a flavor of irony to her words. She did not believe Mairah and Norah were trying to cure a plum blight any more than Mairah believed she had introduced herself merely to be friendly. "I have no intention of forcing myself on you. However, I will be spending some time here learning magic anyway, so if you have any spare time or just need me to translate something for you, you have but to ask."

"Learning magic?" Mairah found herself saying wonderingly. She had never *heard* of a respectable young lady learning magic, and even knowing how different the values of Women's Well were compared to those of Khalpar—and everywhere else in Seven Wells—the thought came as a shock.

Kailee laughed lightly, the sound and the smile somehow bringing light to those sightless white eyes. "It is positively shocking, I know. But if I'm going to have my Mindseye open all the time, then it seems I might as well make use of it, don't you think?" The smile faded ever so slightly. "Though it might be more challenging for me than for other students, as I can't read or see pictures of the elements." She bit her lip, losing some of her easy composure and suddenly looking vulnerable. "Perhaps every once in a while I might ask *you* a question, to help develop my skills?" She glanced over her shoulder at the class of novices, all of whom were poring over primers filled with pictures and descriptions of elements. "I cannot fit well into a regular class."

Mairah had spent too much of her life exploiting her own talent for manipulation not to recognize it when she saw it. Kailee was brazenly attempting to inspire just enough pity to soften the edges of Mairah's resistance. The attempt *should* have irritated her, but instead it inspired a strange feeling of kinship.

"I will help whenever I can," she found herself saying, earning another brilliant smile from Kailee and another lowering scowl from Norah.

Shelvon felt the impact all the way down to her toes when Falcor's sword crashed against hers, and she almost staggered under the weight of the blow. She'd imagined his sword would just barely tap her own in this, her first attempt at a two-person drill, but no. He hadn't put his full strength into the swing, but he hadn't held back near as much as she'd expected, either.

Falcor grinned at her. "Very good. First time I tried this drill at the Citadel, I dropped my sword. I didn't hear the end of it from the other cadets for *weeks*." The grin broadened. "And my trainer reminded me of it until the day he retired."

Shelvon shook her head, not entirely certain he wasn't saying that just to make her feel better. "How old were you?" she asked.

"Fourteen," he replied. "I'd learned the drill from my tutor when I was maybe ten, so I thought I knew exactly what I was doing. Turns out, Citadel trainers hit a lot harder than young gentlemen's tutors. Now move on to the next position."

He was beginning his own swing almost before she comprehended his instruction, his motion such a blur she couldn't follow it. His sword tapped gently against her shoulder before she finally recovered enough to take the second position.

"What, no praise this time?" she teased. She'd have been embarrassed at her lack of skill if she weren't certain he'd never expected her to parry in time.

"No stopping," he said tersely, his sword swinging downward.

She was slow again, and this time his sword tapped her side. She opened her mouth to complain, but he was moving again, back to second position. She scrambled to parry—too late—but she'd been practicing this drill solo for the last two weeks, back and forth between first position and second position, over, and over, and over again, and her body remembered the rhythm of it.

By the third repetition, she was still late, but she was at least getting close. By the fourth, his blade scraped by hers before making contact yet again. But by the fifth, she was fully in the rhythm, and her blade rose to block the overhead swing just in time. The force of the blow was no longer quite so shocking, and she moved swiftly to the second position, blade clanging against Falcor's once again. He grinned his approval, but continued smoothly on.

Sweat beaded on Shelvon's brow and trickled down her back. She was wearing a dress so simple she might have been mistaken for a peasant, and she'd spent enough time in the sun lately that her pale Nandel complexion had turned a golden light brown and her hair had gone from blond to nearly white. There were a handful of other people in Women's Well who had almost-blond hair that said they had Nandel blood in their veins, but no one who looked quite as strikingly different as she.

Breathing hard, she shuffled her feet to take up her next position, feeling almost as if she were following the steps of a dance—although in truth, she'd never had much skill at dancing. Dancing was considered a frivolous activity in the court of Nandel, and so she had not been taught even the simplest steps until she'd married into the court of Aaltah. But this dance with Falcor she seemed to be learning more easily, her body proving that she was not entirely deaf to rhythm after all.

At last, Falcor called a halt, and she groaned as she lowered her sword and bent down, trying to fill her lungs. Her hair had come loose from the simple snood she'd confined it in, and the long strands stuck to the sweat on her face and neck. She laughed a little to herself to remember that she had only last week asked Princess Alysoon to find a husband for her. Just as well she'd been refused; what man would want to marry her if he saw her right now, sweaty and unkempt and muscular from sword fighting, of all things?

"You've progressed quite nicely," Falcor told her when she stood up straight once more. He, of course, was barely breathing hard, and he didn't even seem to be perspiring very much. "I apologize for thinking you would not practice as often as I suggested."

Shelvon shrugged as she picked up the scabbard, which she'd propped against a wooden bench. In truth, she had surprised herself by how much time she'd spent practicing the drills he'd taught her. There was something incredibly soothing about the repetitive motion, about the concentration it required, which made it so much easier for her to forget her worries.

Sliding the sword back into its sheath, she collapsed bonelessly onto the bench, her knees suddenly wobbly with exertion. She honestly couldn't have said how many times they'd just repeated that two-position drill, but it had certainly lasted longer than any of her practice sessions. She wasn't sure how she would find the strength to rise from the bench when the time came.

"And I apologize for any unflattering names I might have called you when you first suggested teaching me to swing the sword," she replied.

He sat beside her on the bench—though he kept a respectful distance—and stretched out his long legs, raising his face to the sun. He was not an especially handsome man. His nose was too large for his face, and his years of military service had left him with some scars, including one across his eyebrow and forehead. Shelvon knew that to warriors, scars were a source of manly pride, but she herself had never found them especially attractive. And yet even as she catalogued his faults, she concluded that there was something quite appealing about the man. He did not make her heart flutter or any such feminine nonsense as that, but she did feel easy in his presence, which was more than she could say for any other man of her acquaintance. Princess Alysoon had declined to arrange a marriage for her, but perhaps she needn't abandon the thought of marriage altogether.

Falcor would certainly be prime husband material. He'd have been considered beneath her in the days when he'd been nothing more than Alysoon's master of the guard, but he was the Lord Chamberlain of Women's Well now. Had Shelvon been unmarried, her father might have at least *considered* Falcor as a suitable candidate for her hand.

Of course Shelvon had no idea how to go about courting a man. Falcor had never shown any overt signs of having noticed her as a woman—although surely his repeated visits to her house and all the hours they'd spent together suggested she held *some* appeal for him. Perhaps his first couple of visits could be written off to courtesy, or even pity, but it had been months since their escape from Aaltah, and here he still was.

"Would you be open to having a couple of other ladies join us for your lessons?" Falcor asked, interrupting Shelvon's flight of fancy.

She hoped her stab of dismay didn't show on her face. How silly of her to think that his time spent teaching her swordplay meant he felt any particular *connection* to her. He'd begun the lessons merely because he felt sorry for her, for her isolation and her obvious discomfort with her place here in Women's Well. And he continued because he felt at least somewhat responsible for her, having helped persuade her to leave Delnamal and upend her life.

"Lord Jailom has offered to teach ladies some basic self-defense techniques," Falcor continued, "but he says no one shows up for more than one or two lessons. He believes they are intimidated by all the men at the Citadel."

Shelvon took a subtle deep breath, hoping to smooth all emotion out of her expression. She could only imagine what it would feel like to attempt to learn something so foreign—and so manifestly unladylike—in the presence of dozens of staring soldiers. Even the thought of it made her want to hunch her shoulders and hide.

"How many ladies are we talking about?" she asked, taking a quick survey of her back garden. There wasn't a great deal of room.

"Just two or three," Falcor replied. "We have drawn a little attention with our lessons, despite the relative privacy. I've been approached by two ladies, and one of them has a sister who might be persuaded to join. I haven't time to give them each private lessons."

Shelvon knew that even teaching just one pupil was something of a challenge; more than once, he'd had to cancel on account of his duties to the royal council. She was not overjoyed at the idea of sharing the most enjoyable time of her day—and her time with Falcor—with other ladies. She had, in fact, made little effort to befriend any of her neighbors or other townsfolk, for she had never been terribly social by nature, and she was well aware that the folk of Seven Wells considered Nandelites uncouth barbarians.

Falcor smiled at her with conspicuous gentleness. "These women admire you, Shelvon. They've seen you practicing and they are inspired by it. They aren't the sort who would make fun of your accent or pepper you with backhanded compliments."

Shelvon was sure her face had gone an unappealing shade of red, for though she had never discussed her social graces—or lack thereof—with Falcor, it was obvious he knew exactly how uncomfortable she was with her place in society. She chewed on her lip thoughtfully.

As far as she could tell, ladies of Aaltah—and very likely of any other court outside of Nandel—spent an inordinate amount of time discussing such trivialities as fashion. Shelvon had learned to smile and nod when necessary, but she couldn't help reading into those conversations a criticism of her own lack of fashion sense—just one more way to make her feel inadequate. At least ladies who came to her house to learn sword fighting were unlikely to spend much time speaking of such things. Actually, considering how rigorous Falcor's lessons were, how much time Shelvon spent panting too hard to talk, the addition of a couple more students might not be much of a hardship, after all.

Shelvon forced a smile she very much didn't feel. "Of course they can join," she said as cheerfully as she could. "It will be nice not to be the only woman here who engages in such shockingly unladylike behavior."

The look in Falcor's eyes suggested he heard every bit of the reluctance she'd tried to hide. "We can try it and see how it works out. Just remember that this is your home, and if anyone who comes here makes you feel bad, you are under no obligation to invite them back."

She nodded her agreement, for there was no point in explaining to him how little this house or even this town felt like her home. She *had* no home, no place where she felt she belonged or could claim as her own. But unless she wanted to crawl back to her father—and find herself shut within the walls of the Abbey of Nandel—she was going to have to find a way to *make* this place her home.

CHAPTER TWENTY-NINE

Delnamal stormed into the council chamber. His entrance always put an end to the chatter that preceded the start of the council meeting, but the cessation was rarely this abrupt, with several mouths snapping shut mid-sentence. Delnamal could only imagine how dark his scowl must have been to have silenced so many men who so loved the sound of their own voices. His mother had counseled him to calm, but then of course she would. She was always making excuses for her cursed brother and his refusal to honor the spirit of the alliance that had formed when she had married his father. Bad enough that Khalvin had refused to provide naval support so that Delnamal could march on Women's Well without leaving Aalwell poorly defended. Now he was sending *gifts* to Alysoon!

His councilors were still halfway into their bows when he ordered them to their seats. The lord chancellor usually began the proceedings with a summary of the agenda, but Delnamal had no patience for the normal routine.

"Khalpar has not only sent its abbess to Women's Well," he said, his heart giving an angry thump at the idea, "but they also sent a chest of jewels! As if they were sending *tribute* to that damned pretender and her paltry excuse for a principality." No doubt the rest of the council had already heard—there had been several witnesses when he'd received the message, and he'd been too angry to bother with discretion.

His councilors shifted uncomfortably, glances darting around the table. None would meet his eyes, which was not a good sign. Every man at the table should be feeling the same outrage that burned in their king's breast, but one look at the sons of bitches was all he needed to see that they would rather accept the insult than take action.

Grinding his teeth, he leaned his fists on the council table and glared at his lord chancellor, who had the seat directly to his right, forcing the man to meet his eyes.

"We will discuss punitive measures to show our strong displeasure at this friendly gesture to our sworn enemy," he said in a tone that left no room for argument.

The chancellor had put on his most neutral expression—one Delnamal knew was meant to hide disagreement.

"Your Majesty," the chancellor began, with the exaggerated caution of a man who was picking his words too carefully, "Khalpar is our closest ally."

Delnamal shook his head and sneered. "They're *supposed* to be, and yet they've given aid to our enemy while refusing to help us. We cannot merely roll over and show them our belly when they've shown such rampant disregard for our alliance."

The chancellor's eyes held a hint of panic as he struggled to find a response, but the lord commander came to his rescue.

"I don't think King Khalvin meant any insult by the decision," he said. "He is merely being practical. I'll wager someone in the abbess's entourage—if not the abbess herself—is a spy, and the jewels were merely a bribe to convince Alysoon to allow the Khalpari to cross her borders."

It was the same excuse Delnamal's mother had given for her

brother, but it was as unconvincing in Lord Aldnor's voice as it had been in the dowager's. "If that were the case, the least he could have done was send word to Aaltah that such was his intention. No. He is flexing his muscles, establishing his dominance. He does not show me the respect he showed my father, and if I don't push back, he will have the measure of me."

"With all due respect, Your Majesty, I cannot imagine King Khalvin making a genuine overture toward Women's Well," Lord Aldnor argued. "He—"

Delnamal cut his lord commander off with an abrupt hand gesture. "I didn't say it was a genuine overture. I said he's testing me. And I'm going to show him what I'm made of so he never does it again."

A flush of red was slowly creeping up Lord Aldnor's neck, visible even beneath his sun-darkened skin. The lord commander was slow to anger, but as his subordinates at the Citadel knew well, he was a force to be reckoned with when sufficiently provoked. "If we take offense when none was meant," he said, his voice level but his eyes flashing, "we could do irreparable damage to our relationship with Khalpar. I must urge Your Majesty—and this council—to consider the consequences before taking any rash measures."

"I will take your recommendation under advisement," Delnamal snapped, making no attempt to play at sincerity. "And we will impose a new five percent tariff on all imports from Khalpar."

The faces of his councilors would have been funny if Delnamal didn't know what those expressions presaged. The flush finished rising up the lord commander's neck and flooded his face with red. The chancellor stared at him with openmouthed horror, and the lord high treasurer looked like he might be in need of smelling salts. Delnamal wondered if perhaps he should have tempered his anger just a bit, maybe imposing something more like a wrist-slap, perhaps only a one percent tariff. Something that communicated his displeasure without being quite so . . . outrageous. But it was too late now. Lord Aldnor's insistence on being "reasonable" had had quite the opposite effect, and Delnamal figured it was his own council that most needed to be taught a lesson in paying proper respect to their king.

"King Khalvin would never accept such a tariff," the treasurer said, his face unnaturally pale.

"He will have no choice," Delnamal said.

"Of course he will," Lord Aldnor said. "He can choose to impose tariffs of his own and send his export goods elsewhere. Our treasury is already strained to the limit from our muster of troops. We cannot—"

"Enough!" Delnamal bellowed, causing more than one council member to flinch.

Why did everyone always have to oppose him like this? When his father had given an order, his advisers had scurried to obey, and yet Delnamal had to fight a battle for every little thing he requested. He understood why his own mother treated him like a child—from what he could see, all mothers did the same—but there was no excuse for his royal council behaving the same way.

"I've given it a great deal of thought," he said, trying to sound calm and reasonable even as he wanted to slap some sense into the cowardly eunuchs who sought to advise him. "The tariff is the best way to prove to King Khalvin that we mean business. It needn't be a long-term measure—if Khalvin shows himself to have received the message." The lord chancellor opened his mouth to speak, but Delnamal cut him off. "The matter is not up for debate. I have decided."

The chancellor's mouth snapped shut for a half second; then he began stammering like an idiot.

"I beg your pardon, Your Majesty," the lord commander said, his face no longer flushed, but his expression stony, "but the council must vote on this proposed tariff before it can be imposed."

It was a fact of which Delnamal was well aware—and part of the reason why he had entered the council chamber angry in the first place. He'd known they would wring their hands and whimper like women. And like women, they would need to see that *he* was in charge. Whenever he raised his voice to his wife, she cringed and quickly backed down—just as Shelvon had done before her—and he hoped his womanish council would react the same way and he could thus avoid a long, drawn-out debate. He was not entirely surprised that Lord Aldnor was not so easily intimidated. The man was, after all, used to imposing his will on his military subordinates. But though he was a member of the higher council—the lord chancellor, the lord chamberlain, the lord high treasurer, and the lord commander—and his vote was weighted accordingly, he was only one man. Delnamal hoped he had effectively set the tone.

"Very well. We vote." He glared at the lord chancellor. "What say you?"

The man visibly quailed as Delnamal stood and towered over him. Which made his barely whispered "Nay" all the more shocking.

"*What* did you say?" Delnamal demanded, sure he must have heard wrong. The man looked about ready to piss his pants. Surely he would not dare to cast a vote in opposition to his king.

"I'm sorry, Your Majesty," the chancellor said, setting his jaw stubbornly, "but I cannot support a tariff on such slight provocation. Aaltah cannot afford to lose Khalpar's support in the current political environment. So I must regretfully vote nay."

In the end, only the grand magus and the marshal—shameless toadies, both—voted to impose the tariff. Delnamal listened to the vote in dumbfounded silence. The rage that had coursed through his blood, that had fueled him through a long and sleepless night as he'd pondered how to respond to King Khalvin's perfidy, drained out of him, leaving a bone-deep weariness behind.

He was the king of one of the most powerful lands in all of Seven Wells. He had taken to wife the woman he had loved since childhood, and his heir was growing steadily in her belly. He had everything he had once yearned for. And yet, somehow, he found himself wishing for the simpler days when he'd been the crown prince and no one had expected anything from him. His marriage to Shelvon had been miserable, and the bitch had lost his heir. But she had never dared to look at him reproachfully as he sometimes caught Oona doing when his temper bubbled over. And no one had dared to defy him so openly as his council had just done.

His head suddenly throbbing, he looked across the table at Lord Aldnor. It was all the lord commander's fault! If the self-important ass hadn't spoken against the tariff, the rest of the council never would have dared to defy him.

"Lord Aldnor," he said in a flat, dead voice. "You are hereby relieved of duty. You may retire with honor, or you can be removed from office, but you will leave the council chamber immediately and your lieutenant will take your place for future meetings."

He was vaguely aware of the expressions of shock and dismay on the faces all around the council chamber, but his eyes remained fixed on Lord Aldnor, whose face might as well have turned to stone for all the expression on it.

The former lord commander slowly pushed back his chair, his posture painfully stiff and proper. "As you wish, Your Majesty," he said, bowing with crisp precision. Then without another word or backward glance, he left the council room.

Chanlix's stomach seized with dread at the soft knock on her back door, even though she'd been expecting it. She had, after all, sent Tynthanal a message asking him to come by during the night. No doubt he was assuming she'd summoned him for an assignation, putting into practice the new, more discreet method of seeing each other that they had concocted now that his wedding to Kailee was less than a week away. If only Chanlix thought he would receive her news with even a fraction of the joy she felt . . .

Smoothing her damp palms against her skirts, Chanlix opened the door to find Tynthanal standing there, smiling at her. It was surely her nerves getting the best of her, but though the smile reached and warmed his eyes, she could have sworn it was dimmer and less confident than what she was accustomed to. A frown line quickly formed between his brows, and he stepped hastily over the threshold with an expression of concern.

"What is it?" he asked, putting his hands gently on her shoulders. "What is wrong?"

Chanlix swallowed the lump of anxiety in her throat and gave him the most reassuring smile she could muster. "Nothing's wrong," she assured him, though he might not agree with her assessment. "It's just . . . I have something to tell you. I have some tea laid out in the sitting room." She turned to lead the way, but Tynthanal caught her hand. No doubt he noticed the dampness of her palms despite her efforts to dry them.

"Please, Chanlix," he said, squeezing that damp hand. "There's obviously *something* wrong. Don't leave me wondering and worrying."

Sighing softly, she turned back toward him. She had spent nearly the entire day trying to figure out how best to tell him and had finally settled on a carefully rehearsed speech to be given over a soothing cup of tea before the comforting warmth of a crackling fire.

It had been a silly plan, an attempt to control that which could not be controlled.

Meeting his eyes, she searched for a semblance of inner peace to help her weather the storm she feared was on the horizon. "It seems one of the fertility potions Alys made for you had a delayed effect," she said, for that was the only way she could explain what had happened.

Tynthanal frowned with puzzlement. "I don't understand. We already knew one of them worked. That's why Kailee and I passed our bloodline test." His voice came out ever so slightly tight, and Chanlix thought that whether he'd consciously acknowledged it or not, some part of him understood immediately what she meant.

"When your bloodline test with Kailee showed you were cured, I assumed that meant the reason our last bloodline test failed was because I was barren," she said, knowing he had made the same assumption. What other reason could there have been? Save one neither of them had considered. "But it turns out I am not barren, after all."

Chanlix put her hand to her belly, hardly able to believe that after she had finally convinced herself that she could never be a mother, a new life had miraculously kindled. Tynthanal stared at her, his mouth open and his eyes wide, but he seemed to find no words for her.

"I wanted to confirm once and for all that our assumption was correct," she said. "I wanted to kill the last stubborn hint of hope that would always have left me wondering if I could have had a child by another man." Pain flickered in Tynthanal's eyes, and Chanlix hastened to reassure him. "I was simply trying to reassure myself. I wasn't planning to leave you."

Still, Tynthanal said nothing as he struggled to absorb what she was telling him.

"I performed a fertility test on my own blood," she said. It was the same test Tynthanal's mother had long ago performed on him, although thanks to society's insistence that childbearing was entirely the responsibility of women, men were almost never administered the same test. "The test showed me to be fertile." She rubbed her belly. "And I realized my monthly was a little late, which I had dismissed as a symptom of stress . . ." She let her voice trail off.

"But it wasn't stress," Tynthanal said, and she couldn't read the emotions in his voice and his face.

"No. It wasn't."

"You're pregnant," he said, shaking his head in disbelief. He cast his gaze around her small kitchen, locating a stool and promptly dropping down onto it as if his knees could no longer support him. His face had gone pale, his eyes haunted.

Not at all the reaction Chanlix would have liked to receive to her declaration, although it was hardly surprising. They had planned to revisit the question of whether he would father a child if and when his inability was cured, but thanks to their assumption that the inability lay with her, the conversation had never happened. He had tacitly agreed to the proposition when he'd first started taking the potions, but never with any great pleasure.

"I will make no demands on you," she said, her voice going hoarse as she struggled not to cry. "You need not act as a father to this child if you do not wish."

"Of course I'll act as a father to my child!" he protested with gratifying speed. "There was never any *question* of that!" He reached out suddenly and took her hands, squeezing tight as he looked up into her eyes. "I just . . ." He sighed and closed his eyes for a moment before catching her gaze once more. "No one will scorn me or talk about me behind my back because I have had a child out of wedlock. Such is almost expected from a man of my rank. But they *will* scorn you, at least a little, even here. And they will pity Kailee and whisper about her and speculate about what inadequacies would send me looking for companionship elsewhere. You know they will. You and she and our child will all suffer for this, and I will be held blameless, and . . . and I *hate* that."

Chanlix wished she could argue, but he was certainly right. She had little doubt that she could withstand the public censure—having been an abigail for more than half her life, she had learned to let the word "whore" slide harmlessly off her back—but her heart did ache a little for Kailee. Having a publicly unfaithful husband was a trial—if a very common one—for ladies of the court, but Kailee had the additional stigma of her blindness. The poor girl had spent her entire life feeling unwanted, and the child Chanlix would bear would be a tangible proof to everyone in Women's Well that Kailee wasn't really wanted here, either. Not in the way she *deserved* to be wanted, anyway. That melancholy realization sucked some of the joy from Chanlix's heart. It had been easier to dismiss the effects her extramarital affair with Tynthanal would have on Kailee before she had met the girl and become so fond of her.

"I'm sorry," Tynthanal said, raising her hands to his lips and pressing a gentle kiss on her knuckles. "I did not mean to cast a pall on your happiness. I know how badly you want this child, and I know you will be a wonderful mother."

She blinked away the tears that had snuck into her eyes, her throat suddenly too tight for speech. Tynthanal smiled at her, and if there was a shadow of sadness in that smile, still there was the welcome warmth of his love.

"We will get through this," he declared. "All three of us." His smile warmed a little more, chasing away the sadness. "All *four* of us, I should say." He let go of her hands to touch her belly, though there was no tangible sign of the new life within her yet. "I'm going to be a father," he whispered as if he could hardly believe it. He sounded amazed and a little frightened, but maybe just a tiny bit glad, as well. Or maybe that was the result of Chanlix's wishful thinking.

"You are," she said, her voice hoarse with the tears she continued to hold back. She cleared her throat. "Would you like me to tell Kailee? She certainly deserves to hear it from one of us before anyone else so much as guesses, and she and I talk every day anyway. We could wait until after the wedding just to be sure she doesn't change her mind, but . . ."

"But then when we told her, she'd be hurt by our lack of trust."

Chanlix nodded. "She's too smart not to guess that we knew before the wedding."

"Yes," Tynthanal agreed. "I'm confident she will still agree to marry me even when she knows. I will tell her."

Chanlix's eyes widened. "You don't have to do that, dearest. As I said, I see her every day."

One corner of his mouth tipped up. "So do I. It's astounding how much time and effort go into the preparation of a wedding. Especially when the bride spends all her daylight hours at the Academy and the work has to be compressed into what little free time she has."

Somehow, in her intense concentration on the vital task of keeping Mairahsol under such close scrutiny, Chanlix had missed what *else* was going on in Women's Well. She knew in an offhand way that the wedding preparations were well underway, and that Tynthanal would need to participate in some of them, but she had not realized he was spending so much time with Kailee.

"But surely your time together is not private," Chanlix protested, for while Lady Vondelmai had somehow been persuaded to allow Kailee to come to the Academy, Kailee had mentioned on more than one occasion how her stepmother overcompensated for that freedom by sticking aggressively to her side at all other times. "This is not a conversation to be had in public." And, though Chanlix failed to voice the thought, it seemed a conversation that might be less uncomfortable between two women than between a bride and her groom.

Tynthanal gave her a wry smile. "Surely you know Kailee well enough by now to realize she can escape her stepmother's scrutiny when it suits her." The smile faded. "We will find time to talk, and I will tell her. I cannot give her the marriage she deserves, but at least I can assure that there is no deception between us."

Chanlix wasn't certain, but she suspected the strange little pang she felt in her solar plexus might be just the faintest hint of jealousy.

CHAPTER THIRTY

Mairah closed her Mindseye as the novices' instructor halted the day's lesson for the midday meal. The young women of the class—the male novices, Mairah had learned, had a separate class with a male instructor, which was only logical thanks to the gendered nature of the elements—began gathering up their belongings and chattering to one another. Everyone all but ignored Mairah and Norah, leaving the room singly and in small groups. Norah took advantage of the room clearing out to move all the way to the opposite side to eat the cold lunch the innkeeper had provided, and Mairah was more than happy for the distance.

To Mairah's surprise, however, Kailee did not file out with the other girls, instead keeping her seat across the table from Mairah and retrieving her own packaged lunch from a bag Mairah hadn't even noticed she'd brought with her. Mairah watched as the girl removed an apple, a hunk of bread, and bite-sized cubes of cheese, laying each item out on a handkerchief on the table.

"You're not joining the other girls for lunch?" Mairah asked in surprise, for Kailee had filed out with the rest the previous three days. Mairah and Norah had never been invited to join them—which was likely just as well given the mutual lack of trust and the formidable language barrier. Even being left alone in the room with their surly escorts, Mairah and Norah were not foolish enough to believe they were unobserved, but it was a refreshing break from the constant blatant vigilance.

Kailee shrugged lightly and popped a cube of cheese into her mouth before answering. "Three meals with the rest of the novices was quite enough for me," she said. "They mean well—most of them anyway—but they don't quite know what to do with me. And they don't seem to understand that because I can see the aura of Rho around them, I can tell when they're shifting uncomfortably and looking away." She smiled, the expression surprisingly devoid of bitterness. "I suppose that while we're all in here working, they can forget that I am blind, but out in the world . . ." She let her voice trail off.

Mairah felt a sudden and unexpected surge of kinship, reaching up to run her fingers over the pockmarks on her face. It hadn't occurred to her until this very moment that part of Kailee's appeal was that she was the only person Mairah had ever met who completely ignored Mairah's disfigurement. And perhaps she was being naïve, but she believed Kailee was the sort who would have ignored it even if she could have seen it.

"I know all about the squirming and averted glances," Mairah confided, wondering if Kailee knew about her face. Surely someone had mentioned it to her.

Kailee nodded. "So I've heard," she said, then shrugged. "I must admit, I don't truly understand what it means that the two of us 'look' different from everyone else, however. Everyone looks just about the same in Mindsight. So why do my eyes and your face make everyone so uncomfortable?"

She sounded genuinely mystified, and Mairah tried to imagine what it would feel like to have never experienced worldly vision. Mindsight was similar in a way, but it had so many fewer nuances. "Do you know anyone who has a really annoying voice that grates on your nerves every time he or she speaks?"

"Several," Kailee replied, then crunched into her apple.

"Well, imagine how you feel about them, how much you want them to stop talking. That's how people feel about my face and your eyes. It's just easier for them to avoid seeing them than it is for you to avoid hearing a voice that bothers you. You would have to leave the room, and they have but to glance away."

Kailee nodded thoughtfully as she chewed her apple. "I suppose," she said, though she sounded unconvinced. "But I'm still capable of liking and talking to someone who has an annoying voice, and very few people seem capable of liking or talking to me."

It was said without an ounce of self-pity—more curiosity and a deep desire to understand—and Mairah admired the girl's calm acceptance of her situation. "Well, I like you," she found herself saying, then blinked in surprise at the admission. She couldn't remember the last time she'd actually *liked* someone. Even Jalzarnin, for whom she'd felt at least some small amount of affection, she could hardly say to have liked, for she'd been too cognizant of the scheming in his heart and of his ruthlessness.

Kailee smiled brilliantly. "We have something in common, then. I like me, too!"

Mairah laughed. Out of the corner of her eye, she saw Norah glower at her from across the room. The old bitch had already told her more than once to be wary of Kailee's overtures—as if Mairah were not smart enough to figure out on her own that the girl had ulterior motives. She let the smile linger on her face just to get under Norah's skin, although she was discomfited to realize that she was unsure if she could echo Kailee's sentiment.

As much as she was coming to enjoy Kailee's company, she had to admit the girl was something of an uncomfortable mirror to look into. She bore her situation with exceptional grace and good spirits, and Mairah could hardly say the same of herself.

Kailee put aside her apple, leaned forward on her elbows, and dropped her voice so that only Mairah could hear. "I'm sure you know that I'm keeping tabs on you, but that doesn't mean we can't be friends just the same."

Mairah shook her head at Kailee's bald admission, but somehow it wasn't surprising. The girl was more than capable of subterfuge, but unladylike bluntness was her most practiced weapon. One that Mairah decided she could wield, as well.

"Why would you want to be friends with me?" she asked. "I have it on good authority that I am a bitter, spiteful, self-pitying bitch."

Kailee snorted. "If your 'good authority' is Sister Norah, I would argue you must consider the source. She fairly radiates bitterness and spite, and I don't doubt a great deal of self-pity lies beneath it. I enjoy your company."

Mairah—who had yet to take even a single bite of her lunch—squeezed her hands together under the table, nails digging into her palms as she fought for calm. How strange and unfamiliar it felt to be defended! Uncomfortable, even.

"That's only because you don't know my history," she found herself saying, her face heating with embarrassment. She'd believed she'd stopped caring what others thought of her years ago, but meeting Kailee had shown her differently. So why was she trying to sabotage the girl's good opinion now?

"You mean because I don't know why you were sent to the Abbey?"

Mairah swallowed hard and nodded, hoping the gesture was visible in Mindsight. She'd survived telling Jalzarnin the details of her ordeal—though he'd obviously guessed more of them than she'd expected—but then he'd known the basic outline of her story before she began. Telling someone who knew nothing about it was very different.

Stop fooling yourself, her nasty inner voice hissed. *She's just pretending to like you for her own purposes.*

"Women get sent to the Abbey for all kinds of reasons," Kailee said. "In every situation, a man could do the exact same thing—be unchaste, be disobedient, be ugly, be blind, be an embarrassment to his family—and he would not be sent away to be hidden behind walls and disowned by society. I don't need to know your history to know you did not deserve to be locked away." There was a fierceness in her face now, a stiffness in her shoulders that spoke of outrage—and spoke of a woman who'd lived her whole life with the specter of the Abbey always looming over her.

"My case is not the usual," Mairah said, then surprised herself by spilling out the entire sordid story of her doomed friendship with Lady Linrai and her unwise dalliance with Lord Granlin. The words came in a frightening, almost uncontrollable rush, flowing far more freely than they had when she had confessed to Jalzarnin. Jalzarnin had admired her for what she'd done, and she'd been so struck by that admiration that she'd somehow missed the absence of true empathy. He had barely reacted to her anguish, and, of course, as a man, he could not comprehend the horror with which women regarded the Abbey.

Kailee understood all too well, and though she did not interrupt the flow of Mairah's words, her empathy was impossible to miss. Her open, guileless face showed every one of her emotions—anger and outrage and sorrow and sympathy—and that just made it easier for Mairah to keep talking.

When she was done, Kailee rose from her bench and felt her way around the table. Reaching Mairah, she dropped down onto the bench beside her and pulled her into a crushing hug. It was the first truly kind touch Mairah had felt in years and, to her shame, she burst into tears. She hated that Norah and their escorts were witnessing this display, hated for them to see her weakness, but something in that frank, unselfconscious hug undid her.

The storm passed eventually, and Mairah pulled away, fumbling for a handkerchief to dash away the worst of the tears.

"If the story itself didn't turn you off," she croaked, "then surely that outburst did the trick."

Kailee smiled gently. "Seems like you needed a good cry."

Mairah hiccuped and wiped at her eyes again. "It would have been more satisfying without an audience." She had her back to the escorts, but she could only imagine the scorn on their faces, for it was a rare man who faced a woman's tears with anything like good grace. And though she refused to look up, she could feel Norah's contempt scorching her from across the room.

Kailee looked stricken. "I'm so sorry! I should not have pushed you like that." Her shoulders hunched.

Mairah reproved herself for the complaint. She hadn't intended to make Kailee feel guilty. It was a churlish response to the girl's kindness, and she hated that she'd been so careless with her new friend's feelings. Mairah patted Kailee's hand. "Don't be silly. You didn't force me to burst out crying. Or to tell you my whole sad story, either." She took a shuddering breath, fighting to restore calm. "But you see now why Norah hates me so much and why our escorts look at me with such loathing. I'm afraid I'm rather infamous in Khalpar."

Kailee made a sour face that looked out of place with her usually cheerful demeanor. "As far as I'm concerned, the punishment—for Granlin and Linrai, at least—fit the crime. What a despicable pair!"

That, Mairah could not argue. Even so, Kailee's acceptance seemed . . . hard to comprehend. "How can someone as naturally kind as you are not scorn me for what I did?"

The sour look was replaced with the more familiar impish smile. "Perhaps I'm not quite as kind as you think me. I've never been wronged as gravely as you were, but I assure you, I have become an expert at avenging myself for smaller hurts. You have no idea how clumsy a blind girl can be. Why, I have 'bumped' into people so hard they've fallen! Only because I couldn't *see* them, of course. And I can't tell you how many times I've fumbled when attempting to hand someone a glass of wine. I come close to their hands, but I'm just a *little* bit off." Her voice dropped to a theatrical whisper. "Once, when a gentleman put his hand somewhere that marked him not a gentleman at all, it was hot tea that I dropped. In a very . . . inconvenient location."

Mairah burst out laughing. Now that Kailee had said it, she could imagine just how innocent those small acts of vengeance would have seemed.

"We are more alike than you think," Kailee concluded. And Mairah had to concede that at least in some ways, she was likely right.

Although Ellin knew she was being mildly petty, she asked her secretary not to show Zarsha into her office until fifteen minutes after his scheduled appointment. She tried to busy herself with paperwork while she waited, but her powers of concentration were nearly non-existent, and all she managed to do was rearrange the stacks on her desk.

She had resisted Zarsha's every attempt to speak with her at social functions, and when he'd protested, she'd snapped at him to make an appointment. She hadn't thought he'd actually *do* it, but then he was nothing if not persistent.

And in truth, she did need to speak with him, even if she'd prefer not to. He was supposedly here in Rhozinolm as a "special envoy" from Nandel, and he had always been far more forthcoming and responsive than the official ambassador, who made no attempt to conceal his unwillingness to treat a woman as an equal, much less as a superior. Whether she married Zarsha or not, she still had an obligation to secure Rhozinolm's trade agreements with Nandel. Those agreements had already officially expired, but Nandel had granted a six-month extension as a "courtesy" to Rhozinolm's "new young queen."

Ellin took a deep breath and searched for calm when her secretary finally opened the door and allowed Zarsha to enter. She intended to keep her attention on the papers for just long enough to make Zarsha uncomfortable before acknowledging him, but it turned out her will was not that strong.

It was rare to see Zarsha without a smile on his face and a twinkle in his eye, but when he rose from his bow, there was no hint of either. He kept his gaze lowered as he approached her desk, and his voice was uncharacteristically soft when he greeted her.

"Thank you for seeing me, Your Majesty," he said.

Her conscience twinged to see him so tentative. Once upon a time, his self-confidence had grated on her nerves, but as she'd gotten to know him better, she'd found it strangely comforting. No doubt it was past time she forgave him, yet she just couldn't seem to make herself do it.

"You said it was urgent." Her voice came out sounding cool and dispassionate, despite the turmoil that brewed in her breast. She imagined she suddenly bore a startling resemblance to her lord chancellor, Semsulin, whom everyone thought was cold and unfeeling.

Zarsha sighed and shook his head, meeting her eyes for the first time. "If you're determined to continue punishing me until the end of time, then perhaps you should just send me home to Nandel. I can present it to my uncle as my own choice, so you need not fear it becoming a diplomatic incident."

Her throat tightened, but she kept her emotions off her face by sheer force of will. "This is what you so urgently needed to speak with me about?"

He dropped any pretension of humble subservience, his blue eyes flashing with anger. "If you've given up entirely on both me and the trade agreements, then I suppose we have nothing urgent to talk about after all. Maybe I was giving you too much credit by believing you were mature enough to put aside your hurt feelings for the good of your kingdom."

She gasped at his harsh words, for though Zarsha had occasionally shown glimpses of annoyance before, she'd never seen him truly angry. It stung to hear that tone in his voice, to see that coldness in his eyes. But he wasn't through.

"I've asked you to forgive me, but we both know I've done nothing to deserve your anger. I had a life before you knew me, and unless and until we are married, you can have my loyalty, but not my *first* loyalty. You forced me to share secrets that were not mine to share, and now you refuse to give up your grievance no matter how unreasonable. You forgave Graesan after he attempted to murder me, and yet you will not forgive me for having had a lover? How is that fair?"

"I *loved* Graesan," she snapped back, feeling a momentary—and very mean-spirited—satisfaction at seeing him flinch.

"And you do not now and will not ever love *me*," Zarsha finished for her. "You have made that abundantly clear. But I did at least believe you *liked* me. Or was that just because you found me useful?"

Ellin closed her eyes and bit down on her tongue. Her heart thudded in her breast, and she reminded herself of all the things Zarsha had done for her over their acquaintance—starting with saving her life on the day of the earthquake that had killed the rest of the royal family. There had always been some hint of ulterior motives to what he'd done, but his support had been unwavering, and she had leaned on him more times than she could count. He was *more* than deserving of her forgiveness.

"I'm sorry," she said without opening her eyes. "I know I'm being unfair . . . but I can't seem to stop myself." She forced her eyes open and looked up at him, at the sternly cold face that had so often warmed her spirit when the rest of the world seemed to conspire against her. "You are the best friend I've ever had, and I've taken you for granted in a shameful manner."

Some of the ice in Zarsha's expression thawed, though he still looked far from happy. "What is it you want from me, Ellin? If it's perfection, then I'm afraid I can't give it to you, however much I might like to."

She sighed and rubbed her eyes. "You've given me more than I could dare ask for already. And I promise I do . . . like you." She could almost hear Star's voice in her head, telling her her jealousy proved her feelings for Zarsha ran deeper than merely "liking" him.

For the first time, he ventured a small smile. "Well, that's a start at least. Now, are you going to offer me a seat, or must I remain standing like a supplicant for the entirety of this conversation?"

It showed something about Ellin's mental state that she hadn't even realized she hadn't offered him a seat. He had more than once during their acquaintance taken a seat without asking first—despite knowing it was a terrible breach of protocol—but she was not surprised he'd refrained from doing so now.

"Please sit down," she said, hoping that time would help smooth things over between them and restore the ease that had once made their conversations so comfortable. She searched for her equilibrium as he took his seat.

"Did you request this audience merely to point out to me that I'm a childish ninny, or was there something else?"

He grinned at her—though the grin lacked its usual brilliance, and there was still that unaccustomed caution in his regard. "Those are your words, not mine." He looked away. "And I cannot claim to be entirely blameless. I wanted to protect Princess Elwynne—and myself—from any possible retaliation from my uncle if he found out I told you. But I could have told you about the affair and my possible daughter without naming them. I was being a coward, and I am sorry.

"However, if you plan to forgive me—or at least look past my bad decisions—then I have information I should share with you before you are blindsided by it."

Ellin all but groaned. "That doesn't sound good."

"It won't sound good to your council in general or Lord Kailindar in specific if they hear about it, but I guarantee you it is just one more bluff."

"*What* is?"

"I've received word that my uncle is in discussions with King Delnamal to establish an exclusive trade agreement with Aaltah."

The blood drained from Ellin's face. For all that she and her council—and her grandfather before her—had been fretting over the renewal of the trade agreements, the fear had always been that they would lose the favorable terms of their present agreement and be forced to accept something far less advantageous. Everyone thought it possible there'd be a temporary iron embargo used to force Rhozinolm to accept the terms, but no one had considered that Nandel would cancel the agreement altogether.

What would King Delnamal do if Aaltah had access to iron and Rhozinolm did not? It might take him a while to stockpile enough weapons to gain the overwhelming advantage, but once he did, he would crush Women's Well, and there would be nothing Rhozinolm could do to stop him. And given how Ellin had already committed her kingdom to that alliance with Women's Well—and made an enemy of Delnamal—it wasn't hard to imagine that he would cast greedy eyes upon Rhozinolm as so many kings of yore had.

"It is a bluff," Zarsha reminded her. "Waldmir is trying to put pressure on you to sweeten our marriage arrangement. He has likely heard about Kailee's engagement to Lord Tynthanal and is unhappy with what that means about your commitment to Women's Well. He likely hopes he can pressure you to give up your alliance with Women's Well in favor of our marriage arrangement and renewal of the trade agreements. He knows the best way to do that is to give you reason to believe he has other, more appealing options."

She frowned at him skeptically. "I may not know Prince Waldmir personally, but I imagine he would find an alliance with King Delnamal much more to his tastes than one with Queen Ellinsoltah. Why should I not believe he is negotiating with Delnamal in earnest?"

"How are Nandelites generally regarded throughout Seven Wells?"

Her frown deepened. "What do you mean?"

"Be honest. What word is most often used within all the other kingdoms and principalities to describe us?"

Ellin squirmed as the obvious answer popped into her head.

"You can say it," Zarsha said softly. "I promise I won't be offended."

She sighed. "Barbarians." She couldn't swear she herself had never referred to them that way, especially in the days when she'd thought she'd be forced to marry Zarsha and live in Nandel as his property.

"Exactly. We're *useful* barbarians—barbarians sitting on the world's greatest source of iron and gems—but barbarians all the same. We dress strangely, we have different color skin, different color hair, different color eyes. Our customs are not your customs, our language is not your language . . . We are unlike any other people in Seven Wells. When my uncle became sovereign prince, no one imagined a daughter of his would be deemed good enough to marry into a royal family outside of Nandel. It was an epic coup when Shelvon was wed to Delnamal and all the world thought Waldmir's grandson would one day sit on Aaltah's throne. He was all set to change our place in history, to make of our 'barbarian' principality a legitimate and well-respected equal."

"And then Delnamal went and divorced Shelvon," Ellin said thoughtfully.

"Yes. That could have been the end of Waldmir's bid for respectability. But if he can't have his grand*son* sit on the throne of Aaltah, he still has a chance for his grand*nephew* to sit on the throne of Rhozinolm." He leaned forward, placing his hands on her desk and staring at her with an almost palpable intensity. "I know my uncle, Ellin. As much as he hates me personally, he is well aware that I can give him the legacy he so desperately wants. He will feign reluctance. He will try to extort any advantage he can get out of a marriage agreement between us. And he will try very hard to scare you into thinking he has the upper hand. But I am confident that in the end, he will agree to our marriage—and the renewal of the trade agreements.

"Assuming *you* agree to our marriage, that is."

Ellin found herself chewing on her lower lip, a nervous habit she'd thought she'd gotten the better of long ago. She was *trying* to forgive Zarsha, was annoyed with herself for the continuing throb of her wounded heart—which had no right to be wounded in the first place—but she had not yet gotten over the idea that he had a daughter. Maybe. A daughter being raised by a man who hated her for her dubious origins and had shown himself endlessly cruel to the inferior beings he considered the female sex to be.

"What happens to your daughter if we marry?" she asked.

Zarsha grimaced and shifted in his chair. She expected him to remind her once again that he was not certain the girl was his—and she expected to counter that the girl was deserving of protection and consideration even if she was not. But she should have known better—Zarsha had never truly acted like a Nandel-born man, never acted as if females were somehow beneath his notice.

"I don't know, Ellin," he said, his eyes filled with anxiety. "But I don't know what will happen to her if we *don't* marry, either. She is only four years old, and I doubt she has spent more than a few hours in Waldmir's presence since she was born. But that will change as she grows older, and I shudder to think how he will treat her when she reaches adolescence."

Zarsha heaved out a sigh and rubbed his hands on his legs. "I make him sound like a monster, I know, but he is more complicated than that. He would happily hurt me in any way he could, but though he will be cold and unfeeling toward Elwynne, he will not actively seek to harm her while she's still a child—unless sorely provoked."

"For instance, if he should find out you've told me about her?"

Ellin asked gently, for the first time allowing herself to accept that he'd had a good reason for keeping at least part of his secret.

Zarsha nodded grimly. "The moment Lord Kailindar broached the subject of our possible engagement, I received a flier from my uncle warning me in graphic detail what the consequences would be should I speak too freely with you. He reminded me that as a member of the royal family of Nandel, my first loyalty must always be to my homeland, even if I should marry outside it."

Ellin tilted her head to the side. "And will it be?"

"I am loyal to people, not places," Zarsha said decisively. "And obviously Waldmir has not had my loyalty for a long, long time. The *only* reason I keep his secrets is to protect Elwynne and myself and the rest of the people I care about from his wrath. I assure you, it is not out of loyalty to *him*." The look on his face was one of disgust.

"And will he believe you if you claim not to have told me?" she asked. "Will he believe you will keep the secret even if we marry?"

He shrugged. "I can be convincing when I want to be. He'd never believe any protestations of personal loyalty, but I can argue that I would not want to risk triggering a war of succession. In fact, I *have* argued that. Waldmir has no surviving brothers or uncles, but except for my father, they were a prolific lot while they lived, and I have scores of cousins who would happily challenge him for the throne if his manhood were to come into question. My little brother would happily cede his own claim—he has always sought after a simpler life—but he would likely be one of the first casualties of any struggle.

"Waldmir will worry. Of that I have no doubt. But however much he dislikes me, and however much he distrusts me, he knows that I am the key to the glorious legacy he wishes to build for himself. I believe he wants that more than *anything*, and that therefore he will eventually agree to our marriage and the renewal of your current trade agreements without any further concessions from you. All you need do is stand firm in the face of his bluster and bluffs."

"I will ask Kailindar to resume negotiations," she said. Her voice came out sounding resigned, which was not how she intended to present her decision.

Zarsha closed his eyes, his expression somewhere between relief and regret. Her conscience grumbled at her, for she was cognizant that she had hurt him yet again, and that he did not deserve it. But she could not take back a tone of voice, and she had given as much ground as she could bear.

She let the silence hang, and hated herself just a little for it.

Mairah glanced over at the other bed, where Norah lay still, her chest rising and falling with silent breaths. She fought against the almost unbearable urge to snatch a pillow and press it to the old bitch's face. Thanks to the sleeping potion she'd slipped into Norah's wine, it would be oh-so-easy to rid herself of her nemesis. But even if tonight's experiment worked, Mairah knew she couldn't afford to draw attention to herself with a mysterious death that could be laid at her feet. She would have to settle for making the bitch sleep through the experiment so that she would not see Mairah's suffering—or witness a failure, if it came to that.

Mairah had always considered herself a careful strategist. Her revenge against Linrai and Granlin had been formed over the course of several months, and she had planned it all out so meticulously that everything had happened exactly as she'd expected. The same was true of her intricately constructed plot to rid herself of Mother Wyebryn and become abbess in the hag's place. But when she had described her fictitious vision to Jalzarnin, she had not realized the position in which she'd placed herself. She'd told him she'd seen herself drinking a seer's poison, and with that, she'd trapped herself. She had no choice but to develop a modified seer's poison, and that meant she had to *test* her handiwork.

Her stomach clenching with nerves and dread, Mairah opened her Mindseye and activated the seer's poison she had formulated over the course of the last several nights. She had started with a base of the weakest seer's poison available—so weak it could not possibly be fatal, even to a non-seer—and then added a new spell for memory enhancement using Ved, a feminine element that existed only in Women's Well.

Mairah smiled faintly even as she shivered miserably in anticipation. Kailee was always careful during their conversations, doing her best not to reveal any contraband information. Mairah had gently pushed a couple of times and been impressed at how artfully Kailee had managed to deflect her inquiries. Even so, the lessons in Continental that Kailee had so kindly offered to provide had turned into an unexpected boon in more ways than one. Mairah had tried—and failed—to re-create a memory potion for which she'd once known the formula, grumbling to herself that she needed a memory potion to remember exactly what the formula had been. She quickly realized that there might be another way to get access to a conventional memory potion that she could use as a jumping-off point for the enhanced version she needed.

It was not hard to pretend to Kailee that she was frustrated with her inability to remember the Continental she had learned in her youth. And she hadn't even had to work very hard to lead Kailee to the idea of giving her a memory potion in an attempt to help her along.

"I couldn't find any conventional memory potions to give you," Kailee told her. "Not without arousing suspicions, at least. But this is a formula they've been working on here in the Academy. It can help you remember your lessons, but you will forget again as soon as it wears off. I figure you can write down whatever you remember while it's active. Or, you can perhaps experiment with it after hours to see if you can find a way to make its effects permanent."

Mairah had forced a smile, tamping down a surge of guilt at so using this young woman whom she had genuinely come to like and admire. She tried to comfort herself with the knowledge that Kailee's offer was borne of more than just kindness. "Hoping to keep me out of mischief when I am out of your sight?"

Kailee's face revealed nothing but guileless innocence. "I merely figured you must be bored to tears being confined to the inn at night."

"Yes," Mairah agreed dryly. "The nights are quite tedious."

The potion proved to work remarkably well, despite its limitations. When Mairah had tested it, she'd found herself able to remember in perfect detail the text her tutor had used in her attempts to teach her Continental, the extensive vocabulary lists so clear in her mind she could remember which pages had creases or ink spots on them. And true to Kailee's warning, within fifteen minutes of having drunk the potion, the memories faded back into obscurity.

Fifteen minutes would be long enough to last through any vision, though even if the potion worked the way she hoped when combined with seer's poison, there was a very real chance the vision itself would fade from her memory when it was all over. Still, the only way to find out was to try.

Mairah bit her lip as she stared at the potion—which she had prepared while out of sight of any possible spying eyes by once again draping a sheet over the writing desk—trying to stave off the dread. If she'd had sufficient time to plan and prepare for this journey—if the king hadn't been in such a damned hurry—she would have arranged for one of the more powerful seers in the Abbey to accompany her. Not Melred, of course. Melred would never be the same after the inquisitor had finished with her. But someone who could withstand a stronger poison and therefore trigger more powerful visions. Yet there was no one else who could test the poison, and she was already almost halfway through the month the king had allotted for her visit to Women's Well.

Twice she raised the potion to her lips, and twice her courage failed. But all she had to do was remind herself how terrible her other options were to finally find the willpower she needed.

Pinching her nose and closing her eyes, she tossed back the potion, grimacing as it burned its way down her throat. She splashed some wine into a cup and gulped it in the vain hope that it would kill the bitterness of the poison. Then she sat down on her bed, back against the wall, as she wrapped her arms around her knees and tried to brace herself for what was to come. If, as Mairah suspected, the room was being watched—either through a spy hole or through magic—her observers would guess that she'd just taken a seer's poison, but she couldn't bear to suffer through the vision sitting on the floor in the smothering dark under the sheet. Besides, she'd likely thrash around so much the sheet would be useless.

Norah would say that the pain of the seer's poison was the Mother's way of preventing Her daughters from overusing their powers for prophecy. To Mairah, it seemed more like a punitive measure, torturing those seers who dared to ask the Mother for help. If Mairah truly believed the Mother existed, she would have cursed the bitch with every foul epithet she could imagine as the burn of the poison intensified, stealing her breath and making her heart hammer as if trying to break out from behind her ribs. With Norah lost in her drugged sleep, Mairah did not have to try to hide the agony, so she let the tears run freely down her face as she huddled on the bed, curled around the pain.

It was so unfair that she should have to suffer like this! All she wanted was to live in comfort, to be free of the cruelty that had been her companion since the moment she'd stepped through the Abbey's gates. If Mother Wyebryn and Norah and their cronies hadn't decided that making Mairah miserable was their life's work, she never would have found herself in this terrible position. She might have been just an ordinary abigail under those circumstances, but she was certain she could have borne that fate with dignity. She gasped out a sob and let herself sink down into the fury and hatred that had helped her survive her years of torment.

She hated Norah, wished the older woman would spontaneously die in agony. She hated Jalzarnin for tacitly encouraging her to eliminate Mother Wyebryn and then failing to convince the king to make her the abbess for the rest of her life. She hated the king for making her only interim abbess and for sending her to Women's Well on this impossible mission.

But her hate ran so much deeper than that, back to those who had caused her to be sent to the Abbey in the first place. She hated her parents for disowning her—though she'd known that was exactly what would happen when she'd planned her revenge. She hated Lord Granlin for using her and promising her marriage then tossing her aside. And most of all, she hated Lady Linrai, who had once been her best friend and had gleefully destroyed her when they had both set their sights on Granlin.

Her mind traveled back to the night of the poisoning, the night that had sent her life careering down the path that would lead to her ruin. Lady Linrai—*Miss* Linrai, back then—had come to Mairah's home before one of the biggest balls of the season, the two of them excitedly preparing together. They'd exchanged fantasies of being swept off their feet by the most handsome eligible bachelors in all of Khalpar, Lord Granlin being the most swoon-worthy of the lot. What Linrai had not known at the time was that Mairah had already won Granlin over—at least, that was what Mairah had believed.

Mairah blinked and shook her head as she realized the pain of the poison had faded to something almost tolerable—and that her memory had come to life before her eyes as the walls of the inn room disappeared.

Mairah sucked in a startled breath as she saw herself as she'd been that night, dressed in a ballgown of rich plum silk embroidered with gold thread, her face young and innocent and unmarred. Beside her stood Linrai in a gown of daffodil yellow, her hair adorned with silk flowers with jeweled centers. At the time, Mairah had thought herself sophisticated and elegant in her dark gown, but with the distance of time she saw clearly that Linrai outshone her with brightness and beauty. If Granlin had favored Mairah as he claimed, it was only because she had granted him privileges a well-brought-up young lady never should have allowed. At the time, she'd been convinced he was deeply in love with her and planned to offer for her—else she never would have granted him that final privilege, never would have given him the gift of her virtue.

"We will have to fight the suitors off with a sword," Linrai burbled, her face alight with excitement and energy. "I pity the other girls who were cursed to come out when you and I are available."

Mairah smiled at her friend with tolerant indulgence. Linrai had always bubbled with high spirits and liked to talk in hyperbole. Mairah agreed that the two of them made a fine pair, and their lineages—and the dowries that went with them—assured them of advantageous marriages, but her own nature was more cautious. They might attract the handsomest beaus at the ball, but if their fathers decided to marry them off to ugly old men, they would have no choice but to obey.

Lord Granlin was a choice Mairah had no doubt both their fathers would be overjoyed with, for it was widely rumored he was a leading contender to be the next lord high priest. No father of the aristocracy could resist the temptation to marry his daughter to such a man, even if his family's fortunes were not what they once were. Granlin's father had reputedly made a number of ill-advised investments and was in rather dire need of a generous dowry for his son—something both Mairah's and Linrai's families were more than capable of providing. All of which figured into Mairah's decision to lie with Granlin, wanting to make certain it was *her* he offered for, not Linrai. In her naïveté, Mairah had assumed a man of Granlin's standing—a *priest*, no less—would never dream of taking a debutante's virtue unless he intended to marry her.

"Stop frowning, Mairah," Linrai scolded, giving her friend's arm a friendly slap. "You worry too much."

Mairah smiled—though she was quite tired of her mother and her father constantly telling her to smile, and she didn't appreciate hearing the same exhortation from her best friend. "I'm not worried," she lied, for though she'd assured herself that Granlin would offer for her, he had not yet done so. She wondered if tonight she ought to belatedly act the demure and proper debutante and not allow Granlin to lure her out of the public eye for a quick tumble. Perhaps she would suggest that she would not be comfortable doing so again until the offer was made. "We'll have offers pouring in before the week is out," she said, genuinely hoping that would be true for both of them. Linrai would no doubt be hurt if she ever learned that Mairah had endeavored to snatch Granlin out from under her, but a beauty such as she would have no trouble securing a marriage nearly as exalted as Mairah's would be.

Linrai clasped Mairah's hands and squeezed them as if she could barely contain herself, her enthusiasm contagious. Young Mairah squeezed back, then cast one last look into the mirror, smoothing a stray fold of lace. Her older self, watching from a distance of more than ten years, saw what she had missed back then, the way the smile died in Linrai's eyes the moment Mairah was no longer looking at her, the flash of cunning and malice that swam behind her usually sweet and friendly mask.

Despite their friendship, Mairah would never have dreamed of telling Linrai that she'd lain with Lord Granlin and was awaiting the reward of his proposal. At the time, she assumed her friend had no way of knowing she had already lost the contest for Granlin's hand. But that one secret, fulminating glare said she knew full well what Mairah had done.

Oblivious to it all, young Mairah grabbed the shawl that was draped over one of the chairs, making the fatal mistake of once again letting Linrai out of her sight. While her back was turned, Linrai opened her Mindseye, plucking an unseen element from the empty air and directing it into the small metal flask she had smuggled out of her father's liquor cabinet. The flask was filled with a strong, smoky whiskey of a sort that was strictly forbidden to proper young ladies such as themselves, who were expected to drink nothing stronger than watered-down wine. "For courage," Linrai had said when she'd produced the small flask from her reticule.

Linrai's eyes had cleared by the time Mairah had settled the shawl around her shoulders and turned back to her. Her face was all innocence.

"We need one more shot of courage before we go down," Linrai said, lifting the flask to her lips and taking a big swig. At least, so it had seemed to Mairah at the time, but she had not been on her guard and never thought to look too closely at her friend's throat to see that she did not swallow, had probably never done more than touched the mouth of the flask to her lips.

Mairah had not much enjoyed her first swallow of whiskey and would have preferred not to take another taste. However, she did not like to think of herself as prim. So she reached for the flask when Linrai offered it, even as the older version of herself screamed futilely for her not to.

The vision faded and Mairah returned to the the inn room and the sound of Norah's snores. She shivered in her sweat-soaked nightdress, her stomach still tight and unhappy from the ravages of the poison. Her mouth tasted foul, and her throat scratched and burned as if she'd been screaming, though she supposed she hadn't been or there'd be people pounding on the door. She rose on shaky legs to down a swallow of wine, her knees so weak she practically collapsed.

Had her modified seer's poison actually *worked*?

What she'd seen had certainly *felt* like a vision, and it remained clear in her mind now that it had finished. She'd regarded the proceedings from what felt like a little distance, very much as she had when she'd seen herself sitting at the abbess's desk. And it seemed that she had directed that vision at the intended memory, just as she'd planned. Not only that, but it had shown her things her younger self had not seen on that fateful night, things Linrai had done while Mairah wasn't looking.

Of course, what she'd seen had been exactly what Mairah had always *claimed* had happened. As soon as the fever had struck that night, as soon as her parents had been forced to whisk her away from the ball while her skin swelled with flaming red, itchy pox, she'd insisted that Linrai had poisoned her. No one—not her parents, not the priests, nor the healers who'd tended her during her illness—had believed her. It was an unfortunate trick of nature, they'd told her. An especially virulent strain of pox that the healers' spells had been able to treat, but not cure. The fact that Mairah had been the only person in all of Khalwell to be struck down by this particular pox was deemed to be nothing but pure bad luck. And the fact that Granlin had taken one look at her face after she was well and immediately offered for Linrai . . . Well, she'd told no one of Granlin's promises for fear that her lack of virtue would land her in the Abbey, so it was no great surprise that he chose the radiant Linrai over her pox-scarred friend.

Had Mairah's vision shown her the truth of what had happened that night? Or had it merely shown her what she was already predisposed to *believe* was the truth?

Frustratingly, Mairah had no way of knowing for sure whether her potion had worked the way she wanted it to. Nor did she know how—or whether—she could make it give her memories that did not belong to her. But, she reminded herself, she did not need her potion to work perfectly, or really even *correctly*. All she needed was a way to create hope, and even if everything the vision had showed her turned out to be false, the potion ought to be enough to create that hope.

Ved was the key; she was sure of it. The other elements in the memory potion were ones she could procure anywhere. All she had to do was find a way to bring some Ved with her when their delegation returned to Khalpar.

Her heart sank at the notion. Not just at the difficulty of smuggling out a supply of Ved, which would be a challenge when their entire delegation had been warned they'd be searched both physically and with Mindsight before leaving. But at the thought of returning to Khalpar at all.

Yes, with her skills, she could likely parlay this potion of hers into an official and permanent position as Abbess of Khalpar. Whether its revelations were true or not, she had faith in her own ability to manipulate the facts. But now that she'd seen what was possible for a former abigail here in Women's Well, it was hard to be satisfied with the prospect of being the Abbess of Khalpar for the rest of her life.

"Get used to it," she growled at herself impatiently.

Unless she could find a way to escape her guards, convince the Sovereign Princess of Women's Well to let her stay, and then disguise herself so well and thoroughly that she would not be immediately captured and sent back to Khalpar for execution, becoming the permanent abbess was the best she could hope for.

Resigned though she might be to the eventuality, Mairah had no intention of returning to the Abbey any sooner than necessary. Only at the last possible moment would she announce the successful testing of her new seer's poison. Until then, she would enjoy the fauxfreedom of her days in Women's Well. And, though she sternly commanded herself not to get her hopes up, she would devote every spare moment to the impossible task of finding a way out.

Chanlix settled behind her desk in the Academy with a cup of mint tea that filled the room with its fragrance. She took a honey-sweetened sip, savoring the flavor while her stomach growled a protest that tea was no substitute for a hearty breakfast. Her stomach had a short memory. The last two hearty breakfasts she had consumed had fled her body before she'd even set foot out of her house and had left her feeling so nauseated that even the thought of downing an anti-nausea potion was enough to make her heave.

Feeling it was prudent to wait and see how her stomach received that first sip, Chanlix put the still-steaming cup down as Kailee slipped into the office, as she did every morning before she joined the abbess and the novices in the back room. Mother Mairahsol no doubt guessed that Kailee was reporting on her, but there was no reason to rub the woman's nose in it, so Kailee made sure to drop by before the start of the day, when there was no chance that Mairahsol would know she had arrived at the Academy.

Kailee took a seat, immediately tucking away the veil that hid her eyes. "Good morning, Lady Chanlix," she said with her habitual good cheer. If the news that Chanlix was carrying her husband-to-be's child in any way upset her, she was a master of hiding her feelings. "How are you feeling?" She sniffed the air. "Is that tea in addition to breakfast or instead of it?"

Chanlix had been unable to conceal her morning sickness during Kailee's previous two visits, and if she didn't get it under control, it wouldn't be long until everyone in Women's Well knew that she was with child. A little sigh—half resignation, half contentment—left her. Even without the morning sickness, her condition would become apparent in another couple of months or so.

"Instead," Chanlix admitted, risking another sip. "If I can avoid making a public spectacle of myself, I will."

Kailee grinned at her. "Does that mean you're going to retire in genteel seclusion for the duration of your pregnancy?" she asked in a tone that said she knew full well the answer.

Chanlix snorted, although for all her happiness at the new life that grew within her, she was finding herself not quite as confident of her place as she'd led Tynthanal to believe. Those of the working classes did not expect their women to hide themselves away while pregnant, but Chanlix wasn't certain how the gentry of Women's Well—what little of it there was—would react to a woman of her station not only being out in public every day but actively participating in council meetings. But that was a trial to be faced later, when she decided to tell others she was expecting. So far, only Tynthanal and Kailee knew, and they were both sworn to secrecy.

No matter Kailee's apparent ease with discussing Chanlix's condition, Chanlix was not similarly comfortable with it, so she changed the subject. Not that she was especially eager to discuss the disturbing report she'd received from those who kept watch on Mairahsol at the inn.

"I'm afraid we made a mistake in giving Mairahsol that memory potion," she said, mentally kicking herself for not putting her foot down. She'd known as soon as Kailee asked that permitting Mairahsol any but the barest minimum of education about and access to the magic of Women's Well was a bad idea, but she'd allowed herself to be convinced the memory potion was harmless.

"Oh?" Kailee asked, her brows arching. "How so?"

There was less concern in her voice than Chanlix would have liked, and Chanlix sometimes wondered if the girl was more naïve than she had once thought. Mairahsol made little effort to hide her unpleasant nature, yet Kailee seemed to be genuinely befriending her. And, perhaps, underestimating her threat.

"She apparently used that potion in combination with a seer's poison last night. Which is not something I believe she would have done spontaneously. I'm afraid she manipulated you into offering it to her."

Kailee showed no sign of being abashed. "Do you truly believe the delegation could not have acquired a memory potion without my help?"

"There's a reason they're all being watched," Chanlix explained patiently. "We will not allow them to go around us to get what they want."

Kailee shrugged. "You're watching them now, yes. But if they decide what they need is a memory potion, they can always hire someone to buy them a potion from Women's Well after they leave. I know our border patrol is doing its best to stop people from smuggling out our elements and our magic, but there's only so much they can do."

Chanlix squirmed, for of course that was true. Every kingdom and principality struggled against smuggling of its unique and rare elements, and it was distressingly easy for someone to make away with a small quantity. "Even so, we should not make things any easier for them. We will give them no more magic, not even the most benign spell."

"Fair enough," Kailee responded. "Do you know what Mairah was trying to accomplish with that memory potion?"

Mairah? Chanlix mused. "Don't you mean Mother Mairahsol?" she asked out loud.

"Don't be a scold," Kailee said, but without any trace of irritation. Of course, she was used to Lady Vondelmai, so Chanlix's gentle and subtle rebuke had no teeth. "I cannot spend so many hours with her and keep using her formal title."

Chanlix tapped lightly on the edge of her teacup, more uncomfortable with Kailee's familiarity with the abbess than she would have liked. "Please be careful with her," she warned. "Remember that she is here on behalf of a man who would love nothing more than to see Women's Well destroyed. She is not our friend."

"I think she *could* be," Kailee countered. "I know she has some very rough edges, but she's been through a lot, and I have a feeling she's known very little genuine kindness in her life."

Chanlix's sense of alarm strengthened. "I suspect I've had as much if not more experience with unkindness as she, but you won't find me trying to take away the first true hint of freedom women have ever known."

"I don't believe she wants to do any such thing. That may be why King Khalvin sent her here, but if she's honestly trying to undo Mother Brynna's spell, then it's because she is being forced, not because she wants to."

Chanlix leaned forward with her elbows on the desk, willing Kailee to understand the gravity of the situation. Her forgotten cup of tea sent a forlorn tendril of steam her way, and instead of welcoming the scent, her stomach gave an unpleasant lurch. "It doesn't matter what she wants," she argued. "It only matters what she *does*."

"Yes, but if she doesn't want to succeed, that greatly reduces the chances that she will. She cannot help but see the kind of life that is possible for women here. I know she admires you and is amazed that a former abbess is now a grand magus. And she sees me, a blind girl who has always had one foot in the Abbey, marrying into the royal family instead of being hidden away in disgrace. She's obviously a talented spell crafter, and it seems she is a seer, as well. She would be a tremendous asset to Women's Well if she can be persuaded to stay."

Chanlix groaned and covered her eyes with one hand. She should *never* have agreed to allow Kailee to make contact with Mairahsol. She was too sheltered to see Mairahsol's true nature, and she was too young to have made peace with the reality that not every person could be "saved."

"First of all, we have no way of knowing if she's so talented a spell crafter. She's not made any progress in her quest to cure that plum blight."

"That's because she's sabotaging the efforts," Kailee said. "She's being very clever about it, but I am clever, too. There are several elements I've convinced her I cannot see, and she very carefully adds those into her potions to ruin her spells."

Chanlix dismissed that argument with a wave that Kailee may or may not have been able to perceive. "And even if she is so skilled, she cannot stay here even if she wants to."

"Why not?" Kailee challenged. "Surely we could make use of her talents."

"She's the Abbess of Khalpar!" Chanlix said with a hint of exasperation she could not suppress. "If we were to offer her a place here, you can be certain her king will demand her return. We are not going to go to war over her."

"So instead of openly making an offer, we help her to disappear instead. I can't imagine the king would be overly shocked to find his abbess had risked everything to avoid being shut up in the Abbey again. We can hide her until the furor dies down, and then she can quietly take a place at the Academy under an assumed name."

Chanlix stifled her first impatient answer, pausing to take a deep breath. Unfortunately, that deep breath brought her another whiff of mint, to which her stomach objected more strenuously. It seemed even the tea was more than she could handle at this stage of her pregnancy.

"Your heart is in the right place," Chanlix said, "but it is simply out of the question." Chanlix would have liked to tell Kailee not to come back to the Academy any more until Mairahsol was gone, but she knew the girl far too well by now to attempt any such foolishness. She believed that Mairahsol was her friend, and she would not hesitate to attempt to maintain that friendship behind Chanlix's back. Chanlix had only to look at how readily Kailee had worked around her stepmother to know that.

"By all means, do what you can to give her second thoughts about attempting to undo Mother Brynna's spell. And continue to tell me about your conversations and what she does with the elements. But don't tempt her with something she cannot have. That would just be cruel."

The look on Kailee's face told Chanlix she was far from convinced, although she offered no further argument. Chanlix swallowed hard in hopes it would keep her gorge down for just a little longer as Kailee rose to leave.

"Please take this with you," Chanlix said, pushing the nearly full teacup away from her.

Kailee grimaced in sympathy as she reached for the teacup, needing only the tiniest sweep of her fingers to locate it. "Is there anything I can get you instead?" she asked, showing her inherent kindness despite having been refused.

"Thank you, but no. I'll be fine."

Closing her eyes and breathing deeply, Chanlix battled the morning sickness for another few minutes before she had to make a sudden rush for the privy.

CHAPTER THIRTY-ONE

Alys laid the talker on the desk in front of her, carefully adjusting it so that it was pointed directly at her face but would also reveal some of the background, which she had rearranged about twenty times over the course of the day. Her council had been of the opinion that she should hold this "meeting" in the throne room of her new palace, but though it might have been more grand than her old office at the town hall, it was not especially conducive to an intimate one-on-one conversation.

Alys wiped sweaty palms on her black silk skirts, wondering if she had made the right decision when she'd insisted on speaking with Prince Waldmir alone. The council had urged her to at least have Tynthanal with her, and it was more than reasonable for her lord chancellor to attend this first meeting with the Sovereign Prince of Nandel. But she feared that if there were a male in the room with her, Prince Waldmir might be less inclined to see her as the true sovereign, and that might weaken her position. She needed to make it clear she considered herself his equal if she had any hope that he would come to consider her one.

But despite all these logical reasons why she had chosen to meet with him alone in her office once he'd responded to her introductory flier, her nerves were buzzing and her stomach was tight with dread. She did not like it when people around her referred to Nandelites as barbarians, and she'd grown close enough to Shelvon that she would never think to use the term herself, but it was unquestionably true that their ways were very different from those she'd grown up with in Aaltah. And it was also true that in her attempts to protect Jinnell from a forced marriage with the sovereign prince, she had built him up into a monster in her own mind.

She wished she could avoid speaking with him at all, and now that it was too late, she cursed herself for sending the talker instead of carrying out any negotiations that might or might not happen through written correspondence. Communication between sovereigns had been carried out via fliers for all of recorded history, and perhaps she should have deemed that good enough for her and Prince Waldmir.

The talker on her desk chirped, causing her to jump and let out a startled squeak. She shook her head at herself, taking a deep breath and letting it out slowly in hopes that it would settle her nerves. The last thing she needed was to show Waldmir any hint of anxiety, or he would lose all respect for her before she even opened her mouth to speak.

The talker continued to chirp as she forced herself to calm—or at least a semblance thereof—and fed a mote of Rho into it to complete the connection. She blinked to close her Mindseye, and when she opened her eyes again, the image of a thin, smiling man was hovering in the air above her desk.

He was dressed all in shades of gray. His doublet was a deep slate gray, and the cloak he wore draped over his shoulders was of a lighter cloud gray and lined with silver-gray fur that was probably fox. Gray hair. White beard. Gray eyes. And a gray crown with no adornment save for a few hematite cabochons.

When she got over the shock of his colorlessness, she noted that in more fashionable garb and with a less fearsome reputation, he would have been conspicuously handsome. His smile was perhaps a little practiced—a court smile rather than a genuine one—but his angular features were pleasing to the eye, and he wore his pale coloring with more grace and comfort than his daughter. Alys examined his face for some clue as to whether the Kai flier carrying Vengeance had ever reached him, but he showed no more sign of hostility in person than he had in his correspondence. Either the flier had never reached him—the mountainous terrain of Nandel and its sometimes violent storms did mean fliers were less reliable there than elsewhere—or he was excellent at hiding his feelings.

Like herself, he appeared to be alone, sitting in an uncomfortable-looking straight-backed chair with a barren stone wall as his only background. Alys knew Nandelites scorned adornment and decoration, but it seemed Prince Waldmir took this scorn to an extreme.

"Princess Alysoon, I presume?" Waldmir said, shaking his head, his eyes filled with wonder.

"Prince Waldmir," she said with a nod of greeting.

"Your invention is . . ." His voice trailed off, and he shook his head again. "I'd heard tell of these talkers of yours, but even when I received one from you, I could hardly credit that they would work as they do. Amazing."

His praise sounded genuine, but Alys had to believe it cost him something. When she had sent him the talker, she had made sure her letter emphasized that the talker was powered mainly by Zal, a feminine element that was exceedingly rare anywhere but in Women's Well. A part of her had been hoping he'd turn up his nose at the use of such obviously feminine magic, but here he was praising it instead.

Of course, considering he had accepted the cargo of trade goods Delnamal had stolen, he clearly was capable of getting over his prejudices with the right inducement.

"The magic here at Women's Well is unique," Alys said. And although her plan was to make this a pleasant and diplomatic conversation, she couldn't stop herself from continuing. "Although if my understanding of the customs of Nandel is correct, your people would be largely unwilling to use any of our spells or magic items because they are women's magic."

Instead of looking insulted at her tone—which admittedly had been less than entirely respectful—his smile broadened. "You do indeed understand our customs correctly. However, I have never seen or heard of a women's magic item that has quite the usefulness of these talkers of yours. They would be especially useful here in Nandel, where travel is rather more difficult than elsewhere in Seven Wells. During the winter months, the roads are nearly impassable in much of our principality, and most communication must be done by flier-borne letters, which naturally have significant limitations."

Alys imagined the talkers would indeed be quite useful in such a mountainous principality. She made a regretful face. "Unfortunately, we have an exclusive trade agreement with Rhozinolm for the talkers, so I'm afraid I cannot offer you a supply. We do have other magic items you may find equally useful, however."

"I'm sure you do," Waldmir agreed, though Alys did not think she was imagining the hint of condescension she heard in his voice. "But before we speak of such mundane topics, I wish to offer you my deepest sympathies on the loss of your daughter."

For reasons that now eluded her, Alys had not expected condolences from Prince Waldmir, of all people, and his words stole the breath from her lungs as the pain of Jinnell's death stabbed through her.

"She was a truly lovely young woman," Waldmir continued in a surprisingly gentle voice. "King Delnamal told me she was being recalled to Aalwell for the sake of her health, and I had no reason to doubt him. It seemed to me at the time that the poor girl would be better served in a land where she had access to women's magic that might have cured whatever ailed her. If I'd known what danger she'd be in, I would have told him that she was too ill to travel."

Alys's hands clutched at her skirts, and no amount of court training could keep her anguish from showing on her face. But when the first shock of pain eased, her thinking mind caught up with what her ears were hearing, and she snapped back into herself.

"Ill?" she said, her heart fluttering in her chest. She had never sought out any information about Jinnell's fateful visit to Nandel and her meeting with her would-be bridegroom. She had not wanted to imagine what her daughter had been through during those terrible days and weeks before Delnamal brought her back to Aalwell to murder her for sheer spite.

Prince Waldmir nodded. "I'd wondered if you'd heard anything about her visit. It seems that you haven't. Jinnell apparently fell ill with a stomach ailment as soon as her entourage left Aalwell. Her illness delayed her progress and necessitated an overnight stay at an inn. Coincidentally, your son and my daughter slipped away from Aalwell at the same time, and thanks to the overnight absence of the king, they were not discovered missing until they had enough of a head start to reach Women's Well."

Alys could do nothing but stare stupidly at the man from whom she'd tried so desperately to protect Jinnell. His gaze was sharp and keen, but not unkind. He did not on the surface look like a man who would marry and discard—or even execute—pretty young women of noble families with the same carelessness with which he would change horses. Alys might even allow herself to think there was a trace of kindness and compassion in his eyes, though she could hardly credit it.

"I cannot say I came to know your daughter well over the brief course of our acquaintance," Waldmir said, "but she struck me as a girl of remarkable courage and spirit." A small smile lifted the corners of his mouth, and his eyes went momentarily distant at some fleeting memory. "I would not be at all surprised to learn that her illness was self-inflicted."

Alys nearly choked on the memory of Jinnell's ill-fated attempt to replicate a healing potion on her own when she got impatient with the pace of their magic lessons. Jinnell hadn't told her about it until well after the fact, but the healing potion she'd created had been missing a crucial element she couldn't see, and while it had healed a small scratch exactly as a normal healing potion would, it had also made her violently sick to her stomach. Alys could almost see her precious daughter coming to the conclusion that making herself ill and delaying her travel to Nandel would give her brother and Shelvon a greater chance of escape. And she could also see Jinnell reaching the grim conclusion that sickening herself might be the only way to escape a forced marriage to Prince Waldmir.

"She made herself sick hoping she wouldn't be forced to marry you," Alys said, in too much pain to keep her loathing to herself. She was no diplomat, and it had been the height of folly for her to think she could have a civil conversation with this man.

Waldmir sighed heavily and with what sounded like genuine regret. "That may be the case. But I believe she and I came to understand each other over the course of her visit. I assured her that I would not wed her against her will. I am too old to risk having yet another wife who cannot bear me a son. I don't know whether she would ultimately have accepted my proposal or not, but of course she did not have the chance to decide before she was recalled to Aalwell. If I'd had any inkling she'd return to a treason charge . . ." He sighed again.

Alys couldn't think what to say, could hardly think what to feel. The wound of Jinnell's death was still open and bleeding, and the most she could ask was that time would ease the sharpness of the pain, for she knew that no amount of time would cause the wound to heal.

"Then again," Waldmir continued, "I'm not sure remaining in The Keep would have saved her in the end. This is pure conjecture on my part, but King Delnamal has never struck me as a man of great courage or strength of will. I am not certain her 'execution' didn't occur *after* her illness had taken her life. She was already so frail when she left here, and the long journey could not have helped."

The savage snarl that rose from Alys's throat surprised her, and she wanted to reach through the illusion in front of her and wrap her hands around Waldmir's throat. "If that's the case, then she died because of *you*," she spat. Diplomacy be damned! She should have listened to her first instinct, which had told her there was no point in establishing communications with Nandel at all, no matter how desperately Women's Well needed more resources. She could not regard him with the eyes of a sovereign, could not quell her maternal rage enough to be prudent.

Waldmir's eyes turned hard and flinty for just a moment, revealing a glimpse of the fearsome creature that lurked beneath the almost kindly façade he'd been showing her. But his emotions were under far better control than Alys's, and the hint of anger disappeared so quickly she might have thought she'd imagined it.

"Perhaps I should have kept my theories and opinions to myself," he said, "but I thought it best we lay our cards on the table from the beginning. We are neither of us fully ready to sit at the negotiating table at this time, but the world being as unsettled as it is, that may not be the case indefinitely. I hope we may speak again when you've had some time to come to terms with what I've told you."

Alys highly doubted such a time would ever arrive.

Chanlix did not really want the cup of tea she held clasped in her hands, and she suspected Tynthanal was equally unenthusiastic about his own, despite having asked for it. They sat together on the sofa in her cozy parlor on the eve of his wedding, and neither of them seemed inclined to suggest a move to the bedroom. Chanlix stared into her cup of tea, feeling shy and nervous in a way she hadn't since the earliest days of their courtship.

"Will it bother you if I come to the wedding?" she found herself asking, still staring into the tea. "Kailee was rather insistent about it, but I don't want to make things any more . . . uncomfortable than they already will be."

Kailee had been more than insistent; she had, in fact, extracted a promise. "You are a part of this marriage, too," Kailee had said earnestly, "even if only we three know it."

"I don't imagine the Grand Magus of Women's Well can gracefully bow out of attending a marriage of state even if it *would* bother me," he responded.

She looked up and met his gaze with a wan smile. "Probably not," she agreed. The gentry of Women's Well all knew about their love affair, of course, and it was possible that Lady Vondelmai and her entourage had heard the rumors by now. Likely no one in attendance would be surprised by her absence, and there would be whispers whether she was there or not. But Kailee's father and even Queen Ellinsoltah were planning to attend, as it were, by means of a talker, and it would not do to offend them.

Tynthanal put down his tea, reaching over to take her hand and giving it a warm squeeze. She squeezed back, her throat tight with emotion. She had resigned herself to this marriage long before he had, but she was far from eager to see it happen. And she was painfully aware that something had subtly changed between them in the time since he had signed the marriage agreement, that a distance had appeared and was growing wider. Instead of cuddling in his arms as she used to, she sat an arm's length away from him on the sofa, and though they had kissed in greeting when he first arrived, this squeezing of hands was the first physical contact they'd had since then.

"Would it be all right with you if . . ." She cleared her throat. "If we don't sleep together tonight? It would feel . . . disrespectful, on the night before your wedding."

Tynthanal sighed heavily, and Chanlix thought she detected a hint of relief in the sound. "Of course it's all right," he replied. His thumb rubbed gently over the back of her hand. "I don't suppose it matters how convincingly Kailee tells us she approves of our relationship. It seems clear to me that neither of *us* approves of it, as much as we'd like to."

Chanlix closed her eyes and laid her head against the back of the sofa, realizing that he had just put into words what she'd been refusing to see. She had told herself repeatedly that their love would continue unabated despite his marriage, and she'd professed not to care about the official trappings of matrimony. And yet in the ceremony tomorrow, Tynthanal would make vows that—being the man he was—he could not help but take seriously.

"You realized all along, didn't you?" she whispered, shaking her head at herself for her unwillingness to see the truth. "That's why you resisted as long and as hard as you did."

Tynthanal snorted softly. "You give me too much credit. I resisted because I wanted to marry the woman I love, not a stranger. It certainly never occurred to me that empty vows might matter to me. To either of us."

Chanlix opened her eyes. Her heart ached, and it was all she could do to hold back tears. "Maybe things will be different once we . . . get used to it." Even fighting tears, she found a smile. "If I know Kailee Rah-Kailindar, she will try to push us together with both hands."

Tynthanal laughed softly. "That she will," he agreed. "It might almost injure my manly pride how desperate she is not to come between us." He shook his head, still smiling fondly. "I've never met anyone quite like her."

"Nor I." She laughed again. "Nor, I suspect, has anyone in all of Seven Wells." Unconsciously, she found her free hand resting on her belly. In the evenings, when she was not racked with morning sickness, it seemed almost impossible to believe that there was a new life growing within her, that she would in just a few months' time be a mother.

Tynthanal saw the gesture and raised her hand to his lips, giving her knuckles a kiss. "She seems truly happy for you," he said, "despite all the nasty whispers she knows she'll hear when your pregnancy becomes public knowledge. She is more than capable of being deceitful—as we've both seen—but I don't think she has an unkind bone in her body."

"It seems hard to believe, given the way she's been treated by Rhozinolm society. But I know you're right. She might chafe under her stepmother's rules and expectations, but she has never in my hearing said an unkind word about her."

Tynthanal nodded. "I complained about Lady Vondelmai's habit of speaking over her, and Kailee leapt immediately to her defense."

"She even likes Mother Mairahsol!" Chanlix said, still wondering how such a thing could be possible. She told Tynthanal about Kailee's desire to rescue Mairahsol from the Abbey of Khalpar.

He raised an eyebrow at her when she finished. "And do you believe she will quietly accept your answer?" he asked in a tone of polite skepticism.

Chanlix wrinkled her nose. "That doesn't sound like her, does it?"

"No, it does not. Keep a close eye on her."

"Of course. Kailee might not have an unkind bone in her body, but Mairahsol is made of them. Not that *anyone* in the Khalpari delegation is a joy to be around."

"I will be more than happy to see the last of them," Tynthanal agreed.

Silence descended, and Chanlix alternated between thinking it companionable and uncomfortable. It stretched impossibly long, their hands still clasped on the sofa between them.

"I suppose I have a big day ahead of me tomorrow," he finally said, and Chanlix regretfully released his hand.

She wanted to ask him to stay, felt somehow that she *should*, and yet there seemed little reason. They had said all that there was to say, and there would be no dramatic, romantic last night together.

"Sleep well," she said, for those seemed the only words her mind was capable of conjuring.

"And you," he replied.

She wanted to throw herself into his arms and cling to him for all she was worth. She wanted to drag him into her bed and make this last night of his bachelorhood last for the rest of eternity. She wanted to scream and rail at the unfairness of the universe—and at the quirks of their personalities that made them draw away from each other despite Kailee's wishes.

But she did none of those things. Instead, she saw him off with an almost chaste kiss on the cheek. She stood for a long time, staring at the door she had closed behind him, before she was finally able to tear herself away and prepare for bed.

Chanlix changed clothes three times before she finally settled on a gown of light blue silk with a deep blue lace bodice and lace trim around the hem. She fingered the folds of fabric anxiously as she studied her reflection in the mirror and tried to recognize herself. She'd bought the impractical gown several months ago, but had never nerved herself up to wear it. She was far more comfortable in simple dresses in subdued colors and with as little ornamentation as possible.

But some occasions required her to dress in a manner deemed appropriate for her station, and she was grimly determined that today of all days, she would dress and act like the Grand Magus of Women's

Well. No matter how many cracks had already formed on her heart and how wide they would grow by the end of the day.

The temple was one of the smallest Chanlix had ever seen. Thanks to the royal council's decision to recognize and accept the worship of the Mother of All, the majority of the religious practitioners in Women's Well favored the Mother of All temple, which was far larger. Chanlix could only imagine how Lady Vondelmai would have reacted to the suggestion of having the wedding there, despite its more accommodating size.

The traditional temple could comfortably seat only around fifty guests for the ceremony, although a much larger celebration was planned for the wedding feast, which would take place in the palace. Chanlix felt as if every one of those fifty pairs of eyes was staring at her as she entered the temple and took her seat at the front with the rest of the royal council. It wasn't true, she knew. There were certainly some who would find her presence uncomfortable—Chanlix was very glad her pregnancy was not yet public knowledge—but based on her day-to-day interactions, she did not believe anyone was especially scandalized. It was only her own self-consciousness that made her feel so eager to flee.

Princess Alysoon arrived almost on Chanlix's heels. The sovereign princess took her seat of honor, with Prince Corlin, decked out in his best dress uniform and looking very much like a young man instead of a boy, to her right. Alysoon then put a talker on the chair to her left, activating it. A small image of Queen Ellinsoltah and Lord Kailindar shimmered to life before the bird's beak. Alysoon greeted the long-distance guests, then pointed the bird toward the altar.

Chanlix caught her breath when Kailee and Tynthanal made their grand entrance. Chanlix had always admired how Tynthanal had looked in his white military shirt, and she had fond memories of the early days of Women's Well, when she would frequently see him with one of those shirts halfway unbuttoned, cuffs rolled out of the way for work. Even when dusty from manual labor, the gleaming white had set off his nut brown skin, and Chanlix had caught many a woman ogling him when he couldn't see.

He looked ever so much more resplendent now, dressed from

head to toe in traditional wedding white. His hair had been combed and oiled into a thick club at the nape of his neck, and no one who didn't know him well would see any hint that he was anything but a contented bridegroom. He smiled at Kailee with what looked like genuine warmth—though she herself could not see the expression— and that smile froze for only an instant when he caught sight of Chanlix. A hint of panic showed ever so briefly before he blinked and banished the expression. Then he offered Kailee his arm and guided her to the altar, where the priest awaited them.

Chanlix sat through the entirety of the ceremony, but she could not have recounted afterward a single word that had been said. She blamed her pregnancy for her constant need to battle against tears, and sometimes she had to actively tune the words out to cling to her mask of stoicism. Just because nearly everyone in the room knew she loved Tynthanal and had hoped to marry him herself didn't mean she had to make a grand display of her grief and pain.

Then the ceremony was over, and it was time for Tynthanal and Kailee to preside over their first feast as man and wife. Chanlix was certain Kailee's invitation—exhortation—for her to attend the wedding included the feast, but she found the ceremony itself was as much as she could bear. Hoping Kailee would forgive her lack of fortitude, Chanlix did not join the knot of revelers who made their way joyfully through the streets of Women's Well to the royal palace.

CHAPTER THIRTY-TWO

When Kailee had decided she and Mairah should take a walk down to the Well to stretch their legs and breathe the fresh air, Mairah had all but laughed at the notion. Every day, she and Norah shuttled back and forth between the inn and the Academy, flanked by their four guards, who refused to allow them to deviate from their path. Within the Academy, two guards were in the room with them at all times, with the other two stationed just outside. If Mairah or Norah should leave the room even to use the privy, a guard would follow on her heels and pound on the door if he thought she was taking too long.

Mairah and Norah might be wearing dresses instead of their robes and might not be shackled, but no one could miss their status as prisoners, no matter how many times the guards declared themselves to be "escorts." Which meant a spontaneous jaunt to the Well was out of the question.

Mairah smiled sadly, surprised at how she longed for the sight of anything other than the walls of the Academy or the inn. "I don't believe I will be allowed such a privilege."

"Nonsense!" Kailee declared, turning to address the two guards who were in the room.

Norah scowled at Mairah and said loudly, "We have much important work to do and must not waste our precious time in frivolity."

Mairah managed not to roll her eyes, but it was a near thing. They were both still playing at trying to cure the plum blight, but it would be a miracle if anyone actually believed that was what they were doing.

Kailee smiled over her shoulder in Norah's direction. "I'm sure your own diligent efforts are enough that you can spare Mother Mairahsol for a half hour." Making it clear that her invitation applied only to Mairah.

One of the guards opened his mouth to voice his own objection, but Kailee spoke first. "You won't have any problem with me kidnapping Mother Mairahsol for such a short time, will you?" she asked with a sweet smile.

A smile that was lost on the guard, who seemed to see nothing but her milky white eyes. Even after three weeks of spending most of their daylight hours at the Academy, there was not one of the guards who seemed to have grown comfortable seeing women with their Mindseye open.

"She is needed here," the guard said shortly.

Kailee put her hands on her hips. "I am sure the ways of Khalpar are very different from those of the continent, but I doubt that our guest customs are so dissimilar. Mother Mairahsol is a guest of Women's Well, and I am sister-in-law to our sovereign princess. You do not seriously mean to interfere with my attempt to show common courtesy to a guest, do you?"

The guard looked momentarily taken aback. Apparently, he'd considered his refusal to be the last word on the matter. But of course their entire delegation had entered Women's Well in the capacity of guests and in an outward show of friendly cooperation, even if neither side believed the show. It would indeed be rude for the guards to refuse Kailee's offer of hospitality if she was going to press for it, which it seemed she was.

Without waiting for the guard's response, Kailee turned back toward Mairah and held out an arm. "Come, Mother Mairahsol. Let us walk."

The guard still looked like he was on the brink of refusing, but Mairah rose from her bench and quickly took hold of the arm Kailee offered. Kailee started boldly forward, practically dragging Mairah with her. The guard had to scramble to avoid having Kailee walk right into his chest. Mairah bit the inside of her cheek to keep from laughing, remembering Kailee's stories of her "accidental" clumsiness.

As Mairah and Kailee started down the hall toward the Academy's front door, the four guards exchanged a few hasty words; then three of them decided to follow Mairah, leaving only one of their fellows to keep an eye on Norah. In case Mairah didn't already know which of the two of them was under the most scrutiny.

Kailee, of course, had her own honor guard now that she was part of the royal family of Women's Well, so the two of them were tailed by a total of five men from the moment they set foot outside. There was some masculine jostling for position and priority that made both women smile, but eventually their little procession made its way down the main street toward the road that led to the Well.

The town was brimming with activity, with people bustling to and fro, taking advantage of the still-pleasant temperature before the sun climbed to its zenith. It was a society unlike any Mairah had seen in Khalpar. Most of the buildings were of wood, and the vast majority of the people on the streets were dressed in unadorned homespun, marking them as commoners. And yet unlike in Khalpar, there was no outward sign that these commoners suffered from any kind of deprivation, and she did not see a single beggar nor any scruffy street children. The mood of the place seemed downright cheerful, people greeting one another as they passed in the street. The few gentry she spotted seemed to share in the general good cheer, and she was taken aback when she realized those gentry were as likely to exchange greetings with commoners as with one another. In Khalpar, it would be considered impertinent for a commoner to speak to one of the gentry without invitation.

The buildings and the bustle tailed off as Mairah and Kailee neared the spring that housed the Women's Well. The land, undisturbed save for a few footpaths, was vibrant and bursting with life, thick with tangled bushes and young trees. Trees that, while small, had clearly grown quite a lot faster than expected, for they were tall enough to provide respite from the sun. The air smelled green and crisp, and a gentle breeze rustled through the leaves. Mairah glanced briefly over her shoulder and saw that even her three brutish guards were intrigued by the place, their gazes wandering to take it all in.

"I love the way it smells in here," Kailee said, taking a deep breath and then sighing with pleasure.

"It's beautiful," Mairah said, realizing the tension that had rested between her shoulder blades and in her neck for weeks had relaxed. "I wish you could see it."

Kailee smiled. "I do see it, in my own way." She turned her head left and right. "So many colors."

Mairah stopped for a moment so she could open her Mindseye and look. She couldn't suppress a gasp at how thick the elements were this close to the Well. She'd found the abundance exciting when she'd first opened her Mindseye in town, but she'd never been this close to a Well before and hadn't known what to expect.

"It's not just beautiful," she whispered. "It's *breathtaking*." And Mairah wondered if Kailee had consulted with the sovereign princess before bringing her here. If *she* were sovereign, she would have forbidden untrustworthy visitors such as her delegation access to the place.

Kailee led her to the edge of a crystal clear spring that gave off a faint hum and made the ground beneath their feet vibrate ever so slightly in a way Mairah would have expected to be uncomfortable and strange. Instead, that hum eased a little bit more of the tension out of her shoulders.

"Give us a little privacy," Kailee called over her shoulder to the guards. "There is only this one path, and you need not be right on top of us to keep watch. We will be discussing female matters that I guarantee you have no desire to hear."

Once again, Mairah had to swallow the urge to laugh. Kailee's honor guardsmen showed no reaction, but the three Khalpari men all looked faintly green and stopped well out of earshot as Mairah and Kailee approached the edge of the spring.

"You are a master of manipulation," Mairah murmured admiringly.

Kailee grinned. "Surely every woman learns at a young age how to repel men with the threat that they might have to hear about female matters?"

Mairah snorted softly and had to concede the point. They stood together in companionable silence for a few moments. Mairah tried to memorize every detail of the place, every scent and every sight and every sound, for she had never before experienced the blissful peace that settled inside her in the healing presence of this miraculous Well. She wondered if King Khalvin would be so bound and determined to destroy it if he had stood where she stood. But all she had to do was take a quick glance at her shifting, uncomfortable guards to realize that not everyone experienced the Well in the same way.

"Do those 'female matters' you wanted to discuss have anything to do with your wedding?" Mairah asked, just in case Kailee's words had had a purpose other than chasing the guards away. Even with her isolation and her poor grasp of Continental, Mairah was aware that Kailee had married into a difficult situation. Considering what was rumored to be going on between Lord Tynthanal and Lady Chanlix, Mairah wondered if a traditional wedding night had happened at all.

Kailee laughed. "No, no. It was just a ruse, I promise."

"So you are . . . happy?" Mairah asked tentatively.

"Blissful," Kailee confirmed. "For the first time in my life, I do not have to ask permission to leave the house, nor give a full recounting of every hour of every day to someone who is sure to disapprove of at least half of it. I have the honor guards, of course, but my husband has assured me he will not question them about my whereabouts, nor will they attempt to tell me where I may go or to whom I may speak. I can't imagine I would have been able to say the same of a man of Rhozinolm, even had one been willing to marry me."

There was an unmistakable glow in Kailee's cheeks, and Mairah was happy for her, even as a part of her worried that the novelty of freedom would wear off and her husband's prior entanglement might cause her pain. She bit her tongue to stave off the impulse to pry, for she was certain Kailee already knew about her husband's relationship with Lady Chanlix. There was very little that escaped her attention, and if Mairah had heard the whispers, then so had she.

"Thank you for bringing me here," Mairah said instead, surprised to find tears prickling her eyes. "It would have been a tragic loss if I'd returned to Khalpar without ever seeing this Well, even though I'd never have known what I'd missed."

Just the *thought* of returning to Khalpar was enough to dispel some of the ease the Well had granted her. Becoming the Abbess of Khalpar had once been her most coveted goal—a goal worth killing for—yet how paltry that prize now seemed.

Kailee pitched her voice so low that the guards couldn't have heard them if they were twice again as close as they were now. "Have you ever considered *not* going back?"

Mairah's heart squeezed with yearning, but she knew she would be a fool to indulge the fantasy. "That is not among my options," she said more sharply than she meant to. Thanks to Kailee's tutoring, Mairah could now understand a reasonable amount of Continental, though her ability to speak it lagged far behind. And yet every other barrier to escape remained firmly in place.

"Perhaps not at this moment," Kailee responded. "But you are a clever woman, and you are not without friends. With a little—"

"Don't," Mairah interrupted. "Don't make me want something I can't have."

"Tell me all the reasons why you must return to Khalpar. Perhaps I can help you eliminate some of them."

Mairah shook her head, wondering if she herself had ever had the kind of optimism Kailee possessed. She could hardly remember who she had been as a young woman. By the time she'd been Kailee's age, she'd been locked behind the walls of the Abbey, any youthful spirit she might have possessed crushed.

"To name them all would take far more than the half hour for which you've claimed me."

"Your escorts are one of them, I presume," Kailee said, undaunted. "I suppose they would not allow you the luxury of refusing to return with them."

If there was one thing Mairah knew about Kailee from their acquaintance so far, it was that she was persistent. She was not about to drop the subject until Mairah answered her questions. "Absolutely not," she said. "If I tried, I would be declared a traitor and condemned to death. Even if I could somehow get away from them, I am not someone capable of hiding. You cannot see my face, so you don't know how painfully easy I am to recognize. My fate lies in Khalpar, and it is not within my power or yours to change that."

"And if it *were* within your power?" Kailee asked. "If you had the choice between being the Abbess of Khalpar or being a spell crafter at our Academy, which would you rather?"

"It's a pointless question," Mairah responded, her voice coming out sharp once more despite her attempt to modulate her tone. "I do not have that choice."

Kailee sighed and bit her lip, tilting her head downward as if looking at the ground at her feet. She looked suddenly vulnerable, in a way she never had before, her indomitable spirit wavering. "All right, then," she said quietly. "Let me ask you a *different* question: do you believe that what your people call the Curse can be undone?"

Mairah's skin prickled with sweat, and she was glad Kailee couldn't see the stricken expression that had no doubt appeared on her face. She knew the people of Women's Well suspected the true reason she was here, but she hadn't considered how having guessed her mission might affect Kailee. How could Kailee even stand to be in her presence thinking that Mairah was hard at work trying to destroy her happiness? It made her kindness all the more remarkable. And Mairah's guilt at having conned the memory potion out of her more severe.

The prudent thing to do was to brush the question off, steer the conversation into safer waters. Kailee was the closest thing Mairah had had to a friend since her confinement in the Abbey, but she was part of the royal family of Women's Well. Technically speaking, the enemy. Yet even knowing that, Mairah couldn't allow Kailee to fear the freedoms she had finally earned would be taken away from her because of Mairah's mission.

She dropped her voice so low that Kailee had to lean closer to hear. "There is no one alive today who has the power to undo the Curse," she confided. "Certain people need to be convinced that every effort is being made to do the impossible, but just because they want to believe it doesn't mean it's true."

A little of the tension seemed to ease out of Kailee's posture, and the worried look smoothed out and became once more a smile. "Thank you. And because I feel certain I know the answer to the question you refused to answer, let me assure you that if there's any way I can arrange for you not to have to go back to the Abbey, I will do it."

Impulsively, Mairah threw her arms around Kailee and gave her a hug. "I will miss you a great deal when I am gone," she said, wishing with all her heart that it were actually possible to stay. "You have been such a good friend to me. The best I've had in a long time."

Kailee hugged her back, but even in the moment of sentimentality, her natural sense of humor came through. "I'm not sure how to take that when your last best friend poisoned you." She pulled away from the hug and smiled, though there was a touch of sadness in the smile. "Until I came here, I had never known true friendship before." She pointed at her eyes. "These meant that respectable families did not want their daughters spending time with me, and though there were servants who were fond of me, they were never *friends*."

"It is *they* who are blind if they cannot see what a treasure you are." Mairah shook her head in frustration at how . . . shallow people could be. "People look at us and see my face and your eyes and they never bother to look deeper, to see us for who we really are."

"Exactly." Kailee nodded. "I believe it will be better here in Women's Well, but that doesn't make me any more eager to lose my first ever friend." Mairah opened her mouth to protest, but Kailee didn't give her the chance. "Do not make the mistake of underestimating me."

Mairah let her protest die, for though she hated that Kailee was getting her hopes up, it was clear the girl had no intention of giving up. "Only a fool would do that. I am not a fool."

Kailee smiled triumphantly. "It's settled, then."

Mairah shook her head, already feeling guilty for the hurt and disappointment Kailee would suffer when she realized this was one battle she could not win.

CHAPTER THIRTY-THREE

Star gave the tapestry a glare that would have melted steel, but that didn't silence the furtive knocking that came from the door behind it.

"I think I liked it better when you two were fighting," the maid muttered under her breath, though Ellin was sure the woman was secretly pleased the marriage negotiations had resumed—albeit with a frustrating lack of progress.

Ellin gently took the hairbrush from her maid's hand and set it on the dressing table. For all that relations between them had thawed of late, this was the first time Zarsha had come knocking on the secret door since their fight, and she found herself ill prepared to meet him in such intimate circumstances. It was scandalous enough to be allowing a man into her bedroom at night, but to let him see her in her nightdress suggested a different kind of intimacy altogether.

Not that he hadn't seen her indecently clothed before, although on that occasion she had let him in only because she thought it was

Graesan at the door—and Graesan's attempt on Zarsha's life had so outshone the impropriety that she'd barely noticed.

"If he's to be my husband, then I suppose there's no harm in letting him in," she said reluctantly.

"I should advise you against it," Star murmured as she went to open the door, "but I haven't the heart."

"Nor the hypocrisy."

Star gave her a mock glare. Ellin grabbed her dressing gown and wrapped it around herself as the door opened.

Zarsha was still dressed in his evening best—a doublet of granite gray over black breeches, so somber that if he were not a man of Nandel, she'd have thought him in mourning. Once upon a time, she'd found the austerity of his color choices off-putting, just as she'd found his blue eyes cold. But the two of them had shared so much over the past year or so—both the good and the bad—that she now saw the inherent warmth of the man behind the colorless trappings. Even when those blue eyes looked troubled and he did not flash her his customary smile. He bowed to her, and he even gave Star a respectful nod.

"Forgive me for disturbing you this late," he said. He shifted uncomfortably, looking strangely hesitant for a man who always made such a great show of confidence. "I shouldn't . . ." He huffed. "I'm sorry. I'll let you get some rest."

Ellin and Star exchanged a puzzled look as Zarsha bowed again, seeming for all the world like he was about to walk right back out.

"You don't honestly think I'm going to let you leave after that," Ellin said dryly, freezing Zarsha in his tracks.

"If you do," Star added unnecessarily, "then you don't know our lady as well you think." She stepped neatly in front of him, firmly drawing the bolts on the secret door and settling the tapestry back in place. She turned to Ellin. "I'll just wait in the sitting room until you're ready."

Ellin gave the maid a grateful smile. There was very little chance anyone—except Zarsha—would disturb the queen at this hour of the night, but just in case, it was nice to have Star on watch. Ellin wasn't sure how vulnerable the reputation of an unmarried queen might be, but she had no wish to test it. Zarsha cast one longing look at the secret door as Star slipped out, then sighed and turned back to face Ellin.

"I really shouldn't have come," he said, and there was a flush of what looked like embarrassment in his cheeks.

"Well, you *have* come, so it's a little late for regrets now." She gestured toward the chairs by the fireplace. "Now sit down and tell me why you're here."

It all came out sounding rather more peremptory than she'd have liked, but it was hard to know how to act around this awkward, uncomfortable version of Zarsha. In any case, he did not seem to mind her tone, crossing to his habitual chair and sitting with a little bit more stiffness than usual. Holding her dressing gown tightly closed, she took her own seat, tucking her scandalously bare feet as far under the chair as possible and hoping the drape of her nightclothes would keep them from view.

"I'm being a selfish ass," Zarsha confided, and a hint of his usual smile flashed briefly across his face before disappearing once more.

Ellin smiled more broadly, unable to resist teasing him despite—or perhaps because of—his obvious discomfort. "You consider this remarkable in some way?"

He drew himself up to his full height and shook his head. "You wound me, Your Majesty."

"And yet *I* am the one set to perish of curiosity. I can't imagine what has made you so . . . unlike yourself." Considering all the scandalous and uncomfortable conversations they'd had in the past, she had no practical guess as to what might ail him now.

Zarsha folded his hands together in his lap, his thumbnails rubbing idly against each other. He visibly steeled himself before speaking. "My—" He cleared his throat. "Princess Elwynne, who may or may not be my daughter, apparently suffered a bad fall while playing on the battlements."

Ellin gasped in sympathy, and against her better judgment, she reached out and touched his arm, giving it a squeeze. "Is she all right?"

Zarsha sighed heavily and seemed to relax all at once. He met her eyes, and the relief in his gaze was impossible to miss. "She will be, though she has a couple of broken bones."

"The poor thing," Ellin said, even as she realized that Zarsha's unease had been caused by fear that her jealousy of his former lover might make her less than sympathetic. She'd have taken offense at the idea, if she weren't so well aware that she'd deserved his caution.

An ugly thought speared through her, and her breath caught in her throat. "Are you sure it was an accident?"

Zarsha winced, but nodded. "Reasonably sure," he said, though she heard the doubt in his voice. "As cold and cruel as my uncle can be, I don't believe he would harm a child. But still . . . The timing is disturbing."

Right after the marriage negotiations had resumed, he meant. "You think your uncle may be trying to warn you of the price of defiance?"

He leaned back in his chair and closed his eyes. "I truly believe it was an accident. But she could have died, just the same, and it's made me realize just how much faith I've been putting in my own judgment." He opened his eyes and sat up straight once more, his jaw set with determination.

"Just because I believe he would not harm a child doesn't mean I'm right. It is unspeakably arrogant of me to act as though my beliefs are facts."

"But what else can you do?" she asked gently. "I'm sure Prince Waldmir has guarded against the possibility that you might want to spirit the child away, so you have no way to protect her other than to try to give him whatever he wants."

Zarsha nodded, his face uncommonly grim as he reached out and took both her hands and looked into her face imploringly. "The only other thing I can do is make plans for what to do if I'm wrong." His hands squeezed hers a little more tightly than was comfortable, but she didn't complain. "If something should ever happen to me," he said gruffly, "might you be willing to help my daughter?"

Ellin was momentarily struck speechless—not so much by what Zarsha was asking of her, but by the thought of something happening to him. They'd spoken about the dangers of his secrets, but she'd taken his assurances at face value and never considered the possibility that Waldmir might decide to kill him after all.

"I think I am safe," he continued, "and I think Elwynne is safe. I don't mean to be alarmist. But that fall . . ." He shivered. "The poor child doesn't have a friend in the world besides me, and I can do next to nothing for her."

Ellin took a deep breath and let it out slowly, trying to calm the racing of her heart. Later, she would think about what it meant that she'd been so paralyzed with fear at the thought of Zarsha's death. But for now, she would try to concentrate on more practical concerns. "What is it you think *I* can do for her?"

"I will cancel the arrangements I've made to release any information that might put her legitimacy—and the legitimacy of Waldmir's rule—in question. As long as she is still recognized as his daughter, you can offer him a future husband for her here in Rhozinolm, and tell him you will provide her dowry."

"She's only four!" Ellin protested.

"But it is not unusual for a child of a sovereign to be promised well before she reaches marriageable age. Surely you can find some nobleman with a young son whom you can tempt with a dowry. And if that nobleman should prefer that Elwynne be raised in Rhozinolm, that would be all the better."

"But . . . why would Waldmir agree to such a thing?"

"The moment I am gone, she ceases to be of any value to him. He feels no paternal affection toward her, and she is nothing more than a weapon he can use against me. He will throw her away like so much refuse, sending her to the Abbey—unless he has a better alternative. Without the need to torment me, I expect he would be happy enough to send her to Rhozinolm. He would never have to see her again, and he would be spared the shame of having his daughter sent to the Abbey."

She regarded him in silence for a moment, until he reluctantly added, "And if he still does not agree, you can admit that I told you I might be her father. And that I shared his *other* deep, dark secret, as well."

"So basically, you want me to blackmail him on your behalf."

"Basically," he said with a pale imitation of his usual grin.

She met his eyes, moved in unexpected ways by his request. "You would forego your revenge entirely for the sake of a girl who may not even be your daughter," she said.

"Of course I would," he answered immediately. "What good does revenge do a dead man?"

She flinched, her heart skipping a beat at the thought. "But he will not act against you," she said with more certainty than she felt. "You are merely feeling vulnerable because of the child's accident."

He nodded. "I'm sure that's true. But I would rest easier if I knew she would be taken care of."

"Can we bring her here anyway?" Ellin asked wistfully, although she already knew the answer.

Zarsha rubbed his face as if weary. "I truly wish we could. But as long as I live, she is his leverage against me, and he will not give her up. Even if I promised never to reveal what I know, he would never trust me if he did not have a hostage."

The pain in Zarsha's eyes made her heart ache, as did the thought of a helpless little girl trapped in the custody of a man who despised her for no good reason. It was unthinkably cruel to hold an innocent child responsible for the sins of her parents. Not to mention that Waldmir might be her father after all.

"Will you make me that promise, Ellin? I know it's a lot to ask—"

Ellin interrupted him with a scathing look. "I know I reacted poorly to what you told me, and I will freely admit that I entertained some irrational jealousy, but unlike your uncle, I would never hold it against a little girl who had no part in it. I will put some thought into how I can best help her. And once you and I are married and Rhozinolm's alliance with Nandel is solidified, we will find a way to bring her here—or at least get her away from Waldmir—without you having to die to make it happen."

Zarsha rose from his chair and came to kneel at her feet, taking her hands in his. He bent and kissed the back of first one hand, then the other, the touch of his lips against her skin making her whole body tingle, though he was not attempting to be seductive.

JENNA GLASS

"You are more than I deserve," he murmured as he looked up into her eyes.

She met his gaze and was surprised by the flush of heat that suffused her. Her body thrummed with a sensation she had not felt since the days when Graesan shared her bed. And for the first time, she allowed herself to admit that this marriage of theirs—should they manage to make it happen—might be about more than just those trade agreements.

Mairah settled on the floor as comfortably as possible beneath the sheet she had draped over the writing desk. Thanks to the success of her test with the seer's poison, she no longer had to spend her nights frantically trying to secure her position as abbess, but since she did not want Norah to know about that success until the last possible moment, she had to keep up the charade.

For the first couple of nights after she'd had her vision, it truly *had* been a charade, and she'd spent the hours in her makeshift tent idle and bored to tears. Then she'd decided she might as well keep herself busy and started trying to improve the memory potion she'd been given.

Perhaps it was an act of arrogance to think she could improve a potion the spell crafters of the Academy had given up on—especially when she had no familiarity with the unique feminine elements of Women's Well—but it at least passed the time.

That was all it was to her at first—passing the time. But the longer she worked on it, the more invested she became. Enough so that she decided to risk testing the experimental potions herself. Of course, before she tested any potion, she formulated an antidote as well. Most potions could be transformed into an antidote to their own effects by adding Grae, a neuter element that, thankfully, was produced by the Women's Well. The number of motes of Grae required for an antidote varied for different potions, and it didn't work with *all* of them. But Grae seemed to work with the original formula, and that gave Mairah reasonable confidence it would work with her variations, should they prove to have ill effects.

It took many nights of trial and error, but eventually Mairah had a potion that could restore old memories and not wear off. She used that potion to help her remember—word for word—a conversation she'd had with the midwife who'd come to help her mother through the birth of her little sister. Mairah had been only six years old at the time—too young to fully comprehend that she was not supposed to talk to the kindly, red-robed abigail—and the woman had not rebuffed her childish questions about magic.

She had long remembered the conversation as something magical and fascinating, despite having forgotten the details, and some part of her had hoped remembering it word for word would offer some useful insight into her current practice. In that, she was disappointed, for the abigail had fed her only the most basic facts—ones that a six-year-old was capable of absorbing. But still, when she found that she still retained that memory when she woke up the next morning, it was all she could do not to dance for joy.

Success was, apparently, a heady drug. As was the freedom to work on the magic *she* wanted to do. At the Abbey, her magical practice had been limited to producing potions that others had invented, doing so over and over and over so that it was nothing but rote, boring drudgery. Then she'd invented the seer's poison, but she had only done that because of the threat of losing her position, not because she actually *wanted* to. And of course there were the many hours she spent at the Academy, willfully sabotaging her own work.

Was it any wonder she had derived no satisfaction from those endeavors?

After her trip to the Well with Kailee, Mairah decided her next nocturnal project should be for Kailee's benefit—as an act of reparation for deceiving her about the memory potion. No matter how much Mairah wanted to believe that Kailee could find a way to keep her from returning to the Abbey, Mairah was too much of a realist to allow the fantasy to hold sway. Which meant that when she was gone, Kailee would once again be friendless. The girl might be better accepted here in Women's Well than she had been in the land of her birth, but those blind eyes of hers would always set her apart. Mairah assumed the spell crafters of the Academy had been assigned the task

of curing Kailee's blindness, but she saw no reason that she herself
shouldn't tackle the problem. What better gift could she give the
young woman who had come to mean so much more to her than
anyone else she knew?

Kailee had made an offhand comment once that she didn't want
to be cured, and that gave Mairah momentary pause. But it was incomprehensible to her that someone who was blind might not want
to see. Perhaps Kailee was merely afraid that if her blindness was
cured, she would lose her Mindsight, which was all she had known.
An easy enough fear to dispel, for it took a concerted effort to make
the effects of any potion permanent, which meant Kailee would always have the option of skipping a dose to use her Mindseye.

Because she'd been making antidotes at the same rate she'd been
making potions, Mairah was struck by the idea that the potion she
needed would be something like an antidote to a potion that already
existed. There were very few people who were born Rho-blind—
unable to see any elements at all even when their Mindseye looked to
be open—but the disability was considered so devastating (at least to
men, who were universally allowed to use magic) that a potion had
been developed to treat the condition. The potion was frustratingly
short-acting, and it only granted the user the ability to see Rho, but
it was better than nothing. With the potion, at least the Rho-blind
could turn on their own luminant or activate a cheval when necessary.

Working with the Rho-blindness treatment—which she had to use
her own memory enhancement potion to remember how to create—
and Grae, she hoped to create a potion that would force Kailee's
Mindseye closed so that her worldly vision would function.

Testing this particular potion was riskier than testing the memory
enhancement potion—the last thing she wanted to do was strike herself Rho-blind—but for Kailee, she would take the risk. After all, the
base potion had the advantage of being short-acting, so as long as she
was careful with her modifications, any effects should wear off in a
few minutes.

Mairah had no way of knowing whether any potion she concocted
would work for Kailee's specific condition, but she figured if drinking

the potion would close her own Mindseye when it was open, it was worth trying. She lost track of how many different variations she tried—in ideal circumstances, she would take meticulous notes, but such was not an option when those notes could too easily be spied—and she was close to admitting defeat when, in the wee hours of the night, she surprised herself by succeeding.

With her Mindseye open, Mairah drank her latest potion, fully expecting it to be as disappointing as the previous ones. But within seconds of swallowing the potion, her Mindseye closed of its own accord. It was all she could do to keep from whooping in joy and triumph. She made every effort to reopen her Mindseye—unable to keep a lick of panic from running through her veins when she could not—but as expected, the potion wore off only a few minutes later. With a sigh of relief, Mairah opened her Mindseye again and took a careful mental note of exactly which elements in what proportions she had put into this particular variation.

She still did not know if the potion would have the same effect on Kailee, and even if it did, it would be of minimal use if she could not make it last longer. But it was a hopeful starting point, and if it worked as she hoped, she would spend the remainder of her time here in Women's Well—as little of it as there might be—trying to make a longer-lasting version.

For a brief moment, Mairah wondered what she could accomplish if only she could remain here and join the Academy, throw herself into her work. Creating new magic was . . . well, the best word she could think of to describe it was *magical*. It was the only work she had ever found herself actively *enjoying*, and to spend the rest of her days doing it . . .

But it was still an impossible dream. One far too dangerous to allow herself to dwell on.

Mairah had assumed her walk down to the Well with Kailee was a one-time treat, but somehow Kailee had managed to make it part of their everyday schedule, a mid-morning break that was by far Mairah's favorite part of the day. Kailee did not bring up again the possibility that Mairah might stay in Women's Well—though Mairah doubted the young woman had given up—and their conversations tended to meander in such strange directions that Mairah never knew where they would end up. She told Kailee more than she ever would have expected about her life at the Abbey, her tongue probably wagging too freely. She didn't come right out and say that her ability to stay abbess depended on her convincing the king she had a chance to reverse the Curse, but no doubt Kailee could easily read between the lines. The only thing Mairah truly held back was her responsibility for the death of Mother Wyebryn. Kailee minimized or forgave every other sin Mairah admitted to, but even her forgiving heart would not condone murder.

For her part, Kailee told Mairah about growing up in Rhozinolm. About the long-ago death of her mother, about what it was like to feel her father's love for her coupled with his shame at her disability. And she told of the joy that had lit her heart when she'd realized she could have a husband after all, as well as the raw ache of marrying a man who was in love with another.

"I don't mind, really," Kailee claimed with a careless shrug. "He never lied to me about it, and he's given me a life that seemed completely out of my reach before." She smiled at Mairah. "I don't think he will ever be as good a friend as *you*, but he is a friend nonetheless. And although I've assured him I don't mind his relationship with Lady Chanlix, he's being so discreet about it that even *I* don't know if and when he is with her."

Mairah snorted, wondering if Tynthanal's ambivalence toward his pretty new bride had anything to do with those sightless eyes of hers. In Mairah's experience, even men who were genuinely in love with a woman were easily tempted by a pretty face, and Kailee should have been tempting enough to lure anyone. Surely Kailee wanted more from a husband than just friendship. And she *deserved* more.

It seemed the perfect occasion to present her with the potion Mairah had been working on. "I've made something for you," Mairah said quietly, reaching into a pocket in her skirts and pulling out a vial. "I cannot guarantee it will work for you, but I *can* guarantee it won't harm you, because I've tested it myself."

Kailee was frowning at the vial, no doubt trying to identify all the elements in the potion. Mairah had been helping her identify those elements they could both see, although Kailee had picked up a surprising amount of knowledge on her own. Kailee tilted her head up in such a way that she'd be making direct eye contact if she could see.

"You have something in there that is . . . unexpected," she said.

Mairah should have known Kailee could see all the elements in her potion—the girl did not have Mairah's ability, but she was nonetheless quite skilled. Which meant that she could see the element Nex, which occurred nowhere else in the world but here and which Mairah should not have been able to identify or utilize. The element was so frequently used in Women's Well that Mairah had spied it in potions and spells that no one had thought to hide from her. It had taken only a few experiments to figure out that Nex seemed to intensify the effects of certain potions and spells, and it had turned out to be the key Mairah needed to make her potion work.

"I know everyone's been very careful to keep me from learning too much," Mairah said, "and I understand why. But sometimes I pick up on things I'm not meant to. A trait that I suspect we share."

Kailee's frown deepened for just a moment before her more habitual smile returned. "That I cannot deny."

"And can you identify the other elements in the potion?"

"Enough to have some idea what you mean it to do," Kailee replied, the frown returning. "I thought you understood that I don't want to be 'cured.'" There was a hint of hurt in her voice.

"I do," Mairah assured her, though of course she couldn't comprehend the why of it. She figured it was enough to understand *that* Kailee did not want to be cured. "But if this potion works, it would not be a cure. A cure would have to be permanent, and this is not. What it is at the moment is a potential *treatment*. Something that would temporarily give you the ability to see."

Kailee was still frowning and did not take the vial. "I'm not broken," Kailee said, looking vulnerable for the first time since Mairah had met her.

"Of course you're not!" Mairah replied.

"Then why are you trying to fix me? I'm so tired of everyone trying to fix me!"

Kailee closed her eyes, and Mairah felt a flutter of panic. She had created this potion meaning for it to be an act of kindness, but apparently her years of scratching and clawing for survival had left her out of practice.

"I'm not trying to fix you," Mairah insisted. "I just want to give you . . . a choice. Something with which neither you nor I have had much experience in our lives. You have never had a choice as to whether to close your Mindseye or not, and if this potion works . . . well, then you will. Even if you decide never to use it, the choice would still be there. And if you *do* use it, and you decide you would prefer eyesight to Mindsight, it's always possible a permanent formulation could be made." She scrubbed at her face, frustrated at her inability to give voice to her own thoughts and feelings.

"No one else need ever know I made this for you," she concluded. "And you need never try it if you don't want to. I made it because I wanted to thank you for the kindness and friendship you've shown me during my stay here."

Kailee let out a shuddering sigh, then took a moment to compose herself before responding. When she turned her face toward Mairah again, her usual smile was back in place, if with perhaps a little less brightness. "Forgive me," she said. "I did not mean to be ungrateful." She took the vial of potion from Mairah's hand. "I hope you will not think ill of me if I take a little time to consider before I decide."

"Of course not," Mairah assured her. "I also wouldn't think ill of you if you decided to show the potion to Lady Chanlix and ask her advice and opinion. Having more experience with the special elements available here, she may be able to improve on my formulation." And assure Kailee that the potion was safe to drink. Mairah had seen no sign that her friend suspected any foul play, but if their roles were reversed, she would have sought a second opinion before trying an untested potion created by the abbess of a rival nation.

Kailee slipped the vial into a pocket, but when she withdrew her hand from the pocket her fingers were still closed. "I have something for you, too," she said. "Something it's best our observers don't see me giving to you. Can you reach over and take my hand and make it look like a natural gesture?"

"Something for me?" Mairah repeated stupidly, for she could hardly believe she had heard right.

The corner of Kailee's mouth twitched. "It's called a gift. I know you are familiar with the concept, seeing as you've just given me one."

At a loss for what to say—and more curious than she could put into words—Mairah slid her hand into Kailee's and felt the small, smooth stone that rested in her palm. The stone was small enough that Mairah could easily conceal it in her own palm when she let go, at which point she dropped it into the pocket that had contained the vial.

"What is it?" she asked, for she didn't know how she could bear to wait until she found true privacy to examine it.

"It's a Trapper spell," Kailee responded.

Mairah could only gape at her young friend. She had heard of Women's Well's famous Trapper spell.

"It's only a small one," Kailee clarified, "but it is big enough to hide a person. You can still give yourself away by making noise or bumping into things, but you can become invisible to both physical sight and Mindsight when it's active." She turned to face Mairah. "I know it's not enough. You cannot live your whole life within the influence of a Trapper spell. But it would help you escape your guards, and it might help you stay hidden long enough to create a spell to change your appearance so that you need not live your life in hiding.

"If you wish, I can speak to Princess Alysoon on your behalf. From what everyone has told me, she has a remarkable ability as a spell crafter, as does my husband. The two of them working together would be a formidable force. If anyone can find a way to permanently alter your appearance, it is the two of them. I feel confident that if I can present Princess Alysoon with a fully formed plan, I can talk her into offering you a place here in Women's Well."

Mairah's treacherous heart leapt with hope, a hope she struggled to rein in. "If I were to disappear, King Khalvin might suspect Women's Well of having helped me. I imagine that might create significant difficulties." Surely the sovereign princess would not risk the well-being of her principality for someone like Mairah. Mairah had exchanged no more than a handful of words with the princess when the delegation had been formally introduced and had scarcely set eyes on her since then, but her first impressions were hardly those of warmth and trust.

"It would be dangerous," Kailee agreed. "For all involved. But Alys means for Women's Well to be a refuge for women like you and me. Women no one else would value or want."

Mairah was a long way from convinced, no matter how much she wanted to believe it was true. "Let me think about it," she said, for though her natural skepticism told her it was wisest not to get her hopes up, she could not resist trying to come up with a plan that felt . . . well, if not *safe*, at least not suicidal.

"Think fast. Your time here is almost up."

Mairah winced, for it was nothing but the truth. In four days' time, Lord Solvineld would pack up their entire delegation and hurry them back home. She surreptitiously touched the stone Kailee had given her through the fabric of her skirt. The Trapper spell might make possible what had once seemed impossible, but there were a great many more hurdles to climb over before she dared allow the stubborn seed of hope that had taken root in her heart to bloom.

CHAPTER THIRTY-FOUR

"Close the door," Delnamal said abruptly when his secretary answered the summons, not even giving Melcor the chance for a polite greeting and bow. Melcor's face showed only a trace of surprise and curiosity before he quickly obeyed.

It was hardly unusual for Delnamal to speak to his personal secretary in private, so presumably Melcor noticed something in his tone or expression that piqued his interest. For just a moment, Delnamal wondered if he was being foolish to put so much trust in an underling. But then he remembered Melcor stepping into the path of the flier that had been sent to attack him, putting his own body at risk to protect his king. It was true that Melcor had already been struck by one of those insidious Kai fliers sent from the witches of Women's Well, and that perhaps he might have thought that being struck a second time would have no further ill effects. Still, he couldn't have been sure what spell that flier carried, and he had risked his own life to intercept it. If that didn't make him trustworthy, then there was no such thing as a trustworthy man.

"I have an unusual request for you," Delnamal said, and saw that Melcor's curiosity was even further aroused. Possibly by the thought that Delnamal would ever bother to *request* something from him when he could simply *order* it. The last time he'd made an actual *request* had been shortly before then-Lady Oona had suddenly and unexpectedly become a widow.

"I am always at your service, Your Majesty," Melcor said. "You know I am open to . . . unusual requests, even when they might have unpleasant consequences. Just as you know I can be relied on for discretion."

Delnamal experienced a surge of gratitude that was almost enough to make him weep. There was not one other person in his life who showed him the kind of loyalty that Melcor did, not even his wife or his mother. *Certainly* not the eunuchs of his royal council. Melcor's usefulness as his secretary made him irreplaceable, so Delnamal could not bestow on him lands and titles that would make him too grand for the position, but he vowed that one way or another, he would reward the man for his selflessness and dedication.

Delnamal swallowed the lump that was forming in his throat as he realized he should *not* have had that last glass of brandy. It was making him maudlin. But it had also given him the courage and the cunning to craft this brilliant and elegant solution to his problem with Prince Waldmir.

By all rights, Waldmir should be falling all over himself at the prospect of seeing his daughter married to Delnamal's son, even if the wedding might not occur within his lifetime. Especially after Delnamal had given him the generous gift of an entire caravan of trade goods from Women's Well with no strings attached. But for all that Rhojal of Nandel had communicated Waldmir's intense interest in the potential match and had dangled the possibility of exclusive trade agreements before Delnamal's nose, there had been no progress whatsoever in getting those agreements made. And Zarsha of Nandel was *still* in Rhozinolm, by all accounts courting Queen Ellinsoltah.

It seemed that Delnamal would be forced to make yet another gesture to entice Prince Waldmir into choosing Aaltah over Rhozinolm. A personal gesture, from one monarch to another, reminding

Waldmir how much more they had in common with each other than with any female pretender with delusions of grandeur.

Delnamal smiled warmly at Melcor as he imagined just how wounded Alysoon would be by the gift he intended to deliver to Prince Waldmir. "Might you still have ways to contact those most excellent mercenaries you hired for me before?" he asked.

Norah had grown increasingly insufferable with each passing night as she saw Mairah's deadline looming with seemingly no progress. More than once, Mairah had had to stop herself from blurting out the truth about the unique seer's poison she had invented, knowing full well that if she did so, their delegation would leave Women's Well the very next day.

She had thought long and hard over Kailee's proposal, and slept scant hours the last two nights in her attempts to figure out how to do the impossible. She'd begun exploring ways to change her appearance, using a few of the most common beauty spells as a jumping-off point, but she needed more time than she had. Kailee had suggested Women's Well could hide her while she—and perhaps even Alysoon and Tynthanal—worked on a solution, but Mairah didn't have as much confidence as Kailee did that she would be offered asylum. She had not in any way demonstrated her magical abilities during her stay at the Academy, so it might be hard to convince anyone but Kailee that she would be an asset. Perhaps if Kailee were willing to show Chanlix the potion Mairah had made for her, it would make a good impression, but Kailee was still undecided about it. The only advantage Mairah had was Kailee's advocacy, and she did not know if she dared put all her faith in that.

Escape from the Abbey seemed at the tip of her fingers, just out of reach. The Trapper spell Kailee had given her meant that surely she could avoid the guards. They no longer spent every night posted outside Mairah and Norah's door; however, there were always two of them stationed in the inn's common room throughout the night, and Mairah could not exit the inn without passing in front of their noses. The Trapper spell would allow her to pass by them unseen, and from there she trusted she could slip out a door unnoticed when someone else opened it.

Escaping the inn seemed entirely doable. It was what came after that still gave her pause. The guards would practically tear the town apart to find her, and though thanks to the Trapper spell, they would fail, Mairah had no doubt that they would lay the blame of her disappearance on the people of Women's Well. It wasn't worth risking everything to stay here if her actions might trigger a war that destroyed her hiding place.

No. She would have to disappear *without* allowing the blame to fall on Women's Well, and that meant she needed someone else to take it. Luckily, the Mother had—for reasons that defied logic—chosen to send Mairah to Women's Well in the company of someone who would be only too happy to see her dead and would therefore be the prime suspect if she were to meet with some mysterious accident. So, all she had to do was escape the inn using the Trapper spell, find some way to convince everyone she'd been murdered, frame Norah for it, remain in hiding until the delegation left, and then hope it was somehow possible to invent a spell or potion that would permanently change her appearance so that she would not be recaptured. If Princess Alysoon could be persuaded to shelter her in the first place!

To say the task was daunting was a massive understatement, and when Kailee gently pressed her for an answer, Mairah had said only that she was still thinking about it. She wanted to stay more than she'd ever wanted anything before in her life, but the risks . . .

If she went back to Khalpar with her new version of the seer's poison, she believed she could craft a convincing argument that it might lead to the reversal of the Curse, and that dangling that hope before King Khalvin's nose would secure her place as abbess. She would be safe and comfortable and, especially with Jalzarnin on her side, she would enjoy a reasonable amount of power. If she attempted to escape and she failed or was later recaptured, she faced a traitor's death. What possible reward could be worth that risk?

The combination of indecision and outright terror that consumed her gave Norah a great deal of pleasure, for the other woman assumed Mairah was thinking about her future in Khalpar as an abigail serving under Mother Norah.

"You needn't worry so much, Mother Mairahsol," Norah taunted, the expression on her face so smug Mairah wanted to scratch her eyes out. "I would never dream of treating you as you treated me when our positions are reversed. The Mother of All teaches us kindness and forgiveness."

"Yes," Mairah snapped back. "That was very obvious when I was serving under Mother Wyebryn. My days were *filled* with kindness."

Norah sniffed disdainfully. "Had you shown a modicum of respect or humility, your time at the Abbey would have been very different. You earned every punishment you ever received. Perhaps you have learned from all your failures, and I will not need to punish you so very often when we return."

Mairah ground her teeth, wishing she could school her expression so that Norah could not see how much the words rankled. It occurred to her that if she found the courage to attempt to stay in Women's Well, it might be easier to frame Norah for her murder if the two of them had a spectacular row. Better to engineer it in public than within the walls of their room, but Mairah's blood was boiling, and she'd never been good at suffering in silence.

"Even if you *were* going to become abbess when we returned," she sneered at Norah, "you would never dare punish me again. Not when I still hold your fate and that of all your fellow heretics in my hands. It's probably just as well for you that I will continue in my current capacity, for you're too spiteful and stupid to restrain yourself if you had the power to hurt me, no matter what the consequences."

Norah's face flushed with heat at the insult—until she absorbed the implications of Mairah's words. They were—naturally—unable to speak freely of Mairah's true mission when they could not be certain they would not be overheard, but there was only one way Mairah could stay on as abbess.

The angry color drained from Sister Norah's face, and she sat abruptly on the edge of her bed as if her knees had gone weak. The bleak despair that filled her eyes was almost enough to make Mairah feel sorry for her, but all she had to do was remember the malicious glee of moments ago to chase that pity away. She crossed the room and leaned over until she was whispering in Norah's ear.

"It seems your Mother of All wants me to be the Abbess of Khalpar after all, else she wouldn't have sent us here." She put a hand on Norah's shoulder in a gesture that might have been comforting under different circumstances and had the pleasure of feeling Norah's whole body tense. "Perhaps that will give you something to contemplate and pray about during the journey home."

"You *lie!*" Norah spat, glaring up at Mairah with undisguised hatred.

Mairah stood up straight and smiled. "Tell yourself that if it makes you feel better," she said. "You won't know for sure until we are back within the walls of the Abbey, now will you?"

Norah, the poor dear, was shaking with fury and fear and perhaps even a sense of betrayal, for if one believed in the Mother, one would have to believe She'd sent that vision with this very end in mind. Tears shone in the old woman's eyes, and when she climbed shakily to her feet, the droop of her shoulders made her look shorter and more frail than usual.

"I-I will go inform our escort that we will be traveling tomorrow," Norah rasped through her tears, then hurried to the door and slammed it behind her. No doubt escaping the room so that Mairah would not have the satisfaction of watching her weep. Norah would be in no more of a hurry to return to Khalpar than Mairah was—not if she believed Mairah might have invented a spell that would lead to reversing the Curse—and Mairah highly doubted the woman was truly speaking with the guards.

Having Norah flee the room in tears was actually a nice touch, Mairah decided. Even if their argument hadn't been observed or overheard by spies, anyone in the common room would see Norah's distress and remember it when Mairah disappeared.

She was going to do it, Mairah realized. She was going to stay in Women's Well. There were still many details to work out in a very short time—even if Norah didn't tell anyone that Mairah's mission had succeeded, their delegation was scheduled to depart in two days—but perhaps once Kailee brought her proposal to Princess Aly-

soon and Lady Chanlix, those three clever women could help Mairah
hone her plan into something that could actually work.

Tomorrow morning, Mairah would give Kailee her answer. And
hope against hope that Kailee was right and she could convince Princess Alysoon to offer Mairah a place here in Women's Well.

Norah had stormed out of the room with no purpose in mind but to
escape Mairahsol's loathsome presence. She certainly had no plan to
run to their escorts and tell them their delegation was ready to go
back to Khalpar.

She made it down to the common room still with no purpose or
destination in mind, then stopped indecisively at the base of the stairs.
The two guards who were on duty at the moment were sitting in a
booth. Both looked up when she arrived but quickly lost interest.
They had made no secret of the fact that Mairahsol occupied most of
their attention. Decades of life in the Abbey had taught Norah how
to put on a show of meekness and pliability around men, and her
advanced age also encouraged the guards to all but ignore her.

Was it truly possible that Mairahsol had succeeded in her mission?
Although the odious woman had never given Norah a detailed accounting of her nighttime experiments, Norah knew she was working
on some kind of modified seer's poison that would—supposedly, at
least—allow her to trigger visions of the past. If she could somehow
see how Mother Brynna had cast the original spell . . .

Norah shuddered with dread and wandered over to the bar so that
the guards wouldn't become curious as to why she was standing there
in a daze. She ordered a tankard of ale that she did not want. If the
guards questioned why she was down here drinking ale—she'd always
made a habit of keeping to her room—she would tell them she
needed time away from Mairahsol, and they would understand, for
the false abbess was every bit as haughty and petulant with them as
with Norah.

The Mother of All wanted us to come to Women's Well, she reminded
herself. Therefore, if Mairahsol had successfully invented a new seer's
poison, it was because the Mother of All wished her to do so. As the

Mother of All certainly had no intention of allowing Her Blessing to be reversed, the seer's poison *couldn't* work the way Mairahsol claimed or hoped.

Norah shivered, remembering Melred's vision of Mairahsol being confirmed as abbess. Whether you believed in the Mother of All or merely in the Mother, conventional wisdom said that a seer would only see visions of fates it was in her power to change. The Mother knew what was in the hearts of Her daughters, knew whether Her seers would want what they saw to occur or not. Therefore, the Mother knew Melred would want to prevent Mairahsol from becoming abbess.

So why had She then shown Melred the vision of Norah and Mairahsol in Women's Well?

The answer, when it came to her, chilled Norah to the bone.

The Mother of All had sent both Mairahsol and Norah to Women's Well because she had known the danger Mairahsol presented to the Blessing. She had therefore arranged for a way to eliminate that danger once and for all.

Norah swallowed hard on a suddenly dry throat.

Even an old woman such as she could manage to kill with a knife in the dark. All she had to do was make sure she ate and drank nothing once she returned to the room for the night—she was fairly certain that several of her suspiciously sound nights' sleeps had been aided by potions slipped into her drink by Mairahsol. Then, when Mairahsol fell asleep . . .

But if Mairahsol were murdered, everyone would know Norah was behind it. Mairahsol had threatened, nay, *promised*, posthumous revenge should anything happen to her. Norah assumed that it was Lord Jalzarnin who was meant to carry out that revenge. Mairahsol had likely left her lover a letter accusing Norah and her sisters of being Mother of All worshippers, and it would be his duty as lord high priest to have them arrested and punished. Whether Jalzarnin would actually do it or not depended on just how genuinely smitten he might be with the pox-faced bitch. Likely he knew that the discovery of so many heretics residing in the Abbey would reflect very poorly on him. But would he care? Was he as vengeful as Mairahsol, willing to hurt himself as long as his perceived enemies were hurt more?

Norah didn't know, and she hadn't the courage to find out. She had to do everything in her power both to stop Mairahsol and to protect her sisters.

Princess Alysoon and Lady Chanlix obviously suspected that their delegation had come to Women's Well for reasons other than to cure the plum blight, but they probably did not know Mairahsol was try-ing to undo the Blessing, and they *surely* didn't know she had a chance of succeeding. If they did, they would never let Mairahsol leave Women's Well with the formula for her potion. Mairahsol—and, more importantly, Lord Solvineld, who was the highest author-ity in their delegation—was convinced they could not sneak any elements or potions out of Women's Well when they left. They would be too carefully scrutinized, their every possession examined in Mindsight, likely by multiple people who between them could see every unique element in Women's Well. But as long as they had the formula, it would be a simple matter to hire an outsider to purchase or steal the necessary ingredients for them once they were gone.

Mairahsol had to be stopped, one way or another, and whoever stopped her would no doubt face consequences. But if Norah played her cards right, it need not be she and her sisters who suffered.

Taking a small sip of her ale, she glanced at the bored and sleepy guards seated in the booth. Each had a tankard of ale in front of him, though they were conscientious enough not to overindulge lest they fall asleep. Even so, they would be unlikely to refuse if Norah gifted them with the rest of her ale before she retired, and Mairahsol was not the only one who knew how to formulate a sleeping potion.

Resting her hand over her eyes as if in fatigue, Norah opened her Mindseye.

When word first got out that Shelvon and a handful of other women were learning swordplay from Falcor, they had drawn an audience of curious onlookers. The whole process was embarrassing enough as it was—not one woman in the bunch had any previous experience, and each was painfully conscious of her awkwardness. It was a strange feeling to be the most confident among any group of women, but her previous lessons with Falcor—and what he continued to insist was her natural talent—put Shelvon in the unfamiliar position of offering comfort and encouragement to everyone else.

When the onlookers dared jeer or laugh, Falcor would chase them off, but even so, the classes dwindled in size as one by one the women decided their dignity was more important than learning to swing a sword. At which time Shelvon had decided all lessons—and her own practices—would occur at night, when there were no casual observers out and about to make everyone nervous and clumsy. Falcor had further decided that the lessons would encompass both swordplay and more general self-defense for women. Sexual violence against women was much less common now that men were aware of the existence of women's Kai. But less common was not the same as nonexistent, so it was still worth a woman's while to learn any self-defense skills she could.

The lessons were irregular, thanks to the demands on Falcor's time, but Shelvon had found she enjoyed the physical activity so much that she practiced the drills—ever more advanced, as her skills progressed—every evening after dinner. She had adapted the garden behind her house into a practice field, creating a good-sized circle of grass in its center while all the bushes and flowers were pushed to the outskirts—conveniently also adding a little bit of cover so that anyone who wanted to peek in could see only through a screen of branches and leaves. It was hardly a perfect barrier, but it was at least adequate for her purposes.

Shelvon always began her evening practice with a set of stretches to limber up. She was in the midst of a series of toe-touches, her sword in its scabbard resting on the grass by her feet, when she was suddenly struck by the sensation that she was being watched. Sure she was imagining things, she stood up straight once more and glanced around the edges of her practice area. She needed very little light for her drills, so she had only two luminants glowing nearby. That light was enough to make the edges of the garden into a wall of near-impenetrable darkness.

Shelvon bit her lip, seeing no movement nor any other sign that anyone was watching. She wanted to dismiss her suspicion as self-conscious foolishness, but one of the lessons Falcor had hammered into her—and to the dwindling handful of students who occasionally joined her lessons—was to listen to her instincts. "Better to feel foolish than to be killed," he'd said over and over, to the point that Shelvon could practically hear him whispering the words in her ear right now.

Already feeling foolish, Shelvon picked up the scabbard by her feet, keeping her eyes up as she drew out the sword. She could combat the feeling of foolishness, she decided, by skipping the rest of her warm-up exercises and proceeding directly to the sword drills.

There was a rustling sound off to her right, and she turned toward it even as she backed closer to her house. *Probably just the wind,* her self-consciousness whispered at her, but she had felt no touch of breeze. *Or an animal.* There *were* small mammals, such as rabbits, in Women's Well, but there was nothing much larger than that.

She brandished the sword in the direction from which the sound had come, angling her body so that the house provided some cover for her back. She continued to feel ridiculous—right until she heard a soft masculine chuckle.

"Who's there?" she cried, her heart suddenly pounding as she caught a glimpse of movement among the shadows. Without taking her eyes from that patch of shadow, she calculated her odds of making it to her door, getting inside, and throwing the bolt before whoever was lurking in the darkness caught her.

She did not like her chances, and if she turned her back to run, she would have no defense. Mouth dry, hands shaking, she assumed a ready position, her weight on the balls of her feet, her stance wide enough to provide a stable base as she angled her body to give her potential attacker the smallest possible target.

A grinning man emerged from the shadows. He was tall and broad-shouldered, dressed in a dirty jerkin. His hair was greasy, and his unkempt rat-brown beard was stained nearly black all around his mouth. Once upon a time, Shelvon could have identified every resident of Women's Well by sight, but the town had grown much too large for that. Even so, Shelvon doubted the slovenly grinning man was a resident. He looked too much like a cutpurse—or a mercenary—to have been accepted as a citizen.

"Aren't you just adorable," he said, the grin turning into a sneer. "But you'll want to put that pig-sticker down and come quietly." He made a big, meaty fist, smacking it loudly into his opposite hand. "I'm no fan of beating women, but I'm not especially opposed to it, either."

Shelvon gritted her teeth and held firm, feeling her suspicion that he was not a resident of Women's Well had been confirmed. If he'd lived here, he'd be unlikely to threaten a sword-wielding woman with nothing but a fist.

Then again, she'd never been in a real fight before, and though she had mastered a number of drills and even tried a little sparring, she knew it would be foolhardy to trust too much in her own abilities. The sword was visibly wavering as her whole body shook with nerves. She sucked in a deep breath.

"Don't even think of screaming," the brute snarled at her, "or I'll make you regret it."

The most embarrassing lesson Falcor had taught his small class of ladies was how to let loose a proper scream, the kind that could be heard over the longest possible distance and that in no way resembled anything playful or humorous. It sounded ridiculously easy—how hard was it to scream, after all?—but Shelvon had been shocked at what a challenge it had been for some of the women. Especially herself.

"Society expects women—especially *ladies*—to be quiet and demure and unobtrusive," Falcor had said when he'd taken them all a mile outside of town for the lesson. "It goes against everything you've been taught to let loose a scream of the sort you need to draw attention unless you've been pressed past your limits—at which point it might be too late."

And then he'd made each woman scream as loud as she could, and their efforts had been almost laughable. Which was why he'd made them do it again and again and again until their embarrassment faded and they put their whole bodies into the effort to produce as much sound as possible.

In the end, they'd all been so hoarse they could barely talk, but each had managed to bring forth a scream that met with Falcor's approval.

Shelvon let loose with such a scream just now, the sound escaping her lips a heartbeat before the villain flung himself at her, hands reaching for her throat as he all but ignored the blade. The sound shattered the quiet of the night and set a neighbor's dog to barking.

Shelvon swung her sword on pure instinct, moving as if to parry the head-on thrust of an opponent's sword. Only instead of her blade meeting an enemy's steel, it met a fleshy arm, biting in deeply until it struck bone.

The man yelled in pain and surprise, jerking away as his blood splashed on the blade. Shelvon felt as if she'd been split into two people—one who was terrified and fighting for her life, and one who was nothing but a passive observer. The observer spoke to her with Falcor's voice, noting that she had slowed her stroke at the last moment, which was why the blade had been stopped by the bone.

"Another lesson you must unlearn if you are to be able to defend yourselves," Falcor had taught his students, "is that women are sweet, gentle creatures who must take pains never to hurt anyone. If you are fighting for your life, you must not only be willing, but *eager* to hurt your attacker."

He was, of course, right about that as well, as Shelvon had learned when she'd tried two-person drills, and later when she'd tried a little light sparring. Instinct commanded her to hold back, to use only the barest amount of force, to flinch away just before her sword made contact. She'd thought she'd overcome that instinct, but again, sparring and fighting for real were two very different experiences.

The ruffian's eyes were wide, his mouth open in shock as blood soaked the bottom part of his sleeve. Shelvon hoped that now that he'd learned he could not take her as easily as he'd thought, he would do the sensible thing and run away. But the look in his eyes hardened, and he made a guttural sound of pain and fury.

Shelvon let loose with another scream as the ruffian surged forward again. His eyes were fixed on the sword this time, and her observer-self noted that he was trying to come up under her swing and grab her arms. She took a couple of quick, shuffling steps backward to give herself more space and time, and once again brought her sword around.

Surprise had given her the edge with her first swing, but her attacker was no longer treating her like some helpless woman with a toy sword, and while she was swinging at his arms, he struck out with his foot, sweeping her legs out from under her.

With a scream that was more like a choked cry, Shelvon went down, losing her grip on the sword. The breath whooshed out of her lungs as the bleeding ruffian kicked the sword out of the way, then aimed a kick at her rib cage.

Something gave way with a sharp crack. Her vision went white with pain, her entire body frozen as she tried to absorb the agony. Her observer-self was still there, urging her to move, to roll, to evade whatever her attacker planned to throw at her next, but her body refused to obey even the simplest command.

So this is it, she thought bitterly. All Falcor's lessons, all the training, all the confidence she had built . . . All of that shattered by one unarmed man who hadn't the sense to run away after she'd wounded him. She did not know what he wanted with her—though the fact that he'd urged her to come with him quietly meant it wasn't just a quick murder or robbery he had in mind—but it wasn't anything good.

"Fucking bitch," the ruffian spat. "I'll teach you to bloody me!"

Shelvon tried to suck in a breath, but the searing pain in her ribs prevented it, and the best she could do to protect herself was to curl inward around the pain.

The ruffian cursed again, and over the pounding of her pulse in her ears, Shelvon heard raised voices coming from the other side of the hedges the intruder had broken through. Someone shouted "Don't move!" in a voice that said he was used to being obeyed.

The white haze of pain faded from Shelvon's eyes just in time for her to see her attacker disregard the order and start to the far side of the garden, no doubt to burst through and keep running. But the order had been shouted by one of the night watchmen who guarded the town's streets, and when it was not obeyed, a crossbow bolt struck the running man in the back of the leg. He screamed and fell, and soon Shelvon's garden was all but swarming with watchmen and concerned neighbors.

CHAPTER THIRTY-FIVE

Mairah had expected Norah to creep back into their room, sullen and angry and frightened, within a half hour or so of storming out, but that did not happen. At first, she'd assumed the old woman was having an epic sulking fit, but when a full hour had passed and Norah still hadn't returned, Mairah felt the first tingle of alarm. There was nowhere for Norah to go but the common room, and Mairah couldn't imagine what she'd do there for a full hour. Abruptly filled with foreboding, she ventured down the stairs.

When she reached the common room, she found that Norah was nowhere to be seen—and both of their escorts for the evening were sitting in a corner booth, fast asleep. The barkeep glanced up at her, then pointedly looked at the guards. The man shrugged and winked at her, which Mairah took to mean he had no qualms about her wandering out of the inn without her keepers glued to her side if she chose. Unless she missed her guess, he would report on her movements the moment she was out of sight, but at least he didn't seem inclined to stop her.

Mairah forced a smile even as her mind raced.

Where would Norah have gone? And what did she plan to do?

Mairah left the inn, wrapping a dark gray shawl around her shoulders to protect her against the chill of the night. It was not especially late, but though Women's Well had grown remarkably in the short time it had existed, it was hardly a bustling metropolis. There was very little nightlife to be had. The small inn and an even smaller public house were the only businesses open at this hour, and the streets were practically deserted. If there were any Women's Well spies watching the inn, they probably had followed Norah when she left. Whether that meant she was unobserved or not, she didn't know.

Having no other idea where Norah might have gone, Mairah found herself heading toward the Academy, which should have been closed for hours by now. But when she turned the corner and the Academy came into view, Mairah could see that lights were glowing in several of the first-floor rooms. Her footsteps quickened, even as she kept an anxious lookout up and down the street to be sure she was not observed.

When she got closer to the Academy, Mairah caught sight of a pair of guards standing by the door, chatting with each other. One of them spotted her, and she forced herself to keep walking past as if she had some definite purpose in mind. One that did not include going anywhere near the Academy. The moon was only a quarter full, and she kept her head down, reasonably certain the guard could not see her face from this distance. Certainly she would attract attention if anyone recognized her, and that was something she must avoid at all costs.

Chewing her lip in anxiety, she rounded the first corner she came to, then pressed her back against the wall in a pool of shadow as her heart pounded.

Norah was gone; the lights were on in the Academy; and there were a pair of guards at the door. All of which suggested to Mairah's worried mind that both Norah and Princess Alysoon were in that building. Which could not be good.

Years of sneaking around the darkened hallways of the Abbey of Khalpar had given Mairah confidence in her own powers of stealth, and after peeking around the corner and seeing the guards once again conversing—showing no sign that they were made wary by the sight of her—she plotted out a route that would take her to the window on the far side of the building without being seen.

Moving quickly, but as silently as possible, she hurried around the block and approached the Academy from a side street, creeping forward until she was pressed up against the wall by the window. A quick and careful peek showed her exactly what she'd feared—Norah and Chanlix and Princess Alysoon were all in that room together. Which meant Norah was even now betraying Mairah, trying to sabotage her one chance at happiness.

Belatedly remembering the Trapper spell Kailee had given her—she made sure to have it on her at all times lest someone discover it—Mairah pulled it from her pocket. Staying out of the light that spilled from the window, Mairah opened her Mindseye and activated the stolen Trapper spell. It was a small one—rumor had it that the Women's Well version of the Trapper spell could be large enough to hide a whole building, but she only needed one big enough to hide her person. She had not had the chance to test it. It was all she could do not to gasp when she closed her Mindseye and realized she could no longer see herself, even when she put her hands up right in front of her face.

Holding her breath, she stepped boldly in front of the lighted window to see Norah crying great big tears as Chanlix and Princess Alysoon looked on in obvious pity. Mairah could not hear their voices, at least not clearly, but she found when she pressed her ear up against the glass she could understand them.

". . . the right thing," Lady Chanlix was saying as she rubbed Norah's back. She was speaking in Parian, as Norah had made no effort whatsoever to learn Continental.

Norah shook her head, covering her face with both hands as her knees seemed to buckle and she collapsed onto the nearest bench. Princess Alysoon and Lady Chanlix shared a look while Norah's face was hidden. The look was full of significance and meaning, but Mairah had no idea what silent communication passed between them.

"My sisters and I will burn for this," Norah was sobbing, her words almost impossible to make out.

"Nonsense," Lady Chanlix said stoutly. "We won't let that happen." But once again she and Princess Alysoon shared a significant look. This time Mairah was fairly certain the message was that they both knew they could not protect Norah from whatever fate awaited her in Khalpar.

Mairah was certain Norah was betraying her, despite knowing she and her followers would suffer unspeakably for her decision. A suspicion Norah confirmed moments later as she raised her tearstained face from her hands.

"If she's truly created a seer's poison that would allow her to see how the Blessing was cast, then it must be destroyed," she said. "The poison and all knowledge of its existence."

Mairah's hands curled into fists even as terror rocked her. Norah was not only actively betraying her, she was suggesting Princess Alysoon and Chanlix *kill* her.

"Mairahsol must not be allowed to leave Women's Well," Norah concluded, and even with the tears and the sobs, even with the distance that separated them and the distortion of the window glass, Mairah could clearly see the flare of malice and hatred in the other woman's eyes. She might tell herself she was trying to protect the Mother of All's Blessing, but what she was really doing was getting her revenge on Mairah for every slight, large and small.

She was willing to be tortured and burned to death—and condemn her fellow worshippers to the same fate—rather than let Mairah win at anything.

"No, I suppose not," Princess Alysoon agreed with what looked like a regretful sigh.

And every traitorous dream of escape that had lit the long-dormant fires of hope in Mairah's heart was snuffed out.

As soon as the door closed behind Sister Norah, Alys turned to Chanlix and said, "What do you think?"

Chanlix frowned, her eyes mirroring the troubled feeling in Alys's soul. "I think that Sister Norah hates Mother Mairahsol more than words can express. Having seen them interact over the past weeks, I have to say I wouldn't put it past Norah to make up a story like this if she thought it would lead to Mairahsol's death. She's never openly said so, but I have the distinct impression that Norah had hoped to become abbess herself and has never forgiven Mairahsol for supplanting her."

"If she's making it up, she's an excellent actress," Alys said, remembering the abject terror in Norah's eyes when the woman had recounted Mairahsol's threats against the Mother of All worshippers in Khalpar's Abbey. "I can't imagine anyone wanting revenge so much that they would submit themselves to torture and death by fire to get it."

Alys shuddered at the thought of what the abigails of Khalpar would go through if Mairahsol revealed them as Mother of All worshippers. The Mother of All cult was frowned upon in Aaltah, but it had never been outlawed, and she couldn't imagine a king of Aaltah ever ordering "heretics" to such terrible fates even if he were devout himself. Then again, the people of Aaltah were not as strict in their interpretations of the Devotional as those of Khalpar, nor did religion hold such a prominent place in their daily lives.

"I might think that of Sister Norah," Chanlix said grimly. "I've seen what can happen to a person when hatred festers. But I have a hard time believing she would condemn her sisters to the same fate, no matter how much hatred she harbors in her heart."

Alys moved over to one of the work tables, sitting on the stool and fidgeting with the empty vials and papers just to have something to occupy her hands. "And do you think Mairahsol has truly invented a seer's poison that will allow her to see how my mother cast that spell? If they were trying to reverse the spell, that would definitely explain why King Khalvin sent them here after he'd made it so abundantly clear he wanted nothing to do with us."

Chanlix sat on a nearby stool and shook her head. "Kailee has certainly confirmed that Mairahsol is a gifted spell crafter, though of course she never witnessed her trying anything untoward at the

Academy. And we know she did something with a seer's poison and a memory potion. But she also told Kailee that she did not think the spell could be reversed, and Kailee believes she was in earnest."

"I can't let the fate of Women's Well rest on one person's judgment. Especially when that person has already shown questionable judgment with regards to Mother Mairahsol."

Chanlix nodded. "I'd say we have to act on the assumption that she has invented some new kind of seer's poison. However, I can't believe it would truly lead to the reversal of Mother Brynna's spell. You've seen the letter she sent out. She and her daughter and her granddaughter were specifically bred—over the course of *generations*—to have the magical powers and foresight needed to cast the spell. A man with no legs might watch an acrobat tumble to his heart's content, but that doesn't mean he can do a cartwheel himself."

"But can we take that chance?" Alys would never forgive her mother for casting that spell, never forgive her for the thousands of innocent lives that were lost or for knowingly sacrificing Jinnell. But that was a far cry from saying she wanted the spell to be reversed. It wouldn't bring all those dead back to life, and the last thing she wanted was to see women lose control over their own bodies once more.

"So you think we should condemn Mairahsol to death without trial and hope we can convince King Khalvin that we had nothing to do with her murder?" Chanlix asked doubtfully.

Alys managed a rueful grin. "Well, no. That doesn't seem like much in the way of a viable option. Especially not when we have only Sister Norah's word to go on. You said Kailee was hopeful that Mairahsol was interested in joining us if we could get her safely away?"

Chanlix lifted a shoulder. "That's what Kailee says. Despite my strict instructions that she was not to make any offers on our behalf."

Alys smiled drolly. "Oh, but Kailee assures us she hasn't made any offers. She merely suggested possibilities."

Chanlix snorted, though Alys was sure her grand magus had not been surprised that Kailee had a will of her own. It was impossible to know the girl and not see that.

"Besides," Alys continued, "if Mairahsol truly has invented a seer's poison that would allow us to see into the past, that speaks of a talent that could be useful to us."

Chanlix did not look convinced. "When it comes right down to it, I don't think Norah's hate is unreasoning. Something about Mairah-sol seems to rub just about everyone—except Kailee—the wrong way."

Alys wrinkled her nose in distaste. She herself had spent very little time with the Khalpari delegation, but with only a couple of brief encounters, she had to admit she had much the same impression as Chanlix. Spite practically radiated from both the abigail and the ab-bess, and if not for the complications, she'd be more than happy to see the last of them sooner rather than later.

"But you also don't think we should allow her to return to Khal-par with whatever formula she's concocted," Alys said.

Chanlix sighed. "No. If there's any chance that potion of hers could work the way she claims . . ." She shivered.

"And you don't think we should kill her."

"Just because Mairahsol is an Unwanted Woman doesn't mean King Khalvin can afford to let a member of his delegation be mur-dered without reprisal. I suspect Mairahsol's death would be all the excuse he needed to ally with Aaltah to destroy us. No, I don't think that's a great option, either."

"So you *do* want to ask her to remain with us. Even though King Khalvin would find that almost as much of an insult to his kingdom as her murder."

"We cannot offer her ordinary political asylum," Chanlix agreed. "But Kailee already had her halfway persuaded to run away, and she would not be so doggedly followed by those guards if there weren't already some suspicion that she might try it. We can tell Sister Norah that we've, er, taken care of her problem and ask her to convince the rest of the delegation Mairahsol has fled. It's possible the explanation could save Norah and her sisters from whatever revenge Mairahsol has planned, so I should think she'd be happy to cooperate."

"Hmm," Alys said, thinking over the proposition. If Sister Norah failed to convince the delegation that Mairahsol had run away, then she was likely to meet with the royal inquisitor when she returned to Khalpar. In which case she would eventually be forced to tell the truth. Having King Khalvin *think* that Alys had killed the Abbess of Khalpar was almost as bad as having actually done it. The crushed flier he had sent back with its unread message said a lot more about his attitude toward Women's Well than the small chest of gems he had sent with the delegation.

"It seems that none of our options is particularly appealing," she said. It was times like these that she was most aware that she was responsible not just for her own fate, not even just for her family's fate, but for the fate of every inhabitant of Women's Well. Delnamal longed to wipe them all out, and he and King Khalvin were natural allies. It was perhaps a stroke of luck that they had not joined forces to wipe out Women's Well already, and the murder—or disappearance—of Mother Mairahsol might negate that stroke of luck.

"Then we must pick the least unappealing of the lot," Chanlix said. "And we haven't the time to wait for the entire royal council to meet and make a decision. If Mother Mairahsol tells anyone else she has succeeded in her mission, then nothing we can do will make her disappearance any less suspicious."

"If Mairahsol can be persuaded to stay and assume a new identity, then I suppose that is the decision with the most potential for a positive outcome," Alys decided, not without some trepidation. "Though I'm not sure how we'll hide her. She is not exactly inconspicuous."

Even if Mairahsol's face weren't so prominently disfigured, she would stand out thanks to her inability to speak any but the most rudimentary Continental, despite Kailee's best efforts. It was impossible to miss her Khalpari origins. Alys was vaguely aware of the lure Kailee had cast—something about inventing a spell to permanently change Mairahsol's appearance—but such a thing would take time to invent.

Chanlix seemed about to offer some suggestion, but she was interrupted by the sudden opening of the front door. Both women jumped, though Alys realized belatedly that she had heard the murmur of men's voices just outside the door, where her honor guardsmen were standing watch.

Her master of the guard stepped into the room with a grim look on his face. He bowed briefly, then apologized for interrupting.

"What's happened?" Alys asked, dread knotting in her gut as she rose from the stool and braced herself for news of disaster.

"She is all right," the guardsman said, "but Lady Shelvon was attacked."

Mairah hurried back to the inn, battling against childish, stupid tears. It wasn't fair! She'd *just* decided to risk everything to stay, just seen her first glimpse of a possible future where she would not be either the Abbess of Khalpar or a despised abigail. She'd allowed herself for the briefest moment to hope that her years of misery might be over.

And Norah had decided to destroy that first delicious glimmer of hope.

Damn her! Mairah hoped the inquisitor would take her apart one slow piece at a time, hoped the bitch would long for her fiery death for days or even weeks before it was granted.

Mairah swiped at her eyes, her whole body shaking with a combination of fury and terror. She had to escape, had to get out of town before Princess Alysoon sent men to quietly murder her. No doubt Norah would volunteer to do the job herself, but Mairah doubted the princess would leave such a vital task in the hands of a doddering old woman who'd never killed anyone in her life.

Mairah's hand was almost on the inn's front door when she checked herself. The Trapper spell had worn off, so she was visible once more. She had managed to sneak out of the inn only because the guardsmen whose job it was to keep Norah and Mairah under constant surveillance had fallen asleep—likely with a little help from Norah. What would they do if they were now awake and saw Mairah creeping back in?

Sucking in a trembling breath, Mairah reached out and opened the door, for she could not just run off into the night with no preparation, and reactivating the Trapper spell would do her no good when she'd give herself away the moment the door moved seemingly of its own volition.

It turned out Mairah needn't have worried about being stopped by the guards—they were still sound asleep, one snoring while the other had his head cradled in his arms as he drooled on the table. Mairah tried to smile at the barkeep when he glanced over at the sleeping men and rolled his eyes with evident amusement. She felt sure her fear showed clearly on her face, but the barkeep didn't seem to notice anything unusual, and he made no attempt to stop her as she hurried up the stairs to her room.

What was she going to do? Fleeing *from* Women's Well was a necessity, but where would she flee *to*?

Her only choice seemed to be to find her way back to Khalpar somehow. She *had* succeeded in her mission, and the abbess's office was now hers for good if she could only return to claim it. Perhaps she could find someplace along the road to hide until the rest of the Khalpari delegation rode by. Solvineld and the guards would no doubt already be poisoned against her thanks to Norah, but they would want to take her back to Khalpar to face justice, at which point she could reveal everything that had happened and triumphantly produce her new seer's poison. It might actually be to their *advantage* if she slipped out of town to rejoin them later, for with the help of the Trapper spell, she could avoid the search that they'd been promised would occur before they were allowed to leave.

She felt little in the way of satisfaction at the thought of that particular victory, not after she'd poisoned herself with hope for a better life. But going home voluntarily was far safer than fleeing and being captured.

Mairah bit her lip, wondering if this plan of hers was as safe as she'd first assumed. With Norah having already condemned herself and her sisters, every moment Mairah lingered in her presence would be dangerous. Even a frail old woman could knife someone in their sleep if sufficiently motivated, and Mairah would be helpless if she was received by the delegation as a prisoner. Not to mention that Princess Alysoon now had more than enough reason to want Mairah not to make it to Khalpar with her information, which meant the delegation would likely be accompanied by some of Alysoon's men, whether they were aware of their observers or not.

No, there were other ways she could find her way home, Mairah decided, and Aaltah seemed the safest route. She could get there easily enough merely by following the road. Though she had seen little on the miserable ride from Grunirswell to Women's Well, she remembered that the road had converged with another, larger one somewhere just short of Women's Well. That second road would be the one that led to Aaltah. Alysoon's troops could not follow her into Aaltah, and despite her still-weak understanding of Continental, Mairah had learned that the Aaltah border was guarded by King Delnamal's soldiers. She would use the Trapper spell to hide herself whenever anyone was near; then she would cross the border into Aaltah and throw herself on King Delnamal's mercy. He was King Khalvin's nephew, after all, and he would surely be willing to send her home. Especially when she told him she knew how to reverse the Curse. (Although, of course, that was a vast overstatement.)

Mairahsol had few possessions, but she grabbed what she could—including the precious seer's poison, which she'd poured into a small wineskin—and stuffed it into the pockets of the red robes she had not worn since her first day in town. She also grabbed the Devotional that she had been given to carry with her to Women's Well. She'd never been devout enough to carry a Devotional, but this one was special, with a thin sheet of hammered gold hidden inside the leather-bound cover. That sheet of gold could store a wealth of elements, and the intention had been that Mairah would use it to smuggle out any crucial elements from Women's Well that she needed to work her spell to reverse the Curse.

That plan had sounded reasonably good, until they'd arrived and been informed they would not only be searched physically, but that they would be examined in Mindsight, as well. They would have no choice but to allow the search, and that meant that they would have to make other arrangements to obtain the elements they needed. But, since Mairah was not going to leave with the delegation after all . . .

She picked up the Devotional and also grabbed another wineskin, which held the potion she'd made to close Kailee's Mindseye.

Delnamal's border guards would be unlikely to believe her claims that she was the Abbess of Khalpar if she arrived at the border dressed like a free woman, but she didn't want to leave the inn dressed in her robes for fear of rousing suspicion. Instead, she shoved the robes and wimple down the legs of a pair of ridiculous pantaloons, which seemed to be the favored undergarment of the women in this principality.

The extra fabric made walking awkward and uncomfortable, but her skirts were just voluminous enough to hide the bulges. Trying not to hurry too conspicuously, she took one last look around the room, hoping to see something that might be of use to her in the journey to come, then slipped out the door once more. If she was right that their room was being watched, she would have very little time to make her escape before pursuit was hot on her heels.

The barkeep gave her a sharp look when she entered the common room once more, and he seemed on the verge of trying to stop her. He thought better of it at the last moment—presumably because he knew there were others watching her—and she hurried for the door.

Her heart was pounding as she exited the inn and wondered how long it would take her to reach the Aaltah border on foot. She had no concept of exactly how far it was, nor did she have with her any food or drink to nourish her along the way. She would have loved to have commandeered a cheval, but they were rare and precious in Women's Well, and therefore well guarded. A horse would have been an acceptable second choice—if only she knew how to ride one.

The streets of Women's Well were still eerily silent, just as they had been last time she'd ventured out. Which made the sudden hew and cry in the distance all that much more obvious.

Dread suffused Mairah's body as she realized that that must be Princess Alysoon's troops coming for her already. They had decided against a quiet murder in the night and were going to storm the inn to drag her, screaming, from her bed.

Sobbing from a combination of terror and loss, Mairah activated the Trapper spell once more, picked up the hem of her skirts, and ran for all she was worth.

Part Three

THE FALL

CHAPTER THIRTY-SIX

Alys was sitting in her parlor, drinking an especially strong cup of tea, hoping it would make her feel more alert, when Honor let her know that Kailee and Tynthanal had arrived and wanted to see her.

"I told them you were resting," Honor said. "Which is what you *ought* to be doing. It's almost dawn."

Alys smiled at the familiar rebuke. Honor had been trying to persuade her to take to her bed, if only for a few hours, from the moment Alys had arrived back in the residential wing of the palace. It was true that fatigue dragged at her, mind and body, but she couldn't imagine lying down and attempting to sleep at the moment.

"Send them in," she said, taking another sip of tea. "And then *you* get some rest. There's no reason you should be up all night just because I am."

"I'll rest when you do," Honor replied, then went to fetch Tynthanal and Kailee.

Alys stood up and rubbed her gritty eyes as her brother and her new sister-in-law were shown in. "I don't suppose you're here to tell me Mairahsol has been caught?" she asked with a wistful note in her voice before she bothered to take a good look at them.

"I'm afraid not," Tynthanal said, and Alys finally noticed the grim look on his face—and the worried one on Kailee's.

"What is it?" she asked, wondering how she could bear more bad news. Mairahsol fleeing Women's Well with a spell that might undo the magic that made their principality possible in the first place was a disaster beyond her imagining. And it had happened because Alys had allowed herself to be bribed by the chest of gems the Khalpari delegation had brought with them.

"Kailee has something to tell you," Tynthanal said, shaking his head ever so slightly at his wife, who bit her lip and stared at the floor.

Alys had never seen anything from Kailee other than confidence and good cheer—despite all the hardships of her life—and this clear show of distress was raising the hair on the back of Alys's neck.

"Go on," Tynthanal prompted more gently when Kailee hesitated to speak. "I promise I'll protect you with my life if necessary."

That brought a hint of a smile to Kailee's lips, and if Alys weren't so worried about what Kailee had to say, she might have been heartened by their ease with each other.

Kailee cleared her throat. "Let me start by saying that I don't for a moment believe what Sister Norah says. Mairah assured me there was no way to reverse what she called the Curse, and she strongly implied that she was stringing her king along with false promises."

"I understand that's what she told you," Alys said, for Chanlix had of course relayed that information when Kailee had shared it with her. "And I understand why you might believe it. But—"

Kailee waved a hand impatiently and cut her off. "I know you all think I'm being naïve. But I spent far more time with her than any of you, and I trust my own judgment."

Tynthanal gave her a subtle nudge with his elbow. "Remember that you're talking to the sovereign princess, not just your sister-in-law," he said, and Kailee blushed.

"Forgive me, Your Royal Highness," she said quickly. "I am . . . out of sorts."

"It's all right," Alys said. "You and I have always spoken plainly with each other."

Kailee let out a relieved sigh. "Yes. But I'm sorry anyway."

"Apology accepted. Now what is it you need to tell me?"

Kailee raised her chin and stiffened her spine. "I gave Mairahsol a Trapper spell."

Alys groaned and sank back down into her chair. Until now, no one had quite understood how Mairahsol had managed to disappear so quickly. The innkeeper had seen her leave and immediately reported it via talker. Making that report could not have taken more than a minute, and yet by the time the innkeeper stepped outside in pursuit, she'd seemingly vanished.

"I was trying to convince her that it actually *was* possible for her to get away from the delegation. And I am sure I succeeded. If Sister Norah hadn't come running to you and scared Mairah off . . ."

Kailee's voice died, and she scuffed one foot against the carpet. Tears glistened in her eyes, but Alys had the distinct impression that they were due to sadness at the loss of her friend—and pet project— rather than remorse for what she had done.

"You gave a woman who is trying to destroy us a way to escape with deadly magic," Alys snapped, suddenly and comprehensively furious with the girl. And with herself, for allowing Kailee to get so close to Mairahsol, for accepting her offer to act as a spy when she had nothing resembling experience.

"She is not trying to destroy us!" Kailee protested. "She couldn't do that even if she wanted to. She is powerful, but not *that* powerful. And one needed to spend no more than five minutes in their presence to know that Sister Norah hates her with a murderous passion. I would stake my life that she is lying."

"You have staked *all* our lives on it!"

Alys rose from her chair once more, unable to sit still. The revelation had done what the strong tea could not, and she was now wide awake and full of restless, angry energy. She wanted to take Kailee by the shoulders and shake her until she saw sense.

"To be fair," Tynthanal said into the tense silence, "Kailee's powers of observation are remarkable. She reads people better than just about anyone I know. If she says Norah is lying, I have a tendency to believe her."

Alys saw the grateful smile Kailee sent his way. And she also noticed when her brother took her hand and gave it a squeeze to express his support.

"So we should just call off the search?" Alys snarled, irrationally angry that Tynthanal seemed to be taking Kailee's side over her own.

Tynthanal's expression hardened, and he retained his hold on Kailee's hand. "There's no need to be nasty about it. What's done is done. It's still possible we'll find her before she gets out of our reach, and then we can examine her spell ourselves to see if it's a true threat."

Alys closed her eyes, trying to contain the rage and panic that roiled inside her. The thought that Mairahsol might undo everything, might doom them all to death, was . . . unbearable. Not after everything she had lost and suffered and endured! Predictably, the image of Jinnell's head rolling in the dust rose to assail her, as it did whenever her emotional walls were compromised. Her breaths came short and fast, and for a moment she thought she might collapse like some storybook maiden in distress.

"Breathe, Alys," Tynthanal's voice suddenly said from right beside her, and she felt his hand on her arm as he guided her back into the chair before she fell. His hand stroked over her back as though she were a child in need of comfort, and in that moment the comparison seemed apt as her world threatened to shatter around her. "We will get through this."

Slowly, Alys pulled the threads of herself back together. She shoved the memory she could not burn from her brain into a dark corner and focused, as Tynthanal suggested, on drawing in one breath after another.

"All is not lost," Tynthanal soothed. "There is a danger, yes, but then there is always danger for us. But I trust my wife's judgment, even if I don't approve of her methods."

Alys sat up straight and swiped at her eyes, embarrassed at her undignified breakdown. Perhaps staying up all night had been a mistake after all. She did not have the resilience she once had, and it was unseemly for a sovereign princess to show such weakness in front of anyone. Even family.

Tynthanal was kneeling beside her chair, looking at her with a compassion that outweighed his still-present resentment of her decision to marry him to Kailee. And Kailee stood behind him, wringing her hands, looking forlorn and miserable.

"If you had it all to do over," Alys asked her with a scratchy voice, "would you do anything differently?"

Kailee took a deep breath and raised her chin once more. "I couldn't have told you or Chanlix what I was planning to do. You would not have approved." Her shoulders hunched. "But I should at least have told you I'd given her the Trapper spell after the fact. I'm very sorry I didn't."

Alys leaned back in her chair as Tynthanal rose to his feet and took his wife's hand once more. Another sign of shifting allegiance? Or just a kindhearted man giving comfort to whomever needed it most at the moment?

Alys's nerves were too frayed to accept the apology as she ought—as Tynthanal said, there was nothing to be done about it now. "I hope by everything that is holy that you are right," she said.

Alys curbed her impatience and gave the man who attempted to kidnap Shelvon a night and a day to think things over in the tiny Women's Well jail that had so far never had more than one or two inmates at a time. There was a stockade at the Citadel for military offenders, but the worst crime Women's Well had experienced so far was the occasional petty theft and drunken brawl.

Truth be told, the delay in questioning Shelvon's attacker had more to do with Alys's need to rein in her own temper than anything else. Shelvon was badly shaken and had required a healer to see to her cracked ribs, but she was otherwise well. But it wasn't only on Shelvon's behalf that Alys's temper teetered on the brink.

When she'd learned of Mairahsol's escape, Sister Norah had immediately changed her tune, all but jumping up and down screaming that Mairahsol's potion had been a fraud all along and that her disappearance proved it. The Khalpari escorts had tried to shush her—on the quaint assumption that their hosts in Women's Well had no idea Mairah had been working on a potion—and had resorted to violence when she'd not heeded them. Alys had no love for Sister Norah, but it had infuriated her to see the old woman's bruised face after the fact.

Sister Norah's new story, however, was a boon to Women's Well, as it absolved them of all responsibility for Mairahsol's disappearance. And she supposed it would help Norah as well, for if Mairahsol had fled of her own volition, then it was possible whatever revenge she had arranged in her absence would not be triggered.

Alys was more than happy to see the delegation depart, but she was still furious at the bruises on Sister Norah's face and was in a foul temper when she arrived at the jail to question Shelvon's attacker. She was met at the door by Lord Jailom, who looked at her with undisguised concern.

"Please, Your Royal Highness," he begged, not for the first time, "let me question him. It is . . . beneath you to set foot in such a place or be in the presence of such scum."

It was not her honor he was trying to protect, she knew, though he would never come right out and put his objections into words. She had no royal inquisitor—it hardly seemed necessary for their tiny principality—but questioning a prisoner was a task more appropriate for her marshal or her lord commander.

"We have already discussed this," she said, letting an edge of annoyance color her voice, though she fully understood his reluctance. He was a good man, and he had adjusted to bowing to a sovereign princess instead of a king or prince with barely the blink of an eye. But he was too accustomed to thinking of women as the gentler sex, and it offended his sensibilities to imagine her taking such a masculine role.

She held up her hands, displaying the selection of rings she wore. Several of them were merely ornamental, but many contained some of the special spells that had been developed in Women's Well. "Women's magic will hold a special kind of terror for a man like this."

Jailom stubbornly remained between her and the door. "You know nothing about this man."

"I know he attacked a woman, expecting her to be helpless. Do you tell me that he's the type to risk being humiliated by a woman yet again?" She shook her head without waiting for an answer. "I may not know this particular man, but I know bullies." She'd grown up with Delnamal, after all. "He will talk to me, or he will pay the price. It's time for you to step aside."

Jailom's body language screamed his continued reluctance, but he bowed his head. "Very well, Your Royal Highness," he said, pushing the door open for her and then stepping out of the way.

Alys took a quiet, steadying breath, hoping she wasn't overestimating herself. If she was wrong and the ruffian refused to talk, did she truly have the appropriate level of cruelty to force him? She could always leave the more aggressive questioning to Jailom if she failed to elicit answers. It was hardly unheard of for a sovereign to leave such matters to others, but her father had always frowned on such abdication of responsibility.

"If someone is to be tortured on my orders," he'd once told her grimly, "then I would feel a coward to turn my eyes away."

It was clear to her that he had not enjoyed the duty, but his insistence that it *was* his duty in the case of crimes against the Crown had made an indelible impression on her. She and her father had had innumerable differences over the course of her life, but now that he was gone, she realized he'd always been an honorable man who had done whatever he thought was best for his kingdom, often at great personal expense.

The Women's Well jail was not as dark and gloomy as she imagined the dungeons of Aaltah to be, but even with its small size and relative youth, she immediately felt a sense of oppression when she stepped inside. The windows were kept covered when there was a prisoner in residence, the only light provided by dim luminants.

Because Women's Well had no easy access to metals—and what metals they had were needed for far more vital purposes—the cells resembled giant wooden crates more than cages. Only the locks and hinges on the doors were metal. The wooden slats were spaced just far enough apart that the prisoners could not hide from view, and the cells were barren except for a single straw-tick mattress on each floor and a covered chamber pot.

Aside from the four cells—three of which were empty—there were a pair of tables at which the guardsmen on duty could sit, and a plain closed cabinet that Alys assumed held weapons. The two guards who were currently on duty rose and bowed as Alys swept into the room, hoping she exuded confidence rather than nerves.

The man who had attacked Shelvon sat in the far corner of his cell, his back against the wall and his arms wrapped around his legs. A stained bandage on his arm revealed where Shelvon's sword had bitten. He had been given only enough healing to ensure he would not expire from infection before being questioned. He glanced up briefly when Alys entered, raised his eyebrows as if surprised, then let his head droop back down as though uninterested in what he saw.

Silently, Jailom picked up one of the guardsmen's chairs and set it in front of the cell. The prisoner pretended to ignore her as she took her seat, smoothing her skirts while observing him from beneath her lashes. His hands were scarred and rough, his clothes were tattered homespun, and she could smell the reek of his body odor from across the room. Whoever he was, he was not a nobleman, nor was he likely to be a professional soldier. Jailom had speculated that he was a mercenary—though not a highly skilled one, or he could have afforded to dress better—and Alys suspected that was indeed the case. And no matter what his usual profession, she was sure someone had hired him to kidnap Shelvon. The question was, who?

Alys had no wish to remain in the jail—or smell the prisoner's body odor—for a moment longer than she had to, so she decided to dispense with any preamble.

"I have already signed your death warrant," she said, and though the prisoner maintained an outwardly stoic, uninterested expression, she heard the faint catch of his breath and saw the tension in his shoulders. "I'm sure you're not surprised to hear that after what you did."

A muscle twitched in his cheek, and the knuckles of his hands went white as he pulled his legs closer in to his body.

"Someone must have offered you an impressive sum of money for committing what you had to know was a capital offense. I suppose you thought it would be easy money, that Lady Shelvon would offer no resistance—or that you could overcome whatever resistance she did offer." She smiled ever so faintly as she thought about Shelvon— meek, gentle, shy Shelvon—fighting off her attacker with a sword. Surely Falcor had never expected such an occurrence when he had first started teaching her.

"Too bad for you things did not turn out how you'd hoped," she continued. "Now the only question is how terribly you will suffer before you die."

Once again, she heard the soft hitch in his breath that belied his impassive face. His eyes were fixed and staring at nothing, and he made no obvious indication that he had heard her, but she was quite sure his pulse was pounding fiercely as he imagined just what creative ways she might dream up to make him suffer.

"The difference between a quick death and a very slow and very painful one is simple," she said. "You tell me who hired you to kidnap Lady Shelvon, and you tell me where you were supposed to take her, and you will be hanged. The noose will be spelled to ensure a quick break so you do not strangle to death, which I imagine would be a great deal more unpleasant."

The prisoner did not respond, and still refused to look at her. But there was enough fear in his eyes that Alys did not feel discouraged. The likelihood of someone as ragged-looking as this man being a zealot with unshakable loyalties seemed very small, which suggested the only reason he felt the need to keep silent was his masculine pride.

Alys looked over her shoulder and gestured to one of her honor guardsmen, who carried a small but heavy stone coffer. He brought the coffer to her, holding it out with both hands and waiting until she had a firm grip before letting go. Even knowing the coffer was heavy, she had to brace a bit to keep from dropping it. She set the coffer carefully on the floor, making sure the prisoner could see it through the slats of his cell. He continued to feign disinterest, but his act wasn't even close to successful.

"You don't strike me as the kind of man who keeps himself abreast of current events," she said with a wrinkle of her nose. "You probably haven't heard of how Queen Ellinsoltah dealt with a traitor she discovered among the members of her royal council."

The prisoner's nostrils flared briefly, and he wasn't able to suppress a small sound of distress, which made Alys smile fiercely.

"Ah, so you *have* heard." It was true that the growth spell Alys had sent to Ellinsoltah had had quite the dramatic effect, so she wasn't entirely surprised that even this lout had at least heard rumors about it. "Well, let me give you a little demonstration of how it works."

She bent down and opened the coffer, scooping up the small handful of seeds that lay in its bottom. She held them out for display.

"You may or may not have noticed that there were quite a number of seeds just like these in your morning meal," she said as she poured them back into the coffer and let the lid fall back down so that it made a loud thump to demonstrate just how solid and heavy it was. She fastened the lid with a solid metal lock.

Brushing off her hands, she opened her Mindseye and plucked a mote of Rho from the air, then loaded that mote into one of the rings she wore. A ring very like the one Ellinsoltah had used to kill her then–lord chamberlain. She moved her chair and waved all the guardsmen as well as Lord Jailom to the other side of the room so that her back was to everyone but the prisoner.

"Everyone stay well back," she warned, and saw how the prisoner drew his legs even closer to his body and pressed himself more tightly into the corner. She gave him a flinty smile. "The force of this spell will be directed forward," she told him. "It may not affect you at all, or you might catch the trailing edges of it."

She was, in fact, certain he *would* catch the trailing edges. Unlike the spell used to kill Lord Tamzin, this one would be targeted by direction rather than toward a named individual. The greatest effect would be on the seeds in the coffer, but the prisoner would feel its stirring as well.

She pointed at the coffer, directing the spell toward it. "Watch, and imagine what it would feel like if all of this were happening inside your body."

Sweat glistened on the prisoner's forehead as he stared at the coffer, and he made another soft whimpering sound as if in pain. Alys took that as a good sign, for the spell started slowly, and he could not possibly be feeling the effects yet. Silently, she prayed that this demonstration would be exactly as convincing as she hoped, because she wasn't sure if she had the necessary cruelty to direct it at a living, breathing human being.

"It's nothing dramatic, at first," she said. "It takes a moment before the seeds' outer shells burst and they start germinating. And, of course, even once they start to grow, there is some resistance. Less when they're growing in flesh than in stone, but still . . . They will take up every spare bit of space that exists, folding over on themselves and pushing outward."

Out of the corner of her eye, she saw the prisoner wince. His hands squeezed together so tightly she thought he might break his own fingers, and then he gasped. His hands flew from around his knees to around his gut.

"As I said, you're only getting the very fringes of the spell. Whatever seeds you have in your stomach may sprout, and I doubt that will be a comfortable experience, but they will not grow as the ones in the coffer will."

"Please stop," he whispered, shivering.

She turned to him, reminding herself what he had tried to do to Shelvon. He was not deserving of any pity, and the spell would not do him any lasting damage beyond some lingering digestive distress.

"I can't stop the spell once it's begun," she lied. "You'll just have to ride it out."

The lock on the coffer made a faint scraping sound as the lid was pushed outward by the raging growth within. Behind her, she heard the shuffling of feet and the occasional clearing of a throat as the guardsmen reacted to what they were seeing. Alys realized she should have warned them all in advance what she was planning, but it was too late now.

The lock groaned and creaked more dramatically, straining to contain its contents as they, in turn, strained to escape. The prisoner continued to whimper, and his eyes were squeezed shut.

"Open your eyes!" she commanded harshly, trying to cover her own discomfort. It wouldn't do to let him know how sickening she found the prospect of inflicting this spell on a human being.

The prisoner's eyes remained glued shut as he shook his head back and forth in denial. Then, there was a loud, explosive crack, which made everyone in the room—even Alys, who was expecting it— jump. The prisoner opened his eyes almost against his will as the stone lid fell away and a teeming mass of greenery boiled forth from the coffer.

"Imagine that happening within your own belly," Alys said, and despite her best efforts, there was a faint quaver in her voice. Not that the prisoner was likely to notice as he gaped in horror—and then turned his head to the side and vomited profusely.

Eventually, she opened her Mindseye once more and removed the mote of Rho from her ring, stopping the spell's progress. The prisoner continued to retch helplessly, and behind her, she heard a great deal of swallowing and throat clearing. She would have to remember to apologize to her men later for putting them through this without warning.

"What did you intend to do with Lady Shelvon?" she asked. "And who hired you? Answer those two questions honestly and fully, and you will suffer the effects of this spell in your imagination only."

The prisoner spat, and Alys's own stomach lurched in revulsion as she caught a whiff of foulness and saw the flecks and stains in his already unkempt beard. He was drenched in sweat and shaking, and he looked at her with such horror that she almost lost her resolve. Never before had anyone *feared* her, and though her half-brother might enjoy being feared, she herself did not.

"I was to take her—unharmed—to Nandel," the prisoner gasped out, all his fight gone.

Alys had suspected that was the case, though she hadn't wanted to mention the possibility for fear of influencing the prisoner's answers. "And who hired you to take her there?"

He stared at the floor, his shoulders hunched. "I can't say for sure. The man who gave me the money and the mission was obviously an intermediary."

She huffed with impatience. "*Where* were you hired? And who was this intermediary?"

"I was in Aalwell," he said, "at a tavern in the Harbor District."

Alys raised an eyebrow. "Not in Nandel, then?" she asked, though she couldn't imagine what a man such as he would be doing in the Principality of Nandel. Though she supposed it would have made no sense for Waldmir to hire a Nandelite to kidnap his daughter. Alys could count the number of fair-skinned blonds in Women's Well on one hand, and of those, only Shelvon was very obviously a full-blooded Nandelite. A Nandelite mercenary would have called far too much attention to himself.

The prisoner shook his head. "No. In Aalwell. And I don't know exactly who the intermediary was. Only that he was a soldier. I'd never spoken to him before, but I'd seen him on the street before when he was traveling to and from the Citadel. He wasn't in uniform when he hired me, but I recognized him."

A soldier. On the streets of Aalwell. Hired to take Shelvon to Nandel. There could be only one man behind such a scheme.

"You were hired through an intermediary by King Delnamal," she said flatly.

And the mercenary, still pale and shaking, did not demur.

CHAPTER THIRTY-SEVEN

"A re you *sure*?" Ellin asked her lord chancellor as her heart sank and her shoulders slumped.

Sitting across the desk from her in her private study, Lord Semsulin nodded. "I am sure the information is accurate," he said. "There is no question in my mind that Aaltah is aggressively courting Prince Waldmir, but that is hardly a surprise. Aaltah is as dependent on Nandel for iron and gems as we are, and now that we've made ourselves their enemy, it seems only logical that they would do everything in their power to persuade Prince Waldmir to trade only with them."

She shook her head. "So much for the prince's great outrage when Delnamal divorced his daughter and condemned her as a traitor."

"Oh, you were under the impression that he is a beacon of paternal love?" Semsulin needled with his customary—and often highly annoying—sarcasm. Once upon a time, Ellin had hated him for it, but it seemed she was growing accustomed to his abrasive manners.

"I thought he might at least make a show of it."

"I'm sure he does, when it suits him. But he is once again being offered the possibility of making one of his daughters the Queen of Aaltah, and it seems that Lord Kailindar was correct when he speculated that Waldmir is not overly fond of his nephew."

It took everything Ellin had to hold her tongue. She very much disliked keeping secrets from her lord chancellor, but she meant to honor her promise to Zarsha. Prince Waldmir might pretend he was interested in a possible future match between King Delnamal's as-yet-unborn son and his own young "daughter," but Ellin was certain he would not pin his hopes on a child whom he suspected was not his. But she could not say that.

"Just because he's talking with Delnamal doesn't mean he's actually going to commit," she argued instead. "Delnamal's son isn't even *born* yet. Waldmir can form a blood alliance with Rhozinolm through my marriage with Zarsha within the year, and that offers far more certainty than a potential match between a toddler and an unborn child."

"True," Semsulin agreed. "I believe, as you and Zarsha do, that Waldmir is merely angling for the most advantageous arrangement for himself and for Nandel. He sees both you and Delnamal as desperate supplicants, vying for his affection, and that allows him to play you off each other at will. I've heard there was an attempt to kidnap Lady Shelvon from Women's Well. The mercenary who attempted it admitted being hired by Delnamal, and his mission was to take Shelvon back to Nandel—a move I am certain Delnamal would not have made had he not been trying so hard to curry favor with Waldmir.

"In any case, Waldmir is making it look like the marriage—and therefore the renewal of the trade agreements—is far from certain. I need not tell you the potential consequences if this uncertainty goes on for too long."

She grimaced, knowing Semsulin was right. She had reduced Kailindar's threat as a potential rival when she'd arranged for Kailee's marriage. But—as both Semsulin and Zarsha reminded her all too often—reducing the threat was not the same as eliminating it. Those trade agreements were the key to securing her throne, and the more doubt crept in, the weaker her position would become.

"You may need to begin entertaining other proposals," Semsulin said gently. "Unless you have changed your mind about Lord Kailindar. We could always arrange to 'discover' new evidence linking him to Lord Creethan's assassination attempt."

"You know I won't do that," she said. "But you also know all the reasons why Waldmir is unlikely to refuse the marriage arrangement in the end, so I don't see—"

"Yes, you *do* see," Semsulin interrupted, which was an unmistakable breach of protocol. "Your mind is too sharp for this pretense, Your Majesty. You are attempting to negotiate from a position of perceived desperation, and you will never get an advantageous deal that way. As long as Prince Waldmir believes you will do *anything* to make the marriage to Zarsha happen, then he will toy with you and play you and Delnamal off each other. You must give him reason to think it possible you'll marry someone else."

If she weren't feeling so agitated, Ellin might have laughed. Not that long ago, she was desperate to avoid a marriage to Zarsha! Now the thought of having another man court her was nearly enough to send her into a panic.

"I'm not saying you have to *do* it," Semsulin reminded her. "I'm just saying you have to seem open to the possibility."

Ellin noticed her fingers were drumming restlessly on the desk before her, her nails making a *tap, tap, tap* that was likely grating on Semsulin's nerves. She might have kept doing it, save that it grated on her own as well once she noticed it. She stilled the tapping by folding her hands together, forcing herself to *think* more and *feel* less.

Semsulin was an excellent adviser. He understood court intrigue better than anyone she had ever met. More importantly, he understood and respected *her*. He could have brought this information—and his advice—up during a council meeting, thereby nearly forcing her hand. But he had brought it to her in private, leaving the choice up to her. The last time she'd ignored his advice, she'd almost been killed. She did not regret the decision—she intended to be the sovereign and protector of *all* her people, not just the rich and powerful—but ignoring it this time seemed foolhardy.

"I can make a few 'discreet' inquiries," Semsulin said. "Nothing overt, but enough to cause a little speculation. Which you can categorically deny, of course, but such rumors have a way of taking on a life of their own."

Ellin sighed. "You are not my lord chancellor," she grumbled. "You are my lord high rumormonger."

Semsulin cracked a rare smile. "My rumormongering skills have worked to your advantage before."

"Until they didn't." She remembered the terrible sinking feeling when Tamzin had taken the rumor of their potential engagement, which Semsulin had started on her behalf, and twisted it into a weapon to use against her.

Semsulin acknowledged her words with a half shrug. "There is a risk to every strategy. However, you have to see that it is to your advantage to plant at least a small seed of doubt in Prince Waldmir's mind. If he sees any chance that he might lose his opportunity to have his kin reign as king in Rhozinolm, he might decide to stop playing hard to get."

Ellin cocked her head at Semsulin. "So you don't think he wants his daughter to marry Delnamal's son instead?"

"As you said, such a marriage would be many years down the road, and there are many ways an agreement could go sour between now and then. Especially when King Delnamal has shown himself to be so erratic and impulsive. But fear makes fools of many men, and the council might take the possibility more seriously than they ought."

Ellin grimaced. "Then I'm sure they'll be overjoyed at the news that I'm entertaining other proposals. They will think I'm giving up on the trade agreements."

"It's a risk we must take," Semsulin said. He regarded her with a sudden and obvious caution. "But we can mitigate the risk if you let *me* make the suggestion and explain the reasoning."

"You mean that if a *man* makes the suggestion, the council will see it as a clever negotiating tactic, whereas if *I* do, it will be seen as a sign of fear." She challenged him with a scowl, but he merely shrugged.

"The world is as it is. I am one of your assets, and you should use me accordingly."

It would not be the first time she had allowed Semsulin to speak

for her, though ordinarily she did so—on his advice—when presenting ideas that were likely to be unpopular, so that he might draw the
council's ire away from her.

"I hope that someday I will have won enough respect to risk
weathering a storm without having to use a proxy," she muttered.

Semsulin inclined his head. "I hope that, too. But until then, you
have me."

It took a long and miserable three days for Mairah to reach the bridge
that crossed over the Endless River into Aaltah. Even on foot, the
journey should have taken her half that time, but thanks to the patrols that regularly scoured the roads, she had to spend all the hours
of daylight in hiding, for the Trapper spell could not hide the dust
her feet kicked up when she walked. Even at night she frequently
had to leave the road to avoid being trampled. Her feet ached, her
stomach howled, and her mouth was parched as the influence of the
Women's Well faded.

For the first few miles after she'd left the borders of Women's Well
proper, the earth was still ripe with burgeoning life, although from
what she had heard the land in this area had been lifeless desert before the Well had sprung up from nowhere. But the farther she traveled, the thinner the elements in the air, and the less life the earth
supported, until the road became but a dusty track and the greenery
turned to nothing but patches of dry and brittle grass.

In her hurry to escape Women's Well, Mairah had brought neither
food nor water with her—an oversight for which she roundly cursed
herself. But she had never traveled on foot before—truth be told, she
had never traveled much by coach, either—and had little concept
how long it might take to get from one town to another.

When she saw the first telltale signs of a town in the distance, she
quickly—though reluctantly—stripped out of her dress and put on
her wrinkled, dusty red robes. The sun was just beginning to rise, and
if she were to stick to her plan as strictly as she ought, she would wait
out the day in hiding and enter town after sundown, but she was too

hungry and thirsty to bear the thought of another torturous day of deprivation.

She hated the very feel of the coarse fabric against her skin, of the smothering wimple that scratched at her scalp and trapped sweat at the nape of her neck. She was reminded of the dreadful day when she'd first entered the Abbey. Although she had known what she was getting herself into, it had still come as a shock how dehumanizing it had felt to lay her fine, fashionable clothing aside and change into the red robes of an Unwanted Woman. She'd felt instantly dirty and diminished, and she'd humiliated herself by crying.

She would not do that this time, though her heart ached and her eyes burned. It was not courage that kept the tears at bay—it was dehydration. She hated to think what her face must look like with layers of sunburn and road dust caking her already unsightly pockmarks.

Reminding herself that she was the Abbess of Khalpar—and that Norah would pay dearly for her betrayal—Mairah straightened her spine and continued down the dirt track toward the bridge.

She was not surprised to see that the road was barricaded just short of the bridge, and that the barricade was manned by a half-dozen soldiers. Nor was she entirely surprised to see that there was a small building that looked like it might be a hastily constructed barracks on the other side, with another handful of soldiers gathered casually in the doorway. From what she had heard, Aaltah's border patrol made it as unpleasant as possible for people to cross in either direction.

All eyes were on Mairah as she trudged closer, and the soldiers who'd been lounging by the barracks house made their way over the bridge for a closer look. She suspected that men posted out here on the very fringes of the Kingdom of Aaltah were excited by the sight of a woman in red robes heading their way, for they were a long way from the Abbey of Aaltah, and the tiny town in which they were stationed seemed unlikely to have a brothel they could patronize. Beneath the heavy robes, and despite the already scorching heat of the early-morning sun, a chill shivered through her at the predatory way in which those men regarded her.

I am the Abbess of Khalpar, she reminded herself, holding her head up a little higher. *They would not dare . . .*

But she found herself unconvinced, for an abbess was generally just an old, used-up whore, and there was little chance the soldiers would hold any respect for her rank. This, she thought with a hint of irony, was one of the few times when her disfigured face might actually work to her advantage.

More than one of the gathered soldiers visibly lost interest when they got a closer look, a couple of them curling their lips in distaste and disappointment. Mairah was caught between relief and despair, for though she didn't want to be regarded as prey, the quick dismissal of men who were no doubt starved for female companionship of any kind still stung. The people of Women's Well had grown accustomed to her looks and gotten most of their staring and sneering out of their systems within the first few days of her arrival. She had almost forgotten what it felt like to have her disfigurement so blatantly remarked upon.

One of the soldiers stepped forward to block her path, looking her up and down most rudely. He looked like just the sort of man she would expect to find stationed at such a remote outpost—big enough to be intimidating, with an ill-fitting uniform with frayed cuffs and several layers of stains. His face was baked practically black from the sun, the skin dry and flaky and cracked, and his eyes were dull with boredom and, perhaps, stupidity. These were not the cream of the Aaltah military, by any stretch of the imagination.

The soldier hawked and spat—just in case she hadn't already gotten the message that he was uncouth and proud of it. "You're a long way from your abbey, Sister," he said. "Do you have permission from your abbess to be traveling out and about?"

"If so, the abbess should have given her a sack for her head to spare the populace this sight," one of his men muttered loudly, much to the amusement of the rest.

Unfortunately, Kailee's tutoring was effective enough that Mairah could understand both men's words. It should *not* hurt her feelings to have this lout insult her looks, and yet Mairah's throat tightened, and it was all she could do not to turn away to hide her face. Anger followed swiftly on the heels of pain, lending strength to her spine and helping her find her voice.

"I am Mairahsol Rah-Creesha," she said with all the dignity she could manage, "and I am the Abbess of Khalpar."

The soldier snorted, and several of his cohorts laughed, though Mairah thought surely her accent revealed the truth of her words. No abigail in Aaltah or Grunir—or anywhere else on the mainland— would have an accent like hers.

"Abbess of Khalpar, eh?" the soldier mused, licking his lips and showing his yellowed teeth. "I'm the Lord Commander of Aaltah, myself. Pleased to make your acquaintance."

He sketched a mocking bow, and his men fanned out around her, surrounding her. One of them said something that made the others laugh again. Mairah figured it was just as well she didn't understand those particular words. Fear obliterated the pangs of hunger and the exhaustion that had filled her mind for the last hours, her heart pattering against her ribs. She wondered if these brutes were familiar with the effects of women's Kai. There was no question that if the Curse weren't in effect, she would soon be beneath them, no matter how homely they might deem her. She didn't much care *what* the Abbess of Aaltah's spell was called, but right this moment "the Blessing" seemed more apt after all.

"You are aware of what will happen if you touch me against my will," she said in as calm a tone as she could manage. "Trust me, you do not want to see women's Kai in action." She said it in Parian—her understanding of Continental might be improving, but she was still a long way from being able to converse easily—but the word for Kai was the same in both languages. She could see from the narrowing of the leader's eyes that he had a good idea what she'd said. And that he knew perfectly well the consequences of slaking his lusts.

There were more comments from the soldiers who surrounded her, none of which she understood, but she was sure they were not complimentary. The leader looked her up and down once more, his nose crinkled in exaggerated disgust.

"You wouldn't have been worth the effort even before the Curse," he sneered. "But you are a witch and a whore, and you belong behind the walls of an abbey."

She heard the scuff of a footstep behind her, and as she tried to turn to see what was happening, someone slammed into her back, shoving her roughly facedown into the dust of the road. She cried out in pain and surprise.

Someone stuck a knee in her back, and her wrists were brutally dragged together and bound with a length of coarse rope. She closed her eyes and offered no resistance, though that didn't make the soldiers any gentler. Rage simmered in her blood, blending with the remnants of fear. She was the *Abbess of Khalpar,* and these brutes were treating her like some common criminal! She imagined what their screams would sound like as a whip tore their backs to shreds, but even as she entertained the pleasant fantasy, she knew they would face no punishment for their harsh treatment.

She should be taken to Aalwell as a visiting dignitary. Or at least an honored guest and emissary from the Kingdom of Khalpar.

When her hands were firmly tied, she was hauled to her feet once more, her robes and skin now thoroughly coated in dust and dirt, which stuck to her sweat. Her knees were shaking, her whole body weak with hunger and exhaustion and despair.

The leader barked some orders that she could not hear over the pounding sound of her pulse, and one of the soldiers grabbed her arm and dragged her, stumbling, across the bridge and into the Kingdom of Aaltah.

Alys had never seen her son looking this angry before, and considering his behavior since Jinnell's death, that was saying a lot. Between his vigorous training at the Citadel and an adolescent growth spurt, he was now almost a full head taller than she, and his shoulders and chest were full of wiry muscles that spoke of strength, if not bulk. His father had been slender and not especially imposing in frame, but Corlin was growing into a different sort of man entirely.

Those wiry muscles of his were all clenched tight with anger as he leaned ever so slightly into her personal space. If it were anyone other than Corlin, Alys would have been intimidated by the aggressive body language—and perhaps she should have been anyway, for her son was clearly not the quiet, reserved boy she'd raised.

"That bastard hurt Aunt Shelvon," he grated through clenched teeth, his voice rough with emotion. Alys wondered absently when Corlin had started referring to Shelvon as "Aunt Shelvon," or if he was doing it now only because he thought she was more likely to give him what he wanted if he demonstrated his deep affection for the woman who had helped spirit him out from under Delnamal's nose. "He does not deserve a quick and merciful death!"

Corlin was not the first person to have objected to her decision to hang Shelvon's attacker, though none of her royal council had been so passionate in their arguments. She didn't doubt the mercenary deserved the worst punishment the law could mete out, but she had promised him mercy, and she feared breaking her word was a dangerous precedent to set. She did not want to become a creature of wanton and casual cruelty, as Delnamal was. But she did not think that argument would hold any sway with Corlin, so she tried what she hoped would be a more convincing tactic.

"Shelvon is far too sweet and gentle a soul to want to see anyone suffer." She allowed a small smile to tug at the corners of her mouth. "Besides, he still has the humiliation—and she the satisfaction—of knowing he was bested in combat by a woman."

Corlin growled in frustration, his eyes flashing. She supposed she was lucky he'd decided to brace her in her office—with a closed door between them and any observers—or she might have had to consider taking him to task for his disrespect of his sovereign princess. Parents and children fought all the time, of course, but when those arguments involved a sovereign, they had to be kept private. On more than one occasion during her rebellious childhood, Alys had been thrashed for daring to argue too loudly and publicly with her father the king. But she wasn't sure she had it in her to punish Corlin for his behavior, no matter how inappropriate.

"It isn't enough," Corlin spat, and though his face revealed only rage, there was a thread of anguish in his voice. "Delnamal killed Jinnell, and you've done *nothing* about it. Now you're just going to let some lowlife traipse into Women's Well and attempt a violent kidnapping of one of our citizens and get away with it!"

Corlin was leaning into her space even more, and no matter how well she understood what was driving him, no matter how much sympathy she might have for his feelings, there was only so much she could tolerate without losing any respect he might still have for her.

"You need to take a step back, my son," she said, staring up into his eyes with what she hoped was an implacable expression.

"Or what?" he asked, leaning in even more until they were almost nose to nose. "You won't even give a scumbag mercenary the justice he deserves, so what will you do to your own son?"

Alys refused to be intimidated or retreat, although the anger that radiated from him was an almost palpable force, and there was some part of her that was no longer sure he had the ability—or the desire— to control himself. She hoped none of her disquiet showed on her face as she continued to hold her ground.

"You may be my son, but you are also my subject and a cadet of the Citadel. If you do not take a step back right this minute, I will report you to Lord Jailom—as I would any other cadet who dared to disrespect his sovereign—and you can see how much my tender feelings toward you soften his punishment."

Alys watched as a storm of emotions twisted her son's face until she could hardly recognize him. Her heart broke for him even as she forced herself to meet his gaze from behind a mask of implacable calm.

"You show mercy to a criminal who would have abducted one of your closest friends," he said, shaking his head. "You let Delnamal sit on his throne unhindered after he murdered Jinnell for pure spite. And yet *me*, you threaten."

"When you're treating me like one of your fellow cadets whom you hope to intimidate with your size and fury, then yes," she said, voice still sounding far calmer than she felt. "Take a step back, and we can talk like reasonable adults. That is the way you want me to view you, isn't it? Like a reasonable, responsible adult rather than like a child throwing a tantrum?"

To Alys's immense relief, Corlin finally took an exaggerated step backward, rolling his eyes and suddenly looking much more like a fourteen-year-old boy. It was like there were two Corlins both living within the same skin—the adolescent boy with a good heart; and the bitter, angry grown man he might someday become. It was Alys's duty as his mother to mold and shape him into the kind of man she could be proud of—and who could be happy—but she was at a loss as to how to accomplish it when his mind and his heart were so thoroughly closed off to her.

"Shelvon's attacker will pay the ultimate price for what he tried to do," Alys continued. "And I assure you, my son, that I have no intention of letting Delnamal sit on his throne unhindered indefinitely." She reached out and grabbed Corlin's shoulders, squeezing them hard as she let her own anger and hatred shine in her eyes. "One day, he will die, if not by my very own hand, then by my order. And I can promise you that for him I will show no mercy. There is no death too slow and too hard for a man such as he."

Unfortunately, Corlin was in no mood to be appeased. He did not pull away from her grip—though she might have expected him to after she'd just made such an issue of him invading her personal space—but there was no softening of his expression, either.

"Those are just words, Mama," he said with no small amount of disdain. "We've yet to do *anything* to threaten Delnamal's rule, and until we do, you can say all the words you want and they will mean nothing."

Alys shook her head and released his shoulders, reminding herself that at fourteen, she hadn't exactly been a bastion of patience, either. It was hard for a boy his age to grasp a revenge that might well be years in the making.

"We are threatening his monopoly on Aalwood," she reminded him. "We are cementing an alliance with Aaltah's greatest rival. And we are helping that rival make it difficult for Delnamal to retain his access to iron and gems. We are continuing to develop new magic that will make us appealing trade partners for others who might otherwise refuse to trade with us for fear of angering Delnamal. We are undercutting him in every way we can. I know these all seem like minor, unimportant things, but if we add enough of them together, his rule will grow less secure. Remember, he *always* has about as much patience and self-control as you've shown me today, and he will not listen to anyone who tells him things he doesn't want to hear. Today, he and Aaltah are an unassailable enemy, but we may find the situation very different a year from now."

Corlin closed his eyes. "I don't want him dead a year from now."

"Well, I don't, either!" Alys snapped, for there was only so much provocation she could take. "I want him here rotting in a jail cell imagining what creative method of execution I'm going to think up for him and dreading it with every fiber of his body. But as that is not among my options, I'm going to do what I can to make it possible in the future. Torturing Shelvon's attacker to death will not aid in that cause." She forced her voice to gentleness once more. "And keep in mind that Shelvon will be present for the execution. Do you think she would enjoy seeing a man tortured to death?"

And for the first time, Corlin actually seemed to listen to her, *hear* her. "No," he whispered, his gaze now dropping to the floor. "She would be miserable."

Alys practically sagged with relief. She felt as if she'd just been in a fight for her life, her body aching from the aftermath of all the tension. Somehow, miraculously, she had gotten through to Corlin this time. But it did not bode well that she'd had to work so hard at it, and she feared this minor victory would do little to sway the tide of the battle against Corlin's demons.

CHAPTER THIRTY-EIGHT

Mairah had thought her journey from Khalwell to Women's Well was miserable, but she hadn't known what true misery was until the captain of the border patrol sent her to Aalwell in chains. She was "escorted" by two ill-bred, ill-kempt brutes who made no secret of the fact that they enjoyed hurting and humiliating her. They traveled by horse—no speedy, convenient cheval-drawn wagon this time—and instead of giving her a mount, they tied her hands to one of the saddle horns and forced her to stumble and stagger in their dust.

More than once on the long, agonizing journey, Mairah lost her footing and was dragged down the road, her robes and skin shredding with the abuse.

At first, they had pretended not to believe her when she claimed to be the Abbess of Khalpar. Ridiculous though their skepticism might be, she'd thought it was her status as a lowly abigail that caused them to treat her with such cruelty and disregard, that if only she could convince them of her true identity, everything would change.

But as the days passed, she began to realize that they were fully aware of who she was; they just didn't care. In their eyes, an abbess was no different from any other Unwanted Woman, and they clearly expected that no one would care that they'd mistreated her.

The guards rarely spoke to her except to mock her and bark orders, and it was hard to hear much of what they said when they were on horseback and she was struggling to keep her feet. But at night when they sat by the campfire—Mairah tied hand and foot and tethered to a stake like a dog—they practically forgot she existed. Most of their conversation was of no interest to Mairah, even when she could catch the words, but she eventually came to understand that she was being taken to Aalwell in chains on the orders of King Delnamal, who had apparently taken grave offense that King Khalvin had sent a delegation to Women's Well in the first place.

Mairah reminded herself multiple times that she was carrying a potion that had the power to save her. (Or, more accurately, her *captors* were carrying it, for they had confiscated her potions and Devotional and thrown the Trapper spell into the river, thinking it was nothing but a pebble.) Surely when she reached Aalwell, she would have a chance to speak to someone of importance, and when she told him about the success of her mission in Women's Well, she would be released. Perhaps she would not be sent back to Khalpar—the continued mistreatment proved how much relations between Aaltah and Khalpar had cooled—but surely she could at least convince King Delnamal to let her perfect the formula and allow her to make use of whatever seers were available in the Abbey of Aaltah. It didn't matter *which* king she convinced of her usefulness, as long as she gained her freedom.

Mairah cursed herself for not accepting Kailee's offer sooner. If she'd had the courage to do that, she could even now be secure and free in Women's Well. That freedom would not have come with a guarantee—if she'd felt sure there was a way to permanently make her unrecognizable, she would not have hesitated as she had—but it would be infinitely more pleasant than being bound and dragged around like a common criminal.

Every night, Mairah fell asleep fantasizing about the terrible revenge she would enact on every single person who'd wronged her, starting with the two soldiers who tormented her. But she had plenty of hatred left—for King Delnamal, on whose orders she suffered; for Norah, who had ruined everything when Mairah had finally seen a future worth living; for King Khalvin for setting this ridiculous burden on her shoulders in the first place . . .

The list was long and varied, and Mairah was fully aware that realistically, she could not easily have revenge against all of them. But on one of her long, uncomfortable nights trying to sleep on the hard ground while tied up, a new idea came to her.

Her tormentors carried with them not just the memory potion she'd made to enhance the seer's poison, but also the potion she'd made for Kailee. It seemed she would never know whether Kailee had decided to try the potion and whether it had worked for her, but she *did* know that drinking it herself had made her Mindseye close. She had not had the time or attention to spare to think about what other uses such a potion might have, but now she had nothing more pressing with which to occupy her mind—and she had a strong desire to lose herself in thought to avoid wallowing in her misery.

Armies depended on magic in times of war—enabling magical shields and increasing the strength and accuracy of their weapons being the traditional precursor to any battle. So what if Mairah's potion could somehow be slipped into an army's water supply?

Mairah's heart leapt at the notion, realizing that such a potion could be used to devastating effect, for a force of magically equipped warriors could prevail against a much larger one who could fight with only conventional armor and weapons.

On the heels of that idea came another one, which was that getting that potion into the water supply of an army encamped on the outskirts of Women's Well would be childishly easy. In the land that had once been part of the Wasteland, there were no convenient wells to be guarded and drawn from, which meant water would have to come from the nearby river. Which meant that the potion, if sufficiently potent—could be poured in upriver, well out of sight of that army.

She was so startled and excited by the idea that she bolted upright, although she instantly regretted it as her bindings dug deeper and one of the guards scowled at her suspiciously.

"Bad dream," she muttered in Continental, then lay back down and turned her back in case her schemes were somehow written across her face.

She had fled Women's Well pursued by an execution squad, thinking her chances of settling there and gaining her freedom were dead. But if she could produce the potion she envisioned, she might make of herself such a valuable asset that Princess Alysoon would welcome her with open arms. If it at least made her hesitate to order Mairah's death, Mairah could explain *exactly* what she'd been doing in Women's Well, how she had never truly been trying to undo the Curse despite everything that Norah said.

Mairah tried not to let her hopes run away with her yet again. There was a reasonable chance she could develop the potion she had in mind—given the time and resources. If she could convince her captors in Aaltah that she was working toward perfecting her seer's poison, she might very well be granted the time she needed, and it was possible she'd stored enough elements in the Devotional to see her through the experiments. But then she would have to somehow escape Aaltah and make her way back to Women's Well, which she hadn't the first idea how to do. She wished her idiot captors hadn't tossed her Trapper spell in the river. And even if she made it to Women's Well, she would still be a fugitive and too easily recognizable.

But any hope was better than no hope at all, and she vowed that she would somehow find a way.

When Mairah—still being dragged along behind the horses, drawing curious stares—finally passed through the walls of the city of Aalwell, her heart lifted, for she was sure her misery was almost at its end. She would finally have a chance to speak to someone with more intelligence and power than the stupid louts who'd been tasked with escorting her, and though she figured she'd have to retell her story many, many times before she would reach someone with real authority, she would finally begin to do her research. Even if King Delnamal insisted on sending her back to Khalpar immediately, she promised herself she would not abandon her quest, though she would have a much easier time getting back to Women's Well if she could endeavor to remain in Aalwell for a while.

But instead of being taken to the palace or interviewed by some petty dignitary, she was taken straight to Aaltah's new Abbey and dumped at the feet of its administrator. Apparently, after King Aaltyn had razed the previous Abbey and sent its abigails into exile, he had decided that the new Abbey should be headed not by an abbess but by a male administrator. Worse, although the disgraced women of the Abbey of the Unwanted were all of noble birth, Administrator Loveland was a vulgar commoner cast from the same mold as the brutish soldiers. His response to her request to send a message to the king was a peal of laughter, followed by the back of his hand.

Mairah lay dazed and aching in the dirt at Administrator Loveland's feet. She tasted the coppery tang of blood in her mouth and felt it dribbling down her chin.

"At this abbey," Loveland said, "whores are to remain silent except when given express permission to speak."

Mairah blinked tears from her eyes and watched his boots as he circled her. Her whole body tensed when his footsteps took him behind her, and she couldn't bring herself to raise her head to keep him in sight. She brought her hand to her cracked lips and wiped away the blood, the red a shocking bright patch of color on her brown skin made nearly gray with the dirt of the road.

"I don't care who you *used* to be," Loveland continued. "You are now an abigail of the Abbey of Aaltah. Which is to say you are *no one*. I don't suppose that even if we clean you up you will be of much use in the pavilion, so you will act as a maidservant for your more profitable sisters. Behave yourself, and you will receive ample food and a comfortable bed in which to sleep. Make any trouble, and you will have me to answer to. Have I made myself clear?"

Mairah lay panting in the dirt, too horrified to speak or move. Had she truly believed her situation would *improve* when she reached Aaltah? She'd thought the worst thing that could happen would be a speedy trip back to Khalpar. She'd never once imagined she'd be shut up in Aaltah's abbey. Tears pooled in her eyes as she realized Loveland was unlikely to hand over her Devotional and the potions she'd brought with her, which meant she would have no chance even to research the spell she'd hoped would win her re-entry into Women's Well.

Mairah shrieked when the toe of Loveland's boot connected with her thigh in a brutal kick. She curled around the pain, clutching her thigh.

"I asked if I'd made myself clear," Loveland growled.

"Yes," Mairah managed to gasp through her pain, but Loveland kicked her again.

"That's yes, *sir*," he corrected. "You will address me with the proper respect, or you will suffer the consequences."

"Yes, sir," she sobbed, wondering if she might have been better off staying in Women's Well, for at least death there would likely have been quick and painless.

CHAPTER THIRTY-NINE

Since the earliest days of her reign, Ellin had made a habit of carving out a few stolen minutes whenever she could between meetings and audiences and correspondence to quiet her mind. On temperate days, those stolen minutes were spent in the Queen's Garden, which was a lovely walled garden so thoroughly warded with spells against intruders that her honor guard could in good conscience allow her to walk in the fresh air in blissful solitude. It was the only time save when she was asleep in her bed that she was free from the pressure of prying eyes and expectations.

She preferred the garden to the solarium, so even when the weather was a little less temperate than optimal, she still chose to spend her manufactured free time outdoors whenever possible. She stepped into the garden and breathed in a deep breath full of the mingled scents of roses and herbs and freshly cut grass. She held her face up to the sun, but it abruptly disappeared behind a thick bank of clouds, taking its warmth with it. Ellin shivered and pulled her shawl a little tighter around her shoulders, but plunged forward anyway, more than willing to endure the slight nip in the air.

She stretched stiff limbs as she strolled around the perimeter of the garden, working out the kinks of long hours spent seated at the council table, trying not to think about the stack of correspondence that was waiting for her attention as soon as she stepped back inside the palace. She would allow herself a quarter hour of blessed freedom before putting both mind and body back to work.

When she finished her first circuit around the garden, her heart sank just a little to see Zarsha standing in the doorway. Her honor guards had barred the way, but they had not forced Zarsha to retreat, and he stood just beyond the threshold in the shade of the hallway, watching her expectantly as she approached.

"Let him pass," she told her guards with a soft sigh of resignation. Zarsha would not interrupt this quiet time if it weren't important, though she was far from eager to hear what new crisis was awaiting her attention.

Zarsha bowed to her as the guards stepped aside, then entered the garden and fell into step beside her. The palace door closed, the guards giving her privacy without a second thought. It showed something of the changes that had occurred within the palace during her rule, for in the beginning, they would have balked at leaving her unchaperoned in the company of a man. But for the most part, they treated her with the same respect they might show a king now, and no one seemed worried she would sully her reputation.

"I hear you've received a marriage proposal," Zarsha said before they'd taken five steps, and Ellin groaned.

She stopped walking, forcing him to stop with her, and looked up into his face with narrowed eyes. "I only heard about it about an hour ago during the council meeting," she said. "How do *you* know about it already?"

Zarsha might now be an influential figure in Rhozinolm politics, but he had no official place in the government and was still just an envoy from Nandel. He had no cause to attend council meetings except for rare occasions when he was invited for specific discussions, and it was hard to imagine how he could be privy to the council's business.

One corner of Zarsha's mouth tipped up in his signature rakish grin. "We've discussed my penchant for nosiness before."

She heaved an exasperated sigh and started walking again fast enough that Zarsha had to hurry to catch up. "I don't appreciate being spied on." She didn't turn to look at him, but she could see the innocent expression he wore on his face from the corner of her eye.

"I would never spy on you, Your Majesty," he said with such a good imitation of earnestness she was almost tempted to believe him. "However, I do a have a couple of highly placed contacts in the Midlands court . . ."

She shook her head at him, not sure if she was more annoyed or impressed. She had never caught him in an outright lie, but she wasn't sure she believed his protestations that he would not turn his illicit eyes on her—even if it was just for the sake of protecting her.

"So how was Duke Stalbok's proposal received?" Zarsha asked with studied nonchalance.

Ellin came to a stop once again, startled by the strange undertone she could have sworn she heard in his voice. Instead of meeting her eyes when she turned to him, he reached out for a rosebush that bloomed nearby, cupping the yellow blossom in his palm and bending to take a deep whiff of its intoxicating scent.

"I'm sure I'm imagining things," Ellin said, "but I could have sworn I heard a hint of jealousy in your voice." She tried for a teasing tone but doubted she succeeded. Zarsha had no cause to be jealous, for of course she had told him in advance that she planned to entertain proposals in hopes of hurrying Waldmir along.

He raised his head from the rose and looked up at her from under his lashes. "I am not immune to that emotion, I'm afraid, whatever I might previously have led you to believe." He turned his eyes to the rose once more, fingers stroking idly over its petals. "A formal alliance with the Midlands would be a desirable jewel in your crown," he continued. "After all, they can be a useful buffer between Rhozinolm and Aaltah."

Ellin made a face, but Zarsha was too fascinated with the rose to notice. The Midlands—a strip of lush and fertile land surrounding a midsize Well—was the single most fought-over strip of land in all of Seven Wells. Oftentimes annexed either by Rhozinolm or Aaltah, it was currently an independent principality and was no doubt highly concerned about the rising tensions between its two large neighbors. If a war came, the Midlands would have to side with one kingdom or the other, and there was some argument to be made that it was worth courting them with a marriage agreement. If she were willing to give up on the Nandel trade agreements, which, of course, she had no intention of doing.

"The council would definitely like to secure a Midlands alliance," Ellin agreed, smiling to herself when the corners of Zarsha's eyes visibly tightened. "And of course there is a great deal less resistance to the idea of me marrying a foreigner now that everyone's gotten comfortable with me retaining the throne."

Zarsha plucked the rose that so fascinated him, perhaps with a little more force than necessary. His eyes remained averted, and there was a flush of pink in his usually pale cheeks. One thing she could say for the Nandel complexion—it betrayed even the smallest flush.

Something fluttered in Ellin's belly, a strange sensation that left her momentarily short of breath as she reached out to touch Zarsha's arm before he could further savage the rosebush. Once upon a time, he'd been perfectly satisfied to share her with Graesan, had evinced no hint of jealousy at the thought of her in another man's bed. But there was no denying that something had changed since then. It was a heady feeling to know she could inspire such feelings in a man, but she was not some coy court maiden who took pride in causing heartache.

"But of course an alliance with Nandel is *far* more valuable to us than one with the Midlands," she said. She quickly withdrew her hand from his arm, but when he took a step closer to her, moving inside her personal space, she found she could not force herself to retreat.

"And what about *you*, dearest Ellin?" he inquired as he gently took her hand, at the same time lifting the rose he had plucked to her nose so that its fragrance filled her head. "Is an alliance with Nandel more valuable to *you*?"

His voice had lowered so much she had to strain to hear. She swallowed hard, looking up into those exotic blue eyes of his and feeling herself trapped in his gaze. Her pulse stuttered then sped, the scent of the rose making her head spin as if she were tipsy.

How many times had she told herself she felt no true attraction to Zarsha? She'd steeled herself to a marriage of convenience, to the prospect of marrying and bedding and bearing children for a man she did not love. But as he stood so close to her, his eyes boring into her and darkening with something she could only call desire, she realized that she'd been lying to herself for some time now.

"Yes," she whispered, eyes still locked with his. "Yes, it is."

He tucked the rose into the lacings at the front of her bodice, then bent his head slowly toward hers, giving her plenty of time to read his intention and rebuff him. Ellin told herself that she really *should* rebuff him, should hold him at arm's length—both for her own sake and his—until such time as their marriage was officially arranged. No matter how convinced he was that his uncle would come around to the match, there was always the chance that he was wrong, and if that was the case, then allowing themselves to get any more attached than they already were was pure foolishness.

But for all her logical objections, Ellin couldn't find the will to turn her head or step away, and when Zarsha's lips touched hers, she all but melted into his embrace, pressing her body tightly against his.

Zarsha groaned and put both arms around her, slanting his head so that their lips pressed together at just the right angle. His kiss hummed through her blood, bringing all her nerve endings alive.

Ellin made an embarrassing mewl of displeasure when Zarsha hastily pulled away. The flush on his face was considerably darker, his eyes huge and his chest rising and falling swiftly with desire, but when she would have stepped back into his embrace, he put his hands on her shoulders to hold her off.

"Not here," he croaked. "Someone could see us, and that might be . . . awkward."

Ellin blinked and looked around, finally remembering that they were outdoors. She glanced up and was relieved to see that the leafy trees that lined the walls blocked them from the view of any of the palace windows that overlooked the garden, but it had still been frighteningly irresponsible of her to give in to her urges like that.

She let out a slow, steadying breath. The rules for genteel maiden-hood might not be enforced for her as queen as much as they were for other women, but there were limits to what she could get away with.

"Maybe you could consider inviting me to your room some night," Zarsha said, his voice now a low murmur. "You can send Star for me if you decide the idea appeals." He allowed himself a slight smile. "It is a service she has provided for you before, after all."

She huffed, wondering if there was a hint of jealousy in his voice now, too. He might not have shown any outward signs of jealousy over her involvement with Graesan, but that did not necessarily mean he didn't feel it.

And with a little distance between them, Ellin's strategic mind wondered if there weren't some calculation to Zarsha's sudden inter-est in seduction. Maybe he thought if they were caught in a compro-mising position, the pressure on her to marry him would increase, despite his uncle's coy attempts at negotiation.

Ellin shook her head at herself. Zarsha was certainly capable of being sneaky and manipulative, but she was doing him a disservice to suspect his motives now. There was a part of her that was afraid to give her heart, afraid he would crush it as Graesan had. But just be-cause she seemed to be giving her heart no matter how much it frightened her, that did not mean she had to give him her body. Even if she wanted to.

She reached up to touch the back of her hand to Zarsha's cheek, then plucked the crushed rose from her bodice, sniffing it one more time before casting it aside. Then, with her emotional armor back in place, she straightened her shoulders and gave him her best coy smile.

"Convince your uncle to agree to the marriage, and I will not make you wait for our wedding to invite you to my bed," she prom-ised. "But until we are sure, it's better for both of us if we refrain."

Mairah gagged as she emptied the last chamber pot into the privy, feeling sick and dizzy despite the rag she'd tied over the lower half of her face to try to block out the stench. She'd had to empty chamber pots when she'd first entered the Abbey of Khalpar, but that abbey was civilized enough to use spelled pots that blocked out the odor. Apparently the Abbey of Aaltah felt such luxuries were too good for its ruined residents, and though Mairah had more seniority than any other abigail in the Abbey—since all the experienced ones had been exiled and later formed the principality of Women's Well— Administrator Loveland declared that she was to take up all the least desirable duties regardless.

It was all Mairah could do not to pitch the pot in the privy along with its contents, but she'd tried that on her first day of duty, and received yet another sign that this abbey was nothing like the one she was accustomed to. She'd expected to be forced to fast and perhaps even beaten with a strap for her disobedience. She had *not* expected to be whipped like a criminal. Nor had she realized how much deeper the whip bit than the strap.

She had never suffered such terrible pain before, and now her back was covered in scars far more vicious than the light ones she had borne before. Much as she would have liked to prove herself un- cowed, the fact remained that she was terrified of Loveland, and for the first time in her life tried to act obedient and pliable.

Well, to an extent. She had no intention of wasting away in the Abbey of Aaltah for the rest of her life. She still hoped that someday she could return to Women's Well in triumph, although her path there would be anything but straightforward now. No matter what, she had to get out of this abbey, and the only way she could imagine winning her freedom was to convince Loveland that one of her con- fiscated potions was the key to undoing the Curse. When she was free, she could pursue her research into her spell to close the Mindseye—and if she could miraculously escape from Aaltah and re- turn to Women's Well without being caught, then her suffering here would be well worth it. And if not . . . Well, she could still hope that her special seer's poison would prove her worth. She did not want to return to the Abbey of Khalpar, even as abbess, but she would greatly prefer that fate to the ones she saw for herself imprisoned in the Abbey of Aaltah.

When she'd found the courage, Mairah had tried to convince Loveland that she had invented a potion that could be key to undoing the Curse, that she only needed a little more time and study to perfect it. He had first laughed in her face, then had her beaten for "making up stories" as he put it.

And so Mairah had realized she had to aim higher than Loveland. Evidence suggested that King Delnamal was as eager as King Khalvin to see the Curse reversed, and if she could somehow get word to him of what she had accomplished, he might well snatch her out of the Abbey and put her to work. She still hadn't the faintest idea how she would escape if and when she created a potion powerful enough to poison the water supply, but she could only face her challenges one at a time.

So Mairah had watched and waited and endured, until at last she managed to persuade one of the Abbey's customers to send a flier to the palace on her behalf. It was a daring and perhaps foolish risk, for if Administrator Loveland were to find out what she'd done, she was certain she'd be whipped again, and she didn't know how she could endure such agony a second time. But convincing the king that she might have the means to reverse the Curse was her only hope of escaping this wretched abbey, and so she sent her message and prayed that it would be heard and believed.

Queen Oona was still pale and exhausted-looking from her hours of labor, and yet when Delnamal stepped into the birthing chamber, her eyes glowed with unadulterated joy. In her arms, swaddled in layers of deep blue cloth, was a tiny, red-faced creature with wrinkled skin, tight-shut little eyes, and no hair. To Delnamal's eyes, it looked barely human, but the midwife had assured him he was now the father of a healthy baby son, and Oona looked at the infant with such adoration that he felt a pang of jealousy. Once upon a time, she had looked at *him* like that, but lately she'd seemed barely willing to meet his eyes.

Today, she looked up at him with that beaming, glowing face and said, "Isn't he just beautiful?" in a reverent voice.

"Yes, he is," Delnamal answered, because that was clearly the only acceptable thing to say, no matter what he might really think. He had never seen a newborn infant before, had never realized how revolting they looked when so fresh out of the womb.

He was standing more than an arm's length from the bed on which his wife lay, and it was all he could do to keep his feet firmly planted when what he really wanted to do was turn away and escape the room. The air felt too hot and close, and he was all too aware of how his wife and the midwife and his mother expected a new father to look and behave. He should be sitting at his wife's side, staring at that tiny bundle with pride and gladness. Not standing halfway across the room trying to persuade himself not to flee.

Only the dowager queen seemed to realize Delnamal's indifference toward the birth of his first child. Sitting on the far side of Oona's bed, the dowager watched him with steady, reproving eyes.

"Come closer and meet your firstborn, my son," Xanvin beckoned.

Delnamal swallowed hard—hoping Oona was too absorbed by the sight of the child to notice—and took several cautious steps closer to the bed. The infant stirred in Oona's arms and made a soft cooing sound before settling more comfortably in the swaddling.

That is your son, Delnamal chastised himself, willing himself to find some hidden depth of paternal love somewhere deep inside. *What kind of father looks at his baby and feels* nothing? He shuddered in revulsion at his own unnatural disinterest.

Oona offered him a brilliant smile, lifting the swaddled infant toward him. "Would you like to hold him?" she asked, as if there were no possible answer but yes.

It was all Delnamal could do not to recoil. Panic rose within him, making his heart race and coating him with sweat. Where had all the air gone? And how had his wife survived hours of labor in this stifling room?

Oona's brow creased with concern, and the dowager gave him a look that combined exasperation with command. *Pull yourself together and hold your son,* the look seemed to say, but he could no more force his feet forward than he could fly.

"Excuse me for just a moment," he rasped, taking first one step backward then another. "I'll . . . be back. I'm just . . . I just need to . . ."

He turned and fled the room before he could stammer like an imbecile anymore. He ignored every courtier and guard and servant who tried to congratulate him with either words or smiles, hurrying through the halls as if pursued until he reached the comfort and safety of his own sitting room, where he abruptly poured a large dose of brandy and downed it as if it were water. Then he downed a second glass for good measure, and poured a third to sip.

The soothing warmth of the alcohol helped ease the panic in his veins, smoothing it out and sanding it down until it was barely noticeable.

Surely, he reasoned, he was not the only man to feel such ambivalence toward his child when it was first born. Caring for and loving babies was *women's* work, after all. Men might feel fondness and responsibility toward their babies, but he'd never seen a man cooing and cuddling one.

He would come to love the child when it was a little older, when it looked more recognizably like a human being. When it had developed a personality he could bond with. Until then, he would let Oona do all the loving and cooing and cuddling, since it was what she was born to do in the first place. Something his first wife had somehow failed to comprehend.

Delnamal breathed out a deep sigh of relief as his seething emotions calmed and settled. He was letting the changes that had rocked the world with the casting of the Curse color his judgment. Always before, there had been clear lines to separate what was a woman's responsibility and what was a man's. Now that there was a woman on the throne of Rhozinolm and a pretender who called herself the Sovereign Princess of Women's Well and a man needed to coax his wife to provide him with children—and might pay with his life for demanding his conjugal rights—the lines had blurred in ways that were naturally bound to confuse a man such as himself.

That damned Curse was to blame for the panic Delnamal had felt in the presence of his son! Fathers were meant to be strong, stoic protectors of their children, not to turn into mush and coo and coddle them. The Curse had fooled him into thinking that his natural male detachment was somehow wrong and abhorrent, and that was why he'd fled the room.

When Melcor had first brought him the ridiculous claims of the former Abbess of Khalpar, Delnamal had refused to even consider hearing the woman out. She was clearly desperate to return home to her own abbey, where she would be coddled and given respect she did not deserve. She would say *anything* to escape the Abbey of Aaltah. But if there was any chance—even the smallest—that she had found a way to reverse the Curse, then he owed it to himself—and all the other men throughout Seven Wells who had suffered so horribly from the effects of this Curse—to listen to what she had to say.

Forgetting for the moment his promise to return to the birthing chamber, Delnamal rang for a servant to fetch Melcor.

CHAPTER FORTY

Staggering under the combination of weight and stench, Mairah carried her stack of chamber pots out into the Abbey's courtyard and filled a trough with water. Emptying the pots was disgusting enough, but now she had to *clean* them. By the end of the task, her hands were wrinkled and cracked, and her scratchy robes were splattered with shit and piss. She wanted to weep, and wondered how long she could maintain her sanity under such conditions.

She rose to her feet, her knees creaking and groaning in protest after prolonged contact with the hard-packed ground, prepared to trudge back into the Abbey for her next menial chore. A well-dressed man stepped out into the courtyard, accompanied by one of the abigails, whose name Mairah hadn't bothered to learn. The women of this abbey were as cold and unfriendly toward her as the ones in Khalpar, and she returned the favor. The man made a dismissive gesture to the abigail, then strode toward Mairah.

She studied him as he approached, and something inside her instinctively recoiled. He was neither attractive nor particularly unattractive, but there was something in his expression and his bearing that gave her the instant impression of cruelty. Or maybe it was the strange twist of his thin lips as he regarded her. His bearing was regal and proud, but he was too old to be King Delnamal. Not that she expected the king to come to the Abbey to speak with her even if he was intrigued by her message.

Mairah swallowed hard and forced herself to bow her head demurely, as an abigail should before any man, noble or common, who crossed her path. She did not speak, did not raise her eyes, barely even breathed. She couldn't imagine how she must look to this great gentleman with her stained robes and her ruined face and her defeated posture. Something deserving of pity, perhaps, although he did not seem like the type of man who was prone to such soft emotions.

"You are Mairahsol?" he asked abruptly, looking at her with undisguised contempt, maybe even disgust. His nose wrinkled as the breeze carried the stink of her stained robes to him.

Mairah weathered a wave of humiliation, then reminded herself of who she was and what she had to offer. She might be forced to feign subservience, but pretending to be a beaten cur did not make her one in truth. Still keeping her gaze lowered, she nonetheless allowed a hint of her former pride to seep into her voice.

"I am Mairahsol Rah-Creesha, the Abbess of Khalpar," she confirmed.

The man looked even more contemptuous. "Don't put on airs with me," he growled. "Here, you are Sister Mairahsol, an inmate of the Abbey of the Unwanted. You should be whipped for having the gall to attempt to send a message to the king. In fact, you *shall* be."

Even with her lowered gaze, Mairah saw the flare of lust in the man's eyes and shuddered. A decade in the Abbey of Khalpar had taught her that some men took pleasure from hurting women, and unless she was very much mistaken, this man was one of them. Fear fluttered in her belly, but she did her best to hide it behind an air of certainty and confidence.

"It is the Abbey's administrator who deserves to be whipped," she said, then silently cursed her lack of proficiency in Continental. By now, she could understand almost everything that was said to her, but speaking herself was far more difficult, and the message she had sent had perforce been written in Parian. She had no choice but to gamble that this dangerous and forbidding stranger would understand Parian. "He kept vital information from the king's ears and confiscated a potion that could lead to the reversal of the Curse. I was sent to Women's Well to find a way to undo it, and when I succeeded, I barely escaped the place with my life. I fled to Aaltah because I knew your king was as eager to see the Curse reversed as my own."

She could tell by the man's sharp and thoughtful expression that her gamble had paid off, and he understood her. Her message might not have gained a direct audience with the king, but whoever had read it had been intrigued enough to send someone who spoke Parian to investigate.

"I am Lord Melcor," the man said with an unmistakable air of self-importance. "I am His Majesty King Delnamal's personal secretary, and my time is of great value. If you have wasted it by drawing me here with falsehoods, a whipping will be the least of your punishments."

"I swear by the Mother and the Creator that I am not wasting your time," she said while inside she quailed with terror.

"And if I allow you access to the king and you waste *his* time . . ." He let his voice trail off and shuddered theatrically. "His Majesty is already most put out with your king for treating with the leaders of this rebellion against the Crown of Aaltah, and he will be more than happy to express that displeasure in some most creative ways. Now, do you still request an audience with the king? Or would you prefer to return to the safety of your existence here at the Abbey?"

Safety? He called this *safety*? Mairah bit down on her tongue to keep a litany of retorts from escaping. She honestly wasn't sure that a slow and painful death would be worse than an entire long lifetime spent in this abbey. She had dreamed of comfort and safety and even respectability as a member of the Women's Well Academy, had been within hours of making that dream come true, which made Norah's betrayal and her own subsequent downfall all the more bitter to swallow. She could not bear to imagine giving up hope of escape, no matter what the risks.

"My king believes it is the will of the Creator that this abominable spell be reversed," Mairahsol said. "I will play whatever role my king and the Creator command of me to return the world to its natural order. Therefore, I must speak to your king about my discoveries. You can be certain I would not have been forced to flee Women's Well in fear for my life if those discoveries were not significant."

Melcor sniffed disdainfully. "I warned you before not to put on airs. You are nothing but a disgusting whore—hardly someone with whom the gods would entrust such a vital mission."

Panic swelled in Mairah's breast as she saw doors slamming shut in her face, saw her last hope turning his back on her and leaving her trapped here in misery. She fell to her knees, hardly noticing the pain that shot through her when kneecaps met packed earth with too much force.

"Please, Lord Melcor," she begged, letting tears well in her eyes. For every terrible thing Mairah had suffered in her life, she had never before been reduced to begging, and her insides shriveled. This was more humiliating even than scrubbing chamber pots. But if there was one thing Mairah had proven about herself time and time again, it was that she was willing to do whatever it took to get what she wanted. If Melcor wanted to see her humbled and begging so he could savor his power, then that was exactly what he would get. But his name would go on the ever-growing list of people she was determined to see destroyed, no matter what she had to do to accomplish it.

"I will bring your ridiculous petition to the king," he said, sneering at her even as his darkened eyes revealed his pleasure at her distress. "If it will entertain him to do so, His Majesty will summon you for an audience at his convenience."

Mairah all but prostrated herself at his feet.

When she had lived in Aaltah, Shelvon had taken pains to avoid as many social calls as custom would allow—which, granted, was very few. As wife of the crown prince and then as queen, any invitation she declined could potentially have unacceptable political ramifications, leaving prominent citizens feeling insulted. She couldn't count how many times Delnamal had made snide comments about her shy and awkward interactions with Aaltah high society, and that had not made accepting the invitations any easier.

While she was a great deal more comfortable in Women's Well, she was very much aware that she still didn't really fit in. She was used to getting only the occasional invitation to attend dinners and balls— most of those invitations coming, no doubt, at Princess Alysoon's urging—and when she accepted, she found herself as socially awkward as ever. She did not know how to talk to other women of her station, her upbringing in Nandel having inculcated in her the importance of being meek and quiet and unassuming. Open, lighthearted conversation—especially when inhibitions were loosened by drink—left her eying the door longingly.

But something changed after the night of the attempted kidnapping.

To Shelvon's shock, instead of being scandalized that she had wielded a sword and actually *wounded* the man who'd attacked her, people began greeting her with every appearance of sincerity when she encountered them on the street. Even people to whom she'd never been introduced would catch her eyes for a moment and flash her an approving smile or nod.

And then there were the invitations. Just a few at first, and she declined them on the assumption that Princess Alysoon was behind them and would not be offended—or surprised. But then they kept coming, and sometimes they were from people who seemed unlikely to have been prompted by the sovereign princess, for they were not inside her social circle.

Eventually, Shelvon accepted an invitation to tea at the house of a young woman named Maidel, who had once been an abigail in the Abbey of Aaltah and now worked as a scribe at the Academy. Shelvon had encountered Maidel a few times on the street, although they had not spoken. Shelvon could recognize in the young woman's body language a shyness similar to her own, no doubt due to the unsightly red blotch that marked her otherwise pretty face. Shelvon accepted the invitation in part on a whim, and in part because she hoped that someone like Maidel would understand if Shelvon was quiet and de-mure and allowed the other guests at the tea to do the majority of the talking. It seemed the gentlest introduction into society she could imagine, and she did not like the feeling that she was being rude or hurting someone's feelings every time she turned down an invitation.

The gathering for the tea party was gratifyingly small, with only three other women in attendance in addition to Shelvon and Maidel, and Shelvon was pleasantly surprised at how they managed to make her feel included and welcome without demanding that she some-how entertain them with her nonexistent wit. Then, just as Shelvon was relaxing into her role as nearly silent observer, sipping her tea and enjoying the feeling of easy camaraderie, her four companions all shared some silent communication via significant glances, and all at-tention suddenly focused on her. Shelvon tensed.

"We all just wanted to tell you how very much we admire you," Maidel said, her habitual shyness showing in the softness of her voice and her demurely lowered eyes.

Shelvon was left speechless as Maidel's companions nodded. "A-admire me?" she finally stammered, shaking her head at the odd no-tion. "Whatever for?"

Maidel's eyes widened in surprise. "Why, for fighting off that brute, of course!"

Heat flooded Shelvon's face and her shoulders hunched forward in a way that she knew was particularly unattractive. "I didn't fight anyone off," she demurred, remembering the terrible feeling of her attacker looming over her after she had fallen, of the helplessness that had swamped her. "H-he knocked me down and broke my ribs. And he would have . . . he would have . . ."

Princess Alysoon had told her exactly what the brute's mission had been, and her whole body shuddered in horror at the thought of what would have awaited her in Nandel. She'd been disgraced enough already, but she would have been considered even more tainted for having spent at least a couple of weeks the captive of some dirty Aal-tah mercenary as they traveled from Women's Well to The Keep.

"But he *didn't*," Maidel said when Shelvon's voice failed. "You defended yourself long enough for help to arrive, and because of that, you are safe and he was hanged." Her three companions murmured agreement.

Was *that* why everyone was looking at her differently these days? Did they actually believe she had done something *admirable*? When she was in the lowest of moods, she'd seen those changes as signs of pity, but even on better days, she had read nothing into it but compassion and commiseration. Certainly she'd never considered that they *admired* her.

Shelvon shook her head, putting down the cup of tea she'd been peacefully sipping. "I got lucky," she said. "There's nothing especially admirable about that."

One of the other women—a commoner by the name of Ruby, who would not have been included at a gathering of respectable ladies in any other place—snorted, though her expression was far from unkind. "Yes, it was nothing but luck. The hours you spent learning to swing a sword and defend yourself had nothing to do with it. I could have gotten just as lucky myself if I'd been attacked." She shook her head. "I don't know if you remember, but I attended one of your group sessions with Lord Falcor. I felt so clumsy handling the sword that I never came back."

"I never had the courage even to attend *one*," Maidel countered. "I figured I'd suffered a lifetime's worth of mockery because of my face, and the last thing I needed was to make a fool of myself."

Shelvon's face was so hot with embarrassment she wondered if she was glowing like a live coal. Her eyes stung, and she feared she was about to humiliate herself by crying, which was unacceptable enough when people were being *mean* to you, but when they were being nice . . .

"We were wondering," Maidel said, a thread of uncertainty entering her voice, "if by any chance you might be willing to teach us. We would pay for the classes, of course."

Once again, Shelvon was stunned speechless.

"I'm sure Lord Falcor is a wonderful teacher," Ruby put in, "but . . . well . . ." She sighed as if exasperated with herself. "Some of us find him rather intimidating."

"And rather male," one of her companions put in dryly.

Ruby grinned. "Yes, that, too. I felt so self-conscious during that one lesson that I couldn't force myself to come again. But if *you* were teaching it . . ."

"I hope you aren't offended by the idea of us paying for lessons," Maidel said anxiously. "We argued . . . er, discussed it a lot before we agreed to pay. I know that for someone who was once the Queen of Aaltah it must seem . . . distasteful to do something that smacks of trade, but, well . . ."

"But in Women's Well," Ruby continued for her, "it is not only men who get paid for their time and effort." She wrinkled her nose. "Besides, I've never understood what it is you highborn folk have against the idea of an honest day's work."

Shelvon blinked frantically, the tears trying harder to escape, and she saw Maidel biting her lip anxiously.

"I promise I'm not offended," Shelvon rasped as she continued to battle the tears.

In truth, she wasn't entirely sure *what* it was she felt. Embarrassed. Flattered. Proud. Terrified.

Yes. All of those, and more.

"We don't expect you to give us an answer right this moment," Maidel said gently.

"Honestly," Ruby said, "we didn't plan to ask you at all today. We were just going to try to plant the seed and see where it led." She gave her friends a somewhat scolding look, although there was a spark of humor in her eyes. "This was supposed to be nothing but a friendly social gathering. Even if we did have an ulterior motive for down the road."

Shelvon dabbed discreetly at the corners of her eyes. "I don't know what to say. I . . ." She swallowed hard. "I'm not qualified to teach anyone. I barely know how to swing a sword myself."

Maidel shrugged. "We don't want to train to be soldiers. We just want . . ." Her voice trailed off and she frowned.

"We just want to learn how not to feel helpless," Ruby finished for her.

Shelvon frantically reviewed the lessons Falcor had taught her, wondering how she could possibly teach what she knew to others. But of course, she *could* demonstrate the various strikes and guards she'd learned. And she'd done the guard drills so many times she felt reasonably certain she could show someone else how to go through them. And of course she was still taking lessons with Falcor, so her own expertise—such as it was—would continue to grow.

"Just let the idea simmer in the back of your mind," Maidel urged. "For now, let's just have some tea and enjoy one another's company."

Shelvon smiled gratefully and grabbed for her cup of tea as if it were a lifeline. But somewhere deep down inside, she knew she was going to accept the challenge. And she realized that maybe—just maybe—she had finally found her place in Women's Well society.

CHAPTER FORTY-ONE

Mairah paced restlessly across the length of the small anteroom, knowing she should sit down and wait in stoic dignity but incapable of doing so. One of the palace guards had entered the room with her, standing by the entrance and appearing to stare straight ahead, although every time she turned her back on him she could swear she felt his eyes boring into her. To say the guards who had escorted her from the Abbey to the palace treated her with a certain level of hostility was an understatement.

She had been allowed to bathe and don a clean set of robes, but the guards had no intention of waiting for her thick hair to dry. It was coiled damply around her head under her wimple, making her feel hot and sweaty and uncouth despite the bath.

The long wait, while not unexpected, frayed Mairah's nerves until she felt ready to jump out of her skin at the slightest provocation. Convincing King Delnamal that she was well on the road to devising a cure for the Curse was likely her only chance of escaping the hellish

Abbey of Aaltah. With so much riding on this one audience, it was no wonder her stomach was churning with anxiety.

Mairah had assumed this audience would take place in one of the palace's formal receiving rooms—either that, or, if he wanted to keep the conversation more private, the king's study—but apparently no lowly abigail was permitted to venture so deep into the palace.

The anteroom door opened so suddenly that Mairah could barely suppress a yelp of alarm, and an enormous, scowling man wearing a gold crown strode into the room.

Mairah curtsied deeply and bowed her head, hoping to keep her first impression from showing on her face. She knew that she herself was hardly a vision of loveliness, but everything about King Delnamal repulsed her. She had seen her fair share of fat men in her life, but most of them carried the extra weight with more grace than the king. His doublet strained over his middle, and his breeches were so tight they revealed every roll of fat in his legs. She wondered how he managed to sit down without splitting them open.

Worse than that was the stink of alcohol that wafted from him even when he stood more than an arm's length away, and the sour expression on his puffy face. His eyes were small and squinty, and his lips protruded unpleasantly in what she guessed was a perpetual pout.

"Your Majesty," she whispered in greeting, keeping her eyes lowered.

"What's all this nonsense I hear about you having developed a spell that will reverse the Curse?" he asked, not bothering with the courtesy of a greeting, though at least he spoke in Parian so she did not have to struggle to understand. "You had better not be wasting my time or I will make you *very* sorry you had the gall to disturb me."

"I would never dream of wasting Your Majesty's time," she said, keeping up her demure and deferential demeanor despite the surge of fury that rose in her breast. How dare this beast threaten her after all he'd already done to ruin her life? He *should* have welcomed her in style. Or at the very least given her comfortable transport back to Khalpar.

"My sole purpose in traveling to Women's Well was to find a cure for the Curse," she said. "My king made me abbess because I am the strongest spell crafter among the women of the Abbey of Khalpar, and he believed that only a woman could reverse the damage that the former Abbess of Aaltah did to the Wellspring."

Delnamal's lip curled in an ugly sneer. "I have no patience with boasting and preening," he growled.

Mairah couldn't help a small flinch at the venom in his voice, but she persevered anyway. "Forgive me, Your Majesty. I did not mean to boast. I meant merely to explain why my king sent me to Women's Well."

Delnamal's sneer remained firmly in place. "And if you have succeeded in this quest set by King Khalvin, then why has the Curse not already been reversed?"

The hostility that radiated from the king convinced Mairah that her only chance at anything resembling safety was to convince him to send her back to Khalpar. The idea made something inside her shrivel, but to try to conduct her research here in Aaltah meant staying within Delnamal's easy reach and being subject to his displeasure at the least sign that she might fail. She had not the courage to do it, even if returning to Khalpar meant abandoning all reasonable hope of winning her way back to Women's Well. Her first priority *had* to be survival, and so she modified the story she'd been planning to tell him to increase the chances that he would send her home.

"I need the aid of a seer stronger than myself," she said. "I have created a potion that will allow a seer to trigger visions of events that happened in the past. I believe a more talented seer would be able to witness the events that occurred on the night the Abbess of Aaltah cast the spell. And that once we know how the spell was cast, we will be able to to create a spell to undo it."

To her dismay, Delnamal laughed. It reminded her of a pack of urchins she'd heard in the marketplace once as they tortured a pathetic stray cat by setting its tail on fire. A laugh that held pure malice in place of any genuine humor.

"So it is as I expected," he said with an unpleasant gleam in his eye. "You are just one more lying whore who thinks to waste a king's time with delusions of grandeur."

Mairah drew herself up to her full height and risked a quick glance into the king's eyes. She quickly looked away again, for she hadn't the self-control to keep her hatred from showing in her expression, and she did not think letting him see what she truly thought of him was in her best interests.

"I believe that with the help of a seer, we can find a way to reverse the Curse," she said, willing herself to sound confident and certain despite her doubt. "If you will return me to my abbey, we have several seers who may well have the talent to see how the Curse was cast, and together—"

He interrupted her with a piggish snort. "You entered my kingdom without permission and you have the unparalleled arrogance to disobey the administrator of the Abbey to send me fanciful claims of power, and you expect to be *rewarded* for it?"

"Of course not, Your Majesty," she hastened to say. Her voice quavered, and she hoped he would interpret that quaver as fear rather than fury. "I seek no reward beyond the pleasure of being of service."

"And yet you expect me to dip into the royal coffers to transport you back to Khalpar."

"I'm sure King Khalvin would be willing to provide the transportation himself when he hears what I have learned. The Crown of Aaltah need not be troubled in any way."

There was a long, aching silence, and Mairah all but held her breath. Surely it was a good sign that he had not already stormed out of the room. For all the accusations and skepticism, he clearly *wanted* her to be telling the truth.

"You are supposedly a seer," he said suddenly. "Why can you not do the work yourself?"

"I have not the level of skill required," she said modestly.

"That is not what your king said when he tried to justify his decision to send you to Women's Well bearing gifts."

Mairah squirmed, because of course she had frequently claimed a great deal more ability than she'd ever shown. It was hardly surprising that King Khalvin would have repeated the lies she'd told, but admitting to telling lies was not a good way to convince Delnamal that she was telling the truth now.

"I'm afraid he is mistaken," Mairah said. "I am considered a talented user of women's magic, and I suppose it was assumed that meant I was a powerful seer, as well." She could see at once from Delnamal's expression that he was not convinced, so she kept talking, with perhaps a hint of desperation. "You see, seers drink poison to trigger visions. The stronger the seer, the stronger the poison she can drink without dying, and the stronger and more significant the vision she will have. My own powers are not sufficiently developed for me to tolerate any but the mildest poisons, and—"

"I have no interest in hearing your excuses," the king interrupted. "I have been told we have no seers in our abbey currently. Except you. If the Curse is to be reversed, it will happen *here*, not in Khalpar. So you have two choices. You can either admit you have wasted my time. Or you can drink a poison strong enough to give you the vision you need. If your vision helps reverse the Curse, then I will send you back to Khalpar in grand style with a suitable reward. But the price you will pay for wasting my time is . . . severe. So will you drink that poison, or shall I consult with my inquisitor for how best to make you pay for your insolence?"

Mairah quailed, her knees going so weak she feared for a moment that she might faint like some helpless maiden.

In reality, there was no telling just how strong a poison she could swallow without dying. Her assessment of her own weakness was based on her lack of willingness to endure any but the mildest seer's poison. Perhaps if she took a stronger seer's poison, she would survive it and achieve exactly the kind of vision she desired. It would hurt more than she liked to imagine, but that pain and possible death would likely be quicker and easier than what Delnamal would do to her if he decided she'd wasted his time. It was impossible to look at him and not see his hunger for cruelty. He would *enjoy* punishing her, and nothing about him said he was the kind of man who abstained from doing what he enjoyed.

"I will drink the poison," she said in a small, shaking voice that hardly sounded like her own.

Jalzarnin entered the abbess's office and suffered an unexpected jolt of pain to find Norah sitting behind the scarred wooden desk instead of Mairah. Despite having been removed from the royal council the moment news of Mairah's flight reached Khalpar, Jalzarnin had wheedled his way in to see the trade minister and tried to convince him to name *anyone* but Sister Norah to the position. Mairah would be *livid* if she ever found out that hateful hag had taken her place. But the trade minister, not surprisingly, was still angry that Jalzarnin had gone over his head to have Mairah made abbess in the first place, so he'd been uninterested in Jalzarnin's suggestions. And though Khalvin had put up a protest about Mairah's capture and detention by King Delnamal, he made it obvious just how little her fate mattered to him when he insisted she be instantly replaced as abbess.

Perhaps it was his imagination, but Jalzarnin could have sworn that Mother Norah looked downright smug when he was shown into her office. Certainly the woman knew about his relationship with Mairah, though she most likely thought it had been one of convenience rather than love. And Jalzarnin had no doubt she was somehow to blame for Mairah's flight, despite her claims that Mairah had run away because she'd known her mission would fail.

"How good of you to come visit, Lord Jalzarnin," Norah said. Behind the layers of smugness and courtesy, he detected a hint of unease she was trying hard to hide. "I can't tell you how sorry I am that Mairahsol betrayed our kingdom and left you in such an untenable position. If I'd had any inkling what she was going to do, I swear I would have stopped it."

Jalzarnin considered himself a man of tact and subtlety, and he'd come to the abbess's office intending to engage her in a complex dance of suggestions and innuendo in hopes that she would reveal more than she realized over the course of the conversation. But faced with her now, knowing she was to blame for Mairah's terrible situation and his own disgrace, he found that subtlety was beyond him.

"Let us not pretend to a cordiality we do not feel for each other," he said, causing Norah to blink in surprise and no small amount of alarm. "I don't know what you did to Mairahsol, how you caused her to flee, but I know you were responsible all the same."

Norah stuttered the start of what was no doubt a denial, but he cut her off with a harsh hand motion.

"She is a captive of the Abbey of Aaltah, which by all accounts has become a place of unspeakable misery, all because of you. If you hoped that claiming she was guilty of a treasonous lie would save you and your sisters from her revenge, you were very much mistaken."

He was not in the habit of bullying old women, but he couldn't deny a glow of satisfaction when he saw terror and comprehension in the new abbess's eyes.

"Oh, you thought I wouldn't reveal the presence of your Mother of All cult in this abbey because I might be tainted by association?" he asked. "That might have been true if the failure of the mission hadn't already cost me the office of lord high priest. But when it comes down to it, right now I have little more to lose."

Tears pooled in Norah's eyes, and she rose from her desk to come kneel at his feet, gazing up at him beseechingly. He wished Mairah were here to see this, for he was sure she would have enjoyed the sight. Just as he was sure . . . well, at least *hopeful*, that she would approve the alternative revenge he had devised in her absence. For in actuality, he *did* still have a great deal to lose by revealing the existence of the heretics. The king already blamed him enough for the failure of Mairah's mission that he'd summarily dismissed Jalzarnin from the royal council. That taint would cling to Jalzarnin for years to come, but at least over time he might hope to win his way back into the king's good graces. After all, Khalvin was nothing if not mercurial. But in the king's present mood, Jalzarnin could not trust him not to lose all sense of reason if he learned about the cult. He might just be angry enough to insist Jalzarnin himself be questioned by the inquisitor, and that was a fate Jalzarnin would not risk. Not even for Mairah.

"Please, my lord," Norah begged. "I swear to you it was not my fault that Mairahsol fled. I won't pretend I did not despise her, but I would never risk the lives of my sisters by betraying her. She *chose* to run because she has been lying to you all along. She has no talent for visions or she would not have needed to force so many of the Abbey's seers to try to solve her troubles for her. She kept up the illusion that she had the talent to undo the Curse for as long as she could, then made a run for it when she realized her time was nearly up. It probably gives her a great deal of pleasure to imagine you condemning us for her disappearance. My sisters and I are blameless."

Jalzarnin snorted loudly. "Even if I believed you were telling the complete truth, you are *not* blameless! You are heretics! And I may not be the lord high priest anymore, but I am still a priest. It is my duty to root out heresy wherever it may sprout."

Norah was too terrified by the threat to question his sincerity, though it would eventually occur to her that his duty to root out heresy had been conspicuously absent from his consideration until this moment. If he were threatening to condemn her because of his great piety, he would have done so long before now. Visibly shaking, Norah prostrated herself at his feet and blubbered.

Jalzarnin felt no pity for her terror. Why should he, when she had never shown an inkling of pity for Mairahsol?

"Please, Lord Jalzarnin," she begged between sobs. "Please do not condemn us. We will do whatever you ask of us. My abigails will service you however you like without charge. We will—"

"There is, in fact, one way I might conceivably be convinced to keep your perversions to myself," he interrupted, and Norah turned her tearstained face up toward him with wary hope flickering in her eyes.

"Anything," she swore, and Jalzarnin had no doubt that she meant it. He suspected in her place, he would have made the same promise, for he could think of no fate worse than being declared a heretic in King Khalvin's court.

In her short stint as abbess, Mairahsol had done only an adequate job of feeding him the information he hoped for. Her abilities had been severely limited by her unpopularity and the resistance she had faced from Norah and the rest of the cultists. But with Norah as abbess—and beholden to Jalzarnin even more desperately than Mairah had been—there was no end to the amount of information he could glean about the fine noblemen who frequented the Abbey. Perhaps enough to restore him to his rightful position as lord high priest in relatively short order. After all, he already knew that his replacement, Lord Thanstal, was a frequent visitor to the Abbey. And just because Mairahsol hadn't been able to learn anything particularly useful or damaging about him didn't mean such information didn't exist.

Jalzarnin looked forward to teaching the ambitious priest just how capricious King Khalvin's high regard could be.

Mairah had hoped she'd be allowed to drink the seer's poison in some semblance of comfort. After all, she would be putting herself through a life-threatening, painful trauma all for the sake of what King Delnamal considered the public good. Surely a sacrifice such as hers—even when made with such great reluctance—deserved *some* compensation.

But no. Instead of undertaking her mission in the royal palace, where they could at least have offered her comfortable servants' quarters, she was forced to trigger her vision in the Abbey in one of the wretched playrooms. From what she'd heard whispered, the playrooms in the original Abbey of Aaltah had been luxurious as the rest of the Abbey was not, in deference to the rich and noble men who were its most frequent customers. However, since the original abigails had been banished and the Abbey razed, the clientele was apparently not so lofty or picky. The room was dingy and airless and smelled faintly of sweat and cum.

Administrator Loveland hovered over her and glowered as she mixed her special remembrance potion with the strongest seer's poison she knew how to make. She did, of course, consider making a counterfeit poison, one that would not cause her such great pain or risk her death. If she'd been in Khalpar, needing only a promising suggestion that she could undo the Curse to secure her position as abbess, that was unquestionably what she would have done. But here in Aaltah, with the king's threats hanging over her head, Mairah feared she would need more than a promising suggestion. She needed something *real*. Which meant her only reasonable option was to down the genuine seer's poison and pray to the Mother she didn't believe in that it would show her a way to save herself.

Mairah held the small vial of poison to her lips, her mouth gone dry and her pulse racing and her skin clammy with fear-sweat. Loveland was still glowering at her, his expression saying he was willing—maybe even eager—to punish her for her hesitation. At which point he would no doubt force the stuff down her throat.

Pinching her nose in the futile hope that she could dull the foul taste, she poured the contents of the vial into her mouth and shuddered convulsively. Willing herself to have a vision of the night the Curse was cast, she swallowed the poison despite her throat's fervent desire to close up and reject it. Her heart tripped over itself in terror as the poison burned down her throat, the heat stronger and more immediate than what she'd experienced with the milder versions.

She was climbing onto the bed, preparing to make herself as comfortable as possible, when a burst of fiery pain, worse than anything she had felt before, bloomed in her chest. It stole the air from her lungs, made her heart thud against her breastbone so loudly she thought sure the sound could be heard in the neighboring room. The empty vial fell from her fingertips. It likely shattered when meeting the stone floor, but she could not hear the sound over her own helpless scream.

The room fell away immediately, her vision going dark as she writhed and cried and tried to escape from the pain. She could not feel the bed beneath her as the fire spread from her chest to her belly then crawled down her arms and legs at a leisurely pace.

She was dying. The poison was burning her flesh away from her bones, consuming her from the inside out. It was the price she had to pay for her hubris in drinking so strong a seer's poison when she had no reason to believe she could withstand it. But this death—as excruciating as it was—was better than the alternative fates that awaited her had she refused to drink.

It went on and on and on until Mairah thought she would surely lose her sanity before she lost her life. And then, as suddenly as it had started, it stopped.

Mairah couldn't feel her body anymore, but the darkness slowly lightened, bringing into focus a humble but comfortable room filled with worn, mismatched furniture and lit by several bright luminants. A middle-aged woman dressed in the red robes of an abigail sat in a shabby armchair by the fire across from a younger abigail to whom she bore a striking family resemblance. The younger woman's body was rigid with tension, her hands clasped together so tightly in her lap that the knuckles were white. The older woman—her mother?—wore a stern expression that carried the undeniable air of authority and perhaps even a hint of impatience.

"Nadeen," said the older woman, whom Mairah now suspected was the late Abbess of Aaltah, "I told you before that our work would require a sacrifice. What did you think I meant?"

The young woman—Nadeen—was visibly shaking, her eyes filmed with tears as she stared fixedly at the floor. "I-I don't know," she said in a quavering voice. "I just . . . I didn't expect . . ."

The abbess's voice softened, although there was too much steel in her expression to make her tone truly gentle. "We have many years yet to prepare. I trust that when the time comes, you will be ready to do what must be done."

A hint of fire flashed in Nadeen's eyes, then was quickly replaced by misery as she shook her head. "I can't, Mama," she whispered. "I am not brave like you."

"Maybe not now," the abbess said, and Mairah winced in sympathy for Nadeen. The abbess appeared not to be the warmest and most nurturing of mothers. "You need time to make peace with your fate. I certainly did not enter the Abbey planning to slash my own wrists for the greater good, and I was not especially receptive to the idea when my abbess explained it to me. But time and maturity have made me see that it is for the best."

Nadeen shook her head again. "And what if I refuse?" she asked. "Will you then slay me with your own hand?"

The abbess made a sound of impatience. "Have you listened to *nothing* I've said? Our willing sacrifice will produce something that is *akin* to Kai, but it *isn't* Kai. At least not the Kai that we are familiar with and that men produce. That Kai is the element of death and vengeance. I can't say for sure, but I suspect thanks to our special breeding, you and I and Vondeen would produce ordinary masculine Kai—and be able to see it—if we suffered a violent death. But that is not what we need to make our spell work. And since our spell is designed to sink through the earth into Aaltah's Well, I can only imagine what damage we could do if we activated it with ordinary masculine Kai. It would almost certainly poison the Well, and it might even spread to the Wellspring. So no, Daughter, I will not slay you with my own hand. Only a woman's willing sacrifice can create the kind of Kai we need. And only the three of us can create motes that can be combined with one another in the way I have foreseen."

Mairah caught her breath. She had heard of men's Kai that was generated on the battlefields, and the new women's Kai that was generated by rape; but she had never heard of a special Kai generated by a willing sacrifice. Her mind reeled at the very thought of this unknown form of Kai. And that it was somehow capable of affecting the Wellspring itself, the source of all magic.

Tears streamed down Nadeen's cheeks. "How can you ask this of your own daughter?" she choked out. "How can you ask me to ask this of *my* daughter?"

"I'm not asking you to do anything I'm not willing to do myself. I've foreseen a future where women are no longer shut up in abbeys or bought and sold like cattle. And having seen that future, I cannot turn my back on it. I believe that when the time comes, you will do the right thing. You and I and Vondeen will lay down our lives to make the world a better place. What better fate and legacy can a trio of Unwanted Women hope for?"

The vision faded, but Mairah's mind continued to whirl as she tried to absorb and make sense of everything she'd heard. Her eyes blinked open, and the physical world came back into focus. She was aware of movement around her, of the dim light of candles, of a man's sharp and impatient voice, and of her body's bone-deep aches and soul-deep weariness. Her vision went dark around the edges, and she allowed her eyes to drift back shut.

There would be time to think later, she assured herself as she sank into an exhausted sleep.

CHAPTER FORTY-TWO

Mairah groaned and lifted her head from her arms, which were folded on her worktable. Her body was stiff and her hands were filled with pins and needles. She hadn't meant to fall asleep, had only meant to rest her eyes a moment, but exhaustion had sunk its teeth into her and dragged her down.

Stifling a massive yawn, she forced herself to her feet in the small, deserted workroom that had become her newest prison cell.

Administrator Loveland had told her she'd been unconscious for two full days after she'd triggered her vision, but she still felt as though she could sleep two or three more without being truly rested. The seer's poison had sapped much of her strength and left her stomach so sensitive she could keep nothing down but broth and gruel. And yet despite the ravages of the poison, she had found—once she'd recovered her wits enough to sort her thoughts—that the vision had granted her a clarity she hadn't even realized she'd been missing.

The vision had told her very little about what exactly Mother Brynna had done to pull off her spell, for it was clear the Kai she and her daughter and her granddaughter had created was used only as a trigger element. But what Mairah had gleaned from what she'd heard was that spells triggered by Kai could affect the Wellspring itself. Traditional men's Kai could apparently have a destructive effect, but such was not the case with the special feminine Kai created by willing sacrifice. A Kai that—as far as Mairah knew—no one but the three women who cast the Curse even knew existed.

The vision had given her no clue how she might go about reversing the Curse. However, it had spawned an entirely new idea. Instead of merely developing a potion to close the Mindseye when slipped into a water supply, what if she were to trigger that potion with feminine sacrificial Kai instead? And what if instead of putting it into the water supply, she fed it into Aaltah's Well?

If that spell were to force the Mindseye of everyone within reach of Aaltah's Well closed, then Aaltah would be so severely crippled they could *never* hope to attack Women's Well! Surely eliminating the looming threat of Aaltah would be enough to convince Princess Alysoon of Mairah's worth and good intentions and would win her forgiveness. Especially if Mairah were also to invent an antidote to her spell so that once Aaltah fell to Women's Well or its allies, she could repair whatever damage was done. Instead of being reviled, she would be a hero!

To achieve her goal, Mairah needed to refine and strengthen the potion she'd made for Kailee. And she had to gain access to Aaltah's Well, for she did not know what Mother Brynna had done to her own spell to make it "sink through the earth into the Well" as she had described it doing.

When Loveland—and after him, King Delnamal—had questioned her about the vision, Mairah had concocted what she feared was an implausible story about how she'd watched Mother Brynna and the others cast the spell and therefore knew how to undo it herself. To provide some verisimilitude to the lie, she'd explained the use of the special motes of Kai the three women had created with their willing sacrifice, and she'd also said she would need direct access to the Well when her spell was ready.

She didn't know whether to be relieved or terrified when King

Delnamal had accepted her story and then given her no more than seven days to research and develop the spell she claimed she needed. She had tried to plead for more time, but whether because he didn't truly believe her or because he was too impatient to wait, he had refused.

Pacing the room, Mairah stared balefully at the worktable, at its scattered clutter of vials and scribbled pages and indecipherable notes. Administrator Loveland poked his head in every once in a while to make sure she was hard at work. Which she always was, although not on the spell she'd claimed would undo the Curse. He had given her back the Devotional with its store of special feminine elements from Women's Well, and though he often tried to watch what she was doing, he could not see the feminine elements at all, and he seemed to have only the most minimal ability to see even the masculine and neuter ones. His attempts to "monitor" her activities were, therefore, nearly useless, and she was free to work on the potion to her heart's content. Even her notes were safe from his prying eyes, for he knew no Parian, but she kept them cryptic anyway.

Of course, she had no one but herself on whom to test the potion—a process she had to approach with the utmost caution, as she could not afford to have her Mindseye unable to open when Loveland performed one of his spot inspections. So she spent the daylight hours tinkering with the formula, then waited until bedtime to perform any tests.

Within four nights, she had a potion that would force her Mindseye closed for hours on end. One version had given her a scare when she woke in the morning and *still* couldn't open her Mindseye. Luckily, she'd had the foresight to concoct an antidote before testing the potion, although it meant spending much of the morning heaving into a chamber pot, for the antidote she'd developed involved the use of a purgative.

For the final version of her potion, she would add the element Sur, which served to make the effects of many spells and potions permanent. Unfortunately, this final version would not be one she dared test, for if it worked and the antidote failed to reverse the effects, she would be doomed.

She would have only one chance to cast her spell on the Well—
assuming Delnamal would provide a subject for the willing human
sacrifice—and she still had no idea how she would escape after she'd
cast it. Feeling she needed every bit of help she could get, Mairah
reluctantly downed another seer's poison in hopes that a vision of the
traditional sort might show her whether her spell was going to work
or not.

She couldn't afford to take a poison that would leave her out of
commission for two days, so perforce she took a much milder one
that merely left her sick and miserable and in pain for a few hours.
The vision it triggered showed her standing in the cavern in which sat
Aaltah's Well. If Aaltah's Well was anything like Khalpar's, the room
would ordinarily have been heavily guarded, but in her vision there
were only four people in the cavern: herself, the king, Melcor, and a
sickly looking woman with dull eyes. Melcor and the strange woman
stood close to the mouth of the Well. Melcor was holding a knife out
to her while Mairah watched. King Delnamal, looking both petulant
and excited, stood apart from them with his arms crossed over his
chest.

The vision showed Mairah nothing more, but it was enough to
help her form some semblance of a plan.

The four of them were alone and unguarded in that chamber.
Mairah could only assume that the sickly looking woman was the
willing sacrifice, and that meant she was no threat to Mairah. Delnamal was standing at some remove, and Mairah already knew that the
Well's cavern was situated below the palace somewhere, which meant
that to exit the chamber would require climbing quite a few stairs—
something she doubted Delnamal could do with anything resembling alacrity. If she fled, he would never be able to catch her. Which
left only Melcor as a potential threat.

Could Mairah outrun him? He was more able-bodied than Delnamal, but her vision had shown there to be a considerable distance
between them. He would surely be distracted when the woman performed the sacrifice, and Mairah could take advantage of his distraction to sprint toward freedom. If she could reach the door first, she

should be able to shut him in, for there was certainly a bar or lock on it.

The plan seemed promising, but still left Mairah with far too many doubts. Would Melcor be sufficiently distracted? Would the door require a key to lock it? How could she escape the palace unnoticed once she exited the Well chamber? And, most important, would her potion work? For if it failed, she knew Delnamal would do everything in his considerable power to find and punish her.

Knowing she needed more answers, Mairah grimly resolved to take as many seer's poisons as necessary to find her path to freedom and glory.

King Delnamal glared around the table at the members of his royal council, hiding the humiliating roil of panic in his belly. The council had been a great deal more accommodating after his summary dismissal of Lord Aldnor, and he'd allowed their complaisance to convince him that they had no more resistance left.

Oh, he hadn't deluded himself into believing his royal council was as steadfast and loyal as a royal council ought to be, didn't believe they respected and esteemed him as they had his father. But he'd convinced himself they'd *obey* him when he made his desires abundantly clear.

There was not a man at the table who was willing to meet his eyes, and that enraged Delnamal even further. If they truly had the audacity to resist a plan that might lead to the reversal of the Curse, they should at least have the courage to look him in the eyes while they did it.

"Is there a man here at this table who does not want the Curse to be undone?" Delnamal snarled.

"Of course not, Your Majesty," his lord chancellor said with only the briefest flick of a glance at his face. "It's just that . . ." Here, his courage failed him and his voice trailed off as he looked helplessly around the table for someone else to take up the cry.

"It's just that it seems a terrible risk to grant the Abbess of Khalpar access to our Well when she has so little reason to think well of us," the grand magus said, causing several of the other councilors to wince delicately.

The council had already more than once expressed a tactful level of discomfort with his treatment of the Khalpari bitch. A displeasure that was all the more evident when King Khalvin had sent an official request to release the woman into Khalpari custody—despite having already named a new abbess. It was as if they *didn't care* that Khalvin had spit in the face of Aaltah by sending a delegation bearing gifts to that band of traitors in Women's Well. As if they expected Delnamal to just bend over and *take it* instead of responding with a firm and unambiguous message.

"I have offered the woman her freedom if she succeeds in her task," Delnamal responded sharply. "She doesn't have to think well of us. She just has to have her own best interests at heart."

There was more shifting and throat clearing and lowered gazes. Delnamal thought surely *some* of the more sycophantic council members would speak a few words of mealy support, but every last man in the room seemed to have lost his voice. Or his balls.

"You can't seriously mean to just *ignore* this opportunity!" Delnamal shouted, banging the table for emphasis. Which turned out to be an unfortunate decision, for the table was solidly built and barely made a sound while it savaged the bones of his hand.

"Let her conduct her unholy experiment on the Well in Khalpar," the grand magus advised. His voice was irritatingly soothing, as if he believed he was speaking with a madman. "She can't—"

"Yes," Delnamal interrupted. "Let's give her everything she wants so that she has no incentive to do anything whatsoever to reverse the Curse. And even if she does still have some incentive, why should we allow Khalvin to have all the glory? Then Aaltah will go down in history as the kingdom that allowed the Curse to be cast, and Khalpar will be the heroic kingdom that restored the natural order. I'm sure that will set the basis for excellent international relations for generations to come."

More wincing and shifting and muttering ensued. Delnamal wondered if perhaps he wouldn't be better served by dismissing every last man on his royal council. Maybe if he started afresh . . .

But angry though he was, he knew that was not a viable solution. The council was made up of members of the richest and most influential families in the kingdom. He'd faced enough grumbling from Lord Aldnor's family already, and he could not afford to make more enemies.

"We cannot risk that the witch might do grievous harm to our Well," the lord chancellor said, and it seemed that he was speaking for every man on the council based on the way they all nodded. "No matter how much every man at this table would like to see the Curse reversed, it is not worth putting our entire kingdom at risk."

If Delnamal had seen even a hint of doubt or disagreement on the face of any man in the room, he would have called for a vote and hoped the dissenters were too cowardly—and protective of their positions—to cast a vote against him. As it was, he was convinced that a vote would not go in his favor.

The truth was, there was no law that said he had to gain the council's permission to take the former Abbess of Khalpar to the Well of Aaltah. There were a great number of decisions codified by law that required at least minimal approval from the council, but the law had never seen fit to cover the unique situation in which Delnamal now found himself.

Delnamal smiled to think how slavishly his council members would kiss his feet, how the common people would worship him, how the kings and sovereign princes of Seven Wells would admire him if he defied the council and the abbess's spell worked.

The smile faded as he considered what would happen if he defied the council and the spell *didn't* work. Even if the failed attempt did no damage, he would lose what respect the royal council had for him, and he could count on all but the most sycophantic of the bunch to resist him more stubbornly. And if something untoward happened, if the witch's spell not only didn't work but in some way harmed the Well . . .

So no. He did not need his council's permission. But cold logic still told him that winning them over was preferable to having the witch cast the spell behind their backs.

The question then became, how could he convince them that trying to undo the Curse was worth the risk?

He didn't yet know the answer, but he was bound and determined to find a way.

Delnamal read over his letter to Prince Waldmir for what had to be at least the tenth time. Ordinarily, his correspondence with foreign sovereigns was written for him by one of his diplomatic scribes, and his only duty was to tell the scribe what to say and then read over the final letter before sending it off. But this particular letter was one he had to write himself, for it was of the utmost importance that no one—not even his most trusted advisers—know about it.

He huffed out a deep breath as he signed the thing, wondering if he had taken leave of his senses. But no. It was his *council* who was to blame. If they had just agreed to let the Abbess of Khalpar attempt to undo the Curse, he wouldn't have *needed* to write to Waldmir at all, wouldn't have needed to undo all the careful work he'd done in building that relationship. He was sure he was on the cusp of luring Prince Waldmir away from his alliance with Rhozinolm.

Rolling up the letter, he sealed it with wax and attached it to a flier. He had done his best not to come across as rude or insulting as he'd regretfully informed the prince that he could no longer offer a future marriage between his heir and the prince's daughter. And he'd included suggestions for other potential ways their two lands could come together in the future, as though he weren't specifically trying to drive Waldmir and Nandel away. But no pretty wording would undo the damage this letter would cause when it reached its destination. Only the hope of his grandson one day sitting on the throne of Aaltah could possibly have tempted Waldmir into the kind of alliance that they needed. With that hope snatched away, in all likelihood Waldmir's nephew would soon be engaged to Queen Ellinsoltah and their trade agreements renewed.

Surely *then* Delnamal's council would see that allowing the abbess to attempt her spell was the only way to keep Aaltah safe. If the Curse would just go away, then Alysoon and her little band of rebels would lose all their power, and all the unholy magic the Curse had brought into the world would be gone. He would no longer need King Khalvin's support to crush the rebels, because they would no longer have the magic that had protected them from his first attack. Rhozinolm might still object—he was well aware that the queen's cousin had recently married Tynthanal—but Delnamal could mercifully spare the girl from her husband's fate and return her to the bosom of her family. Even if the queen and the girl's father were offended, they would be unlikely to find any great support for a war as long as the girl was returned unharmed.

It was a gamble, Delnamal told himself as he opened his Mindseye and activated the flier's spell. If the abbess's spell failed, or if it somehow damaged the Well . . .

He shook the thought off. Great kings took great risks when the reward was worth it. And this one was. If through his actions, the Curse was reversed, then he would go down in history as one of the greatest kings Seven Wells had ever known. If his gamble didn't work, well, it would be a disaster, that was certain. But as long as he had the council's approval to take that gamble—and no one knew he'd sabotaged Aaltah's relationship with Nandel to get it—the blame would not fall on *his* shoulders.

Smiling at the idea of children reading about him in the history books generations from now, he sent the flier on its way.

CHAPTER FORTY-THREE

Ellin was catching up on correspondence—a seemingly endless task on which she was always woefully behind—when her desk drawer began to chirp. She frowned and lowered the letter of complaint she'd been reading from some minor nobleman who felt compelled to tell her that it was not fitting for a woman to sit on the throne of Rhozinolm—as if he had any right to an opinion on the matter. She was not unhappy to toss the letter aside for now, but an unexpected communication via talker was rarely a good thing.

Ellin opened the drawer, fully expecting the chirping talker to be the one that was paired with Princess Alysoon's, and her misgivings strengthened when she saw that instead it was Prince Waldmir's. She had spoken to the Sovereign Prince of Nandel via talker only once, and that occasion had been a brief and painfully formal introduction. For him to attempt to contact her like this without warning boded ill.

She set the talker on her desk, then left it there and opened her office door, asking her secretary to find Zarsha and send him to the office immediately. Then, not knowing how long Waldmir would persist before growing impatient, she sat at her desk and activated the talker.

"Prince Waldmir," she said with a practiced court smile when his image shimmered into life. "What a pleasant surprise."

Waldmir's ascetic face was not made for laughter, but she nonetheless caught a spark of amusement in his usually cold eyes. "I'm glad you find it so, Your Majesty," he said in his rich, deep voice. "My council advised me that I should arrange a more formal meeting, but I felt that in some matters, it was best for two sovereigns to have the freedom to speak to one another in complete openness and candor."

Ellin's lips twitched in a hint of a smile, despite a renewed upwelling of wariness. She was well aware of the Nandelite dislike for the intricacies and deviousness of court intrigue, but though much of Seven Wells considered them to be little better than barbarian warlords, her discussions with Zarsha had convinced her there was a great deal more to them than that. Waldmir's desire to speak with her in private screamed of ulterior motives.

"I have sent for Zarsha," she said. "I assume this conversation will be of interest to him, as well."

The expression in Waldmir's eyes hardened. "I do not wish for my nephew to be involved. This is to be a conversation between two sovereigns alone."

Ellin shook her head. "Am I wrong in assuming the topic will be our marriage?"

"You are not wrong. But if you wish to marry my nephew and retain Rhozinolm's trade agreements with Nandel, you will agree to negotiate with me and me alone. Zarsha does not get a voice."

Ellin stared at the Sovereign Prince of Nandel as she absorbed his words and the implications. Clearly, he planned to propose terms that he felt Zarsha would not agree with, and that was why he insisted on privacy. He might also be hoping that with no one to counsel her, she might make a rash decision that would be to his advantage.

Ordinarily, Ellin would trust her own judgment, despite her relative inexperience. Having sat on the throne only a year and a half, she felt as though she'd weathered at least five years' worth of crises already. But Waldmir's desire to separate her from her advisers aroused a tumult of suspicions. What was Waldmir up to?

"I may be relatively new to the throne," she said with some asperity, "but I am not so green as to believe that either marriage arrangements or trade agreements are ordinarily negotiated between two sovereigns alone. In point of fact, I've never heard of such a thing. I'm afraid it's simply out of the question."

Waldmir pinned her with a steely gaze. "If you want to renew the trade agreements, then you have no choice. I have another offer on the table, and if we end this conversation without making an agreement, then I will insist that you send my nephew home. And our current trade agreements will not be renewed."

Ellin's heart gave an unpleasant thump as the weight of that threat crashed down. She had retained her hold on her throne on the strength of her promise to renew the trade agreements with Nandel. Thanks to Tamzin's death—and the marriage she had arranged for Kailindar's daughter—she had more support on her royal council now than she ever had before. But she was under no illusion that support would last if she lost the trade agreements.

"Do you wish to end this conversation now?" Waldmir prompted with a challenging raise of his eyebrows.

Ellin gritted her teeth. She had little patience for bullies, and she had no wish to give in to one. Most likely, he was bluffing, after all. Then again, he had been unwilling to commit to any marriage arrangement—or renewal of the trade agreements—for half a year now, and the longer he delayed, the less popular her rule would become. Maybe this was her chance to get a firm commitment out of him.

"I'm listening," Ellin said reluctantly. "But there are limits to what I can and cannot agree to without consulting my royal council."

"Of course," Waldmir said with a regal inclination of his head. "But I can assure you that your royal council will have no issue with my offer." He flashed her a wolflike smile. "Though perhaps the same cannot be said of my nephew."

Which was why he'd insisted Zarsha not be included in the conversation, obviously. A page knocked on the office door, and when Ellin beckoned him to enter, informed her that Zarsha was on his way.

"Tell him it turns out I don't need him right now after all," she ordered.

The page bowed and retreated, and Ellin turned back to Waldmir. "Satisfied?"

"Indeed."

"Then what is it, exactly, you propose?"

"I will give Zarsha my permission to marry, and I will agree to renew all of our trade agreements on the existing terms for the duration of your marriage. I am prepared to commit to these agreements in writing. Today."

Ellin was painfully aware of how closely he was studying her face, and she hoped she gave away nothing of what she was thinking. She could almost feel him measuring her, assessing her, deciding just how far and how hard he could afford to push. And how badly she wanted this agreement.

She smiled her most disingenuous smile as she tried to anticipate just where Waldmir was going with this. She wouldn't have believed the deal to be a simple one even if she didn't see the predatory gleam in his eyes—or if he hadn't tipped his hand by barring Zarsha from the discussion.

"I can see no fault whatsoever in such a generous offer," she said. "I look forward to the continued warmth and friendship between Rhozinolm and Nandel and will have my council begin the wedding preparations immediately."

Waldmir's smile showed too many teeth, as if she'd managed to reveal too much despite her obviously falsely optimistic response. "You will agree that this marriage would not be . . . traditional in nature."

Ellin couldn't stop the small frown his words caused as she once again tried to anticipate his intentions. With no luck. "I'm not sure what you mean," she said, choosing honesty as the most expedient course.

"You are the Queen Regnant of Rhozinolm, and you propose to make my nephew your consort. Your subordinate."

Ellin wasn't sure if it was her imagination, but she could have sworn she saw a slight hint of a sneer on Waldmir's lips before he smoothed it away. She regarded him coolly. "I suppose in that way our marriage may be unconventional," she agreed cautiously. "However, I'm sure that you understand that no foreigner can be crowned king, and that therefore this is our only option."

Waldmir's smile hardened. "I have no objection to Zarsha being your bride, Your Majesty. It's a role to which he is well suited." There was no missing the sneer this time. "But if he is to serve the role of a bride, then I will treat him as I would treat any bride of Nandel."

"And just what does that entail?" Ellin asked, although she knew it was nothing good. Women in Nandel were considered possessions of the men in their lives, with no freedom or autonomy save what their husbands and fathers granted.

"A bride of Nandel brings no wealth or property to her husband," Waldmir explained. "It is traditional for her husband's family to provide her father with a brideprice, rather than for her father to provide a dowry. We recognize that this is not the custom elsewhere and are, of course, flexible with our traditions when the bride marries outside of Nandel."

Ellin snorted ever so softly. No man outside of Nandel would pay his bride's family for the privilege of marrying her.

"Have no fear, Your Majesty," Waldmir said. "I will demand no brideprice from you. But if Zarsha is to be your bride, then he will provide his own brideprice by forfeiting his goods and property to the Crown of Nandel."

A cold pit formed in Ellin's stomach.

"His manor house will become mine, as will any servants and retainers he has on staff. I may keep some of them on if I have good use for them, but for the most part they will be dismissed."

Ellin could not force herself to smile or look at ease. Waldmir's expression was too knowing. She had never asked Zarsha whether his uncle knew about her affair with Graesan, who was now one of his retainers living in Nandel. She could not tell from the way Waldmir was looking at her whether he knew or not, whether any part of his malice was aimed at her, or if it was all for Zarsha.

She shook her head. "You cannot expect me to agree to this arrangement without consulting Zarsha."

"As a bride, Zarsha has no say in his marriage negotiations," Waldmir said. "He will marry whom I tell him to marry, or he will be declared a traitor to the Crown."

The pit in her stomach grew bigger and colder. Waldmir was making no attempt to hide his enmity toward Zarsha, and he was still studying her face with more attention than she liked. As if perhaps he suspected Zarsha had told her his secrets.

"Why would you do this?" she asked, hoping she sounded appropriately mystified. "This marriage is to our mutual benefit, so why can we not engage in traditional, reasonable negotiations?"

"Are you sure you don't know, Your Majesty?" he asked with quiet intensity.

"Quite sure," she affirmed. She did not consider herself a naturally good liar, but skillful lying was regrettably a requirement of her position, and she had learned her lessons well. She schooled both her face and her voice to innocence, and she looked Waldmir straight in the eye.

He frowned and shrugged. "Well, even if you don't, be assured that my nephew does. You—and your kingdom—will be getting everything you want out of this arrangement. More, I'll wager, than you believed possible. What does it matter to you if Zarsha should lose some lands and belongings?"

He had a point, but Ellin was distinctly aware there was more happening here than she understood. Zarsha would live in far greater wealth and comfort here in Rhozinolm than he ever would have in Nandel, so the loss of his property would do him no great harm. And he was far less susceptible to insults to his masculinity than the average Nandelite. And yet Waldmir obviously expected this forfeiture to wound his nephew. What was she missing?

"I'm afraid I cannot agree without consulting Zarsha," she said, for surely Waldmir did not expect her to meekly accept his first offer. Especially when she was certain she didn't fully understand it.

"Then *I* am afraid there will be no marriage and no renewal of the agreements. You will send my nephew home to Nandel immediately."

Surely he didn't mean that! It had to be merely a negotiating tactic, one that he expected to frighten her into submission. She sat up straighter in her chair and glared at him.

"Prince Waldmir," she said, "I would advise you to remember I am not a woman of Nandel. I was raised to have a mind of my own, and I would not now be sitting on the throne of Rhozinolm if I were in the habit of cowering in the face of threats."

He spread his hands in a gesture of innocence. "It is not a threat. I'm simply laying out my terms in more plainspoken language than a diplomat would use. I have no intention of granting my nephew a choice in this matter." He reached for something out of her line of sight, then held it before the talker so that she could see a sheet of creamy linen paper covered in neat, precise writing. At the bottom was an angular signature, followed by a wax seal with the Nandel coat of arms.

"I have drawn up the marriage contract with the terms I have laid out," Waldmir said. "As you can see, the document is signed." With his other hand, he picked up a flier, rolling up the paper and settling it in the flier's grip. "I can send it on its way to you right now. Or I can burn it. The choice is yours. But the one thing I will not do is amend it in any way. Will you allow my nephew's potential hurt feelings to stop you from doing what you know is best for your kingdom?"

Ellin sat back in her chair, unable to maintain her polite court mask. She loathed the feeling of being bullied, and yet everything within her cried out that this was not a bluff. She was negotiating as the Queen of Rhozinolm, not as a woman looking out for the best interests of the man she wished to marry. When she and her council had first begun discussing the marriage arrangement, they had all expected that the trade agreements would be renewed on terms that were at least somewhat less favorable than the ones they currently enjoyed. It was a rare negotiation that left one party without *any* need to compromise.

Could she really risk losing this almost too-good-to-be-true agreement to protect Zarsha from his uncle's malice? Especially when

Zarsha had *earned* that malice? He was no innocent victim and had never claimed to be.

"You wish to sour my marriage before it even occurs," Ellin said, though she instantly regretted it.

Waldmir's smile looked convincingly sad. "One thing I have learned time and time again since I ascended my own throne: the world cares not for the happiness of kings."

Ellin flinched inside, although she hoped she kept her expression impassive. Much though she wanted to deny it, Waldmir was right about that. It was her duty to rule in the best interests of her kingdom, regardless of what *she*—or anyone she cared about—wanted.

Instinct told her that Waldmir meant exactly what he said. If she refused the offer, he would cut off relations—no matter how badly he might want the respectability that came with a marriage between the royal house of Nandel and the royal house of Rhozinolm. He would consider it a matter of pride, both for himself and for his principality. There was nowhere in Seven Wells where masculine pride was of more importance than in Nandel.

"Shall I send the contract?" Waldmir pressed. "Or shall I burn it?"

Just because he sends it doesn't mean I have to sign it, Ellin reassured herself. He was asking her to make a verbal commitment right this moment, and even a verbal commitment would be hard to work her way out of if she changed her mind. But at least she would ask Zarsha if he was okay with the deal before signing the paper and sealing his fate.

"One word of warning," Waldmir said, for apparently he read her thoughts as if she had spoken them aloud. "If I send this contract and you choose not to sign it, I will know that it is my nephew who persuaded you against it. Tell him that treason charges will follow, and ask him if he *still* wants you not to sign."

Ellin wanted to scream in frustration. Perhaps Waldmir was merely testing her, hoping to see some hint as to whether she knew the reasons he was unlikely to follow through on that particular threat. But whether he would level a treason charge against Zarsha or not, she realized her decision now would be irreversible. Once she made a verbal commitment, she would make it impossible for Waldmir to grant further concessions without damage to his pride. And it was clear that was something he would never countenance.

Hoping Zarsha would not end up hating her for it, Ellin nodded. "Send it."

Delnamal had started out pacing the length of his office in angry, frustrated strides. But after a few times back and forth, he'd quickly found himself sweating and short of breath. He cursed his ever-expanding girth and wished he could find the self-control to stop overindulging at mealtimes. Pouring himself a generous helping of fortified wine—something he had no interest in doing without, for a day without the soothing blur of alcohol would be intolerable—he dropped ungracefully into his chair.

Discouraging Prince Waldmir's hopes of a marriage between their children had been a calculated risk, and he was hardly surprised to hear that Waldmir had promptly finalized the marriage arrangement between his nephew and the Queen of Rhozinolm. Delnamal had felt sure that disastrous alliance—and all it implied for the future of Aaltah's own trade agreements with Nandel—would finally spur his council into action. They would see that the marriage would put Aaltah in an untenable situation, and they would then—however reluctantly—agree that the only course of action was to take a risk and allow the former Abbess of Khalpar to attempt her spell. After all, if the Curse was reversed, Queen Ellinsoltah could no longer hold her council and her people hostage to her willingness to provide an heir. She could either be replaced by her uncle, or she could be safely married to some nobleman of Rhozinolm, who would then take over the throne as was proper.

When women once again knew their place, when men took over all the important decision making once more and the world was restored to its natural order, Aaltah would no longer be under threat of the unholy women's alliance. And King Delnamal would be hailed by leaders the world over for having had the balls to do what no one else would try.

But even in the face of the new alliance between Nandel and Rhozinolm, the council had been too goddamn cowardly to let the abbess near Aaltah's Well. Delnamal had once again been forced to withdraw his proposal in certain knowledge that it would be voted down. If he wanted to set the world back to rights, he would have to do it without the council's approval. Which meant doing it in secret.

There was a soft knock on the door.

"Finally," Delnamal muttered under his breath, for it felt as if it had been an hour since he had sent for Melcor. "Come in," he said out loud, and his secretary entered the room, bowing and apologizing for his late arrival.

"Close the door," Delnamal interrupted, in no mood for excuses.

Melcor did as told and turned to his king with a politely inquiring expression on his face.

"Can I trust you to handle something for me with the utmost discretion?" Delnamal asked, embarrassed to hear a slight slur in his words. He gave his cup of wine a chiding look, then sighed and took another sip. If he was going to be drunk, he might as well be *properly* drunk.

"Of course, Your Majesty," Melcor said.

The question was a formality after all Melcor had already done for him. Unlike the cowards of the royal council, Melcor was a man of decisive action. Like his king. He understood without needing an explanation that the council had left Delnamal no other choice.

"The witch believes that the spell to undo the Curse will require a willing human sacrifice," Delnamal told his secretary. "A woman. I want you to find one for me. Without letting anyone know what you're about."

"A woman who is willing to die to undo the Curse?" For the first time, Delnamal detected a hint of doubt in Melcor's voice.

"She doesn't have to be *eager*," Delnamal assured him. "And I'm not asking you to find someone with actual *power*. From what I gather, even a Rho-blind woman is capable of producing women's Kai. I'm sure with your contacts in the Harbor District, you can find some old crone—or some impoverished young mother—who would be willing to die so that her heirs might live in a manner well above

their station. You may offer whatever inducement you think is necessary. But find someone, and bring her—along with the witch—to the
palace. In secret, of course."

"Of course," Melcor said, his voice thin and his eyes a little too
wide.

Delnamal glared at the man, daring him to voice an objection. He
was *counting* on Melcor to help him with this most vital of all missions. He hadn't the faintest idea where he would turn if Melcor
proved to be as weak and cowardly as the men of the royal council.

To Delnamal's relief, Melcor made no offers of unwanted advice
or useless warnings, despite the concern in his eyes.

"Disguise the witch when you bring her," Delnamal said, for it
had caused enough rumors and speculation the last time she'd been
brought to the palace. A red-robed abigail in the palace made people
wonder if Oona was expecting again so soon, and he did not want to
face those questions. "And we should do it at night, so there are
fewer people around who might see or interfere."

Melcor swallowed hard, but nodded. "As you wish. It might take
me a few days to find that volunteer, if I'm to be subtle about it."

But Delnamal was through with waiting and being patient. It was
time to end this charade, while he still had a kingdom to rule. "You
have until midnight tomorrow night. I will meet you at the Well, and
I will dismiss the guards so that we might have the utmost privacy."

"I'm not sure—" Melcor started to say, but Delnamal cut him off.

"I've made my decision, and if you want to keep your position,
you'll do as you're told."

Melcor jerked back as if Delnamal had struck him. Delnamal
closed his eyes and took a deep breath to calm himself. Melcor was
the only person in the world who was completely loyal to him, the
only person who never judged him, never disrespected him, never
made him feel like an idiot.

"Forgive me, my friend," Delnamal said, opening his eyes and giving his secretary a beseeching look. A part of him was aware that the
overabundance of alcohol in his veins was making him maudlin, but
he didn't care. "It is my council I'm angry with, not you. But if we

are to undo the Curse, it must be soon, before that gathering of weak-willed old women destroys us all."

Melcor bowed. "I understand, Your Majesty." He shifted as if to take his leave, then hesitated. "I know it isn't my place to say, but I do believe you're doing the right thing. Almost any risk is worth taking if it will free us from the Curse."

Delnamal smiled and gulped down the last of his wine, realizing that whatever Melcor's misgivings might be, he would do as he'd been told. "Who knows?" Delnamal said as he put down the empty cup and told himself to wait a little while before refilling it. "Perhaps when we undo the Curse, the effects of the women's Kai spells will die with it."

The flare of hope in Melcor's eyes told Delnamal he'd been right to put his faith in his secretary. Though they had never spoken about it, Delnamal was well aware that the flier those cursed women in Women's Well had sent to Melcor had made him permanently impotent. It was no surprise he was willing to risk the council's wrath to help Delnamal do whatever it took to reverse the Curse.

"I will find your willing sacrifice," Melcor swore. Then he bowed again, deeply, and hurried off.

CHAPTER FORTY-FOUR

Mairah's heart fluttered in her chest like a wounded bird as she followed Lord Melcor and his sacrificial lamb through the darkened courtyard of the palace. She wore a plain peasant-woman's dress, and a gauzy veil over her face. It was certain to draw some attention, for the custom of veiling the face in mourning was long outdated and had never extended to the peasantry anyway, but she supposed her scarred face was too recognizable for the king's taste. It seemed clear to Mairah that for whatever reason, the king wanted her presence in the palace kept secret, although in her opinion, the veil just drew more attention to her. She could only guess that his royal council had not been privy to—or had actively disapproved of—his plan to let her cast her spell, and he had chosen to do it anyway.

Melcor had failed to introduce the woman who was to serve as the night's willing sacrifice, but he had called her Iris once when he had snapped at her to hurry up. Iris was dull-eyed with drink, and her skin had an unhealthy pallor to it beyond even her obvious Nandelite ancestry. There were deep, bruiselike shadows under her eyes, and her cheeks were hollow with jutting bones. Her breath wheezed in and out of her lungs, and though there was no hint of gray in her hair or wrinkles on her skin, she carried herself like an old woman at death's door. Mairah assumed the woman was dying already and had offered what was left of her life in return for money for her family. Mairah fought back guilt, reminding herself that the woman would have died anyway. Mairah had at least made it so her death wouldn't be in vain.

The numerous visions Mairah had suffered through had refused to give her the reassurance she craved. She had seen herself explaining the steps she planned to perform in order to create the sacrificial Kai, and once she'd seen herself fleeing up the stairs with no sound of pursuit as an unsettling rumbling noise filled the air and small pebbles rained down on her head. She took that to mean that her spell had done *something* and took heart from the sight of herself alone in that stairwell. But in hopes of seeing exactly what her spell had done and how she'd made her escape, she'd downed one more poison, and the vision it had triggered left her even now shaking with nerves.

She'd seen herself trudging along a road she recognized from her forced march into Aalwell. It led through what should have been fertile, verdant farmland, but in the vision, every crop, every tree, every blade of grass, was brown and withered. She passed a pasture in which four horses lay dead and rotting, and even the vultures that picked at the carcasses looked gaunt and half-starved. Mairah herself looked much the same, dressed in the same peasant's clothes she wore today. Clothes that in the vision were filthy and ragged and hung loosely on her skeletal frame.

There were few other people on the road, and all those she saw were as ragged and desperate-looking as Mairah herself. Worse, Mairah hid in the bushes and cowered whenever she caught sight of anyone. A small party of soldiers—whom she barely spotted in time to hide—rode by, grim and vigilant and obviously searching. In the barren landscape, Mairah could only imagine that they were searching for *her*, that she was somehow the author of all this misery.

Mairah tried to dismiss that vision from her mind. After all, though she couldn't say she was an expert on the effects of sacrificial Kai based on that one overheard conversation in a vision, she didn't believe there was any way her potion could have so devastating an effect on the land. In fact, despite all her planning and research, there was some part of her that felt that the most likely effect her potion would have on the Well was none at all.

Doubt assailed her every time she let her guard down, and it would have paralyzed her with terror if she'd let it. But there was one thing of which she was certain: her only chance of survival was to go through with her plan and hope for the best.

Even at midnight, the palace halls were not empty, and she saw more than one curious stare aimed in her direction. Once, a palace guard seemed inclined to question them, but a glare from Lord Melcor silenced the man.

The walk felt nearly endless, and it was followed by an agonizing descent down a long and narrow staircase. Staggering in exhaustion—all those seer's potions she had downed had cost her both strength and sleep—she almost tumbled down the last few steps but caught herself at the last moment.

Of course she had never been near Aaltah's Well, but Mairah was certain the anteroom into which Melcor led her and the woman who had volunteered to give her life would ordinarily be staffed with royal guards. But tonight, the anteroom was empty, just as she had expected based on her visions. She hadn't realized just how much she'd doubted all of the visions until this confirmation that they would be alone relaxed one of the knots in her stomach. She still didn't know if her spell would work or if she could escape, but at least her visions had not been entirely made up of wishful thinking.

"Where is everyone?" Mairah asked, then cursed herself for drawing Melcor's attention.

"His Majesty has seen to it that we will not be disturbed," Melcor said with a curl of his lip, as if it made him feel dirty even to speak to one such as she.

Their footsteps echoed hollowly as the three of them crossed the anteroom toward the open door—a door, Mairah noticed to her relief, equipped with a solid wooden bar that would not require a key—

that led to the Well, where King Delnamal stood impatiently waiting for them.

Aaltah's Well was situated in a gigantic natural cavern, deep inside the cliffs on which the royal palace sat. From what Mairah had heard, Wells manifested differently in the various kingdoms and principalities in which they existed, but this one was a huge crack in the center of the cavern floor, easily as broad as two tall men lying end to end. The floor around the Well was decorated in intricate rows of gold leaf patterns, studded here and there with gems that sparkled in the light of the myriad luminants that circled the cavern. The decorated border of the Well was surrounded by an equally ornate low fence. Only the most well-connected of the Aaltah nobility were allowed within the cavern, and Mairah had heard that ordinarily, the fence was guarded by a circle of royal guards. Benches all along the circumference of the cavern showed where visitors to the Well were expected to sit, keeping far away from the Well itself, which gave off a low hum of energy and power that Mairah felt more than heard. The air felt close and clammy, too thick to breathe, but that was likely only her nerves.

This was it, she realized, fighting to keep calm. The image of herself walking through the dead and dying countryside of Aaltah refused to stop popping up in her mind, triggering a shiver of dread each time. Despite her reassurances to herself that her spell could *not* cause such destruction, she might have chosen not to cast it at all if she'd felt she had a choice. But from the moment she'd first claimed to Delnamal that she might be able to reverse the Curse, she had committed herself, and there was no going back.

"What do you need to do to set up for your spell?" Delnamal asked, bringing Mairah back to herself.

"I just have to put in a few final elements to activate the spell in the potion," she murmured. She could barely hear herself think over the pounding of her heart. If only her mind would stop conjuring images—either from the visions or from her own imagination—of all the ways this could go horribly wrong! With shaking hands, she opened the bag she had brought with her and pushed aside the pages of notes she had stuffed inside so she would have them with her when she fled Aaltah. Beneath the notes, she found the wineskin that contained her potion.

Opening her Mindseye, Mairah added Rho to the potion to activate its spell. The spell was now technically active, and would force closed the Mindseye of anyone who drank so much as a drop of it. But not until she'd added the special sacrificial Kai would it be ready for her purpose.

"You expect me to believe a *potion* has the power to undo the Curse?" Delnamal demanded, not bothering to hide his contempt at the idea. It was true that most potions contained only minor magics.

"It's women's magic, Your Majesty," she said simply, closing her Mindseye and glancing at the frightened woman who'd offered up her life for money. "But truly it is Iris's sacrifice that is the key element to this spell, not the potion. Her sacrifice will create a special kind of Kai that will fuel the spell that reverses the Curse. We need only for her to add her Kai to the potion, then pour the potion into the Well, and the Wellspring will be returned to normal."

Both Delnamal and Melcor frowned at her as she handed the wineskin with her potion to Iris and then backed away.

Melcor rolled his eyes in disbelief, but though suspicion still shone in Delnamal's eyes, he was not so quick to dismiss her claim. He wanted too badly for her spell to work. He would grasp at any straw she offered.

"I don't need to explain again what will happen to you if this spell fails," he said, causing her to shudder.

"No, Your Majesty," she said, lowering her eyes.

"Well, get on with it, then," he snapped.

"Iris will need a knife," Mairah said, and something cold and hard solidified in her core. Whatever the outcome might turn out to be, she was going to go through with this. Silently, she prayed that Melcor would be sufficiently distracted by the proceedings not to notice the distance Mairah was carefully putting between them. Or the furtive glances she kept casting toward the door as she calculated her odds of making it there before him once the spell was cast. "She must stand on the Well's edge and open her Mindseye to be ready to feed her Kai into the potion the moment it appears."

Mairah suffered another twinge of guilt when she caught sight of Iris's terrified face. Willing the woman might be, but she was far from eager. Mairah could hardly blame her, though wasting away in poverty from whatever illness afflicted her did not seem a terribly appealing alternative, either.

Mairah let out a silent sigh. Iris had *chosen* to end her life in this way, and her family would benefit from it. It would be a good death, if there was such a thing. And Mairah's fate if she balked now— or if the spell failed—would be unthinkably awful. The sacrifice was worth it.

Melcor guided Iris to the lip of the Well, stepping gingerly over the gold and gems set into the floor, then handed her the knife.

Ellin had put off telling Zarsha the results of her conversation with Waldmir for three whole days, justifying the decision by telling herself it was best to wait until she'd confirmed that Waldmir had sent and pre-signed the marriage contract as he'd promised. There was no sense, she reasoned, in upsetting Zarsha only to find Waldmir had been toying with her.

Once the contract arrived, she pored over its terms carefully, assuring herself that everything the sovereign prince had promised was covered in the document. The trade agreements would be renewed on their current terms and would not expire until one year after the end of her marriage to Zarsha, whether that end came because of death or divorce. Perhaps, she mused as she signed the necessary papers, Waldmir was hoping her decision to accept the arrangement without Zarsha's consent would destroy their marriage before it even began. She supposed someone like Waldmir might think that fitting punishment for the man who had cuckolded him.

It was with no small amount of trepidation that she finally invited Zarsha to join her in her private study after she'd so neatly avoided him for three days. She'd been convinced he would come knocking on her bedroom door to inquire about her conversation with his uncle—especially after she'd summoned him to join her then dismissed him without explanation. The fact that he hadn't showed an admirable degree of trust and respect—and made her feel even more guilty that she'd waited so long to tell him.

The look on his face after she laid out the terms of the arrangement made her wish she'd waited a good deal longer.

"Please tell me you did not agree to those terms," he gasped, his face even whiter than usual. He was seated on one of the chairs before her desk, his hands gripping the arms as if afraid he might fall.

"I had to, Zarsha. Even with Kailindar's more vocal support on the council, it is very obvious that I am losing support the longer those trade agreements remain in doubt. He offered me the chance to end that doubt immediately, and I took it."

Zarsha shook his head at her, his expression one of mingled anguish and anger. "I told you he was going to try to force concessions! And I told you that in the end, he would break, that he would do whatever was necessary to have a man of his blood on the throne of Rhozinolm. You did not have to give him *anything*!"

She crossed her arms defensively and sat back in her chair, for the anger that radiated from Zarsha was an almost palpable force. She had never seen his eyes flash such fire—not even when Graesan had tried to murder him in his sleep.

"It's possible you are right," she said, "but I don't think so. You didn't see him. Or hear him. He had made up his mind, and once he did, he would never have allowed anyone to change it for him. Especially not a lowly woman such as myself."

"Oh, so now you know my uncle better than I do?"

She almost snapped back at him, but pulled on the reins of her temper, knowing she still did not understand the full implications of what she had agreed to. "Of course not. But I also know my first priority as queen has to be to look out for the best interests of my kingdom. I was in no position to gamble when losing the gamble might mean Waldmir signing an exclusive agreement with Aaltah."

Zarsha pushed back his heavy chair so hard the thing almost fell over. He stood up, putting his clenched fists on her desk and glaring at her so fiercely it stole the air from her lungs. "He *played* you, Your Majesty! He *knew* you would be frightened by his threats, and he used that to his full advantage. You should never have attempted to negotiate with him with no advisers present!"

Ellin rose slowly to her feet, still fighting to keep her temper under control. She had not expected this conversation to go well, but she had also not expected Zarsha to be so angry with her. Ordinarily, he was one of the most even-tempered men she'd ever known, and something within her quailed in the face of his fury. Not because she was afraid of him, but because she feared her decision might have destroyed—or at least seriously damaged—the fragile bond that had been building between them. The bond that had ventured tentatively beyond friendship into deeper territory.

"I did what I felt I had to do under the circumstances," she said, keeping her voice soft for fear it might quaver. She still believed that she'd done the right thing, but it was hard not to doubt herself in the face of Zarsha's anger. "I'm very sorry you've been hurt in the process—"

"You don't even have the faintest clue what you've done, do you?" he interrupted.

Ellin flinched, hating that he was right. "No," she said, her voice now even softer. "I know there's more to it than meets the eye, but I couldn't—" Her voice choked off and she had to clear her throat before she could continue. "I couldn't take the chance that he was bluffing. No matter what."

Zarsha pinched the bridge of his nose and closed his eyes, his chest heaving as though he'd been running for miles. As angry as he was, it was clear that the anger was spurred by pain, and her heart hurt for him even not knowing what exactly had caused it.

"Will you tell me what it means to you to lose your estates?" she asked, and this time no amount of willpower could keep the quaver from her voice. "I know this is far more than a question of male pride."

Zarsha groaned and collapsed back into the chair. He opened his eyes but did not look at her. "Do you think your Graesan is the only person I've added to my staff for unusual reasons?"

She swallowed hard as she, too, retook her seat. "I'd never especially thought about it," she responded. "Although I did realize that Graesan would likely be one of the staff dismissed when your uncle takes possession of your estates."

He grimaced. "Yes. He could end up being a problem again someday. But I might not have thought to hire him had I not taken similar actions in the past." To Ellin's horror, there was a sheen of tears in Zarsha's eyes. "Nearly every member of my staff—every guard, every maid, every cook, every footman—is someone who could find employment nowhere else. I am almost never in residence, so what does it matter to me if my housekeeper is so lame she cannot climb the stairs and must sleep on a pallet on the first floor? Or that my cook is so slow-witted she cannot be allowed near an open flame? Or that my master of the guard lost most of his sword arm to an infection that was treated too late?

"Waldmir will dismiss them all and cast them into the streets." He met her eyes with undisguised anguish. "Do you know how few beggars can survive even a single winter in The Keep?"

Ellin's heart ached. "I can hire them myself."

But Zarsha shook his head. "They would need Waldmir's permission to leave Nandel, and you can be certain he won't grant it."

"You could threaten to reveal his secrets."

He closed his eyes, and his lashes were wet. "That's the special torment of it," he whispered. "He is making me choose between protecting my family and protecting my staff. We both know that if I reveal his secrets, Elwynne will suffer and my brother is unlikely to survive a battle over the succession. I *can't* reveal his secrets unless all hope is already lost." His eyes opened again and he met her eyes. The warmth and affection she was used to seeing in his regard was entirely absent.

"I understand why you did it," he said flatly. "I forget sometimes how young and inexperienced you are."

She bristled at the condescension, but he was, of course, right. Even if she'd grown up as a crown prince, given all the education that a potential heir to the throne might receive, she would *still* be a young and inexperienced sovereign. She might feel as if she'd sat on the throne for half her lifetime, but it had only been a little more than a year and a half, and for part of that time she had considered her reign temporary.

And yet even acknowledging her inexperience, she was sure she'd done the right thing. If Zarsha could have seen the look on his uncle's face or heard his voice, he'd have known the man was not bluffing.

"I am the Queen of Rhozinolm," she said quietly. "I made the only responsible decision I could make under the circumstances. If there is anything I can do to help your retainers—whether in an official capacity or not—I will not hesitate to do it. But the contracts are signed, and the wedding preparations will begin immediately. I hope you can find it in your heart to forgive me, but if not . . ." She sighed heavily. "If not, then that is the price I will have to pay for defending my kingdom."

CHAPTER FORTY-FIVE

I ris stood hesitating on the rim of the Well, her hands shaking, for an eternity. Melcor scowled and loomed over her, growling, "What are you waiting for, woman?"

Mairah held her breath, for the moment of truth was almost upon her. Hope and terror waged war in her breast. Iris looked from one face to another, finally making eye contact with Mairah and making the guilt stab deeper.

Mairah tried for a soft, encouraging smile. "It will all be over soon," she said gently. "You will long be remembered and revered for your heroism."

Iris took a long, deep breath. Then, her spine straightened and the fear left her eyes. She smiled, and it was as though she had suddenly thrown off a mask. The frightened sacrifice who numbed her fear with drink vanished, replaced by a woman who was filled with strength and power despite her illness.

"You really don't remember me, do you, Lord Melcor?" she asked with a shake of her head. Melcor frowned in puzzlement, and Iris chuckled. "No, of course you don't, else you would never have dared to put a knife in my hand. You probably wouldn't have recognized me even without the changes the wasting sickness has made. After all, you've savaged so many women of the Harbor District that you can hardly be expected to keep track."

"W-what?" Melcor stammered, his eyes widening in alarm.

Mairah's mouth went dry as it dawned on her that none of her visions had shown her exactly what was going to happen next. She'd seen the moments before the casting of the spell and after, but never the moment of truth itself. And right now, her sacrificial lamb did not look like she intended to play her assigned role.

Iris laughed, a hint of madness creeping into her voice. "I hardly dared to believe you were truly going to give me this opportunity," she said, hefting the knife. "Unarmed and unguarded." She sighed with what seemed like satisfaction, though Mairah thought there was still a hint of fear in her eyes.

"No!" Mairah cried, stepping forward just as Iris sprang. Behind her, she heard Delnamal's shout of protest as well, but Iris ignored them both.

The knife slashed through the air. With a bleat of alarm, Melcor held his hands up in front of him and hastily tried to back away. Iris screamed like a vengeful demon. It seemed impossible that a woman so frail and sickly could attack with such ferocity. The knife cut into one of Melcor's arms, and he couldn't seem to help his instinctive need to pull away, leaving his chest momentarily unguarded.

Iris took advantage of the opening, plunging the knife into his chest and drawing a howl of agony.

"Melcor!" Delnamal yelled in distress, but he made no move to help his friend and secretary, standing indecisively on the other side of the low fence and flapping his arms about as if he could make it all go away.

Mairah was not at all unhappy to see Melcor in pain and bleeding heavily. It was actually convenient for her escape plan that Iris had already removed him as a threat. But she still needed that special Kai, for she was certain that Delnamal would blame her for this debacle even though it was Melcor himself who had obtained the sacrifice.

She started forward once more, wondering if she could somehow convince Iris to go through with the sacrifice once Melcor was dead. It would be an easier death than whatever execution Delnamal would devise for her.

Melcor had recovered from the initial shock of being stabbed, and when Iris tried to plunge the knife in a second time, he caught her wrist. Blood drenched his doublet and had splashed over Iris's clothes and face. His skin had gone nearly gray, and his knees seemed ready to give way beneath him, but he still had enough strength left to wrench Iris's wrist so hard that the woman screeched in pain. The knife went flying from her hand, and she attempted to twist away from his grip.

Mairah watched in horror as Iris slipped in the splatters of blood at her feet and fell backward. Melcor, his hand still gripping her wrist, fell with her, his body crashing into hers. And sending them both, teetering, toward the edge of the Well.

Mairah reached out a hand helplessly, too far away to reach either one of them. Delnamal screamed a denial, though he had not moved from his place.

For one heartbeat, Mairah thought that it would be all right. Melcor finally let go of Iris's wrist, and she thought they might both somehow regain their footing. But Iris fell, and with a scream of mingled fear and victory, she grabbed a handful of Melcor's doublet and pulled him in after her.

"No!" Mairah and Delnamal both screamed together, for very different reasons. Mairah assumed Delnamal was lamenting the death of his friend and secretary, while also feeling sorry for himself because his plan to "cure" the Curse had gone so horribly wrong.

But Mairah remembered her vision of traveling through an Aaltah-turned-Wasteland, and she knew with a bitter certainty that this was what had caused it. She remembered the late Abbess of Aaltah explaining sacrificial Kai to her daughter, remembered her saying that masculine Kai—the death element—would poison the Well. And she knew with a bone-deep certainty that Melcor was powerful enough to generate Kai as he died, and that he was even now delivering that Kai into Aaltah's Well.

Her plan had failed in the worst imaginable way. The vision had suggested that she could escape this cavern, but it had also shown her cowering in terror whenever she spotted another person. Delnamal might not be able to stop her from escaping, but he would be sure to tell all the world what she had done. There would be nowhere she could go where she would not be instantly recognized. How long could she survive slinking along in the bushes beside the road, diving for cover whenever another person came into view?

Women's Well might have welcomed her back if she had temporarily disabled the people of Aaltah by closing their Mindseye, but even Aaltah's greatest enemy would revile her if they believed her responsible for making a new Wasteland where a once great kingdom had stood.

Sobbing, Mairah turned to look at the cavern's exit. Delnamal was standing stunned and ashen-faced on one side, and she was certain she could easily dart past him. The Well began to make a low, ominous rumbling noise, and beneath her feet, she felt a quiver. The tone of its low hum changed, deepening and somehow taking on a darker tone.

"No," she hiccuped, shaking her head as if she could make everything go away. She turned to run, then came up short, remembering her early lessons at the Abbey about the miracle of foresight. According to canon—and this was true whether one worshipped the Mother or the Mother of All—visions always showed a future the viewer was capable of affecting.

Perhaps that merely meant Mairah could have avoided this if only she hadn't agreed to cast a spell on the Well. But she'd had her vision of the new Wasteland *after* she'd committed to casting it. And if there was a sentience behind the visions, surely it wouldn't have expected her to condemn herself to the slow and torturous death that awaited her if she'd refused at the last moment.

With another gasp, Mairah glanced over at the bag of potions and notes she'd brought with her. The bag that contained both the potion to close the Mindseye and the purgative that she hoped would be its antidote.

The rumbling in the Well grew deeper, the luminants in the cavern dimming as the first bits of debris began to rain down from the ceiling. Delnamal had already turned to flee, though his bulk made him slow and awkward. She doubted he could make it up the stairs without several stops to rest.

Mairah swallowed hard and found herself moving not *toward* the exit but *away*. Toward the knife that rattled against the cavern floor.

The purgative potion would have no effect on the Well as of now, even if Mairah activated it. But what would happen if she added sacrificial Kai into the mix? The late Abbess of Aaltah had proven with impressive efficiency that sacrificial Kai could affect the Wellspring itself. If Mairah could add Kai to her purgative, might it purge Melcor's Kai from the Well?

Mairah opened her Mindseye and let out another gasp of dismay. Moments ago when she'd activated her other potion, the chamber had been aglow with the flood of elements pouring out of the Well. But that glow was considerably dimmer now, the elements no longer so thick in the air. Even in the scant seconds she watched, she could see that the flow was continuing to slow.

She had no choice. She could not let a whole kingdom die just to save her own life.

This isn't fair! a voice within her wailed. *I don't deserve to die!*

But then when had what a person deserved ever mattered?

Mairah had lived with the consequences of ruining Lord Granlin. She had lived with her pangs of conscience at murdering Mother Wyebryn. She had lived with condemning poor Sister Melred to the inquisitor's cruelty. But she could not live with destroying this Well. Especially not if the whole world knew she was to blame.

The knife slashed down and split her wrist open almost before she realized she'd decided to do it. She felt the blood that instantly soaked her sleeve, felt it dripping down her palm. Her heart beat frantically, pumping her blood out ever faster, and she waited for her Kai to form. *Prayed* for it to form, because the only evidence she had that this would work was that one vision of Mother Brynna explaining it.

The elements in the air seemed to be dwindling even more, the roar of the Well getting louder. She was running out of time.

Mairah slashed at her other wrist, a sob of pain and terror escaping her. She shivered in sudden cold as the freely flowing blood stole her warmth. And then, finally, something shimmered to life in the air in front of her. A large, jagged mote that looked like three different crystals fused together: one white, one red, one black.

There was no question that the mote was Kai, for no other element was crystalline in form. Which meant that Mairah was dying even now.

Knees and hands both shaking, Mairah reached out and nudged that mote of Kai into her purgative potion, activating it. She kept her Mindseye open, for she did not want to see the river of her blood, and groped her way blindly toward the rim of the Well, uncapping the potion as she approached.

The cap fell from her suddenly weak fingers, and her knees started to give way. She managed one final, staggering step forward, and her foot came down on empty air.

The open container of purgative still clutched in her hand, she fell into the depths of the Well.

From the moment Iris had first revealed that she was not, in fact, the willing sacrifice he had bought and paid for, Delnamal found himself rooted to the floor, barely able to think, much less move. Some distant part of his mind suggested that he should be trying to help his secretary . . . his friend. Surely two able-bodied men would be sufficient to restrain one desperately ill woman. But he didn't have even a ceremonial blade on him, and everything happened so quickly . . . By the time he recognized the need for action, Melcor's blood was already gushing.

Melcor wasn't going to survive that wound anyway, he told himself to excuse his inaction. Iris's knife had dug deep, and even if Delnamal had rushed to restrain her, Melcor would almost certainly have bled to death before help could arrive. After all, Delnamal had dismissed all the guards who might come to the rescue, and it would take a painfully long time for him to drag himself back up the steep stairways they had descended and find someone else to help. Certainly *he* wasn't capable of carrying Melcor to safety.

It was already far too late by the time Delnamal took a single hesitant step toward the struggling duo. Mairahsol seemed to be running to their aid—almost certainly only because she wanted to preserve her willing sacrifice—but neither she nor Delnamal got very close before Melcor and Iris plummeted into the depths of the Well.

Delnamal blinked and shook his head as if it would wake him from a dream, and even as he did so, he noticed that the Well was making an ominous rumbling sound and that its habitual hum had taken on a darker, deeper note. The hair on the back of his neck stood up, and his heart seemed to stutter in his chest.

Mairahsol had claimed the Kai from a willing female sacrifice would cause her spell to affect the Wellspring itself. But Iris hadn't been bleeding and dying when she fell in, and Melcor had. While Melcor hadn't been gifted enough magically for a career at the Academy, his bloodline had been strong, and he had not been without power. Certainly he was the kind of man who would generate Kai during that knife's-edge balance between life and death.

Kai was the terror of the battlefield, the reason soldiers were trained to dispatch any mortally wounded enemy immediately. A man who possessed a sufficiently powerful Kai spell and had the wherewithal to trigger it while in the throes of death could wipe out half an army if that army wasn't properly shielded. So what might a mote of men's Kai do when plunged into the depths of a Well?

Swallowing hard, Delnamal took first one step backward, then another, as the rumbling from the Well got louder. The earth beneath his feet was vibrating, and bits of debris began dropping from the ceiling.

When the late Abbess of Aaltah had cast her Curse, the changes in the Wellspring had triggered an earthquake felt throughout all of Seven Wells. Thousands had died, and Delnamal was nearly frozen in terror at the thought that the same thing might happen now.

The earth continued to vibrate, but it did not buck and pitch wildly as it had on the night of the earthquake. Even so, there was a loud cracking sound from above Delnamal's head, and a small trickle of dust and pebbles showered the floor.

The trickle was enough to unfreeze Delnamal's feet, and he finally turned and ran—as best his bulk would allow—toward the cavern entrance. There were more cracks and dust and pebbles, and Delnamal could swear the door was receding, no matter how hard he pumped his arms and legs. His breath wheezed in and out of his lungs, and his heart seemed lodged in his throat. A pebble bounced stingingly off his shoulder. Fearing he might die before he reached the door, he stopped for just a moment to open his Mindseye and pluck out a mote of Rho to activate the shield spell in his signet ring.

He meant to close his Mindseye immediately and resume his ponderous sprint toward the exit, but he could not help noticing how much thinner the veil of elements was than it should be. He had no particular gift for magic, and yet even with his middling talent, when his Mindseye was open, the Well chamber was usually awash with motes so thick his worldly vision did not function at all. Right now, the air was so thin he could see the aura of Rho surrounding Mairahsol's body, could see her running not toward the exit, but toward the Well.

Mindseye still open, he saw her throw herself into the maw of the Well.

There was a searing flash of light, followed immediately by what sounded like a peal of thunder. When Delnamal tried to suck in a breath, he could find no hint of air. A cloud of darkness rose up from the depths of the Well. He gaped at it in horror as the cloud shot toward him. With his Mindseye open, he could clearly see the glistening, crystalline motes of Kai that made up that cloud. Hundreds of them, maybe thousands, of all different colors. More Kai than he ever imagined *existed*. Coming toward him!

Finally regaining some hint of his wits, Delnamal closed his Mindseye and rushed toward the doorway once more. Everything within him screamed that he dared not let that cloud envelop him.

The exit was only an arm's-length away when something slammed into him from behind, the impact lifting him off his feet and shoving him through the door. The far wall of the anteroom raced toward him, and he put up his hands in an effort to soften the impact, knowing his shield spell could not withstand the force.

He managed only the briefest scream of pain as his hands splintered and his body collided with the stone wall.

CHAPTER FORTY-SIX

Alys lowered herself heavily into the nearest chair, unable to sort out the riot of emotions that was rampaging in her breast. Tynthanal, the long letter from Lord Aldnor still clutched in one fist, paced the room as if unable to hold still.

This was the first time she and her brother had been alone in a room together since the wedding, and when he had presented himself at her residence and requested a private meeting, she had hoped it meant he was finally prepared to forgive her for arranging the marriage with Kailee. But his purpose had been something completely different—and completely unimaginable.

"He's really dead?" Alys asked in a breathy whisper, her eyes burning with tears she refused to shed. On the one hand, she was fiercely glad that Delnamal had perished, glad that he no longer drew breath while her own daughter was more than a year in her grave. On the other hand, she had now lost all hope of exacting her own revenge. Every lovely fantasy of making her half-brother suffer, of letting him stew in the resentment and humiliation of being defeated and condemned by the woman he had hated for all his life, had vanished.

"*Presumed* dead," Tynthanal clarified. "His body has yet to be found in all the rubble around the Well, but there is little question that he was there when . . . whatever it was happened. He personally dismissed the guards, and it's clear he decided to allow Mairahsol to try her spell on the Well despite the council's objections."

Alys shook her head at the utter stupidity Delnamal had displayed. Even Kailee, who had befriended Mairahsol and hoped to persuade her to remain in Women's Well, had conceded that the woman harbored a chilling level of resentment in her heart. And yet somehow, impossibly, Delnamal had allowed himself to believe her claims and given her access to Aaltah's Well after he'd all but imprisoned her.

"We can always hope the searchers find him alive under there somehow," she murmured. "I can only imagine how the council and the people of Aaltah would treat him."

"Yes," Tynthanal agreed. "Even if he's found alive, he will never sit on that throne again. But Lord Aldnor and the council have already made the presumption of death and voted to instate a regent for young Prince Tahrend."

Alys was startled to realize that Tynthanal was speaking of his former commander as if Lord Aldnor were the Lord Commander of Aaltah. "I was under the impression that Lord Aldnor had been removed from the council."

Tynthanal nodded. "It seems that was one of the least popular decisions of Delnamal's reign, which is saying a lot. He was reinstated the moment the council realized what Delnamal had done—and that he was no longer their king."

"Did Lord Aldnor mention whom the council was considering to act as regent?"

Something changed in Tynthanal's posture and expression, and Alys focused on him in a way she had not been doing for the last several minutes as she pondered all the implications of Delnamal's apparent demise.

"As a matter of fact, he did."

Alys blinked and frowned when her brother did not continue. "Well? Who is it?"

"Me."

Alys's jaw dropped and she stared at him in amazement. "You?" she asked in a tiny whisper.

He nodded and tapped the letter absently against his leg as he finally stopped pacing. "I am Prince Tahrend's closest living male relative. I gather I was not the council's unanimous choice—and Lord Aldnor made clear in his letter that he still considers me a traitor to the Crown, so he was obviously one of the dissenting voices. But I think they hope that by appointing me as the prince's regent, they will mend fences with all the rulers that Delnamal offended."

Alys narrowed her eyes at him. "You mean they think they can get access to the resources of Women's Well if you are regent."

His lips tipped up in a half-smile. "I'm certain that was part of the reasoning." His smile disappeared as fast as it had appeared. "There's one more thing. There's no sign that the abbess's spell reversed our mother's, but Lord Aldnor did confide in me that the Well does not seem to be producing as many elements as before. It's possible that the blockage in the Well chamber is the problem, but I can't imagine that rubble could stop elements from escaping. After all, our own Well is completely submerged in water, and the elements have no trouble escaping it."

Alys shivered in a phantom chill. "You think Mairahsol's spell might have damaged it in some way?"

"Let's just say I wouldn't rule out the possibility, and apparently the council wouldn't, either. Aldnor mentioned that the grand magus was one of my chief supporters."

Alys nodded, for it made sense. Equally skilled at both magic and a soldier's arts, Tynthanal had chosen a life in the military over a life as a spell crafter, but he had tested as an Adept. And he was the only man anyone knew of who was capable of seeing and using feminine elements, thanks to all the special abilities that had been bred into their mother's blood.

Alys's chest tightened as she regarded her brother, and she wished she could return them to the warm and loving relationship they had once enjoyed. She very much wanted to throw her arms around him just now, but she couldn't bear it if he rejected her. There was no question in her mind that he meant to accept the appointment, despite being not only her brother but also her lord chancellor.

"Are you asking my permission to take the regency?" she asked. "Or are you merely informing me that you intend to take it?" The words came out sounding colder and more distant than she'd have liked, but she needed that coldness to keep her true feelings from bursting out. Tears were not a luxury a sovereign princess could afford.

Tynthanal drew himself up stiffly and answered in a similar tone. "I am your loyal subject, Your Royal Highness. I would not presume to accept any position with another kingdom against your wishes."

"Once upon a time, you insisted you had no desire to rule." Of course, that was back when he was trying to convince Alys to declare herself the sovereign princess of a new principality.

"I don't. But my father's kingdom needs me, and I can't see turning my back on it now that Delnamal's gone. If it weren't for him, I never would have become an enemy of Aaltah in the first place."

Alys put a hand to her breastbone, trying to rub away the ache that was forming behind it. If not for Delnamal, she, too, would still be back in Aaltah. She'd be living the simple life of a widowed mother and caretaker of her late husband's estate. How blissful that would have been!

"Have you discussed this with Kailee?" she asked. "A man of Women's Well should not make decisions that affect them both without consulting his wife. I don't imagine she's eager to journey to a kingdom where her blindness will be a source of shame and discomfort once again and where she will be forbidden to practice magic."

"She will practice magic however much she likes," Tynthanal said, "and anyone who treats her poorly will live to regret it." There was a degree of ferocity in his response that raised Alys's eyebrows. "But yes, I will discuss it with her before I give my final answer. I didn't want to distress her if you were going to forbid me to go."

"And what about Chanlix?" She was well aware that something had changed between the two of them since the wedding. "You plan to abandon her to raise your child by herself?"

Tynthanal bristled at her tone, but then seemed to calm himself. "I will talk it over with her, too. But I suspect you know that we are not . . . together anymore. Even with the child on the way, it might be easier for all involved if she and I lived apart. The three of us will make the final decision together, but only if you approve first."

She shut her eyes and thought surely this time she would lose her battle against tears. A tear slipped out from under her closed lids, and Alys blinked it away. She desperately wanted her brother to stay, wanted to find some way to repair the damage she had done to their relationship when she'd arranged his marriage. But she was not so selfish as to keep him in Women's Well against his wishes, and she also suspected their relationship might be easier to repair with distance. Perhaps living in Aaltah, without the specter of Chanlix and her baby constantly paraded in front of their faces, he and his new young wife might make a true start together.

"I will miss you terribly," she admitted, swallowing past the lump in her throat.

Tynthanal's eyes closed and he sighed in evident relief. "Let's not say our goodbyes just yet. Even if Kailee and Chanlix both agree, we'll have to make some arrangements before I leave, and that will take time."

Alys nodded, but her throat was too tight to speak. Yes, he would have to stay just a little longer—at least until they'd decided who would take the lord chancellor's position once he was gone—but she would not wait until he was gone before she would start missing him.

Chanlix sat on the usually comfortable sofa in her parlor and felt as if it were bucking and pitching beneath her. "W-what?" she asked, unable to comprehend what she'd just heard.

"We want you to come with us," Kailee repeated with a gentle smile. Sitting stiffly in the chair beside Kailee's, Tynthanal wore an expression so bland that he was clearly trying to hide what he felt, though his need to hide his feelings spoke volumes.

"You can't be serious," Chanlix said, shaking her head as if doing so would change Kailee's meaning.

Chanlix could not deny that her heart had dropped when Tyntha-nal said he wanted to go back to Aaltah to act as regent. This was the first time he'd set foot in her house since the wedding, and it seemed for all the world that although they both loved each other still, they were neither one willing to carry on an affair. Even with Kailee's ap-proval. Yet the thought of him leaving to reside in Aaltah until the infant king reached majority was bound to leave her weeping into her pillow tonight.

But go with them?

"I am very serious," Kailee said earnestly, and it was impossible to doubt that she meant it. "You are a big part of my husband's life, and you carry his child. I know the two of you have been . . . squeamish because of me, but I never wanted to come between you. And I cer-tainly don't want to come between Tynthanal and his son or daugh-ter. As I said before, there are three of us in this marriage. And that means all three of us should stay together."

Tynthanal shifted in his chair. It was, so far, the only sign he had shown of his discomfort with the whole subject. Kailee's head tilted toward him ever so slightly—just enough to let him know she had not missed the subtle movement and what it meant. Tynthanal froze, barely seeming to breathe.

Chanlix surprised herself with a small laugh. "How on earth did you persuade him to go along with this?" she asked the young woman, who blushed.

Tynthanal turned a rueful—and surprisingly affectionate—smile in Kailee's direction, despite his obvious tension. "You know what it's like trying to say no to her," he said.

Kailee let out an impatient huff. "The two of you will drive me to drink!" she said crisply. "We all know you love each other. And that you both are fond of me, as I am of you. Surely we can find some way to make things work." A hint of melancholy crept into her face and voice. "In Aaltah, I will be alone and friendless."

Tynthanal opened his mouth to object, but Kailee anticipated him and waved him off. "I know I will have you," she said, "and you are an excellent friend. But you will be even busier as prince regent than you have been as lord chancellor. You will not have time to coddle me, no matter what you might like. And while you can force most courtiers to be polite to me, you cannot make them into friends." She turned back to Chanlix. "If you come with me, I will have at least one friend who I can confide in and who I know does not judge me for my circumstances."

"You could stay here, you know," Chanlix said. "You would not be the first husband and wife to live apart." In some ways, Kailee would lose more than any of them, for it was impossible not to see how happy she was in Women's Well. How cruel that she should have this taste of freedom and then have it snatched away so quickly. The court of Aaltah was unlikely to be welcoming, and as the wife of the prince regent, she would not have the luxury of hiding away from the public eye to avoid the scrutiny and disapproval.

Kailee reached over and patted Tynthanal's arm. "Tynthanal already told me he will not compel me to go with him. But he will face enough resistance without putting himself in the socially awkward situation of leaving his new wife behind."

Tynthanal shook his head. "The real reason she insists on going is that she wants a chance to clear Mairahsol's name. She hopes to figure out exactly what Mairahsol did and miraculously turn it into a good deed."

Kailee's jaw jutted out stubbornly. "She has no one else in all of Seven Wells to speak up for her. She was my first and best friend, and I will not let her memory live in infamy until I have seen sufficient evidence that she is to blame for whatever happened at that Well."

The warmth that glowed in Chanlix's chest suggested that she had grown even more fond of this remarkable, exasperating young woman than she'd realized. How she managed to retain anything like faith in humanity given her upbringing was a mystery to Chanlix, and her loyalty was nigh unshakable. Too bad she'd given that loyalty to a woman who did not deserve it. Now that Mairahsol was presumably dead—no bodies had yet been recovered from the rubble, but a mysterious veiled woman had been seen going down to the Well that night, and who else could it have been? Chanlix supposed there was no point in trying to make Kailee see that the abbess had been using her all along and had never been anything like a true friend.

Kailee sighed and shook her head. "I know you all think she was manipulating me, but you are wrong."

Despite her conviction that it was both unnecessary and futile, Chanlix couldn't keep a sarcastic reply from popping out. "Yes, it was entirely coincidental that you thought to give her a gift that would help her escape."

Kailee's hands clenched in her lap, and she seemed to fight some internal battle as she opened her mouth to speak then stopped herself several times. Finally, she unclenched her hands and reached into a pocket of her dress and pulled out a small vial.

"I had not wanted to tell anyone about this," she said, closing her hand over the vial as if to belatedly shield it from view. "I must ask you both to please, *please* not pressure me, to do me the same courtesy as Mairah and let it be my own decision whether to try it or not." Tears shimmered in her eyes, and there was a slight hitch in her breath as she opened her hand to reveal the vial. "*Before* I gave her the Trapper spell, Mairah gave me this."

Chanlix shared a look with Tynthanal that spoke volumes, and she knew without a word being said that they were both alarmed at the very notion of Mairahsol giving Kailee a potion—and relieved that Kailee had not naïvely swallowed it in her trust of her great good friend.

"What is it?" Tynthanal asked. His eyes went white as he opened his Mindseye to examine the potion that Kailee still held clasped in her hand.

Kailee was far too perceptive not to have noticed the tension and suspicion around her, but she ignored it. "Mairah hopes . . . *hoped* . . . it is something that will give me the gift of eyesight, though she couldn't be sure it would work on my particular condition. She tested it herself, and it temporarily forced her Mindseye closed." She bit her lip and glanced down at the vial in her hand. "It was a gift given out of friendship. I'm sure you're both thinking it might be some kind of poison, but she encouraged me to show it to you before I tried it to reassure myself. Not that I ever had any doubt."

Tynthanal's eyes cleared, and he once again met Chanlix's gaze. "I see nothing alarming in it," he said, "but it may well contain elements

I cannot see." Because of his bloodline, Tynthanal was the only man Chanlix had ever heard of who could see some feminine elements, but *some* was a far cry from *all*. "We should show it to Alys."

"No," Kailee said, immediately and decisively. "If I'd wanted the existence of this potion to be common knowledge, I would have told someone about it long ago. I am trusting the two of you to keep it a secret and not to press me to take it. If I were staying in Women's Well, I would not try it at all. I meant it when I said I didn't want to be 'cured.' But it's possible that my life in Aalwell will require me to take the chance, whether I want to or not."

"I know you trust Mairahsol," Chanlix started slowly, trying to choose her words carefully, but Kailee cut her off.

"If it will make the two of you feel better, I'll create my own dose, so I can guarantee that there's nothing in it I can't see. *If* I decide to take it, which remains to be seen."

"We should still show it to Alys," Tynthanal said. "It's very likely she can fine-tune it if it turns out to be as benign as you think."

"No," Kailee said again, just as firmly. "The more people who know about its existence, the greater the chances I'll be pressured to take it. I can't even *imagine* what it would be like if my father ever found out about it." She shuddered delicately.

Chanlix's heart broke just a little on Kailee's behalf. Her constantly open Mindseye was a part of what made her herself, and Chanlix could hardly imagine how much having that part of herself rejected must have hurt. But she could not help thinking that a potion that would force someone's Mindseye closed might have potentially useful—and not-so-benign—applications. It also made her wonder whether Mairahsol had had any of those less-benign applications in mind when she had developed the potion for Kailee, but she knew better than to mention the possibility.

"I'm not sure I can promise to keep this secret forever," Chanlix said, because she refused to lie about it. "I am the Grand Magus of Women's Well, after all."

"Not if you come with us to Aaltah," Kailee countered.

Chanlix shook her head. "Which I cannot do." She leaned forward so that she could pat Kailee's arm in what she hoped was a comforting way. "I appreciate the invitation, and I can't tell you how much your generosity of spirit means to me. But my place is here." What she did not say—and what she suspected Tynthanal knew full well—was that after the things that had happened to her there, Chanlix had no intention of ever setting foot in Aaltah again. She read a combination of sorrow and acceptance in his expression, and she drank in the sight of his dear face while she still could.

"I'm not sure yet how I will manage it," he said, "but I swear to you I will be a father to our child. Even while we live apart."

Chanlix nodded, unable to speak over the lump that had formed in her throat. She had no doubt that Tynthanal would keep his word.

"I wish you would come," Kailee said wistfully.

Chanlix cleared her throat to dislodge the lump, but her voice came out tight with suppressed tears anyway. "I will miss you both more than I can say."

Alys looked down at the boy, who lay too still in the cot, his face too pale despite skin that was tanned a deep, golden brown.

"He lost a lot of blood," Lord Jailom explained, reaching down to run a gentle hand over Smithson's head. As lord commander, Jailom did not spend a great deal of time with the cadets of the Citadel, but he obviously took his role as the boys' surrogate parent and protector very seriously. "The healers say he will fully recover, but it will take some time." He flicked a glance in Alys's direction. "And if Corlin hadn't found a battleground healer within minutes, the boy would have perished."

Alys shook her head, but she could not look upon this suddenly frail-looking boy lying deep in a drugged sleep and deny that the injury had been grave indeed. "He can't possibly . . ." she started to say, but her voice failed her. Corlin had been on his best behavior for the past few weeks, and she had allowed herself to believe that he had finally learned how to rein in his temper. Or at least that he wanted to sit in on council meetings enough that he'd learned how to vent his temper in less obvious ways.

"He didn't mean to," Jailom said, but his voice did not convey a great deal of reassurance. "Smithson was perhaps unwise to try to stop him from hacking up his bed, and there's no question he was remorseful. But still . . ."

Alys had thought Corlin had taken the news of his uncle's death with reasonably good grace, but it seemed that the moment he was left alone, he'd taken his sword to his bed in the barracks house. And apparently to his fellow cadet who'd tried to calm him.

"You understand, Your Royal Highness, that he cannot remain in the Citadel after this," Jailom said gently.

She nodded. Corlin probably would have been expelled from the Citadel before if he were not the heir to the throne of Women's Well. His earlier transgressions had been nothing compared to this, and she could not ask the citizenry of Women's Well to risk their sons' lives at the Citadel, whether Corlin had learned his lesson or not.

"He also can't go unpunished," Jailom said, and this time there was more caution than gentleness in his voice.

Alys swallowed an instinctive denial. It was far from unusual for boys from important families to be excused almost any sin to protect those families' reputations—especially when the victim was a commoner, like poor Smithson—but Alys and her royal council had all agreed that Women's Well would operate differently from the rest of Seven Wells. To expect perfect equity between the classes was unrealistic, but it would be hypocrisy of the highest degree to allow Corlin to nearly murder a fellow cadet with the only consequence being expulsion from the Citadel.

Alys cleared her throat in an attempt to keep her voice from quavering. "If he were anyone else, what would his punishment be?" Her heart thudded heavily, for though she did not have much familiarity with military discipline, she had some idea of how it operated.

"He would be punished like a grown man," Jailom said grimly. "And based on the charters of both Women's Well and the Citadel, I theoretically have the jurisdiction to order him flogged without having to consult you."

It was harder to contain her protest this time, but Alys bit down on the inside of her cheek, willing herself to think before speaking. She did not need to peruse the charters to know that Jailom spoke

QUEEN OF THE UNWANTED

the truth, though she doubted he would do it if she ordered him not
to, charter or not.

Jailom sighed. "To be perfectly honest with you, though, I'm not
sure a flogging would do much to change the course he has set himself upon. Thrashings don't seem to have taught him much, and I
don't see escalation making much of a difference."

Alys closed her eyes. Obviously, Jailom had something in mind
other than a flogging, and that should have been a relief. She didn't
see how she could possibly harden her heart enough to allow her son
to be flogged, but she also couldn't imagine holding her head up in
public if she protected her own son from the discipline other cadets
of the Citadel would face for the same offense. And yet any punishment that fit this crime was bound to break her heart.

"What do you propose?" she asked, dreading the answer.

"Send him back to Aaltah with Tynthanal. Lord Aldnor has always
had a way with troublesome youths." Here Jailom grinned just a bit.
"I'm a prime example. I went to the Citadel of Aaltah as an arrogant,
angry little prick my parents could hardly wait to get rid of. Lord
Aldnor shaped me into a man my parents could be proud of."

"Send him away . . ." Alys whispered. And she was right—her
heart broke just saying it.

Jailom reached out and put a hand on her shoulder, giving it a
comforting squeeze before quickly letting go. It was quite the breach
of protocol for a lord commander and his sovereign princess, but Alys
knew that for that moment, he saw her not as a princess but as a
grieving mother.

"Something has to change," Jailom said. "If he continues down
the path he's on now, he is destined for a short and unhappy life. I
don't know what else to do for him here. Do you?"

She closed her eyes in pain, for Jailom was right. She had tried
time and time again to reach Corlin, and she had failed. "I can't bear
to lose a second child," she said, her heart constricting.

"Then send him with Tynthanal. It need not be forever. Maybe
even as little as a year or two. Then he can return to Women's Well
and take up his place as the heir apparent without the people resenting him."

Alys opened her eyes and looked down at Smithson's sleeping form. "You don't think people will remember what he did when he returns?" She refused to think in terms of *if*.

"I think Smithson is an extraordinary young man who will forgive Corlin for a hurt he knows was unintentional." Once again, Jailom reached down and brushed gently at Smithson's hair, smiling. "He was conscious when I first arrived, and he was very quick to shoulder most of the blame."

"I doubt his parents will be quite so forgiving," she said sardonically. They might well feel that their boy had suffered more than enough as a cadet of the Academy already. This was twice now that he'd almost died in the course of his duties, and Alys doubted any medals or money or land grants would make this episode go down more easily.

"Perhaps we should wait to worry about Corlin's return until such time as the concern is more relevant. And until you've agreed to send him away in the first place."

Alys wanted to scream at the unfairness of life. But her duty as a sovereign princess was to do what was best for her principality. And her duty as a mother was to do what was best for her son.

In this case, she could not help agreeing with Jailom that it was best to send Corlin away.

"He will never forgive me for this," she whispered. *And I will never forgive myself for having failed him so many times.*

CHAPTER FORTY-SEVEN

Alys had never been one to anesthetize herself with alcohol, but a little fortification might help her to see Tynthanal and Corlin off without bursting into humiliating tears. A single dose of brandy had her head swimming just a little as she hesitated in the hallway that led into the courtyard, where her brother and son awaited her. Standing by her side, Chanlix smiled at her encouragingly.

"It will be all right," Chanlix assured her. "When he is older, he'll understand."

Alys closed her eyes and wished she had Chanlix's confidence. She wasn't entirely certain she had the courage not to rescind her order of what was effectively exile if Corlin tugged on her heartstrings in just the right way.

"I will come with you," Chanlix tried again, although Alys had already rejected this offer twice.

Alys took a deep breath and stood up straight and tall. "Thank you." She forced a wan smile for the woman who would be the first lady chancellor in the history of Seven Wells. "But I can manage on my own." *Somehow.*

"You don't have to be so very careful of my feelings or of Tyntha-nal's," Chanlix persisted. "Every once in a while, you should remember to take care of *yourself.* And this will be harder for you than for either of us."

Alys glanced at Chanlix's belly. It was too soon for the new life within her to show, and the pregnancy was still not public knowledge. Alys wasn't sure if she herself would even know yet if she hadn't noticed Chanlix's morning sickness, though she liked to think her friend and her brother would have given her the news shortly anyway. "Soon enough you'll learn how much a mother will put herself through for the sake of her children. I must show my son strength, whether I feel it or not."

Chanlix's eyes shone with sympathy. "I'll be waiting right here for you when you're done," she promised.

Knowing that if she delayed any longer, she would lose the last shreds of her self-control, Alys stepped out into the courtyard.

Women's Well couldn't have afforded the resources to send Tynthanal and Corlin and an appropriate escort all the way to Aaltah on horseback—they still suffered a severe shortage of both horses and chevals—but the royal council of Aaltah had sent a party of their own horsemen and carriages to escort their new prince regent to Aalwell.

Alys spotted Tynthanal and Kailee instantly, standing together with their heads bowed in quiet conversation by one of the carriages. She noted that Kailee's hand rested lightly in the crook of Tynthanal's elbow, and she hoped that meant her brother was treating his bride well. She couldn't imagine Tynthanal being cruel to the girl, but she knew from personal experience that he could be perfectly polite and proper while still freezing someone out. Still, they seemed easy together, and that was a good sign.

Tynthanal looked up when she approached, and Kailee must have sensed her presence, for she turned her body slightly in Alys's direction and smiled her usual warm, friendly smile. The smile was so contagious Alys couldn't help smiling back despite the heaviness of her heart.

Tynthanal's smile was far less genuine, though she had to give him credit for making the effort.

"You will be an excellent regent," she blurted awkwardly, not sure what else to say to her brother who had once been her best friend.

Kailee's smile brightened even further, and Alys wished she could better read the expression in her sister-in-law's blind eyes. "That's what I keep telling him, but he's too modest to believe it."

Tynthanal grimaced. "It's not modesty to know one's own limitations. I was born to be a soldier, not a politician."

"Technically, you were born to be the King of Aaltah," Alys reminded him, for which he gave her a dirty look. "And no one can complain about the job you've done as Lord Chancellor of Women's Well."

She refrained from mentioning that his fairly well-known lack of interest in politics or hunger for power was probably the only reason the Council of Aaltah had felt their infant king was safe in the care of an uncle who would have been king himself had King Aaltyn not divorced his mother. No one who knew Tynthanal would fear he would harm his nephew—no matter how much he might have hated the boy's father.

"Women's Well and Aaltah are two very different beasts," Tynthanal said. "And that was true even before Delnamal made a ruin of it."

There was no denying that Tynthanal would have a long, hard road as regent. Especially if Aaltah's Well failed to recover from the effects of Mairahsol's spell. From all accounts, it was still diminished, its flow of elements significantly reduced, although at least it showed no sign of ceasing altogether.

"I have faith that you will mend enough fences to repair the damage he did." She frowned and glanced around the courtyard. "Where's Corlin?"

Tynthanal's expression turned to one of exasperation. "He's having a sulk in the carriage," he said with a jerk of his thumb.

Kailee's smile faded into a rare frown. "That might be because *someone* suggested he would have ordered both banishment *and* a flogging in Lord Jailom's place."

Tynthanal's jaw locked in that particularly stubborn set of his. "If he'd been a cadet under my command and nearly killed another cadet in a fit of temper, then yes, I would have, given his history of bad behavior."

Knowing Tynthanal's reputation as a disciplinarian, Alys believed him. Likely Corlin had, too. Which was just what the boy needed when he no doubt already felt like his own mother was abandoning him.

Tynthanal shook his head at her. "I can see your thoughts, Alys. But there is only so much that can be excused by the trauma he's been through. At some point, he has to take responsibility for his actions. And that point is well before he actually *does* kill someone."

"I know," she said, gazing at the carriage. The sunlight reflected off the windows, so she could not see inside, couldn't tell if Corlin was watching or even knew she was there.

"Go say goodbye," Tynthanal counseled. "He might not welcome it, but he'll definitely hold it against you if you don't."

Alys nodded and braced herself. Then she went to the carriage, and a footman hurried to open the door for her and hand her in.

Corlin was slouched in the far corner, his arms crossed over his chest. The expression on his face, however, was more thoughtful than sullen, and for that Alys could only be grateful. She settled in the seat opposite him and tried to think of something to say to bridge the terrible gap that yawned between them.

"Uncle Tynthanal says I should have been flogged," he said, his voice soft and subdued.

Alys winced and cursed her brother for making the wound deeper. She met Corlin's eyes, and once again her voice died in her throat. He felt like a stranger to her, and though she felt guilty for thinking it, she wished she could have the old Corlin back.

Corlin sighed and scrubbed his hand through hair that needed cutting. "He's right."

Alys blinked in surprise and gasped out a quick denial.

Corlin leaned his head back against the seat and stared at the roof of the carriage. "If I weren't your son, I *would* have been. I feel like a coward, running away from the punishment I deserve."

Of all the objections Corlin might have had to being sent away, this was not one Alys had imagined. "You aren't running away. You're being *sent* away. There's a difference."

"Explain that to Smithson," he countered. "And his parents."

Alys frowned. "Lord Jailom told me that both Smithson and his parents are satisfied that you are being punished appropriately."

"They haven't much choice but to say that when I'm the crown prince, do they? If the roles were reversed and Smithson had nearly killed me, would you be satisfied with sending him away?"

"Yes," Alys lied, the answer perhaps coming too quickly to be convincing. She'd like to think she would have hesitated to have a fifteen-year-old boy flogged, but it was hard to know what she might have done if her son had been hurt.

Corlin expressed his skepticism with a snort. "I'm being let off lightly, and we both know it. Just as we both know it isn't really fair."

Alys cocked her head and regarded her son more closely. He'd taken the news of his banishment with exactly the sort of poor grace she'd come to expect of him, but something seemed to have changed in him between then and now. She had never been one to pray, but she said a silent prayer to the Mother anyway that Smithson's near death had finally awakened Corlin to what he'd become. And that it was not too late for him to change.

"Maybe not," Alys said softly. "But what Delnamal did to you and to your sister was not fair, either. There is far too little fairness in the world."

Corlin nodded. "But you're trying to change that, at least here in Women's Well." A hint of a smile tugged at the corner of his mouth. "I doubt there is another sovereign in all of Seven Wells—not even Queen Ellinsoltah—who would make an unmarried pregnant woman her chancellor, no matter how deserving that woman might be."

"Probably true," Alys conceded. She suspected that particular appointment was going to be a source of contention in the future, but at least she had the rest of her council's approval, even if they weren't all equally enthusiastic about it.

"When I come back—" Corlin's voice broke, and he cleared his throat. Fear flickered in his eyes before he visibly quelled it with an effort of will and lifted his chin. "If I'm to be the Sovereign Prince of

Women's Well someday, and if I'm to lead us in the right direction, then I should lead by example."

He swallowed hard and met her gaze. "When I come back, I'll take the flogging I should have been sentenced to in the first place. I'll be older then, so maybe you won't feel so bad about it."

For a moment, Alys could only stare in shock. Was this a display of courage, or a sign that perhaps all of Corlin's transgressions were an act of willful self-destruction? Maybe he'd been punishing himself all along for what he considered his failure to protect his sister. She shook her head, but Corlin continued insistently.

"That's how you'll know I'm *ready* to come back. That you can trust me again."

It was impossible to miss the flashes of fear that slipped through the cracks of his stoic mask. Alys decided that even if he was punishing himself, it took genuine courage to make that declaration. And, though she had better sense than to say it out loud, she would never, ever allow her son to be flogged.

Besides, this was likely an impulse of the moment, a flash of pride spurred by Tynthanal's thoughtless commentary. She was perhaps reading too much into it. Easy to say he would take a flogging now, when such an eventuality was at least a year or two in the future.

"Will you tell Smithson and his parents that?" Corlin asked, and there was no question in Alys's mind that whether the impulse was genuine or not, the guilt that lay behind it was.

"I'll tell them," Alys said, hesitating a moment before speaking so that the lie would not be so obvious. If Corlin was serious about this, if it wasn't just a momentary impulse, then they could fight about it later. When he returned home.

Corlin accepted the lie with a sigh. "Good. I'm sorry I've made everything so much more difficult for you. I'll try to do better."

Knowing full well he would not appreciate it—Corlin had been uncomfortable with displays of maternal affection for at least five years by now—Alys moved to the seat beside him and drew him into a hug, her heart near bursting.

"I love you so much," she choked, holding him so tight she was probably hurting him. Corlin endured the hug with the stoicism of a teenage boy and even returned it, if a little stiffly. "I'm going to miss you more than you can possibly imagine."

"I'll be home before you know it," he mumbled against her shoulder, then finally squirmed in such a way that she knew she had to let go.

It took more courage than she knew she had to finally step back out of that carriage.

CHAPTER FORTY-EIGHT

The first thing Delnamal noticed was a pounding in his head so fierce he thought he must have worked his way through an entire keg of brandy. The next was a queasy churning in his stomach, followed quickly by a dozen more aches and pains of varying intensity. The bed seemed to lurch beneath him, and he groaned and opened his eyes.

He blinked in a dimly lit, unfamiliar room. The bed lurched again, his stomach going with it. As he fought to keep his gorge down, he heard the creaking and groaning of wood, as well as the splash of the sea.

The lurching of the bed was not his imagination after all. He was on a ship.

Delnamal barely found the strength to turn to his side before he was thoroughly and miserably ill. He squeezed his eyes shut and retched helplessly over the side of the bed. He heard hurried footsteps, then felt the touch of a cool hand upon his forehead followed by a soothing feminine croon.

The heaving stopped—or at least paused for a moment—and he opened his eyes, trying to remember where he was and what he was doing. Why was he in a ship? And what had he drunk that made him this ill and achy?

He blinked to clear his watering eyes and saw that someone was holding a basin under his chin. The basin was splashed with something thick and black and stinking. He'd suffered enough nights of overindulgence to know that whatever his stomach had brought up, it was far from normal.

His eyes went in and out of focus as he followed the hand that held the basin, using the arm like a climbing aid until he finally found a face staring down at him in concern. His mind felt so thick and wrong that it took him a moment to remember to whom that face belonged.

"Mother?" he rasped as his stomach turned over again.

The dowager queen set the stinking basin down, covering it with a cloth that did little to contain the reek. There was a slight greenish cast to her skin, and there was no missing the misery in her eyes. The ship continued to bob and rock, doing Delnamal's stomach no good—and Xanvin's either, judging by the look on her face.

"What's happening?" Delnamal asked. "Where am I?" He groaned again and flopped onto his back, the effort of supporting his head on his neck too much. "My head is killing me," he complained, closing his eyes as if that would dull the pain. "Fetch me a tonic before I go mad with pain."

He raised his hand to his face, intending to cover his eyes, but something felt . . . wrong. Strange.

He squinted his eyes just enough to see the hand that hovered before his face, and his stomach howled at what he saw. He quickly lowered the twisted ruin of his hand until it was out of sight.

"The healer did the best he could," Xanvin said softly. "When he first saw you, he told me you could not survive. What do you remember?"

At first, he remembered nothing. It seemed like an accomplishment that he had remembered his own name and recognized his mother. But then memory stirred within him, painting a terrifying picture.

It felt like both more and less than a memory. Like he was an ob-server sitting off to the side and watching himself as he made fatal mistake after fatal mistake. Allowing the witch to try her spell on the Well. Tasking Melcor with finding a willing sacrifice when he was so hated by the women of the Harbor District. Allowing that woman to hold a knife when there were no guards around and no one else was armed or prepared. He watched as Iris stabbed his secretary and the two tumbled into the Well. Then he watched Mairahsol throw herself in after them. And at last, he saw the wall of Kai hurtling toward him as he tried to flee.

"Oona and I found you before anyone else thought to look," Xan-vin said, for she could apparently tell from the expression on his face that he remembered. "We took you away and hid you with the help of a couple of loyal soldiers and a healer."

"Hid me?" he mused, uncomprehending.

Xanvin shook her head at him. "We knew what must have hap-pened, what you must have done. You were not especially discreet in your criticism of the council and its resistance to allowing the abbess to try her spell. And the results prove that they were right."

Delnamal would have liked to argue, but not while he lay maimed and weak in the hull of a ship, vomiting black goo.

"If anyone but us knew you survived," Xanvin continued, "you would have been tried for treason against the Crown."

He growled, though it was hard to sound intimidating under the circumstances. "I *am* the Crown."

"No, you are not," Xanvin snapped. "You never were. The king *represents* the Crown, but the Crown is bigger than any one man. You are not some uneducated peasant. History is littered with stories of kings who overreached and were condemned."

Even in his misery, Delnamal felt a sudden burst of righteous in-dignation. "I was the only man in all of Aaltah who had the balls to try to reverse the Curse!" he protested. "My council—"

"Knows only that you very publicly made it known you wished to allow the abbess to access the Well and also very publicly refrained from calling a vote because you knew that it would not pass. The Well is *damaged*. No one knows how badly or if it's permanent, but that wouldn't matter at your trial. You would be attainted, and it would be the ruin of all of us. You would have taken me and Oona and my grandson with you. I could not allow that."

"Where *are* we?" he demanded again, unable to wrap his mind around the enormity of what his mother was telling him.

"We're on a ship," she answered unnecessarily. "Bound for Khalpar. At the moment, I'm not entirely sure how I'll manage it, but I will convince Khalvin to give us sanctuary. And to keep your survival a secret. As furious and vengeful as the council is, I don't believe they will try you in absentia. Not when they can put your infant son on the throne and sculpt him as they'd like."

Delnamal stared at her, aghast. "You left *my son* to be 'sculpted' by that council of hand-wringing old women?" he snarled. Not that he had managed to form any true attachment to the infant over the time he had been a father, hard though he had tried to convince himself to love the bundle of screams and shit and piss. Even the smiles and coos were disgusting, accompanied by drool. The best he'd been able to manage was to feign paternal pride while hoping he would someday figure out how to become a father in more than just name.

"He will have a good life with a loving mother, and he will one day take his rightful place as King of Aaltah," Xanvin said. "That was the best I could do for him. And maintaining the illusion of your death was the best I could do for you."

Delnamal closed his eyes once more so he did not have to see the self-righteous, superior look on his mother's face. She'd had no *right*! He was the King of Aaltah, not some pathetic fugitive bound to live the rest of his life in hiding!

His stomach heaved once more, and this time he could not hold it down. He turned to find the basin ready as more thick, black, oily liquid spilled from his innards, seeming to take the remainder of his strength with it.

When he lay back down, trembling and sweating, he finally realized that the customary bulk of his chest and belly was considerably less than he remembered. He shuddered.

"How long has it been?" he asked.

"It's been three weeks since we found you," Xanvin said. "We wished to see you healthier before we set sail, but there was only so long we could wait. You've awakened briefly before, but this is the first time you've been coherent."

She shook her head and glanced anxiously at the basin and its revolting contents. "The healer isn't sure what's wrong with you. Your wounds all seem to have closed up and your bones have knitted as much as they're going to, but . . ."

"Am I dying?"

The question was asked with little inflection, and no true feeling behind it. Something was clearly horribly wrong with him. His injuries should not have kept him unconscious for so long and could not explain why he was vomiting some mysterious black substance. And yet he didn't feel especially frightened.

"The healer can't say," Xanvin answered. "He fears that something more than the obvious may have happened to you when the Well . . . did whatever it did. He says there are shards of what looks like Kai in your vomit, though they dissipate almost immediately. He's never seen anything like it."

Not surprising. No one had ever thrown a mote of Kai into the depths of a Well before. At least, not that he knew of. Maybe what had happened was the Well had tried to vomit that Kai back out and Delnamal was doing the same in unwilling sympathy.

It was strange not to feel frightened, Delnamal thought as he let his eyes drift shut again. But to be perfectly honest, after a few blips of reaction, he now felt next to nothing. His throne was lost. He was destined never to see his wife or son or homeland ever again. His body was maimed, his hands a ruined mass of misshapen flesh and bone. And he seemed to be wasting away from some mysterious, possibly magical illness.

And yet he felt numb. Almost peaceful. Whatever was happening to him, he had no power to fight it. Honestly, he wasn't sure he truly wanted to. The numbness was surprisingly pleasant. He'd spent a very long time feeling angry and frightened and bitter and unworthy.

He was still alive, at least for now. And if he could live what was left of his life without all that fear and anger and bitterness, then he was satisfied.

The darkness rose in his throat again, and he thought about turning over to spill it out into the waiting basin. But that seemed like too much trouble. So instead he lay still.

And the darkness settled back into his center, seeping into his flesh and into his blood and into his spirit, where he made it welcome.

ACKNOWLEDGMENTS

No book is written in a vacuum, and this book is no exception. I'm extremely lucky to have a wonderful husband, Dan, who is my first reader for every book. He's also chief cheerleader and impromptu therapist, which is something I think every writer should have.

As always, I must thank my fabulous agent, Miriam Kriss. She's always there to help me through the ups and downs of this crazy career. Thanks also to the entire team at Del Rey, who've been unfailingly supportive. The list includes, among others, Scott Shannon, Keith Clayton, Tricia Narwani, David Moench, Mary Moates, Julie Leung, Ashleigh Heaton, David Stevenson, and Alex Larned. And most importantly, I'm incredibly grateful for my editor, Anne Groell. This would have been a very different—and nowhere near as good—book without her insight and suggestions. She is the master of constructive criticism, and I couldn't be more grateful for her.

ABOUT THE AUTHOR

JENNA GLASS made her foray into epic fantasy with *The Women's War*, but she wrote her first book—an "autobiography"—when she was in the fifth grade. She began writing in earnest while in college and proceeded to collect a dizzying array of rejections for her first seventeen novels. Nevertheless, she persisted, and her eighteenth novel became her first commercial sale. Within a few years, Glass became a full-time writer, and she has never looked back. She has published more than twenty novels under various names.

jennaglass.com
Facebook.com/JennaBlackGlass
Twitter: @jennaglass
Instagram: @jennablackbooks

ABOUT THE TYPE

This book was set in Galliard, a typeface designed in 1978 by Matthew Carter (b. 1937) for the Mergenthaler Linotype Company. Galliard is based on the sixteenth-century typefaces of Robert Granjon (1513–89).